1974

Best wishes
James D. Horan

THE
RIGHT
IMAGE

BOOKS BY JAMES D. HORAN

FICTION

King's Rebel
Seek Out and Destroy
The Shadow Catcher
The Seat of Power
The Right Image

NONFICTION

Action Tonight:
The Story of the Destroyer O'Bannon
Desperate Men
The Pinkerton Story
(with Howard Swiggett)
Desperate Women
Confederate Agent
Pictorial History of the Wild West
(with Paul Sann)
Mathew Brady:
Historian with a Camera
Across the Cimarron
The Wild Bunch
The D.A.'s Man
The Mob's Man
The Great American West
C.S.S. Shenandoah:
The Memoirs of Lieutenant Commanding James I. Waddell
The Desperate Years
America's Forgotten Photographer:
Timothy O'Sullivan

JAMES D. HORAN

THE RIGHT IMAGE

**A NOVEL
OF THE MEN WHO "MAKE"
CANDIDATES FOR THE PRESIDENCY**

CROWN PUBLISHERS, INC., NEW YORK

For Pat,
Brian,
Gary,
and Jimmy
who will never need an Image Maker
because they know the image
is the shadow, never the substance

CONTENTS

The characters in this story are completely fictitious; the events in which they play their roles never happened. However, if the residents of any American community feel that my fictitious city of Lawrence, with its official corruption, bigotry, and ignorance, has a familiar echo, I would suggest they examine their consciences.

ACKNOWLEDGMENTS

I cannot allow this book to be published
without publicly thanking two people:
Gertrude, who deserves the credit
for the virtue of this book
and is in no way to blame for its faults,
and Miss Elke Jahn, who helped us type
this huge manuscript with much good humor.

PROLOGUE

Let us suppose that you and your partner were professionals in what should be grimly described as the "game" of American politics—the country's top Image Makers, as *Time*'s cover article put it. Let us suppose further that one of the richest men in the world, a former chairman of the Foreign Relations Committee, offered you both a million dollars a year for four years and a nation's ransom as a campaign chest to elect his son, an obscure congressman, governor of the state and subsequently President of the United States.

What would you do? Sit back and let your numbed mind try to weigh the tremendous odds against such an accomplishment, put your reputation on the scale and see how it balanced against the pile of gold dangling before you, toy with the exciting challenge—or would you just grab those millions and run like a thief, your conscience soothed by promises to turn every trick, to give the last full measure of your talents and energy to transform into reality what you damned well know is nothing but an old man's feverish dream?

Put supposition aside; this really happened to me—Finn McCool, a politician for more than half a century, and Josh Michaels, my partner and dearest friend, whom I secretly regard as a son. Josh is really the Image Maker; his tools are television, newspapers, magazines—anything that carries the printed or spoken word—along with an almost eerie talent for knowing what will catch the imagination of the voting American public. I'm on the bright side of seventy; Josh is still under forty.

What we finally did about this proposition, and how our decision affected not only our lives but also the destinies of many other men and women, some not even remotely connected with us, is the reason for this story.

Some time ago the curator of Columbia's Oral History Department suggested I dictate my memoirs. It can never be said a crotchety old Irishman passed up an opportunity to talk, but somehow I felt that the bare words in that soundproof booth, the whispering tape, could not communicate the human drama, yes, the terror and heartbreak, we all experienced.

Thus, this book.

IM′AGE—A bringing before the mind by language; by representation or description, esp. in a graphic manner . . . a mental conception held in common by members of a group and being symbolic of a basic attitude and orientation toward something (as a person, class, racial type, political philosophy, or nationality) . . .

Webster's New International Dictionary, Second and Third editions

". . . *controversy is important; but in the art of creating political imagery, television is the priceless medium . . . a political unknown placed in a strategic position during a televised public hearing that has captured the imagination of the American public (Kefauver, Army-McCarthy, and so on) can be catapulted into the front ranks of his political party. Should the right image be created, the timing be perfect, he could be thrust into a gubernatorial or even presidential race. . . ."*

An excerpt from the article "The Political Image Makers," by Robert W. Crispin, Ph.D., in the quarterly issue of the National Association of American Political Lore.

(As quoted by Josh Michaels to Kelly Shannon)

BOOK 1

☆☆☆☆☆☆☆

The Shannons ☆☆☆☆☆☆☆☆
of Wexford Hall ☆☆☆☆☆☆☆

CHAPTER ONE: THE SENATOR

IF THERE'S A BEGINNING to this story it should be the wintry day Felix Durant Gentile announced he was quitting as New York's mayor.

For two weeks Gentile had kept the city and country guessing. He had served one full term and most of his second. Would he take another turn at the mayoralty or would he enter the gubernatorial race, which anyone with half a brain knew was the prologue for the Presidency four years away?

There was national speculation; the experts made their predictions, but no one actually knew what Gentile was going to do.

On Sunday night Gentile told reporters he would announce his decision at 10:30 A.M. the following day in the City Council rooms at City Hall. All that Sunday night the solemn experts predicted on TV he would stay in office.

The *Times* even had one of their profiles of "Men in The News" on Gentile, war hero behind the lines in China, former Undersecretary of State, first Ambassador to the African Republic of Gahia, originator of the airlift that brought doctors and nurses to that country when it was stricken by a cholera plague—an act that brought Gahia into the Western fold and defeated a Communist takeover. There were also stories of his trip to Peking to lay the groundwork for the first Vietnam peace talks and how he stood up to Chin Hu. But the *Times* didn't forget the bad marks. His two administrations had been pretty rocky, they were still talking about the school race riot in Brooklyn that left four kids dead; even the cops didn't know exactly how many mothers and fathers, white and black, went to the hospital after that Donnybrook. There were also the usual scandals, none too important, but the school business and the violence in the city's streets had the people on edge.

Although I'm a native New Yorker, born in Hell's Kitchen more years

3

ago than I'll ever admit to, I've been in Washington most of the time since I left the old Harrington Committee, where I was chief investigator, to join Josh Michaels. We've been together over ten years. *Time*'s description of us as political Image Makers, I guess, comes close to what we do. Reach in our sample case of Images and take your pick: The Young and Dedicated American. The Somber Conservative with an Eye on the Bomb. The Great Economist. The Seeker of Social Justice. The Optimist with a Magic Wand. The Greatest Soldier of Them All. The Cautious Yankee. The Great Westerner Who Gets Things Done. The Incorruptible, etc., etc.

Josh insists that before we're done he wants to elect somebody with an image of the Great Lover, and then he goes into his blarney about getting committees of women to endorse our candidate, with the chairlady winning the chance to bed down with him.

It's tough having such a loose young partner.

It was only recently after we opened our New York office that I returned to Manhattan. I hadn't realized how senselessly violent the city had become until I watched the cops kill a bum who was running down Eighth Avenue after robbing and beating an old pensioner on his way home from Sunday-night services.

I can recall that weekend very well. We had been spending most of our time in Washington laying the groundwork for a campaign we were to conduct. It was all hush-hush because the poor fellow we were trying to reelect didn't have much of a chance and we wanted to spring a few surprises.

I had just returned to New York after a week spent in Rhode Island, our candidate's state, to put together a list of his leaders in the cities and towns and an evaluation of each one. This is a preliminary step in any of our campaigns, making a list of our friends.

Our New York headquarters is on the fourth floor of the Woolworth Building overlooking City Hall Park.

I glow with pride whenever I enter our suite of offices, yet feel a bit guilty at the luxurious surroundings Josh insists are part of our own image making. The walls are of the finest Swedish paneling; the huge desks have tops of gleaming onyx like slabs of night sky; the chairs are so deep and comfortable that the moment these old bones hit them I fall asleep. The carpet is as thick and soft as new hay; I picked the color. Green, naturally. Josh and I both have private offices; then there is a conference room with a bar that can equal any in town. The last office is Alice's. She's our secretary, elderly, white-haired, competent, and, more importantly, closemouthed. With Alice our secrets are safe; you couldn't pry them loose with every torture the Inquisition had perfected.

We would be fools to leave our really important files in the office. They're stashed away in a safe-deposit vault in a Maryland bank. So far, our files have been rifled on an average of five times a campaign. Last year we left a cardboard sign in one of our steel cabinets: HELP YOURSELF, and a bottle of laxatives.

By the time I reached the office this Monday morning, I knew I just couldn't go back to those lists. After more than a half century in politics a man just can't miss the action; and today that would be at City Hall.

I started on the lists, but my mind wasn't with it. From the window I could see those sleek, unholy Cadillacs swinging into City Hall Plaza, and I clicked their passengers off as they hurried up the steps: Charlie Saunders, Gentile's brother-in-law, and—as the gossip had it—the second most powerful man in the state, who obviously would run Gentile's campaign for the Presidency; Max Dregna, the Liberal leader and head of the League of Independent Voters and the powerful Plastics Union, and the veteran Queens leader whom I have known for years.

Ah, but the big boy was Barney Mullady, the real kingmaker. Barney and I were born on the same block on Ninth Avenue and Forty-seventh Street, and we both ran the Tuskawana Club, or the Tusk Club, as any professional politician from Maine to California called it. He had taken over after I went to Washington to help the New Deal stay on the tracks, and outside a few hellos in Washington we really haven't seen much of each other. But that's all right with me. I've always thought twice about saying hello to Barney. Even as a kid your eyeteeth weren't safe with him, and from what I have heard in Washington in the last few years, he hasn't changed.

Still, Mullady is a big man on the national scene, and when I saw him step down from that shiny limousine looking like a well-dressed little beer barrel and followed by a sharp young colored man, I knew the lists had to wait. I just couldn't miss this one. . . .

The lobby of the Hall was crowded with everyone heading for the graceful winding staircase that led to the Council Rooms. An old-timer who had lost his scalp to the reformers two years ago carefully licked his chops when he gave me the nod, and I couldn't help thinking of old lady Murphy's big tom who ate the canary she always swore sang like a young seminarian tenor. The district leader from Brooklyn tried to push through to head me off, but I ducked. He always reminded me of Marley's ghost—too many tin boxes dragging after him.

I squeezed in the back of the room, and it was lucky I did, for the guards shut the doors, and no amount of throwing about of names or begging the newspaper boys from Room 9 could get anyone in.

It was a noisy lot, with the Queens boys whistling and hooting when the City Council president, a grand Italian from Flushing, walked up to the rostrum and banged the gavel as though he really had some authority. But even the Queens boys settled down, except for a weird old woman waving some kind of petition who kept trying to force her way down the aisle, probably to force the city to keep stray cats and dogs until they died of old age instead of gassing them. As I always maintained,

5

more nuts attend a City Hall council meeting than there were in all Bedlam. They finally ushered her out, and the Italian from Flushing went into a long, rambling speech extolling the virtues of Felix Durant Gentile, mayor of the city of New York and the Republican great hope for the White House. Even the Queens faithful couldn't take all that hogwash, and I guess the City Council president sensed their discomfort, for he ended with a flourish and introduced Gentile, who came from the rear like a famous tenor about to sing.

But in all honesty I have to admit that Gentile was impressive: iron-gray wavy hair, fine features, and a marvelous tailor. The photographers crawled about the rostrum, and then the television crews took over. The lights blazed on, and in a few minutes all of us in that closed room felt that we were sitting two degrees above the equator. Josh has always insisted that the TV men are more important than the newspapermen, which undoubtedly is true, but they are certainly more noisy.

"Get off those God-damn cables!" one would shout, and then flip the long black snakes like a bullwhacker testing his whip. Gentile took it all in stride; he made voice levels, posed this way and that, then finally raised his hand. The TV crews backed off, and we all held our breath. The announcer for the municipal station, WNYC, dropped his hand, the cameras ground, and Gentile spoke at last in a deep, melodious voice:

"Fellow Republicans and fellow citizens of New York. For more years than I care to remember I have been a resident of this city. I was born here, educated in its schools, and so was most of my family. In fact, my ancestor Robert Durant, who commanded the First New York Line in the Battle of Saratoga, persuaded the city fathers to appoint Marinus Willet, his old commander in the Mohawk Valley, to be our city's first mayor.

"I love this city. I don't think even my political adversaries will doubt that. Therefore, this statement, which relates to my beloved New York, is from my heart. Without boasting I can say that I have served my two terms as mayor with dedication and devotion. How well, I leave to future municipal historians.

"I say this as a prologue to informing you of the decision I have made after long hours of soul-searching. I believe I owe it to all of you, fellow citizens from the Battery to the Bronx, from Queens to Staten Island, to make my position clear. You have a right to know."

Gentile took a deep breath, and even I, old professional that I was, could feel my stomach tighten. All around me men were leaning forward in their seats, intent on the impassive, calm figure towering behind the battery of microphones. He went on:

"Clearly now, with no ifs or buts, I have decided to resign as mayor effective in the next few months. I will not seek reelection; rather I shall actively campaign for the governorship of this wonderful state"—his

6

knowing smile took in the whole room, and his voice assumed a con-spiratorial air—"and then we'll let future events cast their shadows."

His words were lost in the uproar. The faithful went into a frenzy. They whooped, shouted, cheered. The guards ran about like idiots, waving their hands and adding their shouts to the din. Gentile waited for a time, then raised his hands. The uproar gradually died down.

"Thank you . . . thank you . . . but I must continue. I say this without reservation or qualification of any kind. I have not made my decision lightly. My advisers are in full accord. I shall, as I say, end my service in the New York mayoralty in a short time, appointing as my successor the deputy mayor, who is also president of this fine City Council.

"I relinquish this office with much regret but also with the full satisfaction that I have given to these years all my energy, all my hopes, all the talents that I possess. BUT NOW I MUST GIVE PRIORITY to other needs—needs that I believe are at the moment statewide. These needs demand a total and constant priority on the time of any man, any party that has decided to answer these needs."

He paused, and his voice soared in the tightly packed room: "My friends, I humbly dedicate myself, my talents, my energy to those problems, to those needs."

The Council Room exploded again. I settled back. Any professional knew this could be the Republican National Convention, a few years from now.

Gentile went on again for another ten minutes with more soul-searching and reexamination of his record, and how terrible a decision it had been. He ended by suggesting—yet never specifying—the White House, and every Republican in that room lifted his nose and smelled victory. First Albany, then Washington. It's that simple.

Gentile gave us that favorite benediction gesture all politicians have adopted since Sam Adams addressed his warhawks in Boston, and left to a standing ovation.

I watched the boys in Room Nine, those political geniuses without portfolio, leave in a rush. This afternoon their headline stories would be eagerly read from clubhouse to the White House.

The Queens leader tapped me on the shoulder. "Have you met Gentile yet, Finn?"

"The nearest I ever got to him is today."

"Let's go down and meet him."

We pushed our way through the crowd and down the curved stairway to the main floor. I was surprised and secretly pleased at the hands that reached out, the waves, and shouted hellos. With my head two sizes too big for my hat, I said as casually as I dared that it didn't appear as if Josh Michaels and Finn McCool had been forgotten.

"Come off it, McCool," was the reply. "Every mother's son of them is wondering where you guys will fit in the big race. You boys see any-one worth shouting about?"

"Well, certainly New York hasn't given us anyone," I told him. "What the hell's happening to you Democrats?"

"Civil rights, school riots, black backlash, white backlash, taxes, Civilian Review Board"—he threw up his hands—"and a passel of idiots who are cutting each other's throats from the Niagara frontier down to the Battery." He added with an air of gloom: "All we need is a candidate with the looks and class of Jack Kennedy, his family's money, his family's political know-how and their organization—and we'll breeze right into Albany, then Washington." He gave me a tight grin. "Can you image makers supply us with *that* one?"

"What about Gentile?"

"He's going to walk into Albany and then Washington," he said tersely. "The God-damn Republicans are even talking about who will do the catering at the Inaugural Ball. Here we are."

He nodded to the sharp-eyed cop behind the iron rail who reached under his desk and buzzed open the gate, smiled his way past the battery of secretaries, and walked through the half-open door. The beautiful room was jammed with the faithful, all jabbering and trying to make themselves heard while Gentile's aides were firmly but diplomatically trying to clear the room.

Behind his desk a smiling Gentile was shaking hands. There was no doubt he would be a fine-looking candidate. A glance told me the man had enormous self-confidence.

The leader took my arm. "Let's go up—" he started to say, then broke off abruptly. I looked up in surprise, then followed his eyes. Men grouped about the door and the desk were turning. The hum of conversation slowly died away. I could see Gentile's puzzled face; then some of the men in front of his desk stepped aside.

Coming slowly through the door was a man in a wheelchair, a man I could never forget as long as I lived. I remembered him when he had been a big man; now the frame was emaciated, bent over. The ashen, bony face was tight with rage; the eyes hidden under the craggy, thick brows were cold as arctic ice. The big twisted hands skillfully spun the rubber wheels, and finally the chair stopped in front of the desk. The old man took a heavy metal-tipped cane from a socket on the side of the chair, clasped his hands over the large silver knob, and leaned forward, staring at Gentile. For a long, tense moment both men studied each other.

At last the deep, rough voice rang out in the tense silence: "I've just listened to your garbage, Gentile. Listened, and was sick."

Gentile said calmly, "I don't believe we had an appointment, Senator."

The old man glared at him. "I don't need any appointment to talk to you, sir."

8

Gentile licked his lips. "I don't think this is the place or the time, Senator—"

The old man slammed his cane down, emphasizing each word. "What better place, sir, than City Hall, which you have dragged in the mud for all these years?" He shook his finger at Gentile, who stared down at him impassively. "Governor it is now, eh, Gentile? And then the Presidency? By God, the gall of you! I'll say this, Gentile: I'll see you in hell before I would allow you and your gang to walk into Albany and Washington! By God—never!"

The old man raised his cane and crashed it down. The bright tip rolled across the floor and stopped at the foot of a fat reporter holding a notebook. He picked up the tip and self-consciously juggled it in his hand.

The bitter, craggy face thrust forward, and the voice was so harsh and cold it sent chills up my old spine.

"I'm going to destroy you, Gentile, destroy you, and show the people of this state, this country, what you are really like." He slowly turned to the staring faces, studied them, and grunted. If the contempt had been acid, there would have been holes in the thick carpet. Then, without another word, he slowly turned the wheelchair around. The human aisle opened, swallowed the chair, then closed. The door swung open, and a collective sigh rose.

The silence was finally broken by a man's hesitant laugh. Then someone made a derisive remark, and others joined in. But the gay, festive spirit had vanished like mist at high noon. There was a feeling of uneasiness, even apprehension.

"Let's wait until another time," I told the leader. "He has enough on his mind now."

As we walked down the corridor toward the front door, I could hear a reporter excitedly telling the others in the press room the news of the confrontation. More headlines.

"Senator Shannon," the leader said bitterly, "once the biggest man in the country, now the biggest son of a bitch. When the party asked him to help us fight Gentile in the first campaign, he told us to drop dead. Now I wonder what he's up to?" He eyed me. "Your friend, McCool?"

"He was the best damn man the Foreign Relations Committee ever had," I said.

"He was like a buffalo in a tearoom. Christ, I can remember when he was going after State—"

"It's all in the history books now," I said with a last wave. I've always had a delicate nose, and now the bitter smell of big-city politics was getting too strong. Outside, the air was brisk, sharp—and clean. Men in expensive topcoats with the conspiratorial air of political policy makers hurried down the steps to the line of waiting Cadillacs. Just as I reached the bottom step, Mullady's big car drove up and the chauffeur jumped out and held open the door. Barney came from one side, the usual big cigar stuck in his mouth.

"Hello, Barney" I said, figuring that with all the people about' us he couldn't very well reach in my mouth and steal my fillings.

He stopped short, his little eyes narrowed, then lighted up.

"Finn—Finn McCool! It's great to see you, man!"

We shook hands as the faithful crowded about.

"I see you're still light as a feather," he said. He took the cigar from his mouth and said to the idiots surrounding us: "Finn McCool, a grand man from the West Side. And a great politician. And a scholar, mind you." He turned and peered at me. "Do you still read until the eyes fall out of your head, Finn?"

"I've been known to read a book or two," I said.

"Come up to the club and pay us a visit," he said. He leaned over and whispered in my ear. "I'd like to have a talk with you about this one inside."

"Gentile?"

"The same. He's a hot one that can give us plenty of trouble."

"So they say."

"How does he set with the boys in Washington?"

"The President's probably waiting for him on the phone right now."

He stuck the cigar in his mouth and gave me a twisted grin.

"Sullivan's is still on Eighth Avenue, Finn. Let's have some of their grand stew some night."

"I might just do that, Barney."

Now he was looking over my shoulder, and I turned to face a young, well-dressed Negro. I had the impression of a face chiseled out of a block of black marble; deep-set eyes, high cheekbones, and a sharp nose. He was carrying a well-stuffed legal folder.

"Finn, say hello to Gene Abernathy, one of the smartest young fellows around. Gene, this is Finn McCool. You know those big hearings you see on TV? All about the army and Congress and how automobiles should be made safer? Well, Finn here used to organize those hearings. Now he tells the President how to get reelected."

"He's still full of wind," I said to the young Negro as we shook hands.

"I'm happy to know you, Mr. McCool," he said. "I've heard about you."

"Gene was a bad boy once, but we got him straightened out," Barney said.

The young Negro gave him an impassive look, as though he had heard this many times.

"Don't forget Sullivan's, Finn old friend," Barney said as he entered the back seat of the big car.

I walked across City Hall Park, but it was such a fine day I couldn't resist sitting on a bench near the Broadway side. It wasn't lunchtime, and the pigeons and I had the park to ourselves. It had been quite a morning.

Who would have ever thought that Francis Xavier Shannon, once one of the most powerful men in the Senate and now one of the world's richest men, would publicly denounce the mayor of the city of New York?

And then coming upon Barney Mullady, who now had a machine so big he could be called a kingmaker, not only in New York but in national politics. And instead of one of his usual cigar-chewing fatheaded ward heelers following him, he had a Negro at his heels. But I dismissed Barney Mullady and his black shadow and came back to Senator Shannon. It was ten years or more since I had last seen him. It was the Senate investigation into the atrocities committed by the Viet Cong during our big push north.

Shannon then was a bull of a man, never satisfied with pure documentary evidence but always after admissions of guilt. His target at the time was a four-star general, and as senior investigator for the committee I was under his guns. He wore me thin, and one afternoon, in front of the whole staff, he shouted that I was nothing but a cheap New York City tinhorn politician.

I had just finished reading a fifty-page statement, bound together with a heavy clip. I flung it and he ducked. It missed him by a hair. For a moment there wasn't a sound in the room. I can recall how his secretary's eyes grew bigger and bigger until I thought they surely would pop out on the carpet.

Slowly he smiled. "Only an old buzzard named Finn McCool could do that—and get away with it. Mary, give him back that statement. I'll be needing it in this afternoon's session."

After that, we got along fine. I knew he never forgave me, but at least he respected me.

Senator F. X. Shannon, now one of the richest men in the world and, from the looks of him, one of the unhappiest . . .

I went back to our office, but for most of the afternoon I looked out over City Hall Park and wondered what would be the next step of the former senior senator from New York.

A few days passed. The papers were filled every day with news of Gentile's booming campaign. Republicans from every quarter of the state were flocking to his standards. The day after he had announced his candidacy, he began hitting the big cities. The Democrats had been caught napping. No one had really believed that Gentile wouldn't run for the mayoralty again. The Democrats, it seemed, had been only too ready to believe the old adage that the mayor's chair in New York is a political dead end.

The scramble for the job had begun, putting both parties in a bit of a squeeze. The fine young Italian from Flushing, the City Council president, was a poor substitute for Gentile, so the county and state leaders found themselves engaged on different fronts, both for the mayoralty and the governorship.

But my interest in the city's political fight was purely academic. Let the boys fight it out among themselves.

During the next few days I worked on my Rhode Island analysis, made two more quick trips back there to see the state leader, and spent a week-end finishing my report. On Monday I would turn my notes over to Alice, and that phase of the campaign would be finished.

I returned to the office late in the afternoon and, as I recall, was cursing the *Times* for its pompous and inaccurate analysis of Gentile's chances, when the phone rang.

"Mr. Michaels?" a brassy old voice asked.

"And who may I ask wants him?" I said.

"Is Mr. Michaels there?" I knew it was some old wren, and the way she said it ruffled my feathers.

"Ma'am," I said, like I was a prince of the world, "you'll not get a word out of me until I know who is calling."

Suddenly a voice as harsh as a saw cutting through ice broke in.

"Did you get Michaels, Miss Manners?"

"No, sir," she began. "There's a man who insists—"

"Only wanting to know who's calling," I said.

There was a brief pause. "Is this you, McCool?"

I never could forget that voice. Senator Shannon. And I'll be damned if the sound of the old buzzard's rasp didn't make me take my feet off the desk.

"Yes, Senator, it's Finn McCool," I said.

"Where's Michaels?"

I hesitated, but then I remembered it was never any use to keep secrets from him.

"Washington on a bit of business."

He grunted. "What you mean is, trying to fool the voters of Rhode Island so they'll return that blockhead Harrison to the Senate."

There's no getting away from it; he hit me between the eyes with that one. I didn't think there were two souls other than Josh and me who knew the Senator from Rhode Island had hired us to make sure he returned to the Establishment.

"You're not telling me now you're interested in Rhode Island, Senator," I said.

"Get off it, McCool," he said. "You know better than that. I want to talk to Michaels on business. Is he coming in today?"

"Not today or tomorrow and not for a week," I said. "But I'll be going down on the shuttle tomorrow morning."

"You'd better come up, then," he said. "Penthouse, Shannon Building."

In my mind's eye I could see the mighty marble building, gleaming black over the Grand Central area.

"What time, Senator?"

"Now."

And the phone clicked.

The Shannon Building was one of the marvels of Park Avenue. It took in one whole block of the Grand Central area: gardens, fountains, and an enormous glass door bearing the label "Shannon Building." The gold lettering listing the Shannon enterprises took half the door.

The building itself was built of black marble with aluminum windows, a photographer's delight at sunset, as the rays of the dying sun touched the bank of windows and gave the illusion of a black shaft of tree stiff with flame.

The elevator at the end of the corridor simply said "Shannon Ways Color, Ltd." A flunkey in a red uniform gave me a suspicious look. I didn't like the bastard's wavy white hair and whisky color, so I tried to brush past him. But he was too fast, and stepped in front of me.

"Yes?" he said, intoning like a bishop.

"Mr. Shannon," I said, hoping I sounded like a cardinal. "He's waiting for me."

He did a double take but decided to be cautious.

"Is he expecting you, sir?" he asked, sweet as cream.

"That he is," I said, "and smile, man, don't look so unhappy." I walked inside the elevator, pressed the button that said Penthouse, and left Mr. Wavy Hair standing there with his mouth open.

The elevator opened into a fine room, thick carpet red as new blood. There were fine prints in thin black frames, mostly of gentlemen and ladies in Colonial costumes, on horses or dancing to fiddlers. A gray-haired woman, dry as a stick, counted my bones as I walked to her desk. She was content to give me a frozen smile.

"Yes?" she said.

Mrs. Brass Voice over the telephone, I told myself.

When I stated my business she nodded, whispered into a phone, and then showed every one of her upper crockeries.

Shannon was in his wheelchair in front of a big desk. Behind him was nothing but the sullen East River and a ragtag of smog and smoke. There were books, more carpet, and a small table with a silver pot and two cups. I suddenly remembered that the senator liked his morning tea.

He waved me to a chair.

"Where've you been, McCool?" he grumbled. "I've been waiting to hear from you or your boss."

"We were out of town, Senator," I said.

"I told that damn answering service in Washington I wanted you people to call me right back," he began.

I blew the steam from my tea.

"Did you, now?"

He leaned his chin on his cane, and a small smile touched his lips.

"Come on, McCool," he said. "No kicking on the ground, no gouging —and no throwing affidavits at me. Do you remember that day?"

"I do."

He sipped at his tea. "You were a cocky old rooster and the best damn investigator the Senate ever had. You know that job I offered is still open."

"Hell and fury, Senator, I'd only be a gold-plated hatchet man."

"For God's sake, McCool," he said, "you're a brass-plate one now." He held up his hand. "No offense." Clearing his throat, he went on: "I called you, McCool, because I want you and your boss to do a job for my son Kelly."

"And what's that, Senator?"

"I want him to be elected governor next year"—he turned to me— "and his name placed in nomination for the Presidency at the convention." He gave me a sharp look. "Do I make myself clear?"

I glanced at him quickly. "If I'm hearing right, you want us to elect your son governor and then President."

"That's right," he said, cool as a knifeblade.

"Your son is a congressman," I said. "New York."

"A bugtit of a congressman," he said. "He's at every roll call, voting for and against every dam and project from New Mexico to Montana. He made a fine speech for civil rights for which he had an audience of the Congressman from Texas who was making out his expenses and two gentlemen from Missouri who were asleep and his beautiful wife in the gallery."

"Christ," I said, "first governor—"

"Then President," he said. "Look, McCool, you know me, and, mind, I'm not becoming senile by a long shot."

"But, Senator—"

"Finish your tea, and listen," he said. We sipped the brew in silence; then Shannon touched a napkin to his lips, and began: "Do you know of Wexford Hall, McCool?"

"I've seen pictures; a mighty nice place it is."

"In the heart of Westchester County. My grandfather built it after the Civil War. Ever hear of the *Shenandoah*, McCool? Yes, I forgot you're a reading man. Well, as you know then, the *Shenandoah* was a Confederate raider. She wiped out the New Bedford Whale Oil Industry in two afternoons. My grandfather was tipped off by a clerk in the insurance company that held the fleet's policies, and he went around buying up all the coal-oil leases he could. In a year he had a monopoly. Everyone had used the whale oil before the war, and for two years there just wasn't any. A year after Appomattox he was shipping oil to almost every army post on the frontier."

He poured a half-cup. "Wexford Hall has been a part of my family as long as I can remember. I was married there; my children grew up there; and my wife died there. On Thanksgiving and Christmas there are enough Shannons on hand to man a shipyard. There's Kelly, my oldest; Luke, the youngest; and Lacey, my daughter." He grimaced. "She hates politics, and maybe even me." He took a swallow. "But Kelly and Luke are like me; they love it. Luke's been begging me to let him run, and maybe I will—maybe next year."

Maybe I will, I thought, like he owns the Electoral College.

"I want to level with you, McCool. This is no wild dream of an old man. I've had it inside me for years that I want Kelly in the White House, but"—he glowered at me—"I'm not that much of a fool that I think money, even my last penny, would put him there."

"It would help, Senator," I said.

"I'm sure you and Michaels know that better than most," he said.

Oh, you're a sweet one, I told myself, but I took that dandy to the chin and turned the other cheek.

"I've been biding my time, McCool, waiting for the right moment. As I told Luke, there's a timing for everything, even to bedding a woman."

"And now you say it's time."

He nodded. "It's time." He turned and wheeled away from the little table to the desk. "Come over here by the windows; it's a grand sight."

And indeed it was, with the river sparkling in the shafts of the sun that pierced the tattered, dirty-silk haze, and the tiny tugs bucking the fierce tides of Hellgate like laboring beetles. Beyond the fairy tracery of the bridges was the dreary quiet of Queens and its little square windows loaded with silver ice.

We studied the scene for a moment; then Shannon said: "I didn't know the time had come until two weeks ago. It happened on a morning when Kelly drove into Crestview, the nearest village. Outside the post office, a woman named Molly Shapiro stopped him. She'd known Kelly and the rest of the kids since they were this high. In fact, she had horses some years ago, and taught Lacey how to ride. You can see the Shapiro place from our top floor. It's much smaller than Wexford, but she has it furnished like a God-damn museum; I guess you can call it a showplace. The Shapiros have been living there since the 1880's. The old man owned a piano factory, as I recall. I used to see his ads in the magazines when I was a young man in business."

"I remember them," I said. "There was a young girl playing the piano and a young man bending over her."

"You're older than I thought," he said. "Well, anyway, the old man died some years ago, and Molly is the only one left. She's about fifty-five, and lives well. Somehow she met this man who turned out to be a thief. I don't know how they met, probably through some Jewish organization. Maybe she was lonely, how the hell do I know? Anyway, that the background. When she met Kelly this day, she seemed worried. Kelly said he thought she had been crying and asked what was wrong. At first she didn't want to talk about it, but finally agreed to have a cup of coffee with Kelly at Parry's—that's a little drugstore near the station."

He grunted.

"Well, McCool, she told Kelly the story, and it's a whopper."

"Well, come on man, let's hear it!" I said impatiently.

"The bum she met is named Jelkowitz," he went on. "A cheap little thief who apparently has been swindling people since the day he got off the boat from Poland, forty years ago. He's sold everything from bridges to gold bricks. His last job was a fur swindle to the tune of $50,000. The furrier turned him in to the district attorney, and like all those bastards he tried to use the DA's office as a collection agency. Jello—that's what they call Jelkowitz—got up the money in a hurry, but the DA wasn't in such a hurry. For some reason the DA is trying to hang him as a three-time loser."

He gave me a quick look to see if I was getting impatient; although I was, I waved him on.

"Jello now feels he will be railroaded and probably murdered in prison because of what he knows, so he yelled for Molly. Molly listened, and while she's not a brilliant woman, she's not stupid. After every visit she wrote down everything Jello told her. It filled a notebook. This she gave to Kelly, who had it typed."

He picked up a dark-red folder. "Help yourself."

I took the clipped sheaf of almost fifty pages and started reading. By the time I had reached page ten I could feel the goose pimples crawling up my back.

He couldn't wait, and broke in. "That's the bomb I was talking about, McCool. There's a lot more."

"It's big, I know, but is it big enough for what you want?"

"The way I figure it, it could be big enough to help put Kelly in the governor's chair—that is, if we play our cards right."

"I grant you what we have here could be an enormous scandal."

He moved forward from the waist, and I suddenly remembered the power that once was in him.

"An enormous scandal, McCool? The brother-in-law of the man everyone knows could be the next President nailed as a common thief, a dispenser of justice to the highest bidder?" He added scoffingly: "Come off it, man. If the material we had in Washington had been half that good, we would have left the town rattling for years!"

"We'd need investigators, a staff—"

The gnarled hand slammed down on the edge of the chair.

"Damn it, we'll get as many men as we need and then twice that! Now, stop talking about trivia—what I want to know is, will you and Michaels take it?"

"Josh is the one to decide."

"Will you see him tomorrow?"

"Early in the morning, I hope."

"I want you to give him my terms."

"I'll certainly give them to him, Senator."

"I'll guarantee $20,000,000 for the campaign."

"My God, Senator, $3,000,000 is the legal limit for a presidential campaign!"

"We'll double that—triple it if necessary—when we come to getting Kelly in the White House," he said with a grim smile. "Now, what about you and Michaels? How much would you both want?"

"A man should have time to figure out a thing like this, Senator, before he presents his bill."

Shannon just ignored me. "Tell Michaels I will pay him $1,000,000 a year, clear of taxes."

From far off I could hear myself saying, "There's the question of expenses."

"Fifty thousand dollars a month, no questions asked."

The sums spun in my head. More than another half a million.

"And for that you want . . ."

"You and your boss will develop this information and use it to the best of your ability in a gubernatorial campaign you will conduct for my son and—"

"The national convention is three years off, Senator."

"You will advise my son for the next four years and during that time conduct a continuous campaign to assure that his name will be placed in nomination for the Presidency."

"That means we will be working for you for four years."

The thin lips formed a faint smile. "For every year you remain the fee will be the same: $1,000,000 and $50,000 a month for expenses."

The adding machine in my head clicked feverishly. "Good God, man, you will be paying us over $6,000,000!"

"It will be cheap at twice the price if you do the job I think you will do."

"And the campaign fund, Senator?"

"For the governor's campaign, $20,000,000. Twice—three times that for the Presidency. More if you want it." He turned to me. "We haven't got a hell of a lot of time, McCool, but we can make it up in money. Let's face it, big-time politics is a rich man's game. The days of log cabins and country lawyers with shawls and beaver hats walking into high offices are only in the history books."

"A $6,000,000 fee and a $20,000,000 campaign fund just for the governor's race . . ." I let my voice trail away.

For a moment the fire seemed to die inside him as he stared down at his clenched hands that gripped the knob of the cane.

"What would it really mean to me, McCool? $26,000,000, $36,000,000, $106,000,000. What would I do—sell a few companies, shake up the market, get rid of a television network? My God, man, I'm worth more than $500,000,000!" He shrugged. "Do you think I can live many more years in this wheelchair? No. Kelly's the only thing that matters. I've waited a long time for the right moment, McCool, and I know this is it." He reached out and lifted the little silver teapot, but it held only a few drops.

"I'll tell your secretary."

"The hell with it. As it is, I drink more tea than all of London and Dublin put together. I haven't had a drink since Washington." He stared at me as if suddenly remembering. "You weren't in Washington when I had the accident."

"I was out of town when you fell, Senator."

"A pair of new shoes and that God-damn Senate marble stairway," he whispered fiercely. "They picked me up on the bottom, and I haven't walked since. Do you know that in another month I would have had Gentile? One more month and he would have been on the stand."

"What were you getting on him, Senator?"

"There were some wild parties going on. A captain in the DC police tipped me off. The captain said he had a quiet stakeout after some of the neighbors complained, nothing for the record, just for his own information, mind you. He said the report showed there were three black baboons and a Chinaman with DP license plates. He did a check, and found they were from the United Nations. From the looks of it, they were having some wild times."

"You can't bring a man before a congressional committee simply because he's had wild parties in his house, Senator."

"Come on, McCool," he said with a look of disgust, "you know me better than that! I had the Bureau put them through a check. The Chinaman was definitely a Peking agent. The Bureau said he was spending money like it was going out of fashion in organizing those Peace-with-Peking clubs that all those stupid college kids were going for. After Vietnam, the Bureau traced him to Hong Kong, and then he vanished back into China." He slammed his hand down. "That's what I was getting interested in—not a lot of whores! The way I see it, if you're in State you should be like Caesar's wife, or you have no damn business being there!"

"That was years ago, Senator."

"A polecat doesn't change his smell in that time, McCool. He's been doing in City Hall what he did in State. Down there it was fags and high-priced whores and God knows what. Here he's tied to the biggest thief in the country. His God-damn brother-in-law and campaign manager is selling Justice on the barrelhead! Right from City Hall!"

"Why didn't you do something about him before this? After all, he ran for office twice."

"When he left State and came to New York to run for City Hall the first time, the party wanted me to come out against him. But frankly I couldn't have cared less if he won. First of all I had enough enemies—" He gave me a tight grin. "You know that, McCool."

I nodded. How well I knew.

"And I couldn't see any purpose in spending my money and influence fighting him when all he wanted was a political dead-end office. But when his press agents started to drop hints he was ready to run for the governor's office and then the Presidency, that's when I knew I had to stop him." The harsh voice flung the words at me. "Not only stop him but destroy him—destroy him as I will any man who stands in the way of my son winning"—his forefinger shot up—"first Albany"—the next finger snapped into line—"then the White House."

"And you really think your son has a chance for those offices?"

"For years I've sat in this chair waiting for the right day, the right hour." The cane came down with a crash that made me jump. "And dammit, McCool, the right time has finally arrived!"

"How do you know, Senator?"

He tapped the red portfolio, and smiled. "What's in this folder tells me, McCool. It's all in there. Read it!"

I got up. "I guess that's what I had better do, Senator. Read it."

The cold eyes studied me. "You're an old pro, McCool, one of the best in the country. What do you think?"

"I don't know. Frankly, I wouldn't know your son if I fell over him."

"He's a fine boy."

"The country's full of fine boys who wouldn't make a good dogcatcher, Senator, let alone governor—or President."

"You'll know what I mean when you meet him."

"Perhaps. Have you thought of Barney Mullady, Senator?"

"That old thief!"

"Thief or not, he controls the strongest machine in the state."

He spat out the words: "Cubans, niggers, and spicks. He runs nothing but niggers for the head of Tammany Hall. Niggers, mind you!"

"I guess there was a day when someone said the same thing about an Irishman taking over, Senator." I added, "And my mother always insisted a Negro was an Irishman turned inside out."

He chuckled. "My old man said the same damn thing. Well, we'll take care of Mullady, McCool. Don't worry about him."

"You'd better be thinking about him. He's not to be brushed aside so easily."

"I don't worry about a man who can be bought, McCool," he said softly. "I have found that the ones you worry about are the ones who don't care about money or power. They're dangerous."

"There's one thing I haven't brought up: Is this what your son wants?"

He slowly wheeled his chair toward the door, and I followed. "You'll meet Kelly very soon." He looked up. "When will you see Michaels?"

"I'll be on the nine o'clock shuttle tomorrow, Senator. We'll be in touch with you." I paused at the door. "I should warn you—Josh has a mind of his own."

"Tell him if that price isn't satisfactory, we can talk about it—"

"It's not that, Senator."

"Well, then, what is?"

"Josh is one of those you have to worry about—he doesn't give a damn about money or power."

I nodded goodbye and closed the door. Mrs. Brass Voice again showed every one of her fine crockeries, and the door slowly closed behind me. In a few minutes I was out on Park Avenue. I don't take cabs when I can walk, but this time I hailed one. I couldn't wait to read every line in that red leather folder.

I have been living at the General Sheridan Hotel as long as I can remember. Josh insists I'm one of those old New York coots who refuse to leave their neighborhoods even when the sidewalks fall in. I guess he's right. The Sheridan is on West Forty-seventh just off Eighth Avenue and a stone's throw from the tenement where I was born, the high school I graduated from, and St. Malachy's, where I was an altar boy. It's only spitting distance from the Tuskawana Club and Barney Mullady.

Someone once described the Sheridan as the Union Club of the West Side, and I guess that's a fit title. The people who live there are retired engineers, actors, a few old police inspectors, and some of the harbor shipping boys. The place is spotless, and has been run by the same family that had it when General Sheridan was its first guest. Several years ago I took over the living room of the adjoining suite and knocked out the walls to give me a library. As Barney said, I have always been a reading man. I guess that comes from the Jesuits up at Fordham who tried to make a lawyer out of me.

I have a big easy chair in my little library, a fine lamp, the books and a jug, so what else does an old Irishman want? When Josh and I come into the city, he bunks with me unless he has some other ideas.

So it was to this favorite spot that I headed after supper at Sullivan's, where most of us old fellows go to eye the young skirts who come in from nearby shows with their makeup still on and their young laughter and smiles lighting up the whole place.

With a glass of Jack Daniels on the rocks at my side for sipping purposes, I opened the red folder and began reading.

MEMORANDUM #1
INTERVIEW WITH MOLLY SHAPIRO
MONDAY, MARCH 3
KELLY SHANNON

On the Morning of March 2, as I was about to enter the Crestview Post Office, I was approached by Miss Molly Shapiro of Oakland

Road, which borders on the north side of Wexford Hall. Miss Shapiro, whom I have known for many years, asked if she could speak to me. I agreed, and we had coffee at Parry's Drug Store near the Crestview Station.

Miss Shapiro told me she had been keeping company for the last year with a man named Benjamin Jelkowitz, whom she described as a commission man. (Jelkowitz is fifty-eight; Miss Shapiro confessed to fifty-five.) Last month, Jelkowitz was arrested on the complaint of a Manhattan furrier who signed a grand-larceny complaint against Jelkowitz, in the Nineteenth Precinct, charging him with defrauding him of $50,000 in furs. The complaint was later amended in Magistrates Court, where Jelkowitz waived a hearing and was held without bail to await the grand-jury action. The bail action is the result of Jelkowitz's criminal record, which includes two convictions in 1923 and 1941 for larceny. He served time at Sing Sing and Rikers Island.

In many larceny cases, the complainant tries to use the local district attorney as a collection agency; in this instance Jelkowitz, although he swore he was innocent, tried to return the money, but the district attorney refused to allow the complainant to withdraw the case, in fact, threatened the merchant with prosecution if he failed to go through with it.

Miss Shapiro, who said she never knew Jelkowitz had a criminal record but insists she still wants to marry him, told the DA she would put up the bail, but was turned down. She said she talked to Jelkowitz in the jail, and he told her the reason for the DA's refusal to allow bail was because of his knowledge of corruption in high places in government. Jelkowitz insisted to Miss Shapiro that his life is now in jeopardy; if he is convicted and sent to Sing Sing he would certainly be killed on the orders of some mysterious high forces.

Frankly, the whole thing sounded extremely melodramatic and unreal, but because of our friendship with Miss Shapiro and her late father I agreed to file as Jelkowitz's attorney, and see him. I sent the usual formal telegram to the district attorney's office and made arrangements to see him on the 4th.

KELLY

MEMORANDUM #2
INTERVIEW WITH BENJAMIN JELKOWITZ
VISITORS' ROOM, PENSVILLE PENITENTIARY
TUESDAY, MARCH 4

This memorandum is the result of a two-hour interview with Benjamin Jelkowitz. He was born in Poland and came to this country with his mother; his father was killed in an accident when he was twelve. He is now fifty-eight years old. His criminal record is impressive: twenty-three arrests and two convictions, mostly of fraud and grand larceny. He is quite candid in admitting that he has sold more bridges and more goldbricks than any confidence man in the history of American criminology. I am inclined to believe him.

Jelkowitz, or Benny Jello, as he prefers to be called, is obviously frightened. He was extremely edgy in our first meeting, and although I pressed for details, he was adamant in refusing to talk to me. As I was leaving, he whispered he would tell me the reason for his reticence the following day. I left with meager facts but promised I would return the next day.

KELLY

MEMORANDUM #3
INTERVIEW WITH BENJAMIN JELKOWITZ
VISITORS' ROOM, PENSVILLE PENITENTIARY
WEDNESDAY, MARCH 5

Benny Jello, as I now call him, was much more voluble this morning. The reason for his reticence yesterday, he explained, was the presence of the guard in the visitors' room. This guard, he insisted, was an informant for the district attorney.

This may be true. I recalled that when I was talking to Jello, the guard sauntered near us many times. Today is his day off.

Jello spoke to me for an hour. Frankly, his story is shocking, if true. He claims to have paid off numerous city, state, and federal officials during the years of his criminal activities. This has given him the underworld name of Benny Pay Big.

He has detailed information of an alleged $25,000 bribe paid to Charles Saunders, Mayor Gentile's brother-in-law and confidential assistant, by Aaron and Simon Singer, defendants in a hijacking case. (I have checked the basic facts in the Singer case and have attached them to this memorandum.)

Jello claims to have made the original contact with an attorney, who in turn contacted Saunders. Jello was advised how much a "toss out" would cost and how it was to be paid. He claims to have accompanied the Singers to their father's office (the family owns a reputable poultry and egg concern with offices in Connecticut, New Jersey, and on Washington Street, New York City). The father, evidently, is a devoted parent who would do anything for his sons. (Jello's description of the scene in the father's office is very moving.)

He also said he accompanied the Singers' intermediary to a Fifth Avenue office where they paid the money. Jello also detailed other bribes that Saunders allegedly has taken. He has given me facts in five criminal cases. My office has researched the facts, and I have attached memoranda.

Jello terminated this interview with a promise to tell me a "big one" in our next talk.

KELLY

Because of my luncheon appointment with Congressman Elkers, I was forced to postpone my Thursday meeting with Benny Jello. When I arrived on Friday I found him in a frantic state. The suspicious guard was present, and Jello insisted we meet again on this man's day off. When I offered to go to the warden and have another guard substituted, he was almost in tears, begging me not to cause him "trouble." I agreed to meet him again the following Wednesday.

KELLY

This meeting with Benny Jello lasted two hours. He seemed less apprehensive; he claims he has "conned" the guard, and he is not "playing stoolie." He also said money paid to the guard by Miss Shapiro has helped.

His information, if true, is highly explosive. Frankly, it is hard to believe. He has named as bribe takers:

Charles Saunders, Mayor Gentile's brother-in-law and chief administrative assistant. From what Jello claims, Saunders has been conducting an incredible business in corruption at City Hall, using his influence to buy justice, judges, city contracts, etc.

Trevor Remington, a Fifth Avenue attorney, is the intermediary for Saunders, and his bagman. He arranges the deals, and through his hands the money flows to Saunders. Remington was Jello's contact. From what Jello tells me, Remington boasted he could fix anything from an ABC violation to a major criminal charge. Apparently he is a heavy drinker and lives high with his wife, a former showgirl.

Prebel Tucker, Chief Justice of the Federal Court of Appeals. This really stunned me when Jello named Tucker. Everyone in legal circles knows the old man, who has been on the federal bench for years. While some lawyers complain he is crotchety and impatient, I never heard his personal honesty questioned. But after the first shock, I must reluctantly come to the conclusion Jello is telling the truth.

23

Jello claims to know, and has named cases in which Tucker accepted money. Tucker, according to Jello, has taken money, ranging from $20,000 to $50,000, for favorable decisions in federal receivership cases.

When I told Jello this was hard to believe, he became so vehement and insistent that I made a number of notes. Luke's law assistant did the research on this one. Admittedly it isn't too much, just the basic material from documents on file; but the facts, as detailed by Jello, seem to stand up.

Jello has also given me details on widespread corruption in Surrogate Court executor appointments and how they tie in with undertakers and the sheriff's office. A ghoulish business all around, and sickening, to say the least.

There is little doubt that Jello has long been an intermediary between corrupt officials and the underworld. His knowledge is extensive. At present he is a frightened man, and I suppose he has reason for his apprehension. He insists he will be dead in a month after he enters Sing Sing or goes to Rikers Island.

His murderers, he tells me, are a mysterious "they"—this later develops to be politicians and public figures who are engaged in corruption. His point is that they will never allow a no-holds-barred probe of his charges—not in this sensitive election year.

If Jello's charges are substantiated, there is no reason to doubt his fears. Surely such a ring of corrupt officials could not permit exposure of their acts.

I reluctantly agreed with you and Luke, in our discussion of Sunday night, not to turn this information over to a proper federal agency or the local district attorney. I feel a grave responsibility for Benny Jello's life.

I must also caution you about Mayor Gentile's role in these charges. Jello has pointedly told me he has *no* information linking Gentile to any overt act of corruption or malfeasance in office. If Jello's charges are found to be true, Gentile is guilty only of choosing wrong in-laws and not knowing every move and breath taken by the members of his official family. You impatiently dismissed me when I quoted Lord Bryce that America's most conspicuous failure is its biggest cities and the people we elect to run them. However, political ineptitude is hardly an indictable offense. If it was, I am sure our jails would never hold our inmates.

Let us come to an early decision on Benny Jello. I sort of like this little fraud.

KELLY

Attached to the last memorandum were two more sheets labeled:

24

FACTS IN THE SINGER CASE

POLICE REPORT, 19th PRECINCT, DETECTIVE MCFARLAND
AND MOONEY, ARRESTING OFFICERS. SHORT AFFIDIVIT
NO. 456789. DISTRICT ATTORNEY'S
OFFICE, INDICTMENT 453290

At 5:00 A.M., April 17, two armed men, later identified as Aaron and Simon Singer, of 4567 Surf Place, Brooklyn, jumped into the cab of a trailer truck owned by the United States Chemicals, Ltd., with offices in Wilmington, Delaware. The trailer contained lead cases of mercury valued at more than $75,000.

Both men were armed. The driver, José Rodríguez, of Wilmington, was forced at pistol point to drive his truck to Twelfth Avenue and Twenty-eighth Street, where he was pushed from the cab. As he fell, one of the brothers, believed to be Aaron, fired two shots. One grazed Rodríguez's head, and the other tore through his right shoulder. As a result his arm is semiparalyzed.

A night watchman, hearing the shots, looked out his window and saw the driver on the ground. He alerted the police, who arrested the Singers as they fled on foot near the Lincoln Tunnel. Rodríguez later identified them in French Hospital.

The pair was subsequently indicted for felonious assault and grand larceny. Both have extensive criminal records. A study of the docket shows there were numerous postponements of the case. In fact at one hearing, the assistant district attorney, in an exchange with the judge, demanded that the court look into the "maneuverings" of the defendants, as he called it. The judge threatened the assistant with contempt of court.

Several months after their initial arraignment, the police revealed at one of the hearings that Rodríguez, the truck driver, had vanished. The arresting officers told the court they had been informed he had returned to Chile, where he had a commonlaw wife and two children. Although both officers voiced their suspicions that Rodríguez had been paid off, the court did not comment.

Two weeks later the defendants appeared before the court, who agreed to their attorney's request for a lesser charge of assault. The larceny charge was dismissed. The district attorney's office, faced with the loss of the state's chief witness, reluctantly agreed. The assistant demanded that this be noted on the record together with his comments on the court's behavior. There was a further exchange, with the court again threatening contempt.

That afternoon both defendants were arraigned on the lesser charge, and pleaded guilty. The court immediately sentenced them to six months, suspended the jail term, and put them on probation for one year. The assistant again insisted that his comments be placed on the record. This time the judge refused.

Both defendants left with their attorney.

CONFIDENTIAL:

Detective McFarland, now retired and employed by the Pinkerton's National Detective Agency in their Insurance Department, insists off the record that there must have been a "tremendous payoff" in the case.

"We heard all along the Singers had a big rabbi working for them," he said. "Simon is a nitwit, but Aaron is known to have important connections with a Brooklyn district leader. Mooney and I never could pin it down, but Aaron Singer once bet me he and his brother would never spend a day in jail."

Detective Mooney is deceased.

The assistant district attorney in charge of the Singer case refused to discuss it. His only comment was, "It's all water under the bridge."

LUKE

ADDITIONAL FACTS IN OTHER CASES MENTIONED BY JELKOWITZ

Robert Lewis, thirty-two, arrested for fraud, complainant, Pan-Tan Dress Industries, 1780 Broadway: dismissed. Jelkowitz insists the judge received $5,000 for dismissing the case. Police officers agree there was something "smelly" about it. They say the officers of the company and their attorney were indignant about the dismissal. Police and the DA's office say they had an air-tight case.

The Snow Trucks: Jelkowitz alleges Saunders arranged for a Minnesota firm to receive a half-million-dollar contract on snow-removal equipment through rigged bids. In return, Saunders, Remington, and himself shared a $100,000 bribe. For this bribe, Saunders rigged the bids for the city to buy trucks, sweepers, etc., from the Minnesota firm.

LUKE

I put the folder away in my attaché case and had one short nightcap. I was surprised to find it was after eleven. As was my custom, I got into my pajamas, put out the lights, and took a seat by the window that looks out on Eighth Avenue. The theatres had just broken, and the night was filled with cops' whistles, honking horns, and the lilt and laughter of happy people.

I usually enjoy these few minutes, but not tonight. My brain was beginning to spin. If we did take this strange proposition, where would it lead us. To Albany? To Pennsylvania Avenue? To become the laughingstock of Washington, two nitwits striving to turn a dream into reality for an embittered old man who just happened to be as rich as Midas?

I tossed and turned for most of the night. The million-dollar yearly fee and the fantastic expense account could place us both on easy street—but there were other advantages and disadvantages to the senator's proposition. His offer, of course, was an extreme bit of flattery, and sounded as exciting as hell. Didn't Josh say a few times lately, in a casual, almost whimsical way, that now we've elected our clients to every office from city councilman to governor—how would it feel to put a man into the White House?

But on the other side of the coin, there was this boy, so obscure politically that probably half his own constituents wouldn't know him if they passed him on the street. There was also the lack of time. Even if he were known, how could such an important campaign be launched in the brief time left?

Still, there was the Shannon fortune. Not thousands, but millions to spend, and as I've said before, money will help you put a political square peg in a round hole.

But there was something almost as important as money: the information in that red folder. . . .

It gnawed at me so much I kicked off the blankets, turned on the lamp, and went over it again and again. A gray stain was spreading in the eastern sky and the garbage-disposal trucks were growling and clumping on their horrible morning menus when I tossed the folder aside and threw myself on the bed to catch a few winks before I left for the airport.

In my imagination I could almost hear the ticking of the time bomb in that red folder as I dozed off.

I took the earliest shuttle down to Washington, checked in our suite at the Congressional, and started to look for Josh. Our office hadn't heard from him for two days. One of the girls said he had come back from Rhode Island, worked most of a night and a day to finish his report, then left. If I knew Josh, he was on the town.

As usual, I started at the Press Club. Sam the bartender said he had last seen Josh with young Senator Nevins from Florida, and they were both on their way to a wingding thrown by Bea Martinson, the attorney general's wife, who liked gay, young, interesting people.

I caught up with the AG as he was leaving for lunch, and he said he thought Josh had left with a beautiful young blonde, and if I called Bea she would tell me who she was. I found Bea at a tea she was giving for one of her benefits and she said that she had no idea who the blonde was but that for most of the evening Josh had seemed to be edging out the competition.

Over the phone young Senator Nevins, who happens to be a playboy with plenty of money, said he lost Josh after the blonde came in. By four o'clock I had traced them to a small restaurant and motel in Virginia. The owner—who became most cooperative when I told him it was the

White House calling—said he overheard them say they were going on to the Golden Key Club some time this evening.

For me the Golden Key is one of Washington's necessary evils. It's for guests only, one of those dim-lighted, deep-seated places where they bring your private bottle and setups and let you alone to steal the government blind, swing an election, rob each other in a gentlemanly fashion, or seduce your neighbor's wife. In a way it's like those Georgian clubs in London where Lord North's politics and the deadly game of hazard were the only things that mattered in life. In the Key you have Washington politics and roulette. Here, as in Georgian London, men lose their wits over both. In addition to its superb bar, the Key has excellent food, a gambling room, and small private dining rooms. When I was on the congressional committees, the Key was the best place in Washington for making contacts and gathering gossip and tips to all kinds of chicanery.

I called the Key, and Ian, the maître d', told me Josh and his beautiful friend had been sampling the waters for the last few hours and perhaps I had best come and join them for an apéritif and dinner. That's a Limey for you; in other words, Josh was getting stiff with his blonde.

I had been through this before, so the formula was standard; I had a hired limousine and chauffeur drive me over to the Key, and wait. His next guest would be the blonde.

I found them in a corner booth. She was really stunning, a trifle worn on the edges, I thought, but with enough appeal to make the boys at the bar keep looking over.

Before I joined them I studied Josh, perhaps for the first time in years. He is dark-looking, wide in the chin and brow, and with thick black curly hair and dark eyes like the black Irish from the county where the Spaniards from the Armada swam ashore. Well set in the shoulders, although lately I've been warning him that the whisky is showing. He has a nose that had seen trouble in its time—like the lacrosse bat swung by one of those savage kids from that Indian school in the Dakotas where he spent his formative years.

I guess Josh must always be classed with these men who, bored with serenity and stability, rush off to sail uncharted seas in an unpredictable boat; in Josh's case it was politics. Years ago he had left writing a nationally known Washington column to sell—*vend* is his wry term—image making. I have discovered that his confidence can be unshakable, his ingenuity sometimes frightening. Ideas snap from his mind, and while his impatience, temper, even cruelty, over delay or stupidity can be awesome I have found him the humblest of men in the presence of a poor, sodden creature who claimed he once worked with him in some long-forgotten city room. He is the easiest touch in town.

In politics Josh has always ignored the rules of the game, yet after the first burst of anger or resentment, I have seen the most hardheaded machine boss come under his charm and carry out his orders.

He is strictly human in his desires, goals, and weaknesses. In every group—business, war, politics, even religion—there is one man whose subtle genius for organization holds it together—that's Josh Michaels whom I love as a son.

From where I now stood it was apparent there wouldn't be too much trouble this time with his friend. He appeared a bit weary, and while the blonde was leaning forward almost into his drink, he was having trouble stifling a yawn.

Time's been and gone for her, I told myself.

It was the old worn-out routine.

"Mr. Michaels, I have a car outside; he's been waiting for a half hour."

The blonde frowned. "Who's waiting?"

I ignored her, but Josh managed to look stunned. "Lord, I've forgotten! It was for dinner, wasn't it?"

"You know how he is, Mr. Michaels." I gave him a sober look. "He has so much on his mind these days."

By now even the blonde was looking impressed. Josh snapped his fingers.

"Look, suppose your driver drops Miss Reynolds off, and we'll get a lift after I call Senator Nevins."

I gave him a dubious, "Well, I guess that will do. If Miss Reynolds . . ."

Josh leaned over and kissed her, "I'll call tomorrow."

"Who is it, Josh?" she whispered. "Is it—"

"Tomorrow, honey, I'll tell you all about it."

Before she knew it she had her wrap across her shoulders, and I was leading her out the door and into the car.

"I'm sure it must be important," she said, leaning halfway out the window.

"A very grave issue of state," I said. "Very serious."

She gave me a knowing drunken nod and sank back as the limousine gently pulled away from the curb.

"Did you tell her it was the President?" Josh asked me when I returned.

"I never get explicit," I said. "It's more mysterious that way. I'm sure by now she believes you kept the President waiting, and all because of her. Don't tell her otherwise; it would be cruel."

I sat down, and Ian took my order for a Jack Daniels on the rocks. I never could pin it down, but I could swear he sniffed every time I gave him an order. Josh insists it dates back to the time when in a moment of pique I repeated to Ian the old Italian joke that the trouble with England was it had sixty religions and only one sauce. That may be true. A sharp tongue sometimes is an old man's failing.

"I wish you'd get it off your chest instead of giving me that damned injured look," he said. "The truth is, I worked like a horse over the week-end, and jumped when Nevins asked me to go along."

"Good party?"

"Boring as hell. Everyone trying to be young and interesting. Did you see the state chairman in Providence?"

"I flew to Rhode Island twice. The state leaders aren't very happy with our man, but they have promised to go all out. I gave them my word the contributions would come in as he promised."

"Our big pitch is the two shipyards leaving," Josh said, sketching a design in the tablecloth with his stirrer. "I've checked around. One yard will be saved, but the other has to go. The Defense Department never meant two yards to go. They figured that after the initial outcry they would announce one will stay. Our boy will take credit for that. I wrote his speech for this Saturday—"

I shut him off.

"There's something more important than Rhode Island now, Josh."

"Problems?"

"No. A proposition. To elect a governor of New York State and then a President."

He stared at me. "Who gave you the proposition?"

"Senator Shannon. It's his son Kelly. He guaranteed $20,000,000 for the New York campaign. Our fee is a million a year for every year we're with the boy and $600,000 expense account."

The subdued laughter at the bar and the tinkle of ice in the glass were very loud in the stillness.

"Tell me about it," he said, and I did.

It took me over an hour to tell it, and never once did Josh take a sip of his drink or ask a question. When I had finished he leaned back, and the soft whistle came from deep within him.

"That's quite a story, Finn. Why do you think the old man is so eager to get his kid in Albany and the White House?"

"Pride. Ambition. Love of his son. Who knows? Don't forget, he was turned down twice by his party for the nomination. He was a bitter man the last time. But don't have second thoughts about his sincerity. The man wants to go all out."

"When you come down to it, $20,000,000 is a pea in a pod to him," Josh said thoughtfully.

"He admits it. A few oil wells. A few companies. The man has a financial empire."

"What about the stuff they dug up on Saunders? Do you think it will stand up?"

"I believe so. Admittedly they have only scratched the surface. However, buying a New York judge is not new. But—"

"But buying him from the brother-in-law of the mayor of New York, who also happens to be the hottest presidential prospect in the nation, is," he said.

"Let's look at it this way," I said. "Suppose we do develop a big New York scandal."

"Go on."

"Scandals among men in high places in New York are not exactly rare. We could destroy Gentile and make the old man happy, but how would it help the boy become governor?"

Josh gave me a wry smile. "I guess that's what he wants for his million bucks. Do you know Kelly Shannon?"

"No. Somehow we've just missed meeting each other."

"Well, I'm only a nodding acquaintance. He seems like a personable young guy. When he was a freshman I heard he was a bit of a maverick." He shook his head. "But governor—and President!"

"We can turn him down."

"Let's think about it. Do you have any ideas?"

"I always say if you could run Alf Landon and a sunflower, you can run anyone. But I want to see the boy."

"You know the Shannon fortune. And the old man still swings a cat down here."

"Don't forget there are some who still hate him with a passion, Josh. He broke a lot of people when he was running things."

"How long did you work for him, Finn?"

"Four years—four years that made a lot of history."

"Didn't he have that accident when he was trying to get Gentile?"

"He slipped on a marble stairway, and fell. It did something to his spine. He left Washington in a wheelchair, and I don't think he ever got out of it."

"Wasn't he after State at the time?"

"We had been going into the State Department for about three months when he had the fall. Gentile was Undersecretary at the time. He stood up to Shannon and pulled every wire he could to protect his people."

"Did you dig up anything on him?"

"Not too much. We were being fed material by a minor official who had stepped on someone's toes and had been placed in Coventry. He gave us the usual charges of soft policy makers and party-line sympathizers, but nothing concrete. Shannon told me only yesterday that he was getting near to something on Gentile when he had that fall."

"Like what?"

"It appears Gentile favored Chinese ladies."

"That's interesting, but nothing to bring him before a committee."

"That's what I told Shannon. But he filled me in—some of the girls were bringing questionable characters to Gentile's parties—like a Peking propaganda agent. The Bureau had a file on him."

"That's much more interesting. Did he ever do anything about the information?"

"No. He was getting it from a police captain in the DC department with some help from the Bureau. But after he had that fall the investigation was dropped. You know how it is—you only ask for trouble if you go after State or the CIA."

"Wasn't he also having a feud with Tuck Larsen at the time?"

"Larsen knifed him whenever he could in his column or on his TV show. They hated each other. I think it goes back to when we were going into War Assets right after the war, and Shannon refused to go easy on one of Larsen's friends."

"As I recall, Larsen used to call the senator Joe McCarthy the Second."

"He was a hard, ruthless man, but he was no Joe McCarthy," I said. "He never got over the party turning him down twice for the nomination."

"Now he wants to run his son with pots of money in each hand."

"Money is the lubricant of politics, my boy."

"You still need a few other things," he said. "What's the political climate in New York?"

"Gentile is the Republican sure thing. They're counting on him to take the governor's race in a walk. There is no doubt he'll be in the lead for the presidential race."

"That race riot in the school hurt him badly. Four dead kids can't be ignored, Finn."

"That's true, but you know time heals all wounds—even political."

Out of the corner of my eye I saw some shadows moving toward us. Suddenly I was aware of angry voices when they had stopped near the large table that was always neat and pretty with hors d'œuvres. I had started to turn around when there was another sound: a hard slap. One of the shadows spun around and flew across the table. He came down with a crash. Plates, glasses bounced along the deep red rug, leaving trails of deviled eggs, pretty little bread triangles, soft cheese and what have you. I guess it was more of a hard slap than a roundhouse because the fellow on the floor was struggling to his feet, drunkenly dabbing at his expensive suit that was now ready for the best job the cleaners could do. He was immediately surrounded by other shadows, while the one who had done the slapping stood off to one side, looking as though he were ready to continue.

Josh gave a startled grunt, then swung from behind the table toward the lone figure. I was behind him, not knowing what it was all about but ready to join in this blue-blooded Donnybrook.

Josh ignored the one who was trying to brush the food from his tie and jacket; he went straight for the man who stood in the shadows. Two others started for this fellow, but Josh pushed them to one side.

"Get the waiter to clear this up in a hurry," he said to Ian, who had come from the kitchen on the run. Then to the others he had straight-armed he said softly that they had better get their friend the hell out of here before there would be more trouble.

"Get the gentleman's coat, Finn," he said to me. Now, I no more knew than the check girl who this battler was; but before I could ask, a waiter had the topcoat, which I collected. There would never be any hat.

"Good God, did you have to slug him here?" I heard Josh say in a low voice as he helped the fellow into his coat.

The answer was low, almost casual. "I just don't like my father insulted."

"At least I'd wait until he got outside," Josh said. "Who is he?"

"I don't know. I was having a drink with Senator Dolbar when this fellow heard my name and began making cracks. I ignored him until the one about my father."

"Do you have a car?"

"It's in the parking lot next door."

"Good. Let me see if I can straighten out your friend. Good night."

The man peered at Josh. "Well, thanks. Do I know you?"

"Not yet," Josh said, taking his arm and steering him in the direction of the door.

"Perhaps I had better go over and say something."

"I said I'd take care of it," Josh said firmly. "Now go!"

The young man hesitated, then seemed to shrug slightly, and went out.

Ian's team of waiters had the table upright and the carpet cleaned. Most of the food had been brushed from the man's jacket, and Ian was fluttering about him like a mother hen. I also noticed that he kept asking the man for his name and hotel. The man, obviously drunk, kept dabbling stupidly at his tie. His two companions, also loaded, kept up a monotonous string of curses as they pawed at their friend's shoulder.

"I'll take care of him," Josh said.

"I'm sure Mr.—" Ian began.

Josh just stepped in front of him and took the man's arm. "Looks like you fellows are strangers in town."

"South Carolina," one said. "What the hell was the matter with that guy? Jack just said the old senator was the most ruthless son of a bitch he ever met. Nothing new in that."

Josh said, "Look, let me buy you fellows a drink." To Ian, "Let me have their coats."

Their coats were produced as if by magic, and Josh helped them on. I knew Josh didn't have a car, so I told one of the waiters to hail a cab. He returned in a minute and said it was outside. By this time Josh had them laughing; it appeared they were just as happy to leave.

"Take care of Ian," Josh whispered, "before he gets to a phone and tips Tuck Larsen."

"Tips him about what?" I said. "Who is the young John L. Sullivan, Josh?"

"I thought you knew him," Josh said. "That's your Kelly Shannon. We have to move fast. I'll take care of these two jokers. You get on to

Ian." He gave a short, harsh laugh. "And this is the character you want to elect governor of New York State! No wonder his old man wants to pay us a million bucks!"

Then he was gone in a swirl of topcoats, blurred curse words, and jolly good fellowship.

Peace and serenity quickly returned to the Golden Key. At my signal Ian came over.

"I believe this is yours," I said.

It was in my palm, and he went for it as neat as a trout after a fly.

"A hundred, Mr. McCool?" he said. The bastard could see in the dark.

"With this size bill, Mr. Michaels figured you couldn't get change to make a phone call," I said. "Like a phone call to Tuck Larsen, who loves to get these things for his column."

"I never discuss what happens in this club, sir."

"Come off it, Ian," I said. "We know you tip Larsen, and get paid for it." I held off his protests. "Which is fine as long as you don't hurt our friends. Is that clear?"

That white face was iron hard as he started to walk away.

"And just in case you forget and happen to find change," I said, "just remember I know you tipped Larsen to how a certain senator was found by his wife in a motel after he left here. It made quite a story, and the senator will probably lose his election next fall."

He didn't say a word, just turned away. But I knew he would never call Larsen. The funny thing about it is, I never suspected he had tipped Larsen on the raid the senator's wife had made. It was just a shot in the dark, but damn if it didn't hit home.

The next morning, over breakfast, Josh gave me a rundown on what had happened. The two men were simply sales executives in Washington to put in an air force bid. They had been given a courtesy card to the Key by their congressman, who probably was getting some kind of rakeoff. They had been drinking since afternoon and were admittedly potted when they had hit the bar. Somehow one had overheard the name of Shannon. He had been stationed in Washington in the air force at the time of the Shannon hearings and in his drunken way had started to make cracks about the old senator. Kelly had ignored them until the last one.

"They admitted Kelly had ignored them, and twice Senator Dolbar had asked them to shut up; but you know how drunks are—especially in Washington."

"Did they know it was Kelly who slugged them?" I asked.

"No. That's why I hustled them out. They assumed it was just another drunk like themselves. I told them the club had thrown the other fellow out. They liked that."

He looked at me. "And this is the character you want to make President?"

"So he belted a drunk who had insulted his father. I've known a few—"

"My God, he's a congressman!" Josh cried. "Congressmen don't go around belting drunks in a place like the Key!" He glowered at his coffee. "What do you think of him?"

"I didn't see him in the light. That damn place is so dark blind men would love it."

Josh got up and went to the window. It was a beautiful day, and the dome of the Capitol looked like sculptured ice in the clear, cold light.

"I don't think this one is for us, Finn," he said after a while. "I don't care if the old man has a billion dollars to spend. It would be a waste of time." He shook his head. "That damn fool!" As if struck by a sudden thought he whirled around. "Did you take care of Ian?"

"I gave him a hundred," I said, "and told him that if he talked I would tip off a certain senator that he had helped to put in his recent tough spot."

Josh frowned. "What senator?"

"It was a shot in the dark. Just a guilty conscience. I'm sure he won't call Larsen." I joined him at the window. "You're the one who said we should think it over."

"I was half crocked last night when you came in. By the way, thanks for getting me off the hook with Liza. She was all ready to pack her bags and move in. When she calls I'm in London. On NATO business, okay?"

"In the last year, Josh, there seem to be more blondes and more booze. Not that I'm against them—in moderation."

He shrugged impatiently. "No lectures today, Finn."

"Unhappy, are you?"

"Why should I be? I got what I want. I could still be over in the UPI office on rewrite, $180 a week, a wife and a couple of kids, bills, mortgage, driving an old heap and buying out-of-town papers to see who used my by-line."

"I think you're bored."

He turned back to the table, poured a cup of coffee, and stared down into it for a moment. "Maybe you're right, Finn; perhaps I am bored." He put milk into the coffee and stirred it reflectively. "You know, we really haven't had a tough fight in a long time. Oh, I'm not saying they were easy, but the last few times out it seems that after we had the formula set and the machinery going, it was all cut and dried." He took a sip. "Remember when we first started? The only clients we could get were the absolutely hopeless ones, the guys the party had checked off as sure losers. Then came the cover story in *Time* and the *Look* article." He grunted contemptuously, "Image Makers—"

"Well, that's what we are."

"I guess so." He abruptly finished the coffee and put down the cup. "As I see it, we've done all the work necessary for our Rhode Island friend. Suppose you take it all down to Providence to the state chairman. I'm going up to the ranch for a few weeks and get the stink of this place out of my lungs."

"You want me to call the senator?"

"Give him our thanks and tell him we're sorry but we have to pass up this one."

I said, "You're the boss."

"You know there was never any boss between us, Finn. Never was and never will be."

"Maybe it's better this way, Josh," I said. "It could be a great big headache. Don't lose sleep on it. How long will you be gone?"

"Just a few weeks. I'll call you when I'm coming back."

"What plane will you get?"

"I think there's one at five this afternoon. By the way," he said, "did the old man mention Barney Mullady?"

"I brought him up. The senator seemed to think he could handle Barney."

"Did he say how?"

"By making a deal with him or buying him off."

"If he wants this kid to get anywhere near Albany or Pennsylvania Avenue, he'll have to deal with Mullady," Josh said. "He's a no good son of a bitch with bells on, but you can't make a move these days without him."

"He's the new George Washington Plunkett—"

"Plunkett?" Josh gave me a puzzled look. "Who's he?"

"The old Tammany boss. Remember the book I gave you last year? The one I found in that old bookshop?"

"Oh, yes, now I remember. The one written by that *Sun* reporter who took down everything Plunkett said when he was getting his shoes shined. Brother, there was a guy who had an organization! Did they ever catch him with his hand in the till?"

"Never. He was too smart for that. Never bother with the penal code, he said."

"Is Barney as smart as Plunkett?"

"One or two district attorneys tried to nab him, but he laughed at all of them."

"His machine is mostly colored, isn't it?"

"Plunkett had the Irish. Mullady has Negroes, Cubans, and Puerto Ricans. He's put them on welfare, got them appointed assistant DA's, borough presidents, and has been making them the head of Tammany Hall for years."

"The senator better make peace with Barney," Josh said, shaking his head.

"He will. Barney has several construction companies. The Shannon industries are always building. Put the two together and you have a classic example of what George Washington Plunkett called clean graft. Well, Barney Mullady is no concern of ours"—I raised my voice as he was walking into the bathroom—"although you once said you would like to take him on."

"Now, don't try to bait me, you old coot," he called out. "I'll phone you from the ranch."

Then the door closed, and soon there was the far-off hiss of the shower.

Of course I wasn't trying to bait him. There are enough chuckleheaded congressmen in Washington wanting to get reelected without us seeking wild men with dreams of electing their sons President of the United States. Still, something told me . . .

I went down for breakfast, and when I returned there was a note from Josh that he would be having lunch at the Press Club and, later, dinner with Senator Nevins. Two young studs exchanging experiences, I thought.

I spent most of the morning and early afternoon putting together a master report—a report on the survey and vote analysis we did in Rhode Island, the list of loyal county and local leaders and a campaign cost analysis—for the state chairman in Providence. After a sandwich I made my reservation on the afternoon plane and took a break. That hour stands clear in my mind. Twice I had picked up the phone to call Senator Shannon, but each time canceled the call.

Once I had the New York operator, but something made me drop the phone. I did this all day, thinking up excuses why I shouldn't call; then when I saw how late it was I grabbed a cab for the airport, promising myself I would call the senator from Rhode Island.

When I checked in at the airport I found a message waiting for me. It was from Josh. I was to cancel the trip and meet him at the Press Club.

"Mr. Michaels emphasized that you were to meet him in the lobby and not go into the bar until he spoke to you," the clerk said.

"Did he say anything else?"

"He did say to tell you he had been trying to catch up with you all afternoon because he has heard from the Fighting Irishman."

The Fighting Irishman? I stared at the smiling clerk like a ninny; then it came back to me—Josh had to mean Kelly Shannon.

Strange, I wasn't surprised. I guess I had been expecting this development all day. The dark instinct, my mother used to call it, the eerie ability to see the shadows of the future.

Unfortunately, this time my so-called dark instinct didn't tell me the whole story.

The moment I entered the lobby of the Press Club, Josh took me to one side. I was right; it was Kelly Shannon we were meeting.

"I was in Senator Nevins' office exchanging a few notes about the

AG's party when he called," Josh said. "He asked if we could meet him here in the bar."

"But how did he find out it was you?"

"Ian probably made another hundred."

"How did he sound?"

"Young and embarrassed. He sent his apologies to you."

"Accepted. But before we meet him—"

"You mean shall we bring up the old man's deal?"

"Of course. Did he mention it?"

"He said his father had called him right after you had left. So it's no secret. Well, let's go in—"

"You still don't want any part of him, Josh?"

"We'll have a drink and brush him off as gently as we can. He does sound like a nice kid."

"Kid? He's as old as you are."

"Years don't mean anything in our business, Finn," Josh said as we entered the bar. "Who knows better than you? It's all experience."

The Press Club Bar was the opposite of the Golden Key: movement, exuberance, laughter, and light enough to see what the devil you were drinking. We stood at the entrance for a moment, surveying the crowded room, with Josh waving to friends and exchanging insults; then he said, "There he is," and we made our way to a table at the far side of the room.

The man who was standing by his chair was in his late thirties, slender, of medium height, with wavy brown hair, warm brown eyes, and an infectious smile, which as long as I knew Kelly Shannon, always got me off center.

He held out his hand, which Josh took.

"Mr. Michaels?"

"Suppose we make it Josh."

"Fine. Then it's Kelly." He looked at me. "Mr. McCool, I hear you're the brains of this outfit."

"You never said a truer word, Congressman," I said as we shook hands.

"I've been coasting," Kelly said, nodding to his glass. "What will you gentlemen have?"

We gave our orders, then settled back.

"I'm really embarrassed about last night," Kelly said. "Twice over since I found out who you were."

"By the way, how did you know it was us—Ian?" Josh asked.

"Who else?" Kelly said with a grin.

I made a noise in my throat, and Josh blandly explained I was only expressing my great friendship for Ian.

"Seriously, I'm glad Tuck Larsen wasn't having a drink there last night," Josh added. "It would have made quite a column today."

"It was a fool thing to do," Kelly admitted. "But he was making cracks from the moment he came in."

"Just what did he say?" Josh asked.

"Apparently he had been stationed in Washington after the war," Kelly said, "and he was talking about the McCarthy-Army hearings. Then he brought up my father. Once I turned around and told him to forget it, he could read it in the history books, but he kept it up, getting more nasty; then he took off after my father. It wasn't what he said so much as the way he said it."

"What exactly did he say?" Josh asked.

Kelly looked up at him. "He made my father sound like a ruthless old son of a bitch who would frame his mother for stealing his socks, and damm it, he was never that—" He nodded to me. "I'm sure Finn will agree."

"Agreed," I said. "I wouldn't want him on my tail, but he was no Joe McCarthy."

"But he did quite a job on a few people down here," Josh said.

"Most of them needed it," Kelly said.

"They sure did," I said. "I know. I was there."

Josh juggled a few peanuts in the palm of his hand, then threw them in his mouth.

"Well, next time meet them in a dark alley," he said with a grin. "It's too damn expensive to slug them in a club."

"That's a promise," Kelly said laughing. "No more matches in the Golden Key."

"Finn and I have discussed your father's proposition. You're aware of all details, of course."

"The senator discussed it fully with us."

" 'Us'?"

"Luke, my younger brother, and Lacey, my sister. You may recall she was married to Professor Lowell—"

"I remember," Josh said. "There was an accident about four years ago—"

"He was killed near Gallup in a plane crash," Kelly said.

"I remember that," Josh said. "Wasn't it right after he had discovered that Zuñi pueblo?"

Kelly looked surprised. "I thought only the specialists remembered that. Are you interested in archaeology, Josh?"

Josh said laughing, "I'm like Custer—I happen to know a few Indians."

"I guess my father's proposition must sound fantastic to you fellows," Kelly said.

"That it does," Josh said.

"Well, it's nothing new," Kelly said. "It's been my father's dream as long as I can remember."

"But is it your dream, Kelly?" I put in. "That's important."

Both Josh and Kelly turned to me, Josh somewhat surprised, Kelly somewhat thoughtful.

"I'd be a liar if I denied it," Kelly said.

"First governor of New York—then President?" Josh said.

"Far out or not, that's the plan."

"To be perfectly candid, no one knows you outside Westchester County," Josh said, "and maybe not everyone there."

"To be candid, Josh," Kelly said with a smile, "your job would be to correct that."

"But why would you want to be governor—or President? You're a rich man. A congressman. You have a wonderful family, a beautiful home. Why try for jobs that admittedly are the toughest in American politics?"

"Albany is in the mainstream, the heart of the most important state in America—and the crucible for the Presidency. He shrugged. "I know I have all the natural obstacles a man could have: political obscurity, youth, wealth, but my father—and my family—insist I have a chance." He looked at me, and smiled. "I think so too."

"Against the professionals, the machines?" Josh asked.

"Yes. If both of you took me on," Kelly said, "it could be a hell of a fight."

"Interesting, maybe, but with not much of a chance—and I don't go with losers, Kelly," Josh said bluntly.

"Let's get this straight, Josh," was the cool answer: "no Shannon likes to lose."

"In this case it's not what you or anyone else likes. It just happens the odds are against you," Josh said.

"You really think the odds are that much against me?" Kelly asked. "Definitely."

"Is that the reason you're going to turn my father down?"

"Who said we were going to turn him down?"

"You did—not in so many words. But no hard feelings. You would have to be a fool to walk into this one."

"We've walked into worse," I said.

"Not like this, Finn," Josh said impatiently.

"You're right, Josh," Kelly said. "We were only discussing it last night. Lacey said she would bet us all a steak dinner you fellows would turn it down."

"Women should never have been allowed in politics," I said. "It was bad enough when they let them into saloons."

"I keep telling Finn he would have been great in Cleveland's day," Josh said.

"My father always blows his top when Lacey puts in her oar," Kelly said. "But secretly he respects her opinions. She makes a lot of sense most times."

"I think this might be one of those times," Josh said quietly.

"Do you intend to go ahead if we don't take you on?" he asked.

"Definitely," was the cheerful answer. "By next fall there will be more Shannons in American politics than there were Kennedys."

"It sounds like the Shannons stick together."

"Win, lose, or draw. And everyone speaks his or her mind."

"And Lacey doesn't think you have a chance?"

"Not a Chinaman's. But that doesn't make any difference. If we go ahead, Lacey will be one of the hardest workers. As I said, when the chips are down you'll find us all back to back. Like my grandfather used to say, 'It's the only way to fight in an alley or in politics.'"

"Your grandfather was Coal Oil Shannon?" I said.

"Right," Kelly said, nodding. "He lost a leg in the Wilderness, then came back and tried to clean up Tammany."

"Plunkett called him Lace Pants Shannon," I said.

Kelly looked surprised.

"Hey, you know about Plunkett?"

"He knows more about New York politics than five professors," Josh said. "He even got me to read that book on Plunkett."

"Plunkett of Tammany Hall," Kelly said. "It's a fascinating book."

"What did Plunkett say about money, Finn?" Josh asked.

"'I'm in favor of all kinds of money—the more, the better.'"

"We were only saying this afternoon it sounds like Barney Mullady," Josh said.

"There's not much of a difference," Kelly said. "They both manipulated the poor to gain power."

"If you decide to run," Josh asked, "what do you intend to do about Mullady? You know he's one of the most powerful politicians in the country."

"Mullady's a political dinosaur," Kelly said. "He's out of his time."

"He may be," Josh said, "but he still wields a powerful whip. Not only Albany, but Washington jumps when it cracks. The way it shapes up now, he'll be calling the shots at the convention."

"That would be horrible," Kelly said with a shudder. "A man chosen by Mullady running for the Presidency of the United States!"

Josh carefully made a wet circle on the table with his glass.

"Would you make a deal with him?"

"Mullady?" Kelly looked startled. "God, no!"

"Political expediency," Josh said. "You may have to."

"Mullady's not in my plans," Kelly said firmly. "Do you fellows know him?"

"Finn grew up with him on the West Side, so he can tell you all about him."

"Barney will cut your throat if you don't play ball with him," I said.

"Would *try* to cut my throat," Kelly said.

"Oh, he's an expert at it."

41

"It looks like I have to tangle with Barney Mullady," Kelly said with a grin.

"And that's a fact," Josh said. "Well, it's something you'll have to think about. But just as important, Kelly, is how strongly you want to be elected." He leaned across the table. "You know, a man once told me that to be a governor or a President, you must not only want the jobs; you must lust after them. It has to be the only thing in your life. You must love it, fondle it, hold it close to you to the exclusion of everything else. You will have to make deals, compromise, and there will be times when your principles must bend. Is that how you feel?"

"No," Kelly said firmly. "I love politics and I'd be a liar if I told you I didn't want to be President more than anything else in my life. But lust after it, to the exclusion of my wife, my family, my principles, my God? No."

"Then I don't think you'll ever be President of the United States," Josh said quietly.

"I think you're wrong," Kelly said with a smile.

"Perhaps—for your sake I hope so," Josh said.

Kelly held up both hands.

"So now you can see how hopeless this whole thing is. I wouldn't take Mullady's help if he came to me on bended knee. I don't even lust after the job. I'm young; maybe even the people in Westchester County don't know me, and the man I would be running against is intelligent, articulate, and nationally recognized as the Republican's next presidential candidate!" He leaned forward and with mock seriousness whispered, "Gentlemen, my advice to you is run, don't walk, to the nearest exit!"

We all laughed, and Josh waved to the waiter to bring another drink. I wondered what had happened to his quick-brushoff plans.

During the second drink Josh and Kelly argued fiercely about civil rights, housing, and what could be done to straighten out the badly battered poverty program. Then they went into the importance of Stonewall Jackson's tactics to Lee, of the Reconstruction, and the incompetency of the Indian Bureau.

When I looked at my watch, four hours had passed.

"Suppose we have dinner at Ruppert's," Kelly said.

"Fine with me," Josh said. "How about you, Finn?"

Of course it was agreeable to me. I was enjoying not only the conversation but also the gradual change in both Josh and Kelly; they were argumentative as hell and usually at loggerheads, but I had a feeling they now had reached a plateau of mutual respect and liking for each other.

It was about nine o'clock when we came out into the gusty March night. We shook hands and went our own ways in cabs. Josh was silent for most of the ride back to the Congressional. It was only when we reached our suite that he mentioned what was on both our minds.

"Maybe we should take a second look at this one," was all he said.

"Are you thinking of taking—"

"Wait a minute!" he protested. "All I said was maybe we should take another look at the proposition."

"Well, how far should we look?"

"The first thing we have to do is to see this thief Jello, then check his story as much as we can." We walked to the window and stared out over the darkened city. "In the morning I'll call Kelly and tell him to send a telegram to the warden's office notifying him we're coming up to see Jello. He can tell them at the jail we're members of his law firm or any story like that."

"And suppose we believe Jello's story?"

"Then I think we should go back to the senator and tell him we'll look into the proposition further—politically, that is. We can go to New York and sniff the air for a few days. Maybe even have Dyke Short and Frank Shea do a poll on the governor's race and in addition try to find out what kind of man they want for their next President. Then we'll stop in and see Sissy Southworth."

"That drunken bitch!"

"Finn, I'm surprised!" he said, smiling as he turned from the window. "Sissy always spoke well of you."

"That's one hell Dante didn't invent—waking up in the morning and finding her next to you. Do we have to see her?"

"Oh, I know you dislike her, but Sissy and her television show and column are important. Twenty million families every Sunday night and a combined circulation of five million readers! And she likes you, Finn. She once told me you were a miserable old bastard—coming from Sissy that was an accolade."

"I suppose I should be a good Christian and remember to 'bear ye one another's burdens.' "

" 'And so fulfil the law of Christ,' " said Josh warmly. "Well," he added, getting up, "the first thing I had better do is read the stuff on Jello. Then suppose we both go down to Providence tomorrow, see our candidate and the state leaders, give them all we have, then go up to that pen and talk to Jello ourselves."

CHAPTER TWO: THE MAN ON THE THIRD TIER

ELMER MOORE, THE WARDEN OF PENSVILLE PENITENTIARY on the southern boundary of Westchester County, was a young bullyboy in his late thirties with a blond crew cut, a professional smile, and dead fisheyes. He leaned back in his swivel chair and blew gently on the card Josh had just given him.

"I thought Kelly Shannon was Jello's attorney," he said.

The way he said it, I knew he didn't like the Shannons. Josh also sensed it, and played it that way.

"The boy never tried a case in his life," he said. "That's why the firm thought we should come up."

"That's what I hear, Counselor," Moore said. "They say the old man bought his diploma."

"Could be true, Warden," Josh said briskly. "Too damn many young kids running after ambulances these days. When can we see this bum?"

"That's just what your client is, Counselor, a bum!" Moore said roughly. "A no-good, widow-conniving bum! All the son of a bitch has given me is trouble. That old Jew broad he's been romancing, what the hell's her name? Oh, Shapiro. She's been on my back every day. She even called the sheriff and said I was threatening him." He opened and slammed shut a drawer. "The fat little bastard."

"Look, Warden, we don't want to make any trouble for you," Josh said fervently. "Just between us, the only reason I'm taking his case is because some of his friends are putting up some dough."

"Why the hell did the Shannon kid ever get into this?" Moore asked.

"Jello's girlfriend is a neighbor of the Shannons, as I understand it," Josh said. "She met the kid and got him to take the case."

"Well, I guess it's okay."

Josh reached over and held out his hand.

"Thanks again, Warden."

I knew that inside Josh's palm was a crisp century note. The dead fisheyes looked up.

"I'll get him down, Counselor." He touched a buzzer and a guard came in. "Bring Jello down to the lawyers' room. He's on the third tier." He dismissed us with, "Let me know if I can do anything."

"We'll sweat that guy on the witness stand," Josh whispered. "Don't turn on the jammer until we see Jello. They may have an electric eye to pick up any sound equipment."

In the attaché case I was carrying was a small electronic device that sent out a powerful jamming signal to render conversation unintelligible if it was recorded. Both Josh and I were sure the jail's attorney room was undoubtedly bugged, so I brought along the jammer just in case. There is nothing hush-hush about the device; it can be bought in an electronics store for less than a hundred dollars. But in Washington it's a way of life.

The attorney's room was large and sun-splashed. Through the closed barred windows came the distant sound of traffic. We sat behind a long table, and waited. I placed my attaché case next to the table leg and reached in to turn on the switch. A few minutes later a guard swung open the door and Jello walked in. He was a squat, fat man with sagging cheeks and heavy jowls. His deep-set, wavering eyes glittered with fright like a treed fox's; nicotine-stained fingers nervously toyed with a heavy diamond ring on his pinky. His skin was virtually devoid of color. In fact, his whole face reminded me of a well-kneaded pan of dough left by a harassed housewife.

"Mr. Jello, we're from the Washington law firm Mr. Shannon engaged to consult on your case," Josh said. "I'm Mr. Michaels and this is Mr. McCool, my partner." He stared up at the guard, who was hovering nearby. "Do you want to join us, Officer?"

"It's my job," the guard began, but Josh leaned over and shook his hand. "There's a magazine over in the corner, Officer. Why don't you catch up on your reading? We're not going to give him any hacksaws today."

The guard slipped the fifty in his pocket, and grinned.

"Okay, Counselor. Just give me the word when you're finished."

Jello watched the guard as he walked across the room and picked up a magazine. Then he turned back to us. I thought I saw a glitter of respect in his tiny eyes.

"What's the idea?" he whispered. "Where's Mr. Shannon?"

"We're working with him. Did you get Kelly's wire?"

"Yeah, I got it last night. But what's the pitch?"

"Take it easy, Benny; we're on your side. We're from Washington."

Benny swallowed hard. "The Bureau?"

"We're not feds," Josh said. "We're working with Shannon on a committee." He added swiftly, "It's the only way you're going to get out. The DA's ready to send you up. And they'll burn you up there. Right?"

Benny gripped Josh's wrist. His mouth formed the words, "The place is bugged."

Josh smiled and leaned over to him. "Look into that attaché case when my partner opens it."

I casually lifted the case onto the table, opened it just enough for Jello to see the small black plastic case, took out some pencils and a yellow pad, and made some motions as though to take notes.

"It's a jammer," Josh said. "They can have fifty bugs, and they won't register."

I could almost see the pudgy little body relax.

"After the last time the kid was here I got the word they were bugging this room. What do you guys want?"

Josh said, "Everything. We want everything you have on the Saunders payoff and the judge." Josh's voice was cold. "Lie to me and I'll throw you to the wolves. Play ball and I'll get you out of here."

"Guarantee?"

"Absolutely. If we take you on as a witness, you'll have congressional protection. I'll have you sent down to the federal pen on the West Side."

Jello smiled. "The country club."

"But for that, Benny, we want everything. Right from the beginning.

Names. Dates. Places. I want you to describe the inside of offices, homes, everything."

"You want independent collaboration, right?"

"You got it. We have to prove your story is as good as the Pope's."

"Kelly isn't dumping me? I trust that kid with my life. I told Molly—"

I broke in: "Kelly said he was seeing Molly this morning. He wanted to make sure you knew he was still your attorney."

He slowly twisted the diamond ring several times.

"Maybe I'm a *schlomozel*, but if Kelly says so, I'll go all the way."

Josh leaned across the table, and whispered: "You have to go all the way, Benny. If you don't they're going to get a judge to hit you with the book. And when you get up there, they'll be waiting. I wouldn't trust this warden with ten dollars in Confederate money."

"He's a no-good son of a bitch," Jello whispered, first casting a quick glance in the direction of the guard, who was idly skimming through a picture magazine. "He's milking me dry. Ten bucks here, twenty there. He's got his hand out every morning and night. Ask Molly. She gave him fifty only yesterday."

"Do you want to get out of here?"

"Are you crazy?"

"Well, Benny, start talking."

We stayed all that morning and returned in the afternoon. It was the same the next day and the next. Every morning and afternoon we greased the warden and the guard. They were so greedy they were stupid. We could have walked away with the bloody jail if we'd wanted. By the third day we were so accepted the guard automatically put out his hand, took the fifty, and left us alone. Once Jello warmed up he never stopped. He told us the most incredible story of crime, criminals, and official corruption that I have ever heard. I took it down in shorthand as verbatim as possible, and had it typed by Alice.

Later, newspapers here and abroad made much of Jello, that funny and so tragic figure in the events to come. But I believe he never told his story as well as he did in the lawyers' room of the Pensville Penitentiary. Here is Jello's story as I took it down. Ironically, it was Jello who suggested the title. When I asked why he called them "happy days," he shrugged and said that any day a thief is beating the law and milking a sucker is a happy day.

CHAPTER THREE: THE LIFE AND HAPPY DAYS OF BENNY (PAY BIG) JELLO

I'VE BEEN IN THE RACKETS most of my life, since I was fifteen, in fact. I've never been a man with a rod; the confidence game is my line. I've sold goldbricks, phony diamonds, gold-plated brass, mink that ran in the first rain, and so on. There isn't a confidence game I don't know—or didn't invent. At one time I had an organization—I don't like the word "gang"—of more than fifteen of the best swindlers in the country. It helped to give me fifteen of my thirty-two arrests and made me a three-time loser.

It also gave me the know-how to pull a fix with cops, prosecutors, politicians, and judges.

One of the biggest rackets I ran was fur hijacking. This is the way it worked. The furs we used were always stolen. When we had a sucker, like we say in Yiddish, a *schlomozel*, one of our "salesmen" would approach him. We would never select him unless he had lots of coin and was on the make for a fast buck. The salesman would inform the buyer he knew someone who had a truckload of hot furs that he could have for half their value. The customer would be brought to a warehouse in some suburban town or city to examine the furs. How many times have I seen the greedy bastards lick their chops! The deal would be made, the money paid in cash, and he would set out in a car, following the truck to New York. I would be in the truck.

Somewhere along the backroads, suddenly there would be a roadblock. Searchlights would be flashed on, cops with guns would appear, whistles would shrill, and shots would even be fired.

"It's the cops!" my driver would cry. He would spin around on a dime. When he saw the cops running toward the car, blowing whistles and firing shots, the sucker would be frozen with visions of being put in jail. My boys always put on a great show; they would shout to the sucker to duck on the floor, and then they would weave back and forth across the roads with lights out, like a movie chase. They would usually drop the sucker off at a New York bus station and warn him to keep his mouth shut. We even had phony newspaper clippings printed which we mailed to the sucker, telling how the local cops had grabbed a big ring of New York fur racketeers and how they were held in fantastically high bail. The sucker never blew the whistle to the cops; he was usually glad not to be in jail. The "cops," of course, were my boys dressed in uniforms which we rented from a theatrical agency. The guns were blank.

Well, it didn't work all the time. Once a New York furrier, who had more brains than I gave him credit for, jumped out of the car and hid in a field. He waited, then sneaked back to his spot in the road to see me and the so-called cops laughing like hell. He knew he had been taken, and went to the DA.

That's when I put in my first big fix. I paid off the furrier and the local prosecutor in Jersey for a few grand. In fact, after that I put the local police force of that small Jersey town on my payroll. It was so good I even used their jail to pull a few stunts. Whenever I received a beef from a sucker I had swindled by using the paper-in-the-vault trick, I had one of my organization bring the customer over to Jersey to the local jail. Then I was brought into the warden's office, ostensibly a prisoner. This always shocked the customer. All I had to do was remind the customer I had not turned his name over to the local prosecutor who was dunning me for his name. That ended the beef. After the customer ran like a thief back to New York, the warden and I had a few drinks and then I paid him a century note for the use of his office.

I also discovered that it was very easy to buy witnesses. On one occasion I bought eight, all from Coney Island, to beat a case in which I couldn't buy off a cop who had grabbed me on a larceny charge.

The day of trial came, and the courtroom looked like Coney Island. Popcorn men, candy hawkers, guys who sold bathing hats, caps, and pennants, even concession men swore I had been out there at the time the cop said I had pulled a diamond switch on some jeweler. I beat the case, but it cost me more than paying off that dumb cop.

For the next five or ten years I moved about in New York, Las Vegas, Hollywood, Detroit, and Chicago, organizing swindling gangs, putting in fixes of all sorts, and gradually getting to be known as Benny Pay Big.

[At this point in his narrative, Jello went into an elaborate description of the many swindling rackets he had worked about the country: the Gold Dust Switch, the Diamond Fraud, the Bag Switch. He also described his jail terms, one in Sing Sing for manslaughter when two men died in a bar he owned. Jello insists "competitors," as he called them, slipped a bottle of wood alcohol into his stock. Most of his jail sentences were a year or less. Jello claims the "lower the sentences, the more it cost."]

After my last term in Sing Sing I was determined to walk on the right side of the road. One more rap and they would throw away the key under the Baumes Law. I was a three-time loser. I had a nice pile laid aside, so I opened an elaborate Polish restaurant. It became quite a place in midtown, and later I turned it into a Polish discotheque. It sounds funny but it caught the public fancy. It was in the columns, and the so-called Polack Hop was put on by four beautiful Polish girls, buxom as hell and with beautiful blond hair. They were kids from a Pennsylvania mining town, but I never took advantage of them. One even married a

Connecticut stockbroker who had just come in for a night on the town. I think she has two kids now. I still get Christmas cards from her.

Of course, being an ex-con I couldn't get a liquor license, but I had a front. Though I was going straight, I just couldn't shake the people I had known all my life.

After a time I became a sort of official referee for underworld feuds, and then I got to know more and more political figures, a fixer on a big scale. I knew judges, county leaders, out-of-town prosecutors, people big in Washington—and just about everyone worth knowing in the underworld. From the punks to the big boys who never dirty their hands with the Penal Code.

Now I come to the meat and the coconuts, as they say, that is, the Saunders payoff in the Singer case and my relations with Federal Judge Tucker. I will take one at a time.

The Singer matter started this way: One night I was in my office when the girl came in and said a man named Mr. Noodles was outside. I almost broke out laughing. I knew this was Sammy the Noodle, a guy I hadn't seen since Sing Sing. Sammy Feinberg was called this not only because he loved noodles but because he looked like one, thin and flat. But he was a regular *mensch*, and one of the best con men I had ever seen since Little Britches.

As I said, I never turned my back on my friends, so I called in Noodles. We had a lot of laughs about the old days, and then he came to the purpose of his visit. He had two nephews, his sister Jennie's kids, named Singer, Simon and Aaron, both from Surf Place, Brooklyn, who were in trouble. I had heard of them and knew they were rough stickup men, and I told this to Noodles. But he put on a show that his sister was dying of cancer and I had to help him. I should have known he was putting me on, but I fell for it. I guess that's what comes from not being in practice.

He said the Singers had hijacked a truckload of mercury worth $75,000 at Twelfth Avenue and Twenty-eighth Street and had shot the driver. A night watchman tipped the cops, and they were nabbed by a radio car. They were subsequently indicted by the New York County Grand Jury for grand larceny and felonious assault and held without bail because of their previous record.

Noodles said they tried to put in a fix but they couldn't get to the right people. The judge they knew was on the take but wouldn't deal unless through the right connections.

I asked Noodles how much they had to spend, and he said the family had a wealthy produce business and would go for $20,000. Well, that was big coin, so I said I would see what I could do. Noodles said there would be five in it for me. Now, there was no need for me to want the dough, but I guess I'll always have larceny in my heart, so I agreed to take that much.

The next day I called up an attorney named Trevor Remington, who we called the "Judge" because he was once appointed as an interim magistrate for six months. I got to know Remington when he started to come into my place with a few political big shots. Once when an eager beaver ABC agent put a rap on my place when he found a high-class call girl at the bar—I didn't even know it—Remington fixed it for $3,000 so my front wouldn't have a violation against him. Since then Remington has pulled a few fixes for the boys who come in when they are warned the court is ready to hit them with the book or the cops won't play.

[Trevor Remington has offices at 521 Fifth Avenue, and lives with his wife, a former showgirl named Claire Greenway, at Briarcliff Terrace, Darien, Connecticut. His unlisted phone is AA 7-4346. His office number is WZ 7-6556-7-8.]

When I saw Remington he said it could be done through Charlie Saunders, Mayor Gentile's brother-in-law. Frankly, I was amazed. Saunders, he said, could fix anything in town from an ABC license to a murder rap. Only money talked. In fact, while I was there Remington called Saunders and made a luncheon appointment that day for the "21" Club.

[Jello says Remington called CY 4-6112 and asked for Saunders, whom he reached immediately. This is not the City Hall number but a private number. Jello recalls it because Remington asked the girl to get the number. Jello wrote it down as soon as he left the office.]

Three days later Remington came in and said he had reached Saunders and made a deal for the $25,000, the lowest he would touch it for. I asked Noodles, and in two days he was back with the okay from the family.

I recall it was the day before Christmas that Noodles and I took a cab to Remington's office. Noodles had the cash in a valise and we had counted it out on my desk. I insisted on Noodles coming with me to Remington's office. Somehow, for the first time in my life I felt uneasy on a deal. We were ushered into the office, and Remington came out. He shook hands with Noodles and only asked me in. I gave him the valise, and he opened it and counted the money. I remember he looked up and said with a smile, "It's not that I don't trust you, Benny, but let's do it businesslike."

I said okay, but insisted that he come out and tell Noodles that he had got the dough. Noodles, an old con man, might be suspicious, and those Singers were hard-nosed punks and no guys to mess with. Remington did as I wanted. He came out and told Noodles he had received his fee and would file the writ first thing after Christmas. I guess this was a show for the girl in the office.

[The secretary, Jello says, is a blonde Remington calls Nancy. She is about five feet three and is very pretty. Jello thinks she knows quite a bit.]

I forgot to mention that before we left, Remington called that number and told Saunders he had the fee and asked if he would like to share a Christmas drink at "21." From the way he laughed, I guess they had that drink.

I left Noodles and went back to the club. Two weeks later Noodles called and said the Singers had been moved to a better cell on the Island and it looked like the fix was in.

I didn't hear anymore about it until one day Noodles called me and said the kids had taken a plea for a lesser charge and had been sentenced to a year but were let off with time served and put on probation for one year. He was very happy, and said they sent their thanks.

Well, after that, Remington and I did a few things together. I fixed a case through him with a judge for another guy Noodles brought in who had been bagged on a larceny charge. This was a guy named Doxy who owned a dress house and was desperate for money. He pulled a con game with goods but was an amateur and was grabbed. It cost his father-in-law ten grand to get him off the hook. The case was dismissed in Magistrate's Court for lack of evidence. This time not only the judge was reached but the two detectives.

[Jello believes the judge was Magistrate Lamont, and the arresting detectives, Cranks and Lagraw of the Twenty-third Precinct.]

Another big case I took care of through Remington and Saunders was the Blitz Brothers in East Harlem. They ran a policy operation, and were nabbed by the commissioner's Confidential Squad. It was in all the papers how they operated a $10,000,000 ring. It cost them fifteen grand to get off. They took a plea to operating a lottery, a felony but the judge gave them an SS. There was some noise about this one, but it soon died out. That's what gets me: the people in this city get mad as hell one day, and the next day they forget about it. Then they cry about the terrible conditions in the city. Hell, they're to blame. If they want thieves to run their city, they'll have to expect they'll be robbed blind.

But one of the biggest deals I pulled with Remington was the snow trucks we sold to the city. This is really funny. It's hard to believe, but this is the way it started.

One night a group of dress salesmen came in for a good time. It's some guy's birthday. One was the son of a man I knew from the old days, and we got to talking. His name was Manny Summers. I think his house is Paris Best, somewhere in the garment center.

Suddenly this guy gets up and walks to the phone booth. When he comes back he's excited and insists he wants to see me alone. It seems he was having lunch with his cousin, a guy named Stu Saxon, who is working in Minneapolis for a trucking firm, and this cousin was telling him how their head salesman was complaining he couldn't make a sale to the city because he couldn't reach the right people. He said he called his cousin to come down, that maybe I could help him.

Well, the cousin turned out to be a smart kid. He got his boss on the phone—his name is Ken Beering—and persuaded him to come to New York to see me. This Beering guy came in and we had a meeting, and it turned out Beering wanted to sell the city half a million dollars' worth of snow-removal trucks. This guy laid it on the line: $100,000 would be split any way we wanted if the deal went through.

The next day I'm at Remington's office. He jumped when he heard this figure and had Charlie on the phone in five minutes. Only, this time I insisted I meet Charlie. Charlie agreed after a lot of talk, and now I was at "21" having lunch with Saunders. I even bought one of their great cookbooks. I don't think he said three words, just listened. Remington, of course, didn't come out and say anything about dough; he kept talking about his fee, which would be $100,000 for all kinds of writs, searches, and so on. Charlie just nodded, and that was all.

Frankly, I don't think Remington told Saunders who I was; that man looked much too smart to be seen in "21" with an ex-con. But that's what the smell of big money can do for a man with larceny in his heart. Remington just turned stupid.

This deal took time. It went on for about a month. This fellow Beering kept flying in, I kept delivering messages to Remington, who kept calling Charlie Saunders. Then one day I got a call from Remington. The deal had gone through. Beering came in with the dough in cash. I locked the door of my office and we spread it out on the desk. I had never seen so much coin in my whole life.

We took one of the regular cabdrivers who hung out in front of my place, a guy named Louie, to Remington's office, and went in. The valise was simply left on the desk. Remington took it into another room, closed the door, and we waited. In about a half hour he was back, all smiles.

"Thank you, gentlemen," he said, and shook hands. Then to me he said, "Benny, I'll drop down to the club next week."

Outside, Beering, the salesman, and I shook hands, and left. But on a hunch I stayed in the lobby for a while. It was a good hunch; within the hour Charlie Saunders came out. He looked satisfied.

The following week Remington came down and paid me off: $15,000. Out of this I had to take care of the kid salesman and his cousin, who made the first connection. I took care of them with three grand. I broke it down with small bills, and to the kids it looked big. But didn't one make a beef and try to find out what I got! I think the young people today expect too damn much.

I pulled off two more cases with Remington, a case involving a hood named Cummings, who was arrested robbing the Park West Jewelry Shop on Park Avenue, and Joe Americus, who wanted an SLA license. It cost Cummings five grand to get an SS, and Joey was nicked for fifteen grand.

[Robert Cummings, age twenty-eight, an admitted narcotics addict, is now in Dannemora, Jello says. He was arrested three months ago as the cat burglar who robbed many midtown hotels.]

[Joseph Americus is an old-time mobster with a long record. Jello says Remington arranged for a front to get the license for Americus's club, which is the Diamond Tower on Forty-seventh Street, off Park Avenue.]

It was through Remington that I met Judge Prebel Tucker, Chief Justice of the Federal Court of Appeals. I guess it sounds strange that a punk like me could know a big man like Judge Tucker, but sex and greed are great equalizers.

Let me explain: One day Remington came down to the club, and seemed ill at ease. He had been drinking heavily lately, and I knew that wife of his was on his back. Why he never kicked her out was beyond me. But that's what happens to a man who is hooked by a dame. In this case she was meaner and more of a thief than her husband. I knew from Joey Americus she was shacking up with a guy named Francis who owns a club on East Sixty-eighth Street.

You might ask why did Remington, a big Fifth Avenue lawyer, come down and cry on my shoulder? Well, I guess it was the question of being thick as thieves. Maybe he felt we had to trust each other, like hanging together or swinging separately, so he came to me. Besides, the guy drank like a fish, and I never hit him with a bill.

Remington at last got it off his chest. He said he wanted to get next to an old judge named Tucker, who was Chief Justice of the Federal Court of Appeals, a real big man. Through another lawyer he had got word that the old judge could be bought, but only by a few guys. He was very, very careful. The lawyer told him the one way to the judge's heart was dough. It seems the judge just loved to make money. He was always playing the market, and lately he hadn't been doing too good. This guy also told Remington another way to get to know the judge was through dames—it seemed the judge had funny tastes in sex.

Remington asked me if I was interested, and I said why not? He said okay, then he would start maneuvering. He first got in touch with this lawyer who had tipped him off, and we had a few meetings. This guy didn't buy me, but later he met again with Remington, who came back to me and said the lawyer was going to put him close to the judge for a cut of any action that might result from this contact. I think they had agreed on something like 2½ percent.

Remington's lawyer friend then set up the judge. There was a lot of fencing around at first, but gradually they came to talk turkey. This took about two months. Remington said he finally got the judge where he wanted him; this was a day after the judge had a very bad time in the market. He was also financing some new kind of real estate on the Palisades, those big high-rise apartments, and this wasn't going too well. Remington said the judge was the greediest he had ever met—and this guy certainly has met a lot of that kind in his life. Gradually Remington brought around a case involving a big hotel corporation that was going into receivership. It was one of the biggest and oldest in the country, but there had been internal fighting, and the thing was in danger. Remington said he had a tremendous setup planned for us: we would milk the thing and sell the hotel's glassware, rugs, and all that stuff through companies we would own with the judge. As a receiver, and with the judge's okay, this could look like improvement to help a property that went into the millions. It sounded a little too big for my appetite, but I went along. Remington said the judge had agreed I was in with a cut of the loot. I was to act as a sort of link between the judge and Remington or anyone else we had to deal with.

Remington said he wanted to celebrate and we should do it at my club. I said okay, and he winked and said we should have something to make the judge happy. I knew what he wanted: he wanted queer stuff for this old bastard. He kept at me, so I agreed to try and set something up. I contacted a few creeps I normally would have kicked out of the club and let them know what I was looking for. I had to take a lot of kidding, but finally I found a pimp who made a contact with a dame on Central Park West.

The place was a new so-called masseuse parlor. I went up there with this pimp and saw the dame that owned it. She was big as a horse, a German. I could speak the language, so we hit it off. Then she showed me around. There was everything there: whips and chains and mirrors on the walls—everything. I told Remington from now on he would have to do the dealings with Eva—that was the madam's name. He said he would. Later he told me he gave her some money. He thought she would come in handy for other "projects," as he called them.

One night Remington and the judge came to the club. I made sure the old bastard was surrounded by dames. He's a little guy with thin gray hair and a very dignified manner—until he gets a load on. Then he's all hands where the dames are concerned.

It was about midnight when I saw Remington lean over and whisper in the judge's ear. The way the old man was acting, you could see what he wanted. He smiled and nodded and they left. The next day Remington came down to see me—we were in. The judge went through the whole queer bit, and loved it. Even Remington looked sick when he went into the details.

[Mme. Eva Schmidt, Masseuse, 180 Central Park West, unlisted office phone, CH 4-7760; office, CH 4-4532. She lives in the penthouse on the northeast corner of Eighty-ninth Street and East End Avenue. Unlisted home phone: BE 7-3922. Jello recalls she is tall, very blonde, with blue eyes. She speaks with a decided German accent. She told Jello that she was a registered nurse and that she came from Hamburg, where her family was wiped out in the Allied bombing, and has been here since 1955. Once lived in Washington where she had a "lot of customers."]

That was two years ago. From then on, Remington and I were always swinging cases to the judge. The judge never took money. Remington fixed it so we had a phony company with the judge as an officer.

[Transcontinental Trading Corporation, 14 Stone Street, of which Judge Tucker, Jello, and Remington are the stockholders. The bribes they took were put into the corporation and paid out as loans to Jello, Remington, and the judge.]

Frankly, I forget some of the cases we swung to the judge. Some were big, some small. Needless to say, I was rolling in dough. I can tell you I have a well-filled safe-deposit box in Switzerland—and that's where I'm going if I ever get out of here.

Last winter I met Molly and made up my mind I was getting out. But it wasn't easy. Remington hit the roof and made all sorts of threats. But I told him to go to hell. That's when they put this frame on me with this furrier. So help me God, I never met the guy. It's a complete frame. Molly will tell you that ever since I met her I was either at the club or at her place. Weekends we would go up to Grossinger's. With all the dough I got, do you think I would mess with a cheap punk furrier I wouldn't have touched twenty years ago?

CHAPTER FOUR: THE PEOPLE WHO MAKE THINGS
                 GO ROUND

JELLO'S MANNER after the first few hours showed how frightened he was. We discovered he had a phenomenal memory, and he insisted many times he would do anything to get out of the pen.

After we had seen Jello, we checked his story as much as we could without exciting any suspicion or alerting anyone; through Josh's contacts at New York Police Headquarters we checked Jello's criminal record, the police reports on the Singer robbery, and the final disposition of the case in the DA's office. We also checked the insurance company, and an investigator told us in an off-the-record interview that there had to be a payoff in the Singer case. Long before the case had been disposed of, he said he had heard whispers that the Singers had "something going for them downtown."

But to prove it? He shrugged, and threw up his hands.

This, combined with the work Kelly's staff had done, only confirmed my suspicions; there was one devil of a scandal wrapped up in the report in that red folder.

"I agree it could be one hell of a bombshell," Josh said. "But how will it help Kelly?" He hit the palm of one hand with his fist. "What we have to do is use this stuff to create an image for him not only for New York but nationally."

"You sound like you're interested."

"Let me say—just slightly. A lot will depend on the political climate. First we have to see the people who make things go round."

"Like who?"

"Your old pal Max Dregna, the Great Liberal. Sissy—"

"How about the senator?"

"Oh, we'll see him."

"When?"

"Tomorrow. Call him in the morning and tell him we'll be down early. Before we leave, let's stop in to see Shea and Short. I want them to get started on that poll. Even if we don't take the proposition, the results will be interesting."

I called the senator in the morning, and he told us to come down anytime. On the way to the airport we stopped in at the office of Popular Opinion, Inc., the polltaking headquarters of Frank Shea and Dyke Short, the biggest, the best, and the most reliable pollsters in the nation.

We were one of their best customers, and had been since they started. In fact, I think we gave them their first big contract. They were a perfect team, Dyke Short, who fitted his name, was barely five five, a calm, almost glacial intellectual, while his partner, Frank Shea, was a huge, hearty, jovial bear. They had adjoining offices; Dyke's had books, and Frank's the bar. I guess that sums them up.

Popular Opinion, Inc., occupied the entire fifth floor of the Wentworth Building in downtown Washington. Dyke's and Frank's offices were in the front along with the desks of their secretaries and a few clerks. A heavy door marked "Private" hid the banks of enormous IBM's and the rows of glass-partitioned stalls with men and women with earphones, who not only did the polltaking but also took in the results of the street questioning. Their offices were in every major city in the country. Lately they had opened offices in West Germany, France, London, and the Scandinavian countries for their business clients, who relied heavily on the results they compiled about everything from political climate and candidates to a new perfume.

Dyke and Frank were in Dyke's office, and when my name was announced they both came out as usual, Frank with a bear hug and Dyke with a firm handshake.

Back in Dyke's office they sat and listened as I outlined what we wanted.

"No candidate's name yet, Finn?" Dyke asked.

"Not yet. There may be soon," I said.

"Just between friends," Frank said, and winked, "the Republicans are polling."

"For what?" I asked innocently.

Dyke said with a cool smile, "You asked it as though you would expect us to give it to you."

"Not a hint?"

"No. But put yourself in the Republican high command—whom would they be polling for?"

"But Gentile doesn't need any polls," I said. "He's the only Republican on the scene who amounts to anything."

"Just for the hell of it, Finn," Frank boomed, "let's put down Gentile's name in your poll."

Dyke said, "By all means."

Frank mimicked and held out an imaginary pad. "Now, Madam, just how do you rate Felix Gentile as Mayor of New York City? How do you think he will do as governor or President?"

"And let's get one or two reasons, Frank," Dyke said quickly. He turned to me. "I'm thinking of that riot in Brooklyn."

"It's almost two years, Dyke," Frank said.

"Four kids killed," Short said. "That takes a lot of forgetting."

I said, "If something else came up, it might knock him out of the box."

They both looked at me.

"It certainly wouldn't do him any good," Dyke said. "But first let's see what the poll brings out."

"Fine." Though I turned down Frank's plan to join him in a drink, as I stopped at the door I reminded them that this poll had to be on the house.

Frank growled. "Since when did we ever ask you for any dough?"

"Josh said it's because you always got paid on the first of the month."

"I think Josh has a point there," Dyke said dryly. "Look, we'll be in touch."

We arrived in New York at 10:00 A.M., and a few minutes after eleven we were ushered into Senator Shannon's office. He was just the same as I had left him. Instead of a week it could have been an hour ago that I had walked out of the door of his office. He waved us to a chair and nodded to the teapot.

"Tea, gentlemen?"

We said we would have some, and he poured. A few tentative sips, polite comment on the weather, then he got down to business.

"Well, are you interested?" he asked Josh.

"I'm interested but I'm not ready to make a commitment, Senator," Josh said. "Not yet."

The old face twisted into a frown. "Why not? You want more money? You name your terms."

"It's not money—it's politics. Not all the money in the world will help elect Kelly if the time isn't ripe!"

"Don't worry about the time; I know it's right. I've been waiting for years for the right time and the right opportunity. Now we have both."

"You mean Jello?"

"Of course. What do you think of him?"

"He's a thief," was Josh's blunt reply. "A God-damned little thief who would steal his mother's store teeth."

The senator leaned forward. "I wouldn't give a damn if he was Lucifer's handmaiden. All I want from Jello are the facts he has—the facts he can testify to." He slammed his hand down. "That's what I want!"

"There's no doubt you can get that," Josh said. "Like all informers, he's ready to do anything to get out from under."

"Did you check any of his story?"

"We checked as much as we could. There's no doubt a good part of what he's telling is the truth."

"What about you, McCool?" the senator said to me. "You're an old pro. What's your opinion?"

"The same as Josh's. Jello is mostly telling the truth."

The senator leaned back. "Well, what do we do about it?"

"Nothing for the moment," Josh said. "The next thing we intend to do is test the political weather. But I want to make sure, Senator, you realize we haven't accepted the proposition yet."

"Well, dammit, how long will you take to make up your minds?"

"Just as long as it takes to tour the state for a few days. I'm having a poll made."

"Who's doing it?"

"Shea and Short. We use them all the time."

The senator waved a gnarled hand.

"No problem. They're the best pollsters in the business."

"Then we'll see a few people like Luther Roberts."

"Roberts and Clayborne? Another good one."

"Then we'll hit some personal friends in town and head upstate."

"Like who in town?"

"Max Dregna," I said.

"The Great Liberal," he said with a frosty smile, "who's always crying about bosses, but in the past few years since he helped put Gentile in City Hall has found himself surrounded by more darned bosses than Tammany Hall ever had."

"That may be," I said. "But there's one difference—Max and his people are honest."

"Honest people can be awfully boring, McCool," he said.

"Then there's Sissy Southworth," Josh said.

"Oh, God!" the senator said with a groan. "What the hell can she give you?"

"Information and millions of readers and, more importantly, millions of viewers who won't go to the bathroom if they're watching her Immediate Release show."

58

"Garbage," Shannon rumbled. "Garbage."

"Okay, so it's garbage," Josh said wearily, "but you can't deny twenty million viewers."

"Well, see the Devil in hell for all I care," he said, "as long as it helps to put Kelly where I want him."

"Suppose we turn you down, Senator," I said, "What will you do?"

The cold steel-gray eyes flickered over us. "Didn't Kelly tell you?"

"He said you might take it on alone."

"There's no might to it—we will. Luke and I will elect Kelly governor of this state and President if it takes $100,000,000! And we'll do it."

"Luke is your younger son?"

"He's a bastard like me," he said with a thin smile. "He likes to win, and he won't let anything stand in his way. Nothing. Money. Men. Women." Then the cool voice added, "I guess even God."

The way he said it, I believed him.

"I told Kelly to win he must lust after it," Josh said. "Not just want it —lust for it like for a woman."

"Don't worry about Kelly—he wants it bad enough."

"What about Mullady?" Josh asked. "Have you given him any thought."

"Barney Mullady?" The senator shrugged. "As I told McCool, we either can buy him or make a deal."

"Kelly doesn't want any part of him."

"Kelly hasn't been in politics long enough to make a decision like that," the senator said, almost humorously. "Barney's a thief but he's necessary. And we may have to make a deal with him." He shot at me, "You know him, Finn."

"Well enough not to open my wallet near him," I said.

"You open your wallet and I'll have it well stuffed. See him and sound him out." He gave us a quizzical look. "But why all this talk if you're not interested?"

"We're interested—to a point. We don't want to commit ourselves— yet," Josh said. "You know what you're asking us to do will be almost impossible."

"That's why I called you both in," he said. "I could have gotten an army of so-called image makers, but I happen to believe that if anyone can do this, you boys can."

"Thanks for the confidence. But I hope you realize we can fall flat on our faces."

"You won't."

"And we hope you realize there's no time left to pull off a normal campaign."

"I figure that my money, Benny Jello's story, and your know-how will make up for lost time," he said. He held out his hand. "I'll expect to hear from you within a few days."

"Where to now?" I asked Josh after we had left the senator staring out across the East River, his eyes narrowed against the glare of the morning.

"Max Dregna. But first let's have lunch."

We had lunch at Sullivan's, then went down to see Max Dregna in his dusty little office on East Thirty-fifth Street just across from the battered old church where Dubinsky's garment workers have been holding their meetings since the early days when the company goons used to hunt them down with lead pipes.

Max was seated behind his battered desk separated from the rest of his office by an old-fashioned low wooden fence and swinging gate. It was his fondest boast that members of his union could see him at any time on any matter. He had molded his union as he would a piece of plastic, carefully, lovingly, and he knew every member by his first name. Papa Max, they called him, and I know it sounds like a lot of hogwash, but the people in that union really loved him.

Max was a short, rather fat man with a sloping bald head fringed by wisps of gray hair. He wore thick lenses that magnified his weak blue eyes. Sitting behind that desk he reminded me of the man in that science-fiction movie I have seen on late television—Doctor Cyclops. Every time I see him, I expect human beings the size of a paper match jumping about his desk as he peers down at them.

Max had come a long way since he got out of the army after World War II. As Josh said, it was an indication of how dangerous Hitler was getting when they took Max. After the war he went into plastics, built a small factory in New Jersey and, oddly enough, formed the first plastics union. I guess it's not strange when you realize both Max's mother and father were early ILGWU organizers. In fact, his father's death was directly attributed to a beating administered by goons in the early days.

Plastic was new right after the war, but it grew rapidly, leaping from toys to industry. Max gave his factory to his brother, and continued to build the union until it was one of the most powerful in the country. With Max it was plastics first and politics second, so the League of Independent Voters was born with Max as its head. Today it represents the liberal and reform wing of the Democratic Party.

Max is now powerful enough to advise the White House, Albany, and City Hall; he not only knows what is going on nationally and in the state but, more importantly, who is doing what—and to whom.

Three years ago Max came to us—a concession in itself—to ask our help in pushing through a hearing on a consumer's-label bill. As he explained, neither he nor his union could be identified with pressuring the committee. Josh saw a few people, and the log jam was open; the hearing was held. It never really amounted to much, just a few paragraphs in the *Times,* but it meant a lot to Max and his union. When Max talked of a fee, Josh waved him away. Max, he later confided, had done us a great favor by asking our help—now he was indebted to us.

Josh and Max got on well, but Max and I seemed to have more in common. He was a sad little man whose world was his union, plastics and, strangely enough—daguerreotypes. His collection was one of the finest in the country. One day when I was going through some things in storage, I came across a few of those wonderful little portraits on burnished copper. Not knowing who they were, and caring less, I sent them to Max, who acted as if I had sent him a costly present. I have always found that with lonely people who have hobbies, if you give them something connected with their hobby you immediately become a blood brother in their quiet little world.

When Max saw us his face lighted up and he burst through his little gate, hands outstretched.

"Finn, my good friend. And Josh. How good to see you! What brings you to New York?"

"Politics, my friend," I said.

He grinned. "What else?"

He waved us inside his gate and pulled up two large old-fashioned chairs. First came the formalities: a teak box of cigarettes, some kind of Turkish, I recall; tea, a box of cookies Max had been nibbling at, and then he leaned back and made a tent of his chubby fingers.

"So?"

Josh laughed. "So, Max, how is with you?"

He shrugged. "We fight the bosses; they fight us. We threaten; they threaten; and finally we get another contract."

"We're in for a bit of politics, Max," I said. "What's the situation?"

The fat shoulders moved under the shirt. "City Hall? Albany? Where do you want to start?"

"City Hall is as good a place as any," I said.

"There are five Democrats wanting the job," he said, "and as many Republicans. The Republicans are running for exercise, and four of the Democrats are idiots with big mouths. The councilman from the Bronx will get it."

"Is that who you will endorse?"

"He has a good voting record—" he made a face—"as much as you can have in the City Council—he has the backing. He's a good family man"—he raised his eyes upward—"eight kids." The chuckle was deep in his throat. "An Episcopalian yet."

"What about Albany?"

He shook his head. "Gentile is the only one. The Democrats haven't got a chance. They only make noise."

"Will the League endorse him?" Josh asked.

The weak eyes blinked. "Maybe."

"But you're not sure," Josh pressed.

"Maybe."

"You endorsed him before—twice," I pointed out.

"That was last time," Max said. "Before the kids were killed in Brooklyn. And before those other"—he spat the word—"bastards."

"The Birchers?" Josh asked.

Max leaned over and selected one of his long, flat cigarettes from the teak case. He accepted Josh's light and settled back, the smoke curling up from his thick lips.

"They're dangerous, those people. Very dangerous. They're like Nazis. After the riot they paraded around City Hall. There were a lot of cops among them, guns in their holsters. I raised hell with Gentile. Why did you let them march with guns on in your own backyard? I asked him. He claimed the police commissioner said it was the law. Cops have to wear guns even going to the toilet. I hung up on him. He appoints a commissioner; he can kick him out if he wants. We talked about that afternoon a lot up here. Let's say the bloom is off the rose, my friend." He looked worried. "Are you here for Gentile?"

"No," I said. "At this point we are not here for anybody. Just yet."

Josh said, "But we may be back."

Max's face was impassive. "For Albany?"

"For Albany," I said. "And maybe beyond that."

"Do you have money?"

"More than enough," I said.

"So what are you worrying, my friend?" Max said.

"Money can't buy your support, Max," I said.

He smiled. "So you'll come back and we'll talk. Do you have somebody in mind?"

Josh said, "We may be able to answer that in a few days, Max."

"If you take him on, I'll listen," Max said. "But this time, my friends, I'm warning you—we want a liberal. You say your man has plenty of money? That is important, but when he runs for Albany he has to have a hell of a lot more than money. If he doesn't, I'm afraid we can't do business."

"You and Barney Mullady still not talking, Max?" Josh asked.

The weak, magnified eyes behind the thick lenses narrowed. "Someday, somebody will pull a string, and Barney Mullady and his crooks will disappear. It will be a happy day for this city."

"Does he still carry a lot of weight?"

Max sighed. "I would be a fool to deny it. He has votes and jobs to fill. What more could he ask for?"

"We're going to see him in a few days, Max," I said.

He put his arm around our shoulders as he led us out.

"Watch your fillings, gentlemen," he said with a straight face.

"I bet Max got plenty of beefs from his party about Gentile after that school riot," Josh said as he tried to hail a cab. "Christ, we have to have a candidate who's a liberal but who can play with a guy like Mullady; a guy who is rich but who is loved by the poor people, and all we have is a nice kid nobody knows." He whistled with his fingers, and a cab swung into the curb. "I don't know, Finn. I just hope we haven't been put off center by a smile."

"I think we'll find there is more than just a smile. Where are we headed for now?"

"The Onyx Club," he said. Then hastily, as he saw the look on my face: "Look, Finn, we have to see Sissy. There's no way of ducking her. I have to pick her brains for what gossip she might know."

He opened the door of the cab, and I got in. Reluctantly.

The Onyx Club was a small, dim place—why are all these places so dim?—on East Sixty-second Street just off Park Avenue. I guess I'm just a crotchety old gaffer, but I believe that bright lights, a good mahogany bar, a jovial man at the stick, and good friends are all that's necessary for a night of sampling the waters. But in New York it seems as if everyone has to clutch a glass either in the dark or to the accompaniment of some maniac puffing at a tin horn so hard his eyeballs are ready to burst or some skinny young kid in a sweater telling jokes that would make a West Side longshoreman turn scarlet. But as I said, this is only the rumbling of an old man who can remember himself laughing at the old biddies who wanted the corner gin mills closed on Sundays.

We walked into the place, me feeling my way along the barstools like a blind man without his dog, and Josh hurrying ahead to the rear where there were rows of deep booths. In the center, back to the far wall, was a huge round table in front of a bright red-leather seat shaped like a half-moon. The table had a shiny onyx top.

This was Sissy's table. Nobody but nobody ever sat there. Charles the owner saw to that. He had to. Before Sissy made his place the talk of New York and virtually the whole country, it was just another saloon, patronized mostly by husbands cheating on wives or wives cheating on husbands.

One day Sissy, badly in need of a drink, walked in and liked the way Charles made Martinis. From that day on, there was no other place but the Onyx Club. She talked about it constantly in her column and slipped it in on her national television show. There were supposed to be no plugs, but Sissy managed to work it in the news or with her guests.

When I finally groped my way there, Josh had already slid behind the table and had observed the New York ritual of kissing her on the cheek. Then he held her hand like Raleigh and the Virgin Queen.

I just kicked a chair over and sat down. There were the usual six Martini glasses, all lined up. Three were empty.

"Hello, you old toad," she said. "I thought by now you'd withered up and blown away."

"Better than floating away," I said. It was always like this: the poor woman insulted me, and I did the best I could by ignoring her.

"Finn warned me not to light your cigarette, Sissy," Josh said. "He said with all that booze you'd go up like a torch."

The chuckle was deep in her throat, like a man's. Now my eyes were accustomed to the gloom, and I could see her. Poor woman. Homely as sin. And no amount of paint or feathers could hide that. The suit she was wearing was Dior, but for all her figure she could have gone down to Fourteenth Street.

But still, as Josh said, she had an army of twenty million, and who the hell is going to fight that?

"Have a drink, darling," she said, and a waiter materialized out of the gloom with a glass. The six were not to be touched.

"Finn," she said, serious as a mole, "do you have your draft card? The waiter wants to see it."

It was on the tip of my tongue to tell her that if she had a draft card it had been issued at Bull Run, but I held it back and told the waiter to bring me my friend Jack Daniels on the rocks.

Now that the preliminaries were settled, she got down to business.

"Well, what's up?" she said, and with Sissy there was no fooling about; you told her, and if she found out you had lied, off went your head. One thing I'll give the woman: she was honest. Vicious, revengeful, and petty, but honest to her friends. And we were her friends. Even me.

"Finn and I are thinking of electing a governor," Josh said.

"Who?" she said.

"I won't give you the name until we commit ourselves."

"Not pretty-boy Gentile?"

"No."

"A stranger. Someone I don't know?"

I put in, "Young and handsome as the devil on a spring morning—"

"And with more money than Knox," Josh said.

She was alert now; the bright brown eyes flickered over us. By God, I could almost see those damn cogs turning about in her head, faster and faster.

For this meant news. Exclusive news. And to Sissy, news meant more than anything else in the world. News was power. And that was one thing Sissy loved.

"Will I get it—alone?" she asked.

"Don't you always?" Josh said.

The answer was cold. "No. I found out you gave the tip on the federal-judge appointment to that AP man."

I couldn't resist. "I gave it to him—only after you blasted our man from Connecticut." Josh's toe gave me the warning. "With me there's always a two-way street. Now, don't go on blaming Josh, for I'll do it again if you take after us."

For a moment there were just two of us in this dim world. Then the deep chuckle. I relaxed. With some people you have to kick them in the guts before they'll respect you. Sissy was one. I've been saying this to Josh for years, but he'd rather tiptoe like she was surrounded by eggshells. The hell with her. A kick in the rear is what she's been needing.

"Honey, this is a tough old rooster you have here," she said. "Someday I'll grab his pinfeathers."

Then it was back to business.

"I want to know—do I get it alone?"

"Wrapped up in a Christmas package," Josh said, "if we take it. Now look, let's talk. I want to know everything that's going on."

For more than an hour Sissy talked. She repeated the same things Max had told us, but with some refinements. The New York County DA, who was miffed at the county leaders who had reneged on their promise to give him the mayoralty nomination, had subpoenaed some books from the comptroller's office; it looked like a brewing scandal. The Queens group were battling among themselves for the leadership and were threatening to bolt. Bronx also had internal trouble.

The Republicans were cocky as roosters in a henhouse. Eight years ago Gentile had swept into City Hall on a Fusion tide, but now they hoped not only to win City Hall again but also Albany. Max Dregna and his Liberals were disillusioned after the school riot, but all sorts of promises were being made; Max was a great liberal and an idealist, but his policy committee was more practical when it came to patronage— like the surrogate's job. The next few years in Albany would be used to add to Gentile's reputation, then the Presidency. As Sissy pointed out, and I had to agree, there just wasn't anyone else on the national scene. And unlike Rockefeller, there was no divorce in Gentile's past.

What the political scene needed now, Sissy said, was a dynamic figure, someone who could capture the imagination of the public. Gentile was an impressive-looking man and had done some wonderful things for the city, but eight years in City Hall has a way of making the best look ineffectual, callous, exasperating to the voter. The city is just too big, too complex. Gentile's timing in getting out was superb.

"What about Barney Mullady?" I asked.

A sly look from the horseface. "Your old friend Barney's still stealing the city blind and slipping past every grand jury."

"If they had the evidence they'd nail him proper."

"Nail Barney? That's a laugh. He's got a black army of voters from Hell's Kitchen to Harlem, and you know how many that means."

"Tammany in blackface," Josh said.

"He's going to be the loudest voice at the next national convention." She stared gloomily at her glass. "He'll have more black power than ten Malcolm X's."

"Maybe," Josh said. "Look, we have to run. We just wanted to stop in and say hello—"

"You're kidding," she said with a snort. "You wanted to pick my brains. What else can I tell you?"

"We'll be back." He stood up and glanced at his watch. "So long, Sissy. View you later."

Outside, he said: "Luther Roberts told me he would wait for us. We'll see him, have dinner at the Bailiff's Corner, and then—"

"Barney Mullady," I said.

It was old-home week when we entered the busy offices of Roberts and Clayborne, which occupied the entire eleventh floor of a building on Madison and Forty-ninth. As with the pollsters Shea and Short, Luther Roberts and his people have worked with us for years on campaigns. Roberts was one of the finest promotion and public-relations men in the country. After his partner Clayborne had died years ago, Roberts had bought out his widow and kept the name. Public relations, to Luther Roberts, did not mean simply holding formal press conferences and issuing releases to newspapers that would never see print. Rather they concentrated on communities, creating, building them through television, the local press, and the social structure of the area. Luther Roberts was the opposite of the stereotyped version of the Madison Avenue executive. He did not have an ulcer; he was well read; and he had a superb knowledge of national, state, and city politics and how they operate. His organization was expensive, but the best.

Luther was a six-footer, a silver-haired man who spoke slowly, easily. The political picture he drew for us was the same one we had heard from Sissy and Max; Gentile was a Republican shooting for Albany and later the Presidency. Confusion and party bickering were all that could be said for the Democrats.

He did have one additional piece of information: Barney Mullady was beginning to move about the state. Roberts pulled down a map of New York State, and demonstrated.

"Buffalo, Utica, Rome, Lawrence, Albany. We hear Mullady's gang is working their way into the ghettos and making deals with the local machines. Black, brown, or yellow, it doesn't make any difference; if they vote, Barney wants them in his fold," Luther said. "He's a political power now, and you fellows better know it. In a few years he'll be able to put in his own senators, congressmen, and even governor." The map slid up. "And, God help us, his will be the strongest voice at the convention."

"Max Dregna hates his guts," I pointed out.

"You don't have to be a Liberal to hate Barney Mullady's gang," Luther said. "But he was smart. While we were all sleeping, old Barney quietly grabbed control of the black-vote bloc. And gentlemen, these days that's something to reckon with."

"Who will knock him out of the box?" Josh asked.

Luther said firmly: "A black man. It can come anytime, and when it does I think there'll be trouble."

Josh sketched briefly what we were doing, and grinned.

"The old man's going to Pennsylvania Avenue even if it means hanging on to his son's arm."

"He's ready to put twenty million in the pot," Josh said.

Luther raised his eyes heavenward and whistled softly. "With that kind of cash we can run my doorman."

"If we accept, we want the whole organization this time," Josh said.

"With old man Shannon paying the bills," Luther said, "I won't leave a stenographer back here. If you do decide, call me and we'll get down to the basics."

"And now for the Bailiff," Josh said as we left the revolving door for a waiting cab.

CHAPTER FIVE: BARNEY MULLADY AND HIS
                SWEET CHOCOLATES

RESTAURANTS ARE A NECESSITY in the world of politics. There's nothing like towering drinks, fine food, and good companions to thaw a politician and make him reveal the best of the clubhouse secrets. Invariably the places reflect their part of the political world: Sullivan's on Eighth Avenue, in the West Forties, is the old-fashioned type, checkered cloths, thick water glasses, the bar in the front, and a menu laboriously written by Sullivan's wife. The place has been there since Tweed's boys blew the heads from their glasses, and is famous for its juicy steaks, imported beer, and thick slabs of homemade apple pie. There you'll find the rougher leaders, the West Side gang, like Barney Mullady and his old cronies. On the lower East Side off Mulberry Bend is the Little Venice, and there are the lead-pipe gents, as I know them, the Mafia cousins and the champions of the bookmakers. On the East Side is the Rodando, a place of quiet gentility where the gentry of politics gather, the silk-stocking boys who do their politicking on Park Avenue. In Brooklyn there's Tom's at Borough Hall, an elaborate place, crowded to the windowsills at lunch and filled with the county organization's leaders and hatchet men. And let any politician dare not to have his beefsteak dinner party or bar mitzvah in any place but Tom's upstairs lounge, where you get a watery Manhattan included with the meal. Off Foley Square is the Bailiff's Corner, a beautiful little place full of pseudocolonial stuff and satirical drawings of English courtroom scenes. The smell of law is in the air.

The judiciary meets here, from bailiffs to judges, from the Federal Building, the Supreme Court, and the Criminal Courts Building across the square.

This is where we had dinner, and Josh scarcely had time to eat. Drinks were sent over; lawyers and commissioners with the judgeship scent strong in their nostrils dropped by to say hello.

And it was from the Bailiff's that I called Barney Mullady.

If I expected him to sound surprised, I was mistaken; I should have known the old fox. He brayed his greeting like a hungry nanny.

"Finn! Finn McCool, the great statesman of the West Side, now hobnobbing with the gentry and holding hands with the President. A great day it is for you to come back."

As phony as a three-dollar bill with Mr. Lincoln's head all over it.

"Come off it, Mr. Tammany Hall," I said. "I saw you only the day before yesterday and before that last spring at Tommy McGalley's funeral."

"Ah, poor Tom. You'll be glad to know his widow is working down at Municipal in real estate," he said. "Mary always had a head for figures."

"It's a good deed you did, Barney," I said. "They have eight, with one going to Fordham Law." I knew he wanted this pat on the back.

"It was nothing," he said, gracious as St. Joseph. Then, sharper, "Will I be seeing you, Finn?"

"We'll be dropping by," I said.

"We?" he said.

"Josh Michaels is with me," I said.

"Oh," he said, "then it's business, is it?"

Why else would we be seeing your fat little face? I thought, but as casually as I could I told him that it was a little something to discuss and that we would see him at the Tusk Club.

"What did he say?" Josh asked when I sat down.

"Nothing. But he knows something's up."

"Will he repeat what we talk about?"

"No. Not that. It will suit his purpose to make a mystery of it."

There were more judges and more handshakes and several low conversations before we left. They all boiled down to an implication of what we had heard from Sissy, Max, and Luther: the field was open among the bickering Democrats; with Gentile the Republicans were smug as a cat with its whiskers dripping cream.

At nine thirty we paid our bill and left for the West Side to tempt a fox with a pot of honey.

The Tuskawana Club, located on Ninth Avenue between Fifty-third and Fifty-fourth, is a national political landmark. In the early 1850's it was a volunteer firehouse, later a station house. If you look very closely

68

you can see the small holes in the old red brick made by the Minié balls of the rioters who stormed the old station house during the Draft Riots. After the Civil War it was abandoned by the Police Department. In 1872 it became headquarters for the first Tuskawana Club, a sort of West Side annex to Tammany Hall. My father was once its president, and so was I. The Tusk, as it's been called, almost faded away after World War II; but gradually, as the minorities took over the West Side of Manhattan, it began to flourish under Barney Mullady, who, I must give credit, always insisted that the sachems of the Tuskawana would one day again dominate city and state and therefore national politics.

Almost singlehandedly he reorganized the club, kicked out the old guard, or relegated them to minor posts. Instead of the shanty Irish, the club's members were now predominantly Negro. When he felt he had the organization, Barney faced up to Adam Clayton Powell and defeated his candidates. He accomplished what sociologists had warned of many times—whoever organized and controlled the black-vote bloc would have enormous power. Barney also destroyed the illusion that only a black man could control a black organization. Shrewd politician that he was, Mullady selected only Negroes as his lieutenants; he called the shots and they fired the guns. In the last few years, with Castro letting down the bars of his prison, Cuban refugees began to edge into the East Side of the district. Barney was never one to overlook a good thing; he set up a clubhouse, put in a Cuban leadership and began to build another segment of his new black and brown army of voters. He didn't neglect the Puerto Ricans; they also came into his fold under their own leadership.

Mullady was George Washington Plunkett, born all over again, and he was using Plunkett's traditional tools: ignorance, fear, illiteracy, and poverty.

We pulled up to the Tusk and found a small group outside, Latin voices chattering like castanets. We later learned this was a slow night; usually there was a mob, the overflow from inside.

For a moment I gazed upward at the ugly, grimy red-brick building. The heavy green wire screens were still on the upper windows, and the big wooden door still bore the scars of the bullets fired by some hoods in a speeding car in the thirties. We found the riddled body on a Sunday morning. I'll never forget. The corpse was wearing a diamond ring, big as a robin's egg, but it couldn't be found after they put the stiff in the rear of the old West Forty-seventh Street Precinct. "Mysteriously disappeared," the reporters wrote. That gave us all a laugh in the neighborhood. Two cops had it in pawn before *rigor mortis* had set in.

Black faces and brown peered up at us as we moved past the rows of chairs to the wooden stairway that led to the "executive offices" above. It was a large wide open room, the floors scraped clean and varnished. There was a little raised platform in the rear with a tired American flag.

69

The nostalgia was so strong I could taste it. Many a speech to the faithful I had made from that little spot.

In the rear, behind a glass-partitioned office, sat Barney, his round bald head glistening in the hard light as he bent over to speak to an elderly woman. Two burly bullyboys sat just outside the door. Directly in front of the glass-partitioned office was another desk, and behind it was the slender young Negro Barney had introduced me to when I had met him outside City Hall—Gene Abernathy, as I recalled, who once had been a bad boy but who, Barney boasted, was now with him and his gang all the way.

"We have an appointment with Mr. Mullady, Mr. Abernathy," I said as the young man rose.

He smiled and seemed pleased that I recalled his name.

"Oh, Mr. McCool," he said. "Mr. Mullady is expecting you."

"This is Josh Michaels," I said. "Josh, this is Gene Abernathy, Barney's right-hand man."

They shook hands. Then there was a rap on the window, and Barney was ushering out the elderly woman in the faded black coat.

"Bring them in, Gene; bring them in," he boomed.

"This way, gentlemen," Gene said, and stepped aside. The two muscle-men gave us a casual look but that was all.

Barney waved us to chairs, and Gene asked what we would have.

"Any damn thing you want we have," Barney said. "I'll buy a bottle if I don't have it."

"A little brandy," Josh said.

"And I'll have a little Jack Daniels on the rocks," I said.

In a few moments the young Negro was back with a tray and our drinks. Then he smiled and closed the door.

"Nice boy," I said.

"Sharp as a stiletto," Barney said. "Everybody knows Gene on the West Side. The young people listen to him. You know that he has a Master's degree?" He chuckled. "And me with a degree from P.S. 17." Still smiling he said to Josh, "You're Michaels, Finn's partner, aren't you?"

"I'm sorry," I said. "I thought you two had met before."

Barney raised a fat hand with a diamond on the pinky. "To business, men," he said, and sat back.

Josh began, "We've been testing the political air, Barney, and it smells pretty bad."

Barney shrugged. "The boys are squabbling, but I'm sure that once—"

Josh said: "Let's cut the crap, Barney; the party isn't squabbling; it's split. Right down the middle and in four sections. They're fighting for the leadership posts in the Assembly and the Senate. And everyone's jockeying for the party's gubernatorial nomination next year. You know that."

The smile fell away from the tight little mouth. "So you know everything. Why come to me?"

Josh said calmly, "Who do you intend to support?"

The smile returned, and Barney swung to me with a critical click of his tongue.

"Your young friend runs fast, Finn. Did you tell him you have to crawl before you gallop?"

"It's a question we're both asking, Barney," I said. "It won't leave this room."

"That's what you say." He took up a gold lighter and carefully lighted his cigar. "Well, the fact is, I don't know."

"What do you want for your support, Mullady?" Josh said. "And don't give me any crap about position papers or ideals."

"He wants promises," I said. "Promises and money. Don't you, Barney?"

The small, deep-set eyes were cold. "If we weren't old friends, Finn, I'd have your withered ass kicked out of here." He blew the smoke to one side. "But seeing as we are, you're right. The man with the most promises—and the most contributions, so to speak—can be assured he will have my support."

"You mean honest graft," Josh said.

"Call it what you will," Barney said, and this time he leaned forward on his desk, his chin almost disappearing in the upward swell of fat. "But let me tell you, young fellow, there's a big difference between a political looter and a politician who makes a fortune out of politics by keeping eyes and ears open.

"The looter goes in for himself alone, without considering his organization or his people. But the politician looks after his own interests, the organization's interest, and his people's interests. Now take me. I'm a politician, never a looter. I made my pile in politics, as Finn can tell you, but at the same time I served the organization and got more improvements for my people than any living man in this city." He added coolly, "And I never monkey with the Penal Code."

"I'm curious. Just what do you do for these people?" Josh asked.

"I always like to help bright young fellows from Washington," Barney said, "so I'll tell you. What tells about the grip you have on your organization is how you treat the poor people. How you help them in the different ways they need help."

"What about the poverty programs, Barney?" Josh asked. "Don't they—"

"Poverty programs my ass!" Mullady exploded. "They're nothing but boondoggling organizations run by some God-damn do-gooders with eighteen degrees who don't know a damn about the slums except what they read in books! And if they're any good, they're screwed right and left by the local organizations who are fighting for a piece of the pie.

71

Nobody knows how to make the money work. They're all tangled up in red tape, and everybody is cutting everybody else's throat. Now, you take that nice Mrs. Gonzales who left as you were coming in. She and her family were burned out last night. The whole floor in that tenement. A kerosene stove, the cops said. What the hell do I care what started it? She has a sick husband and six kids. Me and my election captains were over there with the first engines. I didn't ask them if they were Democrats or Republicans, I just told them Barney Mullady would take care of them."

He slapped a pudgy hand down on the desk. "Know what those God-damn poverty outfits would have done for Mrs. Gonzales? Made her fill out a hundred forms and give her life's history while the poor woman was going out of her mind. By the time they really did anything, she would have found a place herself or the neighbors would have done it for her. But not me. I take care of them, one two, three. Barney Mullady. The boys mention that name until it comes out of their ears. If a poor family comes into the district and needs welfare, one phone call does it. Barney Mullady. The kids run out of clothes. I got vacant stores all over the West Side with clothes my people collected. We pay women to fix them up, and we hang them neat as in a Fifth Avenue store. We will take care of the Gonzales family until they get on their feet. Hell, I even called her boss down in the garment center and told him to let her off for a few days." He winked. "Even if he is paying the cop on the beat, the captain could make sure his trucks were ticketed."

Josh said, "In other words, Mullady, use the poor."

"On the head," he cried, slapping his fat hand down on the table. "On the very head you hit it, young man! Don't ever think the poor are grateful; they never are. Help them, and they resent it. After a while they take it for granted. What you have to do is make them dependent on you, so if they get out of line you can kick them in the stomach, so to speak. That never fails. They always come around. Isn't that a fact, Finn?"

"That's a fact," I said. I knew it at first hand. I was once poor, and I knew how the machine used us. We sold our votes for a scuttle of coal or a skinny chicken on Thanksgiving or Christmas.

"If there's a family in want," Barney continued, "I want to know about it before the cop on the beat or those high-toned charities do, so me and my men are first on the scene. I have to take care of them. Barney Mullady's people always look up to Barney Mullady as a father and they come to him in their troubles."

I added wryly, "And they never forget dear old Barney on election day."

Another wink. "Right again, old-timer. And there are jobs for the deserving. It's not like the old days of our fathers Finn, before the Civil Service; now they have to pass the tests, but we help them. Down we take them to the school on Forty-third, dear old P.S. 162, where Finn and I had many a battle with the Gilhouley Rabbits, and there they get their learning. Then we take them for the test, and zingo they're sweeping the streets or driving some big truck, or even a boy in blue among the finest saluting the captain in our precinct. . . . Ah, they're my sweet chocolates."

Barney was now in full swing. Eyes half closed and waving his cold cigar, he continued: "And the kids around here. Sweet and loving. *Buenos días* they call out when I come around. . . . I answer—"

"You're a regular linguist, Barney," I said.

"A few words here, a few words there. But who cares? I have their own kind carrying out my orders. See that young fellow outside? Well, Gene is not only educated; he also knows more about the West Side and Harlem than anyone in the city. The young people listen to him, and the old people ask his advice. He got out of line once but he saw the light, as the preachers say. Can't beat 'em, join 'em. . . . Now Gene's my good right hand—that boy's a comer."

"I hear you have about every minority, Barney," Josh said.

"In the old days it was the Irish, then the Dagos and the squareheads," Barney said with a grin. "But they're all gone to the country with their damned power mowers and their snow blowers. Now my sweet chocolates have taken their place, with a few brown ones tossed in."

"Why you, Mullady?" Josh asked bluntly. "Why haven't they selected their own leader?"

"Because the Irish were born to rule, young fellow," Barney said, and without changing a wrinkle, he added, "And they're as honest in politics as the days are long."

Josh gave him the same innocent look.

"How's your contracting business?"

"Booming," Barney said. "Booming all over the place."

"I suppose you have some of your sweet chocolates working for you?" Barney nodded. "Some."

"What do you pay them? Union wages?"

Now the jovial voice was slightly edged with iron. "We have a fine union and they get fine wages."

"Oh, it's your union. Mullady's union."

The swivel chair came down with a slam. "What do you guys want?"

"We're just talking, Barney," I said to soothe him. "Just talking."

"That's right, Barney," Josh said grimly. "Just talking about politics. Your favorite subject."

"What does our union have to do with it?" He began shuffling some papers. "Look, Finn, you come around alone without this guy—"

"What's the matter, Mullady, you afraid of me?" Josh said roughly.

The fat little body pushed against the desk, and the cold, beady eyes fixed Josh. "No, Mr. Michaels, I'm not afraid of you or any top hat from

Washington. That goes for this"—a jerk of his head indicated me—"old rooster. He and I know each other, and maybe that's why we get on. I don't know what you're up to, but don't buck me or put your nose in my affairs or—"

"Or what?" Josh asked.

"Or I'll cut your God-damn throat," Mullady said, "so neat and sleek you won't know it until you turn your head and find yourself looking up from the gutter."

"Look out it's not your head, Barney," Josh said cheerfully.

"I heard of you, Michaels," Barney said. "A real wheeler-dealer down in Washington. But let me tell you—"

"Let me tell you for a change," Josh interjected. "We're going to run somebody. For governor. What do you say to that?"

Barney shrugged. "Good luck to you."

"Would you like to know who it is?" I asked.

"Frankly, I couldn't care less, whether it's Sammy the bootblack down the corner or the good Pope in Rome." He added roughly, "You'll still have to come to me."

"And if we don't?" I asked.

Here a fat finger across his throat. "Neat and sleek, like I said. You'll never get to the convention."

"Kelly Shannon," Josh said in a low, flat voice.

Mullady blinked. He kept staring at Josh, but you could see he was shaken.

"The senator's son?" he asked, as if finding it hard to believe.

"The same," I said.

"Richest man in America," Josh said lovingly. "Contracting companies from here to Brazil. And still able to whisper to the right people in Washington. Like the attorney general."

"Don't threaten me," Mullady said in a tight voice. "I don't scare easy, not by you, Michaels, and all the Shannons put together."

"If Finn and I and the Shannons lean on you, Mullady, you'll never get up," Josh said grimly. Then suddenly his tone changed. "But look, Barney, why look for trouble? We didn't come here to fight."

"What did you come for?" was the blunt question.

"Because Finn said you're the best in the business. An old pro, and you know there are only a few of us left."

"Most of them are radicals and Communists," Barney grumbled. "That boy outside spots them for me, and out they go!"

"I don't blame you," Josh said, "but look, Barney, if we run Kelly Shannon, we'll be around—mainly for advice."

Honey, I had told him, thick, sweet, gooey honey. And I know Barney loves it. He'll be boasting how the two big shots from Washington had to come down and get advice from Barney Mullady.

Well, I might as well pour some too.

74

"I told them they couldn't move a wheel unless they checked with you, Barney," I said with a straight face. "Seeing as we were old friends, I brought Josh down to say hello."

Barney grunted, but the feathers looked less ruffled.

"Maybe we can have some meetings about it," he said. He looked at Josh. "Is the old man ready to put out?"

"Ready and able, Barney," Josh said.

"More business than you'll ever see," I suggested. "For keeping your ears and eyes open and leading your sweet chocolates down the right path."

The chuckle rumbled deep in his throat. Liquor and women thaw some men; with Barney, money.

Then some philosophy: "Like I always said, Finn, men who make a lasting success in politics are men who are always loyal to their friends; men who keep their promises and never lie. Yes, sir," he said heartily, "right down to the last vote."

"We might have to call on your whole organization," Josh told him.

"We're always ready to help our friends." Barney waved his hand grandly. "When I give the word, every sweet chocolate in this city pulls down the right lever." He made a motion of a man pulling down the levers in a voting booth. "Click. Click. Click. Click. Right down the line. Just following Barney's orders."

"Christ, to keep all those sweet chocolates happy must cost you a fortune, Barney!" Josh said with a phony look of awe.

Barney gave him a sharp look, but his ego, big as all outdoors, just couldn't let this one go by.

"Oh, it costs a pisspot full of money, young man," he said. Then he leaned back in his chair and gave us a bland look. "I guess I'm sort of a Robin Hood." He chuckled. "Robin Hood of the Sweet Chocolates, without a bow and arrow!" He winked. "I take from the rich and give to the poor. And there's always plenty where that comes from."

"Well, Barney, I guess we've taken enough of your time," Josh said as he rose. "It was good to see you. We'll be around."

Barney pumped his hand, then mine. Arms about our shoulders, he led us out of his office.

With a flourish, as if he had a pair of kings in tow, Barney said to young Abernathy, "My two great friends, Finn McCool and Joshua Michaels, named after that glorious prophet."

I did a double take; I had never heard anyone use that name. Even Josh seemed startled.

"Good night, gentlemen," young Abernathy said. "It was a pleasure meeting you both."

"Our doors are always open to them, Gene," Barney said.

"Yes, sir."

The two bodyguards yawned and looked sleepy.

An elderly Negress in a housedress rose hesitantly from a nearby bench.

"Mrs. Wilson would like to see you, Mr. Mullady," Abernathy said. "It's about her son who was picked up by the cops last week in that tavern robbery."

Barney nodded. "By all means show the lady in." He slapped me on the back. "Gentlemen, I have to go back to work, taking care of my people. Remember, the door is always open."

I was surprised to see the bitter contempt in the black eyes of the young Negro as he watched Mullady usher the woman into his office.

"Quite a boss you've got there," Josh said.

The lips barely moved and the answer was flat and hollow. "Yes, sir, quite a boss."

When we had reached the street, I asked Josh what he thought.

"He's a tough old bird, but I think he can be bought. Or broken. I bet he has a sweetheart contract with that union and gives his sweet chocolates coolie wages."

"You'd have a hell of a time proving it. A few of the DA's have been after him for years."

"What about the feds? Internal Revenue?"

"They haven't touched him—yet. Let him get on the skids, and they'll check every back return for years."

"Did you get that Robin Hood crack?"

"About robbing the rich? I bet he does. I wonder where he's getting his loot?"

"A politician in power has many opportunities, Josh. I don't have to tell you that."

"From the rackets? Remember Hines?"

"That could be. Every year you hear of a politician milking the rackets. But if Barney is doing it, the money is far removed before it gets in his pocket. The fact that he hasn't been hurt yet in all these years proves he's smart."

"There's a day of reckoning for all of them."

"Maybe the best way is to buy off Barney, as the senator suggested."

"There's a better way."

"Like pushing him off a roof?"

"Not quite as dramatic as that. It came to me when I threw that sweetheart-contract thing at him for size. I caught it in his eyes. Barney's afraid; he knows he has more reins than he can control. Did you see the look that young Negro gave him?" He added thoughtfully, "What did Barney say about him? Something about how he was once a bad boy. One of these days we'll have to look into that."

"You sound like you've made up your mind," I pointed out.

"Almost." He smiled. "The more I get into it, the more possibilities it has: $1,000,000-a-year fee plus a $50,000 monthly expense account and a chance to maneuver someone into the White House! Let's go upstate for a few days and see what the climate is up there."

So we went upstate and saw the leaders; the hard-faced tub of a man who the insiders know controls gamblers and politicians; the old party-line boss who insisted anything would be better than the widening splits in the party on the eve of an important gubernatorial race. Come up with a live one and we'll have dinner, he said.

We dined with the Speaker of the Assembly and the majority leader in the Assembly where the Democrats retained a majority and in the Senate where they lost it, but all we got was the same cry, dissension and disorder. Unity was forgotten.

In a word, there was no strong Democratic candidate for the gubernatorial spot; it was wide open.

On the way to the Albany airport, Josh was silent. I knew him well enough to know he was coming to a decision. As we stood on the windy strip in the lowering light of a gray afternoon, he asked quietly, "What do you think, Finn?"

I answered so quickly it surprised me. In fact, the answer had been dangling on the tip of my tongue for days.

"I think we should take it."

"Why?"

"This might sound farfetched, but I think we may have the next President in our vest pocket."

"An obscure congressman? A political nobody?"

"As Kelly said, our job would be to change that."

"Do you think we can, in this short time?"

"I keep coming back to that red folder. It's a ticking bomb, Josh. Once it goes off, the whole national picture could change."

"But then we have a guy like Mullady—"

"Mullady doesn't frighten me, Josh."

"He doesn't me either, Finn, but put all these things together, and when it comes out you tell yourself you're nuts for even thinking about it!" He bit his lower lip in exasperation. "Yet, something tells me Kelly has what it takes. God, he's certainly likable, if somewhat naïve."

"I think there's something deeper, Josh."

"I think so too, but I'll be damned if I can put my finger on it."

The wind swept between us, sighing like a cat.

"I don't know what it is," I said. "Put it to an old Irishman's intuition or plain sentimentality, but someday we'll see Kelly Shannon walking into the White House."

"Well, we'll see," he said.

I firmly believed what I had told Josh. But what I didn't tell him was the strange, brooding thoughts I had about this smiling, wonderful young man. . . .

THE FOLLOWING AFTERNOON we heard from Kelly. There had been an urgent call from our Rhode Island congressman-client, and Josh had returned to Washington to attend the final conference with him and his state leaders. I was weary of talking to this bumpkin, and decided to remain in New York. It had been an aimless day for me. I just couldn't finish anything; the Shannon business was on my mind constantly. On the trip back from upstate, Josh and I had argued for hours, debating the good and bad points of the proposition. Realistically, there was little logic in our taking it, but we were both finding it hard to come to the decision to turn down the senator. As Josh said, it would be easy to say No to Kelly over the phone, but he just didn't see how he could do it to his face.

Something led me back to our Woolworth Building office, and I was standing at the window, watching the workers from the Municipal Building buck the gusty March winds to the Park Place subway station when the phone rang.

It was Kelly Shannon.

"I'm at the airport," he said, "just in from Washington for the night. I thought you and Josh might have dinner at Wexford."

"You and Josh probably passed each other in the air," I told him. "He had to go back to Washington for a meeting tonight."

"Well, why don't you come along, Finn? No politics. No education scene. Lacey's in and so is Luke. You might like to meet them."

"I'd like to, Kelly. Will you pick me up? The Woolworth Building, fourth floor."

It took Kelly about an hour to reach our office. When I settled in the front seat of his car, downtown was dark, windy, and deserted.

"Did you hear about the fire?" Kelly asked as he swung into the direction of the West Side Highway.

"Frankly, I haven't seen a paper or had the radio on all afternoon. Where is it?"

"The Lawrence Plastics factory. The city's been in a bad way since that strike. As I understand it, the company moved to North Carolina a few months ago. They're working only part time up there now." He suddenly realized that perhaps I didn't know what he was talking about.

"Do you know about this strike?"

"No. We've been in Washington most of the time for the last few years. When we come back to Manhattan, it's usually only for a day or a night."

"Last year the union shut down the plant for months. There were several battles between the police and the pickets. At one point they called in the state troopers."

"Is Lawrence in your district?"

"I wish it was. I always had the feeling that nothing really was done to bring both sides together—"

"What about the district's congressman? Do you know him?"

"He's nearly eighty and has been in Congress since I was a child. Now he's a stumbling old man who does just as they tell him."

"They?"

"The local machine. The same gang has been running things for years in Lawrence. It grew worse when the minorities came in to work at the factory. Now there's a ghetto as bad as Harlem."

"Then it's not a city-management type of government?"

"Anything but," he said with a short laugh. "It's the usual mayor, City Council, and commissioners, all friends of someone."

We were on the parkway when the news came on. Automatically we broke off our conversation to listen.

". . . and a general alarm has been sounded with fire companies from Hudson, Portsmouth, Williams, Edgemere, and almost every community in the county responding to the alarm. Calls also have been made to the New York City Fire Department, and Commissioner Francis has promised immediate assistance. The blaze now has been raging for over two hours and it appears that most of the plant, the scene of many strikes and much violence, is doomed. The bodies of four workers, including two women, have been found. There are five more listed as missing. Fortunately, only a small crew had been employed at the factory, pending a complete shutdown early this summer. The management of the plant transferred its operation to North Carolina only a few months ago. Police Chief Edwards has charged that arsonists touched off the blaze. . . . Here is our reporter at the press conference with Police Chief Edwards, held a few blocks from the fiery plant."

Then, above the wail of sirens and the frantic shouts of firemen, we heard the police chief denouncing the strikers, the "Communists," as he called them, for setting the plant afire, and promising to hunt them down if it took a lifetime.

He sounded stupid and inarticulate.

"What do you think of that idiot?" Kelly said. "He admits he hasn't any evidence but goes on to charge the strikers with arson."

"What sort of place is Lawrence?"

"Years ago it used to be a fair city. Before the war the plant was small and owned by one family, but after the war it expanded until it was a monster. The family sold out to a syndicate, and then the union came in. After that, there was always trouble."

We rode in silence for a while; then there was another bulletin: police had arrested two of the plant's employees, and there was a pitched battle between spectators and the police.

Kelly slowed down as we approached an exit. Under the highway light I could see the sign: LAWRENCE, 5 MILES.

"How about taking a look, Finn?"

"Sure your family won't be waiting?"

"We can always catch up with them. The cook knows me by now." He turned to me. "But look, we don't have to—"

"No, by all means. Let's take a look."

We saw the glow of the blaze in the sky long before we reached Lawrence. There were roadblocks on the outskirts of the town, but Kelly identified himself and we rolled past. A thick pall of smoke hung over the narrow, twisting streets. The buildings looked old, grimy, and forbidding. Faces, momentarily picked up by the glare of our headlights, were tight with bitterness and anger. Finally we came to an intersection blocked by fire hoses and police cars. A patrolman accepted Kelly's identification but pointed down the street.

"The factory's a couple of blocks that way, Congressman, but you can't drive over there—too much hose." He pointed with a flashlight. "Put your car in that lot over there and you can walk."

We bumped our way into a lot littered with rocks and garbage and crowded with official-looking cars, trucks, and radio cars and then began walking. The wind was up, unfortunately coming in our direction, and the yellow smoke made my stomach rise to the back of my throat.

But when we rounded the last block the shocking scene made me forget the smoke.

Fanned by a high wind, the main building was a roaring giant torch with flames licking at the lurid sky. The place was a bedlam of wailing sirens, running men shouting orders that seemingly no one paid any attention to, flashing red lights on the roofs of radio cars, shrilling whistles. Networks of hose laced the ground. As we crossed the wide square a hose burst, the loose ends whipping about like frantic snakes. A fireman who had been holding the hose, spun like a top before he fell. A number of others in glistening raincoats rushed up to drag him to safety.

"There goes another damn hose," a man in a small crowd shouted. "That's the third one that busted. Those thieving bastards at City Hall—"

A passing radio car spun around on a dime and screeched to a spot alongside the shouting man. Two cops jumped out and spoke to the man, who shook his fist in their faces. Then they grabbed him and forced him, kicking and fighting, into the car, which took off. The crowd watched silently.

"What the devil's going on?" I asked Kelly.

"I don't know," he said. "Let's find out.'

We walked over to a handful of spectators who were beginning to drift away.

"Pardon me," Kelly said to a man in a worn leather jacket. "What's happening?"

The man stared at him, then shrugged. "There's a fire, mister—"

"I know that, but what did that man mean about the hoses?"

"Just like you can see: there's a fire and the hose busted," the man said.

"Have others burst?"

"Three so far," someone said.

"Why?" Kelly asked.

"Why don't you go over and look at it if you're so damn interested?" someone else said.

"Who are you?" the first man demanded.

"Congressman Shannon."

"Do you know that silly old fool who represents us?"

"Why, yes, I've seen your congressman in Washington—"

"Do us a favor, will you? The next time you see him, tell him to keep away from Lawrence, because if he ever comes here we'll kick his ass from here to Albany. That old son of a bitch hasn't done a thing for this city in years."

"Let's take a look at that hose," Kelly said in an undertone.

We walked to the corner hydrant, followed by the crowd. They watched as Kelly examined one end of the hose and silently handed it to me. I didn't have to be an underwriter to know it was badly creased and rotted.

"This is shocking," Kelly said.

"It's rotten, just like the whole city," the first man said. He peered at Kelly. "But why are you getting excited, mister? You live here?"

"You don't have to live here to be shocked by a thing like this," Kelly said. "This is criminal."

"What the hell's going on here?" someone shouted, and a man in a raincoat and a white fire hat pushed through the crowd and snatched the piece of hose from my hand. "What are you doing with this? Don't you know it's city property?"

"Rotten city property, I would say," Kelly said.

Two firemen came up on the run, and the fire official—I saw he was a deputy chief by his hat—motioned to the hydrant, and the firemen quickly unscrewed the remnant of hose and walked away under the bitter eyes of the crowd.

"Break it up now," the deputy said, "this is a fire line."

"It won't be unless you get better hose," Kelly said. "Didn't any of your people know that hose was rotten?"

The deputy ignored him and began pushing back the crowd. "Come on, let the firemen work, folks. . . . Move on. . . ."

"I said, 'Didn't any of your people know that hose was rotten?' " Kelly said in a loud voice.

The deputy spun around. For a moment he studied Kelly. Then he shouted to a group of firemen, and policemen gathered about an official car with a revolving rooftop red light.

"Hey, Chief, come over and take care of these guys."

"You better get out of here before the cops start busting heads," Mr. Leather Jacket said. "That's one thing they're really good at."

"Nobody's going to break any heads while I'm here," Kelly said quietly. He turned to the deputy.

"If that's the police chief, please tell him I want to see him."

The deputy stared at him almost unbelieving, then roared out again to the chief that he had better come over.

A squat, stocky man in civilian clothes stepped out of the official car to walk over to us. He was wearing an old-fashioned brown overcoat and a worn fedora. Somehow I knew that underneath the overcoat his suit had to have been ordered from Sears Roebuck along with his shoes, thick-soled and laced to the shinbone. I couldn't help thinking he looked like an awed farmer watching a big-city blaze.

"What are you people doing here?" he asked. He seemed more apprehensive than authoritative.

"Cowshit Edwards," someone said, and the crowd snickered. The chief looked flustered.

"You better get these two guys out of here," the deputy murmured. "They got big noses." He walked back to join the group of firemen.

"You people move along," the chief said.

"May I ask who you are?" Kelly asked in an even, cold voice.

"Chief of Police Edwards," was the proud answer. "Who are you?"

"Congressman Shannon," I said. "We were just looking at your hose."

"Your rotten hose," Kelly corrected.

"Oh. Oh." The chief looked about as if for support. "How are you, Congressman? Terrible fire, isn't it? But we'll have it under control soon."

"I understand three hoses have broken so far, Chief," Kelly said. "That's shocking."

"Terrible. Terrible," the chief said. He added vaguely, "I guess they were just never used. We don't have fires like this every day—"

"Where are the city leaders?" Kelly asked.

"All the boys are down at City Hall," the chief said. "The City Council is holding an emergency meeting." He seemed eager to let us know that City Hall was only a few blocks away.

"I have to get back," he said, now full of vigor. "The plainclothesmen picked up two suspects. Commies. God-damned Commies, Congressman."

"How do you know they are Communists, Chief?" Kelly asked.

"Oh, we've checked," the chief said. "We got them by the short hairs."

"Let's go over to City Hall," Kelly said. "The chief's busy as hell picking up suspects."

The chief smiled, waved, and walked briskly back to his car, which took off.

"That's Cowshit Edwards," the man in the leather jacket said in a bitter voice. "He used to run a dairy farm up here years ago. Then his brother-in-law got big in politics, and they made him police chief. The son of a bitch can't catch a cold." He started to walk away, but turned around.

"Thanks for your interest, Congressman. If you ever see the jerk that represents us, remember what I said about him coming back here."

He walked down the street, head down, his hands stuck into the jacket pockets. The other silently drifted off into the night.

"By God, this city must be worse than I thought," Kelly said. "Let's see what they're doing at City Hall."

The City Hall of Lawrence certainly had been built about the turn of the century. It was only three stories, of ugly red brick, with turrets, wide front steps, and thick glass doors. The lobby was small, bordered by oak doors with gold letterings: MAGISTRATE'S COURT . . . FAMILY COURT . . . WELFARE DEPARTMENT. There were also signs: POLICE DEPARTMENT DOWN-STAIRS . . . COUNCIL CHAMBERS ONE FLIGHT UP.

Men were coming and going. Somehow they reminded me of the old-fashioned political hacks who hovered about Hague and his gang whenever that notorious politician paid a visit to Washington in the thirties. They had the same hard faces and furtive, secretive manners.

We climbed the worn, dusty stairway to the second floor. The hallway was crowded with men in rough working clothes that gave off a strong odor of smoke and burning plastic. Others sat on the railing and stairway, silently smoking, staring morosely at a small knot of men who seemed to be standing guard at two heavy oak doors that bore the legend: CITY COUNCIL CHAMBERS.

"What's going on here?" Kelly asked one of the men at the door who appeared to be the spokesman.

"A meeting."

"Who's meeting?"

"The Council."

When Kelly put out his hand to open the door, the man cried, "Hey, where do you think you're going?"

"Inside," Kelly replied with a faint smile.

"It's not open to the public," the man said.

"It never is," a man sitting on the rail said.

"Shut up, Mike," the first man ordered.

"You going to make me?"

The other looked for a moment as if he might take up the challenge, but changed his mind. Instead he turned back to us. "Meeting's private," he said. "What are you—reporters?"

"This is Congressman Shannon," I said.

"I thought perhaps I could help in some way," Kelly said. "Isn't a meeting like this public? What about the Civilian Defense? Volunteers?"

"Meeting's private," was the stubborn answer.

"We've been trying to get in for the last hour to find out what the hell they've done to the two guys from our union they arrested," the man on the railing said. "They won't give us the right time."

"We're not going to tell any Commies nothing," the man at the door said.

"Who you calling a Communist?" the man said, jumping from the rail and advancing, his face flushed, his fists clenched.

"Easy, Joe," another said, pulling him back.

"No tinhorn politician is going to call me a Commie," the man shouted.

"You and your God-damned union started this fire," the man at the door shouted back. "The cops picked up two of you guys only an hour ago!"

There was a sudden commotion below in the lobby. The men lining the rail leaned over, and someone cried, "Here's Max!"

There were heavy footsteps on the wooden stairs and loud voices; then a crowd appeared on the landing to move down the corridor to where we were standing.

At its head was an angry, scowling Max Dregna. He was almost on top of us before he recognized me. He stopped short and peered at me through his heavy glasses. "Finn! Finn McCool! What are you doing here?"

"I was just passing through with the congressman—Max, this is Congressman Shannon—"

"The senator's son?" Max held out his hand to Kelly. "I'm glad to know you, Congressman. What do you think of these people up here? They have two of my people in jail and say they started the fire."

"We told them, Max, those hicks were smoking in the plastic shop," someone shouted.

"Hicks? What hicks?" Max asked.

"The guys they brought up from North Carolina to move the plastic rolls to the railroad cars. Johnny here belted one guy who threw a butt into the waste—didn't you, Johnny?"

Johnny was an old man with a stubble of beard. He stepped out in front of the others and nodded vigorously.

"That's right, Max. I told 'em it was like throwing a match into gunpowder, but they just laughed at us."

Max pointed to the door. "Who's in there?"

"The City Council's meeting," the man at the door said. "It's emergency."

"The mayor? Is the mayor in there?"

"The mayor and the Council. It's private."

"I insist you tell your mayor or the members of the council to come out and talk to us," Kelly said. "Tell them Congressman Shannon and Mr. Dregna are out here."

"They gave orders the meeting's private," the man said in a stolid, unwavering way. "I can't help it; they gave me the orders."

I know this type; only dynamite can budge them. And money. I reached over and shook his hand, the crisp sawbuck slipping into his palm.

"I'm sure the boys will agree this is unusual," I said softly. "You'll only get in trouble if the congressman is kept waiting."

The man swallowed and put his hand in his pocket. "Well, maybe seein' the congressman's out here," he murmured. He inched open the door and slipped inside.

"Apparently the conditions up here are pretty bad," Kelly said to Max.

"That's an understatement, Congressman."

"Can't something be done about it?"

"This your district, Congressman?" Max asked, looking from Kelly to me.

"No, it isn't, Max," I said.

"What the hell has that got to do with it?" Kelly asked. "Isn't this your union?"

"That it is."

"Well, didn't they arrest two of your men?"

"Why do you think I'm up here?" Max snapped. "You think I left a good gin game to come up to see a fire?"

"I think you should have your union lawyer up here," Kelly said.

"I called him," Max said angrily. "He's out of town and won't be back until tomorrow."

Suddenly the heavy oak door swung open, so unexpectedly it almost knocked over some of the faithful who were standing guard.

In the doorway stood Barney Mullady and behind him the sweetest of his sweet chocolates, Gene Abernathy.

"Finn! Finn McCool, old friend! Come up to help, have you?" He pumped my hand, almost tearing it off at the shoulder. Then he swung to Kelly. "And Congressman Shannon! Our good neighbor who ran up to help poor old Lawrence!" He grabbed Kelly's hand and shook it vigorously.

"Finn, you remember Gene?"

"Of course," I said, and shook hands with the young Negro.

"This is Gene Abernathy, Barney's assistant," I explained. "Gene, this is Congressman Shannon."

They shook hands, barely nodding.

Barney began babbling about how Gene was his good right hand when he caught sight of Max. The smile vanished, and his face became a mask.

"What are you doing here, Dregna?"

Max said grimly, "I can ask you, Mullady—what are you doing here?"

"These people are old friends," Barney snapped. "Gene and I were driving down from Albany when I heard about the fire on the radio."

85

"What about my men they're holding?" Max said.

Barney ignored him, turning to the five men who were emerging from the meeting room.

"The City Council's ordered an emergency," he said loudly. "Every man that lost his job tonight will be on welfare before morning. Nobody's going to starve in Lawrence." He said to a short, stout man, "Isn't that right, Mayor?"

The mayor nodded vigorously.

"Mr. Lewis, the welfare commissioner, will be in his office within a half hour. We'll stay open all night if necessary."

"We don't need your relief checks," Max said. "The union will take care of its people."

"Yeah, I always heard your union has a big fat sock, Dregna," Barney said. "What do you guys do with all that money?"

"We don't give it to tinhorns, that's for certain," Max said. He turned to the mayor, "What about those two men your cops arrested?"

"They're being held for arraignment," Barney told him. "We have to check on them."

"When is the arraignment?" Max asked.

"When the police chief is ready," was the bland answer.

"Where is the police chief?"

"At the fire, telling his cops what to do," Barney said. "Isn't that where a police chief should be?"

"Dammit, you can't keep them incommunicado!" Max shouted. "There's a law against that."

"There are also laws to protect this community," Barney said, "against dangerous bastards like your two buddies. You know they have records?"

"Police records?" Kelly asked.

"Records for trespassing on public property," Barney said. "We found out they were arrested in New York for sitting in the street."

"That was a union demonstration!" Max shouted. "They were dismissed in court the next day. We had more than a hundred arrested."

"That just goes to show how you people pay no attention to law and order," Barney said. "A community has to protect—"

"You can't hold those men on a misdemeanor charge," Kelly said.

"It's more serious than that, Congressman," the mayor put in. "They're charged with arson, among other things."

"Do you have any evidence?" Kelly asked.

"Evidence enough."

"Then you have to arraign them," Kelly said. "My God, don't you know the High Court's ruling?"

"Oh, they'll be arraigned, Congressman," Barney said. "We're not depriving anybody of his rights."

"You are now if you don't arraign these men," Kelly replied. "Have they been advised of their rights?"

"Of course," the mayor said. "Of course."

"Where is the district attorney?"

"He's sending over an assistant tomorrow," the mayor said. He looked uneasily at Barney.

"Leave those guys overnight in jail, and the cops will bust their heads," someone shouted. "Get them out, Max."

"I demand they be arraigned at once," Max said. "At once!"

"Wait a minute, you God-damned plastics peddler," Barney snarled. "Just who the hell do you think you're talking to?"

"Mr. Dregna is right, Mr. Mayor," Kelly said. "You must arraign the defendants immediately." He turned to Mullady. "I'd advise you very strongly to keep out of this, Mullady."

For a long ten seconds Mullady and Kelly took each other's measure in that suddenly silent, crowded hallway. Then Mullady shrugged. "Congressman, I certainly don't want to get into any fight with you, but on the other hand these people are friends of mine and I intend to make sure they get the best advice—"

"Advice, fine. But let it end there."

"I confer with the district attorney tomorrow," the mayor began. "I am sure—"

"If these men are not arraigned within a half hour, I will personally call the Attorney General of the United States and protest that their constitutional rights are being violated," Kelly said softly. He glanced at his watch, then at the mayor. "Twenty-nine minutes, Mr. Mayor."

The mayor licked his lips and looked at his colleagues. They in turn looked at Barney, who waved his hand.

"No need to get all excited, Congressman. We got more important things to think about, haven't we, Mayor? Why don't you arraign those bums, and let's get back to fighting the fire."

"Call Schwartz's home and tell his wife to have one of his partners up here within a half hour or the union will have new lawyers by tomorrow," Max said to one of his assistants. "I think one of them lives in Scarsdale."

"Never mind, Mr. Dregna," Kelly said. "I'll represent your people." To the mayor, he added, "Who has the particulars?"

"The chief has them. I'll get him over here," the mayor said.

"Suppose you tell him we're on our way down," Kelly replied.

"I'll have to call the judge," the mayor said.

"Well, call him," Kelly said impatiently. "That's his job, isn't it?"

"For Christ's sake, Mayor, call the damn judge and get him over here to arraign these bums," Barney snapped. "And let's get on with fighting the fire. Gene, get my coat, will you?"

The shiny black face was impassive, but I thought, for one brief moment, there was resentment in Abernathy's eyes when he nodded silently and went inside the council chambers. But it was gone when he came out and helped Barney into his overcoat.

"Let's get over to that fire, Mayor," Barney said, carefully drawing on a pair of expensive gloves. "Be sure the congressman has everything he needs." He turned to Kelly with a thin smile. "I imagine one of these days we'll be meeting each other, Congressman."

"I don't think so," Kelly said in a quiet, cold voice.

"Oh, can I see you for a moment, Barney?" the mayor asked, and he and Mullady walked back into the council room.

"I don't think Mr. Mullady likes the congressman," Abernathy murmured to me.

"I can assure you the feeling is mutual."

"I can't recall the congressman ever calling on him."

"I don't think he ever will," I replied as Barney came out, gave a jerk of his head to Gene, and went down the hall, followed by the worried-looking mayor and city councilman.

"I called the chief," the mayor said as he passed Kelly. "He's on his way over. You can wait in his office downstairs."

With the buzzing, excited crowd streaming after us, we went down to the lobby, where we waited until the chief arrived, and then were ushered into his office. Edwards was seated at his desk when we entered. He had a bald bullet head, a hesitant smile, and vacant blue eyes. His big hands were toilworn, and I was ready to bet a steak dinner they could still plow a south forty with ease.

"We're here about the arraignment of the two union members," Max said.

"That's right," the chief replied. "The mayor just called me." He pawed at a folder. "I have the charges right here." He carefully put on horn-rimmed spectacles, let them slip down on his nose, and then began reading from an affidavit. In brief, it charged the union members with arson, inciting a riot, resisting arrest, and numerous other matters that I didn't catch.

Kelly placed his card on the chief's desk.

"I'm representing the accused, Chief. I'd like a few minutes with them."

The chief studied the expensively engraved card. "I guess it's all right . . ."

"All right!" Kelly exploded. "Murderers have a right to counsel! What kind of city is this?"

"No need to get excited, Congressman," the chief said. "Come along and I'll see you get in."

"What about the judge?" I asked.

"The mayor just called him. They sent a police car to pick him up. Now, you other fellows will have to wait out in the hall until we open up the court."

We waited in the lobby where Kelly, eyes frosty, lips thin, joined us.

"This is outrageous," he said. "They picked these men up on the basis of an anonymous phone call. One of them has a lump on his head the size of a duck egg. He said the detectives were in plain clothes, and never identified themselves when they entered the house. When he pushed them out, one hit him with a billy." He threw up his hands. "I thought this only happened down south!"

"Maybe you should look in your own backyard, Congressman," Max murmured.

"I'm beginning to think you're right, Max," Kelly said.

The arraignment was brief, and reminded me of a Kafka short story. The judge, obviously irritated at being called from his home, sat behind his desk, drumming his fingers as the affidavit was read. Kelly put in a plea of not guilty, then asked for nominal bail, pointing out that Dregna, head of the union, was present and would personally guarantee the appearance of the two men for trial. The judge listened impassively, then scrawled something across the bottom of the affidavit.

"One hundred thousand dollars' bail," he said. "Counsel will be notified of the trial date." He said to the court reporter, "Make a note of the congressman's address."

"This is outrageous, sir," Kelly began, but the judge swung about in his swivel chair, jumped to his feet, and was gone in a flurry of his robes.

We stood at the bench while two grinning cops snapped handcuffs on the two prisoners and yanked them through a side door.

"I wouldn't believe it if I wasn't here," Kelly said.

"We ought to burn the God-damned courthouse down around their ears," a big Negro said bitterly.

"Remember, no violence," Max said loudly. "If I catch anyone, I'll kick him out of the union."

"What are you going to do—let them rot down there?" someone asked.

Kelly was searching his pockets. He came up with two dimes.

"Give me what change you have," he said.

I dug down and so did Max to fill his hand with nickels and dimes.

"Stay here," he said shortly. "I'll be right back. I have to make some phone calls."

"Where are you going?"

"To get those two men out of jail, what else?"

We waited in the empty courtroom for about a half hour before a man came in and said Kelly told him to tell us he would be back and we should wait.

We settled back on the hard, old-fashioned pewlike benches, listening to the faint wailing of the far-off sirens and studying the faded lithographs of the American Flag, Justice, and Pledge of Allegiance.

Once the door opened and Barney looked in.

"Looks like the fire is under control," he said jovially. "We saved the storehouses. Anybody going downtown? Want a lift, old friend?" he said to me.

"I'll see you around, Barney," I told him.

"You do that," he replied. "What's the matter, Dregna? Can't raise the money for your boys?"

"Better get used to courtrooms, Mullady," Max said. "Someday you're going to be in one."

"Only to testify against you and your bomb throwers," Barney said cheerfully. "I told the cops to give your boys the deluxe suite. The one with a can."

He winked at me and walked out.

"Some day I'll get that bastard," Max whispered.

"Looks like you and your liberals haven't hurt him very much," I said.

"I'm sorry to have to agree with you."

In about an hour and a half Kelly was back. He looked windblown and weary, but there was a triumphant gleam in his eye.

"They'll be out in about twenty minutes," he said.

"They'll be out?" Max said, amazed. "How did you do it?"

"I located a Supreme Court judge I know. I had him sign a reduction of bail. It's down to a thousand. I gave them my check downstairs."

"Man, you moved!" the big Negro said admiringly.

"Well, if I moved so can you and all the other people who live here," Kelly said abruptly. "This place stinks of corruption. The only way it will be cleaned up is by its citizens. Remember that!" He glanced at his watch. "Well, Finn, it looks like you'll have to take a rain check on Wexford."

"You wait, I'll take you boys out to a fine steak dinner," Max said. "I know a place—"

Something told me this was the proper time for Kelly to make an exit. I told Max thanks and walked with Kelly out into the blustery night.

"I would have liked to talk with Dregna," he said, somewhat reprovingly as we entered his car.

"Some other time. Let them chew among themselves what a great guy you are. If you drop me off at the station I'll get a—"

"Don't be ridiculous. I'll drive you back to town. I might as well take a plane back tonight. There's a vote on the President's waterway bill tomorrow, and I have to be there."

"We should be back in Manhattan by midnight. I know a place where we can get a good steak sandwich."

"That makes sense, Finn. Let's do that."

"Just what the devil was Mullady doing up there tonight?" he asked as we swung onto the parkway.

"I don't know. Do you buy his story of just passing through?"

"It's too pat. And the mayor and the others weren't just friends."

"He certainly sounded like the boss of the outfit."

"Didn't he, though! That Lawrence must be quite a place. One of Dregna's boys told me he bought a taxicab in partnership with his son-in-law during the strike last year. The kid used his army pay, and they split the driving. He found out the nearest he could park to the airport, hotel, and the depot was three blocks." He turned to me. "Know why?"

"Traffic?"

"Hell, no. One of the commissioners owned a piece of a cab company, so he put through an ordinance giving his company the monopoly on the three best spots. All competition had to park three blocks away."

"It sounds like a hell of a place to live in."

"That's an understatement, from what I heard. That big Negro in the courtroom told me he sent his wife and kids to his father-in-law's apartment for a vacation last year. His father-in-law lives in Harlem. A vacation in Harlem!"

He was silent for a few minutes as we moved along the deserted parkway.

"How can a city exist like that, Finn? It just doesn't make sense."

"It's not unusual, Kelly. There are many northern cities run like Lawrence. The machine gradually makes inroads, year after year, until they are the absolute rulers. Opposition is stamped out, ruthlessly and immediately."

"It's virtually a police state."

"Not quite. Everything is done nice and legal. If they want a monopoly —like your taxicab driver—they pass a law. They can always think up a phony excuse, even make it sound logical. They have the police in their pocket, and usually the local newspaper is afraid to expose anything because they depend on political advertising and favors. Newspaper owners sometimes have money tied up in other interests, like real estate. It's very easy to raise taxes, you know."

"You think Barney Mullady has his hand in Lawrence?"

"Who knows? But I can tell you one thing: Barney Mullady has his hand in anything that produces money."

"Plunkett born all over again. Something just has to be done up there."

"It's not your district, Kelly. If it was, what would you do?"

"I don't know offhand but I'll come up with something. I shudder when I think of the people in that city represented by that idiot police chief. And that mayor!" He was silent for a moment, then said abruptly, "You seemed to know that young Negro who was with Mullady."

"Gene Abernathy? Josh met him when we talked to Mullady at the Tusk Club, but I had met him earlier at City Hall."

"He looks like a sharp young guy."

"That he is."

"I had the feeling he resented Mullady giving him orders like a valet.

He certainly didn't say anything, but for a moment I thought he was going to kick Barney right in his tail."

"You mean when Barney asked him to get his coat? Strange, Josh said the same thing after we had talked to Mullady at the club."

"I just don't think he's Barney's sweetest chocolate."

For the rest of the ride down to the city, Kelly didn't say much more; he just stared ahead, seemingly going and stopping automatically.

Just before we entered the city's limits he said softly, almost to himself:

" 'Whatever flames upon the night,
Man's own resinous heart has fed.' "

Yeats, "Two Songs from a Play." It was evident Kelly's thoughts had never left the flaming, tortured city of Lawrence.

We had dinner at Sullivan's, where Kelly promptly charmed old lady Sullivan by describing a walking tour he had taken through Killarney when he was in college. Later we walked down Broadway to Times Square and up Eighth Avenue to the Sheridan where I managed to get him in for a nightcap of two fingers of Jack Daniels.

In the next three hours he bitterly, almost savagely, denounced the type of political leadership such as we had encountered in Lawrence. From Lawrence we accidentally drifted into the vast problems of housing and the poverty programs.

I always say you know the expert, not by the facts and figures he can throw at you, but from the logical, forceful answers he gives to your questions. Kelly did just that. It was obvious he not only had studied the problems but also had original ideas.

In between our ideological discussions we swapped stories of Washington, the inside yarns of senators, congressmen, and Cabinet members. We laughed at some or shook our heads in dismay at others.

Suddenly it was after two. Kelly was all for leaving, but I persuaded him to stay over, pointing out that the eight o'clock shuttle would get him to Washington in plenty of time for the House vote. He agreed, and we called it a night.

I never heard the alarm. When I awoke there was a note stuck in the toaster:

"It was a grand evening. Many thanks. I insist you and Josh take a rain check for Wexford—deal or no deal!"

All during shaving and breakfast I reviewed the events of the previous night and the impressive part Kelly had played. Twin emotions shook me: I knew now this was no ordinary young man, and we just had to join him—but at the same time a tiny, almost inaudible voice kept crying out a warning in the far reaches of my brain. But this was no time for dark moods and intangible fears; we had a winner and we had better take advantage of it.

This is what I told Josh when we sat down to dinner that night. I reviewed dramatically and in detail the events in Lawrence and later the long talk and discussion I had with Kelly. He listened, nodding or asking a perfunctory question from time to time. Suddenly I realized he was asking more questions about Barney than about Kelly.

"Mullady's important. It's as simple as that," Josh said when I pointed this out to him.

"How is he important, Josh, if you haven't decided to accept the senator's proposal?"

"The truth is, I've also been doing a lot of thinking."

"About Kelly?"

"Who else?" He shoved the coffee cup aside impatiently. "The guy's got under my skin. My common sense tells me to avoid him like the measles, but something else keeps telling me the guy could be a winner." He gave me an abashed look. "The truth is, Finn, I came back with the intention of talking you into taking Shannon's deal!"

"I think we should, Josh; I really do think so!"

"I like what you told me about last night. It doesn't look as if you can push him around."

"Oh, he has a mind of his own. His father told me that the first time we met. After last night I have no doubt about it."

"Yes, and that's the one thing I don't like," was Josh's wry reply. "You've been in the business long enough to know the headaches that can produce! It's like the guy whose life story you've just written. He doesn't know how to write his own name, but now that the book is published he's an author!"

"I don't think we'll have too much trouble with Kelly. He sounds reasonable."

"Sometimes being reasonable isn't enough. Will he bend? Compromise? You heard him on Mullady. Suppose we needed Mullady and we had to make a fast deal? Christ, this kid could give us headaches!" He walked to the window. "That's what I mean about my common sense putting out warning signals."

"I don't think he'll ever give in about Mullady."

"Certainly not after last night, but there's one ace," Josh said musingly. "We know what the senator's like, and from what he told us about Kelly's brother, Luke, we know they're a fine pair of bastards. But bastards we can talk to." He spun around. "We can keep this up all day! Let's fish or cut bait!"

"Do you want me to call the senator?"

He studied me for a long minute.

"You sure you want to go?"

"More sure than I have ever been in my life," I said.

"Okay," Josh said. "Call him. Tell him we'll be up. Today's Friday. Make it tomorrow afternoon. Tell him we're going to take it, and to have Luke and—what's her name—oh, yes, Lacey there."

He turned back to the window, and I almost didn't hear his comment: "I wonder what *she*'s like?"

BOOK 2
☆☆☆☆☆☆☆
The Buildup ☆☆☆☆☆☆☆☆☆☆

CHAPTER SEVEN: WEXFORD HALL

WEXFORD HALL was marble white with black trimmed shutters, a sprawling Victorian house with gables and turrets set on a rise, majestic and proud as the king's own. The winter-dead lawns were so neat they could have been sheared with a barber's clippers, and the stark oaks lined the way like a papal guard. There were stables and garages, two tennis courts, a large field, a basketball backboard over the door of a large, old-fashioned carriage house, an enormous veranda, swings, chairs, and tables. An incongruous touch was a swing made of an old tire hanging from the oak in front of the house. A scuffed patch of dirt showed it had been put to use. As we drew near we could see, beyond the house, lawns that gradually sloped into a gentle valley where a battalion of leafless trees marched upward to the rim of another hill.

Just beyond the house was an enormous, empty swimming pool and a big corral. A young woman and some children were riding sedately in the corral. Another horsewoman was coming from the valley at a gallop.

She was bent over her horse's neck and heading for a series of hurdles that stretched in the rear of the carriage house to the open field.

"Hey, she can ride!" Josh said admiringly.

The rider soared gracefully over the first hurdle, then the next and the next until she disappeared around the carriage house.

"Whoever she is, she certainly can ride. And that was a damn good hunter she was on," Josh remarked.

"Maybe you can get a chance to do some riding," I said.

"When I think of how I used to live on a horse." Josh sighed.

"As I recall, there was a time you went out every Sunday morning."

"That was only because a particular senator's daughter liked riding," Josh answered quickly, as a beaming Negro in a white coat hurried down the steps to escort us into the house.

My lasting impression of Wexford is gleaming, polished parquet floors, flowers, sun-splashed furniture, a woman's sweet voice calling—and young people. They seemed to be all over the place, laughing, hurrying, arguing. A group was standing or sprawled about the sun porch, trying to make themselves heard over the blaring of that wild, raucous music that all young people today seemed to thrive on. Then Senator Shannon was wheeling across the room with hand outstretched. As I shall always remember, there was a softening in the old man whenever we met him in Wexford Hall.

"It's good to see you, McCool," he said. "Welcome to Wexford Hall, Michaels."

I had a strange feeling that I was in the antebellum age and that the master of all he surveyed was welcoming his guests with juleps and soft words while the darkies sang in the twilight.

Josh must have felt the same, because he praised the beautiful old house as one that is not seen much any more.

"It will stay here as long as there's a Shannon alive," the old man said, and I believed him. "Let's meet the family," he began. Then, "Oh, here's Kelly."

Kelly was hurrying down the wide hall. He was dressed in slacks, a worn sweatshirt, and sneakers. His face was flushed, his eyes sparkling. He looked the perfect specimen of a healthy young man.

"Luke and I just took a run over to Molly's," he explained to his father. "He's driving her over to that historical-society meeting." He turned to us, "Finn, it's good to see you again. And Josh. Welcome to Wexford."

"I was just telling the senator what a beautiful place it is," Josh said.

"We saw a young lady doing some great riding as we came up," I told him.

"That's Lacey," Kelly replied. "She's been working that damned hunter all morning. My wife and kids were the ones in the corral."

"Do you have many horses?" Josh asked.

"We have only five now," Kelly replied. "Four jumpers and a frisky quarter. Do you ride, Josh?"

"I haven't done much in the last two years."

"Let them meet the family first," the senator said, "then give them a drink."

There were ramps throughout the house, and we followed the senator down the hall to the noisy sun porch.

"It's no use trying to introduce you to them singly," Kelly told us. "They're all Shannons, give or take a few." He made a megaphone of his hands and called out: "This is Finn McCool and Josh Michaels. They know everything there is to know about politics."

"That's fine," a big redhead called out. "Come in and join the fight."

"Later," Kelly said. "Where are the others?"

98

"They're either playing eight ball in the billiards room or marking up the field."

"We going to play?"

"Are you kidding?" the redhead said. "I got my lumps last time. Now it's my turn."

"Oh, God," the senator groaned. "Are they going to play again today?"

"A few cracks on the head might give them some sense," Kelly remarked cheerfully. "Lacrosse," he explained to Josh. "We've been having a tournament in the family for years." He pointed to a battered silver cup. "That's our trophy. Whoever wins gets to hold it for a year, and the losers buy a keg and cook the barbecue."

"Lacrosse?" I asked. "The Indian game?"

"The same," Kelly said. "Do you know anything about it, Finn?"

"I know someone who played it."

"Damn-fool game," the senator grumbled. "All they do is chase a little ball with a fishnet and crack each other's head open. The girls are worse than the boys."

"Would you like to see the stables?" Kelly asked.

"Oh, they don't want to see a lot of smelly horses, Kel," the senator protested.

"Really, Senator, I would like to see your horses," Josh said. "How about you, Finn?"

"Well, all horses look alike to me, but I'm game."

"Howard, please get the senator's sweater," Kelly said to the colored servant who was hovering nearby. He hurried off and returned with a heavy coat sweater that he helped the old man put on. Then we followed him outside.

It was a breathtaking view of hills, like rolling brown waves under the startling blue sky, gardens with colored slate walks, and outbuildings painted green and white, gleaming in the bright sun. A striking young blonde woman leading two beautiful children, both dressed in boots and jodhpurs, were leaving the corral when we came up.

"This is my wife, Pam," Kelly said, "and Sean and Tura."

"Pam, this is Finn McCool and Josh Michaels. Kids, say hello . . ."

The two children obediently chorused their hellos, then ran off.

"I'm supposed to be teaching them how to ride," Pam said, "but they keep telling me what to do." She shook her head. "Thank God they start school next fall."

"Sean insists he's going to ride to school," Kelly said with a grin.

"Yes—in the school bus," she replied. "I'm going to clean them up now, dear, I'll see you later."

We dutifully inspected the stables and the four horses. As far as I was concerned, they could have been the nags that hauled O'Grady's coal wagon for years down Ninth Avenue, but Josh and Kelly examined eyes and teeth and ran their hands down the animals' legs like a couple of horse traders. The quarter horse, which Josh called a buckskin, looked to me like a mean-eyed animal, but Josh gently stroked its side and whispered to it soothingly.

"Have you reached your decision yet, McCool?" the senator asked in a low voice.

"We have."

"Well, what is it, man?"

"Let's wait until we get inside, Senator," I said. "I think we should hear it all together."

He made an angry sound in his throat but said nothing.

We were leaving the stables when the black-haired young woman we had seen taking the hurdles rode up. She vaulted out of the saddle and patted the neck of the animal, whose sides were working like a pair of bellows.

"Looks like you really gave him a ride, Lace," Kelly called out. "Come on over and say hello."

She was slender, older than Pam, and not as pretty, but still very attractive, with high cheekbones, clear hazel eyes, and glossy black shoulder-length hair. As she walked over to us I was reminded of a young Katherine Hepburn.

"This is my sister, Lacey," Kelly said.

"Lace, this is Finn McCool and Josh Michaels. We hope they're going to run the campaign."

Her hand was slender, but I got the impression of strength. Though she had Kelly's smile, her manner, while friendly, was a bit aloof. You had to win this one's approval and confidence, I told myself.

"You took those hurdles like a real professional," Josh said.

"I'm glad you didn't see us kick the bars off the last two," she said with a laugh.

"It looks like you have a full house today, Senator," I said as we went back to the house, leaving Kelly, Lacey, and Josh with the horses.

"It's the same every other Sunday. You know, there were ten of us born in this house. Kelly has aunts and uncles, nieces and nephews from the Mohawk Valley to California. Oh, by the way, Kelly tells me you and he had quite an experience in Lawrence the other night."

"It was an experience, there's no doubt about that."

"What do you think Mullady was doing up there, McCool?"

"I haven't the slightest idea, Senator. But this I do know—you'll never get Kelly to make a deal with Mullady."

"We may need that old thief."

"Not your son."

"I'll talk to Kelly when the time comes," he said impatiently. "What's more important, what do you think of him?"

"I liked the way he faced up to Mullady and those other morons in

Lawrence. As you said, he certainly has a mind of his own. Tell me, was he always like this?"

He thought for a moment, then began chuckling. "This should answer your question, McCool. He was in prep school and on a holiday when he came in with a mutt that had been hit by a truck out on the highway. One of the animal's legs had been cut off. He brought the poor thing in here, and I wanted to call the state police and have one of their men put it out of its misery, but Kelly just ignored me. He got the vet out of bed— hell, I think it was New Year's Day—to fix that three-legged hound. Every day I wanted to call the pound, but Kelly wouldn't have it. He argued that the poor thing had a right to live as well as our champion setters. He got Lacey and Luke to join him, and, well—we had that damn three-legged mutt for nine years. He died of old age."

"How was he at school?"

"They almost threw him out of Gardner twice. He was the leader of the misfits. All the kids that didn't belong, well, they followed Kelly. 'Why did you bring this kid home?' I'd ask him. 'Because I happen to like him,' was his answer. Now, Luke was different. He hung out with the kids who played football and went to dances and raised hell. The normal kids. Not Kelly. He was always bucking the God-damn world for someone else. He was popular, though; in senior year he was captain of the varsity football team."

"He went to Yale then, didn't he?"

"Yale wasn't too bad. In freshman year he broke a leg playing football, and that ended that. He met Pam when he was a senior, and they were married a year after he graduated from law school. I had him in Washington for a few years, and he took to it like a seal to ice. Pam didn't like it much, but she'll follow him to the gates of hell if it will do Kelly any good. They're all like that."

"This may be a stupid question, Senator, but why do you—"

"Why do I think he can be elected President?" He turned his chair to face me. "Is that it, McCool? Well, did you ever have the feeling you're dead right about something? That what you're doing is so right that if you don't do it, you'll regret it for the rest of your life? Well, that's the way I feel about Kelly. I know in the marrow of my bones he's going to win Albany and then the Presidency. You know, it's going to be a long way from Lace Pants Shannon who smelled so much like kerosene his wife wouldn't eat with him to my son in a top hat taking the oath on Pennsylvania Avenue!"

"From where we sit here, Senator," I reminded him, "it's a tough road to that spot."

"Sure it is," he said, his gray eyes glowing, "but we'll make it, McCool. Kelly, you, Michaels, me and my family—and my money." He leaned forward, his face grim. "And let's not forget, it—Benny Jello."

"Even put together, it would be a miracle if we win, Senator."

"I've always found out that you can pull off any miracle as long as you have the right connections, McCool," was his curt reply. He nodded to the window. "Here's Luke now, with Molly Shapiro."

Luke, like Kelly, was dressed in slacks, sweatshirt, and sneakers. He was carrying what appeared to be a long wooden fishnet. I immediately recognized it as a lacrosse bat from pictures Josh had showed me of North Dakota.

. Walking next to him, chatting gaily, was a petite woman, obviously in her fifties. Outlandish green stone earrings swayed as she walked. Her hair, dyed a dark red, was cut with bangs, and for a moment I wondered what she reminded me of—then it came to me: a flapper from the twenties.

As they came up the walk they caught sight of us, and waved.

"Molly's been like a favorite aunt to our kids," Senator Shannon said. "When they were young she had the horses. Lacey's her favorite. She's lived alone since the old man died." He shook his head. "She dresses like 1925, but she's a grand person. The kids really love her."

There was a knock on the door, and when the senator called out to come in, Luke entered. He had his father's cold, suspicious gray eyes, a bony face, hawk's nose, and Lacey's high cheekbones. That was Luke. We shook hands when the senator introduced us; then he excused himself, explaining that he had to go out and make sure they were marking the field correctly.

Molly, who had been talking to someone out in the hall, came into the library, bright-eyed and as alert as an inquisitive bird.

When we were introduced she held out a slender, well-cared-for hand.

"That damn game again, Molly," Shannon said.

"Well, Senator, first it was football," she said. "Remember when Kelly broke his arm? What a day, what a day."

"I was out when it happened," the senator said. "It was a compound fracture, and the bone was sticking through the skin. Lacey ran over to Molly, and she drove them all over looking for a doctor."

"Playing golf," Molly said indignantly. "They're never home when you need them."

"Didn't you finally get one?"

"Dr. Lawton over in Blairtown," she said. "He had a nice Hempel chair, but he wouldn't sell."

"Molly collects antiques," the senator said dryly.

"One more antique and I live in the barn."

"Molly," the senator said softly, leaning forward, "Mr. McCool and Mr. Michaels, who will be back shortly, are the men I told you about. They went to see Benny."

"We have to get him out of there, Senator," she said fiercely. "Every day it's getting worse. If I don't pay them, they keep me waiting; they tell me I can only visit him at certain times. . . ."

"We'll do something," Shannon told her. "Don't worry."

She said, biting her lips, "How can I help worrying?" She turned to me, the soft brown eyes shining with tears. "Oh, if you could only help me, Mr. McCool!"

"We're trying."

"Has the senator told you about Benny?" Without waiting for a reply she went on. "I suppose I should be ashamed of myself, an old woman like me worrying about a man like that. When I first heard he was a thief and a no-good, I told myself I would never see him again." She shrugged. "That lasted three days. I guess what they say is right; there's nothing like an old fool."

The senator reached over and patted her hand.

"You don't have to explain, Molly."

But she ignored him, and went on: "I have a big house, a beautiful house, but I'm also fifty-five years old—and alone. I've been living alone since my father died nine years ago. I tell you, I have counted the hours I sat there by that window just staring out at nothing. In the village they say Molly is the busiest woman in the county, with the committees and the antiques. But what they don't know, Mr. McCool, is that sometimes the busiest women are the loneliest. Sure, Benny's a thief, but I love him. What can I say? I told this to Lacey, and she understands—I think sometimes she's the only one who does."

In a few minutes, Lacey, Josh, and Kelly came into the library, glowing with vitality. When Lacey saw Molly she hurried over and hugged her.

"I was just asking your father where the years have gone," Molly said. "It seems only yesterday you were showing me your first jodhpurs, and Kelly and Luke wanted nothing but red jackets."

"That was right after you had taken us to see the horse show," Kelly said. "Luke and I were determined to ride like the Royal Mounted."

"By the way, Miss Shapiro," I said, "this is my partner, Josh Michaels."

"Miss Shapiro?" she said as she offered her hand to Josh, "it always makes me feel like an old bag."

"What do you mean 'old'?" Kelly said. "Didn't I take you to my Valentine dance in high school?"

"That he did," Molly said to us, her voice still tinged with the amazement of it. "It was crazy, but I went."

"And you both won the Charleston contest," said Pam, who had just entered. "Kelly still has that cup upstairs."

Molly smiled, and they all smiled back at her. It was obvious they viewed her with a great deal of affection.

"Where's Luke?" Kelly asked.

"Making sure they're marking the field correctly or some fool thing like that," the senator growled. "Do you have to play that damn game today?"

"Just for a few points," Kelly said. "The others will be disappointed if we don't." He explained to us, "Lacrosse. Did you ever play it, Josh?"

"Oh, I've seen it played. It's quite a rough game."

"Would you like to join us for the laughs?"

"Well, I don't—"

"Perhaps Mr. Michaels could be our scorekeeper," Lacey said brightly.

"It's Josh, Lace," Kelly said, "and if Josh wants to keep score, well, that's fine."

"Oh, no," Josh said easily, "I'm game to try."

To try? I looked at Josh, who gave me a bland, innocent look.

"You're staying for lunch of course?" Lacey said to Molly.

"If I stay for lunch I'll only get involved," she said, throwing up her hands. "Such arguments! It's better I go down to my meeting of the county historical society."

"Are they going to have the house tours again this year?" the senator asked.

"Why not!" Molly said with a shrug. "The Shannons, the Shapiros, the De Witts, Cogwells, Monroes—all the houses, the same as always."

"Every spring the local historical society sponsors a tour of the old houses in the county," Kelly explained. "Molly's is a real showplace."

"Three days a week I have a cleaning lady," Molly said. "But who cleans the stuff? Me. She won't touch it. She says if anything breaks I'll charge her." She got up and shook hands with the senator, Josh, and myself, and kissed Lacey and Kelly on the cheek.

"Luke said he would drive me over to the museum," she said.

"I'll get Howard to run you down," Pam said. "Luke is probably covered with lime by now."

"Did he get the new crosse?" Kelly asked when Molly had left with Pam.

"He came in with it," the senator said. "I think he picked it up at the station when he drove Molly over here."

"Did you talk to Molly?" Kelly asked.

"Briefly," the senator said. "We'll discuss it after lunch, along with a lot of other things. When will you get that damn game over with?"

"Right now," Kelly said. "I'll get the others and we'll meet you at the field. Josh? Lace? Ready?"

"I'm ready," Lacey said. Then, with a faint smile, "Are you *sure* you want to play, Mr. Michaels?"

"Josh," Kelly said firmly. "And I'm sure he wants to play. Let's go."

They went out, and I thought Lacey winked at her father.

I almost laughed out loud.

"Want to watch them, McCool?" the senator said, "or would you rather stay here and have a few more?"

"Oh, no. I wouldn't miss this for the world."

"Those young idiots get a little too rough sometimes on visitors. Maybe I'd better talk to Kelly."

"I'm sure Josh can handle himself, Senator."

"I know Kelly will take it easy, but that Lacey!" He jerked his chair around abruptly and headed for the door. "Since they were kids she's insisted she could do everything they could do—and better!" He stopped at the door and turned around. "You know what?" he asked with a faint smile. "Most of the time she's been right!"

The grassy field was a large one marked off with white lines. The goals were about six feet high, and fitted with a pyramid cord netting, all in an area about eighteen feet square, which they called the "goal crease." The field was also divided by a white line drawn to the center perpendicular to the sidelines. In the center of the field was a white circle. When we reached the field Josh and the Shannons, wearing what looked like football helmets with wire screen, and padded gloves were tossing the tiny sponge ball between them, adroitly catching it in the wooden net that the senator told me was called the "crosse." The object is to carry the ball in the crosse through your opponent's lines and through his goalposts. The senator rattled off the positions: goalkeepers, cover point, first and second defense, center, second and first attack, outside home and inside home. Two of the cousins, over their protests, were elected referee and judge of play. It was evident that the senator, despite his grumbling, enjoyed the game, which he said was wild and woolly.

"I just hope those young idiots don't send your boss home with a shiner," he said.

I chuckled inwardly, but I said humbly, "I hope not." Then I sat back to watch the massacre.

What the Shannons didn't know was that Josh Michaels had been playing lacrosse since he was able to ride—and that was a step from the cradle —with the wildest lacrosse players in America—the young Sioux at Standing Rock Agency, a mile from his grandfather's ranch.

When Pam, Lacey, and a few of the other female Shannons rushed out on the field to take their positions, the senator said, "They can be rougher than men. Watch this."

The game started with the centers, each with his back to his own goal and the ball placed between the reserved surfaces of their crosses and the wood on the ground. This is the ball being "faced," and until it is out of the white circle no other players can enter it. While this is being done each team must confine the goalkeeper and two other players in the defense goal area, two players in the attack goal area, and one player in each of the wing areas. As soon as the referee's whistle sounds, they can be released from their respective areas. At all times during the game each team must have three men on the attack between the center of the field and the boundary of the field behind the goal, the other players being on the defense. Josh and Kelly were on the same team, and on the attack

Luke and a strapping, fiery-haired Shannon cousin were on the defense along with the girls.

As the senator explained, the skill of the game lies in how deftly you can handle your crosse.

The game exploded with the first whistle. Although Josh had described it to me, I had never seen it played or realized what a bloody, rough game it was. It was fast, and only for those in the best of condition.

It was quite evident that these Shannons played to win; when his red-haired cousin muffed a throw, Luke roared at him until the young man's face was the color of his hair.

Even the girls played with a fierce determination, racing up and down and skidding and sliding on the grass until their rears were green and covered with lime. No holds were barred, and once Lacey gave Kelly a crack with her crosse that made him limp.

Josh didn't distinguish himself in the first quarter—there are two periods of fifteen minutes each—apparently he wanted to get the feel of the field and his teammates. But in the second quarter he swung into action. In the first few minutes he scored two goals, once dodging under Luke's crosse and sending the ball into the net with a quick underhand snap that made the ball travel like a shot only a few inches above the grass. The big red-haired cousin received a body check that sent him sprawling in the second goal.

As I recalled, Josh also said that the Iroquois liked long throws but that the Sioux went for short exchanges, flipping the ball between them until one of their teammates was in a better position to start an attack or to shoot it at the goal. This was rough, and required a great deal of skill in handling the crosse.

By the end of the game Kelly and Josh were working well as a team. They moved down the field hurling the tiny ball between them, then passing it to another to try for a goal. Luke was the best player on the other side. Although he had half the strength of his big cousin, he still made him look like an oaf. The girls were uncommonly good, and it was obvious Lacey was out to stop Josh. For her troubles she got cracked on the hands, her crosse was sent spinning, and in the final few minutes there was a great outcry from Pam because Josh had hit Lacey across the rear with the flat end of his crosse. She was a furious young woman, and the hoots and laughter of Kelly and Luke made her angrier. I found myself joining the senator and cheering them on. Finally the whistle sounded, and they came off the field, covered with lime and grass stains, limping and shouting insults at one another.

If the Shannons had used this wild, crazy game as a crucible, it was obvious Josh had emerged with glory. Even Luke seemed impressed, but Lacey gave him a glowering look.

"You didn't say you could play," she said accusingly.

"You didn't ask," Josh said.

"There'll be a next time."

"Any time, Lacey."

"Come on, Josh," Kelly said. "We'll have a shower, a drink in the library, then lunch."

"Your boy surprised them, McCool," the senator said as he returned to the big house. "Particularly Lacey."

"Do your visitors always join in your games, Senator?"

"Sometimes." He looked up. "Why?"

"I thought perhaps it may be the Shannon way of taking a man's measure."

"I brought them up to handle themselves in a fight, sports, politics, and life," the old man said, "and to win as often as possible."

He continued wheeling himself up the graveled path. "And you can't win if you have a weak sister on your side."

"Politics can be a hell of a lot rougher than lacrosse, Senator, as you well know."

"Up here we're all well aware of that. Maybe that's why we wanted to see your boy in action." He paused at the door. "You know, McCool, if your answer is No, you boys are going through a hell of a lot just to be polite."

Lunch was held in the large, sunny dining room, with its old-fashioned windows that extended from the floor to near the ceiling. There were enormous platters of cold meat, salads, and several kinds of chilled wines. The conversation was brisk, ranging from sports to the arts. No politics. That was Lacey's rule, and she banished anyone who violated it. Even the senator.

Pam, Kelly, the senator, Lacey, Luke, Josh, and I sat at one table; the rest of the clan were seated in a smaller adjoining room and the children in the kitchen.

Over coffee and delicious chilled fresh fruit, Kelly asked Josh if he had played lacrosse at school.

Several turned—including Lacey—to catch his answer.

Josh smiled. "Chunkey, we used to call it."

"Oh? Is that what they called it at your school?"

"Dartmouth?" Luke suggested. "They have a good team."

Josh shook his head. "Standing Rock Agency, North Dakota. Chunkey is Sioux for the woman's game. It's something like lacrosse—but much rougher."

Kelly looked startled. "You played with Indians, Josh?"

"I never knew there were white men until I was twelve," Josh said. "I played attack with the daughter of Man-Afraid-of-His Horse." He fingered the lobe of his ear. "Once she almost tore my ear off."

This tickled me. It always did when Josh brought this up. I'm sure by now he secretly knows what effect this stuff has on people when he springs it, deadpan, just as he was doing now. I've watched him do this time and again, say at an important cocktail party. We'd be sitting around, arguing and taking apart Congress or the President, and when there was a lull, somehow the subject would swing around to Indian affairs. Someone would say How do you know so much about this subject? and Josh would answer simply that he had been brought up with the Sioux.

Like he pulled a bloody little wire, all heads would turn to him.

Indians, Mr. Michaels?

I don't know what it is about us big-city people, but just the word Indians fascinates us. Maybe its television. I know that out West they just grunt, and couldn't care less. But not us in the East. I love it when Josh starts telling those Indian stories. When I first knew him, he would drag out a book of snapshots and some yellowing clippings and tell how he grew up with those people and how he wrote stories about them for the county weekly when he was in the state university. But in the last few years he hasn't done much of that. In fact, he hasn't been to the ranch in three years. He wants to go, but he always gets sidetracked. Washington is a busy place for image makers, politically and socially.

Lately for both of us the ranch has become sort of a Shangri-La. For me it's misty, unreal, something blurred by the distorted versions of Hollywood and television. But at any rate, the Indian talk never failed to catch attention, and I can recall even now the details of that luncheon; the gay, sunny room, the far-off sounds of the children lunching in the kitchen, the flicker of interest in Lacey's eyes, and Pam, her pretty face lighting up with delight because her woman's instinct must have told her something was starting, and those cold blue eyes of Luke taking Josh apart and putting him together.

Lacey frowned a bit. "You're not Indian, Josh?"

"Norwegian, Scotch, and Irish," Josh said cheerfully. "No Indian."

"But you said you grew up on an Indian reservation?"

"My grandfather's ranch is on the north border of the reservation," Josh said quietly. "My parents were killed in an automobile accident in 1933, right in the midst of the Depression. My grandfather raised me on the ranch, and I attended elementary school and high school just off the reservation. After the state university I went to work for AP in Mendota, then UPI in Washington, and finally the *Post*."

"They read his column before they ate breakfast," the senator said.

Kelly said with a smile, "So I've heard."

But Josh was still talking to Lacey. "Come on up to the ranch on Nations Day, and I'll show you how lacrosse is really played—fifty men to a side, and no holds barred. There's an old Mohawk—"

"A Mohawk in the Dakotas?" Lacey said quickly. "They're upper New York and Canadian."

"Mohawks have been out West since the eighteenth century," Josh said easily. "The *coureurs du bois* brought them out as beaver trappers."

"Lacey was always interested in Indians, Josh," Pam said. "Wasn't that your Master's thesis, Lacey?"

Lacey looked self-conscious. "The Iroquois Confederacy."

Josh put on what I always called his professorial look. He frowned and and seemed to consider her statement. "You used Morgan, of course?"

"I found Hale much better. He went into Canada and lived at Brant-ford with—"

"Did you run across Joseph Brant in Hale?"

The senator cleared his throat. "Suppose we go into the library," he said, "and leave those poor Indians to the wagon trains."

"Someday we'll realize that the American Indian groups are just as important as the Negro," Lacey said indignantly.

"As far as I'm concerned, they're all pressure groups run by radicals," the senator growled.

"Is Lacey a radical, Dad, because she cares about people less fortunate than herself?" Kelly asked quietly.

Pam put in, "Remember what that Jesuit from the Indian mission in Alabama told us last year."

"He told me he needed money," the senator said. "That lunch cost me a thousand dollars."

Luke looked bored. "Let's go to the library, gentlemen."

"And we'll take the kids for a walk, Pam," Lacey said. "I'm sure these political geniuses don't want a woman's viewpoint."

Josh began, "On the contrary—"

"Let's go while we're winning, Josh," Kelly said.

We all laughed, and the lunch broke up.

"This was a mild one," Pam whispered to me. "You should be here when they're shouting at each other." She whistled softly and raised her eyes upward.

Quite a family, I told myself as I followed Luke, Kelly, Josh, and the senator to the library.

There is one room in Wexford Hall that stands out in my memory more than any other, and that is the library. There were books to the ceiling, large worn leather chairs, a fireplace that crackled cheerily on winter nights, a portable bar, and a deep wall-to-wall carpet. In one of the center shelves were trophies won by Lacey, Kelly, and Luke at all sorts of sports since they were children. I can recall Kelly telling me that he considered the library one of the "happiest" rooms in Wexford Hall. This is where he first discovered books as a young boy when recuperating from an attack of pneumonia. Apparently he and Lacey were close, and they spent hours together in separate parts of the room, reading every-thing and anything.

I sampled a few books and found most to be on political science, biography—there was one of my old favorites, a life of Disraeli, and surprisingly, poetry, with emphasis on Yeats.

"Do you like Yeats, Finn?" Kelly asked.

"An Irishman not liking Yeats?"

He flipped a book from an upper shelf. "*The Lonely Tower*, T. R. Henn's great study of Yeats. Lacey read it first and recommended it to me."

"I'll bet this one is Lacey's," Josh said and held up a thick, heavy book. "Hodge's *Handbook of American Indians* . . . As I recall there are two volumes. We used them as doorstops on the Mendota County *Democrat*."

"Lacey has a whole Indian section," Kelly said.

"What does she do?" Josh asked.

"She teaches retarded children down on the Lower East Side," Kelly said with a great deal of pride. "She's worse on that subject than she is on Indians."

The sullen, cautious March afternoon was filling the valley when Luke closed the door and we took seats about the fireplace. There was a small, cheery fire, the eager yellow flames climbing the sides of the split logs, piled tentlike in the grate.

The senator waved to the bar. "Help yourselves."

Nobody did, and we settled back.

"Well, Michaels," the senator said. "What's your decision?"

"We're going to take it," Josh said. "Finn and I have talked it over, and we feel there's a chance Kelly could win—" He held up a hand. "I said a chance, and frankly that would be your money, Benny Jello's story, and a series of big miracles."

"You don't give us much of a chance then?" Luke asked.

"You want it straight, don't you?"

"Nothing else but," Kelly said.

"The odds are all against you. It's not only going to take the miracles, Benny's story, your father's money, but also a hell of a lot of work, and a fast-moving organization to get Kelly into Albany. In any other year I wouldn't dare tackle this one. But now that the party's split into so many factions—"

"You saw Jello?" Luke asked.

"Finn and I both talked to him in jail."

"What do you think of him?"

"He's a thief," was Josh's quick reply. "I'm sure he'd sell his best friend to get off the hook."

"But he also has dynamite information," Luke said.

"Dynamite has to be touched off properly," Kelly said. "Before we use a line of what Jello told us, I want it checked and double checked."

"I agree with that," I said. "So does Josh."

"And he must have complete protection—"

"For God's sake, Kel, he'll be protected," Luke said. "The way you've been talking, you'd think this thief is an honest, God-fearing citizen."

"I don't care if he's the bad thief," Kelly said firmly. "Once we start to use him, he's our responsibility."

"I wouldn't worry about his safety," Josh said, "but I agree we have to prove everything he says."

"We're not using any state, local, or federal agency, so how would you go about doing that?"

"I have someone in mind," Josh said. "We've used him before."

"He's reliable then?"

"Reliable as the Grand Central clock."

"Hire him," the senator said. "Hire as many men as you need."

"Finn said you made a tour of upstate," Kelly said. "Are conditions the same?"

"Politically, yes. The Democrats are split ten ways. It's the same in Queens as in Buffalo. The way I see it, if they don't get together, they'll lose their majority in both the Senate and Assembly. They're squabbling like hell now over legislative leadership posts."

"It's so bad," I said, "it might even come to an alliance between the Democratic minority and the Republicans."

"Then the field is still wide open?" Luke said.

"That's one of the reasons we're here," Josh said.

"But Gentile is still strong," Kelly said.

"Very strong at this point."

"That's why we have to develop Jello's stuff," the senator said. "We have to knock Gentile out of the box."

"And that won't be easy," Josh said grimly. "He's popular in the city and his strength is growing, not upstate, but nationally."

"That's one thing we must never lose sight of, gentlemen." He leaned forward. "This is not a campaign only for the governorship; we're running Kelly for the White House! And that we must never forget!"

"Kelly gave me a rundown on what happened between him and Mullady up at Lawrence," Luke said. "What do you think about Mullady?"

"There is no doubt he has to be considered."

"He's a blight on American politics," Kelly said.

"Could be," Luke said, "but he's also a practical politician."

"A practical politician is usually the man who doesn't get the right things done," Kelly said. "He's an old Tammany hack, and probably worse."

"A hack who has built a machine, Kel," Luke insisted. "One of the biggest in the country, and all minorities."

"He's doing the same thing they did in the late nineteenth century," Kelly said. "Build a bureaucracy and let it control the city. But these so-called 'practical' politicians use it only for their own gains. What is to show for the Tammany Hall of, say, Plunkett or Tweed's time? A few grimy old buildings? The trouble with the Irish was, they never knew what to do with the power once they had it. They never thought of politics as an instrument of social change. It's the same with Mullady and his gang."

"I told you in Washington you might have to accept Mullady's help," Josh said. "You just can't ignore the fact the man controls a national political organization that dictates not only statewide but also nationally."

"There are not many political bosses left in this country," Kelly said. "The sooner there are none, the better it will be."

Now was the time for an old politician to speak his thoughts, and I did.

"There's one thing you have to remember about New York, Kelly," I said. "It's a fascinating city whether you look at it socially, geographically, economically, culturally, or even politically."

Kelly said, "That New York is fascinating, Finn, you will get no argument from me."

"Fine. But besides fascinating, it's also a bit of an oddball, politically speaking. One night the good people of New York of the 1800's went to their feather beds and awoke to find their fair city had been occupied by the enemy, hordes of them. They poured out of the cargo ships stinking to high heaven, the women in their black dresses and shawls and with their rosaries, and the men in pantaloons, smoking clay pipes and with chips on their shoulders. They were the Irish, and after they got finished digging the canals and building the railroads, they took over politics. How they got to the top is not a tale to be told the grandchildren by the fire nor what they did when they got there. There were graft and violence and evil men.

"But they stayed there for many years. Then came another horde. This time from Italy. And they wanted in—and they got in. And somewhere along the line the Irish and the Italians made peace. They kept their hands out of each other's till.

"One day they went to bed, and when they looked out the window the Democratic town had changed. Last night it was white. Today it is black. 'Sweet chocolates,' Mullady calls them, and they're clinging to every filthy hole and closet in Harlem and on the West Side right down to the tip of the Battery. After a time they got tired of living in broom closets and being kicked in the ass by every shanty Irishman, Sicilian garbage man or poor-white plow horse, so they revolted, and we had a black revolution. During that time they found they could vote and kick someone else's behind, especially the ward bosses. That was when they discovered how strong they were."

I seemed to be talking mostly to Kelly, and he kept his eyes intent on me.

"But somebody had to tell them they had a lead weight in each ballot and that someone was Barney Mullady. When the city was pushing them in the broom closets and not doing a damn thing about the sweatshops that were paying them less than a coolie, Barney was living among them. He helped them, encouraged them, unified them. If a kid on Nineteenth Street gets rapped on the head by a cop, Barney's boys want to know why. If Mrs. Gonzales is trying to get her grandmother out of Havana, Barney's boys drive her down to Immigration to make sure no chowderhead clerk treats her like dirt.

"What happened because of Barney's gesture to his fellowmen? Simple. He formed a machine, and it's colored black, brown, and tan. He has the Cubans Castro let go, living in the Hell's Kitchen closets where the Irish used to live. Above them he has the Puerto Ricans; then across Broadway he has the Negroes living in beds that are never cold because so many shifts use them."

"How does an Irishman talk to a Latin?" Luke asked wonderingly.

"He doesn't," I said. "He's too smart for that. He's the wizard and his Oz is the clubhouse. He has flunkeys, Cuban, Puerto Rican, and Negro, doing his bidding. They control each ethnic group. They're his Tammany Hall. When he whistles they jump—and so does everybody under them, or the welfare check gets cut off. That's why he has a machine so powerful Albany crawls under the desk when the legislature opens, City Hall locks the door when they hear his name, and even Washington hurries to pick up the phone when they hear Barney Mullady is calling."

Kelly said, "But how did Mullady—"

"I know your question, and here's your answer," I said. "Barney Mullady's a smart man, smarter than all those grand Irishmen and Italians who now smoke the best panatelas and eat steaks because they forgot the taste of plain stew and pasta. For years the blacks and the browns were just shades that didn't mean anything. But now they do, and every politician from Brooklyn to Detroit is cursing himself for not being as smart as Barney Mullady. Oh, there were plenty of warnings. Did you ever read Dr. Clark's book on the ghetto? Clark warned the white leaders years ago that the big vote bloc, the important segment of this city and other American cities, would be the black and brown minorities. Whoever controlled these blocs would control city, state, and even presidential elections."

"But that's what I'm trying to find out," Luke said. "How did a white man get such power?"

"You recall that after the state and federal poverty programs fell apart, there was widespread rioting. It seemed that every spring was the signal for some governor to call in the National Guard. Oh, there were stories about the federal government pouring in millions to the states, but somehow the machinery just never worked right, and the people in the ghettos became more frustrated than ever before. They read about the millions, and wondered where the money was going, why they were still living in such places, why their children were getting second-class educations, and so on. They even turned against their own leaders, who only screamed, shouted, and organized picketing, but nothing worthwhile ever seemed to help the individual. That's when Barney moved in. He didn't give them promises or picket lines; he gave them results. But he was shrewd. He didn't show his face at first; he was content to be the man behind the scenes, operating his black and brown puppets. He was tireless; he was never too proud to take care of the humblest family in trouble. I guess he could be canonized for what he did in those early days if he hadn't done it all for himself."

"That's the terrible rub," Kelly said. "Mullady has unified those people for his own gains through misery and hardships."

"Mullady's philosophy is to use the ungrateful poor but keep them in line."

"A man who would use the poor is contemptible," Kelly said.

Luke exploded, "For God's sake, Kel!"

"I got a taste of Mullady the other night," Kelly said angrily. "As far as I'm concerned, he's a no-good bastard who should be in jail!"

The senator said gruffly, "Why worry about Mullady? I can take care of him."

"What will you do, Dad," Kelly asked wearily, "buy him?"

"Let's get off Mullady for a while," Luke said impatiently, "and back on the campaign. There's a lot to talk about."

"That's right," the senator said. "We're running out of time."

"But Mullady's important," Kelly began doggedly.

"He's important, Kelly," Josh broke in, "but there are more important things to consider. We haven't even touched the upstate program."

"Let's get on with it," the senator said. "We'll spend all night talking about that old thief. What do you have on your mind, Michaels?"

"Big miracles. Without the organization, bigger ones."

"Then we'll have to light bigger candles," Luke said grimly.

"What about a blueprint, Michaels?" the senator asked. "Do you have one?"

Josh silently opened his attaché case and handed out the copies of the campaign blueprint we had made up.

"Suppose we go over it very quickly," he said. "Finn and I will fill in the details later. First of all, we're going to recruit a Shannon Inner Circle, so to speak. It will be composed of young, idealistic, energetic professors, lawyers, and liberals. Some of them were once in the New Frontier, and have experience. They have been selected very carefully. All are young and love a challenge. Each man is an expert on a subject from civil rights to taxes. They will supply the outlines for speeches and be available for appearances.

"Next is a list of politicians who are now associated with Gentile but who, I have been told in strict confidence, are ready to dump him if a strong contender enters the ring. I have contacted every man on this list, and a good percentage have promised to join us at a later date if we show any strength."

"But what will they be doing in the meantime?" Luke asked.

"Let's call them the Shannon Double Agents," Josh said. "They'll be in the Gentile camp and can feed us inside information on themes Gentile intends to develop, speeches he will make, and so on."

He turned the pages. "The next five pages are a list of organizations that are big but publicity hungry. Luther Roberts will contact each public-relations man on this list. As you can see, they stretch from Brooklyn to Amsterdam upstate. They are all ethnic in design, from Jewish to the Shriners. Luther will arrange for Kelly to use their monthly meetings, annual charity drives, or carnivals to make an important speech. He'll be given a plaque, honorary degree, or any other gimmick necessary, but he will have a sounding board. Senator, I've already told Luther to hint you will be making a nice contribution to their drives." He added dryly, "Before this is over, Kelly, you'll have more honorary degrees than Eisenhower."

"What about Kelly's image?" Luke asked.

"Young Lochinvar destroying the Old Evil Ways, the Youthful Public Servant dedicated to helping the Little People. He wants only the Young, the Dedicated, the Fearless to follow him."

"God, it certainly sounds manufactured," Kelly said.

"Creating political images goes back to the early days of the Republic," I pointed out. "When William Henry Harrison's people promoted him as the log-cabin, cider-barrel candidate, they knew he owned a two-thousand-acre estate and was strictly a bourbon man. They just wanted to cash in on the frontier appeal created by Andy Jackson."

"And let's not forget Grant's cigar stub," Josh added, "or Al Smith's East Side, West Side brown-derby corn."

"But I want you fellows to back a candidate, not a client," Kelly protested.

"When we back a man for political office," Josh said, "it's for reward, of course—but it's also out of conviction."

"How do you intend creating that image?" Luke asked.

"A hearing plus television that will put Kelly's smiling face in every American living room."

"I assume you mean a congressional hearing," Kelly said.

"You assume correctly."

"In other words Kelly will be on a committee that will expose the Jello material in a series of hearings."

"The Jello material that is confirmed," Kelly quickly interjected.

"What committee do you have in mind?" the senator asked.

"I have one," Josh said, "but until I get Kelly's appointment we'll only be wasting time discussing it."

"The only committee I got on was the Shoring and Timber Mining Act Subcommittee," Kelly said with a laugh.

"And I would use that one if this material came within its scope," Josh replied.

"How do you intend getting Kelly appointed?" Luke asked.

"For the next few days Finn and I will be working on just that—"

The senator leaned forward. "Through whom, Michaels?"

"Ruppert Holmes."

"The Speaker?" Luke was surprised. "You're shooting high."

"Let's say the Speaker wants something we have," Josh said. "As you'll find out, that's the only sure way to get something in politics: the You-Owe-Me Department; it's the biggest in Washington."

"When will you see him?" the senator asked.

"Tomorrow. The Speaker and the investigator are our first two big steps. Without them we're dead before we start."

"When can we start moving?" Luke asked impatiently.

"You're going to start operating tomorrow," Josh said. "Luther Roberts will call you tonight. He'll tell you where and when to meet him upstate. I want you to be in charge of the state campaign; but remember, Luther's an old pro—listen to him."

"Will you be filling in the details on this?" Luke held aloft the tentative state program.

"By noon tomorrow it will be expanded, typed, and sent to you by messenger from Luther's organization. Also, copies will be delivered here. And now I think we'd better head back to the city. We'll be working most of the night."

We slipped into our coats and were at the door when Josh turned to Kelly as though he had suddenly remembered something. "Oh, by the way, Kelly, will Lacey be available?"

"I'm sure she will be."

"Fine. What is she good at?"

"Well, we've both been working on a housing report that I had visions of reading to Congress."

"You're not going to read any report on the floor unless you first get an awful lot of okays," I said.

"I realize that now," he said ruefully. "But I still think it may come in handy."

"Exactly what is it about?"

"Housing, poverty, ghetto conditions. We've gone through the files of almost every federal agency, state reports and city files. We've been working on it for over a year."

"Lacey's a demon on research," Luke said. "I've read some of it, and it does sound impressive."

"Cold facts and figures are rarely exciting to the ordinary voter," Josh said. "Why don't you get us a copy? We'll see how we can use it. Re-

member, we want bombshell stuff. We have only a limited span of time."
He opened the door. "I thought Lacey might work with us, organizing
the women's division. You know they're important as hell in any campaign."

"I don't know," Kelly said doubtfully. "Lacey's not keen on tea parties
and socials."

"Before this one's over, she may get to like tea," Josh said. "Gentlemen,
we'll call you from Washington the moment we get the word."

We were crossing the hall when Lacey started down the staircase.

"Kids in bed, Lace?" Kelly asked.

"Pam just tore them away from TV and threw them in the bathtub,"
she said, then added: "I'm going to the city tonight. I promised one of the
teachers I'd drop by for a few minutes."

"Can we give you a lift?" Josh asked.

"Why, that would be fine," she said without any hesitation. Then to
her father, "I'll stay overnight with her and take the five twelve tomorrow night. Howard can pick me up."

I noticed that Josh seemed thoughtful as his eyes followed her across
the room.

After a few more handshakes we left. I can recall turning around as we
slowly drove down the winding road to the main highway to catch a last
glimpse of the big house in the light of a frosty moon just beginning to
rise.

"Isn't it beautiful, Finn?" Lacey asked.

"It certainly is," I agreed.

"That's quite a lacrosse field you have," Josh said as he inched out unto
the highway. "Do you play every Sunday?"

"Most every Sunday when the others come down from upstate," she
added, and I could swear she was smiling in the dark, "or when we have
visitors."

"God help the visitors who don't know how to play."

"It's always visitors' choice," she said. "Softball. Touch football. Basketball. We even had a chess tournament going for a weekend."

"I'll stick to lacrosse."

"I won't forget," she said, and moved in her seat. "In fact, I think I'll
remember all night."

If that didn't break the ice at least it cracked it.

"Do you like politics, Lacey?" I asked.

"Well, at Wexford I'm a captive audience."

"I don't believe you were in Washington when I was on the committee
with the senator?"

"No. I was in school in Switzerland." She swung around to Josh. "You
know, Finn is a bit of a legend in our family. Father has told the story
many times of how Finn threw that file at him." She giggled. "Only last
night he said he was glad you weren't hammering a nail."

"Those were rough days," I said. "The hearings we were holding or the investigations we were conducting weren't exactly popular."

"I know," she said. "I can still recall crying when I read some of those editorials. That's one of the reasons why I came back. It seemed everybody, even his own party leaders, were against his nomination."

"He lost it twice, didn't he?" Josh said.

"I'll never forget that night in Chicago. It was horrible. . . ." She hesitated for a moment. "I just hope it never happens to Kelly."

In the gloom of the car I could see her studying Josh.

"You're going to take Father's proposition, aren't you?"

"Yes, we are. Did someone tell you?"

"No. I just told myself you could have said No over the phone."

"Kelly said you're not exactly enthusiastic about the idea."

"They know that. They also know I would do anything to help Kelly win."

"You wouldn't like to see Kelly President of your country?" Josh said, half jokingly.

"I think it can be magnificent, yet terrible. I don't know what it is, but from the first time Father called us together and told me—" She looked out the window for a moment at the flashing lights of the passing cars. "It sounds silly, but it felt as if a cold hand had touched my heart."

The way Lacey said this shook me. Another dark instinct?

"Why?"

"I don't know Finn . . . but the afternoon my husband was killed I was sitting in the patio reading just before the maid answered the doorbell. I felt a strange foreboding. I was walking into the living room when the maid came in with a priest and my husband's assistant from the digs. . . . Then I knew."

"Wow, we'd better cheer you up," Josh said.

"I'm sorry," she replied quickly. "You know I'm really not like this, but I can't help feeling depressed when I think of the crowds, the handshaking, the people who really don't care, the dirt that's always flung, and those crummy politicians."

"It's all part of American politics, Lacey," I reminded her.

"I suppose so," she said with a sigh. "And I certainly should be used to it by now. That's all I knew as a kid before I went abroad to school— senators, congressmen, governors—even the President. There always seemed to be big dinner parties or small private ones. And I hated Washington. God, in the summer!"

"That's something I'm sure we'll all agree on," Josh said with a laugh. "But getting back to Kelly, now that we're in can we count on your help?"

"Of course. I'd dance on a knife tip for him. So would Luke. In a way it's always been this way, the three of us against the world."

"We were telling Kelly we hoped you would organize the women's division in the campaign."

"Oh, no," she said with a groan. "Not that!"

"Look, Lacey, it's important as hell," Josh said. "I'd like to get together with you and select a committee—you know the usual junior leaguers, clubwomen, professionals."

"Couldn't I please do something else? Please?"

"But it's important," Josh said. "God, in the last five years the female vote has increased ten times!"

"Suppose I just organize the committee," she said quickly.

"Clubwomen?" I asked.

"Clubwomen, lawyers, and a few socialites with good connections who will work like the devil to get their pictures in the *Times*." She added casually, "I worked with them on Gentile's first campaign."

Josh almost drove off the highway.

"You worked for Gentile?" we both chorused.

"Of course," she said. "He was the only candidate that made any sense. Father wouldn't talk to me for a week, but he finally got used to the idea."

"He won on a Fusion ticket, didn't he?" I asked.

"Yes. The Democrats had an idiot running. In fact, they indicted him only last year."

"What did you do in the campaign?"

"I was in charge of a research bureau. I did the report on why the city's narcotics program failed."

"The report on the Locke Municipal Narcotics Center!" I exclaimed. "You remember it, Josh."

"Oh, yes," he said vaguely. "It was on the money the city spent or something like that, wasn't it?"

"It was a superb report," I said to Lacey. "Didn't you find out the city spent something like $20,000,000 and got only a few cures?"

"Twenty-two five," Lacey said. "And four cures. And they weren't really cures. We traced the social history of the four boys and found that three had been arrested after a single contact with marijuana, which, of course, didn't make them addicts, and the fourth boy's family sent him to a private sanitarium. So they didn't obtain a single cure. The place was horrible."

"The *Times* used the report on page one when Gentile released it," I recalled. "I remember we discussed it, Josh."

"Oh, yes, but Gentile didn't use it very big, did he?"

"They spent their campaign money for an hour on TV on Sunday," I replied.

"I don't think Josh is impressed," Lacey said.

"Oh, it was a great job."

"I think we can forget the tea-and-crumpet tour for Lacey, Josh," I said.

"Don't sell tea and crumpets short," Josh retorted impatiently.

"What's this housing report you were working on with Kelly?" I asked.

"That's a fine report," she said fervently. "I'm sure if I can continue on it—"

"What do you think it could show?"

"The shocking picture of housing on both the state and national levels. It's the hard core of poverty and the ghetto. You know, bad housing was as much the fuse for Watts, Harlem, Philadelphia, and the other cities where they had those riots as unemployment and illiteracy."

"Facts can be terribly boring, Lacey," Josh said.

"But they are facts," Lacey protested. "That's been the trouble all these years: we've ignored the facts."

"We just don't have the time to develop a super-high-level report on a subject like that," Josh went on. "We have the spring, the summer, and part of the early fall—and that's it. Kelly will have to go up like a rocket and stay there all that time."

"Suppose these facts could be dramatized," Lacey suggested.

"Maybe." Josh shrugged.

"I can see you don't consider it very important," Lacey said.

"Every report we make, every move we make, must produce something big for our candidate," Josh remarked. "Suppose you stayed with this housing report for months and came up with a folder choked with facts, figures, and charts. Honestly, now, Lacey, do you think the voters would really care? That they would pull down that lever for Kelly just because of what you dug up?"

"But if I kick them in the guts—" Lacey's voice was edged with sarcasm.

"Kick them in the guts and you can forget tea and crumpets," Josh replied cheerfully. "Is that a deal?"

They shook hands with mock formality.

"I'll start thinking about it tonight. Will you be up at Wexford tomorrow?"

"In two or three days. Finn and I are going to Washington to try to get Kelly appointed to a committee."

"A committee?"

"You know about Jello's story?"

"Yes. Father told me about it, then Kelly and Luke after they looked into it."

"What we hope to do is get Kelly on a committee that will use the stuff. It could mean national exposure."

There was silence for a long moment.

"Don't you agree, Lacey?" I asked.

"I'm sorry, but I don't," she said. "I think you should know I begged Kelly not to touch it. Father was furious, but I think it's wrong to use anything that frightened little man tells us."

"But why?"

"It's dirty. When I heard it I felt as if I had stuck my hand in some slimy water."

"You'd be committing a crime if you ignored it."

"Come off it, Josh," she scoffed. "We'll only use it for our gains, not for any civic good. . . . My father's not that much of a humanist, and for that matter neither is Luke."

"Kelly didn't raise any objections."

"He's the one who insisted every charge be investigated thoroughly. . . . I know one thing: you'll never get any gossip or innuendo past him. I don't care what committee he's on."

"Suppose we investigate Jello's story and find it's all true?"

"Fine," Lacey said promptly. "Then turn it all over to the proper authorities."

It was Josh's time to scoff. "There aren't many I would trust with a red-hot stove."

"The U.S. attorney?"

"This may shock you, but I had dealings with a U.S. attorney who wouldn't make a move until he checked with the attorney general. And the advice he was getting was political, not legal."

"There's always the FBI."

"This is local crime and corruption, and out of their jurisdiction."

"What's wrong with a congressional committee looking into it, Lacey?" I asked. "Congressional committees have done fine work."

"It's not the committee per se, Finn," she said slowly. "It's the motive. The hearing will be held for one purpose—to give Kelly national publicity." Her hand slid into mine. "But if you say it's the right thing to do, Finn, I'll believe it."

"Hey, what about me?" Josh cried with mock indignation.

"I wouldn't trust you, Mr. Michaels, in either lacrosse or politics," she said. "Oh, here's Seventy-second. If you let me off at West End, I can get a cab and—"

"Don't be silly," Josh said. "Where did you say that lady lived?"

We drove her to the address, and as she got out she bent down and said softly, more to Josh than to me: "There's one thing I think you should know—the Shannons have a mind of their own. Father, Kelly, Luke—and that also goes for me."

"You know, I believe her," Josh murmured as we drove away.

"You were awfully vague about that narcotics report she did," I said. "I remember how you kept saying this was a big score for Gentile when the *Times* carried it after his broadcast."

"It was a hell of a report," he agreed, "but if you think I'm going to waste her on a folder of how bad the Negroes have it in Harlem tenements, you're nuts. Women are important in every campaign now, Finn. God, you know that better than I do!"

"Of course they are. But if Lacey can come up with something big on housing—"

"Oh, Christ, what can you come up with that's big in housing? Unless you get the commissioner's hand caught in the till."

"Housing is a big subject these days, Josh."

"Of course it is," he cried. "And important, too! But it could be a pimple on an elephant's ass compared to the shocking stuff we can get out of Jello. If we can get Kelly portrayed as a knight in shining armor, with that damn smile giving every dame in the country an orgasm—who in the hell will need a book of facts and figures on Negro housing?"

"I still think it's important."

"Don't tell me you're going to give me a hard time now—"

"Let's leave it until we see what Lacey comes up with," I said. "I rather think she will surprise us."

"Great. Then let's be surprised. Now for a fast dinner at Sullivan's, then to work."

We were hard at work ten minutes after we arrived at the Sheridan; I made a date for the next morning with the Speaker. Josh had Luther catching the first plane for Albany, where he would meet Luke the following day. Characteristically, now that the decision had been made, Josh plunged into the task. When I went to bed at midnight, he was still typing. He caught a few hours' sleep, then finished it at six. After an early breakfast, we went over the program, adding, deleting, making notes for Luther and Luke to follow through.

In a few hours we had it finished and ready for Alice to type. Luther already had his organization spinning, and a messenger would be at our hotel in a few hours to take copies to Albany for Luther and Luke and for Kelly and the senator at Wexford.

"Let's go over it for a last check, Finn," Josh said and began reading.

"Next month is the Catholic Bishops' Far East Fund Drive, and that should be our first exposure. Kelly has to hit the big dinners here in the city—luckily, they're not all on the same night. I also want him at the big ones upstate—Albany, Rome, and Syracuse."

"All of them?"

"Every one. Luther's contacting the brain trust for an initial meeting tomorrow. I told him I wanted to start tossing around ideas for Kelly's first appearances at these dinners. For example, in Queens I want him to slam home that fear angle, the failure of the city to put more cops on the beat—"

"I wouldn't touch that four-police-shift angle. The police line organizations will be all over us."

He made a note. "Good idea. Make sure Luther knows that. Oh, be sure we check the newspapers before Kelly gives the Queens speech. I don't want some big rape case breaking and we don't even mention it."

"I like this Brooklyn dinner—"

"Isn't it a terrific gimmick? A big Catholic organization and all black. And with that newly appointed African cardinal as the guest of honor. We can really sound off at that one."

"The Bronx is Fordham, of course."

"What else? The dinner at the university is very big. I want everyone who means anything on that dais."

"But the main appearance is at the Waldorf?"

"Definitely. The bishop will be there with every VIP who counts. Make sure we get a shot of Kelly and the bishop. Better yet, have Luke bring the senator down. It will make a better shot: the old man in the wheelchair, the bishop between him and Kelly. I think the senator has an in at the powerhouse. We can suggest he make the arrangements."

"Old Bishop Grant still running the show?"

"Who else? There's a politician we certainly could use!"

"As I recall, he selects two speakers, and keeps them both secret until they're announced at the dinner."

"The old man loves that gimmick, but it certainly has gotten him a lot of publicity."

"Suppose we're too late? Suppose he has both his speakers?"

"That's why I want the senator to contact the bishop. They've always been close. And the senator will certainly bring his checkbook."

"When will we start Kelly off and running?"

"In Washington, at the police chiefs' dinner. He'll explode the Jello story there—not too many details, just enough to shake the Martinis out of the press table and stop the yawns. From then on, I want it to go off like an artillery barrage, one gun after the other."

"Suppose we can't twist the Speaker's arm?"

"You mean not get Kelly on the committee?"

"That's always a possibility, Josh."

"If we can't—then I think we had better wrap this one up and hand it back to the senator. I don't care if he spends a million every hour of the day and night—unless we have national, sensational exposure for Kelly, his campaign won't get off the ground!"

"Holmes will go along if we promise to take on his campaign, Josh. I know the old coot would sell his soul for just one more term."

"This time with Holmes, anything he wants he gets."

"A few months ago you insisted we dump him."

"That was a few months ago—before we met Kelly."

"Are you beginning to feel like I do—that we have a winner, Josh?"

"Remember what we told the old man—we don't take on losers?" He turned back to the clipboard. "Well, we've finished with the Catholics;

let's get to the Jews. B'nai B'rith's spring dinner will be our first one. It's big and important."

"Isn't that West Side rabbi scheduled for our brain trust?"

"Definitely. He's tops. I happen to know he's fed up with Gentile's crowd and will come over to us. He's a good friend of Luther. Let them get together and make arrangements."

He flipped over the pages. "There's also the Daughters of Israel dinner, the Rabbi Trunich Memorial dinner, the Board of American Rabbis Fund Dinner—they're all damn important, and every one is a potential platform. Now take a look at that Founding Day Celebration in that big upstate city. Two state leaders live there. They're dedicating some kind of Colonial fort. Have the brain trust check on the facts and maybe tie this in with today. The encyclopedia makes this fort sound important. By the way, didn't Kelly say one of his ancestors fought in the Civil War?"

"Fought and was wounded in the Wilderness."

He fumbled in his pockets and came out with a tattered clipping.

"This is a piece the *Times Magazine* had on some Union prison they're opening near Elmira some time this spring. I contacted an old friend in the Department of the Interior, and he's going to arrange for Kelly to be the main speaker. Have the brain trust come up with some important civil-rights angle, and we can blow it big up there. By the way, remind me to have Kelly dig up some old pictures of that ancestor—what was his name?"

"Lace Pants Shannon."

"Why the hell did they call him that?" Josh asked, laughing.

"He always wore fancy pants and a fancy vest. Plunkett tagged him that."

"You know, if we ever tangle with Barney, we could use that angle," Josh said musingly. "Lace Pants Shannon fought Plunkett; Kelly fights Mullady—"

"Do you really think we would take on Mullady?"

"Who knows at this point? I have to agree with Kelly on one thing: Barney's a miserable son of a bitch."

"It's better to work with ten devils you know than one you don't."

"We'll really cross swords if it ever comes to making a deal with Mullady," he said. "Well, let's get on with this program."

We finally were all set for the trip to the airport to catch the Washington shuttle when Josh casually said we first had to make a stop.

"A stop? For what?"

"I want to leave word for Willy."

"Willy! For God's sake, Josh, you're not going to use that nut?"

"Now, wait a minute," he said soothingly; "don't get excited. I know you don't like the guy."

"He's crazy!"

"He's also the best wiretapper in the country."

"That means you're going to tap Gentile's phone."

"Saunders, Remington, Gentile. Every damn name that Jello gives us." He added impatiently: "Just how in the hell do you think we're going to prove Jello's story? We have to move, and move fast. I know Willy's a nut, but we need him."

"How do you know where to contact him?"

"I checked with a friend in the Bureau."

"I'm surprised the FBI or CIA didn't pick him up a long time ago."

"You know why they haven't? The answer is simple. They use him. There are some jobs they just can't dirty their hands with, so there's always Willy."

"You going to use his detective agency?"

"Definitely. If he'll go for it, I want to use his people twenty-four hours a day, seven days a week."

"As I understand, the state attorney general's office has picked up his license three times already."

"And each time he got it back. Let's not kid each other; this guy has too many friends in Washington to be without a license too long." He playfully slapped me on the back. "I'm going to take a fast shower, and then it's Wire Willy Williamson. Suppose in the meantime you jump over to get Alice typing?"

With Josh whistling shrilly above the hiss of the shower, I turned to the window. But I wasn't seeing the Eighth Avenue traffic of bums, businessmen, and actors; I was seeing the ugly, menacing face of Wire Willy.

I hadn't seen him in two years, and then only briefly. I had met him in the North Philadelphia Station when he turned over to Josh a transcript of several days of tapping a phone. It was during a campaign we were running for a Pennsylvania senator who was trying to get back into office after having been defeated by a machine candidate who he swore was crooked. Williamson's tapes proved he was right. We never got to use the material; our candidate died in an automobile accident on the Turnpike three months before election. I guess I'm a superstitious old Irishman, but I always linked Willy to death and violence. After that last time, Josh swore to me he'd never use Willy again. That he was willing now disturbed me greatly.

It was true, as Josh said, that Willy would do anything for him, and I know he hated Gentile with a vengeance. The occasion for it showed the madness in the man. When Josh was first starting, years ago, he took on the job of electing a minor New York City councilman. Josh was seeking a political hook when he read a brief news item that a seven-year-old child had been killed by a city dump truck on a Brooklyn street where for years the mothers had been plaguing the city to erect a stop light. The tragedy had taken place in the councilman's district.

The child was Wire Willy's only son, the one thing this man loved. Willy had fought for a light along with his neighbors, and the death of his child almost made him berserk. At the scene of the accident he knocked out three of the cops who appeared, and almost strangled the driver of the truck. Because the reporters at police headquarters simply used the brief facts that came across the police ticker, they missed the dramatic details of the tragedy. But Josh didn't, and he fed Sissy Southworth a story and later a campaign that won her the Page One and the New York Newspaperwomen's top awards. Josh elected his councilman, and won the loyalty of this violent, unbalanced man.

Williamson, an electronics genius, was at that time chief supervisor of the New York Telephone Company. After the death of his son, he became the chief liaison between the city's big gambling rings and the corrupt police. Willy's job was to supervise field agents who investigated complaints. When an agent would report to Willy that there were suspicious activities on the phone, Willy would tip off the gamblers and the cops. The gamblers would change locations—but not before the crooked cops had put them down on their books for a handsome protection fee. Thus Willy collected from two sources—the cops and the bookies.

A new police commissioner's investigator caught Willy, and he was promptly fired. No criminal charges though; Willy was too smart. He told the supervisor who fired him he would turn five tape recordings over to the DA if a complaint was lodged against him. The tapes were of conversations between the supervisor and the newly appointed head of the commissioner's newly organized gambling squad.

There was no complaint.

Willy soon became the darling of the underworld. He had a daily routine of checking the phones of the city's Cosa Nostra leaders and bookmakers. Lawyers and politicians paid him handsomely. Willy hated anything that represented the law, the city, the civic government that had killed his child. And in his twisted mind the mayor was the chief villain —Gentile more than anyone else. I guess because he had been in office the longest. Though Willy kept his small apartment in Queens, he lived like a gypsy in a Volkswagen bus he had fitted out as a workshop, kitchen, and bedroom. He was a huge man, towering well above Josh and me, and had a look of suppressed ferocity that made me uneasy.

Well, it will be worked out, I thought as I slid the pages into an envelope and started for the office and Alice Grady, our secretary, the only one we would trust.

Later, Josh and I took a cab to Second Avenue, and Josh told the driver to cruise slowly when he reached the seventies. We moved at a snail's pace, passing the phony antique shops, the pizza parlors, the taverns. Suddenly he said, "There it is," and paid off the cabbie.

We entered a small, narrow store with a lettered sign, REINHARDT AND MULLER, RADIO AND TV REPAIRS. The place was cluttered with radios, TV sets, tubes, tools, spools of wire, and a cat that sat on the end of the counter, daintily licking its paws. An empty dish lay beside it. Behind the cat, seated in a chair, was a wisp of a man, carefully picking at the guts of a radio. He looked up. Suspicious, weak eyes studied us.

"Can I help you, mister?" His voice was heavily accented.

"I want a radio repaired," Josh said.

"Yes, please. Do you have it?"

Josh said slowly: "It's too heavy. I can't bring it in. You will have to send someone to fix it."

The old man kept staring at us. Then he placed the set he was repairing to one side, carefully lifted the cat to the floor, and faced us. I had the feeling he was weighing us in his mind.

"Yes," he said. "It is a big set. The name of the maker?"

"Scott Pure-Tone."

"The place where you bought it, please."

"Chicago. On Lackawanna Street."

The old man wrote the information on a small pad.

"When can my mechanic come and see the set, mister?"

"Have him call me in two days—three o'clock. Here is my card."

The old man held the card for a long time. "Please, you are a new customer?"

Josh said, "It's the first time I've been here, but I think your mechanic did work for me before."

"Ah, yes." He opened an account book and laid in the card. "I will see that he fixes your set. Two days. Three o'clock. Yes?"

"That will be fine."

We walked out. As I turned to close the door, I saw the cat was back on the counter and the old man was pouring milk into the dish from a container.

"What was all that about?" I asked as we grabbed a cab for the airport.

"It's the only way you can get in contact with Willy," Josh said. "The guy in the Bureau said he was tougher to get to see than the President."

"I still think he's dangerous," I told him, and slid down in the seat and closed my eyes. Josh just gave me an exasperated grunt, and the rest of the drive to the airport was in silence.

CHAPTER EIGHT: THE SPEAKER

RUPPERT HOLMES, the gentleman from Georgia and Speaker of the House, reminded me of a country-lawyer character right out of an early Shirley Temple movie. A shock of white hair hung over one eye, a heavy link watch chain crossed the vest of his traditional blue suit, and to top it off he wore an old-fashioned high-necked detachable collar. He was usually seen in the *New York Times* surrounded by a small army of grandchildren—the caption never failed to mention his ancestor who fought with Boone at Boonesboro. On television he was a superb backdrop for the President when the Chief Executive addressed the nation on vital affairs. To see Holmes was to be assured all was right with the Republic.

That's image making for you—and the old buzzard did it all himself. The truth is, Holmes was a veteran politician, a power in the House, a dedicated party man, and a terror to freshman congressmen who beg for recognition to speak from the floor and get their names into the *Congressional Record* so they can send copies to their constituents. Holmes had been riding serenely for years, a fixture in the House as much as his gavel, but now back home he was in trouble on three scores: the black revolution, his divorce, and his remarriage. As Josh had said, the news that he had divorced his wife of many years to marry a younger woman had shocked the rural parts of his state, where he ceased to be regarded as a mixture of Robert E. Lee and FDR. This, with the Negro groups openly aligned against him, spelled trouble next year.

Once before Holmes's iron rule had been challenged when a strong rebel from his own organization had run against him; that time we had managed his campaign. We had won by a fairly comfortable margin, but it had been a tough struggle. He had always claimed to be in his late sixties, but a reporter had dug up his birth certificate showing he was ten years older than he claimed. Fortunately, the story broke toward the end of the campaign, and didn't do us too much damage.

Twice last winter the judge—Holmes had been a circuit-riding judge in his youth, and clung to the title—had us to dinner to discuss his campaign for reelection. We had never told him, but Josh had come to the reluctant decision we should pass this one up; confidential polls indicated the judge was a loser.

I had known the judge since he had been chairman of the first Senate committee I worked for when I came to Washington—and that was almost a lifetime ago. Holmes was a skillful politician who would slice off your ears while asking your lady's health if you were an enemy, but in our early days he had swung quite a few lucrative campaigns our way. Because of this I had urged Josh to take him on for one more last time, but I always got the answer, Why go for a loser?

And now for Josh it would be the ends justifying the means.

"I told the judge we would consider taking over his campaign under certain conditions," Josh said as he settled down in the Washington shuttle.

"And that is to appoint Kelly to the Jones Committee, of course."

"That came later. I pointed out to Holmes that today no big-time political campaign can do without television. Some of the papers in his state will not endorse him if he runs again, and he knows it. The big one in the capital busted that story last time on his birth certificate."

"I don't see any problem there," I said. "The judge obviously knows he will have to use TV this time."

"Oh, he did," Josh answered. "He went into great detail on how he wants to allocate a big piece of the campaign funds to TV. I agreed. But I also told him there was a problem with TV in his state."

I was puzzled. "What's the problem?"

"Unless we get an in with the local setup," Josh said, "we might have trouble buying prime time. You know how those bastards work: they don't refuse; they just don't have any time to sell you."

"Well, then, let's start moving down there to get that in. I can go down—"

"You don't have to, Finn," Josh said. "I already have the in. I did some checking, and found that Shannon Industries wields a big club down there. If the local networks don't play ball the way New York wants them to, they suddenly find themselves with a lot of problems they never had. So I told the judge how sticky it could be—but I also told him we had the answer." He settled back and closed his eyes. "He sounded very grateful."

"Did you mention Kelly?"

"Not by name. I just said we had a favor to ask, and we would discuss it when we saw him."

"Did he want any details?"

"No. He's a wise old bird, Finn. He asked how big was the contract, and when I told him I thought it was insignificant, he laughed and said no contracts in Washington are insignificant."

"You know, Josh, we agreed Holmes doesn't have much of a chance of getting back in. It's not only the blacks and the civil-rights groups that don't want him; even his own people say he's too old."

Josh turned and opened one eye. "I wouldn't care if he was as old as Moses and was running as a Jew in Yorkville. We'll run his campaign and give him a show for his money—if he'll appoint Kelly to Jonesy's committee." He hit his knee with his fist. "All we need is that committee and blanket television, and Kelly will be on the road. If we don't get national exposure, Finn, it will take years for a buildup."

"Holmes is a bit of a prude. Are you going to tell him about the dirt?"

"No. I'll tell him just what I want him to know. But, frankly, I didn't think even the judge will care what comes out. After it's all over, the National Committee will love him for making Gentile look like a horse's ass. Gentile's running for Albany and the White House, and his brother-in-law, his own campaign manager, is stealing everything but the City Hall carpeting!"

I reminded him: "I think Kelly really means it about not linking Gentile to the mess by innuendo, Josh. In a way he has a point. Gentile's just an innocent bystander who got hit by what was thrown."

Josh groaned. "By God, I'm surrounded by Boy Scouts and choirboys!"

We were in our suite at the Congressional before ten, and while I conferred with Shea and Short, Josh moved around Washington checking with our friends on the Hill and in the Senate Press Room.

I found the polls encouraging. Josh had suggested that the pollsters trail Luke and Luther Roberts and their teams as they moved across upstate New York and make a pilot study in an attempt to find out if the Shannon name was making any impact.

In Kensington, a rundown and jittery upstate city about to be abandoned by its only industry, the pollsters found the residents were definitely beginning to mention the name of Shannon. The community committees Luke had organized, the meetings they had attended, the carefully planted announcement of new orders coming in—thanks to guess who—was making the city talk. From what they told me, Luke and his people were concentrating on young people and making them work. Three polls had been taken; the last one showed 60 percent of those polled knew Kelly Shannon's name.

Later I met Josh at the Press Club, and from there we went on to the Anson House, a beautiful, century-old mansion that had been turned into a restaurant. It was both expensive and exclusive.

I found the judge hadn't changed; there were still the shock of white hair, the trademark of a watch chain, and the shy Will Rogers grin.

Most of the luncheon was taken up with trading of political gossip until, over coffee, almost casually, the judge asked, "Well, gentlemen, what's on your mind?"

Josh said just as casually, "Well, Judge, we thought we might have the right man for that vacancy on the subcommittee on Urban Affairs and Official Corruption."

"Oh, that's the one left vacant by Congressman Wells's death. Fine man, Wells. I remember his father, old Tom Wells, when he was governor. I think he ran for the Senate in . . ."

For ten minutes we listened to a eulogy on the late Congressman Wells. Holmes had a habit of turning to me and saying, "Now heah, Finn, you remember that! Dammit, I know you do," and I would have to play the part of an old crow and join in his reminiscences. But the judge was a shrewd one. This was all part of the act. When he was finished he carefully selected a cigar, snipped off the end with an old-fashioned cutter, lighted it, and waved us on to begin our pitch. I thought he blinked a bit when we mentioned the Shannon name; but I had done some careful research, and as far as I had determined, the old senator and Holmes had never tangled. And I knew Josh had done his homework, for at one point he casually mentioned that one of the biggest television stations in Holmes's state was owned by the Shannon industries. And of course Josh laid it on thick when he pointed out the difficulties that could arise with buying time and getting up news programs on television in Holmes's backyard.

"Well, by God, let's see if we have any friends we can count on, Josh," the judge said. "I'll get my people starting to work on it tomorrow."

Josh said: "You don't have to, Judge. I've already made the contacts with the right people. They'll pass the word to the TV boys in your state."

"And who's that?" Holmes asked.

"Senator Shannon," Josh said quietly. "He owns Shannon Industries, and carries more weight in television than anyone else in the country."

There's one thing about dealing with a wise old buzzard like Holmes—you don't have to ram the message down his throat.

Holmes carefully edged the ash off his cigar. "This Kelly Shannon a bright boy?"

"He's a comer, Judge," I said. "He's going to be a big help to the party."

The old man smiled. "And you boys are going to make sure everybody knows him."

"That's right, Judge."

"Suppose you tell me about it."

Josh outlined briefly and vividly the scandal that had been touched on in New York State, and gradually it was apparent from the quiet nods that the old fox was seeing the picture—the national picture.

"The boys say the Republicans have high hopes on this Gentile," he said. "The national committeeman was saying the other night he's big with the ladies."

"Judge, Shannon could be bigger."

"You think he has a chance for Albany, Finn?" The searching gray eyes swung to me. "A real chance?"

"I think he has more than a chance, not only for Albany but for here." Then, cautiously, I added, "Josh thought you might have trouble with Congressman Jones, Judge, but I told him I didn't think so."

"Jonesy is a good party man, Finn; you know that," the judge said.

"He's still chairman of the subcommittee, Judge," I said.

There was silence for a moment, then Holmes said in his easy way, "Suppose we get the congressman over to my office this afternoon?"

Josh said, "That will be fine, Judge."

The thick, old-fashioned watch came up out of the vest pocket.

"It's two now; when we get back to the office I'll have him over. Say about four." He cocked an eye at me. "Finn, you're an old walker, as I remember. What do you say we walk back?"

"Fine, Judge."

Josh said quickly: "I have to meet someone at the Press Club. Suppose I see you both back at the judge's office?"

"Walking's good for you, Josh," the judge said. "Look at that old fellow Paul Dudley White. He says—"

But Josh was up and had the checks. "Judge, I figure I did enough walking in Korea to last me a lifetime," and then he was gone with a wave.

I had walked with Holmes before, and I knew this one would include the grand tour of historic spots: the house where Kate Chase died a recluse; a small bronze plaque to FDR that brought up a host of memories of those great days. Only at the entrance of his office did Holmes say, "The boys back home tell me I'm going to be in trouble next time up, Finn."

"They're right, Judge. This time they'll be after your scalp."

"If you told me five years ago I would be at the mercy of some Goddamned nigras, I would have held you for a lunacy hearing," he said bitterly. "Now they even have a black boy for Tammany Hall."

"It's the times, Judge," I told him. "It's been a long time coming, but it's here."

"I told them back home I want one more term," he said. "They said they would go along with me. But they're all old-timers, and they're just as scared as I am. When I was in trouble last time you and Josh did fine things for me, Finn. Can I really count on you boys again?"

"Josh gave you his promise, Judge. We'll be on hand."

"Let's go up and get Jonesy over here," he said briskly.

Congressman Wilfred Jones of North Carolina was notable to the Washington press corps for one characteristic; he was as deaf as a post, and insisted on wearing an ancient hearing aid. But he was an expert lip reader, as many a reluctant witness and his attorney soon discovered. He had been chairman of the Subcommittee on Urban Affairs and Official Corruption for years. It seems to me he was always holding hearings on some facet of crime, such as teen-age narcotics or barbiturates, selling guns through the mail, jukebox records, and so on. At almost every hearing he had some known mobster as a witness. They never said anything, as expected, and always took the Fifth, but they were fine for the television outfits. Every hearing was followed by a long and serious report on some particular subject. Oh, the reports were fine and their recommendations superb, but nothing ever happened. The committee's budget was never sliced because Jones's colleagues were frankly afraid of the letterwriting campaign that might follow. What congressman wanted to face the fury of an indignant women's committee demanding to know why he was helping dope pushers destroy the youth of America? The committee had been sailing along for years. No one really paid attention to it, but it was a congressional fixture. Now there was a vacancy owing to the death of the third man on the subcommittee.

Jones, after turning up the volume on his hearing aid, listened to

Holmes extol the virtues of Congressman Shannon, but it was soon quite evident that Congressman Jones had his own ideas of a replacement on his committee.

"Now see here, Judge, I think Congressman Fletcher is the right man for my committee. I was only saying to . . ."

We listened for ten minutes to the virtues of a Congressman Fletcher. Then, when Jones was finished, Holmes slowly puffed on his cigar and eyed him through the thin blue smoke.

"I just remembered something, Jonesy. Dammit, if I didn't forget it until now."

Jones tuned up the volume a bit more. "What's that, Judge?"

"That lunch we had last month. Seems to me you mentioned something about the constituents in the northern part of your state—"

"Since the soap company moved out, the whole damn section's on relief," Jones grumbled. "We offered them a big cut in taxes, but—"

Holmes held up his hand. "That's right. All those poor voters are on relief. Didn't I read something in the *Post* about how some of them came up last month in a bus to see you?"

"That's that left-wing union bunch," Jones cried. "They sat in my office all afternoon, yelling for me to do something."

The Speaker admired the tip of his cigar.

"Now I remember. We had to get the guards to throw them out." He looked at us with shock and indignation. "Do you know that some of these people were lying on the floor of the congressman's office?"

Congressman Jones looked uncomfortable. I knew what was coming, and from his faint smile so did Josh.

The Speaker said: "I was with the Director of the Space Agency yesterday, Jonesy, and he asked me for a list of suggested locations for that new center. Seems he doesn't want any argument over his new budget when it comes up. I know that place is going to cost the taxpayers millions, but it sure as hell is going to make a lot of other taxpayers happy— that is, wherever they build this place. I said to the director, 'How many people do you think this place will employ?' and he said he wouldn't be surprised four or five thousand was a conservative estimate. A project like this is not only going to make a lot of taxpayers happy; it's also going to tickle some state leaders."

The old congressman leaned forward, his eyes now sharp and bright, his face tight with apprehension.

"I told him I was going to give him a location I liked tomorrow," Holmes went on. "Know what place I thought would be just right, Congressman?"

"I'm listening, Judge."

"Your state, sir, your state. That big flattop mountain you have up there right outside the city where all those people used to make that sweet-smelling soap. It's going to take a lot of people to build this place, and when it's finished it's going to take that many more to work it. Wouldn't be surprised the President will come down and cut the ribbon."

Holmes leaned back and reached over to tap the ash from his cigar.

"A $20,000,000 space center right in your backyard, and you and the President to cut the ribbon. How do you like that?"

Jones slowly turned the volume of his hearing aid still higher.

"What's the name of this young fellow from New York?" Jones asked. "The one you wanted me to appoint to the committee?"

After Jones had left, Holmes called Grymes of Utah, the other congressman on the subcommittee, and then the members of the full committee. It seemed each one had a bill, and Holmes pointedly asked them if it was ready for the subcommittee—a bill is dead if it doesn't get out of the subcommittee—and gave them advice and counsel on how to work or rework the bill. Each time, of course, he mentioned in his casual fashion that he was putting young Kelly Shannon from New York on Congressman Jones's subcommittee.

And on the way out the judge said, almost as an afterthought, that he would have the boys back home start sending us memos on what they thought should be the vital issues of his campaign for reelection.

Now with Kelly assured a spot on the committee, Josh and I, with the approval of the chairman, moved in to organize the staff work. As happens many times with a long-time committee that is continually resting on laurels long withered, the staff of this particular committee had steadily deteriorated. The investigators had forgotten how to investigate; the counsel staffs were constantly changing or being transferred to other committees; the minutes showed the meetings were only perfunctory. Most of the material discussed in public hearings was from law-enforcement agencies about the country who willingly turned over their files to the committee with the knowledge that they would receive public accolades at the hearings when their district attorneys or prosecutors testified, and in the final reports. There were three old-time investigators, two former state troopers, and a retired cop. They had been with the committee so long they had moved their families to Washington, had gone through marriages, deaths, and graduations—all because the committee was publicly against sin in any form. Their jobs now consisted of serving subpoenas and obtaining photostats from the National Archives, Library of Congress, or traveling to New York, Chicago, Florida, or Los Angeles to copy material from the files of friendly local crime commissions.

Most of the directing was done by a former New York reporter who was really Jones's private press agent. He knew his way around Washington, but he was a pitiful alcoholic.

The afternoon we settled in Jones's office we paid a visit to the former newspaperman. Josh summed up briefly what was going on, then warned him that if he leaked anything prematurely or got in our way he would be thrown out of the building in addition to losing his job. Josh was completely ruthless in his threats. My heart went out to this middle-aged man with the trembling hands and bloodshot eyes, but it had to be that way—drunks and vindictive women are dangerous to any important plans in Washington.

I took care of the old-timers on the investigative staff. I assured them that their jobs were safe and that under me they would probably get increased traveling time. This they liked, as it's the only legitimate way for committee staff workers to make money from our tightfisted uncle.

Jones wasn't any trouble. As I said, with veterans in politics, the message has to be given only once; Jones knew he would never be hurt by having his grizzled old head thrust into the living rooms of millions of Americans; besides, he had a space center in his eyes.

Grymes of Utah, the other man on the subcommittee, was a shadow of a man in his last term. He had only recently come back from a lung cancer operation, and frankly didn't care what we did.

We spent a day quietly reorganizing the committee's investigative staff. There wasn't much to be done; as Josh pointed out, if we hired Willy, the committee's staff would be used for serving subpoenas and filling routine assignments such as checking police records, researching the files of friendly DA's, and so on.

Josh called Wexford and talked to the senator to advise him of Kelly's appointment. He told us that Luke had joined Luther Roberts upstate and that they both had started to move.

Next came the task of creating the format for the hearing and deciding on the potential witnesses and what they could possibly testify about. To accomplish this, Josh and I returned to the city and went over Jello's statement, line by line, name by name, filling in as much as we could from our contacts in the CIA, the FBI, city and state police, federal agencies, the records of committees long out of existence, the New York Crime Commission, and similar organizations that have extensive files. After years as chief investigator for several Senate and congressional committees, this was fairly routine for me. Josh was also an old hand at steering Washington committees, and between us we had put together the basic material to be investigated. There were twenty-one items listed in detail.

By late afternoon this is the way it shaped up:

1.   WITNESS: Benjamin Jello: complete yellow sheet from the Bureau of Criminal Identification, New York City Police Department, interview with arresting officers on last three cases; reports of Probation Department, General Sessions Court, N.Y.C.; his records from Department of Immigration, check of last address; interview with warden of New Jersey penitentiary who Jello claims helped in marital suit.

2.   WITNESS: Interview with Miss Molly Shapiro, Crestview, Westchester County, N.Y., re Jello.

3.   WITNESS: Singers, Aaron and Simon. Complete police records, Bureau of Criminal Identification, N.Y.C. Police Department. Interviews with arresting officers and night watchman who alerted police in original arrest; interview with the wounded driver (Cross & Co., Baltimore, Md.); report on all arraignments and hearings, General Sessions Court, N.Y.C.; interview with Assistant DA in charge of case (Roger Hope, Assistant DA, Felonies).

4.   WITNESS: Trevor Remington, unlisted home number AA 7-4346, Darien, Conn.; offices at 521 Fifth Avenue, Remington & Penny, office number: WZ 7-6556-7-8. Check his account at "21." (Is it possible to get copies of his bills?)

Check his appearance as attorney of record for Benjamin Jello, owner of the Polish Rendezvous, 1221 Second Avenue, N.Y.C., before State Liquor Authority, State Bldg., Center St., N.Y.C.; Violation allowing a female to loiter for the purpose of prostitution; check standing N.Y. Bar Assn. (any complaints?); political background, associates, schools, family, etc.

5.   WITNESS: Isidore Feinberg (alias Sammy the Noodle Feinberg); address, 1330 Surf Avenue, Brooklyn, phone, SH 4-4578. Check record, N.Y.C. Police Dept. Bureau of Identification; also relationship with Singer Brothers through marriage of his sister Jenny. Her husband, Sam, is owner of the Tri-State Poultry Co., Washington and Chambers St., N.Y.C. (Dun & Bradstreet report on the latter.)

6.   WITNESS: Manny Summers, about 32, son of the late Lou (Frisco) Summers, ex-convict. Young Summers works as a salesman for Paris-Wear, Inc., 212 West Thirty-first St., N.Y.C. No known police record. Said to be heavy gambler. Plays with a local bookie who operates out of his building.

7.   WITNESS: Stuart Collins, known as "Stu" Collins, a salesman for Delafield Motor Supply Corp., 421 Wentworth Ave., Minneapolis, Minn. Manufacturer of municipal automotive supplies. No known police record.

8.   WITNESS: Kenneth Beering, known as "Ken" Beering (sp?) head salesman, Delafield Motor Supplies, Minn. About 6 ft. 3 in. impressive in manner, expensively dressed, florid complexion, jovial, large emerald ring on right hand, said to be graduate of Notre Dame. He boasts of his Washington connections. Has charge accounts: Brooks Bros., N.Y.C., Simon & Craig, Playboy Club. Check AG's office, Washington, Dept. of Justice, FBI.

9.   WITNESS: Eva Schmidt, masseuse, Studio 180 Central Park West; German immigrant. Residence, Eighty-ninth St. and East End Ave., penthouse; about 5 ft. 11 in., heavy German accent, blue eyes.

Home City, Hamburg; check for records: Dept. of Criminal Identification, N.Y.C. Police Dept.; N.Y.C. Department of Investigation; Confidential Squad, N.Y.C. Police Department; Federal Bureau of Narcotics, Department of Hospitals, N.Y.C.; N.Y.C. Assn. of Registered Nurses; phone numbers: Unlisted (home), BE 7-3922; office, CH 4-4532; unlisted office, CH 4-7760.

10.   WITNESS: ——— Francis, no first name, owner of a nightclub, East Sixty-eighth Street and Third Avenue. He is reportedly a friend of Claire Remington. Check records, Bureau of Criminal Identification, N.Y.C. Police Dept., State Liquor Authority, known associates.

11.   WITNESS: Robert Cummings, alias "Cat" Cummings, convicted burglar. Pleaded guilty to 18 counts of grand larceny (N.Y. *Times*, Oct. 3, 1966). Confessed addict. Obtain stenographic report of his last hearing. Check records, Bureau of Criminal Identification, N.Y.C. Police Dept., N.Y.C. Police Narcotics Bureau, Federal Bureau Narcotics; records, North Brothers Island, Narcotics Center (abandoned by N.Y.C. since 1961, but all records are in Dept. of Hospitals Central Record Bureau, Centre Street).

12.   WITNESS: Joseph (Papa Joe) Americus, reportedly old-time hood, associate of Lepke and Gurrah, convicted with them in their first conviction, 1939, Anti-Sherman Trust Act. Also implicated in War Assets Administration scandal, 1950, appeared before Congressional Committee, investigating War Assets (Congressman Hillers, N.C., presiding). Check records: State Liquor Authority (who is his attorney and front?) all credit ratings; Corporation Records, County Court Bldg. Check SLA license, issued to Diamond Tower Club, Forty-seventh Street off Park Avenue.

13.   WITNESS: ——— Doxy, no first name. Charged with fraud. Case dismissed for lack of evidence before Magistrate ———. Get complete copy of stenographer's notes of dismissal. Also talk with arresting officers Cranks and Lagraw, 23rd Precinct. Interview complaining witness. Check DA's files. Was an Assistant DA present at the dismissal?

14.   WITNESS: Nancy ———. No last name. Secretary for Trevor Remington, attorney, 521 Fifth Avenue. Blonde, pretty, about 5 ft. 5 in. Talk to elevator operators in building and cashier in the luncheonette in the first floor of the building. Jello recalls a boy in a white apron bringing in a bag of coffee and doughnuts once while he was waiting. (Cross-section telephone book shows there is a luncheonette in the building. A call to the cashier reveals they serve the building. She may provide last name and information.)

15.   WITNESS: Max ———. No last name. A waiter at "21." Thin, about 60, reserved. Speaks German. (Jello exchanged a few German phrases with him. He said he came from Bremerhaven). He took the

cookbook Jello bought and brought it to the cashier to be wrapped and brought it back to him, with the change. Also gave him cashier's slip. (Does he remember Jello? Show him a picture of Jello, Remington, and Saunders.)

16. WITNESS: Chief Justice, Federal Court of Appeals, Prebel Tucker. We must have a complete family, college, judicial, financial background. He reportedly splurges heavily in Wall Street. Check brokers. Check companies: Transcontinental Trading Corp., office, 5 Stone St., N.Y.C. Must have list of officers, shares, complete D & B report. Check and obtain complete stenographic report Stella *vs.* Frank, Federal Court, patent violation, Eastern District Court. Check all officers of the Frank Company who lost decision. Interview the president and attorney of record. Check files of N.Y. *Times*, *Wall Street Journal*, and *Variety* for newspaper accounts. Check: Tucker is said to engage in perverse sexual activities. We must have a delicate and discreet investigation of his personal life. His law clerk, according to Jello, is a political appointee who usually disappears about 2:00 P.M. He can be found in the Bailiff's Corner off Foley Square about 5:00 P.M. Jello believes he has some knowledge of the judge's activities. Approach must be discreet.

17. OFFICES TO CHECK: N.Y.C. Sanitation Dept. Check records of the sale last February of $500,000 worth of winter equipment (trucks and snow shovelers) to N.Y.C. by Delafield Motor Supply Corp., Minn., manufacturers of heavy municipal equipment. Was it by a sealed bid? Check reported complaint about equipment with workers and inspectors in the Main Sanitation Garage, Tenth Avenue and Seventy-first Street. (Perhaps get known expert on heavy municipal equipment for comment. The equipment is said to be inferior.)

18. RIKERS ISLAND: Check records of Singer Brothers' confinement. Was their cell ever changed from second to top tier? Why?

19. Delafield Motor Supply Corp., Minn., list of officers, corporation papers, stocks, and assets. Complete D & B report.

20. "21" CLUB. Can we get records of book sales and the dates they sold copies of *Recipes of Twenty-one Famous Men and Women?* (Jello insists he bought his book at a display near the cashier's desk. His waiter, Max, brought it to him wrapped.

21. IMPORTANT WITNESS: Charles (Chuck) Saunders, Special Assistant to former Mayor Felix Gentile and his brother-in-law. Must have complete family, political, and financial background. Unlisted office number: CY 4-6112, at City Hall office; home, 62 Bank Street; unlisted home number, WA 3-2346. Clubs: Gramercy Racket Club, The Thespians, The One-None Club, Federation of American Universities, Hampton Bays Surf and Sand Club, Paris Club. Known to dine frequently at Four Seasons, "21," Colony. City car, license CS 1, NY. Was campaign manager for Gentile and was associated

with him in the State Department. Check Washington background. Sources say Saunders was friendly with a television producer who reportedly had a number of "available" girlfriends for the "right people." This is just gossip, no facts.

Saunders' sister, Diana, is married to Gentile. He is a bachelor and has frequently been the escort of socialites in New York and Washington. He is friendly with a number of senators and congressmen and is known to have maintained his friendships with some persons in the State Department.

Complete surveillance is needed. Daily reports are to be made. Photographs if possible. The subject must have no suspicion he is being observed.

We made three copies, all originals, on flash paper, the chemically treated sheets of white flimsy paper that bookmakers use to record their bets. As many sophisticated law-enforcement agencies know, whole bundles of incriminating evidence that could have sent some of the country's largest bookmakers to jail and embarrassed their big-time customers many times over have gone up in flames at the touch of a glowing cigarette to the edge of the flash paper.

What we had on paper was a megaton more explosive than any bookmaker's: if it got into the wrong hands the results could be catastrophic.

"That gives us at least nineteen potential witnesses," Josh said.

"Who did you call in Washington about Saunders?" I asked.

"A former CIA man. He says he is sure that somewhere there is a file on Gentile. He claims he used to be a real swinger when he was starting in State. The senator would love pinning that down."

"Homo?"

"No. Apparently he's strictly a boy-likes-girl type. But this CIA guy says there used to be some real swinging parties in Georgetown when Saunders and Gentile were down there."

"Was Gentile married then?"

"I don't think so. I would love to get that file."

"Any chance?"

"I don't know, but I'm going to try like hell. If I know those CIA files, it should contain a hell of a lot of information about Saunders and Gentile."

"Even though we've only scratched the surface, Josh, one thing is becoming clear. Gentile is clean."

"I'll hold back my verdict on Gentile until Willy gets to work," Josh said. "I don't see how a man who is the mayor of a city this size doesn't know his brother-in-law is a crook. You know how those things work, Finn: there's always a guy in your administration who is too ready to whisper in your ear."

"That's probably true in a lot of cases, Josh," I pointed out, "but

Saunders isn't an ordinary thief. He's discreet, apparently trusts Remington, and hasn't been living outside his budget during all the time Gentile was in office. As an old Washington investigator, I can tell you that's the first thing that trips them up."

"But he made one stupid move—meeting Jello in '21.' My God, how stupid can he be?"

"Wait a minute, Josh, consider this: He trusts Remington; he has been his front all this time, and nothing has ever slipped up. Remington asks him to have lunch with a man Remington claims is important. The luncheon is at '21.' Saunders doesn't have any reason to doubt that this man is important and a New York representative of this Delafield Company. After all, the meeting is held at one of the nation's best-known and most respectable restaurants. Suppose the man does turn out to be not too good. All Saunders has to do is to insist he was simply having lunch with an old friend who was accompanied by a stranger he never met."

"But an ex-con, a notorious fixer, who has spent time in almost every big prison in the country, Finn!"

"So what? Look at the people we have met through old friends and associates. Could you tell me that everyone was what he appeared to be?"

"The guy who will do him in, is Remington," Josh said.

"I believe so too," I said. "Not only is he desperate for money, but he's married to a pretty tramp who can drive him to do anything."

"That's one wire that will produce a lot. I'll bet a tail on her will show she's shacking up with more than one."

"Are you going to give all this to Willy's agency?"

"Every line. Can you see any legitimate detective agency digging into some of this stuff? They wouldn't touch it with a ten-foot pole."

"The committee won't touch it either."

"You can control any committee," he said. "After Jonesy wakes up and turns up his hearing aid, he'll find Kelly all over the headlines. By that time I don't think he'll have any objection to asking a few rough questions himself."

"You'll be playing both ends with Kelly in the middle, Josh."

"Kelly will get nothing but good out of it; I'll see to that," he said. "But I also have another idea in mind—the party. This is a hot election year, and they won't be too sensitive about clobbering the Republicans. If we get the goods on Saunders and Remington, the National Committee will kiss our butts in Tiffany's on Christmas Eve."

"I don't think Kelly will go along with this whoremaster's stuff, Josh. The boy's a politician and he will fight to win, but I don't think he wants to get in the gutter."

"I've been thinking the same thing," Josh said. "There's a lot of Boy Scout in Kelly we'll have to watch out for. We'd better get him moving around upstate when we're organizing the hearings."

"Why not let him continue to work on his housing report?"

"It will take about a month for Willy to really get his teeth into this thing, even if he works around the clock with every man he has. During this time I don't want Kelly protesting every move we make—so maybe we should let him work on that report."

"Lacey also?"

"I don't know about Lacey. I still think she should organize the women's division." He studied the list of witnesses for a moment, tapping his pencil impatiently against the table.

"Let's play that by ear." He glanced at his watch. "Twenty to three . . . Willy's usually on time."

The minutes ticked away; frankly, I was hoping the phone would never ring.

But it did, promptly at three. It was Willy.

Josh scribbled as he talked: "Yeah, Willy. It's me . . . Wait a minute, you're going too fast . . . I know. I know . . . Four o'clock? Where? . . . St. Mary's Cemetery? Where's that? . . . Midtown Tunnel, Long Island Expressway to Grove Street Exit. Left at the bottom. Three blocks, then right. Is it a big place, Willy? . . . Cranford Avenue side. Okay, I got it. Wait a minute, Willy. Why the cemetery? . . . Oh, right. Of course I remember." He spoke low and urgently. "Willy, listen. Who was the guy who went to bat for you? Josh Michaels. Right? . . . Remember how I hit the city on the light? . . . Willy! Will you listen!" Then his tone softened. "Okay, Willy, I know you're my buddy. Can I bring flowers? How about a plant? Right. Okay, Willy, we'll see you . . . Oh, Finn—" He looked over at me and winked. "Okay. We'll see you."

He hung up slowly and kept one hand on the phone as he stared into space.

I said: "He's a nut, Josh. So help me God, he's a nut."

"He's crazy, Finn," he said. "The son of a bitch wants us to meet him in the cemetery."

I almost jumped out of the chair. "In a cemetery! For God's sake, why?"

"His kid was killed on a Friday. Every Friday since that time Willy has gone there to put flowers on the grave." He said wearily: "Look, Finn, what the hell can I do? He's the best in the business." He slapped my report of Jello's interview into the palm of his hand. "How in the hell do you think we're going to prove this? By having Remington sit down with us two God-damned ordinary citizens without power of subpoena, with no power at all—and have him admit he has corrupted one of the biggest judges in the American judicial system or is a partner in crime with the brother-in-law of the man most people believe might be the next President of the United States? Okay. He's a nut! He's the damnedest nut in the whole country! But he happens to be the only son of a bitch with the know-how to help us prove all the stuff we have been hearing for the last three days in a Westchester pen from a frightened little thief who happens to be at the mercy of a thieving son of a bitch who would turn him over to anybody for a buck." He came over to me, and his eyes were blazing. "Am I right?"

"Partly," I said.

"Well, then you give me the answers," he said. "You tell me what we should do."

"We can try that agency downtown. The three guys who run it worked for the Bureau."

He said bitterly, "Sure, they're good for looking up records, putting a tail on somebody, even questioning someone." He leaned over. "But do you think they're going to put in a tap on the private phone of the brother-in-law of Felix Gentile? Or Mr. Remington, a Fifth Avenue attorney? Or the Chief Justice of the Federal Court of Appeals? Are you out of your mind, Finn?" He tore apart a pack of cigarettes. "Dammit, you know I'm right. Williamson is the only man who is crazy enough to do what we want. That's the only way we are going to get the stuff we need for a congressional hearing." He spun around. "Am I right?"

What could I say? Sure he was right—and wrong. Could he turn over Jello's story to a clubhouse hack, a DA on the make? Could he give it to a local U.S. attorney who would have to notify Washington? The cops would slaughter poor Benny Jello. With Josh staring at me angrily as he lit his cigarette, I had to swing to him. You have to break eggs to make an omelet.

CHAPTER NINE: WIRE WILLY

WE CAME OUT OF THE MIDTOWN TUNNEL into the brisk afternoon light. The Long Island traffic was thickening, and it was bumper to bumper for miles. Josh, like a good New Yorker, took it placidly, cursing almost mechanically when we had to slam to a stop.

St. Mary's Cemetery was part of the sprawling acres of tombstones back to back, crosses, squat mausoleums, and marble angels that lined the Long Island Expressway for miles. The thought came to me that in all the years I have been passing them I had never seen a human being, either kneeling or even walking along those crowded marble aisles. They almost appeared to be highway props.

"Grove Street exit," murmured Josh half to himself. "That's right after Stanton Avenue." Then to the cab driver, "That was Stanton we just passed; next is Grove."

In a few minutes we were swinging off into an exit marked "Grove

Street, East Brooklyn and Queens." At the bottom we turned left, proceeded three blocks, and turned right. On the corner was a monument yard and next to it a hothouse. We suddenly swung into the curb.

"Wait a minute," he said to the driver, and jumped out. He was back in a few minutes carrying a bouquet of flowers.

"There's not much you can buy now," he said after paying the cabbie. "The guy says it's too early for plants, so I got some ferns and cut flowers. Willy wants flowers, he gets flowers. The Cranford Avenue entrance is just up the street."

"Josh, do you remember Mary Shelly's *Frankenstein?*"

"Lay off, Finn," he said curtly.

The Cranford Avenue section of St. Mary's Cemetery was a lonely, desolate section peopled only by those monstrous simpering angels, row after row of tombstones, and neatly trimmed grass. We walked from the entrance for some time without seeing a soul, until Josh said quietly, "There he is."

About a block away I could just see his head and shoulders towering above the stones. He appeared in prayer. He never moved as we came near, though the sound of our footsteps on the gravel was loud enough to attract his attention. We stood there like two fools, me clearing my throat and Josh holding the flowers.

At last Josh said, "Willy . . . Willy . . ."

He never turned, but the deep, harsh voice, rough as a saw through oak, said, "Shut up. Can't you see I'm praying for the dead?"

At last Willy made the sign of the cross, and rose. He was a huge man, almost six foot five, but he had gone to fat since the last time I had seen him in the Philadelphia railroad station. His face was a pasty white; the long, black greasy hair had thinned and was ragged and uncut. His belly hung over his belt. Despite the chilly afternoon he was wearing only a ragged dark green coat-sweater with some buttons missing, and dirty sneakers. I remember once Josh telling me Willy could never get the right size shoe, so he wore sneakers. In contrast to his generally nondescript appearance his polo shirt was clean and seemed pressed. That was the true sign of a schizo, I thought, dirty as hell and a clean polo shirt.

His eyes were large, washed blue, and staring. Madman's eyes. His hands were dirty hams.

"I was praying for Robbie," he said. "It's fifteen years ago today they killed him." He shook a huge fist at the distant towers of New York City. "Because of a God-damn street light he's dead all these years." He turned back to us. "He was just a kid, you know that, Josh. Just a kid."

He stood there muttering to himself as he stared at the distant towers of downtown Manhattan.

Josh said quietly, as if humoring a child: "I know it, Willy. It was terrible." He turned to me. "Robbie was a great kid, Finn."

The intense, savage eyes turned on me. "You didn't know him, did you, old man?"

"I told Finn about Robbie many times, Willy," Josh said. Then quickly, as if to swing the attention away from me, he unwrapped the flowers. "Let's put these on, Willy."

Together they unwrapped the flowers, and Willy gently placed them on the grave.

"I like geraniums," Willy said. "There's always a flower. You just nip one off and there's another one. I come here every Friday. Every Friday at this time." He took an old-fashioned pocket watch out of his pants pocket. "It was three o'clock when the truck hit him. The bastards! The no-good City Hall bastards!"

"Willy, I have to talk to you," Josh said.

Williamson looked at us. "Josh," he said, "let's go to the bus."

We followed the huge man several blocks across paths and roads and even through a broken fence and some hedges until I felt like a crazy teen-ager playing follow the leader. At last we came to an empty lot. Parked under some trees was a gray Volkswagen bus.

"I got to do this," he said; "the feds are always on my back."

"Been doing any work for the Bureau lately, Willy?" Josh asked.

"Some." He added with some pride: "They're always wanting my stuff. They know I got stuff they haven't even heard of. Like my sonic spectrum beam."

"What the hell is that?" Josh asked.

The faded eyes became sly. "It's a secret. Even the big boys in the Bureau are after me for that one."

He unlocked the door of the bus and waved us in. This was both Willy's home and workshop. The center of the bus had been converted into a bedroom with a wall bunk and a portable electric stove. There were boxes of canned goods on the floor. In the rear was a workbench that reminded me of the equipment of the old-time knife sharpeners who traveled about the city when I was a boy. There were curtains on the windows, but the place was a mess. Dirty shirts and socks were stuffed in an old laundry bag. There were paper bags filled with garbage and food-littered paper plates. There was an odor of machine oil, decaying food, and gasoline.

"Got to clean this out," Willy said with a grunt and, opening the door, just kicked out the bags.

Willy got into the driver's seat. "We're going to ride around for a while before we go to my office," he said.

"Where's that?" I asked.

"That's what you would like to know, old man," he said, then thrust back his head, and laughed.

I threw Josh a look, but he just shook his head.

"What's on your mind now, Josh?" Willy asked as he started off.

"It's big stuff, Willy," Josh said. "We have to get information for a congressional committee."

"You still working for those phony politicians?" Willy asked. "When are you getting wise, boy, that they're all crooks or Communists? All of 'em. They're all on the take."

"Wait a minute, Willy," Josh interjected. "You don't know who we're looking into this time."

"What the hell do I care? One crook is like another; one politician is like another."

"Gentile, Willy. Felix Gentile."

Willy twisted half about in his seat. "You're after Gentile? The biggest no-good son of a bitch in America!"

"For God's sake, watch where you're going!" I cried as he cut off a car that came within a foot of slamming us in the side. The driver leaned out and cursed us with a vengeance, but Willy ignored him.

"He's running for governor now, huh?"

"And probably President four years from now, Willy," Josh said. "We have a lot of information about some of his friends we have to check out. Good information, Willy. Right from the trough."

But Willy wasn't listening. He was staring ahead, murmuring to himself.

"He was playing with the niggers and the Jews all the time he was in City Hall. He's worse than the rest. I saw him on television begging the niggers' pardon and kissing their asses after the big fight in the school." His voice rose. "Nothing about the poor white people! No, sir! Just begging the niggers' pardon. Like they own the city. Black baboons! Just want to be on welfare and get their checks. They want to work. The hell they do. Ever see a nigger work? Are you nuts? Work? They bust you over the head with a gin bottle if you offer them a job. I know 'em. Guy came in and asked for a job at my place. Said he was a retired cop. Black as a stove cover. You know what he wanted? Two days a week, just checking out ID stuff! He said he had a pension and was hurt making an arrest and couldn't work too long. Black bastard looked healthier than five white men." He gave a short, ugly laugh. " 'I got an office in Birmingham,' I told him. 'You want to go down there, you got a job.' " He slapped his big thigh, and roared. " 'Bring a hambone,' I told him, 'for the police dogs.' Then I kicked him out. No nigger cop working for me."

Josh waited until the outburst was over. "We want you to make some tapes, Willy."

"Where?" he asked.

"In the city," Josh said. "They're all Gentile's friends. We think one's a big thief. We want to bring him before the committee."

"Of course he's a thief!" Willy shouted. "They all are."

"We want your help to prove it, Willy," Josh said quietly. "That's why we want some tape put in."

"I'll tape the son of a bitch for you," Willy said savagely. "I'll get enough on them all to send them to jail so long they'll forget where the keys are."

"You still have your agency, Willy?" Josh asked.

Willy grinned. It was surprising to me what a contrast the strong white even teeth were to the general neglect of his clothes and body.

"Bigger and better than ever, Josh. I do a lot of work—even for the government. They don't want to get their hands dirty. I do. And they pay through the nose."

"There's a lot of stakeout and surveillance and reports to be made, Willie," I said. "Do—"

"Don't worry about my boys. They're as good as any of your boys were down in Washington." He gave us a sly look. "The work comes high, not like it was two years ago."

"Don't worry about the money, Willy. Just give us a bill and you'll get paid in cash," Josh said.

"Where is this office of yours?" I asked.

"You'll soon see, old man," he chuckled. "You'll see."

I gave Josh a look. I didn't care if I was electing King Tut. I could take this loony just so long.

Josh grinned, and shook his head.

We rode around Queens and Long Island until it got dark. I have never heard such mad talk in all my life. There were Communists in City Hall, running the New York City Police Department, running our government; our chief of staff was a decided Red—it was just a matter of time before a whole Red takeover. Remember what Hearst used to say about the Yellow Peril? Well, it was coming. Look what happened in Vietnam. Now the Chinks are making trouble in the Philippines.

Yet between the lines of this nonsense there were some facts, distorted, but facts. I wondered where Willy dredged them from. One day I would find the answer.

We were far out on the island when the lights went on. Only then did Willy start back toward Manhattan, but not on the Expressway. He took side streets and main avenues, twisting and turning as if to kill time. I could sense that even Josh was weary.

"Come on, Willy, we have to get back," he said at last.

"Take your time," Willy grunted. "I'll get you back."

Somewhere in Queens, Willy said he was hungry, but rather than trust those cans and paper plates I proposed we stop at a White Tower. This suited Willy. He came back with a cardboard box that must have contained ten hamburgers, several cups of coffee, and slabs of pie and cake. He went after the food like a wolf. After finishing off most of it, he slapped his belly, kicked out the box, waxed paper and cups, and started off.

146

"Do you live in the bus, Willy?" I asked.

"Best place in the world to live," he said. "Just like the niggers. Throw your garbage out of the window. When I want a woman I pick up a whore hustling along the avenue for guys in cars. It only costs me five bucks." He chuckled. "The specials are ten, but old bastards like you don't have to worry about that. Right, Josh?"

"Willy, it's past nine o'clock. When in the hell are we going to get to this place?" Josh said shortly.

"One hour and we'll be there," Willie said. "Let me tell you about this dame. . . ."

Madam Eva would have a great customer in this poor loony, I thought, as Willy gave us the skin-crawling details of his night with some poor whore he at last kicked out on some deserted Long Island street.

We went into the Queens Midtown Tunnel, then moved up Third Avenue to Forty-eighth Street, where we parked. He was now very businesslike.

"Follow me," he said, "and do just as I tell you. You take a flashlight, Josh. The old man can tag along."

I thought, Someday the old man is going to crack that skull of yours with a hammer, but I bit my tongue and followed Josh.

We walked down Third Avenue to Forty-seventh, then turned west. The street was deserted. Halfway up the block was a small alley. Willy gave a quick look up and down.

"Okay, quick!" he whispered. Like most big men, he was agile and fast. He darted into the alley, Josh and I after him. About a hundred feet in the alley he stopped before what appeared to be a thick mesh gate.

"No flashlights until I tell you," he said.

A key clicked and the gate opened. Willy disappeared, and Josh and I entered. I found myself in a low corridor. A night flash clicked on, and I could see Willy's dirty sneakers in the faint beam.

"Follow me," he said.

The corridor went back about fifty feet, then down ten iron steps to a steel door that warned "DANGER. HIGH TENSION. DON'T ENTER. N.Y.C."

Willy had a key, and the door swung open. We stepped inside; the door closed and I heard the key grate. Now we were in a large tunnel that was warm, almost stifling, and smelled faintly of dust and decay.

"Where in the devil are we, Willy?" Josh asked.

"You're going under Grand Central," he said with a chuckle. "I only have my offices in the best places."

"What about those high-tension wires?"

"Forget 'em," Willy said. "I know this place like the inside of a telephone. Come on."

I should judge we followed this bedbug the length of three city blocks. Twice we came upon tiny red lights glowing in the pitch blackness. Behind each one was a huge console of wires and switches encased in a mesh screening.

"Touch that and you'll wind up a piece of charcoal," Willy said over his shoulder.

After the last warning light the tunnel began to make a wide curve. There were gates and small iron bridges to cross. Once I was petrified; suddenly there was a far-off but gradually rising rumble. Later Josh said it reminded him of a stampede of Indian cattle he had once witnessed. The sound advanced toward us in a gathering wave; then suddenly we were enveloped in a roar that deafened me. The floor trembled under my feet. I felt the tunnel shake and quiver. Dust filled my nostrils. Then, as quickly as it came, it vanished.

"IRT express," Willy said with a grin. He flashed his light toward a narrow niche in the wall. "You're about ten feet from the third rail. You get used to it after a while."

"If we don't get killed, we'll get arrested for trespassing," I said.

"Come on!" Willy shouted. "Are you with me?"

The tunnel curved again, then ended abruptly. We were now at the entrance of a long, narrow bridge, no more than two feet wide, with thin waist-high cables on either side. A loud gushing noise now filled the tunnel. Willy's flashlight caught the rushing, foam-flecked water fifteen feet below us that rushed into a massive concrete tunnel.

"Con Ed's private wells," he explained. "Don't fall; you won't have a chance. A guy I know who used to work for Water, Gas, and Electricity swore there's an alligator down there."

"How do you know about this place, Willy?" Josh asked.

"Don't forget, I worked for the telephone company for fifteen years and ten for the city," Willy said. "I know the guts of this city better than I know my own. Come on."

My heart was in my throat when I stepped onto the narrow bridge. It was only a broad plank, and while it was probably sturdy enough I couldn't help thinking what one false slip could do.

The IRT roared by several more times before we walked the length of the bridge, which led us into a fantastic maze of pipes and concrete corridors stacked in a series of floors beneath us. This, as Willy explained, was New York Central's huge pipe galleries that carried the hot water, cold water, and steam from a midtown powerhouse in the midtown skyscrapers. Willy called the section we were in "Gallery East." He said the tunnels were kept warm and dry by a series of automatic centrifugal pumps that collect seepage and raise it to the level of the street sewers. The place here was fairly well lighted. Every fifty to a hundred feet bulbs lined the concrete walk between the pipe galleries. We finally reached a point where Willy disappeared behind one of the galleries and returned in a few minutes. We followed his light through a small iron gate, then down another tunnel that seemed to go deeper and deeper.

This one was partly brick, seemingly old. It leveled off into a series of brick archways resembling catacombs. Above us a million head of cattle roared across the ceiling. Both Josh and I automatically ducked as dust and plaster swirled in the beam of the lights.

"New York Central," Willy said. "This is part of the old excavation they did in the 1890's." He flashed his light around the immense room.

"You're more than ninety feet below Grand Central now," he said. "How do you like it?"

"Is this your office, Willie?" Josh asked.

Willie's beam shot across the room. "Over here."

There was a large sheet-metal door, like a fire door. Willy unlocked it and clicked on a switch; the glare of the light made us blink.

"Con Ed gives me my light," he said. He pointed to a faucet. "New York Central gives me my water." His wave took in the rows of benches. If Willy's bus was dirty and cluttered, his workroom wasn't. Apparently he respected only electronics. Neatly arranged were telephone bugs, spy cameras, tape recorders, all types of telephones from antiques to the common, of course all bugged; lamps also bugged, a number of what appeared to be physician's stethoscopes, probes, cameras from the tiniest Minox to a stainless-steel barrel less than a foot long.

Willy saw that I was studying the barrel-like thing, and picked it up. In a few minutes he was unfolding it until it was five feet long. When it was unfolded he attached the barrel to a small camera.

"If we were up on the Chrysler Building we could take a picture of a motorcycle on the highway out around Newark," Willy said. "High-resolution photography. It can pick up objects as small as a motorcycle from a hundred miles away." He placed the camera aside. "There are mirrors inside the barrel. This is what the Gemini pilots use."

Gemini pilots. Not astronauts. It was as though Willy considered himself part of their world.

"I have a lot of space stuff," he said proudly. "I have a transceiver that weighs only about fifteen ounces that can take a high quality AM communication at 296.8 mc."

"That's great, Willy," Josh said with a great show of enthusiasm. "But we don't have to bug a spaceship. This is only a routine job: bugging a phone or picking up conversation—you know the bit."

Willy picked up a small black plastic case, no bigger than a matchbox. "Telephone monitor. Just lay it beside a telephone and you can have a two-way conversation without picking up the receiver."

"What are all these lamps doing here?" I asked.

He reached down under the counter and picked up a box filled with spare parts of lamps and bulbs. "In five minutes I can put together a lamp to blend in with the layout of any room," he said. "Knotty pine to wallpaper—you name it. It will pick up any whisper."

"Do you have to be in the next room?"

He snorted. "That's old stuff. I can be five blocks away with this"—
he showed us a small gray box—"recorder. High sensitive recorder. Just
turn it on the frequency, and it will record. Hell, I can leave it on the seat
of my car in the morning and come back at night and it will still be on."
He pointed to a tripod folded in a corner. On the top was what seemed
to be a folded aluminum disk. "Biggest ear in the country," he said. "A
man can sneeze ten blocks away, and I'll hear it." He opened the silver
disk, which spread fanlike, and pointed to a small plug in the back. "Just
plug in a recorder and you're in business. The divorce guys like this one.
You get every squeak of the bed."

"What about that bugged Martini stuff we read about, Willy?" Josh
asked.

"Crap. Just crap," Willy said contemptuously. "Why do I need those
kinds of toys when I have the real stuff?" He turned and leaned against
the bench. "You can't stop me from overhearing something you don't
want me to hear. You can't escape me. I'll get it somehow on tape."

"There's going to be quite a bit of tailing on this job," Josh said quickly.

"Okay. So we have a guy in a car. Easy. I just turn on a transmitter
unit that sends out a signal. I don't care if the guy's car gets in an earth-
quake, that signal will tell us where he is. Look here." He picked up a
black metal case with silver dials. To me the bloody thing looked like
an expensive shortwave radio set. "Four transistors. Four doodos. Two
8.4 Mercury batteries. Once I ran the thing with three separate tapes;
it even has a built-in delay with a sound trigger. This baby was 400 CPS
with an input impedance from a 1-5-0 to 2,000 ohms, and with a—"

"Okay, Willy, we believe you," Josh interjected. "Let's get down to
business. We have about nineteen potential witnesses. Maybe as many
phones to bug. On one man we have to have daily reports. That's Judge
Tucker—"

"The federal judge?" Willy asked.

"The same one. Prebel Tucker. Chief Justice, Federal Court of Appeals."

Willy whistled soundlessly.

"Man, that's big. You know what will happen to me if they find
a bug?"

"Nobody but nobody ever finds your bugs, Willy," Josh said heartily.

"Is he connected with City Hall?"

"It's the same gang," Josh said. "You know the whole bit."

"See? What did I tell you? Federal judges, city judges, City Hall—
even Washington! You know they're in the White House?" The big fist
slammed down. "It's only a question of time before they take over! You
got them in the State Department, stabbing us in the back, making us
kiss the asses of those God-damn Chinks in Peking!"

It was wearing on Josh; I could see that. He nodded, but his eyes were
glazed.

"You're right, Willy, you're right. They're all bastards. Look, here's a report written on flash paper. You know what flash paper is?"

Willy grinned. "Are you kidding? I sold the stuff to bookies fifteen years ago."

"Okay. You know how it works. If somebody picks you up, put the end of a cigarette to it." He said slowly and emphatically: "Willy, listen to me. This can't be found on anyone. Do you hear?"

Willy took the paper. "Nobody finds anything on me, kid. They'll have to chop me out of the bus first." He started reading the report swiftly. Willy might have been a mental case, but he had a photographic memory. "There's a lot of work here. Now let's talk about dough. I think maybe $25,000 to begin. Cash."

"It's a deal, Willy," Josh said. "Do I contact you through that radio store?"

"Forget that," Willy said. "I'll be in touch with you to make a meet. Maybe down in the Village. I know an old broad down there that runs a—"

For some reason the name jumped into my mind.

"Discothèque?"

"Right, old man—a discothèque."

Josh said: "Fine, we'll wait for your call. Now how do we get out of here?"

"I'll take you up," Willy said. "Then I'll come back. I have to work here on my beam."

"What beam is that?"

"Sonic. Maybe I'll use it on your job. You just flood a room with a signal and you can get the conversation without a mike or even going near the place." He took a half dollar from his pocket. "Just a reflector about this big hung on the wall. You just throw a beam of microwaves off it and you'll get anything in that room."

"An Orwellian nightmare," I said, half aloud.

But Willie caught it. "You mean Big Brother, old man? You're right. You just don't know how many Big Brothers are looking over your shoulder every day." He poked his big finger in my chest. "The Commies have this stuff. Five years ago they were bugging our embassy in Moscow." He sounded indignant. "Don't you guys in Washington read the papers?"

"Yeah, we read them, Willy," Josh said impatiently. "Let's get out of here."

The climb back to the street seemed endless. I had the feeling we were ascending from the bowels of the earth in some H. G. Wells nightmarish novel: there were ladders, tunnels, tiny red or stark white bulbs, the systematic roar, faint at first, then louder as you automatically cringe for the impact; then the wave of sound almost as overpowering as an invisible force thundering past. I was staggering with fatigue, and Josh's face was

151

weary in the flashlight beam when Willy brought us to a boiler that towered high in the dim light. In the background were sounds of pumps, turbines, and hissing steam.

"This is the subbasement of the Rendall Hotel," he said. "I'm going to bring you out on Fifty-ninth Street near Lexington. It's dark, and you won't be seen. Just look up and down the street before you walk out. Some of the radio-car guys use this block to catch a few winks. If you're ever caught, act like you're drunk and went into the alley to take a leak." Willy laughed, and climbed a small ladder to a steel platform. We followed him across the platform and up a corridor. Suddenly I could feel the night air. God, how sweet it smelled!

Willy was now cautious. He flicked off his flashlight and moved like a cat through the darkness. At last we faced a large wooden and mesh gate. The padlock—later I learned Willy had equipped each gate or fence with his own lock, which only needed one master key—opened.

"When will you give us the first report, Willy?" Josh whispered as we went out.

"Three weeks—maybe more," was the answer.

I was pushed out, and the gate clicked. The alley stank of urine and dog dirt; the faint dim night-light of a store gleamed at its mouth. The street was deserted as we hurried out. We stopped on the corner of Lexington. The lights were bright; the traffic moved. I took a deep breath; then, as if by silent agreement, we walked across the street to an all-night Automat.

"You boys look as if you were plastering," the cashier said cheerfully as he counted out a dollar in nickels and dimes.

Josh gave me a weary smile. His black hair was white with dust and plaster, and my dark jacket could have been in a snowstorm.

CHAPTER TEN: THE GROUNDWORK

EARLY THE NEXT MORNING we were at Wexford. As before, we met in the library, Josh, myself, the senator, Kelly, Pam and Lacey, Luke and Luther Roberts.

"Give us a rundown on Kensington," Josh said to Luther.

"We have several local committees formed, and the prospects of the company staying are excellent," Luther said, consulting a sheaf of notes. "The union knows it's sunk if the company pulls out, and we've got them on our side. The senator pulled some wires for us, and it looks like orders will start to come in next month."

"Who got credit?"

"My people planted five big stories about the company staying, in five of the biggest papers in northern New York. Without saying so, we put across the idea that Congressman Kelly Shannon had a lot to do with it. We had fifteen telegraph men—"

"Telegraph men?" the senator asked, puzzled. "What's that?"

"Madison Avenue slang for front men, Senator," Luther said. "They move around the community-club circuit—Kiwanis, Elks, Holy Name societies, that sort of thing. These people are usually starved for a speaker, and we supply them. They come with slides, class, good manners, and corny jokes. The clubs love them."

"And they get across the message that it's all Kelly Shannon's work?"

"Definitely. At this time it would be premature to come out and say so outright, but the hints are pretty broad."

"Have you had any queries from any of the other congressmen?"

"Two so far. They wanted to know what the hell was going on. We gave them a polite brush."

The senator looked over at Josh. "You can't keep this sort of thing quiet too long, Michaels. When do you think we should announce Kelly's candidacy?"

"After the hearings. We have to build very carefully, one thing after the other, until the public is so conditioned it accepts as a matter of course that Kelly is running."

"What about the hearings, Josh?" Luther asked. "When do you think they'll start?"

"I have a staff of investigators working on Jello's story now. It's going to cost a fortune, Senator, but I think we can get everything wrapped up in a month."

"Some time in May?" Luther said.

"No later. By that time you and Luke should be organized upstate."

"I have a card file of over five hundred names," Luke said.

"Local newspaper editors, political writers, community leaders, priests, rabbis, ministers?"

"The works," Luke said proudly. "By the summer we'll have a Shannon committee in every town, village, and township in the state."

"Right now we're concentrating on the depressed areas," Luther said.

"Don't make promises," Josh said. "Give them only results."

"What kind of results?" Lacey asked.

"If a factory is in danger of folding, we'll prop it up. If the plant is gone, we'll try to move a new one in." He asked Luther, "Did you get together with the brain trust?"

"Luke and I met every one. Seven will come along with us. Three said No dice."

"Why did the three say No?" Josh pressed.

Luther carefully packed his pipe. "Come out with it, Luther. This is no den mothers' meeting."

"They didn't like the senator's investigation of the State Department after the war."

"What didn't they like about it?" the senator asked calmly.

"They thought you went off half-cocked on a lot of the charges."

"That was Tuck Larsen's stuff," the senator said. "Someone was feeding him. The way he wrote it made me sound like an ogre. Actually, I never gave out a thing. Isn't that right, McCool?"

"That's right."

Kelly leaned over and gently shook his father's shoulder. "We believe you, Dad."

"I hope you do. I'm sure the questions will come up again. That Larsen—"

"Forget Larsen, Father," Luke said. "Let's get back to the hearing. How do you intend to release Kelly's appointment to the committee, Josh?"

"Once Jello's information is checked and confirmed," Josh said, "we start to move. First there will be an exclusive story by Sissy Southworth—"

"That horrible woman with the TV panel show?" Lacey asked.

"That horrible woman has millions of viewers and readers," Josh said. "Don't knock her, Lacey."

"She breaks the story about Jello's charges," I said.

"Right. Just enough to shake up the press corps in Washington. She's going to give us about twelve minutes of her show—"

"I'm sure that will immortalize Kelly," Lacey said grimly.

"Knock it off, will you, Lacey?" Luke said with a frown.

"The next day Sissy will have another story in her column—"

"Won't the newspaper boys be on the story before that?" Luther asked.

"Are you kidding?" Josh asked. "I'm going to have Sissy's staff calling the city desk of every large paper in the country right after the broadcast. Their phones will be ringing all night!"

"What will I be doing?" Kelly asked with a smile.

"Nothing. I don't want you around," Josh said. "We'll take the calls here at Wexford. You'll be out of touch until Monday. Then I'll have an AP man meet you as you're heading for the airport. You'll confirm Sissy's story. This will make Sissy happy and help build the suspense."

"By this time the Washington press corps will be hammering at your door," Luther said.

"They'll be all over the FBI, the CIA, the Department of Justice, the New York cops," Josh said. "I want them to work like hell all weekend, just digging."

"When will we give them some hard facts?" Luke asked.

"One P.M. Wednesday."

"Why 1:00 P.M.?" Luke asked. "That's a peculiar hour."

"That hour the wire-service bulletins will catch the Wall Street editions of the P.M.'s, and we'll have a chance to make Kelly's wirephoto picture along with the story in the final editions. By the way, one of the things I'll have to prepare for you, Luke, is a card file of all the deadlines of every major newspaper in the country, along with that of news magazines. Never call a press conference on these deadlines. Make it at least an hour before. Remember the mechanics of a newspaper; reporters have to call in their facts; the rewriteman has to write them; then his copy goes to the news desk, the copydesk, is stripped down by the copy cutter, made in cold type, placed in a form, molded, matted, then placed on a press. All this takes time. The more time we give them, the more space and better positions on page one do we get from the news editors when they dummy up page one."

"How much do I disclose at this press conference, Josh?" Kelly asked.

"Only a few more facts," Josh said. "Just enough to sweeten the appetites of the Washington reporters. Always let them maintain the illusion they know the whole inside story. It's great for cocktail parties. And remember, some of them don't like to get off their duffs and dig."

"How do you know?" Pam asked.

I quickly interjected, "Because he was once one of them."

Even the senator laughed.

Josh explained that at this press conference Kelly will reveal that he will make an appearance as a principal speaker at the annual dinner of the National Association of American Police Chiefs at the Washington Hilton.

The senator asked, "Do you need any help in arranging that, Michaels?"

"No. The head of the organization is running for Congress next year. He's already approached me to run his campaign."

"So favor gets favor," Pam said.

"That's all part of the Washington merry-go-round, Pam," Luke said.

"In his speech at the Hilton," Josh went on, "Kelly will release a few more time bombs and will promise to name names in his speech on the floor of Congress. I'm sure every congressman will be on hand and the press section filled."

Luke said, "That will be fantastic coverage."

Josh sketched the national popular audience Kelly would have that week, through Sissy's broadcasts, the subsequent TV and radio news broadcasts, the coverage by the wire services and the country's biggest newspapers. Millions would be hearing Kelly's name for the first time.

"Remember one thing," Josh said, "we just have to take over the boob tube. Television has changed politics. Women are voting in greater and greater numbers. And women are not party loyalists; they vote for a personality."

"That's true," I said. "You don't win elections any more by putting up two big signs with the candidate's picture over Main Street.

Even the clubhouse and district leaders are dead—with the exception of Barney Mullady. He has both state and national strength like Pendergast or Hague in the old days."

"What about the Hatch Act?" Luke wanted to know. "Doesn't that hurt him?"

"Mullady doesn't pay any attention to it," Josh said. "He has everything going for him, welfare and the relief-check vote, the civil-service exempts—and they can exempt anything—the minorities, black, tan, brown. Whether he will be controlling them four years from now is a question, but he has them today—and that's what counts."

Kelly said, "I thought I had made my position—"

Josh held up his hands, palms out.

"I know—you don't want any part of Mullady. Let's forget him. Let's get back to one of our many problems—time. We have to go to the people in a hurry and capture their imagination. Once we have captured the public, we'll concentrate on ideas instead of a political organization. Meanwhile, we'll be attuned to the new political forces in the city and state, like Dregna and the liberals, who of course insist they're against the bosses. They always are."

Lacey looked disturbed. "So we're going to use that little man's dirty story," she said.

"Oh, God, you still on that, Lace?" Luke said disgustedly.

"I can't help it; I think it's dirty."

"We're going to prove it all before we use any part of it, Lace," Kelly said. "I promised you that."

"Even if you prove it, I think it then belongs in the hands of the proper authorities."

"I think you should leave that to us, daughter," the senator said angrily.

"No. Wait a minute, Senator," Josh said firmly. "It's best we have this out now, or it will fester."

He lit a cigarette slowly and deliberately and studied Lacey through the thin blue smoke.

"Lacey and I had a discussion about Jello's story while riding down to the city."

"And I told you then what I'm saying now—"

"Okay, it's dirty; so is most of politics. There are times when you have to compromise, make deals, overlook some things."

"Maybe that's why I hate politics," she said.

"Every man to his own opinion," Josh said with a smile. "Just like my opinion on your housing report . . ."

"Are we finished with what we're going to do with Jello's story?" Lacey asked.

"If it's true we're going to use it—big," Josh said.

"You filed a minority report, Lace," Luke said with a grin.

"It will be checked thoroughly, Lacey," Kelly said.

"We were talking about your housing report," Josh said. "Have you decided how to kick them in the guts yet?"

"We have," Lacey said grimly, "but I don't think you're going to like the way we propose doing it."

"Oh, something special?"

"What's this all about?" the senator asked with a frown.

"Do you know about Kelly's and Lacey's report on ghetto housing, Senator?"

"Oh, that thing they've been working on for over a year?" The senator dismissed it with a wave. "Kelly wants to give it to Congress—"

"Well, it could be made important, as I told Lacey, if there was some way to punch the voter in the face—"

"Kick him in the guts," Lacey said loudly.

Pam gave her sister-in-law a surprised look.

"I'm only quoting Mr. Michaels, Pam."

"That's right; that's what I said, and I mean it," Josh said. "Forget the facts and figures—"

"Lacey and I have been talking about a plan," Kelly said quietly. "It's one I like."

"Fine. Let's hear it."

"As I see it, until Luke and Luther get the upstate organization going and your investigators confirm Jello's story, there really isn't very much I can do."

"There'll be appearances next month. The Catholic Bishops' Far East Dinner—"

"That's at least a month off. Is there anything important for me to do between now and then?"

"Well, not really. But I would like you to be around, Kelly."

Kelly, suddenly tense, leaned forward. "As Lacey told you, we have been working on this housing report for over a year. We had meetings with the United Councils, the Federation of City Employees, the NAACP, CORE, the Block Organizations, and just about every organization, official and private, big and small, that has anything to do with city, state, and national housing."

He picked up a thick folder filled with what appeared to be mimeographed reports and fancy brochures.

"Just for background, let me give you some of the facts and figures." He added with a slow smile for Josh's benefit: "I promise to skim over and not bore you. What we have here is broken down in major poverty groups, minority groups that have education and those that do not, race and income, youth education, the dropouts. Listen to this: More than 300,000 families in New York City have an income of $3,000 or less; this represents some 15 percent of all families in the city. In other words, one out of every six or seven families in New York can be classed in the poverty group. In addition, more than 300,000 individuals living alone in New York have an income of less than $2,000."

Lacey said: "They're mostly minority families. I did some of the checking of the city welfare records, and found that almost one half of the Negro families in the city are headed by a female under sixty-five years old. Nearly all of them are on welfare."

"They don't want to work," the senator growled. "Get their welfare check and go to the nearest gin mill. . . ."

Kelly ignored his father; apparently this was an old argument.

"They're not all black," he said. "There are over 50,000 white families in the poverty groups. Almost 100,000 aged white families earn $3,000 or less. There is another 50,000 headed by a white female less than sixty-five in the same poverty class."

Lacey said: "The education figures are almost unbelievable. About 55 percent of all Puerto Rican adults twenty-five or older have not completed elementary school, and only 10 percent have completed high school. I've been having lunch wtih some welfare investigators, and managed to get figures." She looked up. "Welfare won't like this, the figures are confidential: 46 percent of all Puerto Ricans on welfare are unable to speak English; 75 percent are unable to read English; and 76 percent are unable to write English."

Kelly slowly closed the folder. "There's one problem, Josh."

"What's that?"

"These are facts every American should have. But as you have said, they're as dull as dishwater, so who will pay attention to them?"

"We can invite some of the civil-rights people to comment," Josh said cautiously. "But that will be routine stuff."

Kelly shrugged. "They'll shout and they'll plead, Josh. You know that better than I do. But will people pay attention to them? No."

Lacey said, "In the beginning we intended to prepare to show how if the people in the national ghettos are educated they will refuse a tradition of poverty."

Josh said: "I've read it before, Lacey. Let's say I'm on the city desk of a metropolitan newspaper and your White Paper comes in. I tell my rewriteman one-half column. Maybe it even remains on overset and never sees the light of day."

Lacey stared straight ahead. "There are other people in this world besides tired, cynical editors and rewritemen."

"I've seen a million brochures and reports here and in Washington," Josh said wearily, "along with government surveys, state reports, city reports, private reports, Master's theses—you name them; we've been through them, and so has Finn. You just never know how much wasted effort and money have been spent by fumbling federal agencies and do-gooders on our national housing problem until you have chained yourself to a chair in the wonderful quiet of the New York Public Library or

National Archives and read every word and every page of their precious prose. The voters just don't give a damn any more. I think slum housing and poverty are just words to them. Look at this." He reached over and selected a big brochure from Kelly's folder. On the cover was a moving photograph of a child sitting on the bottom step of a tenement. The indignant black type read: POVERTY: OUR NATIONAL DISGRACE.

"I happen to know this is a fine agency," he said as he flipped over the pages. "But who cares?"

"You're right," Kelly said. "No one really cares except the dedicated people who worked on it." He held up the brochure. "Facts. Figures. Graphs. Charts. Photographs. Just as Josh said, an expensive, tragic waste of time." He turned to Josh. "Now I'm going to prove how right you are. I happen to know this report cost a fortune and received exactly a column in the *Times*, a half column in the L.A. *Times*, and less in the afternoon papers. Television ignored it. It was issued five months ago. What has been done about it? Nothing. Where is it now? Somewhere in the stacks of the New York Public Library."

"It's a municipal and government problem," the senator replied, "not the voters."

"But it is, Dad," Kelly protested. "It's your problem—and mine. Particularly mine if I'm running for public office. These people are Americans! Lacey and I agree with Josh that this problem has to be dramatized and brought to the level of the voter's imagination."

"What you mean is, you want to take on an organized political community," Josh said.

"If necessary," Kelly answered. "In the South, the system is purely social, and that goes back to the agrarian way of life. When you break through the social structure you have accomplished the aims of the civil-rights movement. Then and only then can you assume political power and become a part of the community."

"We're not campaigning in the South, Kelly," Josh said. "This is the North."

"That's right. That's why it will be more important for me to join the beginning."

"The beginning," his father echoed, "what beginning?"

"The social revolution in the North," Lacey said.

"Exactly," Kelly said. "It's been edging across the North for a few years now. I wouldn't be surprised if it will explode somewhere near us soon." He turned to Josh. "The North is built on money. For more than a century the control of society has remained more or less the same. A man who is threatened can always hide behind his money, his power, his politics. A mere social change will have an enormous task to accomplish because the people are cynical and disillusioned . . . the barriers are great. . . ."

"Politically, it may be suicide," his father said.

"You're wrong, Dad," Kelly said warmly. "You saw what Barney Mullady has done with his machine of minorities. But in the last few years it's been breaking off, splintering here and there until Mullady's been forced to move into other upstate cities. Somewhere there will be a test case, probably in this state. It could decide the future of the whole civil-rights movement in the North and the future of half the country's Negroes who live in those cities.

"Don't you see, Josh, what could it mean?" he said almost pleadingly. "I could be their champion. I'm sure they would remember that, if I ever ran for the Presidency. It's an enormous challenge, and right now there is no other politician who's doing it. They're afraid of the backlash."

"You still haven't told us your plan," Josh said.

Kelly took a deep breath and glanced over at Lacey. "Lacey and I are going to spend a month in the big ghettos here in the city and all around the state—"

"You mean *live* in them?" Luke cried.

"That's exactly what I mean. Live there. Eat there. Sleep there. If the people are swimming in their own sweat, we want to do the same thing. If they're freezing, so will we. If they fight rats, we want to fight them. We intend to eat and sleep poverty. I want to find out what the people in these places are hoping for, what they expect, why they are bitter and disappointed in the present administration, nationally and statewide. In a month's time we should be able to speak with some grass-roots authority."

"But my God, living in those places!" the senator almost shouted. "It could be dangerous!"

"No more than taking a three-bar jump or the skin diving in those caves off Sand Cay that we did last year," Lacey said.

"How are you going about it?" Josh asked. "You just can't walk into people's houses and say you want to live with them."

"We've arranged a whole schedule," Lacey said, "through some school-teacher friends."

"Can they be trusted?"

"They're not politicians, if that's what you mean."

"We can't afford to have this leak out," Josh said. "It would be seen as a real corny stunt. The son of one of the richest men in the world—and a congressman to boot—living in a slum! It could ruin us."

"Nothing will get out," Kelly said. "These people are not interested in publicity. They're mostly schoolteachers and community workers."

"It could work out," Josh said grudgingly, "but it will have to be planned very carefully. Instead of tipping *Life* or *Look*, we'll take our own pictures and include them in the report." He said to me, "Do we have a photographer we can trust, Finn?"

"Couldn't we do without that—just once?" Lacey asked.

"No—if it means something for our side."

"Suppose we skip the photographer, Josh?" Kelly suggested. "We can make it up later on."

"I'll promise you we'll have something good when we're finished," Lacey said.

"Eyewitness stories of fighting off rats and how cold it is in the front room?" Josh said. "I could write it now."

"My God, you are cynical," Lacey said.

"Cynicism is only experience," Josh said. "That's exactly what I mean. Will you have something that any experienced metropolitan newspaperman, can't sit down and write from memory?"

"If we didn't think so, I wouldn't bother," Kelly said.

"Do you think a month or even more is going to give you a real taste of the slums?" Josh asked.

"I think a week could be enough for someone who is accustomed to buttered toast, hot coffee, and seventy degrees in the living room every winter morning," Kelly said mildly. "How many rats do you have to see?"

"Didn't I read where a professor from California lived on the West Side to write a report on ghetto conditions?" Luke asked. "But he took six years to do it—"

"That's the perfect way to do it. Unfortunately we have slightly less time than that," Kelly said wryly.

"Are you sure you want to do this, Kel?" Luke asked.

"Very sure. Lacey and I agreed that this is the only way to dramatize those dull facts and figures."

"I agree with your father," Josh began. "Suppose something happens to either one of you?"

"I think I can take care of myself," Lacey said.

"Will I be able to get in touch with you, Kel?" Pam asked anxiously.

"Luke and Luther will be upstate. I'll be in touch with them every night." He reached over and held his wife's hand. "There's really nothing to worry about, Pam. Lacey and I know the people we'll be staying with."

"Will you keep a diary—day to day?" Josh asked.

"By the hour if you want," Kelly said.

"Suppose the word gets around the town where you're staying and the cops decide to find out who you are?" Luke asked. "After all, a white man and woman—"

"Our friends have arranged a regular underground railroad," Kelly replied with a laugh. "We'll be on the move most of the time. We not only want to avoid the police but also the NAACP, CORE, or any of the regular organizations. This is to be strictly a private, unpublicized survey. It was only on that basis that our friends agreed to arrange it."

Josh looked at the senator, and shrugged. "Well, in the meantime, we'll wrap up the material for the hearings—"

161

"—while we work upstate," Luke added.

"Senator, I wish you'd start contacting your people for the television coverage," Josh said. "By the way, we'll have to hire five planes and pilots—"

"Five planes?" Pam asked.

"Once the campaign has been launched, Kelly will have to be on the move day and night, Pam, and sometimes with you."

"If you can't hire them, buy them," the senator told Luke.

"Well, I guess that's it for tonight," Josh said.

"We'll be leaving first thing tomorrow." Kelly sighed a little as he spoke.

Josh turned to Lacey: "Please, no risks."

"You want me to kick them in the guts, don't you?" she asked innocently.

"What do you think of Kelly's idea?" Josh asked me on the way home.

"It could work out. At least it's sincere and original."

"It's risky as hell," he said. "Not only could they be discovered by the cops; dammit, they could even be hurt. A couple of goons could find out who he is and—"

"You're the one who wanted it all dramatized, Josh."

"Christ, I didn't want Lacey risking her fool neck!"

"I think she's a girl who can take care of herself."

"She's a damned opinionated woman with more nerve than common sense," he fumed. "I don't know why the hell I didn't insist she stick to organizing the women's division."

"For the main and simple reason, as Penrod used to say."

"What's the main and simple reason?"

"She would have probably hit you with the tea and crumpets and walked out."

He drove in silence for a few minutes, then laughed shortly. "Maybe you're right, Finn. Anyway, this takes Kelly out of our hair for the next few weeks while dealing with Willy. If there's any problem, we'll talk it over with the old man."

"Did you tell him about Willy?"

"He didn't want to know who we're using. All he said was, he didn't care if we tapped the Vatican as long as we got the goods on Saunders, Remington, and Gentile. Getting back to Kelly and Lacey, we have to figure how we can use their stuff. It could be dramatic."

"It's not new, you know. Kelly's not the first rich man in politics who went to live with the poor to get material for legislation."

"Who was the other one?"

"Isaac Newton Stokes."

"Wasn't he in La Guardia's time?"

"He was in government long before La Guardia's administration. He was battling slums and poverty back in the 1890's. And just like Kelly, he went to the tenements and lived in them. No publicity; the people never knew who he was. But Teddy Roosevelt heard about it and had him write the Tenement House Law—I think it was about 1901. Roosevelt later said he picked Stokes because he was the only one who really knew anything about tenements and poverty, even though he was a rich man."

"Isn't that the old-law Tenement Act?" Josh asked.

"That's correct. Stokes' work was the biggest help Roosevelt had in solving the scandal of minimum-income housing. And Tammany fought and ridiculed Stokes at every turn." I couldn't help but give him a bit of a dig. "Stokes received national attention. Had he been a politician he could have gone far."

"If he didn't enter politics what did he do?"

"Next time we're up at the house," I said, "remind me to show you six volumes called *The Iconography of Manhattan Island,* which he edited. It's the classic work in the field. And by the way, you'll find it in the Shannon library. It's evident someone's been reading it."

CHAPTER ELEVEN: THE TAPES

IN THE NEXT FEW WEEKS our Woolworth Building office became so busy we moved up to the Roosevelt Hotel and took a large suite under a tool company's name. If there were any questions, we were preparing the company's annual report and laying the groundwork for the big annual meeting. I've found that all you have to do in a big city is have ready and logical answers. Be evasive, and the average city dweller becomes suspicious. We put on some people, mostly from Luther Roberts's Madison Avenue firm. The majority had worked with us before on other campaigns, and could be trusted.

The first polls from Dyke Short and Frank Shea confirmed not only what the others told us—it was a wide-open race—but also indicated it would be a difficult task to get Kelly elected. While the polls showed that Gentile's charm had worn thin, they also showed he still maintained his popularity among the female voters. The males mostly shrugged their shoulders when his name was mentioned, and said Who else is there?

The significant and startling fact to emerge from our analysis was the reaction of the young voters; they couldn't care less for Gentile. They seemed to feel he had failed them, and they were seeking a new leader.

Josh just smiled when he finished reading the analysis.

"If you say 'I told you so,' I'll flatten you," I warned him.

"Pick up the dinner check tonight, and I won't say a word. But seriously, Finn, we have to keep developing this theme—the young, fearless, imaginative fighter against not only crime and corruption but anything that smacks of conformity. He's got to be the maverick."

"What's better than what he's doing right now?"

"You mean this ghetto survey?"

"Exactly. We can milk it for days: magazine layouts, TV appearances, dinner speeches . . ."

"I think you have a damn good idea," he said thoughtfully. "By the way, how are they doing?"

"I spoke to Pam last night. She's worried, of course, but Kelly calls her every few days."

"Is he keeping in touch with Luke and Luther?"

"Every night. Luke said Kelly is now an expert at taking a bath in the kitchen sink, and Lacey knows how to wash bedsprings with kerosene to kill bedbugs."

"Christ, what pictures we're muffing!"

"That's the way he wants it, Josh. The boy's sincere in what he's do-ing—"

"Sending a photographer along with them wouldn't make it any less sincere."

"It would smack of the worst kind of publicity stunt; you know that."

"What about the groundwork upstate?"

I gave him a rundown on the latest report I had received from Luther only that morning:

Upstate the various teams under the direction of Luke and Luther were accomplishing great things. Some county chairman had called, indig-nantly asking who was this young bird—meaning Luke of course—and what was he doing? But Luther Roberts was an old pro. Every time Luke cold-bloodedly cut some backwoods politician to shreds, Luther pasted him back together with kind words, pats on the back, and promises.

Later, when Luther called he told us how Luke was proving to be a shrewd, ruthless political strategist. Sleep and food meant little to him. Luther said he was worn to skin and bones but seemed to thrive on late hours and backwoods creamed-chicken dinners. He was also versatile as hell, Luther told me; he held meetings on ski slopes, in back-country bars, in city political clubs, in ice-skating clubs.

"The kid's good," Luther said. "One of the local glamour boys was skiing. Luke hired a pair of skis and went looking for him. He even entered a jump contest!"

"He didn't win, I hope."

"A few weeks ago he would have," Luther said with a chuckle. "This time he let the local boy win. But they're impressed with him. This place had a problem with the railroad. Luke found out some guy he went to school with had an old man who's a big wheel on the railroad. He got him out of bed and got an introduction to his father. They're having a meeting in Albany tomorrow."

"Is he getting Kelly's name across?"

"He first started to ram it down their throats, but after we had a few shouting matches he calmed down. Now he gives them Kelly's name in easy doses. But he's getting the message across."

"What about the leaders?"

"They're asking questions," he said. "I'm just dodging; the only thing I ask for is their problems. And brother, do they have them!"

"You might hint that Kelly Shannon is the man to solve them," Josh said.

"Come on, Josh," Luther said in an aggrieved voice. "What do you think we're up here for?"

Luther filled us in on their problems, suggestions, obstacles, and accomplishments. I'll never forget how he summed up Luke just before he hung up: "If you understand the old man, you can understand Luke. The question is not whether Luke is in your fold, but whether you are in his."

We were spending money as we never had before on any campaign. We were able to hire only three big planes, so we bought the other two. They not only came with pilots but were equipped with everything from the finest bar to banks of typewriters for the press. Every plane had a professional stenographer who could also use the stenotype, and any speech Kelly made could be typed up with copies in minutes after he had finished.

Upstate, Luke and Luther were leaving behind a trail of bills that staggered me and would have ruined any other embryo political campaign. But not this one. We just sent the bills to a dummy corporation the senator's legal brains had established, and forgot them.

Strange, there weren't any leaks in those first hectic weeks. Once a Washington *Post* political columnist wondered about Congressman Kelly Shannon's future plans, and upstate a veteran political reporter wrote a political dope story about the strange stirring upstate on behalf of Kelly Shannon. But his paper missed it; they buried his story deep inside. Josh eagerly checked every edition; it was dropped after the first. I've always wondered about this quirk of fate. Suppose there had been an astute, politically minded editor on that big metropolitan daily's night side. A phone would have rung in the bedroom of his old political writer some time during the early hours of the morning (it was an evening paper), and the editor would have questioned him closely about his story. Where did he get it? What did it mean? Wasn't it politically significant in this politically significant year?

The editor, satisfied there was a big story in this brief dope story, would have turned the political writer over to a rewriteman and together they would have come up with something stronger. The editor, praising himself for his own astuteness, would have spread it on page one and sent a clip to the publisher. The city desks of other newspapers would have followed it up. Somewhere upstate a disgruntled politician would have spilled the beans, and the story would have been all over the country; Senator Shannon's son is running wild. Such a story would have been dangerous—but fortunately the story never registered on this night side editor's mind (there were probably too many columns to check for libel; too many fashion pages to send through) and the phone never rang in the old-time political writer's bedroom. . . .

It went on this way for three weeks. We met with the senator several times, and Pam told us that Kelly called almost every day. We had postcards and brief letters; the tone was that everything was going fine. Once, Lacey had written Josh a note suggesting he check into a rumor an upstate powder factory was going to be shut down by the Defense Department. The shutdown would throw fifteen hundred men and women out of work and destroy the entire community. Josh checked and found Lacey's information was correct. The shutdown would come within a year; this was given high priority on our list of things for Kelly to do.

In the middle of a Sunday afternoon in the fourth week, Josh and I were in the hotel suite, checking and rechecking our card file on upstate county and local leaders. We had been working since early in the morning. Our lunch had been ham sandwiches. The phone rang. Josh casually picked it up and swung around in his swivel chair to stare out the window at the deserted city below. Suddenly he stiffened.

"Yes, Willy . . . Right . . . Where? . . . Nicky Minolli's Tet? The discothèque in the Village? . . . What time? . . . Closing? Two? How does it look?"

He slowly took the phone from his ear. "The bastard hung up."

"What does he want?"

"What we've been waiting for—he has the tapes."

"Do we have to walk down to the center of the earth again?"

"He wants to see us in this discothèque in the Village. Nicky Minolli's. From what I know of it, it's a swinger. By the way, be sure and take a notebook. I want to study what's in those tapes."

We worked until early evening, then had dinner and took a cab down to Greenwich Village. I hadn't been down to the Village in years, and I was shocked at what I saw. There was no more of the self-conscious air of rebellion; there now seemed to be an air of suppressed violence and anger in the faces of the young people I saw.

One pair who hopped from a motor scooter passed us with large buttons on their suede jackets. They reminded me of political buttons; only, these had large block letters on a white background:

WE LIKE PEKING

When I mentioned that this seemed pretty strong, Josh nodded. "I suppose I should be nearer their generation, but I find I can't get through to them," he said.

I stepped aside to avoid getting a kneecap slammed with a guitar. "I know someone who will get through to them."

Josh said, "Kelly?"

"Somehow I believe he'll have a big following among them. I don't think they'll feel alienated."

"There it is—Nicky Minolli's Tet. The swingiest place in the Village."

"What the hell is a *tet?*"

"It's an Asian word for a holiday of many moods—a carnival. From what they tell me, it's aptly named."

It was. The wild pulsing sound of a rock 'n' roll band greeted us as we entered. To the left was a dance floor the size of a subway token, and on it were, it seemed, a thousand young couples, bobbing back and forth or throwing up their hands and wringing them in the best manner of the Aztecs worshiping their sun-god. Pretty Oriental girls with deep low-cut décolletage and slit skirts weaved between tables, skillfully balancing trays of beer bottles and glasses. The bar was crowded with slim young men with lacquered hair and tight collars who appraised each newcomer through the haze. They didn't bother with me; Josh got several smiles. We took a seat at a table as big as my hand and had a gin and tonic, which was mostly bad tonic. The noise grew louder and louder.

"Real camp," Josh said in my ear, and held up an ashtray. Embossed on it was Gainsborough's Blue Boy smoking a cigar.

"What are we waiting for?"

"Willy said to just sit by the bar and he would send out word. Enjoy yourself."

Fags. Noise. Smoke. Phony red velvet drapes and walls of pictures of arrogant actors who were kind enough to scrawl their autographs across the bottom. We had just ordered a second gin and tonic—the waitress lifted her wonderfully curved eyebrows when I suggested she put the gin on the side—when a waiter whispered in Josh's ear. He nodded to me, and we followed the waiter. Now the music was ear-splitting, and the dancers were in a frenzy. One pair of teen-agers were shaking on their knees as though they had the ague.

We found Willy in the rear stockroom surrounded by wine and liquor bottles. He was wolfing down the last of a pizza.

"This is a hell of a meeting place, Willy," Josh said, waving aside his offer of a drink.

"I check their wires every night to make sure they're clean."

"Who would bug a crazy place like this?" I asked.

"There's racket money in this one, old man," Willy said. "They've been pushing horse out of here for a year. The feds have a sniff of it now, and they're trying to pin it down. I found one of their bugs last week."

"Got something for us, Willy?" Josh asked.

A smile spread over the pudgy face. "Damn right I have, kid. Real good."

"When are we going to hear it?"

"Right now," he said. "In my office."

"Jesus, do we have to walk to the core of the earth again, Willy?"

He got up and belched loudly.

"If you think I'm going to play the stuff I have anywhere else, you're nuts. Do you want to hear it?"

"Let's hear it, Josh," I said. "I have a hunch it's important."

"You're so right," Willy grunted. "Important! It will raise your God-damn hair."

"Okay," Josh said. "Let's go."

This time we descended from a gate in the rear of the station. The noise of the subway was still terrifying; for the few moments that it lasted I felt I was swallowing the sound. Deep in Willy's cavern the thunder of the New York Central trains were just as bad. I unconsciously reached out for support as the ground shook under my feet and the dust sifted down in the narrow, yellow flashlight beams.

It seemed better inside Willie's workshop; here at least the boxes, wires, and tubes gave me a sense of reality.

"Who did you get on tape, Willy?" Josh asked impatiently.

"I got them all," Willy shouted as he swung a recorder up on the bench. He plugged it in. "Who do you want to hear first?"

"Let's start with Saunders," Josh said. "Finn, you take notes."

It was one of the strangest scenes I have ever witnessed: ninety feet under one of the largest and busiest railroad stations in the world, with an unbalanced electronics genius and a man who talked to Presidents and political titans, I listened to a series of taped telephone calls that would eventually help to decide the fates and careers of our country's most important political leaders.

I made shorthand notes until I thought my fingers would drop off. I didn't get everything—that was left to the experts in Washington—but what I did get would shock the country in the months to come.

Willy first turned on a conversation that Saunders had had from his private unlisted phone at his Bank Street apartment with a New Jersey attorney who had a "contract." The attorney was representing the parents of a teen-age boy who had been arrested for attempted rape of an elderly widow in upper Manhattan. The boy, apparently drunk, had followed the woman into the hallway of her apartment house and had beaten her unmercifully when she resisted his advances. Her screams had attracted a foot patrolman, who was forced to subdue the boy by force.

The attorney told Saunders he had "taken care of the cop, who was cheap," but the judge needed a nudge from City Hall.

The bargaining was simple and to the point:

SAUNDERS: Who's his old man?

ATTORNEY: He owns a big soap factory in Jersey.

SAUNDERS: If he's got the dough, what's the rub? Rape and felony and a tough judge? Our fee will be high, Counselor.

ATTORNEY (*laughing*): Don't I know. Will I deal with Remington as usual, Chuck?

SAUNDERS: The same arrangements. I'll call Trev tomorrow.

Then Willy put on two more tapes, one of Saunders talking to Remington at the attorney's private unlisted phone in Darien, Connecticut, and another of Saunders talking to Remington at his Fifth Avenue law office. Apparently when Saunders had called Remington at home, he found him thick-tongued and obviously drunk. In his second call he bitterly lashed out at his partner for being a fool and a lush. Remington was contrite, and mollified Saunders with many promises to "ease up on the bottle"; then Saunders detailed the Jersey attorney's case; the "fee"—$5,000.

One of the most shocking tapes was one of Saunders talking to Remington at his Connecticut home in which both men discussed a proposition from Kenneth Beering, the man Benny had told us represented the Midwestern firm named Delafield Motors, to sell the city steel for a new $15,000,000 school program. The bids were to be rigged, and the concern would pay "twenty big ones" for each fixed bid. It was also the first time Benny Jello's name was mentioned by Saunders. As he told Remington, he wanted to make sure Benny was "sent up" for a few years "to keep his big fat mouth shut."

"And if that doesn't stop him, we'll have to look for stronger medicine, Trev," he said. "This bum could be dangerous."

There were also calls from Beering, the crooked attorney from Delafield Motors, calling Saunders' private phone and insisting on a luncheon date so he could be paid off for arranging a Sanitation Department deal; a call from Saunders to Remington bitterly accusing him of being drunk when he had met Beering, and a frantic call from Remington back to Saunders, pleading to meet him for lunch at a place called Erma's.

"Your boy at City Hall is worried about his lush pal," Willy said. He threw a strip of photographs on the table.

"We got a photographer in a hurry and posted him in a car across the street. This strip shows Saunders and Remington going into that place. You can see the sign."

Saunders was easily identifiable standing under a small canopy with the name "Erma's." His companion, a tall, thin man, was gesturing. Willy passed over several more strips.

He held a strip of negatives to the light. "I didn't have a chance to

169

print these. They show Beering and Remington coming out of a downtown restaurant. When he went in, Saunders wasn't carrying anything; Beering had the attaché case. When they came out, Saunders had the case and the dough."

"It will be hard to prove money was in that case, Willy," Josh pointed out.

Willy waved his hand. "He later gave it to Remington, who brought it to a bank and put it in his account. A few days later a share went to Saunders, who doesn't trust banks—he takes it out to a safe-deposit vault on the island."

"What about the judge?" Josh asked.

"Coming up," Willy said. "Judges, whores, City Hall thieves. You name it—we have it."

The taped conversations of Judge Tucker were with Remington regarding the receivership of the Lucas Theatres, an old-time theatre chain. It was evident that the judge, as senior judge of the Circuit Court of Appeals, could appoint anyone as a receiver by designating himself as a district judge and then making the appointment. But there was a catch. The judge hinted to Remington that he should buy stock in his phony real-estate company. Remington promised he would, then called Saunders to curse the old man as a cold-blooded thief!

Later the judge called Remington and said he had to take another loan from the company—Transcontinental Trading, the dummy they had set up—because he intended to take a European trip. In this conversation Remington reminded the judge he had not called "Madam Eva," who had some "great surprises" for him. The judge promised he would.

Remington, the tapes showed, immediately called the madam and warned her not "to turn the old man off."

"Satisfy the old bastard even if you have to buy a bullwhip," he told her.

As the tapes played on, it was evident Remington's phone was extremely busy that night; Saunders was notified the judge wanted another loan from Transcontinental but would swing the Lucas receivership their way; Beering called to alert him that another attorney from a Chicago company was on his way to New York to "make a deal" and would show him half a calling card as identification; Eva Schmidt, the German madam, called—as a client in case Remington's wife answered—to let Remington know Lily Steuben, who had just arrived from Hamburg, would be the judge's companion for the next Saturday night. Her fee would be $500.

"How do you like those coconuts?" Willy cried as he lifted the reel. "A couple of whores entertaining one of your biggest judges. And $500 the old bastard pays to be whipped by a whore!" His eyes gleamed in the hard white light of the naked bulb. "You wanted whore stuff, brother, you got it! I got five hours of this bitch on tape. Your judge isn't the only customer. I got a few boys you'll recognize. And not all Republicans."

Josh said, "What about City Hall? What about Gentile?"

"Nothing on him yet," Willy growled. "But"—he lifted two reels of tapes—"this is his boy Saunders; you know that Jersey lawyer? Well, it's on here how the whole thing was taken care of, and he wants to make a date with Remington to pay off. The guy from Chicago calls Remington and asks to meet him for lunch so he can sell trash baskets to the city. He's willing to pay. We got a tinhorn lawyer calling and slobbering over the phone how great it was to be named a magistrate and how does he pay his fee?"

He slammed down the tapes; now his voice was a roar: "Corruption! It's in every damn office in the city! This is what I told you—weaken us like this, and bang! There we go and the Commies move in! You think the Party's dead? You're crazy! They're underground. They're in the army. Overseas. At City Hall. Washington. Who do you think is putting those kooks up to that picketing? The Commies. This is the proof of it, Josh. I told you—"

"Okay, Willy," Josh said smoothly. "I guess you're right. Look, do you have a report on the surveillance?"

Willy, mollified, said, "Sure I have reports." He threw a few more snapshots across the table. "There's the judge going into that whore's apartment on Central Park West. There's the dame."

He spread some small snapshots on the table. "And here's the Jersey lawyer who wanted Remington to fix the rape case parking his car outside Remington's office. See that attaché case? That's the payoff."

"How did you establish it's the Jersey lawyer?" Josh asked.

Willy stabbed one of the snapshots with a thick finger. "His license plate. We checked Trenton. It's registered in his name. We checked around his neighborhood in Westview and in the building where he has his office in Englewood. There's no doubt it's him. He's a big man in Jersey. Besides, we taped a call when he told Remington he would be over at 3:00 P.M." He pointed to a clock in the window of one of the stores near the car. "See. Ten minutes to three."

"Too bad we don't have a recording of that meeting," Josh said.

Willy silently took a reel from a box. "Stop the crap, Josh; you know I got it. When that lawyer called and said he would be over the following day, I got in Remington's office that night. Remember the small disk I showed you? It looks like a light shield? I put that up and used the sonic beam from the next roof. Every word they said went into the recorder."

He fitted in one end of the tape and clicked on the machine. The voices were as clear as a telephone tape, with a sort of echo-chamber effect:

REMINGTON: Much traffic, Counselor?

JERSEY ATTORNEY: It's starting to thicken a bit. How have you been?

REMINGTON: Fine. They took care of your boy, didn't they?

ATTORNEY: Wonderful. I got my fee and here's yours.

REMINGTON: You don't mind if I count it, Carl?

ATTORNEY: Not at all. (*Pause*)

REMINGTON: All accounted for. Did you have to take care of the complainant?

ATTORNEY: I got her to take three. I told her if she played games I'd produce witnesses who would swear she was the neighborhood whore. She saw the light. How about a drink?

REMINGTON: Fine with me. Wait until I give this to my secretary to deposit.

Willy said: "We took his secretary to the Midtown National Bank, then home. She lives on West Twenty-eighth Street. Remington gave her the rush when she first worked for him, but she cooled it. She's going to get married next summer to a guy in the navy. This came from a dopy old dame who runs the corner liquor store. The secretary's name is Nancy Devlin. She could be a good witness."

He put on another reel. "It was tough getting Saunders and Remington together, but we finally got them. They only sit in Saunders' car on South Street near the Downtown Heliport. Good spot. Nobody around, no witnesses."

"So how did you get them?" Josh asked.

Willy slapped him on the back.

"You know me, kid—I always get them! We took his car to his garage and bugged it with a sonic plate. Then we fixed one of the windows so it wouldn't roll up all the way. I hired a hot-dog stand and put the recorder on top of the rollbox like it was a radio. A couple of jerks that work on the piers bought hot dogs, but nobody paid any attention."

He switched on the recorder, and the echoing voices filled the room:

REMINGTON: Your share is in the attaché case. Do you want to count it?

SAUNDERS: Here? Are you crazy?

REMINGTON: The way you sounded this morning, you don't trust me anymore.

SAUNDERS: I don't trust you when you're on the booze, Trev. You're half loaded even now. Christ, can't you lay off for a while?

REMINGTON: After Beering gave me the twenty gees, I couldn't take him to the Automat. So we went out and had a few.

SAUNDERS: How is he?

REMINGTON: He said you took care of him with five gees, but next time he wants more. He wants to know what's going to happen after your blood brother gets out.

SAUNDERS: Tell that greedy bastard not to worry about it. I told you we were going to Albany.

REMINGTON: Business as usual during alterations?

SAUNDERS: Right.

REMINGTON: But that won't help Beering on a city contract.

SAUNDERS: I'll take care of downtown; don't worry about it.

REMINGTON: Beering wanted to know if he would be welcome up in Albany.

SAUNDERS: Welcome as the flowers in May, tell him.

REMINGTON: Is Gentile really in, Chuck?

SAUNDERS: In like Flynn. After Albany, it's Washington. We're going for big stakes, Trev; that's why I want you to straighten out.

REMINGTON: You're right, Chuck. I'll cut down.

SAUNDERS: When do you see Beering again?

REMINGTON: Delafield is going to put in another bid next month.

SAUNDERS: Then he pays us another twenty?

REMINGTON: That's right. But he wants a bigger slice.

SAUNDERS: We'll talk about it. Feel like some fish at Sweet's?

REMINGTON: No, thanks. Just drop me off where I can get a cab.

SAUNDERS: Jello taken care of?

REMINGTON: Don't let it worry you, Chuck; you can trust me.

SAUNDERS: When I can't we're both in trouble. Do you get that—we're *both* in trouble.

REMINGTON: I get it, Chuck; don't worry. (*Sound of motor starting.*)

Willy threw a yellow film box on the table. "One of my people got a film of them getting into the car and Remington getting out on Broadway and Chambers. Then he tailed Saunders to Hitchcock, on the island, near Westbury."

"I thought he lived in the Village?"

"He does, but he does his banking in Hitchcock. It's a little bank."

"Under an assumed name?"

Willy snorted. "He's not that dumb. Safe-deposit vault. Every summer he takes off for Europe. He's got the guard in the vault a little curious. He says Saunders comes in maybe once a month. But in June he leaves with a valise. We checked. That's when he takes his vacation." He gave us a sly grin. "Get it? Do you get it?"

"He takes the money to a Swiss bank," I said. "Not very original."

"But effective," Josh said. "Will you have a report for us, Willy?"

Willy consulted a list. "We checked out every name you gave us. That Joe Americus who owns the Diamond Tower Club paid for his license. I'll get the name of the SLA contact. There were sealed bids when the city bought that $500,000 worth of snow trucks from Delafield Motors, but they were rigged. We hit the other companies, and they're sore as hell. You know that old German waiter who waited on Jello? He remembers Jello. We have an affidavit from him. We told him Jello was in bad with his boss for an expense account."

"What about the Singer brothers, Willy?" Josh asked.

Willy glanced at some notes. "We have five tapes on their phone. They pulled a hijack last week in Passaic. Cigarettes. The truck is in a garage on Ninth Avenue near Sixteenth Street. I'll get a picture of it this week. On Monday they were talking with some guy in Philadelphia who wanted to put in a fix for his brother who was grabbed in a stickup here. They told him they would get a name of a guy who could help. The next night they told this guy in Philadelphia to tell their lawyer to get in touch with Remington. That salesman for the dress company who made the first contact for Delafield is a young punk. No previous record. But he's up to his ears in markers with a bookie named Lightning who works out of his building on West Thirty-first Street." He tossed the notes aside. "We'll give you a complete rundown on every bastard you listed. I had to send a man out to Minnesota on that Delafield company, but it was worth it. We put a tap on the phone of that guy Beering."

"What did it show?"

"He's paying off everybody in the country," Willy said. Then, raising his voice: "Just what I told you. The whole country's falling apart. Payoffs, whores . . ."

"Okay, Willy," Josh said. "Give me a call when you have everything wrapped up. Now, how do we get out of here?"

Willy's big fist slammed down on the table. "I tell you, Josh, this is important! The Commies are in!"

"Okay. Okay. I heard you, Willy. I'll get to the committee tomorrow morning."

"If you don't we're dead," Willy cried. "And then the only thing left to do is hunt for the bastards with these!" He ran across the room, bent down to fumble with a lock on a heavy metal cabinet, then rose and turned around. My heart skipped a beat. He had an armful of revolvers with long, tubelike barrels—silencers—and two rifles with scopes. He kicked open the cabinet door. Inside, neatly arranged on the shelves, was an arsenal of guns and ammunition. I swallowed hard and looked at Josh, who was putting on a fine show of looking calm.

"You've got more guns than I ever saw in Korea, Willy," he said, smiling. "What are you going to do—start a private war?"

"This is no fooling, Josh," this nut said, coming over to us, the guns held tenderly in his arms. "If we lose this fight we have to take action ourselves!" He shifted the revolvers to one side and squinted along the barrel of one of the rifles. "I can pick the buttons off the coat of any son of a bitch I want at half a mile."

Still keeping up his weird line of Commies under every bed and politicians selling out the land, Willy put away his arsenal, and then, between shouts over his shoulder, led us through the torturous maze.

We came out in a small alley between a hotel and the post office on

Lexington Avenue. I didn't realize how the hours had fled. A gentle pink stain was spreading across the sky; it was nearly dawn. I was staggering with weariness, and Josh had a smear of grease on his coat and a torn pocket. Rust-colored water stained a pants leg, and we were both coated with that fine dust. Back at my place I just tumbled into bed and left Josh at a table making notes. In the early afternoon, when I got up, Josh was asleep on the couch. On the table was a list of potential witnesses.

To Start Hearings

Benny Jello, his complete story. (He'll be on for about three days.)

The Singer brothers. (Get rogues' gallery photographs and yellow sheets to be distributed to the press when they appear.)

Father of the Singer brothers, who agreed with Noodles to pay the bribe.

Photographs of the hijacked truck in the garage on the West Side. (Make preparations for TV to make shots of this truck when the Singers take the stand, before notifying the New York State Police. Could be dramatic films.)

Kenneth Beering, of Delafield Motors, Minn. Subpoena all contracts of any city department he had dealings with. Subpoena his superiors. (Check comptroller's office for records of all bids, when they were advertised; check with the companies who lost out; we may get a beef.)

The New Jersey lawyer who put in the fix with Remington for the rape charge against the teen-ager from Jersey. (Make sure he is warned before he takes the stand that a complete transcript will be forwarded to both the Disciplinary committees of the New York and New Jersey Bar associations.)

Eva Schmidt and Lily Steuben, the two whores. (Check Immigration for their complete records, also Interpol and Hamburg police for possible records. FBI may have compulsory-prostitution record on Eva.)

Trevor Remington. Make sure we get all his bank records, deposits, withdrawals, etc. Check IRS for his last five years' returns.

Charles Saunders. He's bound to deny ever having met Benny. Make sure we get statement from the waiter who served them; have him identify all three pictures. Also get their luncheon check if possible. Remington signed it.

Get statement from bank guard Willy said was curious about Saunders' comings and goings. Check dates of his appearances at the Long Island bank against Remington's withdrawals in the Manhattan bank. (If necessary, IRS will seal his vault.)

(We may use films of Remington and Saunders; however, they don't prove much. But the film of Saunders going to and entering the bank on the island may fit in with the documentary records.)

Things to do: One of the first subpoenas will be for Noodles, who first came to Benny. Have the investigators check with N.Y.C. Police and the agent in charge of the N.Y. FBI to help find him. If he doesn't show, request a 13-state alarm be sent out for him.

We will also need the Blitz Brothers, the policy guys in East Harlem Willy says paid off through Remington. We may only get a Fifth from them, but Willy insists they're hot and may talk. (We can always hit them with Internal Revenue.)

All records of Transcontinental Trading Corp., the phony company Remington, Saunders, and the judge set up. D&B report.

We must have Justice go over the decisions of Judge Tucker on the cases Willy told us about. Have investigators contact the losers in the suits.

Remington's secretary. She can identify Willy and describe how he appeared at Remington's office with that valise and Noodles. When she is interviewed initially have the investigator show her Noodles' picture. She also brought money to the bank. Get bank slips. (Also get copy of her driver's license and have professional handwriting expert compare both signatures in case she gets cute with us.)

Willy said he had the regular cabdriver who had the stand in front of his place drive him up to Remington's office. He said the driver first drove him around a bit while he held the valise of money between his feet. Perhaps minor witness, but still future corroboration.

Check the background of that lawyer who paid for his magistrate's job, and subpoena him. Was he recommended by the Bar Association? Who were his sponsors? What club does he belong to?

(These are the principals. We will have to sit down with the committee's investigators and go over the other witnesses Benny mentioned, such as the fellow in the dress business who helped bring Beering into the picture. I don't think we'll have any trouble with them. They can be frightened easily by a subpoena and threats of either federal or DA prosecution.)

After dinner we went over the agenda for the hearings and the TV coverage.

"We must have complete coverage," Josh said. "I want every housewife from Maine to L.A. to tune in and drool over Kelly. When the old man gets home they'll bend his ear until he tunes in for the night reruns." He snapped his fingers and made a note. "Night sessions. Don't let me forget to bring that up with the senator."

"I'm still worried about Willy and how he got his stuff, Josh. Wiretapping is still illegal. Remember the explosion when that committee found the Internal Revenue boys had been using wiretaps and bugs?"

"I'm with the old man on that: Bug the Vatican if we have to."

"It may be okay with the senator, but what about Kelly?"

"Simple. Kelly won't know how we dug this up. If he wants to know we'll tell him, private investigators." He slapped me on the back. "Stop worrying, Finn; we're on our way! If we bring out half this stuff before a committee, Kelly will be known nationally within a week!"

He locked his hands behind his head and studied the ceiling. "Just how in the hell is Tucker, Chief Justice of the United States Court of Appeals, ever going to explain a whore like Eva?"

He suddenly leaned over and underlined Eva's name and Immigration on the list of potential witnesses. "I want Immigration to get on her back day and night. They don't have to tell her what it is—just twist her arm. I never saw a whore who wouldn't become a state witness to save her own skin. Tom Dewey will tell you that." He made another note.

"Do we really need that whorehouse stuff?" I asked. "The evidence of corruption is shocking enough to damage Gentile even though we still haven't linked him to any wrongdoing. But this woman and the whips and mirrors . . ."

"Corruption makes headlines, but sex and corruption make bigger ones," he snapped. "I know; I covered enough of them. Remember Bobby Baker in LBJ's time? Remember how big it was when it first broke? But do you remember when they brought in the real dirt, the good-looking women and that gal who fled back home to Germany? That's when TV began to get interested. Let's face it, Finn; this is what they want. And, brother, are we going to give it to them!"

"I don't think Kelly will go for it."

"As I said before, we'll do this sort of dealing with Luke and the old man. We can plant questions with Jonesy or the other guy on the committee. Once it's out, they can't stop."

"Even with the senator's influence, the networks might get squeamish."

"Squeamish?" He threw back his head, and laughed. "Not on your life. It's no secret television is scraping the bottom of the barrel these days. What do you think will happen when our hearings start and who comes to the stand but the brother-in-law of the man many Americans believe will be President, followed by one of the most important men in the American judicial system and those German bitchs, not forgetting our friends the Jersey lawyer, the guy from Delafield Motors, Jello, and a few others? A whole new generation has grown up wondering what the Kefauver hearings were all about. They will tune in. Come on, Finn, you know there won't be a word spoken in a hundred million living rooms across America!"

And the tragic thing about it was—he was right as rain.

THE REASON BEHIND Kelly Shannon's vast popularity was his love of the underprivileged, the misfits of society, and what he called God's unforgiven—the poor. This was no pose for political purposes; this was no manufactured image. Sure it was square, politically unrealistic, and Boy Scoutish; but dammit, it was real, and the public knew it and loved him for it.

Too often the word "love" is alien to American politics, but with Kelly it was sincere. He really felt for the underprivileged. The day I located him in that decaying tenement in Lawrence, I recalled what his father had told me that first day at Wexford House; even at prep school Kelly was leading and caring for the misfits, the unpopular, the kids with two left feet who never made the teams he always seemed to be elected captain of with such ease.

Few know the real story behind Kelly Shannon's classic paper on poverty and state and national housing, which someone once said had been truly written in blood. The final report, with a long chapter on Lawrence, mostly contributed by Josh and Lacey, was a cool, detached analysis of what had gone wrong with so many federal and state programs, and ending with its tragic, final result. It is history now that it helped to influence Congress in all future programs, but how it came to be written with such authority has never been told. It is this authenticity that makes the Shannon Report unforgettable. True, there are numerous facts of housing, unemployment, hatred, and discrimination; but they were translated into human beings against the backdrop of flaming terror that shook the nation—I guess that without exaggeration I could even say the world—because I have before me a variety of news reports quoting articles published in Moscow, Paris, Germany, and other European countries.

Josh and I were intimately connected with this report from its very beginning. The part we played in it really began on the evening when we had finished going over the agenda for the hearings. We agreed Josh should go back to Washington to start tying together all the loose ends while I would go upstate, liaison with Luke and Luther and find Kelly and Lacey to alert them that their report had to be finished and that Kelly must join us in Washington to start familiarizing himself with the material we had gathered.

I met Luke and Luther in Syracuse. They both looked haggard and worn. Luther said they were averaging less than three hours' sleep a night, and he estimated they had crossed and crisscrossed the state several times. But their charts and reports showed they had formed the hard core of a statewide organization. A series of small red circles, each representing a group dedicated to Kelly Shannon, dotted a map of the state; they were in farm districts, small towns, and large cities.

"What do you think, Luther?" I asked.

"We're going to make a hell of a fight."

"We're going to fight—and we're going to win," Luke said as he restlessly prowled the room. He stopped before the map. "By this time next fall we'll have twice as many circles on this map."

"What about Kelly?" I asked. "When did you hear from him?"

"Last night," Luther said. "He's been in Lawrence."

"In Lawrence? Why?"

"Ever since the night of the fire he's been itching to get back there and do some digging."

"Did he find out what Mullady was doing there that night?"

"Frankly, I didn't ask him. He just said they had come up with some great stuff. Lacey said the city's ready to explode."

"He wants to get together with you and Josh as soon as possible," Luther said. "Apparently he feels they can stop researching and start writing."

"That's good news. Josh wants Kelly back in Washington as soon as possible. How do I contact them?"

Luther scribbled a name and address on a memo pad. "Here's the address. Kelly said they're living in the apartment of a family named Jones. It's in a bad section of the city—so bad they call it Potter's Field. When will you be leaving?"

"First thing in the morning. I want to get him to Washington as soon as possible."

"I wish to hell they picked a city that was Republican-controlled," Luke observed.

"Lawrence has been Democratic for years," Luther said. "Their machine is very powerful. The upstate people said they can pull a lot of strings."

"Clobbering Lawrence may hurt us with the party," Luke said gloomily.

"It might go with the younger voters," Luther said. To me he added, "You know we've been following Josh's suggestion and concentrating on the young voters."

"Any reaction?"

"It was good upstate. Gentile's lost some favor up there, especially among the minorities."

"We have black committees?"

"Black, brown, yellow, even some Indians who feel they've been screwed by their Brooklyn basket manufacturers," Luke said with a laugh.

"You really think we have a chance, Luther?" I asked when Luke had gone to the bathroom.

"We have a chance, but we'll need some of those big miracles Josh first talked about," was his answer.

I left early the next morning for Lawrence. It was a bitter day, with a raw wind that made old men like me cringe inside their overcoats. The gray, dismal day certainly didn't enhance Lawrence. It made it twice as depressing. It was a long ride from the airport to the address Luke had given me, and I got a good view of the city as the cab took me along the narrow, twisting streets. It appeared to be an old city, the usual upstate industrial center that had been virtually built about a factory. There seemed to be a large number of men, aimlessly wandering about, with heads bowed or tucked into the folds of their overcoat collars or huddled together in doorways of tenements staring out on the littered streets and rows of battered garbage cans.

"Not a pretty place," I observed to the driver.

"It's a dump," he said bitterly. He pointed to some men in a doorway, "and they're the garbage; we're all garbage."

I suddenly remembered Kelly telling me on the night of the fire about the politically owned cab monopoly, and when I asked the cabbie he just gave me a startled look and kept silent for the rest of the drive. He seemed glad to drop me, and took off like a racing driver.

The tenement I was studying was as old and grimy as any in Harlem or in the Negro sections of Washington. Windows were cracked or broken; torn newspaper was stuffed into the openings. I was conscious of faces peering through curtains, but no one was visible.

The hallway smelled of urine. As I started up the gloomy stairway, a cellar door opened and an old man stumbled out. The smell that followed him almost made me sick.

"My God, what's that?" I asked.

"Sewer pipe," he said. "The damn thing's been broken for three weeks."

"Why don't you call the landlord?" I said. "You can get sick from that, man!"

"A couple of kids died last week, mister," was all he said as he entered the apartment and softly closed the door behind him.

There weren't any names on the second-floor apartment doors. I knocked on some but there were no answers, although I could swear I heard rustling and breathing behind them. On the third floor I thought I heard the faint sound of a typewriter. I knocked. There was no answer, and I knocked harder.

The door opened a few inches, and I could see a black face.

"I'm looking for the Jones family," I said.

Then it suddenly opened wide and a cool young voice was asking, "Slumming, Mr. McCool?"

It was Gene Abernathy, Barney Mullady's sweetest chocolate.

"My God, what are you doing here?" I asked.

"It's a long story," he said. "Too long for now. Please come in."

"We'll fill him in, Gene," someone said behind him.

Lacey was smiling and holding out her hands. She looked tired but still trim. When I kissed her cheek, I smelled soap instead of the faint, expensive fragrance she had on the night we had driven back to the city from Wexford.

"Kelly's inside," she said. "We were going to call you or Josh tonight."

"Josh is back in Washington on the hearings," I said.

Abernathy interjected, "I'm sorry, Mr. McCool, but I have to run. It's good seeing you again."

His slender, bony hand gripped mine. Then he was gone.

"What was that all about?" I asked Lacey.

"Come on in and we'll tell you."

Kelly was typing on a portable perched on a kitchen table. The room was painted a nauseating green; the linoleum was worn, but scrubbed. The old-fashioned windows with the low sills had clean but faded curtains. A sagging sofa and a few chairs completed the room's furnishings.

Kelly looked thinner, but his smile was still the same. It lighted up his face when he saw me. "We were just typing up some notes," he said. "Did Lacey tell you. We're about finished."

"I didn't have a chance to tell him anything," Lacey said.

"First, let me get you a beer," he said. "It's the only thing we can drink here; the damn water's polluted."

"I know. A man downstairs told me. He said two children died."

"Two died and five are still in the hospital. The whole block's been without water and heat for days."

He handed me the beer, and Lacey brought out some cheese and crackers.

"I'd be lying if I told you I wasn't ready for a big roast-beef dinner," she said. "We've been living out of cans for weeks."

"What about Abernathy? What's he doing here?"

"Hold your hat," he said. "He's with us."

"With us? What do you mean?"

"Just that. He's been helping us for weeks." He tapped a folder filled with typed pages. "We have enough here to blow Barney Mullady to bits along with his whole machine."

"Wait a minute; you're going too fast. How did all this happen? And why?"

"Suppose we start from the beginning," Lacey suggested.

"Fine. Let's go."

"First of all, let me give you some of the background of Lawrence,"

Kelly said. "It's hard to believe it isn't the South and not the North. First of all, the minorities here make up more than 50 percent of the city's people. They have had some economic power for years. But the political and economic power were organized by the machine and under the machine—never against it. In the past twenty-five years not one Negro has led a fight or social movement against the power structure. What the Negro community has received came as a gift from the Democratic Party leaders. Lacey, put up the map for a moment and show Finn."

Lacey carefully pinned a well-worn city map of Lawrence to the green wall. On it were crayon circles of different colors.

Kelly pointed to several squares. "These are the most crowded schools. All are Negro. The classrooms are bursting. Narcotics are rampant. Kids no more than twelve drink wine under the stairwells. There have been fifteen rapes this year so far. The teachers, all Negro, will leave the schools only in small parties. Negro unemployment in Lawrence is twice that of whites. Negroes uniformly pay higher mortage payments than whites. They pay more for their terrible flats. They must pay 10 percent more for a comfortable place, yet their income, according to government figures, is more than one quarter below that of whites."

He made a wide circle with his finger. "They live in this ghetto, covering about fifty miles. They have been controlled in the past by a variety of Negro appointments, all arranged by the machine: aldermen, sheriff's assistants, city poundkeeper, park attendants, a few in the legislature, a few on the fringes of the power structure. These men formed an élite and led the whole Negro community for years. They have access to the white leadership; they drive nice big cars; they live in nice houses—and they turn out the voters on election day."

He turned around and said grimly, "Now formed against this group in a small secret organization, almost a warlike resistance group that is moving against the old-line political power and economic structure. When there were signs the plastics factory might shut down, the administration didn't do a damn thing to help the unemployed, who just wander the streets or sit on stoops. And listen to this: The mayor is dominated by a gambling syndicate, and the chief of police hasn't raided one of the ten local whorehouses in five years. In every little candy store there's a pinball machine put in by the local hoodlums. It costs $4,000 to get on the local police or fire departments, and the bastards have a loan company set up across from the town hall for the poor suckers to get the money. You don't get on welfare unless you vote the right way, and the director is a notorious drunk. The federal funds for the antipoverty program has been drained into the salaries of the directors—their meeting hall is a subbasement, so dark the lights are on in midmorning."

"Is this just Republican propaganda?"

He returned to the table. "Propaganda, hell!" He held up a thick folder filled with papers clipped together. "We have affidavits, photostats of police reports that were filed away and forgotten, copies of municipal salaries, eyewitness reports on the poverty program—building department reports, slum clearance reports which are covered with dust, and as for schools—Alabama has a better program."

He threw the folder back on the table. "Sure, the corrupt judge and Gentile's brother-in-law and all the stuff down in the city is shocking, but I think if we took this city apart, we could give the hearings much more fiber and more meaning." He took another swallow of beer. "Maybe I'm wrong, Finn, but I think it could have one hell of a national impact."

"You realize, of course, Lawrence is a Democratic stronghold."

"A *corrupt* Democratic stronghold," he emphasized. I think that any Democrat, whether he's in New York or Missouri, will be ashamed of his party when he hears what's going on here."

"Any decent human being would approve of exposing this rathole," Lacey said fiercely. "The leaders of this city are incredibly corrupt."

"There's an old rule in politics: Never wash your dirty linens in public," I said.

"I refuse to underestimate the voting public," Kelly said, "and there's many a historic precedent to back me up."

"Besides, we can hang them all together," he added. "The mayor is a Democrat and the three city councilmen—the jokers we saw that night of the fire—are Republicans. They share alike."

"How does Abernathy fit in?"

"I believe it was Josh who pointed out that Mullady seemed uneasy with so many factions to control."

"We made that observation after we had met Mullady at the club."

"Well, he's right. Mullady's stretched thin, and now there are people in his organization who are boring from within, so to speak."

"And Abernathy's the leader."

"Right. Gene heads the opposition, and it's growing every day."

"How can you trust him? Maybe he's a clever plant."

"We thought of that and we checked—"

"Checked? With whom?"

"You'd be surprised the friends we've made, Finn," Lacey said. "All kinds. And they have one thing in common: they want to get rid of Mullady."

"All black?"

"The opposition is mostly Negro, but there's a good percentage of whites who have joined them, mostly liberals and reform Democrats."

"I still don't get Abernathy leading any opposition to Mullady," I said. "It's obvious Barney trusts him completely—and knowing Barney, he'd think twice before he'd trust his mother."

"That's what puzzled us in the beginning," Kelly said, "but after we found out some things about Abernathy it made sense. Lacey did most

183

of the research into Abernathy's background. Why don't you give Finn a rundown, Lace?"

"It came to us in bits and pieces," Lacey explained. "Gene was born in Harlem, rumbled with a street gang called the Apaches, one of the worst fighting gangs in the city. His story is typical of a Harlem boy, a drunken mother, part prostitute, and a schizoid father who would beat him with anything he could lay his hands on. He later died in a strait-jacket in jail on Blackwell's Island. Fortunately, his aunt had gone to high school and, as he put it, 'licked me 'til it started raining' whenever he missed school. Somehow he got through the first two years of high school. Something happened in the third year. Gene believes it was the death of a close friend by OD—overdose of narcotics—that shook him up. He made fair grades in junior and good grades in senior year. By that time he had left the street behind him. He went to CCNY at night, working as a push boy in the garment center during the day. He graduated *summa cum laude* and went on to get a Master's in social science. But the best he could get was a senior investigator's job in Welfare.

"He tried politics, and was making a reputation when he was beaten by Mullady's strong-arm men. He realized he could never beat Mullady in a fair fight, so he decided to join him and bore from within. He said he swallowed every insult and indignity that Mullady handed him. Apparently this went on for a few years until Mullady felt he could be trusted. For the last two years he has been quietly building a counter-organization to Mullady's."

"Are these facts or just gossip his boys gave you?"

"Facts," Lacey said firmly. "When Kelly was in Syracuse I took a trip down to the city and checked with some friends—"

"For example, when she says he was a member of the Apaches," Kelly said, "Lacey got that from the files of the Youth Board. She even got his records from CCNY."

"His school and Youth Board records are one thing, but what about his political maneuvering? You didn't get that from any records."

"Of course not," Lacey said. "That came from the people who were at the meetings."

"What meetings?"

"The meetings of his organization," Lacey said. "For example, last week we attended one upstate. It was held in the rear of the most horrible tavern I've ever seen. Frankly, I held on to Kelly's arm all night."

"And I held on to Abernathy," Kelly said with a grin.

"You're crazy," I exclaimed. "Suppose you had been hurt?"

"At all times we had four of the biggest men I have ever seen on all sides of us," Kelly said. "Every meeting was brief and to the point. We were brought to the meetings, saw and heard what went on, then were taken back to where we were staying."

"Where were these meetings?"

"They're being held in almost every large city in the state," Kelly said. "The people who attend roughly represent thousands of embittered voters who are violently anti-Mullady. They are organizing, and organizing fast. They've kicked out the Black Muslims and some Commie fronts who tried to take over before Gene arrived on the scene, and they are strictly an organization that will soon take on the machine." He said earnestly: "Finn, these people are Democrats! They are ordinary Americans who just can't see being kicked around by a God-damned machine that's robbing them blind!"

"What kind of people are they?" I asked. "Mostly Welfare?"

"Don't be so cynical, Finn," Lacey said. "Sure, a lot are on welfare. But then again a lot are not. At last week's meeting there was the former head of the poverty program in Lawrence who quit because he just couldn't stomach what was going on. Another was a former city councilman who was clobbered by the machine in the last election because he asked too many questions at the City Council meetings. Then there are voters who have gotten together out of desperation. For example, the man who owns those cabs that can't get near the Lawrence airport or terminal—remember him?"

"One of his drivers took me here. When I asked him about the monopoly, he took off in a cloud of dust."

"Of course; they're frightened."

"You can't count on frightened people to buck a machine," I cautioned him.

"Frightened—and desperate, Finn," he said. "And desperate people with their backs to the wall can be dangerous. Mullady knows that."

"If he finds out what's going on, Abernathy could be in trouble."

"Gene knows the risks. He's prepared to take them."

"When do they plan to come out publicly?"

"The plan was to stage a sit-in on the first day of the gubernatorial convention when Mullady runs his candidate. But now Gene is talking to his people about joining us."

And that will be the end of any deal with Barney Mullady, I told myself. Josh has a few surprises in store for him.

"How do you feel about that, Finn?" Kelly asked.

"I think we had better play it by ear. Let's wait until they really come out—"

"That sounds like Josh," Lacey said. "Believe nothing until you see it."

"Sometimes that's not a bad policy, Lacey."

"But you have to believe somebody!" she cried. "If you keep doubting everybody's word—"

"There's no written contracts in politics, Lacey," I told her. "And damn few bargains kept."

"One thing you can count on," Kelly said grimly, "This city is a time bomb, and when it explodes, God help the people!"

185

"What you propose to do is combine the corruption in Lawrence with the Jello story?"

"Exactly. It all comes under the committee's scope, and instead of exposing only a bunch of thieves in high places, we would also be letting the public see a horrible mess of injustice."

"Where would you hold the hearings?"

"Break it up into three areas: Washington, New York City, and Lawrence."

"In their own backyard?"

"Of course. Once we demonstrate we're not afraid of the machine, I'm sure the people would come forward with more shocking disclosures than we have now."

"Did Abernathy ever tell you what Mullady was doing up here the night of the fire?"

"We'll get the answer to that one tonight," Kelly said.

"Why tonight?"

"That's why Gene was here," Lacey said. "We've been talking about it now for a week. He's holding a meeting with his people this afternoon. If they agree, he has promised to tell us the whole story of Barney Mullady's connection with Lawrence."

"Then there is some connection?"

"Absolutely. The more we dug up here, the more evident it became Mullady has some kind of power over these people. But it's like quicksilver; you just can't put your finger on it. Even our friends just shake their heads when we mention his name."

"In other words Abernathy has told you only half the story?"

"I guess you can say that," Kelly said.

"Then he must want to make a deal."

"From what Josh said only a few weeks ago, deals are not unusual in politics," Lacey said.

"But I also remember how strong you were against a deal of any kind, Lacey," I reminded her.

"In this case I guess I have to agree with Josh that there are times when the ends can justify the means."

"How will Abernathy let us know what his decision will be?"

"If he agrees to tell all, I asked him to come to Wexford tomorrow to meet us. I think that's the best way."

"Josh will need you in Washington, Kelly. There are piles of affidavits and reports you must study."

"We can listen to Abernathy and decide in a few hours. I'll go back with you in the evening."

"And your report?"

"Lacey and I have been working on it every day. We have a tentative first draft almost ready now." He turned to his sister. "How long will it take you to finish the first draft, Lace?"

"No more than a week."

"Would you call it a blockbuster, Lacey?" I asked.

"There'll be those dull facts and figures, but we have numerous case histories."

"Narcotics?"

She searched through the folder and handed me several snapshots, clear, but unmistakably taken by an amateur. They were of several boys and an elderly man in a schoolyard.

"One of Gene's groups made these pictures from a truck. These are pushers selling drugs to the children at lunchtime recess. They identified the pusher and got his rogues' gallery picture."

She handed me a small rogues' gallery picture of a swarthy-faced, middle-aged man with the usual police number across his chest.

"It's a ghetto school," Lacey said. "My schoolteacher friend obtained five affidavits from teachers and mothers."

"Where is this?"

"Lawrence," she said. She pointed to one of the boys in the snapshot.

"He died of an OD two days ago. The people in the neighborhood marched to City Hall to demand that something be done. Two of them were arrested for disorderly conduct. That was the action they received."

"That's what we mean, Finn, when we say this is a time-bomb city ready to explode," Kelly said. "The people are seething."

"When will you be leaving?" I asked as I slipped into my coat.

"This afternoon—just as soon as we see Abernathy."

"Then you're going directly to Wexford?"

"Wexford, a bath, clean sheets, and a roast-beef dinner," Lacey said wearily. "I'll never forget these weeks, never."

"You could have been killed—both of you," I said. "The more I think of it, the more I know we were fools to agree to this crazy scheme."

"Perhaps," Kelly said, "but I can assure you, Finn, we have material we would never have got any other way." He looked around the horrible little railroad flat. "If I'm elected to nothing but dogcatcher, at least I can look in the mirror without being ashamed when I talk about the poor or the poverty program!"

I flew back to Washington late that afternoon and told the story to Josh in detail. He listened intently, interrupting only to shoot a question.

"In other words what they have is a pilot study of an American city ruled by a corrupt machine and how that corruption has affected the minorities and the poor. Do you get that?"

"I do, but frankly I didn't see it as an isolated instance."

"But we will," he said as he began pacing. I knew something was coming; I could almost hear the gears turning.

"What's your idea?"

"Suppose we took an American city apart, piece by piece, kicked over

187

the rocks, and show how the human scum works, making the welfare clients vote right, taking dough for putting a kid on the cops or the fire department, junkies in the schoolyard—with pictures."

He stopped and looked out the window. "What did Kelly say about Lawrence, something about it going to explode?"

"He said it was a time bomb."

"Lawrence, the Time Bomb City," he said, spinning around. "Christ, what a hell of a hearing that would make!"

"I think we would first have to send some investigators up there. Kelly's stuff is good, but we need some professionals—"

"We'll give it to Willy," Josh said shortly. "If the place is so wide open, his people can wrap it up in a week."

"Every time I hear his name a shiver runs up and down my back."

"Put on a sweater," he said with a grin. "When is Abernathy going to give them his decision?"

"This afternoon. I told Kelly we would be at Wexford by noon."

"That black boy must have something big on Barney. Whatever it is, we have to get it."

"We can't get it if he won't give it."

"We'll get it if we have to promise him he can be Secretary of State. Do you think he wants to make a deal?"

"That's what Lacey thinks."

"So Lacey finally decided it isn't a felony to wheel and deal?"

"She admitted the end might justify the means in this case."

"You're God damn right it would," he said shortly. "But I want the stuff Abernathy has on Mullady for another kind of deal."

"I hope what I'm thinking isn't true, Josh."

"I'm afraid you're right, Finn."

"You want to make a deal with Mullady?"

"What else? Keep the lid on, and have Barney's sweet chocolates pull down the right levers. Remember how he told us he did it?" He made a series of swift motions as if pulling down a lever. "Click. Click. Click. Right down the line."

"You couldn't, Josh!"

"You can bet I can—and I will if Abernathy gives us anything strong enough."

He returned to the table from the window and bent down, his face on a level with mine. "We have shockers Kefauver would have given his right arm for. But we need more and more. Frank and Dyke gave me their latest poll last night. This is going to be a rough campaign, and we just can't squeak through! We have to come out big, take over the state party, be the big voice at the convention! That's why we need Barney's sweet chocolates, Finn."

"You'll never get Kelly to agree to make a deal with Mullady, Josh. Never."

"First let him get a taste of the hearings and the campaign—then let's see how he feels."

He opened a folder and threw me several typewritten pages clipped together.

"Let's get back to the hearings. That's a draft of a summary. Give it a read and see what you think."

We arrived at Wexford early the next day. They were all waiting in the library, Luke, the senator, Lacey, Kelly, Shea and Short, Luther Roberts and, sitting off to one side, Gene Abernathy.

So now he was with us all the way.

Howard brought in a pot of coffee, and after finishing a cup and getting rid of the amenities, I opened my attaché case and distributed copies of the fifteen-page résumé of the hearings we had prepared.

"Shall we go into the hearings first or shall we talk to Mr. Abernathy?" Josh asked.

"Did Finn give you a rundown?" Kelly asked.

"He told me all he knew. As I understand it, Mr. Abernathy and his people were to make a decision."

"That's right—they did," Lacey said.

"And that is—"

"Gene has volunteered to be a witness before the committee," Kelly said.

This produced a stir in the room, and I could see from Josh's face he was taken aback. "A witness—about what?"

"Barney Mullady," was Abernathy's reply. "Remember, Mr. Michaels, I'm still his sweetest chocolate."

"What can you testify about?" Josh asked Abernathy.

The even teeth were startling white against the dark skin. "Quite a bit, Mr. Michaels, quite a bit."

"Like what?"

The young Negro said: "I've been with Barney for eight years now. There isn't much I don't know about him or the organization."

"Do you have anything that can hang him?" Josh asked.

"I've been his bagman for three years," was the calm answer. "As I told Mr. Shannon, I even bring down the collections from Lawrence."

There was a gasp in the room. The senator leaned forward and asked eagerly: "Illegal money, of course?"

Kelly broke in: "It was payoffs from gambling combinations that had been turned over to the local organizations. Two years ago Mullady sent Gene upstate to organize local machines that would cooperate with the existing organizations. Now Barney has his hand in almost every ghetto upstate. In Lawrence they first threatened Gene, but Mullady sent back word he would force a gambling investigation through the Investigation Committee for City and State if they didn't play ball. The Lawrence people knew Barney could do it, so they agreed to give Mullady a percentage of the monthly take."

Josh asked, "How much is it?"

Gene said, "No less than $25,000. The combination gives our local boys an accounting, then takes it off the top."

"What does Barney do for that?"

"Stops trouble and gives favors. He's helped to make two upstate judges already."

The senator cried, "That means we can hang the old thief!"

Kelly raised his hand. "It won't be as easy as that, Dad. Gene will explain."

"It's all in cash," Gene said, "and I don't even know where it goes after I deliver it to a construction office on the West Side. I leave a valise with an old hatchet-faced woman who doesn't say a word. I have never seen Barney in the place."

"Where is this place?" Josh asked.

"Forty-eighth Street, just off Tenth Avenue," Gene said. "It's a small red-brick building with no name on the door. There's only this woman in a small office with some telephones, typewriters, a few desks, and some files. It looks like it's been there for years."

"How do you know it's a construction office?"

"There are rolls of blueprints on the desk, and once I heard the woman talking to someone on the phone about a contract for fill for a construction site."

"Don't you talk to Barney about it?"

"He never mentions it, and neither do I. The money is delivered; that's all he cares about." He smiled. "I guess that makes me the perfect assistant."

"Suppose it wasn't delivered?" I asked.

The answer was a flat, "No one steals from Barney Mullady."

Josh gave the Negro an incredulous look. "Wait a minute. What you are saying is, you are willing to testify before a congressional committee that you collected payoffs from a gambling combination for Barney Mullady?"

"That's right. But there are a few strings connected with the package, Mr. Michaels."

Josh said, "There would have to be."

"I didn't come here as a crusader," Gene said. "That's not my role. As I told Mr. Shannon, I'm interested in only one thing, and that's my people —black people, not white. I think you have more than enough on your side now." He said to me: "Do you remember, Mr. McCool, the first time I met you outside City Hall with Barney? I don't know if you recall, but when he introduced us he said something about how I was once a bad boy but he brought me back in line."

I said, "I remember."

"I guess the inference was that I had been some kind of juvenile delinquent and he had made me respectable, but what he really meant was that I bucked him some years ago in Harlem. I had a small organization going and was making some headway with a candidate for City Council when four of his musclemen greeted me in the hallway of the apartment house where I lived. They worked me over for more than an hour." He lifted his chin and touched an ugly jagged scar. "I almost became the black Scottoriggio."

Luke said, "I don't recall reading anything . . ."

Gene gave him an ironical look. "You don't think the daily press would carry anything about a Negro being beaten in Harlem, do you? Oh, two detectives came over to the hospital and took a statement. When I got out, I had lost my city job and the election was over. My organization had gone up in smoke. The boys wouldn't even talk to me, and my candidate walked to the other side of the street when he saw me. I was down on the bottom rung when Barney sent word he wanted to see me. I went down to the club, and he greeted me like I was the prodigal son. Nothing was ever said about my busted head, broken arm, and caved-in ribs. He just said he had heard great things about how I could organize and that he wanted me to join him. By this time I didn't have much in sight, so I took what he had to offer. I gave him good service, and in a few years he moved me inside. Then one day I was carrying the valise."

Josh asked, "What are the strings, Mr. Abernathy?"

"I'm coming to that. About two years ago, Barney heard that two young fellows had opened a club on the West Side. They were going up and down the avenue making speeches about how Barney was using the black people for political capital. This was around the time white cops down South killed those women in the march, and feeling was running high. It's not like it was when Barney first took over. A lot of young people don't want any part of Barney or his stooges. I know Barney was worried. Well, they did the same thing all over; some of Barney's musclemen walked in on those two kids and messed them up and just tore that clubhouse apart. One kid lost an eye.

"I couldn't sleep much that night, and in the morning I went up to see the kids in Bellevue. They were both college kids who were trying to change the world. Well, I didn't get anywhere that day. They didn't say anything; they just looked through me. That hurt. I kept going back.

"It took a long time, but I kept arguing that I was taking my life in my hands just meeting them, and what good would I get out of it? The people were frightened and wouldn't talk to them, and their clubhouse was gone, so what could I gain? It took a long time, but finally they bought this: I helped them plan another organization. I fed them the names of all the people who hated Barney. I gave them money and, more important, information that could be used to hurt Barney."

"Does Barney know about this rival group?" Luther Roberts asked.

"He's aware of it, but he can't put his finger on it. It's an underground organization. There's no clubhouse. We're working through families and groups. Except for a handful, no one knows that I'm connected with it. When the time comes we'll announce ourselves."

"Tell them about upstate, Gene," Lacey said.

"Last year we branched out, statewide," he said. "In every ghetto in New York State we have a working organization. Albany, Buffalo, Syracuse—you name it, we have a group. They range in numbers from two hundred to five hundred."

"All Negro?" the senator asked.

"There aren't many white ghettos, Senator," was the answer.

"What about the Negro organizations?" Luke asked. "You can't open a paper that one isn't organizing a march or sitting in the mayor's office or picketing someplace."

"You don't sound exactly enthusiastic about them," Abernathy said.

"Frankly, I'm not. I think now there are just as many black demagogues as there are white."

"Not quite," Abernathy said with a grin. "You still have a big edge on us for demagoguery. A hell of an edge."

"Luke has a point," Josh said. "What about the black groups? Shouldn't they be part of your movement?"

"I'm sure they have enough work to do bringing the message to you people. There's always room for one more group, especially in the North."

"This is purely a political organization?" Josh asked. "No picketing— no peace marchers?"

"Just politics," Abernathy said. "That's what we dig most."

"Let me get the map," Kelly said. "Maybe we can pinpoint Gene's ideas much better."

He walked to a side of the library and set up an easel with a large map of the state marked with circles in red crayon.

"Seems every time we meet, Finn, we have a map," Kelly said with a smile. He pointed to the circles. "These are the groups Gene is talking about. Lacey and I have met most of them, and I can tell you they are active, politically savvy, and real workers."

"What are they, Democrats, Republicans, Greenbackers, or Federalists?" Josh asked.

"All Democrats," Gene said, "who are sick and tired of being run by white ward heelers. They simply want a voice in their own organization." He pointed to a red circle. "This is a typical city. On Election Day they suddenly discover the Negro vote. They wheel out their cars to bring them to the polls. They supply baby-sitters; they call them by their first names. They promise they'll get the housing inspectors on the job first thing in the morning, along with the exterminators. Housing plans are suddenly presented in the daily paper that loves the local machine because they get the political ads. There are great editorials painting rosy pictures of the bright new kitchens and sweet bedrooms.

"Then Election Day is over. The inspectors never appear; the rats multiply; and the housing projects remain on the drawing boards." He added emphatically, "We intend to change that by one thing—an organization that will really work for the individual, particularly the minorities."

"You were going to talk about strings," Josh said.

"Very simple," Gene said. "We'll announce the existence of our state-wide organization when Mr. Shannon announces his candidacy. In every city there will be a public statement endorsing him. I can promise you that thousands of Negroes from Manhattan to the Canadian border will be working for him day and night." He smiled slightly. "And they're not all Pullman porters."

"You still haven't told us what you want," Josh said bluntly.

"Money," Gene said just as bluntly. "Money, and lots of it for our groups. We want money for rent, stationery, telephones, placards, local radio and television time, for speakers, automobiles, gasoline—you name it, we want it."

"And for that you and your people will do everything to help us?" the senator asked.

Gene said promptly, "Day and night, Senator."

"But there's more to it, isn't there, Mr. Abernathy?" Josh asked.

He nodded. "There is. And that is why I want to throw in with you. I feel Mr. Shannon has a good chance of being elected." He said wryly, "One reason is, you have more money to spend than the government." He added hurriedly, "But there are other reasons, and more important ones. Mr. Shannon is the first white politician I know of who has seen at first hand what conditions are really like in some of our cities. I think his programs are fine, even if he gets only half of them working." He hesitated and stared at Josh. "But the main thing is, we intend to run a Negro candidate for mayor, and we want Kelly Shannon's endorsement, whether he wins or not."

I was startled. "A Negro mayor of New York City?"

Gene shrugged. "You make it sound as though it's impossible. Cleveland came within a few hundred votes of electing a Negro mayor."

"Cleveland isn't New York," Luther Roberts said. "For one thing, you would never get it past Mullady. He may be a thief, but he still controls the biggest combination in the state—if not the country!"

"I hope he may be indicted by that time," Abernathy said. "Then perhaps the same thing will happen to his organization as happened to the Hines machine when Dewey threw Jimmy Hines in jail—someone else took over."

"And that someone will be you," Josh said.

"Plans have already been made for the takeover," the young man said with an air of supreme confidence.

"What about you, Kelly?" Josh asked abruptly.

"I told Gene that if his people put up a man of integrity and an outstanding background, I would endorse him."

"You might have asked my—our—opinion."

"I probably should have," Kelly said, "but I can tell you right now the answer would have been the same."

"In a town like this, that could be political suicide."

"They used to say that about a candidate's religion."

"We have a Negro senator from Massachusetts, Josh," I said.

"A senator from Massachusetts is a hell of a lot different from the mayor of New York City," Josh said. "If this gets out—"

"Don't worry, Mr. Michaels," Abernathy said cheerfully, "It won't. There will be no public announcement from our people until next year."

The senator said, "Let's go back to the hearings."

Josh said, "I intend to. Now, Mr. Abernathy, you say you are willing to testify."

Gene said firmly, "I will testify to everything I know about Mullady's operation: how his nephew's construction company received the major part of the $10,000,000 Pier Renewal program; how a pistol local on the waterfront made a political contribution of $10,000 after one of its officers was put on parole in a larceny case—courtesy of Barney Mullady, of course—"

"And how you were a bagman for Mullady in Lawrence?" Luther Roberts asked.

"Chapter and verse," Abernathy said. "But I want to make it clear that while you'll shake up Barney with my testimony, you will still have a hell of a time putting him in jail. Barney's the new type of political crook. If he's a thief, he's a legal thief. If he discovers he's outside the law, he'll have someone put through a law or a code to cover him. Like a tract of land some millionaire owned on the West Side three years ago. He wanted to make a park out of it, but some real-estate guys got Barney's ear, and he had new zoning laws put through. After about a year of wearing him down with bureaucracy, the millionaire said the hell with it and sold the land to the real-estate syndicate. Someone in Barney's family has a real-estate brokerage office, so who do you think represented the syndicate and got a fantastic fee? Now Barney has a deal ready to close in Lawrence: there's some kind of phony Urban Renewal program. Barney's construction company will throw up some houses that will become shacks in a few years, and reap all kinds of money. Poor Lawrence. It's certainly being milked."

Josh said: "Don't worry about Lawrence; the committee will take care of that. But let's get this straight, Abernathy—you'll testify. But you are aware of the risks?"

194

Abernathy stood up. In the soft light his face reminded me of those dark wood carvings you see in the windows of African airline offices—all cheekbones and nose. From where I sat I could see a faint sheen of perspiration on his forehead.

"All of us here are three times seven, Mr. Michaels," he said. "No one has to spell out what could happen to me after I spill my guts about Barney Mullady. But it has to be done. One of these days a Muslim group will move in to take over Barney's organization, and then there will really be a hot summer in this town." He shook his head. "This is the only way to do it. For months we've been wondering how to get Barney, and then suddenly Mr. Shannon appeared. When we heard about the committee going into Lawrence, we all agreed this was the fastest way to hang Barney." He shrugged. "I'm the only one who can tell the story, so I'm it." He turned to Josh. "You're running this show, Mr. Michaels—do you want me?"

Josh said, "We'll take you."

Lacey asked, "With the strings?"

Josh looked at Kelly.

"With the strings," Kelly said. "If your people will put up a candidate who will satisfy us with his background and integrity, I will endorse him, whether I win the governorship or not."

"It's a deal." He gave a quick glance at his watch. "I'll have to be downtown, so I'll say goodbye now."

"We'll have to get together soon on your testimony," Josh told him.

"I'll be evailable any time you say," Abernathy replied. "I've been putting together something on paper you might care to read."

"Watch that paper," Josh said. "God help us if it got into the wrong hands."

"After the years I spent with Barney Mullady?" The Negro gave him a quick smile. "Never."

When he had gone, the sound of Luther Roberts closing the zipper of his tobacco pouch was very loud in the still room.

"Well, what do you think of that sweet chocolate?" Josh asked.

"Please don't call him that, Josh," Lacey said.

"What do you think of that black patriot?" Josh amended with elaborate sarcasm.

"Do you have to make it sound so cheap?" Lacey asked angrily.

"That's what I think it is, politically cheap," Josh snapped. "You heard him say so himself; when he kicks Mullady off the throne, he takes the crown. If he gets a Negro to run for mayor, he can make himself the political voice of the blacks! Who are we kidding?"

"He's not an opportunist," Lacey retorted angrily. "He's a sincere man who's trying to do something for his people. Do you always have to be so cynical?"

"Remember what Machiavelli said: Cynicism is only experience."

"I agree with Lacey, Josh," Kelly said. "Gene is a sincere man. He knows he'll be putting his head on the chopping block when Mullady finds out what he's done."

"You only had to be up there at those meetings," Lacey said almost pleadingly, "to know how much he's risking!"

"Someday we'll find out how sincere he really is," Josh said.

"Anyway, now we know why Mullady was in Lawrence," I remarked.

"I thought something smelled that night," Kelly said.

"So besides Gentile we're going after Mullady?" Josh asked.

"I'm not after Gentile," Kelly said quietly. "We haven't anything to connect him with corruption, but we certainly have on Mullady."

"My God, Kelly, we have Gentile's brother-in-law selling court sentences and robbing the city blind!" Luke protested.

"That's his brother-in-law," Kelly said, "not Gentile." He turned to Josh. "By the way, Luke tells me your investigators confirmed Benny's story."

"Not only confirmed it but dug up more details. With photographs. They also found Saunders' private safe-deposit vault out on the island."

The senator snorted with triumph and slammed his hand down on the arm of his wheelchair.

"Great stuff! You'll probably find Gentile's money there!"

"Have your investigators linked Gentile to this vault?" Kelly asked.

"To be candid—no. It's Saunders' and his alone."

"Until we get indisputable evidence he has taken money or has knowingly allowed Saunders to operate, he's clean as far as I'm concerned." Kelly gave his father a level glance. "And as far as this committee is concerned—or I'm not sitting with it."

"He's a thief," his father shot back.

"We don't know that, Dad."

"Then he's an idiot if he doesn't know what's going on in his own official family," Josh broke in roughly. "Let's bend over backward to be fair, Kelly, but let's not break our own backs doing it."

"I just want to make sure we don't hurt an innocent man, especially a man with Gentile's reputation," Kelly said. "My God, this man was former Undersecretary of State!"

"You should have read some of the stuff we had on the State Department," his father replied.

"Was it legal proof, Dad?"

"No, but I was damn near proving Gentile wasn't the saintly patriot you think he was."

"I'm coming to realize there are few men in politics who are saints," Kelly remarked dryly. "But I believe in calling a man a thief only if you have the proof."

"In this case we don't need the proof," Josh said. "He will be identified as Saunders' brother-in-law by every news medium in the country—and in Europe."

"Well, then I think the committee should make some formal announcement clearing Mr. Gentile of any wrongdoing," Lacey said.

"The next thing we'll be doing is not identifying Saunders," Luke retorted. "You're talking like a ninny, Lacey!"

"I think Lacey has a point," Kelly said. "I'll discuss that with Jones when we get back to Washington."

"Dammit," Luke cried, "you could take the backbone out of the hearing!"

"I don't care what I take out of the hearing, Luke; this is the way it's going to be." Kelly's voice was hard, and for the first time I sensed the iron in him. He and his brother glared at each other, but it was Luke whose eyes dropped.

"Let's get back to your report, Kelly," Josh said quickly. "When will it be ready?"

"I hope to have the first draft next week."

"Don't forget your eyewitness account. That's the freshness of this report. You have to tell what you—"

"I don't want to sensationalize it, Josh."

"Who wants to sensationalize it? The fact that you and Lacey were there, that you saw the real life in the ghetto, saw the horrible conditions under which those people live—that must be the heart of this report! Facts, figures, fine. But they must be underscored by your personal experience. This is what will capture the imagination of the voters! That you, a rich man's son and a congressman, had enough dedication actually to live in the slums! Okay?"

"Well, if you think that's important—"

"Believe me, I do," Josh said impatiently. "Now let's get back to the hearings. As I understand it, you want them held in three stages—Washington, New York City, and Lawrence."

"That's correct. I thought we could close in Lawrence. In fact, we were just discussing that phase when you arrived."

"I have some ideas on that," Josh continued. He nodded to the papers I had distributed. "You'll find it in the résumé; the hearings in Lawrence will be a pilot study of the decline and fall of an American city due to corrupt politics and how it has affected that community's poor and minorities."

"That's an excellent theme," Luther said. "Take the city apart piece by piece."

Josh turned to Lacey: " 'Lawrence: The Time Bomb City' might be the heading for your chapter. We can release the report just before the hearings end, and base the Lawrence hearings on that chapter."

"That sounds impressive," Luke said. "Is the stuff Kelly and Lacey brought down strong enough?"

"It's a damn good start, but I'm sending investigators up there to dig deeper."

"The same ones you used on Jello?" Kelly asked.

"The same."

"What about Benny Jello?" Kelly asked. "With all this Lawrence business, I haven't had a chance to see him or Molly. Lace, have you heard from Molly?"

"She's called three times. She's very nervous. I'm going to drop over there this evening."

"Has she seen Benny?"

"Almost every day. She says the guards are getting more hostile. We were going to talk about his protection after he testifies."

"Lacey is concerned about Jello's safety, Josh," Kelly said, "and, frankly, so am I. How will he be protected?"

"United States marshals. He'll have plenty of protection."

"What happens to him after he testifies?" Lacey demanded.

"I guess he goes back to jail," Josh told her.

"In other words. ter we use him we discard him?"

"What would you have us do, Lace?" Luke said impatiently, "decorate him on the steps of City Hall?"

"Isn't there any reward for assisting the law and helping to put guilty men in jail?" Lacey asked indignantly. "Is it only a one-way street with Justice?"

"After the hearings the head of the committee makes suitable recommendations either to the local district attorney in charge of Jello's case or to the presiding justice, Lacey," I said.

"Thank you, Finn," she said quietly; then, accusingly to all of us, "I still think it's obscene to use anything this man told us."

"Oh, Christ, Lacey's on her white charger again," Luke groaned.

"I can't see the difference between Jello and Abernathy," Josh remarked, an edge of impatience in his voice. "They're both informers; they are both turning in former friends and employers."

"That man is desperate, facing life in prison, but no one forced Gene Abernathy to come to us."

"No one but a big fat opportunity to—"

But Lacey was on her feet, glaring at Josh. "I'm sick and tired of all this cynicism," she said. "Do we have to suspect everyone? Isn't there anyone we can trust according to your standards?"

"I trust only those you have proved can be trusted," Josh said. "And Mr. Abernathy hasn't filled that bill yet, Lacey."

"Well, he has my trust," she snapped, and walked out of the library.

"That's the trouble with letting women in politics. They swallow the damnedest stuff." Luke asked Josh, "How do the hearings shape up?"

"We'll start off with Jones reading a brief statement for the purpose of the hearings," Josh said, "then he'll—"

"He'll talk for an hour," the senator said impatiently. "This is all prime time. We want to hook the housewives right away or they'll scream all over the country about their soap operas!"

"I wrote the statement, Senator," Josh said. "It's very brief and to the point. Frankly, Jones is just as important to us as the housewives are. He's still the chairman, and we have to keep him happy."

Luther asked, "You're getting an early start, Josh?"

"Ten A.M. on the nose."

Shea said, "I've been watching the papers; there hasn't been a thing, not even in the columns."

"After Sissy Southworth's show there will be," Josh replied. "Let's get back to the agenda. Benny Jello will probably take up most of the first day and the second."

I said: "I think we should cut down on his early life. Benny likes to talk, and I don't think the ladies will care a curse for that."

"I don't want to cut him off too soon, Finn," Josh said. "The guy's a hell of a storyteller."

"Prime time again," Luther pointed out. "He may be funny as hell to listen to, but he's still a fat little thief. Remember Joe Valachi? Those rambling, disjointed sentences and old-hat crime stuff?"

"Jello isn't a tough-looking mobster with marbles in his mouth," Josh said patiently. "He's been a con man most of his life and he knows how to talk." He looked over at me. "What do you think, Finn?"

"The man can talk a donkey out of his shoes, but a little goes a long way."

"Let's do this," Josh said as he made a note. "If he gets boring we'll send a note in to Kelly, who will have to steer him to the first explosion as soon as possible. By the way, I've arranged to have a room down the hall from the hearing equipped with two big TV sets. I'll be there, and so will the senator, Luther, and whoever else isn't directly concerned with the hearing. You'll be getting notes from me. If the hearings are boring, I'll tell you. Remember, we have to keep every housewife from New York City to Montana and down to Louisiana glued to her set. If she switches channels, we're dead."

"Housewives in Montana don't vote in New York," Luke said.

Josh gave him a sober look. "We're going for broke, Luke. We're not only rolling for New York, but for Washington four years from now." He turned to Frank Shea and Dyke Short. "You fellows all set up? No problems?"

"No problems," Short said quietly.

"How about Molly—will you use her?" the senator asked.

"Benny's own statement is enough," Josh said. "She has no independent corroboration. And as for bribing the warden and his guards, a committee investigator went to the pen last week supposedly with a message from us to Benny. He paid both the warden and the guard, so he can testify. Next comes Manny Summers, the owner of Paris Best; his cousin, Stuart Saxon, who works for Kenneth Beering, the purchasing agent for Delafield Motors in Minnesota. This will corroborate Benny's story and lay the groundwork for the bribery conspiracy."

"Will they talk?" Luke asked.

"We will subpoena the company records and the records of the bids in the New York City budget director's office," Josh said. "With the Department of Justice and the New York DA breathing down their necks, I don't think either Beering or his bosses will take the Fifth. By the way, I've arranged for Jones to make sure each witness knows that two IRS men will be present."

"What about those hijackers?" Luke asked. "The Singer brothers?"

"They'll undoubtedly take the Fifth," Josh said. "But we'll introduce photographs of the last truck they hijacked that's now in a West Side garage—with copies, of course, for the press. I intend to tip off the TV advance men to have a team on call on the corner of Canal and Lafayette in New York. When the testimony is heard they can shoot the team over there before the cops get there."

"Should make a great strip of pictures," Kelly said. "How the devil did you ever get that, Josh?"

Josh said blandly, "Some of the investigators got lucky."

"Well, I guess Benny will be the main witness in Washington—"

"And Saunders, Remington, and the judge in New York," Josh said.

"This could be the bombshell hearing," Luke said, and I could swear he smacked his lips.

"It will be, even if it lives up to only half its billing. After Benny lays the groundwork in Washington and we have those other independent witnesses testify, I don't see how Saunders or Remington can explain it all."

"The first witness will be that Jersey lawyer who paid Saunders for the fix for the kid in the rape case?" Luther asked as he consulted the typed résumé.

"He'll be an excellent witness," Josh said. "We'll crucify him if he clams up."

"How?" Luke asked.

"Before he takes the stand, he will be notified that a member of both the New York and New Jersey Bar associations' disciplinary committees will be present along with observers from the New York County DA's office."

"That guy in New York County will have a grand jury convened twenty-four hours after we spring this stuff," Luther said. "That first assistant is fanatical on grabbing crooked lawyers."

"He'll wet his pants when we hit him with some of the stuff we got," Josh said.

"Won't that Jersey lawyer plead lawyer-client relationship?" Shea asked.

"Let him," Josh said. "We'll still get the questions on the record. And he knows the New York DA will get a copy of all we have."

"Then there's the boy's father," Dyke Short said. "He's a big businessman in Jersey—he's not going to lie."

"Not unless he wants to be indicted for perjury," Josh said.

"Have the investigators found those policy racketeers who paid off?" Luke asked.

"The Blitz brothers? We're trying to serve them, but even if we do they'll probably take the Fifth. But a few gangsters are good for any hearing, especially on TV."

"We're going to have a fight on that score," Luther said. "Remember Costello's hands and Bobby Baker?"

"We'll keep audio on, and I have a few tricks in the bag," Josh said. "Don't worry, TV will get everything that's possible to get on camera."

"Josh, do you think Remington will talk?" Luke asked. "It says here he's a boozer."

"I think he will," Josh said. "I don't think he will be able to stand the pressure."

"And Saunders?"

"He'll play it cool. You won't get him to admit anything right off, but I think he'll change his tune when the walls start to fall in." He closed his folder and looked at all of us. "Don't forget, Saunders is our main target— outside of Gentile, of course. Everything that is said on the stand must be tied in with him. If we can't get anything on Gentile, Saunders will have to do."

"I'm not out to destroy Gentile, Josh," Kelly said firmly. "I want that understood."

"You don't have to," Josh said quietly. "Any rewriteman or broadcaster who doesn't mention that Saunders is the brother-in-law of Felix Durant Gentile, the man most people agree will be the next governor and perhaps President should be fired." He nodded to Luther and Luke. "Any problems upstate?"

"None," Luther said.

"What's the schedule now?" Luke asked. "When do you think—"

"Two weeks from this Sunday night Sissy Southworth will break the first big story. After that, forget about sleeping or eating until Christmas." He glanced at his watch. "I'd like to get the eight o'clock plane, Kelly."

BOOK 3
☆☆☆☆☆☆☆☆
The Hearings ☆☆☆☆☆☆☆☆☆☆

CHAPTER THIRTEEN: WASHINGTON

For the next two weeks we worked around the clock preparing the hearings. During this time I caught a good glimpse of Kelly under pressure, and he impressed me.

Josh is the opposite of Kelly: intense, impatient, many times dogmatic, wildly enthusiastic one minute and maddeningly casual about it a few hours later—and, like Kelly, he possesses a mind of his own that could be iron-strong.

And God how they clashed!

In the beginning there were skirmishes, then forays, and finally pitched battles between them; Josh was for throwing everything but the sink into the hearings; Kelly was coldly legal and factual—nothing was to go into the record that couldn't be proven by document, eyewitness, or independent corroboration.

"For Christ's sake, this is not a criminal trial!" Josh shouted late one night as we discussed some minor witness's closed-door testimony. "Let him tell his story!"

"It's not a criminal trial. That's exactly the point," Kelly said. "I don't care who the witnesses are—Saunders, Remington, or a racketeer—I will not be any part of a smear! They're not going to be digging me up like McCarthy ten years from now!"

Usually I was the peacemaker who suggested an agreeable compromise, but I could see the tension growing between Josh and Kelly. Someday there wouldn't be a compromise acceptable to either one, I told myself, and that would be a tragic day for all of us.

While we were working on the hearings in Washington, Willy and his gang—"researchers" is the usual Washington euphemism—were in Lawrence. At Willy's request we had met him again in his hole under Grand Central, and he gave us more wiretaps and surveillance reports. He was a nut, but as an investigator he was tops. At first he refused to have anything to do with Lawrence, but after the payment of another $25,000 and a cock-and-bull story of how it would eventually be linked to Gentile, he went up there.

When he returned, Willy said it had been a piece of cake. He and his people had stolen records from the Lawrence Police Department; they had got the local madam drunk enough to admit she was paying the police, who hadn't raided one of her places in ten years; the police chief kept a small fortune in a tin box, of all places, in his wife's bedroom; the Lawrence Welfare boss was using elderly cleaning ladies on the welfare rolls to clean his tenements as a reward for keeping them on relief, while relatives of the local politicians were running the federal poverty program at enormous salaries.

Willy and his team stuck only to crime and corruption in Lawrence; but Abernathy and his organization kept us supplied with reports on racial incidents that had erupted since the fire but had been kept under wraps by the police and the local newspaper, which depended on the county political machine for its legal advertising.

There was one disturbing note: Benny Jello. Josh and I had seen him in the Pensville Jail to prepare him for the day when he would suddenly be taken from the pen and transferred to the federal detention pen on the lower West Side, as nice a place as you would want—if you have to be in jail. Benny just shrugged when we told him. He seemed dejected and obviously afraid. It took a great deal of wheedling but Josh finally found out what was wrong. He had received a message written in black crayon on the bottom of a plate: "Talk and you're dead."

Molly, he said, had received the same warning in an empty milk bottle placed on her porch. We did our best to cheer him up, and promised him complete protection, but Benny's answer was, "What? For the rest of my life?"

We had seen Molly twice in her beautiful home, just west of Wexford Hall. It was a smaller building but utterly charming. The place was cut off from the main road by towering hedges; the walls of the house were of a beautiful purple-and-white-streaked stone, called "pudding stone," which had been shipped by barge from a New Jersey quarry. The living room was large, with an enormous fireplace and rough-hewn beams. One, which Molly proudly showed us, still had its original bark. Antiques were everywhere: glowing cherrywood tables and dainty Hitchcock chairs, primitive American paintings, an original Audubon that he had made during a visit.

"He said he didn't want to stay at Wexford," she told us. "He said the old man smelled of kerosene; that was Kelly's grandfather."

She went to the kitchen and came back with three tall glasses, each one topped by a slice of cucumber.

"Pimm's Cup," she said. "I serve this to impress my neighbors." She sat down with a sigh. "Now what about my *umglicklach* friend?"

"We saw him yesterday. He's getting more protection than a state guest," Josh said. "What about you—do you want a marshal to stay here?"

"Who needs a big goof with a gun knocking over everything?"

"Just say the word, Molly."

"Lately I started to look over my shoulder," she said, for the first time betraying a sign of nervousness, "after I got that note—"

"Benny told us. What did it say?"

"Just a few words, stuck in the milk bottle: 'Tell your boy friend to keep his mouth shut.'" She added anxiously, "Tell me, would they hurt him?"

"Well, he's certainly not going to be the most popular guy in his circle," Josh said cautiously. "Benny's been around; he knows that."

She threw up her hands in disgust.

"Why did I have to fall in love with a man like that? You tell me."

"You're the only one who can answer that, Molly," Josh said with a smile.

"You should live so long for the hours I have tried," she said. "Do you want me to talk to him?"

"It would help. If he backs out now . . ."

"He won't," was her firm reply. "He takes the stand and gets out or he looks for another mama. Like I told him, 'Benny, when you get out, you as much as look at a furpiece that isn't on me and you get this cherry-wood on the head.'"

"Then you'll go and see him?" Josh asked.

"Tomorrow," she said. "I'll give the bums in the jail $25; maybe they'll let me stay a few hours longer."

At the door she said, "Too long the bums of this world have been scaring us. Don't worry about Benny—he'll do what you want."

"She has a lot of moxie," Josh said as we walked down the twisting, flower-edged path to the main road. "That God-damned thief doesn't deserve her."

"We have to make sure the DA drops those charges," I warned him. "It would be a terrible blow to her if they put him away after all this."

"Don't worry about it," he said impatiently.

"I *am* worried about it."

On the ride back to Wexford, I tried to get Josh to agree to call the DA to plead for Benny or have Jones do it, but he brushed me aside.

Our next step was organizing a secret national polling system that would tell us within minutes what impact the hearings were having on the country's TV viewers, but more importantly what the country thought about Kelly Shannon. It was the biggest, most expensive idea born in Josh's fertile imagination.

The plan was this: Dyke Short and Frank Shea in the West, and Luke and Luther Roberts in the East, had organized hundreds of survey teams.

The Midwest, South and Central states and all those west of the Mississippi were controlled by Short and Shea, with headquarters in Washington and Chicago. Luke and Luther were assigned New York State. Shea and Short had teams posted in countless cities, towns, and even villages; Luke and Luther had established a network of teams that stretched from the Niagara frontier to New York City. In New York's larger cities, tagged "Indicator Cities" by Josh, there were both polling groups who used the phones and street-canvassing teams. Every phone group had a particular ethnic contact; operators with German accents called areas that were traditionally German; Negroes called the Negro ghettos, and so on. There were even Chinese- and Russian-speaking teams.

This national polling system had three goals: It could tell us almost immediately if the majority of housewives had found the hearings boring and were turning the dials back to their soap operas. It could also tell us what impact Kelly Shannon was having in his first contact with a national audience.

The network, as Josh explained, could also be used in the gubernatorial campaign for Kelly right up to Election Day. Our nerve center on that fatal and final day would be at Wexford Hall, Josh told us. There we would be receiving initial reports of polls taken by teams in the Indicator Cities.

The results would be fed into computers that would tell us what trends and "voters' thinking patterns" were developing. If they were adverse to Kelly, Luke and Luther could set in motion their high-pressure telephone groups or standby teams composed of attractive, articulate young men and women who could counteract or even change the trend or developing voting patterns.

It was a plan in which modern electronics, high-speed communications, and old-fashioned legwork teamed together to keep us abreast of what America was thinking when they saw Kelly Shannon for the first time. On Election Day its help would be invaluable.

Accompanied by Luke and Luther, Josh and I made a flying tour across New York State to inspect the network, which was hidden in motels, lofts, barns, abandoned factories and office buildings. There was little doubt a large part of the senator's millions had gone into this venture.

"Damn good job," was all Josh said to Luke. The tired, bony young face never changed expression, but I could see a gleam of pride in those icy blue eyes. I felt like whispering in his ear: Stop playing the role, young fellow; it's not a sign of weakness to show emotion.

After Washington our next stop was Chicago, one of my favorite cities.

It's a great town for politics, and I spent some memorable days there during the conventions. Sure it was a rough place during Prohibition, but so were New York, New Jersey, and a lot of other places, including some quiet western spots where they blew people to pieces with bombs. Not many people realize Chicago took so much, then said This is enough. Their Crime Commission is one of the best in the country, and once they kicked the thieves out of the Police Department, it had no peer.

Chicago was to be the heart of our national polling system. The teams posted north, south, and west were equipped with batteries of telephones and the names and telephone numbers of hundreds of families owning TV sets in their localities. Every hour they were to poll these families and ask if they were watching the hearings and if not, why not. The results were to be phoned into the Chicago headquarters, where we had leased a huge loft and equipped it with the best computers we could get. Frank Shea and a staff of veteran assistants were to phone the results to Josh in his room down the hall from the hearings.

The states east of the Mississippi were in charge of Short, who had the same arrangement. His headquarters was his firm's offices in Washington. He also would phone in the tabulated results hour by hour.

The giant loft in Chicago was deserted when we inspected it with Shea and Short, and our footfalls on the concrete were the only sounds. Banks of gleaming computers lined one side of the loft. The other side had row after row of tiny booths with headsets dangling from hooks.

"Reminds me of the days when I was a kid reporter covering the election at police headquarters in New York," Josh said.

"Only here we will be getting the results faster and more accurately," Short said.

"So what we will be giving you will be a national TV Gallup poll," Shea said.

"Every hour on the hour," Short said.

"We must gear these hearings to the likes and dislikes of the people," Josh said. "If they are bored"—he slapped his hands together—"off goes the witness or we move him into a more sensational subject. I want a God-damn bulletin out of this hearing every fifteen minutes! I want to rock them, and I want to shock them! And every minute and every hour they will be hearing the name of Kelly Shannon and looking into that handsome kisser."

On the plane back to New York and on the ride to Wexford Hall, Josh was bubbling with last-minute details: press arrangements for the hearing room, the statement Jones would read for the TV cameras, with enough mimeographed copies for the working press; someone had to tip off photographers when the witnesses left by a side door; biogs had to be prepared on each witness for the press; Jones, who had trouble with an upper plate, had to be warned to speak slowly, and Congressman Tom Grymes had to have a prepared statement so he wouldn't be lost in the shuffle.

"The main things are the reports on each witness," Josh said, "and the suggested questions. I've gone over and over them and I can't think of a thing left out. Kelly has copies; I hope to hell he does his homework."

"Will TV be up in Lawrence?"

"TV will be with us every minute of the way," Josh said. "An advance man from every network will be down next Monday."

"The rumor mill is starting in Washington," I said.

He laughed. "Jonesy said he's being buttonholed every day on the Hill, but he and Grymes must be following orders to say nothing and saw wood. There hasn't been a line in the papers."

"Is Sissy set?"

"As set as she can be with all that booze in her." He shook his head. "After that blast on her program, Finn, we'll have to be with Kelly day and night."

Our juggernaut was finally set in motion on Sunday night at 10:00 P.M. when Sissy Southworth, in an atrocious evening gown—and cold sober— swished from behind the studio curtains to take her place at the head of a large half-moon desk while millions of Americans, in beds, bars, living rooms, and paneled dens sat back and smugly waited for her to shake up Washington, Albany, the Department of Justice—or sometimes the middle-aged wife of some public figure who never suspected her husband was about to dump her for a slender young thing who would in turn dismiss him in a year or two.

The name of Sissy's show was "For Immediate Release," and it was a wow. Her newspaper column might be filled with press-agent trivia, but when Sissy was on the air she gave her fans nothing but the best.

Sissy's format was simple: she had two regular members of the panel. A young man named Dick and a young girl named Jane. She was ribbed plenty about the Dick and Jane bit but they simply asked the questions that led Sissy into her sensational disclosures or comments. To illustrate her subject, Sissy would sometimes have stills or a movie strip flash on a screen behind her.

We had spent most of Wednesday afternoon with Sissy at the Onyx Club. This time it was a different Sissy—no Martinis, no jokes, all business. She and Josh plotted their moves like bank robbers. Josh had the deadlines of the city's morning newspapers and a carbon copy of the story he would slip to the news editor of Sissy's network early Sunday evening. This release, based on Sissy's broadcast, would lead off the regular 11:00 P.M. news. In return for the advance story, the news chief had agreed that a still of Kelly would be shown.

Both Sissy and Josh had contacted friends on wire services, alerting them to an important release that would be delivered to their city desks simultaneous with the broadcast. It was a hard news story, written by Josh, and had an 11:00 P.M. embargo. On the top of the page were three unlisted phone numbers where a "spokesman" for Congressman Shannon could be found to verify the story. That spokesman, of course, was Josh at Wexford Hall.

"For God's sake, Sissy, be sure you're around when the wire services call you," Josh said.

"You couldn't tear me away from that studio telephone right after the broadcast," Sissy said. "By the way, I'm having fifty mimeographed copies of the broadcast ready for reporters when they call."

We also arranged for Sissy's staff to be at a bank of phones set up in her office. Each staff member would have a list, which I had compiled, of the names and phone numbers of the night editors of the nation's leading morning newspapers.

"Have your people turn it in like they were handling a news story," Josh said. "Be sure and tell the city desks you're giving them the story before they'll get it on the wire services. They like that."

Sissy gave him a look of scorn. "Come off it, Josh, I was working for a city desk when you were still chasing Indian girls in grammar school." She yawned. "When will you have the press conference with Shannon?"

"Monday or Tuesday."

"Remember—he confirms my broadcast."

"Absolutely. And maybe next week we'll give you another one."

I could swear her ears pointed up like a rabbit's, but Josh patted her hand. "Next week, Sissy—don't push."

"You'll have to give it to me by Friday. Those damn network lawyers—"

"Guaranteed. Will you cover the press conference?"

She looked indignant. "Of course. It's my story."

"Fine," said Josh. "Then I'll plant the big questions with you."

"He'll be primed?"

"Of course. I'll call you the morning of the conference. Let me have your home number."

She gave it to him.

"And for God's sake, get down in front."

"Did you ever see me anywhere else but down in front? Even Jack Kennedy and Eisenhower knew that!"

"What about art on Kelly?" Josh asked.

"I'll have my staff dig out some good stills," she began, but Josh held up his hand.

"We'll get the art to you, Sissy. And a nice one-minute film of Kelly at Wexford."

"Christ, you want the whole half hour!"

"The other crap you're going to have on won't make a two-head in any paper in the country, Sissy, and you know it. We'll give you something on film that you'll be bragging about for the next twenty years that you were the first to show."

"Well, maybe," she said grudgingly. "Send it down by Friday. What about the art on those two bums, the Singers?"

"Have your man at police headquarters get their yellow sheets and rogues' gallery pictures," Josh said. He searched in his pocket and took out a penciled memo. "This is their B number so the cops can't give you a stall about two many cons by the name of Singer in their files."

Sissy frowned. " 'B number'?"

I explained: "Bureau of Criminal Identification file number."

Josh grinned. "When were you working for a city desk, Sis?"

"I covered the big ones while you were chasing fires," she said. "Anything else?"

Josh held out his open hands "You name it and we'll deliver."

"Nothing—at this point."

We stood up, and she gave him a warm smile. "Good luck, Josh."

"Thanks, Sissy. We'll be in touch."

Josh and I spent the rest of the afternoon in the file room of the Associated Press, the United Press, and the old International News Photos. There wasn't much on Kelly, and only one or two bad shots of Pam and the kids.

There was a lot on the senator, and Josh let out a whoop when he spotted a shot of me and the senator walking out of the Caucus Room after one of the Harrington Committee Hearings on State Department policy.

"God, you haven't changed a hair, Finn," Josh said as he studied the picture, "but the senator . . ."

He was a powerfully built man then with cold, searching eyes that upset many a witness and even their attorneys.

"Who does he look like, Finn?"

"Luke," I said. It was an older Luke who stared out at us from the faded photo.

"There's nothing of Kelly there," he said and tossed aside the photograph. "Frankly, I wish there was." He looked at me. "Finn, Kelly hasn't got his heart in this hearing."

"He said as much, Josh. He's not a Rudy Halley or a Bobby Kennedy. It's just not his world."

"Well, it had better be," he said savagely. "If he doesn't go out and eat those guys up, millions of Americans will turn back to their soap operas and forget he ever existed."

Later in the day Josh hired a young photographer whose work had been featured in *Life* to make stills, and an expert television team to do a brief documentary of Kelly and his family at Wexford Hall. It was short and wonderful. Kelly was superb on film: handsome, vibrant, articulate, and with the camera catching those wonderful little gestures, the wave, the flashing smile that couldn't be manufactured, the grace, the complete lack of artificiality so evident in most American politicians.

"That's what I mean about television," Josh said after we had viewed the film in a private midtown studio. "It can capture a boor, but it can also capture class, and that's what Kelly has lots of, thank God. Can you imagine what TV would have done in the twenties or thirties for a candidate, say, like FDR with that smile, cigarette holder, and that Groton accent?"

We were to watch Sissy's show in the library. At Luke's suggestion Kelly and Pam spent the evening with friends. Josh insisted he wanted no one but me or himself to take over the calls from the newspapers or networks.

The hours dragged and the tension increased. Lacey and Josh played Luke and Luther endless games in the billiards room while I remained with the senator in the library, reminiscing about our days in Washington. Finally it was ten to ten, and Howard summoned the others, who gathered about the huge color TV set. As the credits for Sissy's program flashed on, Lacey's hand found mine. I held it tightly, my throat dry as a weed.

Sissy's show was deceptively simple but shrewdly plotted. It lasted a half hour with a series of explosions getting bigger and bigger. There was a scandal in a Broadway hit show with the cashier the object of an eleven-state police alarm; a big city official would submit his resignation the next day because of ill health; the Board of Education's report on bussing contained several new plans that would give it national attention; the State Department was recalling one of its career diplomats. In between, the young man would ask when she was ready to disclose the big one, but Sissy would give him only an enigmatic smile.

The fifteen minutes had passed, and there was a brief commercial break. Josh murmured that this was it as Sissy and her panel appeared again on the screen.

"Sissy, we heard you have a big one tonight," the young woman said.

Sissy smiled and shuffled some papers on her desk. "Yes, a real big one, Jane, one of the biggest exclusive stories I have given to our listeners in years. Do you know of Congressman Kelly Shannon from New York?"

"That must be Senator Shannon's son," the young man said.

"That's right," she replied. "Kelly is the oldest son of a man most Americans recall in the postwar years. The senator, as you know, had that tragic accident in the Senate Building and retired from politics, but Kelly has been carrying on. . . . Here he is now."

A still of a smiling Kelly Shannon appeared on the screen, then another one and another.

"He has a wonderful family," Sissy said, "and they live in that fantastically beautiful old mansion, Wexford Hall, near Crestview up in Westchester County. Let's look at a few shots. . . ."

"It's obvious, then, that your exclusive has something to do with Congressman Shannon," Dick said.

Sissy gave him a sweet smile. "Very much so, Dick. I'll get to it in a minute, but first I do think we should know something about him . . . oh, here they are. . . . Aren't those children marvelous?"

213

Josh said the TV team had cost him an arm and a leg, but I could see it was worth every penny. The camera had done a wonderful job. Kelly, Pam, and the children were superb, and Wexford Hall, with its lawns and gardens, even in brief glimpses, had a character all its own. Finally the scenes faded, and the camera zeroed in on Sissy. The smile was gone, and her voice was cold and crisp.

"What I am going to disclose now, Dick," she said, "is one of the most shocking scandals I have ever encountered in all my years on television and in the newspaper business. Through a series of strange events, Congressman Shannon uncovered the scandal, and the people not only of New York but also of the nation should take their hats off to this fine young man who, I predict, will go far in the ranks of his party.

"Congressman Shannon has discovered that one of the most powerful men in this country has been selling justice for a price. This man has sold judge's appointments and court sentences; he has rigged city contracts—to the tune of millions—and in return he has collected a fortune in bribes."

Sissy was at her best. Every word clanged like a bell in that silent studio. Although they had known what was coming, the young man and woman seemed to be caught up in the excitement of the moment.

She picked up two rogues' gallery pictures of the Singer brothers, and the camera zoomed in.

"These are the Singer brothers, Aaron and Simon," she went on. "They are hijackers from Brooklyn. They have been arrested many times by the FBI and the police of five cities over the last ten years." She said in a tight, melodramatic voice, "They were arrested last year for hijacking a truck and cold-bloodedly shooting down its driver. But they got off with suspended sentences." Slowly, emphasizing every word, "A suspended sentence! The price—$25,000 paid in cash to this fixer!" A pause, then: "Ask Congressman Shannon—he knows."

She held up her hand. "And this is not all. There is a Fifth Avenue lawyer who is the bagman for this fixer. I hope this man is listening, because I would like to let him know Congressman Shannon has the details of that Department of Sanitation contract—you know, the one you fixed for that Midwest firm."

The young woman asked, "Is this fixer—would I know his name?"

Sissy nodded. "Any newspaper reader or TV viewer knows him, and I might add, he's high in the ranks of his party, and at this very minute is making plans to put a man his party regards highly right into the White House!" She paused, stared into the camera, and said slowly, carefully enunciating each word, "And he may succeed unless he is stopped by Congressman Shannon's investigation."

"In other words, he's a politician?"

"Let's say a crooked politician, Dick. But wait, there's more. Congressman Shannon has caught a few more fish in his net: one is a high ranking

214

Federal Judge who has sold, not one, but many of his federal court decisions."

Another pause, then: "Ask Congressman Shannon—he knows."

She took a dramatic sip of water, and continued:

"Congressman Shannon also has uncovered the payoff to a member of the State Liquor Authority Board by this same fixer to grant a liquor license to a man who owns a well-known East Side nightclub. I won't disclose the name of this place because it would only hamper the continuing investigation, but I can tell you that this place has been in every Broadway column—including mine—for years. But what I never knew, the owner is a convicted panderer who served five to ten years in Atlanta for white slavery. Yet he obtained a liquor license—for a price. How did he do it?"

She looked up, and the camera caught her grim smile.

"Ask Congressman Shannon—he knows."

The young man asked, "Does Congressman Shannon have only gossip or does he have proof of these allegations, Sissy?"

Sissy snapped: "I wouldn't put it on the air if I knew he had only gossip. He has proof, concrete facts!"

Jane asked, "I believe you said before that this fixer was closely connected with a presidential campaign?"

"That's true, Jane."

"But, Sissy, there aren't any presidential campaigns going on now. The President still has a few years more to serve in office."

Sissy smiled. "Presidential campaigns are started long before they are ever announced to the public, my dear, and this man, this despicable fixer, is close to one that already is off the ground."

Dick asked, "What will happen to the proof that Congressman Shannon has gathered together?"

This time Sissy spoke directly to the camera and to her millions of listeners: "I predict there will be a series of public hearings on these revelations that will rock the country and have a significant effect on the important national elections.

"I predict you will see this fixer on the stand and you will be shocked by his identity. I also predict you will see a number of public figures trooping to the same witness stand to make admissions that will sicken our country."

For the first time she smiled: "I also predict that before this year is out the name of Congressman Shannon will be a household word to millions of Americans from New York to the Golden Gate. Remember, you heard it here first, on—'For Immediate Release.' "

There were more commercials, and then Luke leaned over to click it off, but Josh stopped him.

"Leave it on for the news."

Josh's story was number one on the announcer's list:

"That a New York politician connected with a forthcoming presidential candidate has been named as a fixer and bribe taker in evidence gathered by Congressman Kelly Shannon of New York was the highlight of a sensational broadcast tonight by Sissy Southworth on her network show 'For Immediate Release.' Miss Southworth also disclosed that Congressman Shannon has the evidence. . . ."

There were pictures of Kelly, Wexford Hall, and Sissy.

Josh spun the dial, and there was another announcer describing the broadcast. Luke switched on the radio, and another announcer was describing Sissy's charges.

Then the phone rang.

"Let Howard take it to see who it is. I don't want anyone else answering the phone," Josh snapped. "I'll take care of all the papers and press associations."

There was a knock, and Howard was at the door.

"Senator, there's a reporter from the Associated Press asking to speak to the congressman."

"I'll take it, Howard," Josh said. "Make sure I get all the calls from the papers." He went to the extension phone and picked it up.

"Hello. Yes, this is a member of Congressman Shannon's staff. Right. We know about the broadcast. I have a statement here from the congressman, who was just on the phone. Do you want to take it? Okay, start the quote:

" 'Several months ago information came to me regarding the alleged taking of bribes by an influential member of the New York City government. The charges were so shocking that at first I was inclined to disregard them. However, I had members of my staff interview the source of the information, and the charges were repeated to them in detail. In subsequent interviews the names of members of the judiciary, underworld, and municipal government of the city of New York were given to us as alleged bribe takers . . .' "

Josh paused, listened, and said impatiently, "If you wait, I'm coming to that. Pick up the quote:

" 'It would have been unfair to turn those uncorroborated charges over to a local law-enforcement agency. Had I done so, and had there been premature publicity, the reputation of these officials could have been ruined. Instead, we continued our own investigation. To my dismay many of the original charges have been confirmed by independent witnesses and documentary evidence.

" 'Appropriate action will now be taken.' "

Josh paused again, then said shortly, "No. I can't name names at this time."

He had just hung up when Howard was again at the door. UPI was waiting on the phone, and so was the Washington *Post*.

Josh went over the statement for both. Then the calls really started to pour in. Everyone wanted the names. Some even made guesses and asked for confirmation. But "no comment" was our policy. Within an hour the local reporters were at the door. Luke brought them into another room, and I read them the statement. This was followed by TV news crews who took Luke and his father.

Kelly called and spoke to Josh. He said he had seen the broadcast and thought that he should be at Wexford for a press conference, but Josh was just as insistent he remain out of sight for the rest of the evening.

"He said he felt like a fool, having someone else speak for him," Josh said. "I had a hell of a time convincing him to stay where he was and let me handle it."

"That won't happen too often," Lacey said.

"What won't?" Josh wanted to know.

"Someone else speaking for Kelly—"

"I know exactly what I want in the papers tonight," Josh said.

"But does he?"

"Lacey, you're bugging us again," Luke said. "Lay off, will you?"

"Don't say I didn't warn you," she said to Josh as she started to leave.

"About what?"

"The Shannons. Sometimes they like to think for themselves."

"That's fine," Josh said, "but there will be times when the Shannons will have to listen to me."

"Want to bet?" she asked sweetly as she left.

He glanced over at me and shook his head angrily. "How did it go?" he asked Luther, who returned with the senator after a TV crew had televised a short interview with the old man.

"Fine. No trouble with TV, but Luke just received a disturbing call."

Josh spun around to Luke. "What about it?"

"It was a call from a young local fellow who is a stringer for one of the New York papers. I know him from the Village—"

"Well, just read him a copy of the statement."

"He said his office got the statement earlier from the wire services; he wanted something else. He wanted to know if our source is a swindler in the pen named Jello. Apparently someone in the jail tipped him off that Kelly had been in to see Benny."

"Where is this guy now?" Josh snapped.

"He left his number."

"Let's get him on the phone—quick!"

As soon as he got the young reporter on the phone, Josh changed like a chameleon. Instead of the brisk, impatient, snappy spokesman, he was jovial, soft-spoken, calling the young reporter by his first name from the very beginning.

Yes, it was true that the congressman had represented Mr. Jello some time back, but it was only because a neighbor had asked for help. In fact, he suggested, if the reporter wanted, he could get the name of the attorney who had taken the case at the request of the congressman, who didn't practice criminal law to begin with. Josh was, oh, just so friendly, and before he was finished he had given the newsman an exclusive story of how this very minute Congressman Shannon was secretly talking to his source in a motel room somewhere in Maryland. Josh made a great show of reluctantly parting with the information, protesting again that the reporter was getting more than he had told the others. I could hear the eager young voice on the phone pressing, badgering, demanding more facts.

When Josh hung up I could see a sheen of perspiration on his forehead.

"The story's a phony, but it won't hurt anyone and it may get that kid off that track," he said. "He must have gotten a tip from one of the guards." He asked Luke, "Does he cover the jail?"

Luke nodded. "He covers the county courthouse and the jail for the city papers. He's always calling Kelly, looking for news."

"Hire him tomorrow," Josh snapped. "Tell him you're reorganizing your brother's public-relations staff. Tell him anything, but get him upstate or to Washington or anywhere."

"I don't see how it would hurt us if he does pin down that story," Luke said. "After all, Benny will be on the stand—"

"For Christ's sake!" Josh exploded. "He hasn't been transferred yet to a federal pen! There are only rumors from the grapevine that he might be talking, and he's already gotten threats. Even Molly. A few more threats, and that bum will shut up like a clam! That's why I want to get this kid off that angle!"

"Give him to me," Luther said. "I can use him."

"That kid's an eager beaver," Luke said. "His family has been running a weekly up here for years, and he's dying to get on a New York paper—"

"Tell him you'll get him a job on any paper he wants—after Election Day," Josh said. "Tell him anything."

"Pay him double what he's getting now," the senator put in. "I never saw a reporter that didn't like money!"

"There are a few, Senator," Josh said. "Still a few." Then, to Luther: "Do your best with Luke to get this kid off our backs. My God, do you know what would happen if they blew this story of Jello very big? He wouldn't give us the right time!"

Luther said quietly, "If they didn't kill him first."

Josh didn't say anything. He just turned and went out of the room.

It was quite a night: reporters, telephones ringing, television crews snaking their cables over the floor, Jones wondering from Washington when the committee would be mentioned—Josh reminded him it had been agreed Kelly would break the news about the committee hearings when he addressed the Police Chief's Association dinner, and for God's sake have your statement ready so we can give it out to the press that night, all of which mollified the old buzzard—and finally the call to me from Max Dregna. It would be a quiet drink at his apartment. When? Tomorrow night.

Josh said with a grin, "I bet he made sure not to invite me."

"He says you run too hard, Josh," I said. "And besides, you don't like daguerreotypes."

"I'll personally lead a movement to canonize Mathew Brady if he would help us," he said. "Did he give any indication—"

"Max doesn't indicate anything," I said. "He either tells you Yes or No. Maybe we'll get him; maybe we won't."

"Do you think the liberals would want to back Kelly?"

"Who knows? But Max will tell us, plain and simple. One thing Max is that a lot of politicians are not—honest."

"It would be a hell of a coup if we could get Max in our camp. The last time out he got Gentile the uncontested liberal support."

"Whatever it is, we'll soon find out."

We stayed overnight for the first time at Wexford Hall. Few of us got much sleep. At 4:00 A.M. we were still in the library, with Josh on the phone spending a fortune in tolls talking to old friends in bureaus all over the country and all over the world, trying to persuade them that this story in America would make wonderful reading for their readers. Italy declined with regrets. Paris asked Josh to cable a brief dispatch, but London bought Josh's angle that now the United States would soon have its own Profumo case.

Josh's aggressiveness and endless energy and ideas once a campaign got under way was an old story to Luther and me, but for Luke it was new. He soaked up everything, and I could see his memory absorbing every idea like a sponge, every move, every alibi, every sales pitch, neatly cataloging them for future use. In five years, I predicted to Luther, Luke would be one of the best political campaign managers in the country.

"And the most ruthless," Luther observed.

I returned to the city the following afternoon, and after a leisurely dinner at Sullivan's, walked leisurely over to the Dakota Apartments on Central Park West where Max had lived for as long as I could recall. He had confessed very readily it was pure egotism that made him stay there.

"What old man can say he met Lauren Bacall in the elevator on Christmas Eve and kissed her?" he said. "Once when I met Douglas Fairbanks in the elevator he stood on his hands. *That* you can't get on East End Avenue."

He met me dressed, as always, in pajamas, an old blue bathrobe, battered leather slippers, and smoking a cigar. On a desk were three beautifully leather-bound daguerreotypes.

"Later," he said. "I got them last week in a little junk store upstate. One of a Confederate soldier—just a little boy with a gun."

He pointed to the movable bar, but I shook my head.

"When we were young, with cast-iron livers, we couldn't afford the whiskey," he said. "Now we have all the whiskey in the world, and a liver that demands seltzer. Take a rest, my friend."

I sank into the soft sofa, and he took an easy chair.

"All last night and today I have been hearing about your boy."

"What do you think, Max?"

He shrugged. "Statements are one thing. Do you have anything good?" He held up a hand. "No names, please."

"It's big, Max. There's going to be a congressional hearing. We want him on the committee."

"What committee?"

"The Jones Subcommittee on Urban Affairs and Official Corruption."

He put his head back and groaned as if in severe pain.

"Jones! That *umglick!* With his phony hearings on guns that you buy in the mail and those schnooks he has on the stand telling why little kids take dope!" He slammed his fist on the armrest. "Never once do they say that maybe the stinking tenements or the lousy jobs or crummy bosses —that may be the answer. No! They put up a chart with a lot of shaded areas, and Jones looks like Solomon and tells us this is the answer!"

"I know he's a boob, Max," I said, "but we needed a committee with a vacancy in a hurry."

He went across to the bar and poured himself a drink. "Between Jones and this whiskey I'll be eating Tums forever. Tell me, will your boy control the hearings?"

"Josh has him primed. We have enough to make headlines every day."

"Who cares about headlines?" he said, slumping down. "What about television?"

"The senator has guaranteed there will be daily coverage—nationally."

"And what if the witnesses put up a squawk?"

"We'll do something like Costello's hands. And get the witnesses on the way out. The testimony will be important."

"Real big?"

"Very big."

"He impressed me that night in Lawrence. I've told a few important people the story, and they liked it."

"Did you tell the boys who count?"

"Who else?"

"I'm going to let you in on a secret, Max. Kelly and his sister, Lacey, went back to live in Lawrence for a while."

"They lived in Lawrence?" he asked, frowning. "Why?"

"They lived in tenements."

"For a gimmick?" he said. "For publicity?"

"Definitely not. He refused to let us give him a photographer."

"But it has to be a gimmick!" he protested. "The son and daughter of one of the richest men in the world—the former chairman of the Foreign Relations Committee!" He waved his hand, unbelievingly. "Come off it, my friend—"

"Maybe after all these years we find it hard to recognize a sincere man, Max," I said.

He studied me for a moment, then shook his head. "You I've known for a long time, and if you say it's true, it must be. But you'll never get my boys to believe it."

"Maybe they've forgotten how the tenements smell, Max."

"Their wives wear mink perhaps, and they have their shoes handmade, my friend, but they will never forget the smell of a tenement hallway. The stink remains in your nose until you die."

"Well, then, let them talk to Kelly—he can tell them the best way to kill a rat, and his sister knows how to use kerosene on the bedsprings."

"Kerosene," he said. "I can close my eyes and remember my mother using it for the bedbugs." He asked abruptly, "Why would he do a thing like that?"

"He said he wants to know poverty at first hand. He insists you can't learn it from a book or pamphlet."

"There are millions right here in the city who could tell him that."

"But he found something more important in Lawrence than just rats and bedbugs."

Max held up his hand.

"Is it politics?"

"Yes."

"Don't tell me, then, my friend. If it's a secret, and it leaks out you will never trust me again."

"I don't have any reason not to trust you, Max."

"What I don't know won't hurt me. Will it come out?"

"It will."

"Will we like it?"

"Definitely."

"Well, let's leave it like that. When it comes out I'll be in touch." He squirted some seltzer into his empty glass. "What about Mullady?"

"Kelly refuses to have any part of him."

"Why?"

"He called Barney a blot on American politics."

"Your boy sounds more interesting every minute. Suppose his old man wants Mullady's help?"

"Kelly would never stand for it."

"That's one strike your boy has against him—"

"The senator?"

"My people hate his guts. They said he almost ruined the State Department with those God-damn hearings and investigations."

"I can tell you, Max, they weren't all saints and patriots in State those days."

"Maybe not. But with all the trouble we were having, he shouldn't have acted like a cop running up and down parking meters trying to give out tickets!"

"The senator never gave out half the stuff that appeared in the papers. That was mostly Tuck Larsen's hatchet job."

"Maybe. But people forget the details—they only remember the headlines." He paused. "You people going into Lawrence?"

"Very big, I can promise you."

"There are a lot of my union people up there."

"They must like what Kelly did that night. Remember, no one asked him to go up there. It was purely voluntary. That's what I mean about his sincerity, Max."

"All right, all right, so he's sincere. Granted."

"I think you should point that out to your people."

"They weren't there that night. All they know is he's the senator's son. Very rich, a nothing in Congress."

"Then you had better tell them to look at TV."

"Who would miss it now?" he said with a wry smile. "Josh Michaels is a mover, Finn."

"That's an understatement."

"Tell me," he said suddenly, "what's this I hear about some kind of an organization started in Lawrence?"

It was my time to be cautious. "Organization? What kind?"

"Come on, my friend. You're tiptoeing around."

"You're the one who's been tiptoeing, Max."

"Does your boy know about this organization?" He cocked an eye at me. "Some of my people say it's got Mullady worried."

There's always a time to enter, always a time to leave, in politics. This was my time to leave. Max was on a hook, and I intended to leave him dangling.

"Max, will you support us or not?"

"Me, I'd go along if only from what I saw in Lawrence that night." He shrugged. "But there are too many others on the committee. Some of them spit when you mention the name Shannon. Besides, we're a small party, Finn; you know that. Before we jump we must look on all sides. If we back the wrong horse, what happens? It takes four years again to get Washington on the phone. You win, that's great. Everyone loves you. Then they call me Max the Kingmaker. When we lose, what do they call me—Max the Bum."

"We're spending money like it's counterfeit, Max."

"Don't I know that? Don't you think we could use some of that Shannon dough for our campaign? Liberals, talk, talk, talk. Ask them for money and what do you get? Talk, talk, talk." He drew a deep breath. "There was a meeting of the policy committee the other night. Some want to back Gentile; some want to run our own man. . . ."

That was bad news, and it was an effort to keep my voice casual. "If you run your own man it will mean you'll drain off three hundred thousand votes. A defeat at the top could mean the Democrats might not control the Senate and constitutional convention. It would be better if you didn't endorse anybody, Max."

"There was a lot of talk about endorsing Gentile again," Max said gloomily. "When I said No, they asked me who else."

"Did you mention Kelly's name?"

"The guy from the Hatters' Council said I must be smoking marijuana—" The seltzer squirted into his glass with an angry hiss. "You can't blame them, my friend. When they ask, What will he do for us?—what can I say?" He took a sip and smacked his lips as if the bubbly water were the finest he had ever tasted, but I knew he was weighing his next words. "But if your boy had something on Mullady and went after him, that would be something." He lifted his hand in a resigned way. "But who can hurt that old thief? When you have a machine that brings in the vote, do they care in Washington? They're politicians; they only want to win."

"A lot of things can happen in the next few months, Max. Why don't you ask the policy committee to hold up their endorsement until after the hearings?" I added, "Something could even happen to Mullady, who knows?"

"In the garment center you hear many stories," he said. "Some you listen to; some you laugh at. Lately I hear stories from Lawrence." He measured his drink with the eye of a careful pharmacist. "You boys after Mullady?"

"Let's say there might be a few surprises."

"You take on Mullady, my friend, you take on a lot of weight."

"I know Barney better than most, Max; he has a glass chin." I couldn't resist adding, "And I'm surprised you great Liberals never tried to find it."

Max held up a protesting hand. "Remember that DA we elected five years ago? And who was his big target? First the big press conference, then the big headlines. Then nothing. Who would talk? Nobody. What did the witnesses do before the grand jury? Tell them what a great man is Barney Mullady. End of investigation. But Barney didn't forget. A whole year it took him to find an assistant in the office who wanted to be a judge so bad he sold out his boss. Barney finally got what he wanted. It wasn't much. The DA had recommended that an old man in a fraud case get a suspended sentence. What nobody knew was that the old man was related to the boss of the Cutters' Union who also happens to be big in our party. The governor happened to have a bill he very badly wanted passed. And who do you think could get that bill passed? And what did Barney want in return? The DA's resignation, or charges would be preferred before the Judiciary Committee."

"I always wondered why he resigned."

"For years the DA had a bad gallbladder. Go in the hospital and have it taken out, I told him; then put in your papers. What could I do? They had us by the short hairs."

I knew now was the strategic time to go.

"Well, my friend," I said as I got up, "tell the boss of the cutters he should watch TV. It might be interesting."

"I'll walk you to Sixth Avenue," he said abruptly. "I'm going to suffer tonight, so let it be with corned beef on rye with a pickle."

Max knew that I knew he had been hooked. I waited while he dressed, and then we walked over to the Sixth Avenue deli. It was a wonderful walk, not only because the weather was fine but also because I had a wily old pro on the hook and I had to play him for all I could. I deliberately gave him a few tiny nuggets, then retreated into doubletalk, naïveté, and plain stupidity. Max was too smart to lose his temper; he just backed away after each question, probed gently, and tried again. By the time I left him, he knew there was a possibility a no-holds-barred assault had been launched against Barney Mullady for the first time since he had assumed the role of national kingmaker.

I made sure when I left him that the questions lay on Max's mind as heavy as the corned beef would rest on his stomach. How much did we have on Mullady and how far were we going to fight him? And should he, Max, persuade the Liberals to jump on our bandwagon? He knew that if we destroyed Mullady, or even badly dented his organization, Kelly would have a strong voice in the national convention, and it was politically obvious that we would look with favor on the Liberals if they joined us when the battle lines were forming and not after the fields had been littered with the wounded and the dying.

But on the other hand, if he did persuade the Liberals to join us, and this charming, wonderful young man emerged from the crucible of the campaign as only a charming, wonderful nothing—what then? Max knew he would be back to making plastics. There would be no judicial or Surrogate Court patronage for his party, and the message from Pennsylvania Avenue would be simple but firm: Don't call us; we'll call you.

Josh was still at Wexford when I found him. I sensed his impatience when I began to describe my meeting with Max; halfway he cut me off.

"We'll have to take care of Dregna later, Finn. There's something more important. It didn't pan out with that kid reporter."

"The one who had the tip on Jello?"

"Right. He turned down Luke's offer of a job. They even went to $500. The kid was no fool. He knew something was up. The *Daily News* has it in 120-point type on page one. Switch on the eleven o'clock news tonight and catch it."

"What about Benny?"

"As soon as Luke called me, I went over there. He's frightened stiff. That son of a bitch of a warden is openly calling him Shannon's stoolie. Benny said one of the trusties threw in a message from the Singer brothers —it was written on the inside of a match cover—'Remember Abe Reles proved stool pigeons can't fly.' "

"Did you show it to the warden?"

"He put on a big show of calling in the chief keeper and warning him that Jello must be guarded at all times—you know, all for the record. Hell, if anything happens to Benny he can bring me in as a witness to prove he had tightened security measures."

"Can't we get him out of there?"

"I had Jonesy on the phone three times. God, I'm hoarse from shouting at the deaf old bird, but I think we have Justice moving. They're sending down two marshals to bring him to the West Street Federal House of Detention in the city. I had a hell of a time with Kelly. He wanted to bring Molly down to the jail, but I told him the place is crawling with reporters. I finally got Lacey to go instead."

"That was a victory."

"It's a funny thing with these Shannons; they fight like hell among themselves, but it's shoulder to shoulder when the outsiders start to move in."

"How was Molly?"

"She's starting to crack. That's why I wanted her kept away from the reporters. Nothing like this ever happened to her before. But when Lacey finished talking to her, she was okay. Lacey called us from the pen a few minutes ago. She said that Benny was shaking like a leaf in the wind but that he got hold of himself after he talked to Lacey."

"Don't forget Sissy."

"God, how could I forget! She's been on the phone every twenty minutes. At least she's happy. The network informed her this morning the coverage has been fantastic. I told her I didn't want Kelly to say too much, but I planted two good questions with her for the press conference. I wish you'd get there early, Finn, and check on the arrange-ments. Make sure Sissy has a seat down front. I'll be there early, but I want Luther to front for us. No use showing our hand until we have to."

I walked over to Times Square and picked up the News and Times, along with the Washington papers. The tabloid had it exclusively; on page one there was an old picture of a much thinner Jello taken at his East Side Club. The story was wildly sensational, hinting at all sorts of revelations. It couldn't have been worse for Jello. The Times and the Capital's dailies had page one stories about Kelly and the mushrooming scandal but nothing about Jello. There was one nice touch: the Times had Kelly for its Man in the News profile. It was well researched and excellently written. It was a welcome sober note in all the melodramatics.

The 11:00 P.M. news had a still of Jello, an interview with the warden, shots of the prison, and a still of Kelly.

The impact of the television news broadcasts and the morning papers left little doubt this was the beginning of some enormous national scandal.

I felt our juggernaut starting to move . . .

The press conference with Kelly the following day was a tumultuous affair. The conference room was so crowded we had to move to a small ballroom. That created all sorts of problems with the heavy TV equipment. Men with lights, tripods, cables, and cameras cursed savagely as they broke down their equipment and hauled it to a freight elevator and up two flights. Then there was the usual fight between TV and the newspapermen, who kept shouting "writing press." The TV people wanted their shots first, and the daily press kept shouting them down.

Luther's calm, easy manner, backed by experience of countless press conferences, restored order. Under the glaring TV lights it began. Kelly first read a prepared statement that actually was only what we had given out the night before. But Josh had written it so cleverly it appeared to be brand new.

"On a story like this you create a drought of news after the initial break, then give them a statement," Josh murmured as the reporters scribbled. "It doesn't matter if it's an old statement as long as you don't insult their intelligence. . . . It's not hard to make old news look new—the papers do it all the time when the night side rewrites the A.M.'s for the P.M.'s. . . . There's Sissy."

Sissy now was on her feet. She had received information the congressman would address the Association of International Police Chiefs next Sunday at the Hilton in Washington. Was that true?

It was, said Kelly, smiling.

And at that time would the congressman disclose what he intended to do with the information he had received? And would that disclosure have any connection with a congressional hearing?

No comment, Kelly said, which any reporter knew was confirmation of Sissy's question.

She looked pleased and flushed. The TV cameras had let Sissy score another one.

It was Kelly's first big press conference, and from where I sat he did fine. Some of the questions were stupid, as they usually are, but some were barbed, probing, and filled with carefully laid traps. But Kelly never lost his good humor. He joked with the reporters, refused to lie, and while he answered all the questions and spoke quite a lot, he didn't give them any more information than we had agreed to beforehand—a pro's old trick, and not easy to handle. It was quite obvious he had enormous personality, which attracted the newsmen. They laughed with him, exchanged quips, and listened intently when he was serious.

"He's cute," one lady from a wire service said as she went to a telephone.

"You mean he's a cute politician," an elderly political reporter said. "I have a feeling this guy has something big cooking."

Josh said, "That's the way I want them to leave—satisfied but guessing."

After the conference we joined Kelly, Luke, and Luther in an upstairs suite.

"Lacey just called, Josh," Kelly said. "She's with Molly. There's been two phone calls. Both warned her to tell Benny to keep his mouth shut."

"If she bends we're in trouble," Luke said. "She's the only one Benny will listen to."

"Don't worry—she won't," Josh said.

Luther said, "She's a courageous little woman."

"Dammit, we just have to make sure these people who help us won't get hurt," Kelly said. "I told Jones their safety must be the responsibility of Justice." He added disgustedly, "What has kept him around so long?"

"Indignant mothers, mail-order guns, a few pathetic addicts who testified with masks to bring in the TV guys; some law-enforcement officials who got some badly needed publicity after they predicted that soon every school kid would be on LSD and junk, and a parade of Cosa Nostra mobsters who refused to testify and took all Jonesy's screaming about God, country, and the American way of life. And don't forget, Congress knows this old phony for what he is, but is afraid to do anything about him or his two-bit committees when the vote on the Budget comes up."

"I guess that includes me," Kelly said, "but frankly I never gave their committee a second thought. I suppose I should have been suspicious of those idiot Americanization awards Jonesy is always getting and J. Edgar's annual appearance before his committee to warn us the Apparatus is in full swing. By the way, does Jones really know what he's in for?"

"The only thing Jones can see now is some marvelous publicity," Josh said cheerfully. "He may try to shut it off if the going gets rough—"

"If he tries to back away from Lawrence and Mullady, I'll crawl all over him," Kelly said. "Just remember—after Abernathy testifies I want Mullady subpoenaed."

"And you just remember we warned you—subpoena Mullady and you'll have the National Committee on your back," Luther said.

"As far as I'm concerned, Mullady is just as much a thief as Remington or Saunders," Kelly said.

I noticed Josh studying Kelly. "We probably could make a sweet deal with him."

"Not subpoena him?" Kelly said. "Never. And I want that understood.

By the way, the 'Today Show' called the house. They want me in the morning. Shall I take it?"

"By all means," Josh said. "You're also going to be on 'Spotlight' on Sunday afternoon. Luke, you'll have to make sure we have the plane waiting at National. It will be a tight schedule all day Sunday."

"Finn," Kelly said abruptly, "you've been around longer than any of us, physically and politically. What do you think about subpoenaing Mullady?"

"He'll cut your heart out," I said. "And he will twist the arm of every county and state leader to kill your chances. He'll put up a dogcatcher before he takes you."

"And if I don't?"

"Subpoena him and destroy him—or take his support."

"It's something to think about, Kelly," Luke said. "Even Gene admits he can't directly connect him with the actual taking of the money."

"But we know he does." He looked around at us. "Is there any question in your minds that he didn't send Gene Abernathy up to Lawrence to get a rakeoff?"

The muted sound of the traffic below was the only sound in the room.

Then Kelly said quietly, "I think we ought to go over what I'll say in Washington."

I don't know why it is, but I think most people can spot a policeman anywhere. Josh insists it's my natural Irish aversion to policemen, but I insist that after a man puts on a patrolman's uniform something happens to him. It leaves a peculiar air about him—God knows it's not humility— maybe arrogance. I believe it is done by osmosis; whatever it is just seeps through the pores to set them apart. Most of them believe in the same things, observe the same rituals, even adopt the same language. Did you ever see one of them interviewed on television? "I apprehended the defendant after observing him in the act of jostling the gentleman who is the complainant and thereupon charged him with an 872. . . ."

They even slip into categories: the young ones in their thirties are usually going into fat and have crew cuts; the older ones become cold-eyed, white-haired, and dress with the sharpness of a bookmaker. And they always seem to be whispering when they're in a group. A retired inspector once told me they're usually telling each other they are going to the bathroom.

Their politics are conservative. They dislike and will fight to the death the winds of change. They admire the Legion, the PBA, the "House"— their precinct—and they are suspicious of politicians (except those who kill any bills in Albany which might change their shifts and do away with overtime).

The minute I entered the Hilton that Sunday evening, I spotted them in the lobby, elevators, dining room, and cocktail lounge. It appeared as if our town of clerks, stenographers, and politicians had suddenly been taken over by big burly men who looked as if they were suddenly going to ask you for your identification.

The organization is one of the largest in the country, and important. When an issue affects policemen anywhere, their voice is loud and clear, and politicians and city fathers had better listen. One thing they do like is a speaker prominent in the news at the time of their convention. I know Josh had a devil of a time persuading the head of the speaker's committee to accept Kelly, but once the news broke he was constantly on the phone, urging us to have Kelly come out with another news blockbuster.

Cops don't like talk of corruption and official action; sometimes it strikes too near home, but they were willing to listen as long as the organization got the headlines.

The dinner was in the main ballroom of the Hilton, and Luther reported they had to add another press table. Kelly got some kind of bronze plaque before the dinner, and posed with the committee who presented it.

As Josh said, you can always gauge a man's news value by the way photographers take such a commonplace picture; usually they act bored and sleepy-eyed, but now they were alert, pushing and shoving, flashbulbs winking, posing Kelly this way and that.

"He's a hot subject tonight," Josh murmured. "Wait until after he gets through."

Gradually we were to learn that you shouldn't write out anything for Kelly: notes are sufficient; his delivery was natural. He had a gift for turning a phrase, and his flashes of humor tickled any audience.

The dinner finally ended; there were the usual motions and reports read, and then Kelly was introduced. The photographers again leaped into action; the reporters leaned forward. The applause was polite; then Kelly began.

Those of us who were there will never forget it. He started off by warning his audience that it would be a short speech because as a teenager he had had to visit so many Communion breakfasts that he soon lost any sympathy he might have had for the speaker, who, he soon discovered, was only the interruption between the scrambled eggs and the forty-yard-dash for the parking lot.

To the chowderheads in the audience who sat back expecting the usual long, rambling, cliché-riddled banality, Kelly was finished before they had tossed away their cigars. The speech was almost brutal in its denunciation of those politicians who would betray their constituents for gain, for others who would close their eyes to the misery of the less fortunate. He urged the cops themselves to discard the cry of the finest. Make it instead, he said, the boast of the most charitable, the most fair, the most eager to stand between evil and the good.

Then he ended by simply telling them that he would appear on the floor of the House of Representatives to report to that body his discovery of certain charges of corruption existing not only in New York City but in other upstate communities.

He stood there for a moment, a poised, handsome young man, obviously sincere. He seemed to be reaching out to every man in the room— then he simply thanked them and sat down.

The applause was scattered, gained a bit, then died out as a buzz filled the room.

"He hit them where it hurts," Josh whispered, "but I think it's good. Look at the press table."

The reporters were nodding and talking. Then one scribbled a note and beckoned a waiter over.

"They're going to grab him after the dinner," Josh said. "Let's get Luther with him."

But Kelly didn't need us. He was corraled by the reporters as he was leaving the dining room, and answered their questions with candor. Yes, he said, he had received information of corruption in a certain New York Police Department, and while he thought many metropolitan departments were admirable in times of municipal crisis, he believed they were archaic in their handling of minority and civil-rights problems.

"Well," said Luther, "there goes twenty-six thousand police votes in New York City."

"I wouldn't be too sure," Josh said. "The only ones who are going to howl are the old-line cops who have been trying to perpetuate their dynasties. But lately that new commissioner has been bringing in the better educated, and they all realize the days of skull busting have gone, and something tells me Gentile is going to be mad as hell after we bring up this police issue."

As Josh had predicted, the Washington and New York City papers devoted a large amount of space to Kelly's speech, with the *Times* starting it on page one. But what was more surprising was Gentile's statement a few days later at a Police Academy graduation ceremony: the theme could have been taken right from Kelly's address of the week before. When I pointed this out to Josh, he said Wire Willy just happened to have big ears on a day Gentile was checking his speech with Saunders.

The next few days were hectic, with Kelly on 'Sunday Spotlight,' the 'Today Show,' Johnny Carson's 'Tonight Show,' and others. Invitations to appear on radio and TV were coming in every hour, and Josh insisted we accept as many as possible.

"We can always be choosy," he told Luke and Luther. "Let's get as much exposure as we can before he goes to Washington."

Kelly's appearance before the House of Representatives was for the following Monday. That week was the busiest I had experienced since we had joined Kelly's campaign. While Josh worked with Kelly, I went to Washington to arrange with Holmes for Kelly to take the floor. The Speaker agreed to allow him five minutes sandwiched between a request from the Subcommittee on Mines and Mining to sit during general debate and a gentleman from North Carolina who wanted to read a tribute to a well-known artist from his state who had recently died.

Ordinarily this would be a routine affair—have you ever sat through an afternoon session of the House of Representatives and heard the banalties read for the benefit of the *Congressional Record?*—but the mounting publicity that began with Sissy's broadcast made this very special. I also had to assure Jones he wasn't being ignored. In fact, I wrote his release, which would be issued immediately after the Shannon speech, setting the date and schedule for the hearings; paid a visit to the national chairman, who wanted to know just what the hell was going on; saw the AG and made sure the Department of Justice was arranging Jello's transfer to the Federal Detention Pen in New York City; and paid a visit with Congressman Tom Grymes, the third man on the subcommittee. Grymes, a wisp of a man who was still terribly ill, said he would probably attend the opening session but would then return to the Naval Hospital at Bethesda for another major operation.

So it would be only Jonesy and our boy.

Monday was a tense day. We all traveled to Washington early Sunday. With Shannons coming in from all parts of the country to pay homage to the senator and Kelly, we had to take most of a floor at the Hilton. A few apprehensive congressmen from New York dropped by to see if they could worm out any advance information—which they didn't—the assistant director of the FBI offered the complete cooperation of the Bureau—how could he refuse? Josh wondered—and a number of old-time senators and military men came by the hour to see the senator.

Luke had his first taste of Washington politics, and he made the most of it with Luther, who buttonholed the important and neatly sidestepped them into an adjacent and very private suite. It was a beautiful day, so Pam and Lacey took the children to see Lincoln's Memorial, the Iwo Jima Flag Raising Memorial at Myers and to Ford's Theatre. Later Josh took Lacey to dinner. It was about midnight when he returned. I was ready to boot him down the hall for leaving me to have my ears bent by our congressman-client from Rhode Island, who demanded to know why we couldn't get him this much publicity, but when I saw his face I held off.

"You and Lacey still arguing?" I asked.

He sighed as he poured himself a nightcap. "She's with us all the way —but only because she feels there is nothing else she can do. She's dead set against these hearings."

"She still frightened?"

"That and the idea that we are manipulating human beings." He finished the drink. "Christ, I tried to show her that's a big part of politics! You plan, you move, you manipulate—if you can't win, you compromise." He yawned and threw his jacket on a chair. "She should know about the call I got this afternoon."

I looked up. "How could she know about it when I don't?"

"I didn't get a chance to tell you. Willy called. He got the Gentile file out of the CIA. How he does it I don't know. I could hardly understand him. When I told him we couldn't come to New York tonight, he blew his top and hung up."

"I'm afraid of that file, Josh."

He turned, surprised. "Why? It might be just the icing on the cake."

"Maybe. But something tells me, go easy."

"It's Willy more than the file you're afraid of."

"Perhaps. But when you have that nut shouting on the phone about how great this file is—well, that makes me suspicious right away."

"The only thing that worries me is I might have made him mad." He turned to me. "It's funny, but you know he sent chills up my back?"

Monday was a jewel of a day, sparkling with the promise of spring. During lunch hour, gossiping and laughing government workers, all glowing with the freshness of youth, crowded the streets and parks when we walked into the House of Representatives. Before Kelly had disappeared into the well of the House, he had been stopped every foot of the way. Such is the power of publicity. A few weeks before they would have nodded, and in answer to a question would have said, Oh, he's the young fellow from New York, the son of . . .

The public gallery was packed; there wasn't a vacant seat in the press section. If we were jittery, Kelly was the calmest. While waiting for the Speaker he visited around, shook hands, and laughed and joked with the reporters about his desk.

"You'd think the guy was doing this every day of his life," Josh said. He nudged Lacey, who had her eyes closed. "No sleeping—that's only for congressmen."

"I was just saying a prayer," she said, "and I'm not too proud to admit it."

The routine business below us continued; water glasses were filled, copies of bills distributed, the sergeant at arms and the clerk of the House quietly debated some point; Jonesy and the majority leader were whispering, with the leader's mouth practically inside the old man's hearing aid; Grymes came in to take his seat, and was immediately surrounded by solicitous colleagues, while the tourists above them buzzed and pointed. Now the Speaker took his place and the roll call began, the clerk's dreary, monotonous voice filling the big, dark-paneled chamber. The gavel banged, and an eager-looking young minister from somewhere in Pennsylvania offered the prayer and put God right in with the tempo of the afternoon as his voice rose to end with: "And may God bless every effort of this great body this afternoon to find justice and peace for all whom

Thou hast fashioned after Thyself . . . and to send those who have violated Thy laws into eternal damnation . . . through Jesus Christ, our Lord, Amen."

The Journal of the proceedings of the day before was read and quickly approved. The gentleman from California asked and was given permission to address the House for one minute to extend his remarks on Peking. This sort of thing went on for almost an hour, with the various congressmen rising to speak on everything from trade with Red China to a plea to adjust the pay rates for postal workers.

Then the gentleman from Indiana made a point of order to the Speaker that a quorum wasn't present. Speaker Holmes was obviously annoyed, because it was clearly evident that the House was packed, but ordered a call of the House. The bored voice of the clerk began the roll, 380 members answered and, by unanimous consent, further proceedings under the call were dispensed with.

The tension in the House was at a peak. The gentleman from Nevada hurriedly asked the Speaker for unanimous consent that his Subcommittee on Mines and Mining of the Committee on Interior and Insular Affairs be allowed to sit during the afternoon's general debate and without any objection raised; it was so ordered.

Finally the gentleman from North Carolina, a rambling old coot who knew what was coming right after he sat down, read a long tribute to a famous artist who had just died in his state. He ended by reading a three-column obit in the state's leading newspaper—which he just happened to own.

Then Kelly was standing, asking permission of the Speaker to address the House. Such a buzz and twittering arose that the Speaker banged his gavel, glowered at the galleries, and then gave Kelly five minutes to address the House.

"Mr. Speaker," Kelly began, his voice loud and clear in the hushed House, "some weeks ago I was the recipient of disturbing information in connection with the conduct of certain New York public officials. The charges were so shocking that at first I refused to believe them. My first inclination was to turn the matter over to the local law-enforcement agency. Yet I realized that if I had done so, and had there been premature publicity of an investigation connected with the names of the individuals, their careers and reputations could have been badly damaged. Instead, I had my staff conduct at least a superficial probe to ascertain the truthfulness of some of the basic facts.

"To my astonishment, these facts proved to be true. The deeper my staff dug, the bleaker the picture became. It was soon apparent that Justice was being sold on the barrelhead in New York City and in other cities in our state. . . ."

" 'Justice on the barrelhead'—that's the eight-column line in today's Wall Street edition," Josh whispered.

The Republican minority leader leaped to his feet. "Mr. Speaker, will the distinguished young man from New York yield?"

Kelly smiled. "I yield to the gentleman from Oklahoma."

The minority leader snapped: "Mr. Speaker, I would like to ask the gentleman from New York if the crooks he has uncovered are only of the opposite political party."

Kelly said, "I regret, sir, they are from both parties."

Josh nudged me. "There they go."

Across the room reporters ran toward the glass doors at the top of the press gallery that leads to their press room. In a few minutes frantic bells would sound in the wire rooms of most American newspapers and copy boys would leap to tear away the bulletin announcing that Congressman Kelly Shannon disclosed to the House of Representatives today that he had uncovered a "shocking" scandal in both the Democratic and Republican parties in New York City and New York State where Justice, he said, was sold on the barrelhead. . . .

Now the questions were really flying. Indiana, Illinois, Wyoming, and New Jersey were demanding that Kelly yield to their questions. He answered each one calmly and straightforwardly. Yes, he had prima facie evidence. Yes, the judiciary was involved very seriously. No, he would not disclose any names. Then he went on to describe Lawrence without naming the city, giving the House a hair-curling account of the rotting tenements, the listless, heartsick unemployed, the growing hate and discontent.

Every eye was fixed on this slim young man whose voice now rang in the huge, silent room.

". . . I can tell the Congress it is a sad, disillusioned city; its people live in constant fear and dread; fear of hunger and want, dread of their children's futures, the menace of narcotics and other evils that hang over their rotting homes like a shroud. But still they cling to their hope, their faith in their government, though fear and heartbreak are their daily lot."

He ended with a fierce denunciation of the lawmakers and the politicians who would sell themselves.

"We of the government must fight these traitors with the cold spotlight of disclosure. We must fight their corruption with laws and truth. We have laws in plenty, truth in abundance . . . let us expose this official filth; let us bring hope to this community of despair and tell its citizens they have not been forgotten by their government, whose programs are from the ideals of angels but whose execution has been in the hands of imbeciles. . . ."

At this point he paused, and then, in a grim, loud voice, made the prediction that would be repeated again and again in the tragic months to come:

"We must do something for these Americans. We must drive the thieves from their city halls and their marketplaces. We must accelerate our poverty programs, repair broken promises, and give them truth, not grandiose political dreams of glittering kitchens and dollar cigars." His voice rose and his forefinger stabbed them all: "If we fail to do this, a human eruption will take place in this city that will be volcanic, and instead of ashes, blood will flow down their streets. . . ."

In the days after Kelly's speech more than fifty subpoenas were issued; number one was for Remington. Somehow, as it always does, word had leaked out that Remington would be called. By the time he was served he was on his way to Federal Court with his attorney to challenge the legality of the committee and the validity of the subpoena.

It didn't do any good. The committee pressed for a ruling and it soon came down, denied "in all respects," as the judge put it, pointing out that official corruption is a matter clearly affecting the public peace, public justice, and public laws and should rightly be examined by a branch of Congress.

That same afternoon Remington tried in Supreme Court for a writ, but again was refused.

By now the papers were having a field day. Remington had a wild press conference in which he denounced Kelly, the committee, and the witch hunters in Congress. We had carefully avoided issuing a subpoena for Saunders, and if word was seeping to City Hall via the political grapevine there was no evidence from Gentile. He pointedly issued a statement from his campaign headquarters, emphasizing that it was an election year.

At a time when we thought Willy would be filling us with reports of what the tapes were disclosing about Gentile, there was only silence. I once called that crazy discothèque in the Village, but a woman just told me I had the wrong number and hung up.

A week before the hearings were to open I returned to New York to pick up a Dun & Bradstreet report on one of the companies we suspected had bribed the judge for a favorable verdict, and a confidential report on the case from an old Wall Street friend. After lunch I went to our office in the Woolworth Building to read them. The D&B was interesting, but the inside report was so startling I forgot everything else.

Suddenly I became aware that someone was in the room. I looked up and almost jumped a foot from the chair.

Wire Willy, back to the door, was staring at me. It was a surly, mean-looking Willy, still wearing the bedraggled sweater and sneakers.

"How the hell did you get in here?" I blurted out.

He gave me a twisted grin. "No lock keeps me out, old man. I can pick any in the city. Where's Josh?"

"In Washington. The hearings start tomorrow."

"Yeah. So I read. You subpoena Gentile?"

"What for? You didn't produce anything on him."

His face twisted with rage. "You old son of a bitch! Don't tell me that!

I got plenty on Gentile. He's a no good whoremongering bastard." He came over to the desk and slammed down his fist. To me it looked the size of a big-league catcher's mitt. "Why didn't Josh come up to see me when I called? Maybe he doesn't want anything now on Gentile. Maybe you guys have sold out to him and all those damned Commies he has in City Hall!"

I tried to keep the tremors from my voice. "Wait a minute, Willy; don't get excited. Josh has been working on Gentile night and day. You know we want him just as much as you do. The committee would love to have something on him. . . ."

My voice trailed off, and those little eyes buried deep in the flesh studied me.

"I still think you're lying, old man," he said, but momentarily at least his rage seemed to have passed. "I still think you sold out to them." He walked over to the window and looked out across City Hall Plaza. "I got stuff that will curl your hair about this guy, stuff that took place down in Washington when he was pimping for the big shots in the State Department. How would you like to talk to a nice little Chinese broad that used to tickle his belly? How would you like to get her to testify how a TV producer used to send the dames down to see Gentile every Sunday for some nice hot parties?" He turned and gave me that crazy grin. "How would you like those apples, old man?"

"Going to bed with a callgirl isn't exactly the job of a congressional committee to investigate, Willy," I pointed out.

"It's a crime if he was pimping for those damn Chinks and black Commies!" he shouted. "That's how they get our secret stuff—whores and booze!" He pointed out at City Hall. "You tell Josh I want to see him. You tell him I got this stuff that can pin this guy to the wall. You tell him —hear!"

"Okay, Willy," I said, "I'll tell him."

He stamped to the door, making the floor shake.

"You tell him one more thing, old man . . . you tell him if he doesn't use this stuff, maybe there won't be any hearing."

"Don't be silly," I said, "it's all set."

He gave me that grin again. "Maybe it can be unset."

"Where did you park your bus, Willy?" I asked, hoping to get him back on the track, "You usually don't like to move around in the daytime."

"There's a lot of ways to get into this building besides the front door," he said. He yanked open the door. "You just tell Josh . . ."

Then he was gone. I hurried to the windows, alternating between the one facing Broadway and the one facing Park Place. But Willy never appeared. I suddenly remembered how he had boasted to me he could travel about the city from the Battery to Coney Island without once walking on a sidewalk.

The day before the hearings opened, Benny Jello, guarded by two Department of Justice marshals, was brought down to the Washington Penitentiary, where Josh and I saw him. He obviously had lost a great deal of weight, and was jittery.

"I was a schnook to get involved with you guys," he said nervously. "Better I should have taken the bit up the river." He glanced around the conference room and said in a whisper: "I got three warnings last week. One of the trusties kept telling me they were going to poison me. He said I wouldn't know what hit me, one swallow and they would be putting me on ice."

Josh took out a pencil. "Give me his name, Benny."

Jello looked terrified. "Are you crazy? Please—don't give me any more trouble! You don't know what it's like in the pen. I come in here this morning, and some guy tells the marshals over there he hopes they will keep a good eye on me because they don't want to be responsible. What kind of talk is this? I help a government committee and put my life on the line, and nobody can protect me?"

"Wait a minute, Benny," Josh said. "You were crawling like a snake when we first talked to you. All you wanted to do was blow the whistle loud and clear so they wouldn't send you up the river."

He shrugged. "So now the trip up the river wouldn't be too bad, maybe."

Josh said bluntly, "You trying to tell us you're not going to talk?"

"Sure I'll talk," Benny protested. "I'll talk for a week, but you got to guarantee I won't get hurt."

Josh said promptly, "Guaranteed. You'll have more protection than the President."

"And look, what about that charge? It'll get dismissed, right?"

"Guaranteed also," Josh said. Then, with a great show of heartiness, he slapped Benny on the back. "Forget it, Benny. We'll take care of everything. After the hearings we'll get you an SS, get you married to Molly, and send you on a trip for a while, okay?"

Benny looked mollified. "What can I say? I'm at the mercy of you guys." He added nervously: "You sure they'll have plenty of guards around? You know those Singer brothers are crazy. And that damned Saunders has a lot of connections with some tough guys."

"Forget him," Josh snapped, "and let's go over the story from the beginning."

We spent four hours with Benny. Josh made him go over the story again and again, suddenly shooting questions at him like a harassing district attorney, then twisting his answers, snarling at him until the sweat broke out on Benny's dead-white face.

"Let up, will you!" he shouted at last. "Whose side you on?"

"Easy, Benny," Josh said wearily, "I just want to make sure, that's all."

On the way out we stopped at a Coke machine in the lobby of the jail and bought a cup. It was sweet, but ice cold.

"I didn't know the committee got the DA to give Benny an SS," I said.

Josh shook his head. "He didn't. One of the investigators said the DA's ripping, and wants to send Benny up for life. The warden also got two warrants, one from Illinois and New Jersey. They want Benny for grand larceny."

"My God," I said, "and you promised—"

"What do you want me to do," he asked, "tell him they're going to throw the key away after he testifies tomorrow."

"Does Kelly know this?"

"No," he snarled. "And for Christ's sake get off my back!"

I was stunned. It was the first time he had ever spoken to me like that. We've had our fights and loud arguments, but this was different. Now a lie lay between us, and we both knew it. Later in the day he said he was sorry and let's forget it.

I felt like Benny Jello. What could I say?

The hearings were held in the new Senate Building, that $5,000,000 monument of overwhelming mediocrity.

The committee sat behind a half-circled dais with the witness table directly in front of them.

The press section was crowded, with every last chair taken. I saw some familiar faces, including Sissy Southworth's and—this gave me a start— Tuck Larsen's. Well, we could be sure his "Washington Desk" column, read by every politician and officeholder in Washington, including the gentleman on Pennsylvania Avenue, would not give us the best of it. When I had known him, Larsen was a peppery little man who always wore his trademark, a blue polka-dot bow tie. He still wore the bow tie, and while his hair was grayer he still looked his old vicious self.

I deliberately walked past him to see if he remembered me. He did.

"Hello, McCool," he said. "Still stooging for Shannon, I see."

"And I see your heart is still as big as a flaxseed," I replied. "Going to do a hatchet job on us as usual?"

"Nothing would give me greater pleasure."

"I better remind myself to go over our list of witnesses again," I said. He gave me a puzzled look. "Why?"

"Well, the last time you did a hatchet job on us, one of your friends was a witness. Is he still in Leavenworth?"

That's why I like this great big beautiful city, I thought as he spun on his heel and walked away, so full of goodwill and love of country.

In the hearing room, off to the right of the dais, were the television and radio sections with their usual jungle of thick black cables, cameras, tripods, reflectors, and young, nervous producers in desert boots and Gant shirts. The radiomen were more sedate. They seemed content to whisper confidentially into their mikes and to toy with their black boxes with numerous dials.

Outside in the corridor, lines had been forming since the building had opened. Television cameras were set up, with reporters interviewing some of the spectators who were abandoned as soon as Kelly, Jones, and Grymes appeared. Jones read his statement and gave some off-the-cuff comments. Grymes was brief, and Kelly simply said the primary purpose of the hearing was to throw a spotlight on an urban situation, and should any evidence of a criminal act be established, it would be promptly turned over to the city, state, or federal authority in whose jurisdiction the crime belonged.

Then, as Josh had suggested, he ended by disclosing that "observers" from the IRS, the DA's of the five boroughs in New York, the FBI, and the Department of Justice were present.

Josh, the senator, Luke, and Luther were stationed in the locked room down the hall where we had two huge black TV sets.

"Josh is really manipulating today, Finn," Lacey said quietly as we left the "TV rooms," as we called it, to walk down the corridor toward the hearing room.

"It's all part of politics, Lacey," I said. "We just want to make sure as many people as possible see, hear, and like Kelly Shannon."

"Kelly could get hurt."

"He may well lose some of his political baby fat, Lacey, but I don't think he'll get hurt very badly."

"I don't want him to get hurt at all."

"That's impossible—either in life or in politics."

"What about the people around him? You can't tell me someone won't suffer before this is over. I know it. I feel it in my bones since I saw Molly so frightened. And that little man who was shaking so much he couldn't hold a cup . . ."

"There will be marshals all over the place watching out for Benny. In a few weeks it will be all over for him and Molly."

"And then what?"

I hesitated, and she stopped and looked at me.

"And then what, Finn?" she pressed. "Remember, I'm not Molly. I just won't swallow this story Josh is telling them about the law letting him go and they'll be married and everything will be roses and antiques for the rest of their days."

"The committee will give the DA an excellent recommendation, Lacey," I said lamely. "I personally guarantee they will."

"Will you also guarantee the charges against him will be dropped and he will go free?"

I tried to say it but I couldn't. The words stuck in my throat.

"That's what I mean, Finn," she said sadly. "You and Josh are making an image for Kelly—with other people's lives. And you're telling me this won't hurt him or change him inside?"

She walked along in a brooding silence. At the door of the hearing room I stopped and took her hand. "I'm an old man, Lacey, and I've been around these halls and hearings for more years than I care to remember. Remember always—we may be the means, but Kelly is the end."

"But will it be worth the price, Finn?" she asked. "That's the question."

"Frankly I can't answer that, Lacey," I said. "We haven't received the bill yet."

"I hope it doesn't stagger all of us," she said, and went inside the hearing room.

When they entered, Kelly, Grymes, and Jones were immediately swallowed by the press, including Sissy Southworth. At the insistence of the "writing press" a brief conference was held, in which Kelly—again as suggested by Josh—dropped another little morsel of news to keep them happy and on our side: the committee had uncovered evidence of bribery and corruption in the prison where Jello had been confined in New York, and the warden and his guards would be subpoenaed by a local grand jury.

That was a little kick to the warden's butt to pay for some of the weight Benny Jello had lost.

Every hearing takes some time to settle down the first day. The TV people have to be taken care of along with the writing press, spectators seated, the first witness—this would be Benny Jello—pampered and soothed in the witness room, papers sorted, Jones's hearing aids tuned to the proper volume, windows opened or closed.

Then Jones, as chairman, read the opening statement, ending with: "This morning's hearing will be presided over by my colleague, Congressman Kelly Shannon of New York."

Jones, no fool, realized Jello was Kelly's witness. Rather than stumble along, he could always follow Kelly's lead in the questioning.

"We now open the first of these hearings in Washington," Kelly said. "Subsequent hearings will be held in New York City and in the upstate city of Lawrence."

The reporters didn't miss it: Lawrence was the city Kelly had meant in his speech on the floor of the House of Representatives. . . . I could see the AP and the UPI man scribbling bulletins. Within minutes the governor in Albany would be holding a press conference, denying that this fair city was a swamp of corruption as Kelly had described it.

Then Kelly went on to welcome the representatives of the various New York district attorneys, the IRS, and other agencies.

"Let me repeat what Chairman Jones has stated," he said. "This Committee is not a prosecuting body. Those witnesses who appear before it should not be viewed as defendants. Its role is an investigative one whose purpose is to bring to light corrupt forces in our urban society. Should evidence of any criminal acts be established, the record and transcripts pertaining to that act will immediately be made available to the proper law-enforcement body, be it city, state, or federal. Are you ready to proceed, gentlemen?" he asked Jones and Grymes. When they nodded, he said quietly, "Call the first witness."

A door off to the right of the dais opened, and Benny Jello, blinking and wan, dwarfed by the two burly marshals, walked to the witness stand. Thief that he was, I felt sorry for him, and sorrier for us who were using him. How right Lacey was.

He was sworn, and gingerly sat down. Under Kelly's quiet questioning he began sketching his early life, the boyish crimes, the stern father, and the harsh times. Gradually the room seemed to relax. Benny was naturally witty, and some of his wisecracks convulsed the audience. I could see the reporters chuckling and nudging each other. This was the comedy relief. Benny likewise thawed. He now had an audience, and he loved their tittering and laughter. Jones put on a good show of pounding the gavel, but no one really paid any attention to him.

The whole morning was spent on Benny's reminiscences. By the noon recess I caught some yawns, and the TV crews seemed to be paying more attention to Jello as a comedian than as a witness. Josh was furious. He sent a note to me: "Wind him up. Get him to the club and the mob; polls just came in housewives are starting to go back to their soap operas. I told Kelly we have to catch the Wall Street editions with something good."

For lunch we shared sandwiches and soft drinks in the "TV room." It reminded me of a newspaper office in miniature; phones never stopped ringing. Luke or Luther, looking harassed, were either making notes or snapping out suggestions to Shea and Short in Washington or Chicago. By the end of the lunch period Luther gave us a gloomy report of the morning's TV coverage. It had started off with complete coverage, but toward noon housewives in the Midwest area were switching on "Richard Arlington, Country Doctor" or "Sally Winters." As Chicago warned, we were competing with Sally Winters having a baby or undergoing some damn crisis in her maudlin, fictitious life.

"My God," was all Lacey said.

Josh just gave her a look and finished his soda. Frankly, I was glad Kelly had left to spend a few minutes with Benny Jello. Then a clerk came in, and once again we were off to the bloody races.

After the noon recess Jello seemed grim and tense. Kelly slowly took him along his story, from the beginning of the East Side Hungarian Club, skillfully letting Benny paint a verbal picture of how the underworld had slowly adopted the place, the meetings, the deals, the characters. By two o'clock, every one knew about the Polish Rendezvous and how Benny had gradually taken on the role of the old-time mediator, a fat, jolly referee whose word and decisions were respected by the underworld, especially the established mobsters with European backgrounds.

There was a noticeable change in the audience. The restlessness had disappeared. The TV men were once again training their cameras for close-ups on Jello, and the wire-service men were sending out running stories, as they call them, by way of Western Union messengers who flitted in and out of the hearing room, awkward with self-consciousness.

At 2:10 P.M., Kelly leaned across the dais and asked very quietly, "Mr. Jello, are you acquainted with the Singer brothers?"

Benny wet his lips, and nodded.

Kelly said to the stenographer, "Please note the witness has indicated Yes." Then to Benny, "Please tell us the circumstances under which you first became acquainted with them."

This was my clue. I already had rogues' gallery pictures and a brief résumé of the Singer brothers' yellow sheets from the New York City Police Bureau of Identification and the FBI. I sent a clerk to distribute them to the press section along with a separate set of prints for the still photographers and TV people.

Benny now was nervously describing each step of his story, as he had first told it to us in the pen, about the old-time hood Noodles (as his name was put in the record) who paid him a visit and asked him to try and arrange a fix for the hijackers. (I also distributed Noodle's rogues' gallery picture and yellow sheet to the press.)

Q.   What did he say to you, this man Noodles?
A.   He said the old man, the boys' father, was frantic. He didn't want his sons to go up for life. He said the family was willing to pay a a lot.
Q.   What business is the family in?
A.   Poultry. On the lower West Side. They got a nice business. A couple farms in Jersey, and they do a good egg business. Noodles said the old man always had trouble with these two bums but the family always got them off.
Q.   Did you attempt to help this man?
A.   Yes, sir.
Q.   What did you do?
A.   I contacted a lawyer named Trevor Remington.
Q.   Where is he located?
A.   On Fifth Avenue and Forty-first Street. His home is in Darien, Connecticut.
Q.   Was this for the purpose of arranging counsel for the Singer brothers?
A.   Oh, no, sir.
Q.   What was it for, then?
A.   To put in a fix.

Q. (Grymes) What made you think this fellow Remington could put in a fix?
A. I had used him before to fix a case. I think it had cost me five skins.
Q. (Jones) What the devil is five skins, Witness?
A. Five thousand dollars.
Q. (Grymes) How did he fix it—with a judge?
A. No, sir. (*Hesitation*) With some connection he had in City Hall.

I could almost reach out and feel the frozen silence. The wire-service reporters waved wildly at the Western Union messengers, who took the sheets of paper and ran out of the room.

Q. (Shannon) Did you know who this alleged contact was at City Hall?
A. Yes, sir. Mr. Saunders.

The name hung in the room. There was an audible gasp from the audience, and whispering arose until Jones was forced to pound his gavel. Grymes, the Republican, bore in on Benny to try to establish that he had never seen Saunders, but Benny, now visibly nervous, kept nodding and saying, "Yes, I did. . . . I did. . . ."

Q. (Jones *bellowing*) You did what, Witness?
A. I met him. Mr. Saunders. We had lunch at "21." I was with Remington. It was the day I paid him the $25,000.

Bulletins flew from the room. Benny reached over for a glass of water, and dropped it, the splintering glass sounded like a bomb in the room. With the guards hurrying to mop up the water and shattered glass, the TV men moving in for close-ups, Jonesy pounding his gavel, and Grymes and Kelly trying to calm Benny, the place was a bedlam.

Two notes were passed to me; one from Josh:
"They're putting bulletins on the air. Shea says Middle West back on. Keep it up."

And a note from an AP man I knew: "My office says Saunders claims Jello is a liar and that he never saw him in his life."

I couldn't help feeling a bit smug. How would Saunders explain the statement from the waiter who had served them, and the copy of the dining check? Mr. Saunders would be an interesting witness.

The hearing was back on course. Benny's face had taken on a gray hue, and the handkerchief between his hands was a twisted wet ball.

Q. Why did you pay him $25,000?
A. For fixing the case. For getting the Singer brothers an SS.
Q. (Grymes) An SS is a suspended sentence, I gather.

A.   Yes, sir.

Q.   (Shannon) Was the judge in on the fix?

A.   No, sir. I think he did it as a favor to someone. At least that's what Remington said.

Q.   (Jones) But you said you fixed judges, didn't you?

A.   I not only fixed them, Your Honor; I made them.

There was a burst of laughter, and Jonesy threatened to clear the courtroom, which he wouldn't have done in a million years.

Q.   (Shannon) When you first met Remington and asked him if he could fix a case, what did he say to you?

A.   He said he could fix it through Chuck Saunders. He said Saunders could fix anything in town from an ABC license rap to murder. I think I can still remember what he says. Yeah. He said only money talked.

Q.   Did he ever talk to Mr. Saunders in your presence?

A.   Yes. The first time we talked about the fix in his office he called a number. It was CY 4-6112.

Kelly nodded to one of the investigators, who produced a telephone tracer. He read into the record that the unlisted number was officially listed in the name of Saunders and was located in City Hall. There was another flurry of bulletins.

Q.   (Grymes) Was a deal made for a fix?

A.   I saw him about three days later when Remington came into the club. He said the best he could do was for $25,000. He would take ten. I was to get five. The rest was for grease. You know, the fix.

Q.   (Shannon) And did you deliver the money?

A.   Noodles came with the loot. I put ten in an envelope for Remington and five for myself. The rest I put in another envelope. I insisted Noodles come with me because I didn't want any trouble from those two bum nephews of his. So we took a cab and went to see Remington.

Q.   This man Noodles accompanied you?

A.   Yes, sir. We saw Remington in his office. And I gave him the loot. He took it into his office and then came out and told Noodles he he had gotten his fee and thanks very much. Then he wished us a Merry Christmas.

Q.   Did the fix work?

A.   Two weeks later Noodles called me and said the boys were put into the top tier on the island—that's Rikers Island. Then I didn't hear anything for a while. One day, I think it was about a month later, Noodles called and said the boys were out. They had copped a plea to a lesser charge, and the judge gave them a year but gave them an SS.

Q. (Grymes) Did you say a secretary in Mr. Remington's office saw you and the other man?

A. Yes, sir. She even saw me give him his Christmas present. (*Laughter*)

(Shannon) We have the girl under subpoena, Congressman. She will be called.

Q. (Shannon) Was this fix the end of your relationship with Mr. Remington?

A. Oh, no. We did a lot of business after that.

Q. Please describe your activities.

A. Well, one day Noodles came in and said he had a friend named Sam Doxy who owned a dress house. Sam was grabbed for trying to work a fur switch, and indicted for grand larceny. Now, this guy was a jerk. Like I said before, when you do a fur switch you need three arms and five eyes, and this guy only had the regular two and two. So I was not inclined to help this schnook. But Noodles kept pestering me. Finally I said okay and sent him to Remington. I got three iron men out of it, and Sam got an SS.

Q. (Jones) "Three iron men"? What's that, Witness?

A. Three gees, Your Honor.

Q. (*Shannon informs the hearing that Doxy was subpoenaed and will appear.*) Anything else?

A. Yeah. The Blitz brothers. They were in numbers in Harlem, around 138th Street, and were going real big. They were busted by Downtown.

Q. (Jones) What Downtown, Witness?

A. Downtown. That's the cops downtown. The commissioner's confidential squad. They'd bust their mother.

Q. (Shannon) Continue, please.

A. They were busted, as I was saying. So one day Noodles comes in and says they need a new lawyer. The one they got can't fix a flat. So they need one who can. I called Remington, and he puts the bite on them for ten—$10,000—and they get an SS. There was a lot of talk about it because the DA had them indicted for a felony. You see, the cops busted their bank and grabbed them with the slips and the ribbons. It was open and shut. I don't know. I asked Remington, and he said he just called Saunders. He was a little mad. He said Saunders wanted $7,000 as his share. Remington got $2,000. I got only a grand, which was peanuts. I think he gave me the shaft on that one, but I didn't care. A grand for making a phone call was pretty good percentage, as I see it.

Q. Did you arrange any city business with Mr. Remington?

A. I sure did.

Q. Please describe it.

A. Well, this one I did through a guy—a man—named Manny Summers. He was one of my customers. I think his house is Paris Best. He says he had lunch with his cousin, a guy named Stu Saxon, who works for a big firm named Delafield in Minneapolis, and this guy says he can't do any business with the city because you have to have a connection, and a connection this guy ain't got.

Q. (Grymes) What was the nature of this firm's business?

A. They made snow-removal equipment. This particular time they were trying to sell the city half a million dollars' worth of stuff. You know—shovels, salt, trucks, all that stuff.

Q. Did you meet anyone from this firm?

A. Yeah. I'm coming to that, Your Honor. Well, I tell him to bring in his cousin, this guy Saxon. The next day he did, and we had a talk. He says he wants his boss, a guy named Ken Beering, to come in to town. I said, Fine, come in, the water's fine. So he calls him, and Beering is as hot as a three-dollar pistol to put over this deal, so he flies in that night. The next day we all meet at this guy's hotel. We have a coffee and we talk about the weather and how bad the traffic is in New York. Then we get down to the meat. He says he wants to make a deal with the city for over half a million dollars' of snow-removal equipment. Maybe it's more like $700,000. He shows me all kinds of fancy brochures telling how good his stuff is, but I told him the last time I shoveled snow was in Poland, so I'm not interested; but I am interested in what his proposition is. He is a cool guy and lays it on the line. One hundred thousand clams for us if we can swing the deal. This is no small potatoes, so I called Remington from this guy's hotel room and I rush up to his office. When Remington hears about this figure, he gets all excited. He called Saunders—

Q. (Shannon) Were you present when he did this?

A. Absolutely.

Q. (Jones) And it was the same telephone number, Witness?

A. Absolutely.

Q. (Grymes) How do you know? Did he ask his girl to get it?

A. No, sir. He dialed it. He has a private number in his office. But he hung up right away. He said Chuck—that's what he called Saunders—had someone at his elbow. In about a minute the phone rang, and he was calling him Chuck and telling him about the deal and said he had better see us for lunch. So we made a date. At "21."

Q. (Shannon) You met Mr. Saunders then?

A. Yes, sir.

Q. Did you know of your own knowledge whether Mr. Remington told Mr. Saunders you were an ex-convict or a fixer?

A. No, sir. He didn't. But he certainly knew I wasn't Lily White's father.

Q. How did he introduce you?

A. Just Mr. Jello, that's all. Personally, I thought he was stupid for bringing me along and for Saunders meeting me; but that's what happens when you have larceny in your heart: you just can't wait to get that buck.

Q. And you had a meeting with Mr. Saunders and Mr. Remington?

A. Yes, sir. We sat and talked. I could see Saunders liked the smell of that $100,000. But he kept calling it our "fee."

Q. (Grymes) You mean by that he indicated this would be an attorney's fee.

A. That's right. Sure, but I had to laugh to myself. Here was a guy trying to make me believe he was taking a lawyer's fee—a guy at City Hall representing a company doing business with the city? I said to myself, This guy must think I'm a hick! But I didn't say anything. If this is what he wants me to believe, so I'll believe it. He kept talking about writs and searches and estimations and all that stuff, and then he said he would see what could be done. I think by this time he was getting a little jittery with me there because all he ate was scrambled eggs and coffee. I just sat there like a little saint, saying nothing. I even left them for a few minutes to buy a cookbook.

Q. (Shannon) Did this deal go through?

A. Like a dream. Beering kept coming in with stuff like brooms and shovels and models of trucks and going up to Remington's office. Then one day he comes into my place with two other guys. They looked like private dicks, and gave me a valise. He said it was the material we had agreed on. I took it into the office and almost fell down. It was loaded with dough. I never saw so much coin in all my life. We had a drink, and then I took one of the regular cabbies that hung outside my place and we drove up to Remington's office. I felt so good that I told this cabbie to drive through Central Park. I wanted to feel how it was driving around the city with one hundred grand between my feet. I know it sounds nuts, but that's what I did.

Q. Did you see Mr. Remington?

A. I had called him, see, so as soon as I entered he almost jumped through the door and practically carried me into his office. He locked the door, and we spread the stuff out on his desk. You'd think the bum was a teller. He counted every buck. Then he just kept smiling and looking at the door for so long I got nervous. Then he counted ten gees for me and put the rest into a valise. He said he had to see Saunders for dinner. He was getting stoned because he was knocking them off in his office. I warned him to go easy on the booze because it would be a hell of a thing if he left the valise in a cab. Remember what happened to Costello's $25,000 that was left in the taxicab? So I got up to go as he was dialing Saunders. Just as I opened the door, he was making a date with him for dinner.

Q. You didn't see him hand Saunders any money from this deal?

A. No, sir. But later he told me he had taken twenty-five and Saunders got the rest.

Q. (Jones) That was sixty-five left for City Hall, wasn't it, Witness?

A. (Shannon) Not for City Hall, Congressman! Allegedly Saunders —but the witness didn't see him receive any of this money.

Q. (Jones) You heard him talking to Saunders when you left, didn't you, Witness?

A. Yes, sir.

Q. And he told you later Saunders got the rest—after your ten and his twenty-five, didn't he?

A. Yes, sir.

Q. (Grymes) But you didn't see Mr. Remington personally give Saunders the money?

A. No, sir.

Q. (Jones) But—

A. (Shannon) I think, gentlemen, the charges are so grave and so shocking, there should be no question of our fairness.

Q. (Jones) Well, let's get Saunders up here—

A. (Shannon) We shall give Mr. Saunders an opportunity to answer these charges, Congressman.

Q. (Grymes) Did you have any more dealings with Mr. Remington, Mr. Jello?

A. Yes, sir. Plenty.

Q. Please describe them.

A. Well, by this time we knew we had something going good. Word was getting around among the boys that I could put in a fix, so they began coming to me. One was a friend of a guy named Cumings. He was called the cat burglar. The dicks nabbed him on a big jewelry job, and the insurance outfit was pushing for the judge to hit him with the book. It cost them five to get to the dick but he watered down some of his evidence and they had to let him take a plea to a lesser charge. Then there was Joey Americus.

Q. (Jones) He sounds like a gangster.

A. He was, Your Honor. He owns a club on Forty-seventh Street.

Q. A club? What kind of club?

A. A nightclub. The name is the Diamond Tower. It's off Forty-seventh and Park Avenue.

Q. (Shannon) What did you do for him?

A. Fixed it so he got a license.

The name of the Diamond Tower wasn't lost on the reporters even though they were based in Washington. The Tower, as it was called, was now the water hole of society, and frequently appeared in the Broadway gossip and society columns. Again bulletins went out.

Q. Did Mr. Remington help in this case?

A. Yes, sir. He certainly did.

Q. How were you approached?

A. I got a call one day from a guy who wanted to know if I had any connection with the SLA. I said personally I didn't, but I knew a guy who had taken care of a rap for me.

Q. What do you mean—for you?

A. Well, that's how I first met Remington. The SLA put a rap on me when they found a young dame—girl—at my bar. I thought she was okay but it turned out she was working with the bartender, hustling. I canned the bartender, but the rap still stuck. Someone told me about Remington, and I went to him. It cost me three, but they dropped the rap for lack of evidence. I told it to this guy, and he said come up and see Joey.

Q. That's Joseph Americus?

A. That's right. Joey said he wanted to buy the club but because of his yellow sheet he couldn't get a license—

Q. (Jones) Yellow sheet, Witness?

(Shannon) Criminal record, Congressman. Go on, Mr. Jello.

A. I knew Americus from the old days. He used to pal around with the big boys in that coffeeshop near police headquarters.

Q. (Grymes) Wasn't that the one they took films of a few years ago and showed those gangsters on the sidewalk?

A. Yes, sir. That's the one. Some cop took the pictures from a building across the street.

Q. (Jones) Mafia, Witness?

A. Personally, Your Honor, I think that Mafia is a lot of—stuff. They got an organization and they know each other. New York, Chicago, Detroit, Canada—like gambling. You meet the same bums in New York or Vegas.

Q. (Shannon) Was Americus prominent in the underworld?

A. Very big. He used to work for Joey A, and he was one of the guys they caught at Joe Barbara's cookout years ago. I wanted to do him a favor because I didn't want him to think I wouldn't.

Q. Did you put in a fix?

A. Yes. I took the money from Joey, and he and one of his boys went with me in a cab to see Remington. I made Remington tell this guy he got the money and word would get to his boss soon. About three weeks later Joey called me and said that Remington put the arm on him for another five but that he got some guy to front for him for the license and it was worth it.

Q.   Did you get any money for that fix?

A.   Remington gave me three.

Q.   Three thousand, of course.

A.   Yes, sir. Three gees.

Q.   Did you fix any other case with the aid of Remington?

A.   Yes, sir. Through him and the judge.

Q.   (Jones) Judge, Witness? What judge?

A.   Judge Tucker.

Q.   (Grymes) Justice Prebel Tucker? Chief Justice of the Federal Court of Appeals?

A.   Yes, sir.

Q.   (Shannon) And you fixed a case with him?

At this point Jello got the shakes, took another glass of water, and looked beseechingly at Kelly, who ordered a ten-minute recess. It was growing late, and I saw Kelly look up at the clock and lean over and whisper to Jones and Grymes. They nodded, and Kelly then announced they would recess until noon the following day. As soon as Jones slammed down the gavel, the room exploded. Reporters and TV men made a dash for the committee and for Jello, who was walking toward the door of the witness room.

One thrust a mike over the shoulders of the marshals into Jello's face, shouting, "What fix did you put in with the judge, Benny?"

Benny said solemnly, "It was a fifteen-dollar parking ticket. I got it for ten."

Then the door slammed in the face of the fuming TV reporters.

The press swirled around Kelly, Jones, and Grymes. Questions flew in from all sides.

"What was the fix Jello made with Justice Tucker?"

Kelly said, "It will be brought out in testimony."

"Did the judge take money?"

"The circumstances of the case will be explained by Jello's testimony."

"What about Remington? Will he testify?"

Grymes said, "Gentlemen, will you let me pass?"

It had been too much for the congressman, who was obviously very ill. His face had a grayish tinge. Kelly motioned to an attendant, who pushed his way through the throng. Then he and Kelly began to lead them out. The reporters hung on their flanks like a pack of worrying terriers.

"Is Saunders subpoenaed?"

"What about this guy Americus? Are you going to bring him in, Congressman?"

Kelly turned and said something. Then I saw Tuck Larsen move in front of Kelly, making him stop. He said something to Kelly, who turned and pushed him aside. Apparently Larsen slipped on a cable and fell against another reporter, and both tumbled backward into a seat. It was more ludicrous than serious. By the time they got up, Kelly, Grymes, and the others had gone out; but the TV cameramen, who had got everything, were hurrying after the furious Larsen, who had dashed out into the corridor.

Josh and Luther came in a few seconds later.

"What the hell did he push Larsen for?" Josh demanded.

"I don't know, but if I know Larsen it was for some vicious Larsen crack. But how do you know he pushed him?"

"It was all on television," Josh said. "Christ, that's not going to do him any good!" He gestured to where Jones, in a sea of reporters, was shouting answers to questions as the crew climbed all over them with mikes and lights.

"That's where I wanted him to be. He's letting this old bastard steal the show."

"It looks like Grymes was taken ill," Luther said.

"Sure. But the attendants could have taken him out," he snapped. "Sissy! Do you have a minute?"

Sissy, who was across the room comparing notes with a few reporters, hurried over to us.

"It looks like you boys have a hit," she said. "But what's with Kelly Shannon? He almost slugged Larsen out in the corridor." She chuckled. "Not that I'm against that, mind you. As far as I'm concerned it should be open season on Larsen any time. But I thought Shannon would be giving us a good fill-in—"

"That's what I thought," Josh said grimly. "Why did he tangle with Larsen?"

"Larsen asked him about Gentile, and your boy said he didn't have any evidence of any wrongdoing on Gentile's part. Then Larsen said it looked like it was going to be a typical Shannon kangaroo court. Kelly went for him, but his brother was out there and stepped in. No punches thrown. No knockdowns. But it was great for TV. It will go real big tonight on the six and eleven news spots." In a lower voice she asked Josh, "Anything I should know?"

When Josh hesitated she said quickly: "I'm guesting tonight on 'The National Scene.' They're going to give me fifteen minutes. Eight o'clock. Prime time, buddy, and national coverage."

"No cracks about Larsen?"

"I want exclusive stuff, Josh, none of that country-bugle crap."

He nodded. "Okay, you can hint call girls were used in some of the fixes. At least one will be subpoenaed along with a madam."

"From New York? L.A.?"

"New York. They operated out of a swank place on the West Side. You know, with all the trimmings—whips, chains, mirrors."

She was writing furiously. "And they were used in the fixes?"

"Definitely."

"With Remington?"

He patted her on the back.

"Just a little more," she pleaded.

"You can say one of the principals in the fixes helped to set her up to ease the way when they had a big thing going. Now, that's all. . . ."

"But you're going to bring her in?"

"That I can promise you."

"Here or in New York?"

"New York. They will both testify."

For years I have marveled at these people; the worse things they are told about someone, the happier they seem. I guess it proves the old saying: Who wants to read happy news?

"You'll go all out for us tonight, Sissy?" Josh asked.

"All out, Josh," she said. "I'll really give him a big blow on the show."

"You're going to have trouble with Kelly, Josh," I warned. "He just won't take this dirt."

"He'll have to," he said. "We've got a big one going, and I want to milk it for all it's got." He said to me, "Get some word to Jonesy about this angle before he reads her story or hears it on TV. He'll blow his batteries for sure if he does."

"The office read me the AP from Albany," Luther said. "The governor's boiling mad. He cited something about some rehabilitation program for Lawrence—"

"Did your people distribute those unemployment and welfare figures from Lawrence to the press at Albany?" Josh asked.

"Just before the hearing started, we had someone in the pressroom at the State House with copies of the statistical breakdown over the past five years on unemployment and the rise in welfare cases," he said. "Did you know it developed they have more cases per capita in Lawrence than anywhere else in the state?"

"Good," Josh said. "Then the reporters had the background when the governor called the press conference."

"They hit him with some tough questions," Luther said. "The way the AP sounded, he fumbled pretty badly. He ended by saying he intended to call in the mayor and City Council of Lawrence."

We had our dinner and our first postmortem in the Shannon suite against the usual backdrop of ringing phones, messengers, and the old senator glued to a big color television set and chuckling with satisfaction after every news broadcast. The floor of the suite was littered with the late edition of every newspaper we could buy.

Fortunately for us, it had been a slow news day, and the hearing dominated every page one from New York to L.A. As Josh had predicted, Jello's first big revelation had caught the Wall Street editions of the big-town papers. Evidently the very late editions managed a bulletin on Jello's disclosure of the judge. The A.M.'s would develop that. But in addition on the late TV show, there were shots of Kelly pushing Larsen aside and the little man flying into the seat, then running after Kelly. The shots in the corridor were jerky and confused. It showed an infuriated Larsen shouting something at Kelly; then Luke's jacket moved before the lens and a door was closing behind Kelly and Grymes. We caught the full fury of Larsen's 6:00 P.M. "Washington Desk." He denounced Kelly, Jones—even Grymes, and called the hearing a typical Shannon pillory. He quoted at length Remington's statement that he knew Jello only as a petty thief who had been a client, and Saunders' statement of amazement that he had never seen Jello, knew Remington slightly, and vehemently denied any wrongdoing.

Gentile appeared briefly in a City Hall press conference in which he stoutly defended his brother-in-law and attacked the committee for not contacting the local district attorney.

"We'll take care of you—and Larsen too," the old man growled at the TV screen.

"Larsen is no prize package, Kelly," Josh said, "but wait until after the hearings, will you?"

"I know it was childish to do," Kelly said, "but to stand in front of me when I had this poor man on the verge of collapse . . ."

"What the word on Grymes, by the way?" Luther asked Luke.

"They're removing him to Bethesda this afternoon," Luke said. "The doctor said he wants to come back, but they won't allow it for at least a week."

"He won't come back," Luther said. "He's out of it. I don't give him six months the way he looked when he left that room."

"That's just what I mean about Larsen," Kelly began, but Josh held up his hand.

"Agreed, but we have to live with these people. Ignore him. Say 'No comment.' Refer him to me, but Christ, don't belt him. Not now, anyway. By the way, where's Lacey?"

"Molly came in this afternoon," Luke said. "She said she couldn't stay home after watching TV. We arranged to let Benny have dinner with her before taking him back to the pen tonight. Lacey is with them." He glanced at a notebook. "This is the number of the room."

Josh took it. "I think I'll give them a call."

He went inside and came out after a few minutes. "I talked to one of the marshals. Benny's nervous as a cat. He won't eat, and keeps telling Molly he won't live until the end of the hearing."

"Luke, check with Justice and make absolutely sure everything has been done to give him complete protection," Kelly said. "Will you be back, Josh?"

"Give me an hour. We'll go over tomorrow's stuff when I come back."

"Let's arrange to have Molly stay here at the hotel," Kelly told Luke.

Luke nodded and walked inside the bedroom to make the arrangements.

I walked Josh to the door. "Sissy's on at eight," he said. "You might as well turn her on. If Kelly blows, tell him to wait for me. I'll be back right after eight."

I did turn on Sissy, and we listened in silence to her account of the hearing, interspersed with stills and bits of film. There was no doubt about it: Sissy was an old pro. She gave a vivid description of the growing tension in the hearing room as Jello began making his disclosures; and, true to her word, she praised Kelly until he squirmed. Then she turned on the heat and described her exclusive. She ended by smiling into the camera and reminding the audience to tune in tomorrow for more disclosures that would shock the nation.

I clicked it off. We might as well face the music.

Kelly gave me a surprised look. "Just where the devil did that come from?" He turned to Luke and Luther. "Did you know about this?"

"It's something the investigators dug up," Luke said lamely.

"But what is it all about?"

I moved in and gave him a brief description of Eva and how she operated with Remington and the judge as one of her customers.

"But what does it have to do with official corruption?"

"Josh said to wait until he comes—"

"The hell with waiting for anyone," Kelly snapped. "What I want to know is just what do these whores have to do with official corruption in New York City?"

Luther said: "He used these women to placate the judge. God knows what else he used them for."

"Is there any evidence that Tucker dispensed judicial favors in return for what these women gave him?"

"Well, it's all part of the setup," Luke said.

"Let's get Josh over here," Luther said. When I nodded, Luke silently gave him the number, and Luther went into the bedroom to call.

"Nothing to get upset about, Kel," Luke said. "If the women are parts of Remington's operation, they should be brought in."

"Let's wait until Josh gets here," was the quiet reply.

We waited for over an hour before Josh returned. I noticed for the first time that he looked tired. There were lines in his face; his dark beard was showing and his eyes were dull with fatigue.

"They had to give Benny a sleeping pill," he said shortly. "I arranged with Justice to let him stay in the suite with the marshals. Molly's not coming over; she's got a room next to him." He walked to the portable bar and poured a stiff drink. "Lacey's staying with Molly. She won't leave her."

"Lacey's always around when the going gets rough," Kelly said. He looked up at Josh, and for a long moment they studied each other.

"I gave that story to Sissy, if that's what's on your mind," Josh said. "The reason is simple—she was on network, and because you made an ass of yourself with Larsen." He took a swallow. "I told you we had to live with these people. If you want to belt Larsen, wait until the damned hearings are over, and then you can throw him into the Potomac for all I care."

"If Larsen makes another crack about any member of my family, I'll shove him through a wall," Kelly said tersely, "and I don't care if he represents a thousand papers from New York to Alaska. But Larsen's not important tonight—Sissy Southworth's story is. Where did it come from?"

"I told you I gave it to her," Josh said calmly. It's all part of the investigation. Remington used this madam as a fringe benefit for Tucker."

"I know every line of the reports on Tucker, Remington, Saunders, and the Transcontinental Trading Corporation in New York. This man sold his verdicts for money, not sex!"

Josh gave him a cold smile. "Sex helped."

"Do these women have knowledge of corruption on Tucker's part?"

"I don't think he's that stupid."

"Then what's the purpose of bringing them in to testify?"

"Headlines," Josh said bluntly. "In two days there's going to be a shoot for Venus from Cape Kennedy. The papers will start building it up tomorrow. Let's face it: if we have to compete with Venus—let's do it on her own ground."

"I don't want any whores in this hearing," Kelly said flatly. "The facts are shocking enough. I don't want any cheap sensationalism. I think it will take away from what we're trying to do."

"I think you're wrong, Kel," Luke said. "These women are part of the case—"

"Prove to me they know something about Tucker, Remington, or Saunders' corruption, and I'll put them on," Kelly said. "I'm not going to put them on for just what Josh said he wants—headlines."

"Don't be a choirboy," Luke said testily. "It's just as Josh said—Tucker is stupid but not that stupid, and neither is Remington. He used this whore to set the stage. . . ."

"Remington didn't need a whore," Kelly said. "All he had to do was wave money in front of the judge. The man was helplessly in debt playing the market when Remington appeared. Tucker would have sold his robes at the time if Remington asked him to."

255

"But Remington didn't know that," Josh said. "That's why he got Jello to contact Eva."

"She's an alien, isn't she?"

"She's here six months from Hamburg. So is her girl."

"Have someone make up a report and turn it over to Immigration," Kelly said. "I don't want any part of it."

"You have to," Josh said. "Jones is not that high-minded. He likes girls on the stand, testifying."

"If he brings them in, I'll leave the hearing," Kelly said.

Josh stared at him. "You're kidding!"

"Then try me," he said softly. He rose and stretched. "Let's go over the hearing for tomorrow; then I want to turn in."

Josh finished his drink and carefully set his glass down. "Is that the way you want it?"

"That's exactly the way I want it, Josh," Kelly said evenly.

"You're making a mistake, you know."

"Fine. Then it's my mistake, not yours."

"Let's talk about it tomorrow," Luke said tersely.

"We're not going to talk about anything tomorrow—we're going to talk about it tonight," Kelly said, still studying Josh.

For a tense moment I thought, This is it; this is the blowoff. But it wasn't. Josh just waved his hand nonchalantly.

"Okay. If that's the way Kelly wants it, that's it—no whores. Now, who's going to be the first witness in the morning?"

Luke gave me a look of wild relief and hurried to get the pile of folders on the table across the room.

"We ended with Benny introducing Judge Tucker's name for the first time," Kelly began. "Suppose we just let him lay the foundation."

Within a few minutes they were deep in a discussion of Jello's testimony for the next day. It was as if nothing had happened.

The storm had passed, but in a tiny corner of my mind its angry growl could still be heard.

Until the early hours we went over Jello's statement and subsequent reports on Tucker, Remington, and the D&B report on their company. Then, as the whine of the early shift filled the corridors, we tumbled into bed.

"What are you going to do about Jones?" I asked Josh as I eased my old bones between the sheets.

"What about him?"

"The reporters will mob him tomorrow about Sissy's story."

"I'll tell him we want to steer clear of that angle for a while."

"You'll have to give him an excuse."

"The best in the world." He yawned, and turned on his side. "We found a black book in the dame's apartment that contained the unlisted phone numbers of certain members of Congress."

That did it, of course. Jones was eager to have Eva testify, but when Josh told him why he couldn't he swallowed hard and quickly agreed there was no point in making the hearings unnecessarily sensational. Josh wrote out a brief, ambiguous statement for Jones that, while confirming Sissy's story, double-talked about how that phase of the investigation wasn't complete because another federal agency was helping us, and because of that the committee could not comment.

Investigation that isn't complete is the greatest. You give it out knowing it will never be complete, and in a few days the reporters will have forgotten about it anyway.

Jello was visibly nervous when he took the stand at noon the next day. He was pale and sweaty, and continually rolled a handkerchief between his hands. Molly was in the audience now, with Lacey at her side. Grymes, of course, was not present. The hospital bulletin said he would be confined for some weeks.

In the hearing room there were the usual starting clamor and running barrage of questions by the reporters, with Sissy and Tuck Larsen snarling and spitting at each other like angry cats. Then Kelly leaned over to whisper assuringly to Benny, and the day's hearing started.

Q. Yesterday, just before we recessed, you were discussing a Justice Prebel Tucker.

A. Yes, sir. Judge Tucker.

Q. Did you know him as Judge Prebel Tucker, presiding Justice of the Federal Court of Appeals?

A. That's right. He was a real big-shot judge.

Q. How did you meet him?

A. Through Remington.

Q. Describe your first meeting with Judge Tucker.

A. Well, one day Remington came down to the club, and he was looking bad. He had been belting the booze a lot, and when I asked him what was wrong he said his wife was on his back. He said they had a big fight because she wanted him to buy a nightspot in Miami. He said it wasn't in his line and that those guys who operate down there were in the mob, and he didn't mind making a buck with them but didn't want to be their partners. Somehow partners either wind up broke or in the river. I didn't say anything to him, but I knew what the score was with his wife.

Q. What was that?

A. Joey Americus told me. She had gotten friendly with some guy who owned a joint on East Sixty-eighth Street, and it was this guy's club she wanted Remington to buy into. From what he told me she was a real bitch—pardon me—a mean woman. I didn't blame the poor guy for getting stoned. Like I said, when you marry a woman make sure she has lots of kids and a lot of work.

Q.   (Jones) What was that?

A.   (Shannon) The witness said, Congressman, that his philosophy is that when you marry be sure you have plenty of children to occupy your wife's time.

(Jones) I can't argue with that, Witness.

Q.   (Shannon) How did this lead to Judge Tucker?

A.   Well, we got to talking, and Remington said he had a lead that could eventually mean a lot of money for both of us. He said he wanted to get next to a big judge named Tucker, Chief Justice of the Federal Court of Appeals, a real big man. Through a lawyer he had heard the judge could be bought but that he would only deal with a few trusted lawyers. He was a very, very careful man.

Q.   And was a contact made?

A.   Yes. Remington got in touch with this lawyer who had tipped him off that the judge loved money. Then this lawyer set up the judge for a meeting. It took a long time, but finally Remington called me and I met the judge.

Q.   Where was this?

A.   The Bailiff's Corner restaurant on the east side of Foley Square, where all the judges and lawyers go.

Q.   What was discussed at this meeting?

A.   Nothing much the first time. The judge just sat there and ate; he eats like a horse even though he's a little skinny old guy, and didn't say much. But later, as we got to know him, we talked more. He let on he didn't like to talk dough in front of both of us, only with Remington. Then Remington would come in and tell me what happened.

Q.   What was the first case you were involved in with the judge?

A.   There was this big hotel corporation that was going into receivership. They owned a hotel on Fifth and Fifty-second Street and others in Chicago, Philly, and all over. They also owned a chain of motels across the country. There was sort of a family stock fight going on, and the places were slipping. Then they had a big fire in Chicago, and that didn't help things. Somehow Remington made a connection and found out everything and had the case shifted to Tucker. Remington sold the judge on appointing him trustee, then setting up some phony company that would sell the hotels' things like rugs, silverware, chairs, and all the stuff that a hotel would need. We would do it through a company Remington called Transcontinental Trading Corporation, with a hole-in-the-wall office on Stone Street. Because I knew a lot of guys in the linen and supply companies that usually worked with the restaurants owned by the mob, I was elected to set up the companies.

Q.   And did you set up the companies?

A.   I did. I had about ten names with box numbers all over the country, but even they eventually came back to Transcontinental Trading.

Q.   That was the parent company?

A.   That's right.

Q.   And what about the supplies? Were they really sold to the hotels?

A.   Yes. It was—it was poor stuff. One time we set up a deal in which the Fifth Avenue hotel was to get carpeting in the lobby and on every floor, corridor, and room. I went up and looked over the carpet. It wasn't bad, but out it came. Then we ordered $75,000 worth of new carpeting from our own company. I contracted for the cheapest I could find. It was so cheap that three months later the manager said the nap was coming off in the maids' vacuum cleaners.

Q.   What did you do with this complaint?

A.   We had all kinds of letterheads. Remington just had a nice letter sent from our phony carpeting company promising to send an inspector around to look the carpet over. We always did that: just be nice; promise them everything but give them nothing.

Q.   What other companies did you establish?

A.   The judge didn't overlook a bet. One day he said he had eaten in the Fifth Avenue hotel and that the prices were the highest he had ever seen. Imagine this guy! He's robbing the place blind and complaining about the prices! (*Laughter*) Like I told Remington —we can take lessons from this crook! We had a meeting in the Bailiff's Corner, and Remington said that maybe we could take over the food bills for all the hotels. This went into hundreds of thousands of dollars every month. I said this looked like it might be too big for us, but both the judge and Remington talked me into it.

Q.   By this time, I gather, you and the judge were on friendly terms.

A.   We were buddies.

Q.   Now he didn't seem reluctant to talk money or bribery?

A.   Well, he never came out and said it that way. He always talked of fees and things of that kind.

Q.   Please continue.

A.   Well, I knew guys in the markets, mostly chickens who worked with restaurants and joints the mob had taken over. Maybe for a loan a guy couldn't pay to the sharks they would take his restaurant. I went to them and we set up another company. All we did was arrange for these places to deliver meat and poultry.

Q.   Was it foodstuffs of good quality?

A.   It wasn't prime like they had before, I can tell you. Maybe the steaks could be used by a shoemaker, and the chickens were on Medicare. (*Laughter*)

Q. (Jones) But didn't you people realize you were destroying an old and reputable business?

A. We were milking it, Your Honor. Right down to the last pretzel.

Q. (Shannon) And you didn't get any complaints?

A. Complaints you never heard! We sold them silverware that came from Hoboken and we had them stamped Sheffield. The kitchen help could never get the stains off them, and the knives were so dull they couldn't cut cream. When they squawked we sent them one of our sorry letters, and that was that.

Q. Didn't any of the executives of the hotels complain?

A. We had one guy in Chicago that threatened to blow the whistle. But I got one of the meat boys to make a few calls to Chicago. This guy received a call and was told to come to a certain chicken market on Chicago's West Side. When he said he wasn't going to visit any chicken market, he was told if he didn't he would be plucked like a hen. So he went over there. They just told him he would be dumped in the river if he kept talking; so he saw the light, and left.

Q. Were there any other projects similar to Transcontinental Trading?

A. Oh, yes. The judge suggested to Remington that maybe Saunders could tip us on some big cases that were ready to go into court and we could be ready for them.

Q. (Jones) That was your man at City Hall, wasn't it?

A. That's right, Your Honor.

Q. Is that the first time he was brought into this new arrangement?

A. Yes, sir. Remington had a meeting with Saunders and the judge. I wasn't there because Saunders seemed to be leery of meeting me.

Q. Why was that?

A. He knew I knew what the score was, and this he didn't like.

Q. And did Saunders bring you any new business?

A. He tipped us off that a suit was going to be filed against a big bus company by some stockholders who claimed the chairman of the board had been given some fantastic bonuses. This looked good to us. I guess the chairman was a thief like we were, but with some more class. Tucker managed to get the case, and after a few months I got a call from Remington. He said he wanted me to go to an office on Broadway and Forty-fifth Street and pick up a valise. He said to be very careful; it contained $240,000 in cash. I almost fell over. He said to bring it to the judge's chambers right away. Remington said he and the judge had arranged a phony loan from the bus company, and the judge in the next few weeks would dismiss the suit.

Q.   (Shannon) And did you pick up the valise and give it to the judge?
A.   I did.
Q.   What was the office where you picked it up?
A.   It was Quick & Best, a public-relations firm. I was to ask for Mr. Best and he would give me the valise.

Kelly gave me a look, and I nodded. This was a new name, and I sent it into the pool of investigators who were standing by for such developments. By now Benny was visibly nervous. The words poured from his lips. The only sounds in the room besides his harsh, guttural voice were the muted description of the radio announcers, the muttered orders of the TV crews, and their shifting and moving of their rubber-wheeled cameras.

I had received a few terse notes from Josh: Benny was coming over great, but try to calm him down; the polls were showing our audience was growing by the hour. It seemed many a kitchen was being left unattended. Josh also pointed out that Kelly was beginning to catch on, particularly in the Midwest. Once I slipped into the investigators' room. It was a fascinating experience. The blinds had been lowered to shut out the blinding morning sun, and there was Benny in the semigloom, nodding and smiling as he spun his tale of official evil.

When Kelly appeared on the screen, I could see in an instant why the housewives were leaving their dishes and mops. Something came out of that glass tube that just captured the viewer. The set was surrounded by rows of chairs, occupied by members of our committee, clerks, stenographers, investigators, and employees of the building.

"Any good?" I asked one man.

"Kefauver was never this good," he said. "This Shannon's a hell of a boy."

I said cautiously, "I remember his old man."

The man gave me a grunt of disgust. "He was an old bastard. This kid's nothing like him."

Score one for our side, I told myself as I went back to the hearing room.

At the point where Jello was about to tell how he picked up the valise of money, an attendant handed Kelly a note. He read it quickly, nodded as if in agreement, then whispered to Jones, who apparently agreed. Kelly then banged his gavel and ordered a recess until the next day. It was perfect timing. We now had an audience of millions who would rush back to their set the following day.

Before Benny left the stand, sweat streaming down his face, he leaned over to Kelly and said something. He seemed to be pleading. Kelly nodded and patted him on the back. There was the usual press of reporters about Kelly and Jones, but although I kept an eye on Larsen he didn't do much but glower. Now I noticed a change in the attitudes of the newspapermen toward Kelly. It was clear that his personal attractiveness was beginning to tell. It was noticeable, too, as we walked down the hall to the TV room. Stenographers, clerks, and secretaries were beginning to smile at him; men called out and waved. Washington's invisible telegraph was tapping out a message that said Kelly Shannon had the smell of success; and in this city that loves only success, and despises and fears failure, the message was being listened to. Before the night was ended, it would be repeated over tables in the Senate Restaurant, in bars, in the Golden Key, in buses, taxicabs, and over dinner tables. The outline of the Image was finished. Now must come the gentle shading.

"I want your people to continue polling all night long if you have to," Josh was barking into a telephone when Kelly and I entered the TV room. "I want to split the questions. The hearing, fine, but I also want to know about Kelly. What do they think? What do they like about him? What don't they like? Okay? Fine. You can get me at the hotel all night."

He picked up another phone. "Hey, John—how you doing? Fine. Great. Yeah, it's a hell of a hearing. Wait until we really get going." He listened and grinned at us, then said: "If you send your writer and photographer—who's going to do the piece, by the way? Oh, good. He does a good job. Have them come down and ask for me. We'll set it up."

He hung up and grabbed a sandwich from the buffet set up against the wall.

"You were great today, Kelly," he said. "Benny was really rolling. I'm glad you cut it off as I suggested. Remember, always leave them hanging."

"I'm going to see Benny," Kelly said. "Just before he left he whispered to me that he really cooked his goose today."

Josh frowned. "Why today?"

"Apparently those hoods in the meat or supply houses don't care for publicity," Kelly said dryly. "Want me for anything before I go?"

"That was *Look* on the phone," Josh said. "They're sending one of their writers down with a photographer over the weekend. They want to do a cover story on you and Benny."

"Do we have to? By the weekend Benny may be ready to climb walls."

Luther said, "He did look a little jittery."

"He begged me to see him," Kelly said. "Is Lacey still with Molly?"

"They just went back to Benny. They're having dinner together again."

"I'm going to join them," Kelly said.

"We have a hell of a lot of things to go over, Kelly. I want Luke and Luther to go back upstate tomorrow and start preparing for the announcement of your candidacy. And don't forget, next Sunday is the Bishops' Relief Dinner." He turned to me. "By the way, Finn, did the senator make that call to the Power House?"

"Oh, two weeks ago."

"Then it's all set?"

"Queens, Brooklyn, and the big one at the Waldorf with the bishop."

"We want to make hay that night," Josh said. "I think we should start kicking around what you're going to say."

"I don't think I'll have any trouble," Kelly said quietly. "We can discuss it tomorrow or the next day."

"We won't have a damn minute with this hearing going the way it is?" Josh snapped. "Let's grab a bite here and shoot right back to—"

"I told you I'm going to see Benny," Kelly said.

"Christ, do you have to hold his hand every minute?" Josh said angrily. "Lacey has to wet-nurse this old dame, and now you're running over there every time he starts to weep! We have a campaign coming up! Or isn't that more important than a miserable little thief?"

"Molly's a dear and valued old friend of Lacey's," Kelly said quietly, "and as for Jello—I told you before, Josh, I consider him my responsibility. I brought him here. I don't think it matters what he is—the man's on the verge of hysterics. After all, he's helping us, and the least we can do is talk to him."

"Let's talk to him all he wants," Josh growled, "but not on my time."

"Your time, Josh?" Kelly asked thoughtfully. "I thought it was *my* time."

CHAPTER FOURTEEN: TROUBLE IN THE HEEL OF
THE HUNT

MY MOTHER ONCE TOLD ME, when the rains came just as everything was looking rosy, that it is always best to expect trouble in the heel of the hunt; it's a time when the horse never clears the stones or the hounds lose the scent or some member of the gentry falls on her glory and has to be carried to the big house. Mother got that from her father, who was the best poacher in the county and, as the saying went, took more skins from under the landlord's nose than there are bogs in all Ireland. He came across one jump from a warrant and stayed with us when I was a child. He was really the first McCool in New York politics: he was sheriff, alderman, and a power on the West Side. But he was a rebel, always fighting the organization or refusing to go along with things. He'd come in the house on Election eve shaking his cane and roaring that there was trouble in the heel of the hunt but that, by God, he'd lick it.

Trouble in the heel of the hunt. The words drifted back to me when our troubles began. In the beginning they were minor compared to the future. It started in the early hours of the morning. Investigators had been coming and going all night; they had found Roger Best, president of the public relations firm of Quick & Best, and it developed they had handled public relations for the bus company. Best had made some damaging admissions to them; in fact, he identified Benny's picture as the man he gave the valise to, and after a great deal of squirming he also admitted he knew it contained a large sum of money that was to go to "some judge," but denied he knew it was Tucker.

Josh snapped to the investigator on the phone: "He's a lying bastard. Tell him he's going to be indicted. Do you think he'll bend if you lean on him? Right. You gave him a subpoena, of course? Good. Returnable tomorrow? Fine. Now go back and scare the hell out of him. Make him give. Tell him that we know the whole story and that if he lies we'll turn his testimony over to the U.S. Attorney's office by Friday and he'll be indicted for perjury. Got that? Good luck, and call us back as soon as you leave him."

Kelly had returned to the suite about ten o'clock; though this had Josh fuming, he said nothing. The senator had gone to bed, and Luke and Luther were on the phone in the adjacent room, running up an enormous phone bill to find out how America's TV viewers liked the hearings—and Kelly. They did. The reports had been wonderful all night; we now had an audience estimated at more than twenty million. Kelly had clicked. He was a new, fresh face, and was catching on. The reports were so good Josh had the senator send word along to the proper channels that orders were to be given to the TV crews to move in on Kelly for more close-ups when he was conducting the questioning. After Kelly finally arrived, we all went to work on Jello's testimony of the next day. Josh and Kelly examined the story of the bus-company scandal in minute detail, with Josh suggesting questions paced to arrive at Tucker's shocking decision dismissing the complaint against the board chairman.

It was then the call came in. Josh answered it in the next room; he was casual enough when he came out, but I knew him well enough to know something had happened.

"An old friend from Dakota is in for a convention and wants me to run over to the Congressional for a few minutes."

Luke got up and rubbed his eyes. "I don't know about you guys, but I've had it for tonight."

"Why don't we call it quits?" Kelly suggested. "It's almost two o'clock in the morning."

"Suppose we hop over and see my friend," Josh said to me. "It will only take us a few minutes."

It was on the tip of my tongue to suggest that any friend who called at this hour could jump into the drink when I caught the warning look in his eyes—something was up. "Let me get my coat," I said.

"We'll see you in the morning, Josh," Kelly called out as we were leaving.

"Bright and early," Josh said as he stood in the doorway. "Luke, you and Luther get together when you want to leave for upstate."

"As soon as the hearings here are over," Luke said. "Probably Saturday."

"Fine. Good night."

Once the door closed, I asked him what was wrong.

"That was one of the marshals," he said, jabbing savagely at the elevator button. "There's trouble over at the hotel."

"With Benny?"

"With Benny, with Molly, with the whole God-damn mess," he snarled.

"But what's the trouble?"

"All I know is, the marshal wants someone over in a hurry; that old bitch is screaming like someone put lye in her coffee."

In a few minutes we arrived at the hotel where Benny and Molly were staying, and hurried to Benny's suite. When Josh pushed the doorbell button I thought I heard muffled sobbing, but then the door swung open. It was one of the marshals, looking troubled and anxious.

"What happened?" Josh demanded.

"Just before I called, a lieutenant on the New York State Police phoned for Miss Shapiro. I didn't want to give her the call, but he said he had permission from the department because it was personal and urgent. I thought it had to do with some accident in her family, so I gave her the call." He arched his neck nervously. "She listened for a few minutes, then dropped the telephone and screamed like a stuck cat. If Miss Shannon wasn't here, we'd have had our hands full with her yelling around and Benny shouting he was going to dive out the nearest window."

"What happened, man?" I said. "Tell us."

"The state trooper called to tell her someone had burned down her house. According to what he told Miss Shannon, there isn't a stick left."

"Where is she now?"

He nodded to a door. "She's in there with Miss Shannon"—he jerked his head to a door across the room—"and Benny's in there."

"What's Benny doing?"

"He keeps saying he's not going on tomorrow. He kept shouting he wants to tell Congressman Shannon. That's why I called the congressman when you answered the phone."

"I'll take care of them both," Josh said.

"I think perhaps I had better talk to the congressman," the marshal said hesitantly. "Or maybe the chairman."

"I said I'll take care of everything. Is Miss Shannon in with her now?"

"Yes, sir. She's got the old woman calmed down a lot. But before—"

Josh slowly opened the door and walked into the adjacent room. I followed him.

Molly was sitting in a chair near the window. Now there were no skillfully applied cosmetics, no expensive hairdo, no skin-tight girdle or fine dress. This was a frightened middle-aged woman. Standing beside her was Lacey, an angry, bitter Lacey when she turned to us.

"Hello, Molly," Josh said softly.

"Did you hear what happened?" Lacey said.

"The marshal just told me. I'm terribly sorry."

"It was all I had," Molly said, moaning and clasping and unclasping her fingers. "It was all I had."

"I'm sure something can be done," Josh began, but Lacey turned on him.

"What would you suggest, Mr. Michaels?"

"I don't know, offhand, but I'll think of something."

"Yes, you always do—don't you?"

"How's Benny?"

"Fine. He's not going back on tomorrow, and I'm taking Molly home."

"Molly can go where she wants to, but Benny's going back on that stand, Lacey."

"What do you intend to do, drag him back on?" Lacey asked scornfully.

"No. He's going to walk on," Josh said, "just as Molly's going to tell him to do."

"Molly's not going to tell him any such thing—"

"You know what will happen to Benny, Molly," Josh said in a low, level voice, speaking directly to the pale, drawn face and frightened eyes. "They'll throw him into the pen, and in a month he'll either be in the hospital or in the morgue. You know that, Molly; you've known that from the very beginning; that's why you came to us."

"My God, how can you torture her?" Lacey cried.

"Why don't you get off your God-damned high horse for a change?" Josh snapped. "Forget the bleeding hearts and the do-gooders. That's an ex-con in the next room, a three-time loser who's blowing the whistle on some of the biggest men in the country. Did you hear what he said yesterday about that hotel manager in Chicago? He called some of his boys and they went over to pay this manager a visit. 'Keep quiet or find yourself in the river,' they told him. That's not me talking; that's quoting Benny and some of his friends! Come off it, Lacey; this is no social tea we're at. Benny goes the limit, or by Christ I'll throw him to the hogs!"

There were only the blood pulsating in my ears, the faint whirr of a descending elevator, the rapid breathing of Molly, who stared up at Josh.

"I never thought you could do this," Lacey whispered. "Never."

"Maybe someday you'll understand," Josh said. We turned to the marshal. "Get him in here."

The marshal opened the door a few inches, whispered to someone. There was a mumble of conversation, followed by a squeak of bedsprings; then Benny was standing in the doorway.

"Get in here," Josh said roughly.

"I don't want to talk to you," Benny said. "I want Shannon."

"Get in here and shut up, you crawling little bum," Josh said.

"Benny," Molly sobbed. "Benny."

"Can't you see you're tearing her apart?" Lacey cried.

"I told Molly that if you don't get back on that stand tomorrow, I'll have the DA come down and get you," Josh said. "I'll make sure the judge throws the God-damn book at you so hard you'll never get up." He walked over to Benny and asked in a low tone, "You know what I mean, don't you, Benny?"

"They burned down her house," he whined.

"So be glad you weren't in it," Josh snapped. "Just remember what I said—go back on the stand or go to the pen. . . ." He nodded to the marshals, who gently nudged the pudgy little man. Benny licked his lips, looked from Molly to Josh, and without a word walked back into the other room.

"Get him a sleeping pill," Josh told the marshal before he closed the door.

"Does Kelly know about this?" Lacey demanded.

"I'll tell him about it," Josh said.

"Don't worry—I'll tell him," Lacey said. "Molly, will you be all right?"

"Sure. Don't worry about me, Lacey. And thank you."

"Where are you going?" Josh asked as Lacey reached for her coat.

"I'm going to see Kelly."

"You're only going to wake up Kelly, and besides, Molly needs you," Josh pointed out.

Lacey stood in the center of the room, one arm in her coat and obviously fighting back angry tears.

"Who do you think you are, twisting and bending people's lives just to help yourself?"

"It's not to help me," Josh said quietly; "it's to help your brother."

"Well, I don't want you to help my brother—not this way," she cried. "Don't you understand?"

"You're the one who doesn't understand," Josh said wearily. "We're all at a point of no return. You just can't go in there tomorrow and turn those hearings off like a faucet."

"He's right, Lacey," Molly said in a dull voice. "Benny started it; he must finish it. Maybe someday it will help."

"They can't give you a guarantee the law will let him go," Lacey said. She whirled on Josh. "Can they? Tell her the truth."

"When the hearings are over, the DA said he'll let Benny take a plea to a lesser charge," Josh said evenly. "Then it's just a formality before he gets out."

"So we'll have to wait a few more weeks," Molly said. "Mr. Michaels is right, Lacey. It's the best way."

"You'd better stay with her," Josh said. He took Lacey's coat and draped it across a chair. "Why don't you both take something and get some sleep?" He glanced at his watch. "We'd better shove off too, Finn; it's almost four o'clock."

We left them as we had found them, Molly beaten, dejected, staring out the window, Lacey holding her hand.

We rode back to the hotel in silence. The only time Josh spoke was when he said: "I had to tell her that, Finn. I just had to."

What could I say—that it was a cruel lie, that we both knew Benny would never get out, and her pitiful, middle-aged dreams would never come through?

In the morning, as usual, we all had breakfast together to go over the agenda for the day's hearing. After we had sat down, Josh lost no time in telling Kelly and the others what had happened.

"Trying to intimidate a congressional witness by arson—that's incredible!" Kelly said. "What's being done?"

"The New York State Police are investigating, of course."

"What about the federal agencies? Justice, the FBI?"

"The AG's office is handling it."

"This makes me believe they might try to harm Jello," Kelly said.

"He's well protected."

"God, losing that house will break Molly's heart," Kelly said. "Who would do a thing like that?"

"Who knows?" Josh replied. "Benny realized from the start the syndicates would never vote him the man of the year if he testified."

"But to burn a woman's house down!"

"The house is burned, Kel," the practical Luke said. "Now let's decide what we can do for her."

"We'll build her a bigger and better house," the senator said. "It will still be the showplace of the county."

"Money can't replace the priceless items she had," Kelly pointed out. "How can you replace that Kentucky long rifle she used to show us when we were kids?"

"They make replicas of everything these days," the senator said. "Even those old Civil War guns."

Kelly gave him a look of exasperation and turned to Josh. "That must have shaken up Benny."

"It did. He didn't want to go back on."

"Did you talk to him?"

"I did." Josh sipped his coffee. "He'll be back today."

"Come on, Kel, let's get back to what you're going to say Sunday night," Luke said impatiently.

"I'll work on it over the weekend."

"Do you want Finn and me to contribute anything?"

"Of course." He added slowly, "Suppose we announce that the committee will subpoena Mullady?"

"You might hint at that without naming him. But I wouldn't go all out. Give yourself a fire escape. It could still sound like dynamite."

"Why not just come out and name him?"

"Because I don't think we've reached that point."

"When do you think we will?"

"I haven't seen that memorandum Abernathy promised."

"Still seeing is believing, Josh?"

"When it comes to Abernathy blowing the whistle on Barney Mullady? Yes. In spades. I want it all down on paper, notarized. And then under oath."

"I never doubted for a minute he would give it to us."

"Fine. When he does, let's talk about Mullady."

"Suppose Benny refused to go on today?" Kelly asked. "What would we have done, Josh?"

"Cite him for contempt and throw him back in the pen." He looked at Kelly intently. "You're getting at something, Kelly. What is it?"

"I'm worried about Benny's safety. If I thought for a minute he would be harmed, I'd excuse him as a witness."

"That would mean the end of the hearings as far as I'm concerned," Josh said coolly, evenly, directly to Kelly.

"Don't be a fool, Michaels," the senator said gruffly. "No one's going to end these hearings."

"The hearings must continue until Jello finishes preparing the way for the judge's appearance and then identifies Remington and Saunders in the courtroom," Josh said. "He's the informer, the accuser, the committee's main source of its charges."

"A confrontation?" Luke said, surprised. "Benny identifying both of them?"

"Just like Chambers and Hiss," Josh said. "I want Benny to walk down from the witness stand and tap them both on the shoulder while twenty million watch him do it. Then if we can get the judge, I want him to do the same thing."

Luther said: "That will polish it off very nicely. This is all in New York?"

"Before Remington and Saunders take the stand. That's why he's needed—"

"Suppose I excused him?" Kelly pressed. "Suppose the man's life was in such danger it wouldn't be human to let him continue?"

"As I said, that would end the hearings. There wouldn't be any more need for me to stay."

"You mean you'd walk out?" Luke said. "Leave the whole campaign?"

"As fast as my two little feet will carry me," Josh said cheerfully. "As far as I'm concerned, this hearing with all its implications is a hell of a lot

269

more important than the fears of a thief who's been crying from the first day he found himself in a police station." He said to Kelly, "If you're going to excuse him, Kelly, tell me now."

All eyes turned to Kelly, who was idly making circles in the tablecloth with the prongs of a fork.

"I have no plans to excuse him—now," he said at last. "But I warn all of you—if I receive information—information that I consider reliable, that there is a plot to kill Jello, I will excuse him as a witness before this committee."

"Stool pigeons are always afraid," the senator growled. "It's their occupational disease."

"It's not unbelievable that something could happen to him," Kelly said. "Didn't they kill a Kefauver witness to keep him quiet?"

"Can we arrange it?" Luke asked with a grin.

"That's nothing to joke about, Luke," Kelly said sternly.

"Anything can happen," Josh said. "They even shoot Presidents. Don't worry, Kelly; no one's going to get to Benny."

"I don't know. They burned Molly's house down, and if you told me yesterday that that would be done I would have laughed at you." Kelly pushed the fork aside. "I don't know about you people, but to me human life means a great deal—even a criminal's."

"What a nice morbid breakfast," Luke said.

"Well, is Jello going back on?" Josh asked Kelly.

"You really don't think there's any danger?"

"Not while he's a congressional witness. He has marshals with him day and night."

"He's as well guarded as the President," the senator said.

"That's the irony of it," Luther murmured. "A petty thief guarded as carefully as the President."

In the tiny interval of silence the phone in the next room rang. Luke answered it and came back, glum-faced.

"Well, Benny's not going to take the stand today—whether we want him to or not—"

"Why? Who was that?"

"The AG's office. Jello's had an attack of kidney colic. It's painful, but nothing serious. They just took him to the Washington Hospital. The doctor said it's from tension—"

"Molly?"

"Lacey and Molly went with him. The marshal said he had a message from Benny for Josh."

Josh looked up and said sharply, "What is it?"

"He told the marshal to tell you he was going on just one more time."

"That's all we need him for," Josh said. "When will they let him out?"

"The marshal said over the weekend. He'll be out by Sunday."

"But what do we do today?" Luther asked anxiously. "Dyke said last night they expect fifteen million viewers."

"I suppose we'll have to call it off," Luke said.

"Make an announcement that Benny is—"

"We can't," Josh said shortly. "The edge would be taken off. We have to go on."

"Why? A man can get sick, can't he?"

"That story about Molly's house being burned down is bound to get out," Josh pointed out, "and a bastard like Tuck Larsen will walk all over us in the papers and on his show. A great big congressional committee canceling its hearings because the house of the principal witness' girl-friend was burned down!"

"But if we prove that Benny's sick?"

"That will only be a paragraph in the story. Nobody will believe it."

I could see Josh's point. While Benny's illness was real, the burning of Molly's house would be a sensational story, and if the hearings were shut off so abruptly, the image we had been creating of Kelly, the crusader, the dedicated foe of evil, would be badly tarnished. Although no one would really say so, the inference would be that he was frightened or his witnesses so intimidated he had called off the hearings.

"Do you have any ideas, Josh?" Luther asked.

"I have one cooking. Just give me a minute," he said, half to himself. He automatically stirred the cold coffee as we watched him. Then he spoke, slowly, carefully, as though he were letting the thoughts come out as they flickered across his brain.

"We can still make today's session exciting by putting on the Singers along with some other witnesses."

"The Singers?" Luke asked dubiously.

"Their appearance would be only part of the show," Josh said. "This is what I have in mind. From our investigators' reports we know the Singers hijacked a truck from Philly and that they stashed it away in a garage on West Sixteenth Street, just off Ninth Avenue in Manhattan. We know that, but the cops don't. We also know the Singers are waiting for things to cool down before they contact a fence. It's the only truck in the place with Pennsylvania plates. What I propose to do is tip off the networks something big will break in the city today and that they can get in on it if they assign some crews to stand by with one of our people. Luther, you'll be that contact. What I want you to do is gather those TV crews and park, say, two or three blocks from the Sixteenth Street garage. Hire a Sony to keep track of the hearings. When the Singers take the stand, one of the questions Kelly will ask is, What do you know of a truck hijacked three weeks ago on Route One near New Brunswick, New Jersey? That's your cue, Luther. Get the crews over to Ninth Avenue and into that place. After they get their shots, call me and I will tip off the deputy police inspector who's sitting in on the hearings as an observer where the place is. Don't let the crews go, because the cops will knock it off right away. It will make some great shots."

"The garage is private. They may tell me to drop dead," Luther said.

Josh said impatiently, "I thought of that." He took a black wallet from inside his jacket and flipped it open to show an impressive legal-looking document with a bright gold badge.

"You're now a member of the Jones Committee, a representative of the United States Government."

Luther took the wallet. "Who'll follow the Singers to the stand?"

"Their old man. As I get it, the family is frightened to death, and he'll probably lie, but we may get something out of him. Finn, did they ever find Benny's pal Noodles?"

"No. The New York cops say he's still among the missing."

"You gave out his yellow sheet and rogues' gallery pictures, didn't you?"

"When he was first mentioned."

"Okay. Give them out again. We'll have Kelly announce New York has a thirteen-state alarm out for him."

"That sounds like enough excitement to satisfy them," Luther said. "Do you think there's time to arrange it all, Josh?"

"The hearings don't start until afternoon," Josh said. "Senator, you can make some calls to New York and get the networks excited before Luther gets down there."

"Well, that saves the day," Luke said, slapping his hands together. "What about tomorrow?"

"Pick up the minor witnesses, have a short afternoon hearing, and recess until Tuesday. Let Jones announce the hearings will continue in New York in the Federal Building. After the hearing tomorrow, Kelly can hold a press conference and hint something big will come off in New York. Over the weekend, I'll slip Sissy another story and get everyone excited. Senator, do you want to start making those calls?"

"Right away," the senator said and wheeled himself into the bedroom. He called out, "Where will I tell them to have the crews meet Luther?"

"Tell them Luther will call from the airport."

"I'll grab some breakfast when I get to the city," Luther said as he slid into his coat. "Keep your fingers crossed."

"Don't worry about it. You'll have to make a big score when those cops kick in the doors," Josh said. "Just make sure the cameras are set up. Good luck."

With a wave Luther was gone.

"I think we should start going over those Singer reports again, Kelly," Josh said. "You should crawl all over them when they get on the stand."

"Don't you think someone should go over and see Benny?"

"Finn and I will run over to the hospital before the hearings start,"

Josh said. He picked up a thick report and thumbed through the pages. "Here's the part where it tells how the Singers hijacked that truck."

Around noon Josh and I visited Benny in the hospital. The doctors confirmed that the attack was painful but nothing serious and that he would be released on Sunday. Molly was there with Lacey, and Benny, drowsy from sedation, whispered to Josh as he leaned over: "I told them to tell you one more day—right? One more and that's it . . . right?"

"Don't worry about it, Benny," he said. "After next Monday you'll be free as a bird."

Those words would stay in my memory forever.

There was a bit of a stir in the press section when Jones read the announcement explaining Benny's absence and revealing that because many of the other witnesses had pressing business, the committee would hear them this day. But I saw that the pressing-business nonsense didn't impress Larsen. He leaned over and whispered to one of his young legmen, who nodded and hurried out.

Trouble from that quarter, I told myself. I sent a note back to Josh and got one in return: "The hell with him. Don't forget the yellow sheets for the press section."

The first witnesses were the Singer brothers. They looked hard and dangerous. Both were dressed in dark, conservative suits and appeared to be businessmen instead of criminals with long and impressive records.

They were accompanied by a lawyer who always seemed to be present wherever mobsters were summoned before congressional committees or being arraigned in court. He knew his way around, and before his clients took the stand, he objected violently to the TV cameras. Kelly had to agree. The Rules Committee had handed down a decision protecting the rights of witnesses as far back as the Bobby Baker case, so he had no alternative to ordering that the TV cameras be shut off. The radio could and did stay.

But Josh had anticipated this, and pulled what I have always thought was a neat trick: he had the TV crews keep on the audio; for visual he had them focus on the door of the hearing room, where he hung a card that gave the name of the committee, who was doing the questioning, who were the witnesses, their rogues' gallery pictures, and what they were being questioned about. The lawyer for the Singers raised hell when he discovered it later, but by that time his clients were off.

As it was, the Singers didn't lend anything to the hearing. All they did was drone the usual: "We respectfully decline to answer on the grounds that, etc., etc. . . ."

But Kelly's fast questions made them start. Did they have any knowledge of a truck hijacked on Route One, near New Brunswick, New Jersey, that had been bound for New York City from Philadelphia?

The oldest brother was testifying when he was hit with it. He licked his lips, smoothed his jacket, glanced at his brother and lawyer, then gave his usual little speech. But it was clear he was so rattled that he could barely get the words out.

After Kelly had finished, Jonesy jumped in. Gangsters were his meat. He ranted about Democracy, the Law, Justice, the Common Man, Decency, and ended up by shouting that he would make sure they were cited for contempt and would spend at least five years in jail.

The brothers gave him an amused look, which said, simply: Who are you kidding, Congressman? Don't you know the Supreme Court threw out all those contempt citations against the boys years ago?

Their father was next. He was a frightened little man who had held onto his wife's hand all the while he was sitting in the audience. It was clear to anyone he was lying; he recalled he had paid a large fee to a lawyer named Remington who had been hired through a friend of a friend. . . . No, he had never met Benny Jello, nor had he ever heard of him. And as for Noodles, all he knew was that he had been born in the neighborhood and was once a chicken plucker.

The note from Josh was brief and to the point: "Get him off." They were tuning us out all over the Midwest.

A short time later another note came from Josh: "Luther called. They got the pictures. I just tipped off the inspector. He seemed upset. There should be some action soon."

The only explosive witness of the afternoon session was Roger Best, president of the big New York public-relations firms Jello had fingered as the drop where he had collected the huge bribe for Judge Tucker in the bus case.

Best, a small nervous man who wore dark glasses and an elaborate wristwatch that seemed to have more dials than an airplane cockpit, apparently had been warned by his attorney to tell the truth, because he seemed almost eager to answer Kelly's questions.

A few minutes after he had taken the stand, Best stirred the hearing room by testifying he had received the bus-company contract through Saunders after only one call to City Hall by Remington.

Q. Did you pay Mr. Remington anything for getting you that contract?

A. Yes, sir. Ten thousand dollars. He said most of it had to go to Mr. Saunders. I believe he called it the usual fee.

Q. Did you see him pay Mr. Saunders?

A. No. But when I was in his office he called Mr. Saunders and said I had just given him the money.

Q. How do you know it was Mr. Saunders he was talking to?

A. Trev—Remington—was a little high when I got there. After he talked to Mr. Saunders he handed me the phone and said to say hello. I did.

274

Q. Was it Saunders?

A. Yes, sir.

Q. Had you met Mr. Saunders before?

A. Yes, sir. When I was first trying to get the bus contract.

Q. And you know his voice?

A. I could never forget it.

Q. What did he say to you?

A. Not much. He seemed annoyed that Mr. Remington put me on the telephone. In fact, he slammed down the phone.

Q. And Remington brought the valise of money to your office for Judge Tucker?

A. Yes, sir. He said someone named Benny Jello would pick it up and deliver it to the judge's home.

Q. And did Mr. Jello pick it up?

A. Yes, sir.

Q. (Jones) Answer me this, Witness, did you peek inside that valise?

A. Yes, sir.

Q. What did you see inside that valise?

A. Money. It was stuffed with money.

At this point Best was shaking. He leaned over and took a sip of water. When Kelly suggested they take a short recess, Best shook his head. "I'm not afraid of testifying, Congressman," he said, the words coming so quickly they sounded jumbled. "My attorney advised me to tell the truth; tell them the truth, he said, and they'll accept that. Lie and you might go to jail. Well, I don't want to go to jail, that's why I'm here."

His voice rose and he slammed his fist down on the side of the chair. "But I demand protection! So far I have received three calls, one at home that almost frightened my wife to death, one at my office, and one in the hotel only this morning before I left. It was—" His voice broke, and he sat there nervously rubbing his face and looking beseechingly at Kelly and Jones.

"Do you know who made the calls?" Kelly asked.

"No. It must be some kind of a nut. He had a booming laugh. He said that if I went on I could expect a bomb in the cellar. He said he could have it all arranged so that if someone rang my doorbell or someone lifted the phone it would go off and me, my wife, and three kids would be blown to bits. He said he would fix it so I wouldn't know what to expect. I could even start the hi-fi and this thing would go off."

He reached out and took another swallow of water.

"Did he make the same threats on every occasion?" Kelly asked.

"He kept saying the same thing every time he got me on the phone," Best cried. "I don't know who he is, but he seems to be able to read my mind. After the first call I called a detective sergeant I know, but he wasn't in, and I said I would call him back. About fifteen minutes later this nut called again and said if I got the cops—"

"Maybe it's someone in the police station," Jones suggested.

"How could they?" Best said. "I didn't leave my name."

A few minutes later the messenger handed me a small note from Josh. It said: "It has to be Willy."

They kept Best on the stand only a few more minutes, then excused him with promises from the FBI of protection.

Joey Americus was next. He was a deeply tanned, expensively dressed man in his late fifties. Like the Singers, he was represented by a rackets lawyer, and profusely apologized to the committee every time he took the Fifth. Outside in the corridors he forgot his role as a dignified, polite businessman, and belted a photographer who took his picture. It was a brief but furious bit of action for television.

Jones ended the day's hearing by reading a statement announcing the recovery of the hijacked truck in a New York City garage and the arrest of the Singers as they were about to board a plane at the National Airport.

In our "TV room" Josh excitedly gave us a rundown on the action that had taken place in New York.

After the TV crews had grabbed their shots of the hijacked truck inside the garage and Josh had alerted the deputy inspector, who called New York headquarters, plainclothesmen raided the place. The attendants, who were probably members of the Singer hijacking mob, refused to open the garage doors, and the cops smashed it in with crowbars. A pitched battle between the police and some of the young hoods then took place. When the TV crews moved in, the hoods attacked the crews, and a wild melee followed. With tire irons and police clubs swinging, one of the gang ran out of a rear door to a parking lot and got into his car. Shots punctured the car as it roared out of the lot and crashed into a pole. The man, gun still in hand, staggered out of the battered car and raised his pistol, only to be cut down by a fusillade of bullets.

The TV films were breathtaking. Before the afternoon had ended, Dyke Short and Frank Shea reported we once again owned every channel from New York to the West Coast.

But it wasn't all cake and ale. We were back in the "TV room" watching the reruns of the films of the cops raiding the garage and the cameraman, blood streaming down his face, rolling around in the street with the young hood who was wielding a tire iron, when suddenly there was a knock on the door and an attendant said someone was waiting for Josh. I caught a glimpse of a small, dapper man with a polka-dot tie: Tuck Larsen. He could only spell trouble.

Josh was back in a few minutes. Face grim, he threw down the late edition of a Washington afternoon paper.

"They're also using it big in New York," he said.
The headline read:

SHANNON HEARINGS DOWN THE DRAIN?

HOME OF COMMITTEE'S WITNESS BURNED
SHANNON MAY CALL IT OFF MONDAY

The so-called Shannon hearings into urban crime and official corruption that have been shocking the nation with their charges—all made by a petty thief now in jail—may go down the drain over the weekend.

This was learned today by this reporter as the committee's chief witness, ex-convict Benny Jello, was stricken with a kidney attack and put in the Washington Hospital under twenty-four-hour guard. He was later removed to the Washington Penitentiary.

This took place shortly after Jello's elderly girlfriend, Miss Molly Shapiro, daughter of the late New York industrialist and philanthropist Israel Shapiro, had been notified by the New York State Police that an arsonist had burned down her home, one of the showcase homes near the Shannon estate of Wexford Hall. Miss Shapiro had given incriminating evidence to the committee early in the investigation.

Jello, it was learned, told Congressman Shannon's staff he was through. The congressman admitted to this reporter that he was ready to cancel the hearings, which are scheduled to continue here in Washington and then move to New York City and Lawrence, the industrial city upstate, the recent scene of a disastrous fire that swept through the well-known Lawrence Plastics Factory.

There have been hints that Congressman Shannon would explode a "blockbuster" in the Lawrence hearings, although the mayor and recently the governor have scoffed at the idea that the congressman would expose corruption on a wide scale in that city.

"Maybe a few bookmakers," the mayor said last night, "but outside of that I don't think the congressman has anything. I think it's going to be a political smear. After all, I am sure we can recall the hearings conducted by another Shannon—and isn't this an election year?"

The fire that swept through the Shapiro estate apparently had been set by professional arsonists, Inspector Pope of the State Police told this writer.

"Obviously the fire had some connection with Jello's appearance before the congressional committee," he said. "We understand Miss Shapiro is his girlfriend. We had contacted the Department of Justice last night to report the fire. As we understand it, Miss Shapiro once before had received a death threat in the form of a note stuck in a milk bottle.

"She did not notify us or the local Crestview police of the note. We had to learn this through our own sources. If the committee had seen fit to let us know she was in danger, proper protection would have been provided both to Miss Shapiro and to her property."

The story went on to tell how frightened both Jello and Molly were, how he wouldn't eat, and so on. Then the story went on to recap the many "unconfirmed disclosures, many only hearsay and bits of gossip . . ." he was making before the committee.

Under it was the wire-service story of the Washington hearing.

"It's a typical Larsen hatchet job," Josh said. "He got the local cops, who couldn't catch flies in the first place, to sound off. Then he throws in cracks like 'gossip and hearsay,' and makes sure he frightens Jello to death." He threw the paper on the table. "With Benny afraid to go to the can by himself, this couldn't have come at a worse time."

"Someone in Justice must have tipped Larsen," Luke said bitterly.

"It's the old story," Josh said. "Cops, whether they are in the Justice Department, the FBI, or some hick-town police force, hate stool pigeons. Call him what you like, that's what Benny is."

"Any chance of Benny not seeing this?" Luke asked.

"Not a chance. Larsen will make sure he gets a copy of the paper." He turned to Kelly. "Did you tell Larsen you were ready to cancel the New York hearings?"

"Not that way," Kelly said. "He grabbed me in the hall this morning and started to shoot questions at me. One of the things he asked me was, would I cancel the hearings if I knew that Benny Jello was going to be killed."

"And what did you tell him?"

"I simply said that I would do anything in my power to prevent another human being from being killed—and that would include a thief or a man charged with a capital crime. I knew what he was trying to get me to say, and I was as formal as I could be with him." He glanced at the paper. "I don't suppose there's any use of calling up the editor and protesting."

"None at all. But there's one thing we have to do on Monday."

"What's that?"

"Make this God-damn hearing sensational. We have to shove this down Larsen's throat."

"The confrontation," Luke said.

"You're damn right. Benny coming down from the witness stand and tapping Remington and Saunders on the shoulders—it could start the New York hearings off with a bang." He said to Kelly, "You should hint at that Sunday night."

"The Bishop's Dinner?" Luke said. "Will the bishop be there?"

"Are you kidding?"

"He certainly knows how to make news," Luke said. "His dinners are always on page one of the *Times*."

"Why do you think I want Kelly there as a speaker?" Josh said. "The filet mignon isn't that good."

"You going to announce Mullady will be a witness?" Luke asked.

"No," was Josh's firm answer. "Hint at it, yes." He said to Kelly, "We must be absolutely sure when that announcement is made. There can be no turning back once you give it out."

"I agree with that," Kelly said. "Will you and Finn give me your ideas?"

"We'll have it up to you at Wexford by Saturday morning. Oh, by the way, Finn and I are going to New York to tie up a few loose ends."

I gave him a startled glance; this was the first I knew of it.

"Where will you meet us for the dinner?" Luke asked.

"Suppose we see you in the lobby of the Waldorf about seven thirty. There are three or four private cocktail parties Kelly should look in on."

"What about Benny?" Kelly asked. "Who'll take care of him?"

"The two marshals. They'll bring him down to New York sometime Sunday or Monday."

"Let's make sure he'll be put in a hotel and not the pen."

"I'll talk to the AG's office," Luke said. "How about Molly?"

"Lacey's bringing her back Saturday," Josh said.

"I want Molly to stay at Wexford," Kelly said. "We'll have one of the best architects in the country preparing plans for a new house. We'll have him look up the original plans for the house in the county historical society. That's the least we can do."

"We'll get a million antiques for her," Luke said.

"It will be something for them both to be occupied with," Kelly said, "after Benny gets out." He said to Josh, "Did you call the DA yet?"

"No, but I will tomorrow."

"That's important, Josh."

"Don't worry about it. I'll call him tomorrow."

"Maybe we can ask him to talk to the committee. It might help things."

"Fine. I'll ask him. Mull over the material for Sunday night, will you?"

Outside, Josh flagged down a cab.

"While you were with Molly I got a call from Willy. He wants us to meet him in that damn cemetery Friday at three o'clock. He insists it's a matter of life and death. We'd better see him before he frightens any more witnesses half to death."

"There was no doubt he called Best."

"Of course. He had the guy's phone tapped."

"That's what he meant about upsetting the hearings if we ignored him. Do you think he—"

"—burned down Molly's house? No question about it. The mob doesn't go in for burning houses unless it's for insurance. You said Willy was mad when you saw him in New York."

"Violently so."

"I wonder what he's so upset about now?"

"He has the Gentile file, and he thinks we're ducking him."

"Maybe it could come at the right time," Josh said musingly. "If it's dynamite we could certainly use it."

"Things are becoming uncontrollable. I'd be afraid of anything more he gives us, Josh."

"Don't be."

"How far will Kelly go Sunday night?"

"Just far enough to make Barney keep running to the bathroom."

"In other words you want to make sure Barney sees the handwriting on the wall?"

"Obviously."

"So there won't be any question he will make a deal?"

"Right again. He'll come crawling to us."

"I was hoping you'd forget it, Josh."

"Why should I? It's a perfect setup."

"You'll lose Dregna and the liberals. I'm sure they'll support Kelly if we take off after Mullady."

"The liberals are great for letting someone else fight their battles. Where have they been all these years Barney was making it with his sweet chocolates?"

"Max said they tried, but Barney was too smart for them."

"You can bet your ass he was. Barney understands one thing—if he knows you have a horseshoe in your glove and can clobber him, he'll wheel and deal. If he's not afraid of you, watch out."

"And you feel you have a horseshoe in the glove, Josh?"

Josh put his head back and smiled faintly at the cab's grimy ceiling. "Not only one, but two. If Abernathy comes through with that affidavit, Barney will jump through a hoop if we ask him to. And Max Dregna and his liberals can go screw themselves."

"If they run their own candidate it could drain off 300,000 votes."

"Barney has one last big election left in him, Finn, and that's going to be Kelly's. By the time the national convention comes around in a couple of years, he may be in trouble from guys like Abernathy. But if the lid is kept on until November, he will be able to deliver every sweet choc- olate from the Battery to the Bronx line, and they could give Kelly one hell of an impressive plurality. Impressive enough to make him the most attractive candidate at the convention."

"I can see now what Lacey means when she says we're using other people's lives—"

"Sometimes I think all Lacey wants is Molly married to that bum."

"Lacey only wants to see the woman happy. What did you tell her at the hotel?"

"I finally convinced her the DA is going to squash the charges against Benny and we could get him off."

"For the love of God, Josh, how can you lie to her? To Molly, even Jello?"

"I'm going to make another pitch with that phony DA," he said quietly, "if only we could scare the hell out of him."

"The Republicans put him in, and he knows he has us over the barrel."

"Maybe I'll put Willy on his tail. Get something on him or his office."

"If that hearing ends and they put Benny back into jail, Lacey will never talk to you again," I warned him.

"I know it," he said fiercely. "Don't you think I realize that? It took me an hour to convince her I was getting him off."

"Don't hurt her, Josh; please don't."

He turned to stare out the window.

"I would cut off my right arm before I would hurt her," he said. "But I would cut them both off before I would let the hearings be canceled. We have a President of the United States in our pocket, and I'll be damned if I'm going to lose him!"

CHAPTER FIFTEEN: WILLY'S FOLDER

As Josh had predicted, the TV films of the police raid on the New York City garage topped the Washington hearings; by late Thursday this thirty minutes of film, more exciting than any manufactured melodrama, was the talk of the country. Every station had repeats, and you couldn't flip a dial that you didn't see all the fireworks.

When Josh saw how the films had captured the attention of the country, he got the senator to take to the phones; the first reruns that evening had an epilogue of Kelly Shannon interviewed by TV's top reportorial team.

Josh also insisted that highlights of previous days of Benny Jello and the other witnesses, of close-ups of Kelly, be distributed to the networks, and although it cost a fortune it was done. Again Josh was right. Every network had news specials on the Manhattan gunfight, and used the clips.

It was evident from the bale of newspaper and magazine stories starting to pour in from the clipping services and from the polls that Kelly Shannon was starting to make a national impact. Europe, too, was beginning to take notice: BBC had asked for TV prints; *Paris Match* was sending a famous writer-photographer team to cover the rest of the hearings;

Der Spiegel wanted all the stills they could buy from the wire services; and *Pravda* had a piece, pointing out, of course, that Kelly Shannon was the son of the rich capitalist and that traditional foe of Communism the former Fascist, Senator Shannon.

The New York papers had solid picture pages on the gunbattle—and, as Josh jubilantly pointed out, Larsen's story now rated only a paragraph or two, buried in the accounts of the hearing and the garage battle. While we waited for our Friday-afternoon date with Willy, Josh and I worked on a draft for Kelly's Sunday-night speech, which we sent up to Wexford. Later we mapped the moves we would make upstate following the announcement of Kelly's candidacy.

Friday at two we started in a cab for the cemetery to meet Willy. It had been a gray, sullen morning; then about noon a steady, cold rain began to fall. When we got out of the cab at the entrance, I nudged Josh and pointed to the small greenhouse on the corner.

"To hell with flowers today," he said shortly.

Heads hunched down in our raincoats, we started up the winding, muddy road.

"There he is," Josh said suddenly.

He was kneeling in the mud at the edge of the tiny grave, a huge lump, barely discernible through the curtain of rain.

"Let's get this over with," Josh said. "This place gives me the creeps."

We hurried to where Willy was kneeling. As before, he ignored us, although the sucking sound of our shoes in the mud was loud enough. There wasn't anything to do but wait. And like two idiots we waited. He was dressed the same, with the exception of a huge raincoat that had a big ball-peen hammer sticking out of one pocket. A few more geraniums were planted, with the empty pots neatly stacked by the headstone. For the first time I read it:

"Robert W. Williamson, Age Nine, Murdered by the City of New York."

Despite my distrust and fear, a surge of pity went through me.

At last he rose, looking wilder and more haggard than before. Rain ran off his stubbled cheeks and chin, down into the tufts of white hair visible in the *V* of the open shirt.

"Where the hell have you been?" he demanded.

"You mean where have *you* been," Josh said. "Haven't you been watching TV?"

"Yeah. I've been. You're going easy on Gentile. What's the story?"

Josh gave him a look of manufactured amazement.

"Going easy on him! Come on, Willy, didn't you hear Benny? Everybody's talking about City Hall!"

"I mean Gentile," Willy shouted. "Not City Hall. Who gives a damn about City Hall! I want Gentile! Put his name in the record! Tell the people what he is, a God-damned fancy pants whoremonger!"

"Wait a minute, Willy," Josh began, but Willy was in full swing.

"Wait a minute, my ass! You're protecting this bum; that's what you're doing! You sold out to the Commies and the whores!" He glared at us. "What about the whore on Central Park West! Why didn't you call her!"

"But Willy," Josh shouted back, "Gentile was never there! Only Saunders! You never gave us Gentile going to Eva's place!"

Willy went into a rage, shaking his fist in Josh's face. "I gave you the picture of Gentile going in there with that other guy," he shouted. "What did you do, sell it to them?"

It was obvious Willy was now confusing Saunders with Gentile.

"Sell it to whom?" Josh said desperately.

"To Gentile and his gang," Willy roared. He suddenly yanked the heavy hammer from his raincoat and, eyes blazing, started to advance on Josh.

I was frozen, my feet like stumps of lead stuck deep in the muddy road. I don't know how I did it but I managed to blurt out, making it sound almost casual: "That's why we're here, Willy. We want you to wrap up the case against Gentile."

Willy slowly turned to me; he seemed to have difficulty focusing his eyes. "What the hell you doing here old man?" he said, seemingly surprised.

"Like I told Josh, we need you to really wrap up Gentile, Willy; you know that picture you gave us of Gentile going into Eva's place was too blurred. You couldn't introduce it; nobody could make out Gentile's face."

Willy frowned. "I told that stupid bastard to use the Jap camera, not that Big Bertha. . . ."

Out of the corner of my eye I could see Josh, his face strained and pale, studying Willy.

"We have to get Gentile, Willy. Gentile!" He almost shouted, "Gentile!"

Willy stared at us for a long moment. My heart froze as I looked into those feverish eyes. Whatever Josh was up to, I hoped it worked, and fast.

Slowly the name of Gentile seemed to penetrate Willy's shadowy, tortured mind. He kept nodding and licking his lips. "Yeah, Gentile," he mumbled. "Got to get that bastard." Suddenly he raised his fist and shook it violently in the direction of City Hall. "You pimps and whoremongers!" he shouted. "We'll get you yet!"

The only answer was the hiss of the rain and the gurgling of a tiny rivulet that flowed down the path.

He shook his head a few times like a fighter recovering from a staggering blow, then rubbed his eyes. Now he was brisk and businesslike.

"Let's go. I got something for you guys." He walked away in the rain.

Josh pursed his lips and whistled softly. "Christ, that was close."

283

Single file we followed the towering, plodding, drenched figure through the wavering shawls of rain.

We drove around all afternoon in Willy's smelly bus as he talked us into a stupor—Communism, thieves in office, crooked politics, Hitler was the right guy, niggers and Jews and Catholics (no offense, old man) who have to be put in their place; City Hall and the bums with their hands out; no-good women who should have their heads shaved and their asses kicked from the Bronx to Coney Island. . . .

It went on and on as he drove through the rainy streets of Queens. Josh fell asleep, his head to one side, his body swaying with Willy's erratic twists and turns. I went to sleep too, to awake with Willy shaking me and holding out a gooey piece of pizza.

I hate this damn symbol of today's young, but rather than touch off this maniac again I accepted it, curving it in the middle in the best accepted style, and eating it. Josh did the same. I looked at my watch. It was almost eight o'clock. We had been traveling for hours.

"We through the tour now, Willy?" Josh asked.

"We'll head back for the barn now," Willy said. "Then I'll show it to you."

"What is it?"

"You'll see. You'll see."

It was still raining; the traffic had thinned when we arrived in Manhattan to park on East Forty-ninth Street. As before, Willy entered by an alley grating. This time the warm darkness was welcome after the chilly hours in that cramped bus.

We went down the various levels with me frozen as always when that damn subway express roared out of nowhere.

"Don't they ever come across you, Willy?" Josh asked.

"Never," Willy said emphatically. "I could lose the best of them in ten minutes."

"Why couldn't the experts find you down here, Willy?" he asked.

"Because I know this place like I know the back of my own hand," he said. "Back in the thirties when I was a kid I used to come down here. When that God-damned Communist FDR got in I spent a whole winter down here, neat and cozy as a bug in a rug. In the morning I'd go out and get me a few rolls and milk; then I'd spend the day exploring. Experts! Hell, they'd get lost after ten minutes down here. . . . You ready, old man?"

"Ready as I'll ever be," I said, and we pushed on.

We finally reached his headquarters, as he called it. I grabbed a wooden box and sat down, my legs trembling as though I had been dancing a jig for hours. Willy laughed, but he brought out a bottle of whiskey and gave us a stiff hooker. It went down like fire, but it was welcome.

"You're not going back to Washington tonight," he said suddenly. "You and the old man are going to Hollywood where all the pretty girls are."

"Hollywood!" I cried. "What the hell for?"

But Willy was serious now, and very lucid. He walked over to a section of the wall, carefully removed several of the old-fashioned red bricks we used to call "Murphys" on the West Side, reached in, and took out an envelope.

"This is Gentile's file," he said. "I did a personal job for some guy down there last year, and this is his payoff."

It was a black folder, and on it was the title "Gentile, Felix Durant, Undersecretary Asian Affairs, State Department, Washington, D.C."

In the center of the folder was a red stamp: RESTRICTED.

From another envelope he took two snapshots, one of a beautiful Chinese girl, the other of a handsome, rugged young man in his early thirties, dressed in a sport shirt. When I studied his face closely, I could see traces of the Oriental.

"The girl is Suzy Chu; she's a bit player and goes under the name of Suzy Lake," he said. "Her married name is Forest. She's Gentile's sister-in-law, so to speak."

"Sister-in-law!"

"Wait a minute, Finn," Josh said quietly. "Keep talking, Willy."

"In World War II this Gentile was first an observer with the Nationalists; then he was behind the lines in East China, where he developed an underground railway to help Allied personnel to escape."

Giving us Gentile's background seemed to help calm Willy. Except for an occasional snarl or oath, his voice was almost controlled as he went on: "He was in command of the first mission to reach Shanghai when the Japs surrendered. He got a lot of publicity and had his picture on the cover of *Life* when he was the first one into that big Jap prison in Shanghai. He stayed on in China and got to know a lot of big people in government. One was General Chu, who had twin daughters, Suzy and Nina, and a son, Ching, who was educated at Harvard or some other fairy place like that. Then the general was sent to Washington, and Suzy, Nina, and Ching came along for the ride. By this time Gentile was in the State Department and had a lot of friends. The bastard was always making friends. When Nina arrived they started shacking up. When the old man was called back after the Commies got going, Nina stayed behind. I understand she had a hell of a row with the old general, but they made him keep it quiet because they didn't want any trouble with Washington at the time. Suzy went back, but Nina and Ching stayed on. Ching got into television when it just started, and became a producer."

He picked up the picture of Ching and tossed it at me.

"He became a pimp for the guys down in Washington and at the UN. He could get you anything, white, black, or yellow." He pointed to the folder. "You read it and see how this Chink operated. He had a hell of a big thing going, and only big customers—and I mean big: State Department, UN delegates, even those big black baboons.

"By this time Gentile was starting to back away from this Chinese dame. Then she had a kid, and that did it. Gentile ran. As I understand it the girl really kept after him, but no dice; this highfalutin bastard really gave her the brush. Then one day she turned on the gas. The cops found her and the kid."

"Suicide?"

Willy shook his head. "There were no notes, so the cops said it was an accident. Being who she was helped, because State sent somebody down to talk to the cops."

"Maybe it might have been an accident," I said.

Willy gave me a look of disgust. "You know better than that, old man. Besides, that's why you guys are going to Hollywood—"

"Why, Willy?" Josh asked.

"Suzy is married to some jerk actor named Forest. From what I hear he's just a big hambone. He latched on to some idea of a spy series, and is putting a company together in Hong Kong. He needs dough to make the pilot film, and I guess the letter is all Suzy has to sell. She wants five grand."

"Her sister's suicide note!" I said in disgust to Josh. "For God's sake, are we vultures?"

"That's pretty small potatoes for five grand, Willy," Josh said. "Besides, putting in a thing like that would hurt us more than help us. You know that."

"The suicide letter is only one part of the package." He gave us a shrewd look. "Maybe you could get word to this bum that you have the letters and if he doesn't pull back you're going to let them go. I bet you could place them somewhere."

I just grunted. I couldn't say anything.

He laughed, a wild braying laugh. "Look at the old man. He doesn't like this dirty stuff, Josh." Then, seriously, he pointed to the picture of the young man. "He's the important angle."

"What's important about a TV producer?"

"I said he was a pimp. And he pimped for a long time for the baboons at the UN. Then he went to Washington and pimped for the boys down there. One day the feds grabbed him, and he was indicted for transporting. The bail was $50,000. Someone got it knocked down to ten, and he skipped to Moscow. Suzy will tell you where he is now."

"Where?"

"Peking. He just finished making a documentary on the life of Chou En Lai. He used to go to Moscow every six months. When the Chinks started to move into that new African country, Ching was down there in charge of running the guns. He's a real red-hot Chink Commie—and the reason why he's in Peking and not in jail is Gentile." He slammed

286

his fist into his palm. "Gentile twisted the arm of the U.S. Attorney and had him lower the bail. Then he made sure the feds weren't trailing Ching so he could skip. How do you like those apples?"

"Wait a minute, Willy; that's an awful lot to prove," Josh said.

Willy nodded. "I know it." He pointed to the file. "It's all in there, and for that five grand Suzy will give you letters from friends in China, smuggled out through Hong Kong, who can tell how Ching is operating."

"How can you prove Gentile put on the pressure to let this guy get off the Mann Act charge?" I asked.

He eyed me sternly. "For an old guy who's been around you certainly can be stupid! Number one, you go down to the U.S. Attorney's office and see if you can find Ching's file—you won't, someone has lifted it. Even the indictment's gone. Then you read this file I'm giving you, and you'll see someone got the U.S. Attorney to give a statement as to what Gentile did; he even quotes Gentile. I guess he didn't want to be left holding the bag for Gentile if it ever got out. Then Suzy will give you a sworn statement how her brother told her Gentile was arranging to let him skip and that he intended to go back to China because it was now a new China and someday it would rule the world. He even tried to get her to come back with him, but she turned him down."

He eyed me sternly. "For an old guy who's been around you certainly want? You want me to go over to Peking and bring back this Chink?"

Josh held up a hand. "Easy, Willy. Let's not get excited. When are we supposed to see this girl?"

"Tomorrow afternoon." He burrowed deep in his raincoat pocket and came up with a crumpled bit of paper.

"Here's her address. It's over in Benedict Canyon. I'll call Forest and tell him you're coming out."

"So you saw her?" I asked.

He gave me a sly look. "Yeah, I saw her, and just between us, that jerky husband of hers will let you bang her in Macy's window for another hundred."

"Did she show you her sister's letter?" I asked.

"Still doubt me, old man?"

"We don't want to buy a pig in a poke, Willy," Josh said.

"Pig in a poke!" he shouted. "Sure I saw the letter. What do you take me for—a rookie!"

"Willie," I said abruptly, "have you been in Westchester County recently?"

His madman's eyes were narrow and cold. "What do you want to know for?"

"Somebody burned down the house of Benny Jello's girlfriend."

Josh gave me a quick, imploring look, but I ignored it.

"Somebody burned her tail, eh?"

"Was it you?"

"Suppose it was, just what could you do about it?"

"Why would Willy want to do that?" Josh said quickly. "Come off it, Finn."

Why, I wanted to shout, because he's a God-damn nut—

"Did you make those calls to that man Best, Willy?" I asked.

He gave me one of those crazy smiles; he seemed to be enjoying it. Josh looked worried.

"Why? Somebody make some calls?"

"To someone called Roger Best, the man who owns that public-relations outfit—and threatened him—"

"So somebody made that fag change his underwear. So what?"

"Benny Jello almost didn't go on. He was frightened to death."

He reached out to slap me on the back. "So a fag and a punk crook got scared—who cares?"

"They're important witnesses, Willy—"

But Willy was working himself up again. "Important! Shit they're important! Gentile's the guy who's important." He turned to Josh. "He's the guy the country has to worry about—not a Madison Avenue jerk and a con merchant!"

"You're right, Willy," Josh said soothingly, "so right."

The way he said it made Willy flare up, and he stabbed Josh with a stubby, dirty finger. "You're God-damn right I am! But you guys don't care—you want to brush me off!"

"Willy, we have these hearings to take care of—" Josh said desperately.

But there was no turning him off.

"Sure, I know all about the hearings," Willy continued, "but I also know when I'm getting the brushoff." He waved a finger in Josh's face. "Don't do it, Josh! Just don't! It's too important to the country now. You're not dealing with just whores and crooks anymore—now we got the Red Chinks in it! Bastards like Gentile would let them take over the whole damn country!" He slammed a fist into his open palm. "Letting a creep like that Ching escape back to Peking! I always said so, but nobody would listen—they're going to sell us out! Piece by piece! We got to wake up this country! Show what Gentile is really like! Don't you realize he could be President? What would we do then?"

"Okay, Willy," Josh said, ignoring the madman's last outburst, "We'll be on the first plane in the morning, and we'll see Suzy. I think maybe we can make a deal with her. This stuff sounds great, doesn't it, Finn?"

"Great," I said with a big show of enthusiasm.

Willy slowly rubbed his hand across his face. I noticed that after these sudden outbursts he seemed momentarily bewildered, almost dazed. He kept nodding as his eyes slowly cleared.

"Yeah, okay," he mumbled. "You guys be on that plane and see Suzy. . . ."

"You're going to take us up now, Willy?" Josh said softly.

Willy rose and for a moment fumbled with the collar of his raincoat. "I get these damn headaches," he said. "They keep pounding like hammers inside."

"Have you seen a doctor?" Josh asked.

"Doctors? They're all quacks," he said. He shook his head like a fighter recovering from a stunning blow.

We followed Willy up that torturous maze again. He said little on the way up, just grunted or ignored Josh's questions. He himself seemed eager to leave the place behind.

We came out into a chilly, dripping darkness. The rain had stopped, but a mist hung over the city. Before we left, Willy said he would call us and not to call him. Without another word he turned and walked toward his parked bus.

The automat was open, but I told Josh I wanted Jack Daniels, not coffee.

We found a gin mill on Third Avenue and took seats at the end of the almost deserted bar. The mirror told us we both appeared to have been dragged in out of the rain; our suits were shapeless and soggy, and I was sure I left a wet trail.

As soon as he sat down Josh began skipping through that folder. He drank his whiskey absentmindedly, never once looking up, just waving to the bartender when he wanted his glass refilled.

"It sounds like a McCarthy hearing," he said at last. "There's a lot of secondhand gossip and hearsay. Apparently Gentile was quite a swinger in those days right after the war. He had some wild parties in his place; there's a few cracks about homos and Reds, but the best part is this business of Ching. The U.S. Attorney's statement could be devastating; he claims Gentile put on the pressure to get him to agree to lower Ching's bail. He says he warned Gentile that Ching would skip, but Gentile insisted he would be available for trial."

"Is Ching just a pimp or could he be an agent?"

"There's a quote from a report, maybe from the Bureau—you know how they steal each other's stuff—that Ching had been seen in the company of a Chinese they were sure was directing the organizing of those Commie clubs that want us to hold hands with Peking."

"Did Ching take part in any pro-Peking activities?"

"No. That's why he could be dangerous; the ones who do the most screaming at the rallies or in the parades are local talent. The ones behind the scenes, who never get into the FBI files, are the dangerous ones."

"Could Ching be in that category?"

He shrugged. "On the face of it"—he patted the binder—"it looks devastating. Who could swear Ching isn't an agent? Just on these facts alone, Gentile either was the damnedest fool or—" He hesitated.

"Or a young guy in a hell of a spot," I pointed out. "This Chinese girl kills herself and his son. If it comes out, he's finished. Then Ching is nabbed. If I'd been in his spot, I think I'd have wanted that Chink somewhere at the South Pole."

He tossed off his drink. "That could be. But there's one thing I know" —he patted the binder again—"Benny Jello can drop dead now for all we care."

"Are you seriously thinking of using this, Josh?" I asked. "You just said it sounds like a McCarthy hearing."

"I don't care what it sounds like," Josh said bluntly. "We're going to use it. I want this New York hearing to be the biggest and most sensational in years. Kelly's caught on now, and I want it to continue. After Lawrence the hearings will be over, and we have to leave on the highest note possible. When we announce his candidacy, the ball will really open!"

I warned him, "You'll never get it past Kelly."

"If we show him Gentile made it possible for a Peking agent to skip and return to China, he can't ignore it."

"So far he's just a pimp who was indicted after violation of the Mann Act."

"But Suzy is going to help us prove he was more than a pimp."

"I guess we really will be on that plane tomorrow."

"You never made a better guess. Don't forget we have to be back Sunday night for the Bishop's Dinner." He glanced at his watch. "It's almost ten o'clock. There's an early-morning flight from Kennedy. I'll phone for reservations."

He slid off the bar stool, phoned, and returned in a few minutes.

"I got the reservations," he said. "I also called the Beverly Hills for a suite. We can get a few hours' sleep before we talk to Willy's Chinese girlfriend." He slid a tip across the bar. "Let's go."

The night clerk at the Sheridan had two messages for us, one from Shea, the other from Max Dregna. While Josh talked to Shea, I made us each a cup of instant coffee, then called Dregna. While he admitted he had been impressed with the hearings, Max wanted the answers to the questions: Were we going after Mullady? Would he be called to testify?

"Shea says the polls are getting better every hour," Josh said as he poured a cup. "He thinks we should score big with the confrontation scene on Tuesday. Benny, Remington, and this stuff on Gentile! It's going to be one hell of a week for our side, Finn! Oh, by the way, what did Dregna want?"

"Something we have to discuss—Mullady."

"What about Mullady?"

"You still want to make a deal with that thief? For God's sake, forget it, Josh!"

"I don't intend to forget it. In fact, it's in the works now. I've already talked to him."

"To Barney? When?"

"On Tuesday in Washington. He came to see Holmes. The Speaker called me. Barney was there. He's worried and he wants to make a deal. Holmes hinted it would be good all around."

"Holmes is in no position to dictate to us. He's in the fight for his life!"

"That's true, but he's still the Speaker, and he could help us in November, when we'll need all the friends we can get."

"Kelly will never go for a deal with Mullady; you know that. He'll walk out."

"After the Monday hearing, Shea and Short expect the polls to show he's in millions of homes of voting Americans and in the image we hoped for. After the Lawrence sessions, and when the campaign starts, he'll be the talk of the country. Don't worry—Kelly won't walk out. Incidentally, I talked to Luke and the old man. They're all for it."

"You talked to Luke and the senator without telling Kelly?"

"This is a time for practical men and rough decisions, Finn. I don't want Kelly around tripping over his heart."

"What about Abernathy? The man's put his life on the line for us."

"That's a crock. He's just a damned jig political opportunist who wants to hang on to our coattails. He can con Kelly and Lacey, but not me—"

"It will never work, Josh. Never."

"The hell it won't. Mullady's playing scared money. He knew it was the beginning of the end when Kelly announced the Lawrence hearings. He said he doesn't give much of a damn, he's loaded and ready to call it a day; but he also admitted he can't stand any digging."

"And Lawrence? What happens there?"

"Actually, it won't be too bad. Mullady was down to get the okay for a $10,000,000 federal rehabilitation program. He said he's going to throw money around like a drunken sailor up there. Before it's over, there'll be more projects and more Negroes singing Hallelujah to Barney Mullady than there are relief checks cashed in Harlem."

"Abernathy will never keep quiet. What about that affidavit he promised to prepare? Suppose he gives that to a newspaper? Or a DA?"

"A newspaper would never print it, too libelous. And even if a DA went into it, the investigative job would take months. He would have to send in undercover men, comb the records, put a small army of accountants on the job. Besides, it smells of politics."

"It didn't take Willy long to come up with proof."

"Willy used tapes and bugs and reached the records and the witnesses before Barney sent up his orders to lay low. As he told me, they're burning more records in the basement of Lawrence's City Hall than the Nazis did in Berlin before the Russians got there."

"But what about all those people who put their necks and jobs on the line to join Abernathy? You heard what Lacey and Kelly said about them. You can't just push them aside, Josh. You just can't!"

"It will have to be part of their education in politics, I guess." He shrugged. "When you have only a few months to elect a man governor and make him a presidential candidate, you can't wet-nurse a lot of moony reformers. Once that federal dough starts flowing around Lawrence, watch how fast they forget their ideals."

"I wish you could have been with us that night in Lawrence. You might have seen what Mullady really is."

"Look, I know what he is. No one has to tell me. All I want from him are those levers going down. Click. Click. Click. Sweet chocolates from the Battery to Syracuse, and all loving Kelly Shannon."

"Then you don't want Max?"

"Couldn't care less now. Let his cloak and suiters put up their own candidate, and watch us slaughter him."

"They'll be a threat at convention time."

"The hell they will! They'll be begging to jump on Kelly Shannon's bandwagon. It's God-damned hard for politicians, whether they're Democrats, Republicans, Greenbackers, Federalists, or liberals, to keep polishing their ideals when the parade is passing them by."

"Perhaps I shouldn't mention it, but why didn't you tell *me* about your meeting with Mullady?"

"Because I really hadn't made up my mind until tonight, Finn." He tapped the folder Willy had given us. "This is what made the difference."

"You said yourself it sounds like a McCarthy hearing—half truths, gossip—"

"Most of it is, but don't forget that the hard core of truth is there. Gentile put the arm on a U.S. Attorney to get the bail reduced for an international pimp who now is in Peking! Who cares about the other stuff? I believe Willy when he says this part is true. The excerpts quoted the U.S. Attorney's name, this dame we're going to see in Hollywood— it all can't be phony, Finn."

"That may be true, but there's one thing you forgot. Lacey."

A shadow fell across his face. "That's one thing I didn't forget—"

"And what do you intend to do about her?"

"I have to go through with it," he said. Then to me, "Maybe she'll see it my way after we—"

"She'll never see it your way, Josh. You'll only break her heart. If you care about her, don't go through with the deal."

"I feel stronger about her than any woman I've ever known," he said slowly. "And I've told her that." He smiled. "In fact, I told her in the coffeeshop she was the only woman I would ever consider taking back to North Dakota."

"And what did she say?"

"She just sat there with two big tears rolling down her cheeks, and so damn mad I thought she'd slug me."

292

"And knowing how she feels about you, would you still go ahead? Please, Josh!"

He slowly removed the shirt from its plastic laundry sheath.

"I'm sorry, Finn," he said slowly, "I'm truly sorry. I'm sorry about Molly's house. I'm sorry about that little thief who is hoping he will be canonized for selling his former partners down the river so he can skip a jail term and marry a lonely old woman who has spent most of her life polishing pieces of Wedgwood or Paul Revere tankards. I'm sorry for Abernathy, who hopes we're going to help him reclaim his lost dreams of becoming the political leader of his race." He leaned over and gripped my shoulder. "I'm sorry most of all if I have to hurt you or Lacey." His voice hardened and sounded cold and foreign. "But all the regrets in the world will not change my mind. I believe Kelly Shannon has a greater potential for this country than all the other candidates put together who we know or have helped to put into office. If I have to sacrifice you, me, Lacey or all the others to put this man over I will do it gladly." He leaned down and added in a low, fierce voice. "And if I have to make a deal with that conniving thief, Barney Mullady, to accomplish this, I will do it gladly, even if I have to sign it in blood!"

And, God help us, he did.

BOOK 4

☆☆☆☆☆☆☆

The Gung-Ho Girl ☆☆☆☆☆

CHAPTER SIXTEEN: HOLLYWOOD

As many times as I have visited Los Angeles, I have never really become accustomed to the place. For me it's a place of transients—little old ladies from Kansas or Missouri with hesitant smiles and sun-dried skin; old men in horribly gauche sport shirts; hard-eyed drifters with Beatle haircuts; and religious fanatics. They all seem to be looking for something: the old people, eternal sunshine and peace in their last years; the drifters, easy money; the religious fanatics, a soapbox and converts. The old people usually find smog, high prices, and perhaps a small, pink stucco house with lizards and fleas; the drifters, thirty days in the workhouse; the fanatics, an audience of three bleary-eyed winos.

We checked in at the Beverly Hills early the following morning, had a few hours' rest, then hired a car to drive to the address Willy had written on the piece of paper. It was on the rim of Benedict Canyon, a beautiful one-story stone and redwood house surrounded by a small stone wall. As we pulled up, I noticed a battered sports car in the garage. This day the smog hadn't appeared, so we had a breathtaking view of the entire countryside with its beautiful toylike homes clinging to the sides of the rolling hills.

"Well, let's hope Suzy is in," Josh murmured as we walked to the front door.

We didn't get a chance to ring the bell.

The door was opened and a burly bearded young man of about twenty-five was standing in the doorway. He was dressed in Levis, pale from many washings, dirty sneakers, a black, sleeveless turtleneck that I believed he wore more to show his impressive biceps than anything else.

"Looking for someone?"

"Yes. We're looking for Miss Suzy Chu."

"You mean Forest," the young man said. "That's me. My wife is inside. You from New York?"

"Yes. We were told Miss—Forest was waiting to see us."

"You from that guy Williamson?"

"That's right. We were with him last night."

He stepped aside and waved us in. "Come in, my wife's inside."

We followed him into a beautiful sunken living room. There was an enormous fireplace, as well as a few low tables and chairs, a curved sofa that ran the length of the windows that looked out into the valley, and a set of weights in the middle of the floor.

"I was just finishing my situps," he said. "This is my wife, Suzy."

She was tiny and beautiful, with dark hair, grave dark eyes, and an alabaster skin, a delightful little Oriental cameo. She was dressed in a long yellow sheath slit up both sides.

"You fellows have a drink?" the bearded one asked.

"No thanks. Too early," Josh said.

"Tea perhaps?" she asked. Her voice, like herself, was tiny and musical.

"I would love some tea," I said, and she smiled and went into the kitchen. She returned shortly with a teapot and two handleless fragile cups. The tea was fragrant, hot, and delicate.

"Did Williamson tell you the deal?" Forest asked.

"He spoke to us about it," Josh said cautiously. "But we'll have to talk first."

"Like I told Suzy," he said, "I think we can go to *Life* and get a big chunk of dough and maybe good publicity. I can use it to help me in this new series." He bent over and picked up a heavy weight with ease and put it to one side by the fireplace. "It's spy stuff with schmaltz. Lots of action shot right in Hong Kong."

Josh gave him a steady look. "Mr. Forest, if you give this to any newspaper or magazine, I'll personally guarantee to subpoena you before the committee. I don't think your backers would like that sort of publicity."

The young bearded boob opened and closed his mouth a few times, but Josh's quiet threat had thrown him. He mumbled something about how they had a right to use their material any way they saw fit, and Josh nodded.

"You certainly have, Mr. Forest; but remember, this isn't a movie or TV scenario. Your wife has information that touches on the life of a man extremely important in American politics at the moment."

"I have been watching the hearings," Suzy said. "It is terrible, these things in New York. Did Felix know all about this?"

Felix. The ease with which she used the name brought Josh back to her immediately.

"That's what the committee is trying to determine, Mrs. Forest. Did you know Mr. Gentile for a long time?"

"Sure she did," said her husband. "She told me all about her sister and how she—"

"Suppose you let your wife tell the story, Mr. Forest?" Josh said. Then, to temper the bluntness, he added cheerfully, "You know, just to get it from the horse's mouth, so to speak."

"Okay. You're paying the dough."

Josh turned back to Suzy.

"My sister Nina, myself, and my brother, Ching, came to Washington with my father, General Chu, who was then head of the Nationalist Air Force. That was before the Generalissimo moved to Formosa. We were happy in Washington. There were many parties, and twice I met the President and his lady. Nina was happy. She had Felix, and they went everywhere together. Ching went to Harvard to finish his college and then to photographers' school. He was very good with the camera. Twice he won prizes for his pictures. Then the *hsien-fei* came down from the north—"

Her husband put in, "That's what they call the Commies."

"Border bandits, it means, but that is what the Communists are," she said. "My people have to leave the mainland, and there was much trouble. My father is ordered back. Nina does not want to go. She says she loves Felix and will stay in the United States. I tell my father I will go. My brother is now very busy in television and also says he will stay here with Nina. There was much trouble in our house. Father wanted to go to the State Department—"

"Mr. Gentile was in State at the time?" Josh asked.

"Oh, yes. He would soon be Undersecretary in Charge of Asian Affairs."

"Please go on."

"My father's people told him he should not go to the State Department because it would be bad for our country. Now we needed all the help we could get from the United States. There was a hearing at the time about the China lobby, and my father's friends were afraid such a scandal would be used to hurt us. My father told Nina she was no longer his daughter, and we left. I received many letters from my sister. In the beginning she was sad because she was not with us, but said she loved Felix and was happy. But soon the letters changed. She said Felix had met an American girl who was very pretty and very wealthy, and the newspapers said they were going to be married.

"Then one day she wrote and told me she had a child. This upset me greatly, and I told my father I wanted to go back to the United States, but he would not hear of it. I didn't hear from my sister for a long time. Then one day this letter came. It was from her and said that when I received this letter she would be dead and so would her son. She said Felix would not see her anymore."

The dark eyes became misty. "That night we received the cablegram. The police said it was an accident, but it wasn't! Nina killed herself and the baby because Felix would not see her anymore."

Her husband snorted, "How do you like that kind of a guy?"

Josh's hand waved him to silence. "What happened to Ching, Suzy?"

"In New York he disgraced my father," she said. "He used many women for money. One day a letter came from the State Department. It told my father Ching had been arrested for using these women. A few weeks later my father had a heart attack, and died. Then I came back to the United States and saw Ching. He was very different. He took me to the United Nations and introduced me to many people. Some were black people; some were Chinese. I told him I did not trust these Chinese, but he said they were very good friends."

"Did he sympathize with the Communist regime in China?" Josh asked.

She nodded. "Yes. He told me many times the new China would some-day rule the world."

"Was he still friendly with Mr. Gentile?"

"Yes. He said he and Felix were still very good friends. He said he got many women for Felix's friends. When he was arrested by the police, he said Felix would help him. After I arrived he was indicted by the grand jury and was taken to the jail because the bail money was so high. But the next day I saw him. He said Felix had arranged for small bail so he could leave the country for Russia, and then he would go to Peking."

Josh said quickly, "Your brother said Gentile had fixed it so he could go free."

She nodded.

"And did your brother say that Gentile did this so he could skip to Russia and Peking?"

Another nod.

"You're sure, Suzy?"

"So sure."

"And you would give us a statement to that effect?"

"She's got nothing to hide," Forest snapped.

Josh ignored him. He was talking to Suzy.

"Yes, I would give you the statement," she said. "I will also give you letters from relatives who were smuggled out. They tell much about my brother in Peking." She looked up at her husband. "Then you will give us the money?"

"Five thousand," Josh said. He looked at the bearded man. "In cash. No tax. On the line. Tens, hundreds, thousands. You name it."

Forest wet his lips. "Hundreds. It will be easier. You want the statement and the other stuff now?"

"Let me make a call back at the hotel and we'll return within an hour."

"Okay. Not earlier," he said. "I have a reading to listen to down the road at my agent's house. We're having trouble with the female lead." He made a grimace and shook his head. "She has to be right, just right."

Good Lord, I thought, how low can you get?

300

He must have sensed the disgust I felt, for he said lamely that what his wife was going to give us would probably help the government.

"She's real gung ho," he said.

We found a small restaurant on one of the main boulevards where Josh made a call to the senator from a pay booth. No one was going to find a toll call listed from the Forest phone to either the committee or Wexford Hall.

He came out all smiles. "The old man's hot as hell about this. He told me to pay her anything I want, even double it if she will testify."

"She said she's going to Hong Kong with that bearded jackass."

"That's just fine," he said. "The fact is, I don't want her to testify. Her statement and the documentary evidence are enough. We can get the former U.S. Attorney to testify, and that will be real big."

"Why don't you want her to testify?"

"I don't trust that jerk husband of hers. The only thing left he has to sell is how we came out here and paid his wife $5,000 for her letters and statement. Don't tell me Gentile wouldn't use it. Come on, let's get back up there before Forest starts to think about raising the ante."

"We've been through a lot together, Josh, an awful lot," I said. "And we've done things, God help us, which I don't think we'll ever be proud to say we did. But this makes me sick. I feel I'm reaching in the grave of that poor girl."

"Let Kelly have the humility and scruples," was his short reply. "We just don't have the time. Come on, let's get back to that big jerk."

It took more than three hours to get the statement, even though I put her through the grinder, as we used to say in Washington in the old days, questioning her like a DA, while Josh took it all down on a portable. Anything she didn't see or hear herself, I discarded. When she quoted Gentile, I insisted that the entire quote be used. Actually, when it was finally finished, it was a devastating statement. The letters showed Ching held a trusted position in the Chinese inner circles. Reluctantly I began to feel that perhaps Josh had a point. Gentile was either an incredible fool or a Communist sympathizer. The latter was just too fantastic to believe, but still—I leaned to the theory he had been a frightened young man on the brink of a brilliant career, who may have been blackmailed into doing what he did by Ching, whose own sister was now painting him as a young procurer who used women both for money and to gain position.

The trouble with gathering statements—and I have heard this scores of times from men in all phases of law enforcement, local, state, or federal—lies not only in persuading the subject to talk but also in having at hand trivial things: a typewriter, pencils, pens—and finally a notary.

Luckily, Forest had the portable, but the notary was another thing. It was late Saturday afternoon, and we had a devil of a time finding one.

Forest sullenly abandoned his weights to accompany his wife, and we drove around until we found a real-estate man who was just finishing with a client. The fifteen-page statement finally signed and notarized, we drove to the airport to make a late New York plane. Forest kept hounding Josh for some kind of note that the money was coming to him, until finally I could keep quiet no longer and gave the young pup a tongue-lashing that brought a flush to his face. I felt sorry because of his wife, but she listened with Oriental impassiveness.

One day I would regret my sharp tongue.

CHAPTER SEVENTEEN: THE TWO MEN WHO CAME
TO DINNER

As SOMEONE ONCE SAID, Bishop Farley Grant might look like a lovable little cherub in clerical robes, but he also used a dirk as a bookmark for his breviary. And he was an expert with it as he gained souls for the church, favors for his diocese, schools for his children, and housing for his poor. He was the most astute real-estate dealer in New York, and could have taught Hetty Green a few things about the market. He was just as astute in politics as he was in real estate and finance. When the bishop liked a candidate, word went humming through the city. The leaders listened, and not many wanted to risk the old man's fury. By the time of this dinner he was a legend, a stout little man on tottering legs, almost eighty but still clinging to his shiny black cassock, heavy rosary, and time-worn crucifix. This was his image, God's Little Shepherd who never left his humble East Side flock, the shy little priest who seemingly was so awed by the tall, strong, sophisticated men of the city.

When it came to image making, the old man made me shake my head in admiration.

Once a year Bishop Grant held a dinner, ostensibly for the benefit of his little church located on the lower East Side since Civil War days. In reality the dinner was a stage for the political blessed, the stars slowly rising, the men with the sweet smell of success. No has-beens or failures ever addressed the dinner. After the war there were the giants of the military: MacArthur, Nimitz, Holland, and Ike in his first year at Columbia. Dewey, smiling in the triumph that never came, and scrappy Truman also made headlines for the Bishop's Dinner, along with the Kennedys —Jack, Bobby, then Ted; Rockefeller, Wagner, and LBJ. The faithful of all parties and of all faiths were never absent. After every dinner the Bishop's Relief Fund was always richer, and the state or city leaders left with another problem; in his traditional brief speech of welcome the bishop always hinted at what he wanted. It could be anything from a few more scholarships to help in building the new community center.

The senator had known the bishop for years, but it had taken a personal visit—and a fat contribution—to make sure Kelly received an invitation to be one of the speakers. There were usually two, and until they appeared no one knew their identities. The politicians just shrugged and called it another one of the old bishop's eccentricities, but it was much more subtle than that. The old man was a pro when it came to promoting his dinners, and not knowing what friend, foe, or dark horse would appear on the dais just whetted politicians' appetites and filled the press table.

The glittering affair was always at the Waldorf, with the VIP's flitting among the numerous private cocktail parties held before the dinner. While we shaved and slipped into our evening clothes, we discussed Suzy's statement. Josh insisted we not disclose it to the others until the next day when we gathered at Wexford.

"But didn't you tell the senator when you called him from the coast you were getting the girl's statement?"

"I did, and I told him to keep it quiet until we all met tomorrow," he said.

"But why?"

"Abernathy will be there. The senator said he has something for us. I hope it's his affidavit."

"Of course. How else would you make a deal with Mullady?"

Josh just wouldn't get mad. Even though he had only a few hours' sleep in the last forty-eight, he appeared alert and brimming over with confidence.

"My, don't we have big claws tonight! The truth is, I want to do some more checking."

"Why be so cautious? We have Suzy's statement."

"I want it to be as ironclad as I can get it when I hit Kelly with the Mullady deal. His God-damned love of truth could have us all qualifying, amending, and stalemating ourselves."

"What do you want checked?"

"The indictment, whether or not the Bureau ever sent out a flyer for Ching. The usual stuff."

"Will you tell Abernathy you don't want Mullady subpoenaed?"

He turned slowly from the mirror with a look of amazement. "Are you nuts, Finn? Why should I do that?"

"I think we should start by being honest with him."

"Well, I'm in no honest mood these days. Let him find out for himself." He ran a comb through his hair. "Let's go. It will be murder getting a cab now."

We met the senator and Luke in the corridor outside the old bishop's suite shortly after the photographers had taken the pictures Josh had staged of the bishop, Kelly, and the senator. But Kelly had already left, telling his father and Luke he intended to visit as many of the private parties as possible before the dinner.

"You'll both be up at Wexford tomorrow?" the senator asked.

"You couldn't keep us away, Senator," Josh said, and they smiled at each other.

"Did Kelly get our draft of the speech?" Josh asked Luke.

"He did," Luke said, "but I don't know how much he's going to use of it. He was writing and rewriting it all last night."

"Did Lacey come back with Molly?"

"We talked to her a few hours ago. She was still on the turnpike. She said the traffic's incredible."

"Is Molly going to stay at Wexford?"

"No. She doesn't want to. We made reservations for her at the Burning Oak Motel. It's less than a mile down the road.

"Any word on Benny?"

"They brought him down this morning. Kelly spoke to the AG himself. He wanted no part of a hotel, but we persuaded him to let Benny and the marshals stay at the Commodore. It's near the East Side Drive, and they can be down at the Federal Building in twenty minutes. Benny keeps asking the marshals to call Kelly and remind him this is the last time he's going to appear. By the way, Kelly was going to call the DA who's handling Benny's case and ask him to come down and talk to the committee—"

"Did he?" Josh asked quickly.

"No. He said it would be better if you handled it."

"I suppose we should hit some of those parties," the senator said.

"It won't hurt," Josh said.

As we started down the corridor, an elevator opened and a man carrying a camera with a heavy black bag over his shoulder hurried out. As he passed us, Josh suddenly whirled around and called out a name. The man stopped, stared, then rushed back to shake Josh's hand. Apparently they were old friends. Suddenly I saw the smile fade from Josh's face as he waved goodbye to the man who entered the bishop's suite.

"That's an AP photographer I knew in Washington," Josh said when he joined me. "He just tipped me off who's going to be the other speaker besides Kelly. Guess who?"

"I couldn't guess. Who?"

"Gentile. He just went in to get the bishop to ask them to pose for a picture."

I stopped in my tracks to stare at him. "Gentile!"

"You know how the old guy likes to keep his speakers secret until the last minute? I should have suspected he would stage something like this. Let's tell Luke and the old man." We hurried to catch up with Luke and the senator before they reached the elevator. The senator slammed his hand down angrily when we told him.

"That old conniver!" He looked up at Josh. "Well, there's nothing we can do, is there, Michaels?"

"We certainly should alert Kelly," Josh said. "I don't want him posing with Gentile at this stage of the game." He asked Luke, "Where do you think he is?"

"I guess at one of the private parties."

"Which one was he going to?"

"He said he was going to hit all of them," the senator said.

"There are four that I know of," Luke said. "The newspapermen have one; then there's the Catholic Charities, the Knights, and the Gaelic Society—"

"Suppose we split up," Josh said. "The suites of the different cocktail parties are on the mimeographed sheet they gave us. Let's each take one. Whoever finds Kelly is to bring him to the foyer outside the grand ballroom. I'm also going to try to find out what Gentile's speech is all about. Let's go."

My cocktail party was the one held by the Gaelic Society, an old and powerful organization, once composed of Irish-American municipal employees, but now numbering among its members Irishmen, Jews, Italians, Poles, even Russians. To qualify for membership you had to be a municipal employee, a foe of automation, and a stern advocate of shutting down all city offices at 4:00 P.M. during the summer months.

I found the party in a small ballroom that was packed to the doors. I squirmed inside and made my way through the noisy, laughing crowd. The bar was packed ten deep, and a noisy five-man band desperately competed with the din. There were round, red faces, jowls hanging over stiff collars, cigar butts, cigarettes, braying laughter, intent, jabbing voices, conspiratorial whispers. But no Kelly Shannon. I finally gave up and fought my way out of the room to head for the Grand Ballroom foyer. I made my way into a crowded elevator and turned to the panel of floor buttons when someone reached over my shoulder and pressed number twenty—going up.

I looked up into Kelly's smiling face. Some men can buy the best evening clothes in Brooks and still look uncomfortable and rumpled, while others can take the jacket and pants from a pipe rack and look born to them. Kelly was the latter.

"I've been looking all over for you people," he said. "I just missed Josh at the Catholic Charities party."

"What's upstairs? Another party?"

"We have a date," he said. "I'll tell you about it when we get off."

We got off at the twentieth floor and started down the tomblike silent hall.

"I was just leaving the last party when one of the bishop's aides found me with a message from the bishop," Kelly explained. "Gentile's the other speaker, and the bishop wants us to pose for a picture."

"That's exactly what Josh doesn't want you to do, Kelly. That's why we've been trying to find you."

"I don't see how a picture of us together will hurt—"

"Prosecutors don't pose with defendants, Kelly."

"I thought we had agreed some time ago—I'm not a prosecutor, and I'm not trying to destroy Felix Gentile. Besides, I already told the bishop I would pose."

"What about Gentile? Does he want to pose?"

"I just spoke to him on the house phone. He has no objection. Incidentally, he sounds like a nice guy."

"You're not playing it according to the script."

"Oh, balls," he said warmly. "Here it is."

The buzzer sounded, and the door was opened by a stony-faced young man who glared at Kelly, then silently stepped aside.

As we walked into the living room, Gentile came out of a bedroom smiling and with hand outstretched. He looked older, and I thought the splendid air of confidence he possessed that day in City Hall was not so strong. He was still an impressive-looking man. I thought to myself that if Hollywood needed a man to play the role of a Secretary of State, they could cast this handsome man with the perfect evening clothes and iron-gray wavy hair who looked so poised and dignified.

"I understand we're supposed to pose for a picture, Congressman," he said. He turned to the younger man. "Did the photographers call, Harold?"

"They're on their way up."

"This is Harold Knox, one of my advisers," Gentile said with a smile. "He doesn't think I should pose with you."

"And this is one of my advisers, Finn McCool. He doesn't think I should pose with *you*," Kelly said.

"Let's forget politics tonight, shall we?" Gentile said. The buzzer sounded, and the photographers crowded into the room. As photographers have undoubtedly done since the days of Daguerre, they criticized the lighting, brusquely ordered Kelly and Gentile this way and that, took a fantastic number of pictures they could never use, accepted a drink, and then were gone, leaving behind the debris of their brief visit, cigarettes, used flashbulbs, disarranged furniture.

"Harold, will you tell the bishop the pictures were taken?" he asked his aide, who nodded and with one last bitter look at us, left.

"We have about a half hour," Gentile said. "Would you gentlemen care for a drink?"

Kelly had a Scotch and water, I had a rye highball, and Gentile a short Scotch on the rocks.

"I guess we're the evening's surprises," Gentile said. "Did you have any idea I was to share the dais with you?"

"I didn't. Frankly I thought it might be someone from Washington."

"Wait until you hear that buzz when we walk in," Gentile said with a laugh. "Trust the bishop to make it an interesting evening."

"This is my first Bishop's Dinner," Kelly said, "but I've heard about them."

"This is my second," Gentile said. "The last one was almost eight years ago, when I first ran for mayor. I'm glad City Hall is behind me, although campaigning is no joke." He raised the glass and studied Kelly over its rim. "Do you intend to enter the race, Congressman?"

"I've been told in politics it's bad form to give previews unless you have a press conference or an audience of no less than ten thousand," Kelly said, smiling.

"I can see you have expert advisers," Gentile said with a laugh. Then, almost casually, "By the way, the committee's doing a fine job—"

I held my breath and gave Kelly a warning frown: Stay clear of the shoals.

"I'm sorry it had to hit so close to you," Kelly said. "Have you asked Saunders about any of the charges?"

I could only close my eyes and hope for the best.

"The day after your witness—the fat little man—"

"Benny Jello?"

"That's the one. After he testified he had those deals with Chuck, I called Chuck in. He swore up and down—as he's done many times since—that he doesn't know Jello, never met him, and knew Remington only as a lawyer who has had difficulties with booze." His voice became strained, and it was evident the tension inside him was slowly building up. When he lifted his glass his hand trembled slightly.

"Have you known Saunders long?"

"We were roommates at Farrington, then roommates at Yale. We were in the army together, went overseas together, and both served in the Asian theatre. A year after I joined State, he came to Washington and worked with me in the China Division. We shared an apartment for years until, as you know, I married his sister. I don't think there has been any man closer to me than Chuck Saunders." He shrugged. "So what can I say? I would put my life in his hands without question—even today."

Who are you kidding? I told myself as I clamped my teeth tight to keep from asking the question. What about Nina, Suzy, and Ching? And the visit to the United States Attorney with the plea to have Ching's bail reduced?

I said, "How long were you in Washington, Mr. Gentile?"

"Several years. You were down there at the same time, I think—with Senator Shannon's committee, wasn't it?"

"I was with several committees: War Assets, Highways, Consumers, the Vietnam Atrocities, Peking Propaganda—and the Shannon Committee. I was with the senator for several years. It was strange we didn't meet. . . ."

"I imagine we would have, had the senator continued his investigation into State," Gentile said almost gently.

"I would suppose so," I replied, and our eyes locked.

"Did you like it down there?" Kelly asked.

"I loved what I was doing, but the town—no. Sometimes I thought it was a place of sharpshooters instead of lawmakers. And sometimes I wish I had never left State," Gentile said. "I always felt as if I was doing something worth while."

The words popped out before I could stop them. I knew they sounded blunt and slightly contemptuous: "Well, why did you leave?"

"The party felt I could win if I ran for mayor," he said, unruffled.

"If you had to do it all over again?" Kelly asked.

"I would never leave State," was his prompt answer. "You may be a deer down there, but at City Hall you're an elephant, and they never miss."

He said it so ruefully, with such sincerity, it made Kelly laugh and, frankly, it did raise a smile with me.

The thought I had voiced aloud to Josh began nagging me again. How could this smiling, distinguished American betray his country by dealing with a Peking agent? It just didn't sound logical. Then suddenly I remembered what a wise old statesman had told me many years ago: It wasn't the grubby, the crude, the ill-educated who were the villains of our history, but rather the genteel, the ones blessed by education, breeding, affluence, who betrayed their country for motives often shockingly commonplace. . . .

Like Gentile. Caught in a vise of scandal and a brilliant future?

Kelly and Gentile were busily exchanging reminiscences of Washington and some of its personalities when I put down my glass with a sharp finality.

"It looks like we have to go," Kelly said, standing up. "It was wonderful meeting you."

"I'm sure we'll be seeing a lot of each other—or at least hearing about each other before November," Gentile said as they shook hands.

"Perhaps," Kelly said. "Well, to the dais . . ."

The three of us took the elevator to the small foyer off the ballroom where we were greeted by the bishop, who put on a great show of tottering over to them and linking his arms to Kelly and Gentile. Of course, there were photographers who began shooting more pictures. The foyer was filled with political VIP's, and from the looks and out-of-the-corner-of-the-mouth whispers I knew the town would be buzzing with the news before the dinner was over.

The senator, stony-faced, ignored Gentile, while Luke studied him as closely as a butcher might a newly arrived steer as it hung from a hook. If someone touched Josh with a match, it would ignite, I thought, as I inched my way to his side.

"For Christ's sake, where have you been?" he whispered.

"I met Kelly on his way to Gentile's suite. He had promised the bishop to pose with Gentile."

Josh groaned so loudly a startled woman turned to peer at him.

"Let's get out of here," he said as he pushed his way from the room. Outside, he lit a cigarette and turned to me furiously. "I hope you didn't let him pose with that guy."

"I asked him not to, but he said he didn't see why he shouldn't."

"Why he shouldn't? For Christ's sake, Finn, he'll be all over the papers posing with a guy the committee's slowly destroying as his political opponent! After all we've done—"

"Dinner's starting in a moment, gentlemen," a waiter whispered as he stuck his head out the door.

"—————— the dinner," Josh said savagely, and the startled man hastily shut the door.

"I gave him all those reasons," I said. "I told him prosecutors don't pose with potential defendants—"

"And what did he say to that?"

"He said he wasn't a prosecutor and he had no intention of destroying Gentile."

Josh said fiercely, "Him and his God-damned sincerity will sink us all yet."

He ground the cigarette into the rug. "Let's go."

It was a superb but tense dinner. Those who didn't stare whispered. After we sat down, the photographers stalked the dais so much the bishop had to order no more pictures until after the dinner.

Gentile made an excellent speech. It was obvious his people were very much on the ball: the whole thing was aimed at page one of *The New York Times*. Gentile went on to disclose an elaborate housing program aimed at wiping out the main ghettos of the city. He said that he had secretly set it in motion several months before his resignation. Now the surveys had been completed.

Of course, the artist's conception of the project was available for the press table. There were blocks of stores, squares of flowers, fountains and no traffic, high-rise housing projects—a dream city where now there were only rat-ridden tenements. As a plan that had been conceived while he was mayor and that had been kept secret for all these months, this was cold, hard news, and no reporter could ignore it.

But Kelly, on the other hand, had not worked all night to bring forth a mouse of a speech. Like Josh, he had a knack for turning a phrase, and what he borrowed from Josh and what he invented himself made an im-

pressive and at times startling half hour. He made the press table sit up
when he quietly told the intent guests that one of the most infamous men
of American politics, a man who had dealt in injustice and human indignity, would be summoned by the committee. With a cold quirt of a
voice he went on to lash his fellow Americans and the nation's leaders in
Washington for the ghettos that lay across the land from the Empire
State to Watts.

"The *Times* will have to twin them both up on page one," Josh said.
"The man on Pennsylvania Avenue isn't going to love him after tonight."

Finally it was over, and we were leaving with the bishop's farewell,
"It was a grand night, boys, and God walk with you!" in our ears.

We returned to the senator's suite, and there Josh and Kelly met head
on.

"Didn't it occur to you, Kelly, it might be harmful to pose with this
guy?" Josh said, minutes after the door closed behind us.

"No, it didn't."

"Didn't you realize the average newspaper reader or television viewer
might find it a bit incongruous for you to be shaking hands with Gentile?
As Finn told you—"

"I know," Kelly said shortly, "the prosecutor and the potential defendant. But that's not true. I'm no prosecutor, and Gentile's no potential
defendant—as far as I can see."

"Don't be too sure," Josh said roughly.

"Then you know something I don't," Kelly said.

"Perhaps I do. Don't you realize Gentile could have had that room
bugged?"

"I'm sorry, Josh, but I just can't view every man having ulterior motives and every phone or room bugged. That's a hell of a way to go
through life."

"Maybe. But sometimes it's the safest." He turned to the senator. "Senator, I think we should get something straight once and for all."

"Michaels is right, Kelly," the senator told his son. "There are times
when you must listen to his experience—"

"Experience, yes. But please let me make my own judgment."

"And what's yours of Gentile?" Luke asked.

"I think he's a nice guy. He'd probably make a hell of a good governor."

"Holy Christ," Josh said.

"This man is not my personal enemy," Kelly said angrily. "He has
never harmed me or anyone of us! I don't want any vendettas! I don't
care for personal attacks! If we find Gentile has done wrong, fine. Then
expose it! Then hand it over to the proper authorities! But for God's sake,
don't try and push me into hurting or hating a man I scarcely know
simply because he stands in the middle of my political path."

He tore off his cummerbund and tie and began removing his studs.

"You want to get something straight, Josh—well, so do I. I'm not out to destroy Felix Gentile by innuendo, gossip, hearsay, or character assassination."

"You don't have to do it," the senator said grimly; "his thieving brother-in-law has done it for him."

"What has been brought out in the committee's hearings have been facts, cold hard facts," Kelly protested. "Thank God I insisted on that—"

"Let's say we do get something on Gentile," Josh said. "What do we do —forget it just because he's a nice guy?"

"You know better than that, Josh," Kelly said. "If I caught Luke here guilty of any wrongdoing, and it came within the committee's scope, I would bring him before the committee. You know that."

"Is that a promise?"

"It's more than a promise—it's an obligation!"

"That's all that I wanted to know," Josh said. "What time do you want us at Wexford, Senator?"

"How about eleven?" Luke put in. "We should see Benny, Molly—and arrange for that confrontation on Tuesday—"

"Have you spoken to Lacey?" Josh asked.

"Only once when she was on the Turnpike. I imagine she's got Molly bedded down at the motel."

"I was wondering if we should have a marshal with them," Kelly said.

"She's not a government witness," Luke pointed out.

"But they burned her house down," Kelly snapped.

"Suppose we arrange that in the morning," Luke said, yawning.

Josh said, "Well, we'll say good night."

"Will you fellows see about that marshal for Molly in the morning?" Kelly called out from the bedroom as we opened the door.

"Sure," Josh said, "first thing in the morning."

But we never did.

CHAPTER EIGHTEEN: DECISION AT WEXFORD

We arrived at Wexford shortly before eleven and were immediately rushed into the library. Everyone was there: Luke, the senator, Lacey, Luther, Shea and Short—and Gene Abernathy.

Josh casually threw copies of the *Times*, *News*, and the Washington papers on the coffee table.

"You're in all the papers, Kelly."

Kelly glanced at the Washington *Post*, which had the picture of him and Gentile on page one. The overline read: "Beloved Enemies?"

He grinned, but the senator glanced at it and threw it to one side.

"Oh, come on, Dad, where's your sense of humor?" Kelly said. "If we can't stand a little thing like this—"

"Let's forget it," Josh interrupted. "Tonight they'll be wrapping fish-heads in all of them."

"Dad said you had something important to tell us, Josh," Kelly said.

"Very important," Josh was emphatic. He glanced at Abernathy.

"Gene came down to give us some news," Kelly remarked evenly.

"It's not that I don't—"

"Forget it," Abernathy said cheerfully. "You boys have your secrets. Me, I'm better off not knowing them." He handed Josh a folder. "This is the statement I told you about. It gives names, dates—chapter and verse on Barney's activities. I signed it and had it notarized."

"You realize this may implicate you legally?" Josh asked. "A party to a conspiracy?"

The young Negro held up his hands.

"So what? If I go, man, I go all the way or not at all."

"Gene was just telling us what's happening in Lawrence when you arrived," Kelly said. "There have been two more incidents. The cops shot a young kid they said was driving a stolen car. They insisted he had pulled a gun on them. The car turned out to be his uncle's, who had given him permission to use it, and the gun was a wrench the boy had in his pocket. The boy was an honor student who won the plastic union's full college scholarship last year. A Muslim group raised hell last night, and there was a fight. A cop had his arm broken, and they overturned a radio car."

"I didn't hear anything on the news broadcast," Josh said. "Did you, Finn?"

I shook my head.

"You wouldn't have," Kelly answered. "They covered it up. The local police chief called it a fight between a group of drunken Negroes, coming home from a wedding, and the police. Gene said his people are straining at the leash. They want to break out now; they don't want to wait for my formal announcement."

"It's too soon," Josh said. "I said it should be done right after the Lawrence hearings. The impact will be much greater. If we do it now with the New York hearings not even started, we'll scatter our shots. As I said—"

"You calling Barney soon?" Gene asked abruptly.

"First come the New York hearings, then Lawrence," Josh said earnestly. "You've been watching TV, Gene—you know what a job we're going to have to do to catch up with Remington, Saunders, and the judge. It's going to be a hell of a week!" He turned to Luther. "Any word on Remington or Saunders? I thought Remington was going to be on 'Spotlight' this afternoon."

"We all did," Luther said. "I tuned in, and there was this guy from some consumers' outfit discussing that new bill. I called up to ask how come, and the producer said he got a call this morning from Remington's wife that he had a virus. He said he tried to get Saunders to take Remington's place, but there was no answer at his number. The City Hall operator said she tried, but no luck."

"We have someone keeping track of them?"

"There are two men covering Remington and Saunders. All we can do is tail them."

"The *Times* caught up with Saunders outside a restaurant," Luke said. "They quote him as saying he never saw Jello, and furthermore that he wouldn't be seen in the same county with such a cheap thief. He also told the *Times* if Kelly wants to make the same charges outside the committee hearing room, he will instantly sue for $5,000,000 in damages."

"Fine," Josh replied. "Kelly will repeat all the charges in a press conference. In fact, he will repeat everything that Benny has charged and challenge Saunders and Remington to dispute them on the witness stand under oath." He said to Luther, "You make the arrangements, Luther. Make sure we send out a note to all editors on AP and UPI tonight, advising them of this conference, and also make sure all TV knows it. Now let him put his testimony where his mouth is."

Gene stood up. "Well, I have to get back. I just wanted to let you know—"

"By the way, Gene," Josh said, "Barney still doesn't know anything."

"About me?" Abernathy asked. "Hell, no. If he did I wouldn't be here. Maybe in the morgue."

"When it comes out it can be rough," Luther said.

"Could be," Abernathy replied. "Could be."

With a great show of sincerity, but with an obvious note of dismissal, Josh said: "This statement should be important as hell. It's great of you to come down. This new thing, as I said, is really not—"

The young Negro flashed us all a smile. "No problem. I'll be in touch if there are any new developments." He turned to Josh: "Be sure and let me know when you subpoena Barney."

"You'll be the first to know."

When he left, Kelly asked angrily, "Now what the hell was so important we couldn't discuss it in front of him?"

Josh slowly removed the black leather file on Gentile and Suzy's statement from his attaché case.

"Just this," he said. He opened the file. "This is a secret government report on Gentile. Why it was made I don't know. Perhaps he just came to the attention of the agency and they began building up a file on him. It covers his career and personal life from the time he returned to Washington with General Chu, Chiang Kai-shek's Air Force Minister, to recently. I will grant you a large amount is uncorroborated, garbage, a mess of gossip, probably obtained from hostile sources, as much of the information in these files is; however, there is one aspect, one shocking aspect, which I don't think any of us can overlook." He paused dramatically and said, "I think it may have something to do with our country's present conflict with Peking over Vietnam."

The senator remarked impatiently, "Let's hear it, Michaels. Let's hear it."

"Suppose I read you excerpts, which I will carefully document as to the sources; then we will go into the more serious charges."

Oh, the boy was putting on a good show.

For more than an hour he read excerpts from the report, and as he promised, he carefully put each charge in its proper perspective, gossip, enemies of Gentile, half truths, documentary evidence, excerpts from secret documents, such as FBI or CIA reports, and so on.

There wasn't a sound in the library when Josh slowly read the story of the tragic romance of Gentile and Nina, and Suzy's explanation of her sister's death and the subsequent suicide letter.

Then Kelly exploded. "By God, that's the dirtiest, filthiest accumulation of garbage I ever heard!" he shouted. "Do you expect me to bring this out in open hearings, Josh? Have we no sense of decency? Are we—"

Josh's voice was cold and cutting. "Just who the hell are you to say I don't have any decency, Kelly? I'm reading from an official United States Government document! I'm not the source of what I'm reading. Our government is!"

"But you yourself described it as garbage."

"Perhaps what I have read so far—there's more."

"Well, come on," the senator said. "Let's have it."

"Let me get one thing straight," Josh said, turning to Kelly. "Just so there is no misunderstanding about this file. I never intended to smear Gentile with half truths, gossip, or unconfirmed scandal. In fact, that is exactly why I wanted Abernathy out of here. We all know and trust one another. We all like Abernathy and we honor what he is doing. But he's a black politician, and for my money he's as human as a white one. Maybe more so. Maybe this election they'll know they'll be throwing the punches, not taking them, so we must expect them to be on the lookout for every opportunity. What we discuss here must always remain in this room." He ticked us off, man by man. "Is that agreed?"

We all nodded.

"I didn't mean it that way," Kelly offered. "I'm sorry if it sounded like that."

Josh's smile was wide and friendly. "No harm done, Kelly. Let's get to the heart of this thing."

He slowly read them a capsule description of Suzy's statement, and held it up to show her signature and the notary's stamp.

"My God," Shea cried, "that's dynamite! He may be an agent!"

"Don't be ridiculous," I snapped. "He was a prominent young man in a tight situation, and probably did it because he was panicky. Let's not bring in espionage. It will make us all look foolish."

"Finn doesn't think nice dignified young Americans can be enemy agents—or sympathizers," Josh said wryly.

"If he wasn't a Communist sympathizer or an agent, he was a complete fool," Luke put in.

"Granted," I said. "A fool, yes—an agent, no."

Luke said roughly, "I think we should take him apart on this."

The senator pounded the arm of his chair. "Why are you even hesitating? You have the statement from the girl who quotes her own brother!"

Shea said: "We could have every housewife in the country hanging on every word! It will be bigger than anything that ever hit television! The guy they said would walk into the White House helping a Peking agent get out of the country!" He slapped his hands together and whistled softly.

"Let's go slow on this," Kelly told us. "How do we know Ching is in Peking?"

Josh said: "I agree with Kelly. We have to check out every detail before we spring it. I'm going to Washington the first thing in the morning and see what I can get from my sources in the Bureau and the CIA." He turned to me: "Finn, you check the Federal Building and see if the indictment is on file. Also Ching's bail slip. Talk to his bondsman. Also the local Bureau to see if they ever sent out a flyer on him."

"I just can't see Gentile—" Kelly began, but Luke broke in.

"If the facts add up, Kel, what can you do? This is too big to let go by the boards. I think the country should know about it."

Luther, who had been silent, spoke up for the first time: "If this is true and, as Luke says, the facts add up, then it is shocking and should come out. But, on the other hand, if it is a half truth, that's something else." He shook his head. "I agree with Finn. It just doesn't ring. Something's missing."

I said promptly: "I told Josh the same thing. Gentile might have been a fool, but he's no man to shake hands with the Devil."

The senator bellowed, "You can't have a fool running for Albany and Washington, McCool!"

Josh said: "The senator is right. That's a point that has to be considered. Would you want a man foolish enough to have done this in the White House? Or Albany? Or even City Hall?"

"Suppose we let the complete facts tell us the whole story," Kelly suggested.

"We can't hold this too long, Kelly," Josh warned. "Finn and I will clean up the facts, and if they add up as I think they will we should disclose them to the country as soon as possible."

315

Shea said: "That means you'll have Remington, Saunders, the judge—and then this? That'll be the week that was!"

Josh said, "We'll be back here late tonight—with the facts, as many as we can gather. Then I think we should decide what to do."

Luke said: "I say go all out. Gentile would have to withdraw. Out completely."

The hatchet man, I thought, the complete young hatchet man.

"It will be the biggest week in television," Shea said. "I'm going to call Dyke and tell him."

Kelly held up both hands, almost pleadingly. "Please, Frank! Go easy." He looked around. "Just as Josh said, this has to stay in this room. One word, one slip, and Gentile would be ruined in the most horrible way possible. It would be worse than McCarthyism."

"Oh, come on, Kel," Luke said. "Nobody's going to shout it from the church steeple, you know."

"I'm aware of that," Kelly replied. "But I think we should all realize what we have is still only one side of the story—"

The senator slammed down his hand impatiently. "An official report! The girl's sister's statement!"

"I still say it's half the story, Dad," Kelly told him sharply. "I agree with Finn and Luther—there's something missing."

"We'll find it," Josh said. "One more thing before we break up. Did you talk to Benny?"

"He's absolutely frightened to death," Kelly said. "He keeps insisting I call the DA and get something in writing that the charges against him will be squashed."

I looked at Josh, who was as tense as a coiled spring.

"Forget it," he said. "I'll take care of it. But you'll never get a DA to put anything like that in writing. Benny knows that."

"He's terribly frightened, Josh."

"I realize that. I just don't want to queer anything at this point."

"Jones and I did agree we should ask the DA to come down at the end of the week and talk about it."

"I think that's a good idea," Luther said. "Let him come down after the hearings have rocked everybody. He might get the message faster. Don't you think so, Josh?"

Josh gave him an indifferent look. "Maybe. Let's see how it goes. Frank, how did we do last week?"

"We reached almost 35 percent when Benny was telling about his deals," Shea said, consulting his notes. "It hit 50 plus when they discovered the hijacked truck and the TV crews made those great films. The east was almost 80 percent. And they all stayed with it, right through the news broadcasts, six to eleven. Coverage in the press was just fine. The late papers in New York, Chicago, L.A., Washington, and other major cities made a splash with the wirephoto shots of the fighting in the streets and the hijacked truck. Now what do you plan for tomorrow?"

"It won't be hard to maneuver Remington into repeating the statement he made on TV, that Benny was a client and nothing more," Josh said. "We open the hearings with Benny in the witness room. Let Saunders and Remington briefly repeat their statements for the record. Then we bring Benny out and ask him to identify both of them and repeat some of his deals with them."

"Hiss and Chambers, all over again," Luther said.

"Exactly," Josh replied. "We have Benny stand up and identify them" —Josh suddenly stood up and dramatically pointed his finger at Kelly— "then slowly walk down"—he walked to where Kelly was sitting and tapped his shoulder—"and tap each man on the shoulder."

"Beautiful," Shea breathed. "Just beautiful."

There was a shadow on Kelly's face, and his eyes were troubled. "When the charges against him are dropped, how soon will they let him go?"

"It's not that easy, Kelly," I told him. "He'll probably have to be used in other trials. If Saunders and Remington are indicted, as they surely will be, Benny will have to be the people's witness."

"That's right," Josh replied quickly. "He'll have to testify. But that's not a hard life. They treat the state's witness with kid gloves."

Kelly shook his head.

"I just hate to—"

The door opened and Lacey stepped in. She looked weary.

"Lace, you look beat," Kelly said with concern.

"We drove back," Lacey said. "I didn't know it until I got on the phone with the airline that Molly wouldn't fly if St. Peter was the pilot. So I hired a car and we drove. That shore traffic on the Parkway was unbelievable." She flopped in a chair. "Now if some kind soul would give me a cup of hot coffee." She looked at Josh, and smiled.

"Hello, Wet Nurse," Josh said with a smile. "I saw a friend the other day. He wants us to go to Basin Street East. It's Peggy Lee."

She leaned her head back on the chair and gave an exaggerated groan. "You mean one night without staying up with this poor, frightened woman?" She opened her eyes and accepted the cup from Luke.

"I know she's little and dumpy and wears ridiculous jewelry, but she also has the most fantastic courage I have ever seen! She's been like a mother to that stupid little thief! And do you know what she talked about all the way up from Washington? How she and Benny will go out to Los Angeles on a honeymoon and see her niece who's a registered nurse!"

"Did you leave her at the Burning Oak?" Kelly asked.

"She took one of their little cottages. She was sleeping when I left—"

"Oh, Josh, did you see about the marshal for her?" Kelly asked.

Josh snapped his fingers. "Damn, I forgot. I'll do it the first thing after we get back to the city."

"If not a marshal, a Pinkerton guard or something," Kelly said. "I just don't feel right leaving her there alone." He turned to Lacey: "Did she want to go over and see the house?"

"No. She cried when I told her it would be rebuilt. I think the poor woman's in a daze." She turned to Josh. "Please, Josh—let that little man go on tomorrow and no more! Please!"

"I promise. After tomorrow, no more."

"And the district attorney will help him?"

"Absolutely."

I wondered how he would face her after tomorrow.

"He'll be terrified facing those two men. He told Molly that Saunders knows a lot of awful people."

"After tomorrow Saunders will have only one thing in mind—how he will explain it all to the grand jury," Josh said.

"Do you think the DA will act?" Luke asked.

"Absolutely. Also the U.S. Attorney. But we have something more important than Benny right now, Lacey." He handed her the Gentile folder. "Suppose you go over in the corner and read it."

While Lacey read the contents of the folder and sipped her coffee, we discussed the agenda of the next day's hearing. Along with Saunders and Remington there would be the waiter who would identify them as the men who ate with Benny Jello, the introduction of their luncheon check, Remington's secretary, the Jersey lawyer who paid Saunders and Remington to fix the case of the executive's son charged with rape, the arresting officers in the case, the boy's father. Also subpoenaed were Beering of Delafield Motors, his superiors.

"They'll need three grand juries." There was a glint in Luke's cold eyes. "They'll be handing down perjury indictments by the fistful."

"Then comes Lawrence," Kelly said grimly, "and Mullady."

"We'll come to Mullady," Josh replied quickly. "Let's not forget Gentile. That's going to rock the country."

Lacey came across the room and silently put the folder back on the table.

"What do you think, Lace?" Kelly asked.

"I guess I could repeat that horrible cliché about nothing being sacred," she said. "That poor girl."

"We're not interested in their love affair," Josh told her, "if that's what you're getting at."

"Are you telling me it will never be mentioned?" Lacey asked in a bitter, sad voice.

"We're interested in one thing—did Gentile get Ching's bail reduced, and why?"

"If it's true, Lacey, it should be brought out," Kelly said.

"I suppose I'm just naïve," she went on, "but I find it hard to believe Mr. Gentile is a Chinese agent or even a fool. It appears something is missing."

"Before anything is brought out it will be first confirmed," Luke said. "Nobody wants to crucify him, Lacey."

"After what I've seen these last few weeks I wouldn't be surprised to find you boys pulling wings off butterflies." She walked to the door. "I called the school and told them I would be in this afternoon."

"Wait a while and we'll drive you down," Josh urged.

"No, I'll drive down myself. You have too many butterflies to take care of today," she said, and left.

Josh hurried after her and came back a few minutes later.

"She give you a hard time, Josh?" Luke asked with a grin.

"She's tired," Josh replied impatiently. "I tried to get her to let us drive her down, but it's like talking to a stone wall." He returned to his clipboard and notes. "Well, I think that takes care of the New York hearings." He turned to Kelly: "I'll get the shuttle for Washington, and Finn can move around the city."

"Can you check it out all in one day?" Luther asked.

"Definitely. We'll be back tonight, but late. Will you all be here?"

"I'm going to see Dyke in Chicago this afternoon," Shea said, "but I'll be back for the hearing in the morning."

"Try to call us late tonight, Frank," Josh replied. "You and Dyke should know how it comes out."

"Definitely. I'll call tonight."

"By the way, be careful how you use these phones," Josh told him. "We don't know who might be tapping our wires."

"Wiretapping?" Kelly said. "That's illegal."

"So is bookmaking, but it's a multimillion dollar business," Josh retorted.

"You can't go very far with wiretapping these days," Luther said. "Even Internal Revenue got knocked down on the use of bugs."

"Don't believe it. Wiretapping and bugging still go on. They're big business today." Then Josh added, with a faint smile, "The only crime is getting caught."

We all rose, stretched, and started to gather our things.

As we walked to the car Kelly suddenly turned to Josh.

"By the way, Josh, where did you get this file on Gentile?"

"From a source."

"Reliable?"

"As I said once before—reliable as the Grand Central clock."

"You couldn't tell me who it is?"

Josh put his arm around Kelly's shoulder. "Who gave it to us is not important; that we have it is."

"I don't like to keep repeating myself, but Lacey and I agree—something's missing in the Gentile story, Josh," Kelly said.

I added, "That's my feeling."

"I just wonder what Gentile's explanation for all this could be," Kelly murmured.

"It had better be good," Josh remarked with a wide yawn. "It had just better be good."

Kelly turned to Josh. "Two more things and I'll get off your back: you're going to call the DA on Jello's case and then arrange for Molly to have some kind of guard. If not the marshals, then the Pinkertons."

"I'll take care of both of them this afternoon. We'll see you tonight."

As we moved out into the highway, I asked Josh: "Did you ever call that DA again?"

"I talked to him at home while you were shaving."

"And—"

"No dice. He couldn't care less if Jello turned in Benedict Arnold. He's going to throw the book at him as soon as he gets him back."

"What will you tell Lacey?"

"I don't know," he said roughly. "Now, for Christ's sake let's forget about Jello for a few minutes! We'll work out something! The old man told me he'll get him some high-priced lawyers, buy off the complainant, the cops, anybody. First it's Kelly, then Lacey—now you. Let up on me about this bum!"

I let up.

It was clear that the room clerk in the United States Attorney's office, Eastern District, in the Federal Building, was disturbed when I asked to see the indictment on one Ching Chu, indicted by the Federal Grand Jury, Eastern District, for violation of the Mann Act. He fumbled around for a minute getting his answers ready in his mind, then asked, in the solemn way of all file clerks, to see my credentials. He examined the committee's badge, mumbled something about checking the files, and disappeared.

I knew he was on the telephone in the back room, so I wasn't surprised when a young, smiling assistant appeared at my elbow and said the U.S. Attorney would like to see me regarding my request.

Fortunately, he wasn't a total stranger. He had been a young assistant on the AG's staff some years ago in Washington, and we had at least a nodding acquaintance. I blandly informed him the committee was doing a survey of the bail system and needed a breakdown of defendants who have skipped, all for the purpose of legislation. He didn't believe a word of it, of course, but just as blandly assured me of the complete cooperation of his office.

And the Ching file?

He was sorry, but at the present time the FBI had it; as I was undoubtedly aware, the Bureau periodically went over the files of all fugitives.

When I asked if the Bureau had sent out flyers on Ching, he hesitated, but quickly informed me flyers indeed had been circulated, after I had slyly suggested that if they had not been issued someone had surely goofed, perhaps in his office.

He had been in Washington too long not to get the message. Everything, he said, was up at the Bureau, and if I wanted he could call the acting agent.

I thanked him, and before an angel could sneeze, was out of his office. I didn't want to get involved with the Bureau, who would be sniffing about my heels like a coon dog on the scent. I did the obvious. I visited the Main Post Office on Eighth Avenue.

Sure enough, there was Mr. Ching's picture on the FBI flyer. No one was looking, so it was in my pocket and I was out the door in a matter of seconds. One line in the flyer was significant: "The fugitive is reported to have left the confines of the continental United States. American citizens abroad are requested to" . . .

Willy was right thus far: the indictment and vital papers on Ching, all public property, were important enough to have been lifted from the files of the U.S. Attorney's office by orders of someone big in Washington. And Ching had fled the country. I hoped Josh would get some of the answers through our Washington friends.

To find the bail bondsman was simply a question of going from door to door of the bailing offices that are scattered about Foley Square. The third one was paydirt. He was a little gray-haired man with the face of a rodent. His feet came crashing down off his desk when he heard the name Ching.

"You know where he is, mister?" he asked eagerly. "There's 10 percent in it for you."

I showed him my credentials, and his feet went back up with a grunt.

"Me, I don't know nothing about this Chink. One day his sister comes in and we make bail for him. Five thousand. Mann Act charge. First it was fifty; then they knocked it down. He just signed the papers and paid, and that was it. The trial date comes up, no Chink. Then the FBI comes around and asks me if I saw him." He said indignantly: "If I saw him? I'd call the nearest cop! The insurance company's on my back every month about this guy. One day an agent comes down and says he skipped the country. Where? Who knows? Maybe Mexico. A lot of thieves go there."

"Then he's a fugitive?" I asked innocently.

"Are you kidding?" he demanded. "They gave him thirty days to show; then the grand jury hit him with failing to appear for trial and leaving the jurisdiction of the court. If they ever catch up with him they'll throw away the key, buddy."

That evening when we had all gathered, waiting for Josh, I described what I had found, and passed around the flyer. The senator kept nodding, as though he knew he had been right about Gentile all along. Over the phone Luke said Shea had whistled softly at the prospect of his biggest week in television. Luther just smoked his pipe and shrugged as though to say that this was it. Only Lacey and Kelly listened impassively.

I had reached my interview with the U.S. Attorney when Josh came in. I did a fast recap, then went on.

When I finished, he said he had had a devil of a time getting anyone to discuss the case—even off the record. His shirt was rumpled and grimy. He had a dark beard; there were black circles under his eyes, and his irritability was plainly only below skin surface.

He reported gruffly that Ching definitely had skipped the country. The FBI and Interpol were looking but had not caught up with him. He seemed to have dropped out of sight. One source did tell him that there had been a brief mention in *Variety*, the theatrical trade journal, that London had heard Ching was making Communist documentary films in Peking and had been seen in Hanoi, then Geneva, when the peace treaty talks had begun. He showed us a photostat of the article he had copied in the Library of Congress.

"Well, that's that," Luke remarked. "He's either a fool or an agent. We'll nail him on either one."

"Gentlemen," Kelly said softly, "we are not going to use the Gentile file. In fact, I want all of you to promise me on your word as gentlemen we will never discuss what we know."

He could have fired a shotgun, and it would have had the same effect.

"You're kidding, Kel?" Luke asked.

"I'm not," was his brother's solemn answer.

"But why, Kelly?" his father shouted. "Why? All you have to do now is reach out and you have him!"

Josh said angrily, "Yes—suppose you tell us why?"

Kelly looked over at him. "I can't tell you," he said. "You will just have to trust my decision."

"But you just can't leave us hang like this, Kel," Luke said. "If there is some fantastic reason why this stuff on Gentile should not be used, let us know!"

"There is a reason, but for the time being I must keep it to myself."

"This is crazy, Kelly," his father said. "Just crazy."

"Perhaps, but that's the way it has to be."

"You realize, of course, what this means?" Josh said.

"I guess we won't get Frank's total viewing audience," Kelly said quietly.

His father wheeled closer to his son. "I don't know what your reasons are, Kelly, but we're doing something wrong here by suppressing these facts. This may be a traitor, an enemy agent!"

"For one thing," Kelly said shortly, "I don't believe all the facts are in."

"But here it is!" his father cried. "An FBI flyer, the statement from General Chu's daughter, every sheet of paper on the case is missing—what more do you want?"

"Kelly has his reasons, Father," Lacey said. "I don't think we should badger him."

"Do you know his reasons, Lacey?" Josh asked.

She hesitated. "Yes, I do."

"And do you believe he's right?"

"I most certainly do."

"And you believe he has a right not to tell us what these reasons are—the people who have been working for him?"

"Yes, I do—I'm sorry, Josh."

"Why be sorry?" he snapped. "After all, I'm only supposed to be running this campaign. The whole thing is crazy, absolutely crazy!"

"Well, where do we go from here?" Luke asked.

"Back to the hearings," Luther said. "They still go on tomorrow. Right, Kelly?"

"Of course. I talked to Benny this afternoon. He's all set for the confrontation."

"Well, at least that's not down the drain," Luke remarked.

"And it's definite we're not going to touch Gentile?" Josh pressed. He seemed to be slowly emerging from a slight state of shock.

"It's definite, Josh," Kelly told him. "I'm sorry, but I have my reasons. You just have to trust me."

"I'd trust you a hell of a lot more if you told me what they are."

"I can't—at this time." He said with a faint smile, "I didn't press you for the name of your informant who gave you this file, did I?"

"I told you it was from a reliable source."

"And that was enough. It ended there. Can't you have the same faith in me?"

"Michaels has more experience, Kelly," the senator said. "He's been through this before—you haven't."

"Let's say my education has broadened within the last few months, Dad."

"Do you know your brother's reasons for not using the Gentile material?" Josh asked Luke.

"No more than you do."

"Is Lacey the only one?"

"The only one," Kelly said firmly.

"Let's get back to tomorrow, Josh," Luther suggested gently. He gave Luke a look. "What time do we want the confrontation?"

"Two o'clock," Luke said quickly. "Frank says that way we can still catch the Wall Street editions and the afternoon housewives."

"What plans do you have for calling Mr. Mullady?" Lacey asked.

"Probably just before the start of the Lawrence hearings," Kelly started to explain, but he stopped short after looking at Josh's angry face.

"Now I have a surprise for *you*," Josh said in a tight, hard voice. "We're not going to call Mullady."

It was sure a night for the unexpected. Luther slowly put down his pipe to join Kelly and Lacey in staring at Josh. Only Luke and the senator didn't seem surprised. I remembered Josh telling me he had discussed the deal with them.

"Did I hear right, Josh?" Kelly asked bewilderedly. "We're *not* going to subpoena Mullady?"

"You heard right."

"Why? Is he ill?"

"We should have his health. He'll probably live to a hundred."

"Well then, why?"

Josh leaned forward to fix him with his eyes. "I have my reasons, and I'll tell them to you. We're not going to call Mullady because we're going to make a deal with him. We're not going to subpoena him, and in return he will support you at the convention and in the campaign. With his help we can roll up the biggest plurality this state has ever seen. You'll be the undisputed head of the party. You'll be on a paved road to the White House."

"No, Kelly," Lacey said faintly. "No."

"Yes," Josh said fiercely. "I'm sick and tired of this head-in-the-clouds politics. Let's get back to earth. Sure we can win without Mullady. I'm not thinking of Albany now; I'm thinking of the national convention and the White House. If we can bring Kelly home with a big score, not only the county and state leaders but the National Committee will know we have a winner. There's no one on the scene now but Gentile. That's why I want to knock him out of the box—fast and forever. If you don't want to touch this file, fine; you have your reasons. It must be your responsibility. But I'm a practical politician. I'm willing to make deals with anybody as long as it helps my man."

"Josh—Mullady's an evil man!" Lacey cried.

"So, he's a crook," Josh said roughly. "The political woods are full of them. Shady political leaders have always been here; they always will. Someone once said it was a flaw in our democracy. I don't know. Maybe it is. I just know we need Mullady's sweet chocolates—every last one of them."

"You would become partners with a man who uses the poor, the illiterate, the people on welfare to help him gain political power?" Lacey asked.

"He's not unique, believe me," Josh told her. "It's not our problem how he got what he has—our problem is how we can use it."

"Just as Gene Abernathy warned us this morning," Kelly said, "Mullady's getting more dangerous. He's on the phone every day telling the

324

Lawrence police chief to throw the pickets in jail. Communists, he calls them. My God, they're anything but Communists! One man they arrested yesterday has two daughters who are nuns."

"I knew a Communist who once studied for the priesthood," Josh said. "When he was in Spain he executed prisoners who had their hands tied. Beware of anyone with noble motives, Kelly; they always let you down. I know Mullady for what he is—a thief whose hands have been in the pockets of the poor since he was stealing packages in Hell's Kitchen. I wouldn't trust him with a red-hot stove. But neither do I trust Abernathy. Only, in this case to quote Finn, I believe it's better to walk with ten devils you know than one you don't."

He turned to the senator. "When you came to us you had grand plans for Kelly, Senator. First there would be Albany, then the Presidency. I don't have to tell you what that takes. If Kelly just manages to squeak into Albany, they'll say it was just a freak because of those hearings. I don't want a squeak-in vote; I want the biggest landslide this state has ever seen! Then they'll come running to us. Why? They'll know Kelly could be the next man in the White House, and they'll want to get on his bandwagon early. From next January until the national convention there will be one name—Kelly Shannon. We can't lose!" He smashed his fist inside his cupped hand. "But dammit, we can't do it without votes! Votes! More votes! Those black hands clicking down the levers." He took a deep breath. "Next year. Two years from now, this couldn't happen; Mullady's finished and he knows it. He has one more big election in him—and it's this one. We need him."

The room tinkled with silence when he had finished. The senator was looking anxiously at his son.

"He's right, Kelly. Mullady's machine could give us a landslide."

"You're wrong, Josh," Kelly said slowly. "If I thought I needed Mullady as much as you say, I would never announce my candidacy. You're right when you say Benny and the others are thieves and crooks who should have been in jail years ago, but Mullady is a bigger thief than all of them. He not only stole money; he stole people's lives. He has stripped them of the barest essentials of living, of decency and self-respect. He has used poverty, ignorance, and fear to gain his power." He paused, then added: "Unless he is subpoenaed I will not appear tomorrow morning on the committee."

"You could be making the biggest mistake of your life, Kelly," Luke said.

Kelly looked at him. "Luke, do you agree with Josh?"

"I certainly do, and so does Father."

"Then Josh spoke to you both before tonight?"

"After Josh saw Mullady he told us—"

Kelly swung quickly to Josh. "You saw Mullady!"

"I saw him in Washington," Josh answered. "He's running scared.

When it was announced Lawrence was on our agenda, he knew something was up—"

"Does he know about Gene Abernathy?"

"No, he doesn't. He thinks he could be sold out by the local crooks. He just can't afford to take a chance on that stand. That's why he's willing to make any kind of a deal. I told Luke and your father. They couldn't agree more."

"You didn't give him an answer, I hope."

"I told him I would have to talk to you."

Kelly looked relieved. He reached into a folder by his chair and came up with a small square sheet of paper. A committee subpoena. He quickly scrawled his name on the bottom.

"Fill in Mullady's name," he said firmly. "I want him on the stand this week before we go to Lawrence."

"Kelly, we're not going to subpoena Mullady," Josh said softly. "We can't. We need him."

"Please, Josh, we don't need that terrible man," Lacey pleaded.

"This is a political decision that I believe rests with me, Senator," Josh said. "Do you agree?"

The old man, his face pinched and worn with fatigue and emotion, looked pleadingly at his son. "Michaels is right, Kelly."

Josh turned to Luke. "What do you say, Luke?"

"I say make a deal. Let somebody else get him after the hearing."

"Luther?"

"Let me pass this one."

"Finn?"

I took a deep breath; there were a lot of years between Josh and me, but I had to look in the mirror tomorrow morning, and I knew Josh would want the truth.

"I have to go with Kelly, Josh. Mullady should be subpoenaed."

He turned to Lacey. "I guess there's no doubt about what you want, Lacey."

Her eyes were bright and wet but her voice was firm. "There shouldn't be, Josh."

"Well, we're speaking our minds tonight. Perhaps we should have done it before this," Josh said, cool as ice. "As I understand it, Kelly, you will not appear at the committee hearing tomorrow if Mullady is not subpoenaed?"

"I'm sorry, Josh, but that's the way it must be."

"We're all tired and edgy," Luther said. "I say we leave this for a few days."

"No. It must be resolved now," Kelly said.

"Leave it lay for a day or two, son, as Luther suggests," the senator said. "We would regret any decision we made at this hour." He gave Josh a look of desperation. "Isn't there any other way?"

Josh had been studying his clasped hands. He slowly raised his head. I could almost see the gears turning.

"This thought has just come to me, Kelly. Would you put it up to Abernathy? Lay it right on the table."

Kelly frowned. "Why Abernathy?"

"He has the most to lose," Josh said. "Or maybe to gain."

"I don't understand."

"I think as part of the deal we can get Mullady to support Abernathy's candidate for mayor."

"Mullady supporting Abernathy's candidate? Wouldn't he want to cut his throat after he finds out what Gene has been doing?"

"Not necessarily," Josh said. "Mullady's a hardheaded politician. He's already seen the cracks in his wall. I think he might go for it."

"Then he would probably want to make another kind of deal with Abernathy and his people," Lacey said. "Where does it end—unless there's no beginning?"

"Wouldn't that be Abernathy's problem?" Josh asked. "Why don't we let his conscience be his guide? He's a big boy now."

Luke said firmly: "That's a great idea, Kelly. Let Abernathy decide about Mullady."

"He'll laugh at me," Kelly said.

"How do you know, Kelly?" Josh asked. "How do you know he won't go for it? Politics is the art of the possible."

"I like to think of politics as the art of accomplishing things through people," Kelly retorted.

"I believe Gene Abernathy has the same philosophy," Lacey said firmly. "He hates Mullady and all he stands for."

"Let's see just how much he hates Mullady," Josh challenged.

"There's no question of it," she said heatedly.

"You're afraid, Lacey," Josh told her with a smile. "You're afraid that maybe this sweet chocolate will go for it."

"You'd like that, wouldn't you?"

"I'd love it. White or black, they're all politicians. Let them get a smell of success, and they'll bargain away their shoes." He said to me, "Will you go for that—putting it up to Abernathy, Finn?"

I had to go along with it not only because it was a shrewd play and not unreasonable but also I couldn't go against Josh any more.

"I think I will."

The others chimed in, and one look at Kelly's face and I knew Josh had won again. Except Lacey. She sat in her chair tough and straight as a country squire's riding crop.

"Will you go up there with me, Lacey?" Kelly asked.

"I'll go—but I think it's wrong."

"What about the hearing in the morning, the confrontation?" Luther asked. "Will that go on?"

"I'll take care of it," Josh said quickly. "We'll make it brief. Put Benny on, then have him confront Remington and Saunders right in the hearing room."

"But what about Jonesy?"

"Kelly, you'll have to call him in the morning," Josh said. "Just tell him we've found a highly important witness who won't talk to anyone but you. He won't put up too much of a beef after he realizes he'll be alone for the big scene."

"Are you really going to Lawrence, Kelly?" Lacey asked.

He hesitated for a moment, and we all hung on his words.

"I must, Lacey. Josh deserves an answer and so do I."

"But why you?"

"Because if I didn't go I would never be sure that I hadn't made a mistake in Abernathy." He turned to Josh. "One thing more, Josh. If Abernathy turns down your deal—will you agree Mullady must be subpoenaed?"

Ah, there we had it.

"Agreed," Josh said, surprisingly. "Does that satisfy you?"

"We'll leave first thing in the morning," Kelly said. "Now I think we all ought to get some sleep."

We started out of the library, but I heard Josh say to Lacey he wished some kind soul would show him to the kitchen so he could perhaps scare up a sandwich, even toast. As he explained, he hadn't eaten since breakfast. Lacey said that was an idiot thing to do, and if he would come along she would fix him something—only on the condition he would not talk politics, hearings, or elections. Josh said he would tell her about the letter he had just received from the man who rented his ranch describing the wild stallion a neighboring rancher had recently caught.

On that note they said good night, and left.

But I think the talk of wild stallions was finally replaced by politics. As I came out of the bathroom I could hear them below, arguing.

Well, at least they were able to argue; that was one good sign. And then I heard Lacey laugh—there was a note of resignation in it, but at least she laughed.

But as my head touched the pillow it came to me: Was Josh down in the kitchen to try to find out the reason why Kelly won't use the Gentile file?

It was a distasteful thought, but, knowing Josh, probably correct.

I had been asleep for what I thought was hours when I awoke abruptly; the thought came to me that I hadn't called the hotel to see what messages had been left for us. It was a habit I had been following for years, and not to follow it every day was like not brushing your teeth.

The moment the old night clerk recognized my voice, he interrupted me excitedly.

"You've had a number of calls and there's been a man here all evening who has been demanding to see you, Mr. McCool," he said. "He started calling early and then came over to the hotel, insisting I was lying to him."

"What did he look like?"

"He's a strange-looking fellow, big as a house and wearing an old sweater. He looks strange."

How better to describe Willy?

"Did he say what he wanted?"

"He kept insisting it was important. He sat here in the lobby after I refused to let him in your place."

"Is he there now?"

"No, sir, he left about an hour ago. He said to tell you and Mr. Michaels he would be waiting for you in his office at Forty-ninth and Second Avenue. He said you were to meet him there, no matter what the hour. You didn't want him in your apartment, did you? He kept insisting, but he looked so weird."

"No, thanks. You did right. Good night."

"Good night, sir."

I sat on the edge of the bed for a few minutes debating whether I should wait until morning and contact Willy or tell Josh and go down to the city and see him. It was just possible he had uncovered something more—it wasn't like Willy to come out of his hole and try to find us so desperately.

I decided that at least Josh should know. The kitchen was quiet, and I cleared my throat several times very loudly as I came down the hall. But they must have been oblivious to everything, for when I stood at the doorway they were at the window overlooking the dark valley; her head was on his shoulder and he was whispering, earnestly and intently. They jumped as lovers do, and Lacey flushed when I cleared my throat again, this time loud enough to dislodge my tonsils.

"I'm terribly sorry, Josh, but I just called the hotel and there's an important message for you."

"At this hour, Finn?"

"There's an old friend of yours, probably from Dakota, who's waiting to see you. He says he has only a few hours before he has to leave."

I spoke slowly, and he quickly caught the message.

"Maybe I can pick him up in the morning before the hearings."

"I don't think so. The clerk said he would be gone by then."

"Why don't you see him, Josh?" Lacey said. "He probably has to get an early flight."

"Did he leave a phone number?" Josh asked impatiently.

"No. He's waiting in Grand Central . . . he's between trains."

"Oh, Josh, you should see him. The poor man has probably been waiting in that station all night."

"He just doesn't seem important now."

She touched his cheek, and smiled. "Kelly and I will be back tomorrow —tonight."

"Lacey and I have a bet," Josh explained. "She's promised to visit the ranch after the hearings are over."

"Have you been there, Finn?" she asked.

"No, but I've heard a million stories about the place. It sounds awf— wonderful."

"Finn says the farthest west he wants to go is Chicago for the convention," Josh said with a laugh. "Well, all right, let's go."

"There won't be any traffic," she said. "You should be down there in an hour." Almost automatically she placed her hand on his arm. "Be careful," she said gently.

"Your wish is my command. I'll see you tonight—"

"We'll be back," she said firmly, "with Gene Abernathy's refusal."

"You want to bet?" he asked scornfully.

"We'll see tonight. Goodbye."

She leaned over and kissed him lightly. Josh held her hand, and they smiled at each other.

"It's three o'clock," I said.

"Okay," he said, "I'm coming."

I felt it was my cue, and said I was going to get dressed. I came down to find Josh in the front hall with Kelly in dressing gown and pajamas.

"I'm terribly sorry if I got you up," I said.

"I just couldn't sleep," Kelly said. "I came down for some milk and found Josh. Too bad you have to drive down at this hour."

"This fellow is only going to be there for a short time," I said. "He sounds terribly anxious to see Josh."

"Of course. We'll see you back here."

"Has Lacey gone to bed?"

"She just went up as I came down." He added abruptly, "I'll be glad when it's all over."

"Nothing will be over until Election morning," Josh said, "and that's when we'll all sit down and curse each other for the mistakes we made." He shook Kelly's shoulder gently. "And we'll make plenty."

"I'm sure a lot will be mine," Kelly said with a smile. "We'll see you tonight. Do you have the keys for the Thunderbird?"

"Right here. Good night."

"For Christ's sake, Finn, do we have to see this guy at this hour?" Josh asked as he drove down the road to the highway.

"The desk clerk said Willy was in the lobby all night insisting it was a matter of life and death. I don't see how we can ignore him at this point. It must be something important. He's never done this before."

"I guess that's true," he said, "but I sure hate to leave what I was doing to go down to the city to talk to that character!"

"Yes, I could see that."

330

"I'm going to ask her to marry me, Finn."

"Oh? Are you sure?"

"More sure than I have ever been about anything."

"Do you think she'll accept you, Josh?"

"I'm going to try like hell."

"What do you think she'll say when she finds you lied to her about Benny Jello?"

"I'm going to pull every wire I have to get that little crook off the hook," he said savagely. "I've spoken to Jonesy. He's already started to make some moves."

"From what you told me, that DA isn't going to budge."

"When I was in Washington I found out he hopes to run for Congress next year. He'll come around."

"Do you really think Abernathy will accept a deal with Mullady, Josh?"

"As I said before, he's only human. There are damn few heroes in politics; you know that." He slowed down and stopped at a tollbooth. As he waited for change he said slowly, half to himself, "I wonder what Willy wants."

"No doubt it's something to do with Gentile."

"I hope so. If he's dug up any more it might persuade Kelly to use the stuff." He shook his head. "I'll never understand why he refused."

"I thought that was what you were trying to get out of Lacey."

"Oh, I tried," he said with a grin, "but she wouldn't give."

As the miles slipped past, my eyes grew heavy and I dozed. The next thing I knew we had left the West Side Highway at Forty-second Street and were going crosstown. We parked on Third in the fifties and walked down to Forty-ninth and Second. The Volks bus was parked in the middle of the block. We were passing the mouth of an alley, a few car lengths from the bus, when Willy's voice stopped us.

"Is that cop still on the corner?"

Josh looked up and down the street. It was deserted.

"No cops, Willy."

"Get in here."

We followed his huge bulk down the alley. On either side were barred doors and windows. He stepped into one deep recess, and faced us. A dim night-light from the store caught the wild glint in his eyes. I was so close to him his strong body odor, almost like an animal's, made me gag.

"So you sold me out!" he snarled.

"What do you mean, Willy?" Josh asked quietly.

"You know God-damned well what I mean," he said, his voice rising. "You sold me out; that's what. Sold me out to that God-damn Commie Gentile!"

"How did we sell you out?" Josh asked.

Willy pulled a handful of crumpled newspaper clippings from his pocket and thrust them in Josh's face.

"Here it is in the papers. Gentile and Shannon shaking hands, like they were asshole buddies. Smiling and laughing at each other—you know why?" His voice was so full of menace it petrified me. "Because they made a deal on the stuff I gave you—a nice big fat deal!"

"Don't be silly, Willy, nobody made a deal—"

"Don't give me that crap; you're not going to use anything on Gentile."

"Who said so?"

"That son of a bitch Shannon, that's who said so—"

"When did he say this, Willy?"

"In his God-damn house last night, and you were there."

"Do you mean to tell us you had our meeting bugged?" I asked.

"You're damn right I did," he replied savagely. "I heard every word. Shannon doesn't want to use my stuff on Gentile because he made a deal with him. He's just like the others—he's sold out to the Commies and the whoremongers, sold his God-damn country—"

"Wait a minute, Willy," Josh said. "Don't get so excited." He put out his hand, but Willy flung it savagely to one side.

"Don't give me any of your bullshit," he snarled. "You and this old bastard are just stooges for them. I should have known better."

I saw the gun in his hand, and froze. Josh casually looked down at the weapon, then ignored it to keep on talking, softly, intensively, soothingly.

The Gentile file definitely would be used, he promised. It was only a temporary decision, and with the additional material we were getting . . .

But Willy wasn't buying any explanations. What would have happened in the next few minutes is anybody's guess—had it not been for the cop's voice at the head of the alley demanding to know what we were doing.

For a moment I thought Willy would turn the gun on the cop, but instead he quickly opened the barred door of the store and slid inside. "Okay—you screwed me and the country—now it's my turn," he said hoarsely. The door clicked shut.

"Come out of there!" The cop's voice was angry. "Come out with your hands up. . . ."

"Play along with me," Josh whispered as he zipped open his fly and staggered up the alley.

Fortunately the cop was an old, bored veteran. He gave us both a fast frisk, then stepped back with a frown.

"What the hell were you doing in there?"

"So help me, Officer, I had to go—so bad I could taste it."

"What's the matter with Grand Central? There's ten men's rooms over there."

"Ever since I had that damn malaria I can't hold it," Josh mumbled.

"Why don't you see a doctor?" the cop asked. "And what were you doing?" he asked me, "holding the candle?"

"He's the son-in-law," I said, trying to act embarrassed and nervous. "He and my daughter had a big fight this afternoon, and the old lady sent me out to find him."

The cop studied us for a moment. "Got any identification?"

We showed him a host of cards, including one from the Washington PBA.

"Where were you going?" he asked as he returned the cards to us.

"I thought I'd get him to the Commodore," I said, "and go home in the morning."

"Well, maybe when your old ladies get you, you'll need all the breaks," he said with a grunt.

We walked to Third Avenue with as much dignity as we could muster. After we turned the corner, we hurried to our car.

"That was close," Josh said as we pulled away from the curb.

"In more ways than one. Josh, we'd better do something about Willy. There's no telling what he'll do."

"He's just talking."

"Josh, he has a gun! For a moment I thought he was going to shoot that cop!"

"Well, he didn't. I was more afraid of what the cop would do. Suppose he had pulled us in for committing a public nuisance? Christ, we would have to wait until day court."

"Forget what the cop would have done—it's Willy I'm worried about."

He snapped, "Let me take care of Willy—"

"How?"

"He'll be on the phone. We'll meet him again and give him another $25,000."

"But Josh, that nut doesn't care about money!"

"Then we'll tell him the FBI is investigating Gentile and we'll have him off our backs."

I just couldn't impress him with my fears and apprehension. He refused to listen. At the hotel he took a shower and tumbled into bed, leaving me fearful and full of prayers as the garish dawn slowly spread across the night sky.

BOOK 5
☆☆☆☆☆☆☆
The Blackest Page ☆☆☆☆

IN THE LIFE OF ANY MAN, there's always a day to remember, a day so terrifying the smallest details are etched in memory.

This day, the most dreadful of my life, began with the wail of a siren. It would end the same way.

Josh and I had just finished a hasty breakfast when we heard it. Sirens on the West Side of Manhattan are commonplace, so we ignored it even though it wailed outside the hotel. A few minutes later the door buzzer sounded. When I opened it, a patrolman was in the hallway.

"Mr. McCool?"

I swallowed hard; maybe that old cop had had second thoughts.

"That's me. What is it?"

"Is Mr. Michaels here?"

"Right here," Josh said. "Is anything wrong?"

"The lieutenant wants me to take you both over to Central Park West in a hurry," the cop said.

"What for?"

"You got me. My partner and I just arrived in the house when the lieutenant grabbed us." He flipped open his notebook. "Central Park West and Seventy-second. Can you come now?"

"Right away."

We slipped into our topcoats and followed the cop into the elevator and past the curious desk clerk to the street. Another cop was at the wheel. "That them?" he asked.

The cop nodded, and we squeezed into the rear seat of the radio car, which took off with a screech of tires and the frantic wailing of its siren.

"Do you fellows know what it's about?" Josh asked.

"I think it's a homicide," the cop at the wheel called back over his shoulder. "You got any friends over there? Maybe the detectives want you for identification."

"Not that I know of," I began, then stopped. Josh and I looked at each other. "Eva," he whispered, "the German whore . . . "

In a few minutes we were entering the luxurious lobby of Eva's apartment house. A uniformed man escorted us to the eighteenth floor where three plainclothesmen identified themselves as from Manhattan Homicide West.

They opened the door a crack, and two other men with Immigration badges pinned to their jackets peered out. "Mr. Michaels?"

"I'm Michaels. This is Mr. McCool."

"Thank God you're here," one of the Immigration men said. "This is a mess." He opened the door. "They're in there."

"They?" Josh asked.

"Eva and a young girl. We think she was one of Eva's girls."

The detective consulted his notebook. "Her name is Lily Steuben."

Lily, the young prostitute on Willy's wiretap.

"Where's she from?"

"Hamburg. Like the madam. She's probably a new hustler."

He looked up as a short, stocky man with a granite face walked in.

"Oh, Inspector, these are the men from the committee. Michaels and McCool, isn't it?"

"Josh Michaels and Finn McCool," Josh said. "We're on Congressman Kelly's staff."

"Immigration said you people had this woman listed as a witness," the inspector said. "What about it? I have to make a report to downtown."

"They were *not* witnesses. We had them under investigation," Josh said. "The committee was forwarding a report this week to Immigration," Josh said. "By the way, did you find anything?"

"Like what?" the inspector asked.

"Like anything," Josh said.

"We found a few letters, some in German."

"Let's cut the crap, Inspector," Josh said sharply, "Did you find her book?"

The inspector suddenly became very formal.

"The DA's man is on his way up. You'd better talk to him. . . . You people have a copy of that report on her?"

"I think you had better speak to the committee, Inspector," Josh said briskly. "We have a hearing to attend to. Just make sure you don't tell the reporters they were committee witnesses. They were not."

Outside on the sidewalk a large crowd of reporters gathered about a plainclothesman who was reading off some details from his notes as the newspapermen furiously scribbled. Off to one side a TV reporter was asking the superintendent of the building about the last time he had seen the murdered women. We walked hastily past and crossed the street where the police were starting to erect barricades.

"He's started, Josh."

"Who's started?"

"Willy. We have to do something, and fast."

"What do you have in mind?"

"We must notify the police. There's no telling what he might do next."

"How do you know it was Willy?"

"Who else would do a thing like this? Two women?"

"Did you ever talk to a whore? The weirdos they get would make your hair curl. How do we know it wasn't some guy who went off his trolley? You didn't pay Eva a visit just to get laid. This was a dame who played some rough games." We both watched a TV cameraman making a panshot of the building with a hand camera. "Let's say we tip the cops it was Willy and it turns out it wasn't?" He turned to me. "We just can't afford to have Willy grabbed by anyone—not now."

"We should have done something about him last night, Josh."

"What?" was his scornful reply. "Call the West Forty-seventh Street Precinct and tell them there's a guy walking around with a gun who has tapped the wires of City Hall and dug up a scandalous file on the man who someday may be President? Come on, Finn, use your head."

Of course, what he said made sense. I could only imagine the cold, suspicious voice of a detective who would only tell himself he either had an imaginative drunk or a psycho on the phone.

"Well, what do we do?"

"I'm worried about Jonesy all by himself in the Federal Building. The reporters are probably crawling all over him. Let's get down there."

We found Jones with some of the committee's investigators in the witness room. He had his ancient hearing aid tuned to its highest volume and was yelling into the phone, apparently at one of the servants at Wexford Hall. When he saw us he slammed down the phone and sank back into his chair.

"My God, where have you boys been?" he shouted. "There's a million reporters outside shouting questions all morning about some whores who were murdered on Central Park West."

"What did you tell them?" Josh demanded.

"What could I tell them?" Jones replied. "I don't know a damn thing about those women. Were they murdered? Was this the woman with the black book?"

Josh patted him on the shoulder. "I have all the facts, Congressman, and if you give me five minutes I'll have a statement that will be on page one and on every television show across the country. Just relax." He said to one of the investigators, "Let's have some coffee and tell those guys outside that Congressman Jones will hold a press conference in a half hour. Make sure the networks are notified. Also call up AP and UPI and ask them to send out a city-desk memo on the conference." He took off his jacket and draped it on the back of a chair. "Jonesy, we have a real big one today."

I have attended countless congressional and Senate hearings in my years, but this one was the wildest I have ever witnessed. It was really a disgraceful circus. Josh wrote a two-page statement, describing how the committee had received information regarding Eva's activities and had submitted a report for Immigration. Then one of the batteries in Jonesy's hearing aid went dead and that added to the confusion. While photographers and TV crews fought each other for the best shots, reporters, both TV and the writing press, surrounded Jones like a band of Indians circling a wagon train. They shouted question after question; some Jones heard, others he didn't, and gave the wrong answers or answers that had nothing to do with the subject. Meanwhile, I had two investigators racing about the city trying to locate batteries for Jones's old machine, which must have been manufactured at the turn of the century.

Benny was brought down, and for a time it appeared that perhaps he might just refuse to go through with the confrontation of Remington and Saunders. He had obviously lost weight and was worried why Molly had not appeared.

"I looked in the courtroom, but she isn't there," he said. "Is she sick?"

"She never felt better in her life," Josh said cheerfully. "She's probably delayed by the traffic. You know the West Side Highway in the beginning of the week, Benny."

"Did you talk to her?" Benny asked.

"Sure. She's at the Burning Oak Motel. You can spit in their swimming pool from Wexford."

"Is Lacey with her?"

"Of course. She's bringing her down."

I looked at Josh. He was smiling as he lied like a trouper.

"This is it," Benny said. "After today—"

"Just today, Benny," I said. "No more."

"What about the DA? He's going along, right?"

"Don't worry about it, Benny," Josh said abruptly. He said to the two marshals, "You boys taking care of Benny?"

"We're watching him like he was our father," one said. They were both young, perhaps in their thirties, and seemed to like Benny.

"Only, he's a lousy pinochle player," the other said.

"So lousy you guys owe me three bucks from last night," Benny said.

"Have you seen Molly?" Josh asked after the marshals had taken Benny to the courtroom.

"No, I haven't. You didn't talk to her, did you?"

"No. I only told him that. Keep an eye out for her. If you see her, pass the word along to Benny."

"Were any arrangements made to pick her up this morning?"

"Dammit, no. I saw Luke, the senator, and Shea in the corridor. They were all excited about Eva and the other dame. They said it's all over radio and TV."

"What about Molly?"

"When they heard the news about Eva on the radio, they probably rushed down and forgot about Molly. Maybe she's still sleeping. Let's get back."

I forgot Molly the instant I entered the courtroom. There wasn't a single seat left; one of the investigators said papers all over the country and Europe were calling Jones about Eva and Lily. In fact, the hearing was held up while Jones completed a televised interview.

"That old bastard's lapping it up," Josh said. "He's read that statement a hundred times if he's read it once."

In the courtroom I recognized Remington and Saunders from newspaper photos. Remington was tall and lean, with puffy eyes and apparently with his insides wound tight. He kept tapping one foot and nervously glancing about the room. Saunders was older, calmer, and looked more at ease. As soon as they entered they were surrounded by reporters. Their attorney was one of the most distinguished members of the American Bar.

The hearing started with Jones announcing that it would be brief because of Congressman Shannon's absence. But the full hearings would resume the following day with Congressman Kelly Shannon present. The purpose of today's hearings, he said, was to allow Mr. Remington and Mr. Saunders to confront the committee's witness.

"Bring in the witness," he said.

The door of the witness room opened, and Benny Jello walked in, his face dead-white. He looked frightened, and his eyes swept the audience. I knew who he was looking for—Molly, who wasn't there.

"Mr. Jello," Jones said, "you have testified before this committee that you had seen Mr. Remington on many occasions and at least had lunch with Mr. Remington and Mr. Saunders. Is that true?"

"Yes, sir."

"And you would know them if they were present in this courtroom?"

"Yes, sir."

"Are they here now?"

Benny looked over at Remington and Saunders, and licked his lips.

"Yes, sir."

"Will you point them out?"

Benny's trembling fingers pointed at Remington, whose foot tapped faster than ever, and at Saunders, who stared at Benny impassively.

"Will you go down and touch these men on the shoulder and for the record identify them?" Jones said.

Then Remington and Saunders' attorney was on his feet. "Mr. Chairman, at this time I respectfully request that all television cameras be covered," he said. "I believe it would be prejudicial to my clients if . . ."

It was a long and legal argument, with the attorney quoting from a host of precedents.

Jones at last agreed with him and ordered the cameras covered. Then a trembling, shaking Jello got up, walked down and touched first Remington, then Saunders on the shoulders. It was truly a dramatic moment.

Jones was an old pro and didn't need any instructions from Josh how to milk this scene dry. Slowly and distinctly he asked Benny what was the name of the man he was tapping on the shoulder, where he had met him, and under what circumstances. Poor Benny virtually had to repeat his whole story of his corrupt dealings while standing in front of the men he was accusing. Once, Josh left the courtroom and came back all smiles.

"Frank said we're going big all over the country. We have 90 percent of the poll."

"What about TV?"

"I did the same thing we did in Washington. I told them to keep audio on and have a camera focused on the outside door. I have a sign telling what's going on—I just saw it—it's coming over great."

It went on for an hour more. Remington and Saunders briefly took the stand to deny emphatically and vigorously that they ever had any crooked dealings with Benny. Remington admitted Jello had visited his office, but only as a client who had received a complaint from the State Liquor Authority. Saunders coldly dismissed Benny as a thief and an unmitigated liar whom he had never seen before in his life.

There was no further testimony. Thus the foundation had been laid for the perjury indictment of both Remington and Saunders after our independent witnesses, such as Remington's secretary and the old waiter, had testified.

It was about noon when Jones banged his gavel and announced the recess. The reporters immediately surrounded Jones, Remington, and Saunders. I saw Jello walk toward the witness room flanked by the two marshals. I waved, but he didn't see me.

"I wonder what happened to Molly?" I said to Josh as we left the courtroom.

"I haven't the slightest idea," he replied. "I'm going to write something for Jones and have him give it out this afternoon. Then I think we should all head back to Wexford."

It was then that the court attendant handed Josh the grimy envelope. Josh tore it open and took out a torn sheet of ruled paper, the type schoolchildren use. He read it and handed it to me wordlessly.

The note was badly typed. It read:

"I got those two whores. Now I get your fat little stoolie Jello. From now on, your hearings are dead."

I looked at Josh, who was tense and tight-lipped.

"He's going to try and kill Benny, Josh!"

"I'll notify the cops and the Department of Justice," he said. "They can—"

Then the thought hit me with the stunning force.

"Josh! Molly!"

He had started to turn away, but he spun about. "Have you seen her?"

"No. I looked over the crowd outside a few times. She isn't here." I grabbed his arm. "Would Willy—"

"How would he know where she is? Lacey took her to the motel."

"But he bugged our meeting! He heard everything that went on."

Without another word Josh ran back into the courtroom. Remington, Saunders, and their attorney were still hemmed in by a crowd of newspapermen, TV cameramen, and reporters. He flung open the door of the witness room and looked in.

"Where's Jello?" he asked the court stenographer, who was putting away his stenotype machine.

"The marshals just took him out the side door."

"Do they use the regular elevator?"

"I think so. They use the exit at the back of the lobby. It goes down to the marshals' office in the basement. I think one of them wanted to call his wife."

Josh wheeled and ran. A reporter who reached out to say something was hit by a shoulder and bowled over. Someone called after us, but we were out of the courtroom and running down the hall. Josh punched the elevator bell savagely. Overhead the tiny green lights ticked off the floors, thirteen . . . twelve . . . eleven . . . The doors opened. The car was filled, but Josh jumped in with me right behind him.

"Take us down to the lobby fast!" he snarled to the young operator.

"I'm sorry, sir, but I—"

"God damn it, take us down fast!" Josh shouted. "It's an emergency!"

The young woman, her eyes wide with surprise, pushed her lever forward and the car descended. To go down those ten floors seemed an eternity. As the door slid back on the lobby, Josh jumped out. It seemed the whole inside of the elevator pushed forward and I was caught in midstream. I had just elbowed my way out when I heard Josh shout, "Willy! No!"

The lobby was fairly crowded, mostly with lunchtime stenographers, clerks, and attorneys returning to the courtrooms. Josh was standing near the elevator at the end of the lobby nearest the front door. Benny, between the two marshals, was halfway, walking east to the end door that led to the basement where the file rooms and the marshals' office are located.

Just as Josh shouted, I saw Willy. He was just coming out of a phone booth at the far end of the lobby. In one hand he had a paper bag; the other was raised. As Josh shouted he turned, startled, and his hand went out.

Almost immediately there was a dreadful racket, like a burst of fire from a machine gun. Women screamed, while men just stared foolishly in the direction of the noise. In the quiet high-domed lobby it sounded like a miniature war had just begun.

Involuntarily both marshals turned in the direction of the noise—it later turned out to be a handful of firecrackers Willy had tossed—with one marshal pawing for his gun.

Benny, pale as a newly laundered sheet, just stood there, welded to the floor with fear.

"Willy! No!" Josh screamed again.

My heart almost stopped. Willy had dropped the paper bag. In his hand was one of the silencer-equipped revolvers he had showed us.

I never heard the tiny cough of the gun. One of the marshals had run toward the exploding firecrackers. The other had automatically started to follow, but stopped in his tracks a few feet from Benny. A man with a briefcase was hopping about as the firecrackers exploded about his feet. Two other men near him watched, foolish smiles on their faces. A young stenographer who had screamed was laughing now, and holding her ears. I saw Willy raise the gun. A man who was just emerging from another phone booth dived back in and slammed the door. Another man held up a brief-case as though to shield himself.

Suddenly, directly in front of Benny's forehead, was a gaping hole. Blood slowly oozed out of it. Then one eye disappeared in another hole. He sagged, rather than fell, slowly, as if in a clip from an old-time slow-motion film. When he reached his knees he fell backward, his skull smashing on the marble floor with the sickening sound of a bursting melon.

Then Willy half turned. I thought for a moment he was going to shoot Josh, but he didn't. His twisted mind may have told him Josh wouldn't suffer if he was killed. I saw the madness in his face, and then he was running across the lobby, headed for the rear door.

The marshal who had run toward the exploding fireworks had his gun half out when he heard Josh's shout. When he turned, Josh pointed to Willy. A glance took in the situation. He pulled his gun free, and fired, just as Willy reached the door. I could see the chips of marble fly. Willy turned and fired almost without aiming. The marshal was dead before he hit the floor. The other marshal, who now had his gun out, also fired. But by this time Willy had yanked open the door and was racing down the steps.

I can only describe the lobby as chaotic. Women shrieked hysterically; men shouted and ran aimlessly about. The marshal swung open the door and followed Willy. Josh was at his heels, and I, like a fool, was behind them. As I skirted Benny's body I could see a pool of blood edging out from under his head.

I had taken two steps when gunfire exploded in the stairwell. I heard Josh shout Willy's name, and I reached the basement as the big door was slowly closing. As I came out into the basement corridor, two shots crashed out almost simultaneously. At this point, the corridor is long and narrow and makes a sharp bend to the right that goes on for about another hundred feet, ending at the revolving door that leads to Foley Square.

Willy had reached the bend in the corridor when the marshal came out of the stairway. As Willy turned, both men fired. I saw Willy stagger as if hit, but his bullet spun the marshal off his feet. But the brave young man rolled over and got off two more shots that sprayed the paint from the wall above Willy's head as he rounded the corner. Josh's cries trailed after him in the corridor, which still echoed with the crash of the guns and now smelled of acrid gunpowder. The marshal was staggering to his feet when we reached him. He had been hit in the shoulder, but he pushed us aside. Blood was staining his shirt as he stumbled down the corridor.

At the end of the corridor was a strange sight: two window cleaners had been at work on the panes of the locked revolving door. Willy had swept them from their wooden platform and hurled it against the thick glass. Using it as a battering ram, he was enlarging a hole in the door. The marshal leaned against the wall, aimed, and fired, as glass crashed. As Willy spun around, gun up, Josh hurled himself against the marshal, and both fell to the floor. The bullet plowed through the plaster where the marshal had been standing. Then, shouting something unintelligible, Willy crawled through the smashed door while the two terrified window washers crouched in the corner. One, who had some sense, jumped up and slid back the lock on the revolving door. With Josh helping the marshal, we went through the door and left it spinning wildly.

By the grace of God the major part of the lunchtime period was over, and most of the employees of the nearby courts and State Building had returned to their offices. But there were still a number of pedestrians walking about the square and enjoying the afternoon sunshine in the small park that lies like a green triangle in the center of the square.

Willy was already running across the street when we came out of the building. As we reached the front of the Federal Building, men and women were streaming down the long flight of steps, shouting and pointing to Willy, a fantastic giant in an old-fashioned coat sweater and sneakers. He still held the gun in one hand. A police officer who had been directing traffic at Worth Street was running toward him, his gun drawn. Without a break in his stride Willy fired, and the officer went down. At the edge of the park Willy paused and turned. The marshal fired, and Willy staggered. When he raised his gun, Josh and I pulled the marshal down behind a bench, and the top wooden slat splintered from the impact of the bullet. When we got to our feet, Willy was hobbling across the park.

"He's hit!" the marshal gasped. His left arm dripped blood; his face was chalk white as we started across the street and into the park.

Foley Square was an incredible sight. Men and women lay flat on the ground, covering their heads or crouched behind automobiles. One woman had put her child in a wire wastepaper basket. The only person standing was an old hot-dog vendor at the curb on the north end of the square where Willy was running. The old man was calmly daubing mustard on a hot dog as he watched Willy run past. His customer was in a tight ball at the old man's feet. Incongruously, two tiny Greek and American flags hung from the big yellow umbrella.

It was plain that Willy was headed for the Worth Street subway station. For Willy the underground would be home. At the entrance he turned and fired again, but now we were crouching behind parked automobiles, and his bullets only crashed into metal and shattered windshields. Then he disappeared into the subway.

"Wait a minute! Don't go down there after him!" Josh told the marshal. The marshal tried to stumble forward, but collapsed at our feet.

Within seconds the area was flooded with cops and echoing with the wailing of sirens. Policemen with drawn guns rushed down into the subway station; emergency-squad men and transit police ran about, giving orders to have the power shut off. Wooden barricades were erected to dam the growing sea of curious. The reporters and television crews who had been at the hearing were everywhere. The young marshal was now unconscious, and Josh and I had stripped off his bloodstained shirt. There was an ugly hole in his shoulder, but Josh, the old soldier, said it looked as if it had gone clean through without breaking any bones.

A red-faced police sergeant puffed up the subway stairs. "There's a couple of guys down on the platform. We don't know who they are. Will you have a look at them?"

We went down and assured the cops that none of the four or five frightened-looking men was the gunman they were looking for. Someone shouted that the power was off.

The sergeant jumped down into the trough and looked up. "They say he's a big guy."

"I'll go along with you," Josh said.

"I don't want to get involved in any suits against the city," the sergeant said. "Just give me a description of the guy."

Josh ignored him and jumped down. I followed.

"He was winged, Sarge!" a cop shouted up ahead. "Here's blood."

At the end of the platform several drops of blood were bright against the glittering steel rail.

"Hug the walls," the sergeant shouted, "and watch out for track workers." He gestured with his gun. "Where does this lead?" he asked a transit motorman.

"Up to Canal."

"Let's go. Everyone fan out."

We moved ahead in the darkness, steel ribbons gleaming in the beams of the flashlights. The only sounds were our heavy footfalls and the rumble of the traffic overhead.

"Here's more blood, Sarge!" a voice shouted up ahead.

"Just keep your eyes open."

We had moved up past the Canal Street station, now crowded with the curious, when somone called out they had found blood on a ladder. The flashlight showed where Willy had climbed to the street.

"Well, that's that," the sergeant said. "He's on the street now. But he can't last long; he's hit. Collins, call Communications and tell him this guy is out of the subway."

He turned to us. "You better give me a complete description of this guy. He's dangerous as hell."

The understatement of the year.

Even with the sergeant escorting us, it took a long time to get back into the Federal Building. Now it was ringed solid with policemen. On every floor, every corridor, plainclothesmen, badges pinned to their lapels, demanded identification. The bodies of Benny and the marshal were still in the lobby, covered with the usual grim shroud of big-city crime—a newspaper. As we entered, a police photographer had finished setting up his camera. He waved, and a policeman gingerly removed the paper.

"Good God," Josh whispered.

From across the lobby it seemed that Benny's half-opened eye studied us almost roguishly. The pool of blood about his head had widened considerably. One hand reached out, clawlike, as if clutching the smooth marble in one last desperate attempt to escape. The marshal, a young man in a blue suit, looked to be sleeping. He had been shot through the heart, and died instantly. There was almost no sign of blood.

The Homicide detectives carefully outlined the bodies in chalk, then, using tapes, measured the distance from the phone booth where Willy had hidden, while others photographed the chipped marble and dug the slug from the heavy oak door. Newspapermen and photographers, held back by a barricade at one end of the lobby, were intermittently calling someone "Chief," a calm-faced man who ignored them.

After consulting the detectives in the lobby, the sergeant brought us to the thirteenth floor and into the U.S. Attorney's office, which seemed to be a sort of command post. Here were gathered the city's leaders, the mayor, some federal judges still in their robes, the police commissioner, the local heads of the FBI.

They surrounded Luke, Luther, and Shea, all of whom looked stricken. As we came in, Jones, trailed by a reporter with a mike, rushed from another room. "Terrible, terrible," he said. "I had the Speaker on the phone, Josh; he wants you to—"

"Later," Josh said wearily.

"This is unbelievable, Josh," Luther said in a low voice. "Are you all right? We heard you and Finn were in the lobby when he started shooting."

"We were there. What's happening here?"

"The Bureau is raising hell all over the place because we won't turn everything over to them. They want all our records," Luke said. "We told them Willy was an informant, nothing more."

Josh nodded. "Stick to that story. Is someone trying to raise Kelly?"

"We've been calling all over Lawrence," Luther said. "The phone number we have for Abernathy doesn't answer. One of the investigators called the Police Department, but all they did was shout they're too busy and hang up. I guess we have to expect that."

"Maybe there's some kind of a big accident or a fire," Shea said.

"Is the Bureau handling this one or the cops?" Josh asked.

"The police are going right ahead as if it's a homicide with no federal jurisdiction," Luke said. "There's a sharp guy named Marrick, chief inspector, who's taking over. He was looking for you to get a description of Willy."

"Where's the senator?"

"I sent him back with the chauffeur. He's terribly shaken."

"Have any of you seen Molly?" Josh asked swiftly.

Shea said, "Not today. She usually sits down front."

"We'd better find her—and fast," Josh said grimly.

A look of horror spread across Luther's face. "What's wrong? Are you trying to tell us something, Josh?"

Josh closed his eyes for a moment, then took a deep breath. "We don't know," he said with an obvious effort to keep his voice calm. "We know Willy's gunning for all our witnesses—"

"He bugged our meeting last night at Wexford," I said.

Luther grabbed Josh's arm and shook it violently. "For God's sake, let's do something!"

"Keep your voice down," Josh said in a low, savage tone. "Don't panic now, for Christ's sake! Luke, you know Burning Oaks. Call the manager and tell him to get her out of there! Tell him to take her over to the local police station and keep her there until you and Luther arrive."

"Suppose Willy got to her—" Luther began.

Josh gave him a steady, unblinking stare. "All I can tell you, Luther, is to say a prayer they find her sitting in the sun, knitting."

"Inspector Marrick just came in, Josh," Shea said.

As Luther, Shea, and Luke hurried out, I heard Luke say, as though to himself, but loudly, "The ratings definitely should hold. . . ."

Luther gave him a gray and startled look. I guess he felt there wasn't need for an answer.

348

After they had left, a swarthy-skinned, athletic young man dressed in conservative gray came up to us.

"Mr. Michaels?"

"That's me."

He put out his hand.

"Tom Marrick, Chief Inspector. I understand you're handling things for the committee?"

"In a fashion. I'm attached to Congressman Shannon's staff."

"You saw the shootings?"

"Yes." Josh turned to me. "My associate, Finn McCool." Marrick nodded. "We both saw it."

"Do you know the man? The killer, I mean?"

Josh hesitated for a fraction of a moment.

"Yes. His name is Willy Williamson. He's off his trolley."

"That's obvious," Marrick said dryly. "Is he connected with the committee?"

"No. He simply gave us some information which we are still in the process of checking out.

Two young men whose appearances shouted FBI, had joined us. "What information did he give you?" one asked.

"It's congressional information, and confidential," Josh said. "Are you from the Bureau?"

"It's important that we—" one began, but Marrick held up a protesting hand.

"Wait a minute, fellows; wait a minute! First let's get a description out! He's armed. He's on the street. Let's do something about getting him before we start talking about secrets!"

"We'll see how confidential that information is," one of the two said coldly, and they hurried out.

Marrick stared after them with a look of disgust. "Give me a fast description of this man," he said. He turned to one of the group of plain-clothesmen who surrounded us. "Steve, get this out to Communications right away. Also give it to the TV and reporters."

"I gave them one a few minutes ago—"

"What's the difference?" Marrick said impatiently. "Give them another one!"

Josh rattled off a minute description of Willy, and the detectives hurried out.

"What about addresses for Williamson?" the inspector asked.

"He has no address—he lives in a bus."

The inspector gave him a startled look.

"I told you he was a nut. It's a blue Volkswagen with dirty curtains on the windows. He has it fixed up like a camping trailer. He parks it anywhere on the East Side from Forty-third to Fiftieth streets, or on Second or Third Avenue."

"Get that out fast," Marrick said to his aide. "Tell Communications to have every available radio car hit that area."

"I have an idea where we might find him. . . ."

"Let's have it. Where?"

"He has a hideout under Grand Central."

"A what?" One of Marrick's aides said incredulously. "How the hell—"

The inspector glared at him and he broke off.

"Get that captain from the Transit Authority over here," Marrick ordered. "Then get the Grand Central people to round up their experts on the station. Tell them to bring some maps of the station. We'll be up at the stationmaster's office in fifteen minutes."

"Here's the Transit Authority captain, Inspector."

"Fine. What's your name? McCarthy? Fine. What I want, Mac, is for you people to get every available transit cop you can round up. This guy is out on the street now, but he may go back into the subways if the heat's on."

Josh broke in. "He knows the underground of the city intimately."

"That's why I want Transit to get going," the inspector said. "Do you have that transit map?" he asked one of the plainclothesmen, who handed him a large, folded portfolio.

The acting mayor, who had taken over Gentile's job the day Gentile resigned, hurried over, escorted by the police commissioner.

"Now look, I want everything done to get this killer," he started to say, but the inspector gave him a brief nod and a cool look.

"Everything possible is being done, sir."

"Shut down the subways! Do anything to get that maniac!"

"You can't shut down the subways, Mayor," the inspector said patiently. "In a few hours eight million people will be using them. We're having every mile of the subways patrolled. Now, if you'll excuse me . . ."

He nodded to Josh and me, two of his aides, and the Transit Authority captain.

"There's a small room over there. Let's use that. I want to go over this map."

In the room he spread the sheet out on a table. "Here's the entire subway system," he said. "I want every mile of it covered." He looked up at the Transit captain. "How many men can you raise?"

"Six hundred, more or less."

"Fine. You have trackwalkers, maintenance men, and so on, don't you?"

"They're not cops, Inspector."

"They have eyes haven't they? Let them call a cop if they see anything suspicious. They don't have to be heroes. You people divide the system into sections, so many cops to a section. Our Communications will set up trucks, and in that way we'll be in complete contact with you. Can you get them on special trains and spread them out fast throughout the city?"

"We're making up some trains now," the Transit man said. "We'll move in five minutes."

"Make it three," the inspector said. "Let's get up to Grand Central. Tell the Bureau where we're going. We'll be in the stationmaster's office."

As we reached the corridor the elevator door opened and Luke and Luther leaped out. They were both deathly pale, and visibly shaken.

Before they could say a word I knew what had happened.

"Josh," gasped Luther, "they found her. The manager's hysterical."

Marrick spun around like a guardsman. "What's this?"

Josh said, "Benny's girlfriend. Willy must have gotten to her—"

"Where is she? What's her name? Quick!"

"Molly Shapiro. She's at the Burning Oak Motel, near Crestview. Last night—"

But Marrick was already dashing back into the room. He yanked up the phone and told the operator to get him the state police barracks at Crestview. In a moment he was barking into the phone:

"Lieutenant, this is Inspector Marrick, down in New York. We've just been notified of a homicide at the Burning Oak Motel. It's a woman named Molly Shapiro—" He listened, then held the phone against his chest. "Is that the woman whose home was burned down a few days ago?" When we nodded, he returned to the phone. "The same one, Lieutenant. You know what's happening down here? Right. No doubt yours is connected. Yes, I'll have two men starting immediately. Right."

He hung up and waved to two of his assistants. "Get up to the Burning Oak Motel right away. It's outside Crestview. This crazy man has killed a woman up there. Her name is Molly Shapiro. She's the girlfriend of the guy in the lobby. Get going. Let me know what the score is as soon as you can."

The two men left the room on the run.

Marrick turned and gave us a bitter look.

"Any more people you know who may be the target of this maniac?"

"Who knows?" Josh said dully. "Who knows?"

The unmarked police car that would take us to Grand Central eased out of Foley Square and headed toward the East River Drive. The wounded traffic cop had been removed to the hospital, but the army of curious had increased, it seemed, by the thousands. In addition there were heads at every window.

Josh and I were numb. The impact of what had happened in the past thirty minutes or so was just beginning to sink in. Benny, Molly, the young marshal who had gone to call his wife—dead. Another marshal and an elderly police officer wounded . . .

While the inspector and his men discussed their plans, Josh stared straight ahead. A smear of grease stood out against his pale face.

"Josh," I whispered, "what about Kelly? We have to get to him somehow."

"I have to get Willy first," he mumbled. "I've got to get him before he does it again." He leaned his head back on the seat.

"God—if I had only realized . . ."

"Let the cops go after him, Josh."

He just shook his head and kept staring straight ahead.

A group of Grand Central officials were waiting in the stationmaster's office when we arrived. A short, stout white-haired man who looked as if he would be more comfortable in overalls than in the white shirt and carelessly knotted tie was introduced as the station's expert. He had rolls of charts, many of them stained with age, of Grand Central.

When Josh and I described the way Willy had brought us down into the depths, the old man nodded. "He used the old New York Steam systems," he said. "Some of those tunnels haven't been used since the thirties."

"We'll have to block off the entire station," Marrick said briskly. "I want every passageway, every corridor in this place covered."

The old man gave him a dubious look. "There are a thousand different ways to get in and out of this area," he said. "You have Con Ed, the subways, New York Steam, Water, Gas and Electricity." He threw up his hands. "Few people know there's a whole city under this city!"

"Okay, so we have to patrol that city," Marrick said.

"It will take a thousand cops—"

Marrick slammed his fist down. "Look, don't tell me how it can't be done! It must be done! There's a maniac that has a gun somewhere down there, and he can shoot! For some damned reason he's out to kill people! My job is to see that he doesn't. I want to take him alive, but from what he did downtown, there's going to be a hell of a lot of shooting; and when bullets fly around, someone is bound to get hurt. Now, let's start from the beginning." He looked up at me and Josh. "Suppose you tell exactly how you got down to that place."

As we told him, he ran a pencil along the route on one of the charts, then asked the old man how many tunnels and passageways he knew of that could match this route. When the old man told him, he marked off the places for his aides to cover.

Meanwhile phones were ringing madly. Uniformed police and plainclothesmen hurried in and out of the stationmaster's office. Word was spreading about the city that the killer was trapped in Grand Central; and when the TV crews appeared, that did it. From the reports coming into the office, the streets were jammed from Forty-second to Fiftieth, from Madison to Third.

All traffic was now diverted from the Grand Central area. Subways were running on a curtailed schedule, and this increased the confusion. The special subway trains were moving through the city, dropping off

352

transit police, some armed with high-velocity rifles, every second or third station.

From Thirty-eight to Forty-ninth streets patrol wagons were parked on side streets, filled with policemen armed with rifles and tear gas. Every fifth man had a walkie-talkie. Communications trucks were now posted about the city, in constant touch with the transit policemen moving underground.

Marrick was in the middle of issuing an order when a detective looked up from a phone.

"They found the Volks bus, Inspector, on Forty-fourth, off Second. There's blood in it. A woman said she saw a man get out of it and start toward Forty-ninth Street. She said he was staggering like he was drunk. She said he had a paper bag."

"The gun is in the bag," I said. "That's what he used in the Federal Building."

"Then he must be headed for his hole," Marrick said. "Let's get these men started down." He stabbed the map. "I'll take this entrance. You fellows start down the other entrances. Now, for God's sake, be careful! Tell those cops not to shoot unless they're sure it's Williamson. Has Transit, Con Ed, or New York Steam anybody down there?"

"Everybody's up," the old man said. "There are only rats down there."

Marrick murmured, "Let's go." He looked at us. "You'd better stay here."

"I'm going along," Josh said.

"No civilians," Marrick said firmly. "You get shot, and I'm in hot water with the commissioner and the city."

"I know this man," Josh said. "I may be able to talk him into sur-rendering."

Marrick hesitated. I could see the idea appealed to him. "We have a bullhorn. Okay. Bring it along." To me he said, "You too?"

"Me too."

Marrick looked as if he were about to say something, then changed his mind and stalked out. We all followed.

There were five emergency-squad men armed with rifles and wearing heavy wire mesh masks and awkward-looking breastplates that reminded me of baseball catcher's vests. One man had two powerful German shepherds that he said the State Police had rushed over. The dogs might be useful in the darkness, Marrick explained.

We started down, and the dry, warm gloom triggered a picture in my mind's eye of how we had followed Willy the first time. One of the men had a walkie-talkie, and was constantly receiving and sending out orders, while another man marked a map showing the locations of the other police teams that were virtually sealing off the entire Grand Central area on the streets and underground.

The night-lights used by the cops gave an eerie effect of a line of

353

shadows moving up and .down the twisting tunnels and corridors. At one point near the huge water-filled room, we stopped for a brief halt.

"You mean you came down here with this nut and never told the police?" Marrick demanded.

"He wouldn't talk to us any other place," Josh replied. "He had vital information, and we needed him."

"Well, you and your people will have an awful lot of explaining to do," Marrick said shortly. "For your sake, I hope his information was worth what happened downtown." To the others he said, "Let's go."

We had passed through the room with the thunderous, gushing water when the man with the walkie-talkie stopped. He listened for a moment, then turned to Marrick.

"He's back underground. Henderson's men said they caught a glimpse of him. He hit one of them."

"Serious?"

"He got a cop in the hand."

"Tell Henderson to get the cop upstairs right away." He consulted the map. "It looks like he's coming down from Forty-ninth Street toward us. Keep your eyes open."

We had just started up again when I heard the far-off sound of the approaching train. Marrick nodded when I told him what it was. That roar had just enveloped all of us when one of the officers suddenly clutched his shoulder, and fell against the wall.

"Spread out!" Marrick shouted. "He must be just ahead."

The next shot broke the single overhanging light. We were now in almost total darkness.

"Watch for his muzzle blast," Marrick ordered.

The almost indistinct cough of the revolver was practically simultaneous with the whine of a bullet overhead; then the tunnel was filled with the crash of rifles.

"Move up easy," Marrick ordered, "but stay down."

We had started to inch forward when Marrick told the dog handler to release the shepherds. Both dogs, tails down, ears back, took off in a crouching run. In a minute they were gone. Then we heard their savage, snarling barks, followed by a sharp yelp.

"The dogs are at him!" Marrick shouted. "Move up!"

He had his revolver out and started forward, hugging the wall.

The tunnel curved, then straightened out. Far ahead I could see a faint light and the outline of a large platform. I remembered the chamber with dials and wires and the narrow bridge Willy once had called his escape hatch. I recalled how he had pointed to it and rocked with laughter. There was no doubt this was what he was headed for.

Suddenly I saw the figure move out of the shadows into the dull yellow light of the naked bulbs. Again the roar, the rattle, the earthshaking sound of the passing subway train. Then silence again, broken by the abrupt yelping of the hurt dog. We could see one of the animals clinging to Willy's arm as he frantically battered at its head with the butt of his revolver.

Josh snatched the bullhorn from the policeman and ran ahead.

"Come back, you fool!" Marrick shouted.

Josh was now outlined by the light of the overhead bulbs as he raised the horn to his lips. It was as if a giant were speaking. The words bounced back and forth between the walls like invisible rubber balls.

"Willy! Willy! It's me, Josh! I want to talk to you!"

The sound of Josh's voice must have given Willy some superhuman strength, because he suddenly raised his arm, the animal still clinging to it, and fired. The dog dropped. Then he turned and raised the revolver. I remember shouting, but I don't know to this day what I cried. Josh was a perfect target. It was an unforgettable tableau: Josh standing in the faint light of the tunnel, the horn at his side; Willy, half bent over, one arm across his stomach, the other aiming the revolver at Josh.

Then, inexplicably, he shouted something, ran across the small iron bridge, and into the narrow tunnel.

"You damn fool!" Marrick shouted at Josh. "What are you trying to do—get killed?"

Josh silently handed the horn to the patrolman. "I wanted to make the business downtown worthwhile," he said quietly.

"Don't play hero with me," Marrick said angrily. "Where does this tunnel go?"

"We don't know," I said. "Willy once said it was his escape hatch."

"Tell Henderson and the others where he's headed." He looked at the map. "West, I guess. Nobody knows where the hell this thing ends. Tell them we're going in, too."

The tunnel was worse than any we had traveled with Willy. It was narrow, twisted, and totally black. There were piles of debris, pipes, stacks of ancient wooden piles, and rusting lengths of tracks. We barked our shins, stumbled and fell, expecting any moment to hear the cough of that gun. It seemed we had been walking for an hour—the walkie-talkie had faded because of the narrow confines—when we heard the rumble either of a train or of a subway. It grew louder, and from the frequency of the noise we took it to be the subway.

It was.

The tunnel finally ended in an abandoned spur that led to a main track. Marrick decided it was too dangerous to walk the tracks to the nearest station; instead, with the walkie-talkies again in working order, we contacted one of the other teams, who in turn called a communications truck to notify the Transit Authority. It was a terrifying experience while we waited. The subway trains were virtually at our fingertips, roaring past in a kaleidoscope of flashing lights.

Trackmen finally guided us to an exit. There were more ladders, more climbing. At last we saw daylight through the grating. It was pushed aside, and we stepped out onto Sixth Avenue just off Bryant Park. A group waiting for a bus studied us with the typical stolid indifference of veteran New Yorkers.

"Hey, where you going, a masquerade?" a teen-ager called.

I guess we looked it: the cops with their iron masks and steel mesh and leather aprons, all cradling shotguns or rifles, and the rest of us with torn trousers and jackets smeared with grease and dirt and covered with dust and cobwebs.

The teen-ager, who was holding a transistor radio which the others were listening to, called out, "You guys looking for the killer?"

"Beat it, kid," a weary cop murmured.

"What are you guys squawking about?" the boy asked. "You should be up in Lawrence!"

"What happened up there?"

"Riots," a woman said. "It's terrible. They're burning and killing all over the place."

"They went nuts," the man holding her arm volunteered. "The governor just announced he's sending in the National Guard. I think there are fifteen dead already."

"And there's a congressman trapped up there," the woman went on eagerly. "They say he can't get out. He may even be killed."

"That guy Shannon who's been holding the hearings," the man added. "The radio said he and his sister went back there when the riots broke out."

"Even the President's been on the phone," the woman said.

"That's right." The man turned to us again. "The President was holding a press conference when he heard about the riots and how the congressman was up there. He got upset and said everything should be done to get him out. It was all on TV. They even had air shots. The whole damn city's burning!"

"The country's crazy," the woman said with a sniff. "Imagine a man killed in the courthouse and then this!" She looked down the street. "Here's the bus. Louie, you got the transfers?"

The man nodded gloomily and held up the transfers. "They cut out everything for the special broadcasts on the riots and the search for that killer," he said. "Even the late results they didn't give."

The crowd pushed its way into the bus. The wide-eyed teen-ager, radio to his ear, turned to us from the bottom step.

"The guy on the radio says they just threw a cop off a roof up there!"

"Crazy, that's what they are, just crazy," the woman informed the whole bus.

"Lady, if you get in we can beat the light," the bus driver called out impatiently.

"The light's so important?" the woman asked indignantly.

"See if you can get the late results, will you, kid?" the man asked the teen-ager as the bus doors closed and the heavy bus lurched forward, driving back the few pedestrians who had gingerly stepped off the curb like cautious bathers reaching out a foot to test the water.

Apparently our day of reckoning had only begun.

CHAPTER TWENTY: THE TIME-BOMB CITY EXPLODES

INSPECTOR MARRICK GAVE US a radio-car escort to the Bronx County line. From there the state police brought us to Wexford. Programs were constantly interrupted by bulletins giving the latest details on the hunt for Willy and the rapidly growing riots in Lawrence.

There was no news of Kelly or Lacey. Evidently they had been on their way back to New York City when they heard the first news of the riots and had returned to Lawrence in the company of three Negroes. One was an elderly clergyman; the other two were said to be connected with some civil rights movement in Lawrence. I wondered if one was Gene Abernathy.

The superintendent of the state police, interviewed at his command post on the outskirts of the city, described the riots as the worst in the history of the country. He predicted the loss of lives and property damage would far exceed the riots of Watts, Harlem, Philadelphia, and Cleveland.

"The city is in the hands of uncontrollable mobs," he said. "A large number are armed and intoxicated. From the reports we are receiving inside the city, all stores are being looted and burned, whether they are owned by whites or Negroes."

"What about Congressman Shannon and his sister?" the reporter asked.

"We fear for their safety," was his blunt answer.

The other bulletins described the hunt for Willy, who police now believed was trying to escape from the city. Roadblocks had been set up at all tunnels and bridges; there were enormous traffic jams at the Lincoln, Holland, and Queens Midtown tunnels and the George Washington Bridge, where police and state troopers were checking every car that passed. The area from Thirty-fourth to Fiftieth streets, Fifth to Twelfth avenues, was locked in by fleets of radio cars and unmarked detectives' cars. Pairs of heavily armed foot patrolmen had started a block-by-block search with orders to shoot to kill.

Subway schedules were back to normal, but squads of track workers were guiding groups of armed city and transit police up and down the

East Side subway system just in case Willy returned to his underground world.

A trail of blood had led from where we had emerged on Sixth Avenue down two blocks to a parking lot and a groggy young attendant who had been knocked out. One car was missing. It was feared that within the short time when we had last seen Willy in the tunnel and when he had emerged to slug the attendant and steal the car, he had escaped to Long Island or New Jersey before the roadblocks could be set up.

In New Jersey and on the island, every town, village, and city had issued police alerts. Loudspeakers in train depots, bus stations, terminals—in fact, every large public place within fifty miles of Times Square—had loudspeakers blaring out Willy's physical description.

"He's as big as an elephant, and badly wounded," Inspector Marrick had said. "He can't hide forever."

There was no question of where we should be—Lawrence. From the moment he had heard Lacey was trapped in Lawrence, Josh was like a man possessed. We almost had to use physical force to get him to accompany us to Wexford. There we found the senator and Shea sitting before the huge TV sets with the screen shifting from the blazing ravaged city of Lawrence to elevated shots of the monstrous traffic jam at the Lincoln Tunnel and grim-faced cops, guns in hand, cautiously entering a cellar.

"We have to get Kelly and Lacey out of there." The senator's haggard, sunken face turned to us. "We have to get Kelly and Lacey out of there," he kept repeating, almost mechanically.

"We'll find them and get them out of there," Josh assured him.

While he fumed with impatience, Luther and Luke made a series of fast phone calls to the state police command post in Lawrence and the AG's office in Washington. Of course, they made promises, but all admitted they had no news of either Kelly or Lacey.

"I'm not going to wait here any longer," Josh snapped. "I'm leaving now."

"I don't think there's anything we can do up there," Shea observed. "These phones are ringing like mad."

"You answer them," Josh said. He started to walk out.

I picked up my coat and joined him.

"I'm going into that place, Finn," he said.

"So am I." I wasn't being heroic, because I'm not particularly a brave man, but it seemed to me unthinkable to stay behind.

"I'll drive," Luke said.

"There should be a lot of things to do up there," Luther said as he picked up his hat.

"I guess Howard can answer the phones," Shea remarked as he reached for his coat.

"Frank, you'll just have to stay here with the senator," Josh said.

"Luther, I think you should also. Keep the reporters and TV people out of here. Tell them we're going to hold a press conference as soon as we possibly can."

"They're asking what Kelly was doing in Lawrence," Shea pointed out.

"Tell them he was interviewing one of the most important witnesses of the whole hearing," Josh said. "He had to go there himself because the man wouldn't speak to anyone else. Put it in a formal statement. You can hint this witness was ready to expose every scandal existing in Lawrence. Come on; let's go."

"You'll be in touch?" Luther said.

"As soon as we get Kelly," Josh said.

"Then you think—"

"Do I think he's alive?" Josh said. "Of course I do! Kelly Shannon wasn't born to die in some God-damn gutter with the walls falling in all around him! He's going to be part of history. You people should know that by now!"

We had a state police escort to Lawrence, and as we made our way up the parkway, weaving in and out of the traffic, we listened in silence to the radio reports. The most accurate accounts of the riot were coming from a young radio reporter representing a small Westchester station, WZRA. The reporter told how he had learned of some sporadic incidents that had been taking place during the morning in several sections throughout Lawrence: a truck driver had been beaten and his truck overturned and set afire; a band of Negro teen-agers had stoned a local white high school. When the police appeared, the youths turned on them.

Police had insisted over the phone to the reporter that the incidents were isolated, mostly teen-age gang rumbles, but the reporter had driven to Lawrence to investigate the stories, when suddenly it erupted—a terrifying human volcano.

As Luke skillfully followed the wailing radio car—I was startled to discover he wore glasses—we listened to the reporter's young, eager voice fill the car:

"I am in the center of the Nelson Memorial Ball Park, on the outskirts of Lawrence. On all sides of me are police from Lawrence, Jefferson, Hamilton, and Spendrock, all neighboring cities and townships. They have just been issued tear gas and shotguns. Across from me are the bodies of the police officers who were killed less than a half hour ago when the mob fired at a contingent of police. The police returned the fire, and I have counted the bodies of six rioters. Ten minutes ago a sergeant from Hamilton was brought in, suffering from a bad concussion. He said the mob has started fires in some tenements and the whole block is now ablaze. A fire truck has been overturned and put on fire along with a radio car. What I saw I will never forget. The people are like raging animals. They are running up and down the streets shouting, laughing, and whistling. Every store window in Lawrence has been

359

broken. They have liquor now, and many are drunk. Sporting stores have given them guns. When they saw me they came for me. I made a run for my truck and made it—thank God!

"It's getting worse by the minute. The governor had better act, or there won't be any Lawrence left by morning.

"This is Don Keith, WZRA Special Events Department. I am now going back into the city. If all goes well, I'll come back with another report. . . ."

A half hour later he was back, his voice breaking with excitement: "Lawrence is in flames, ladies and gentlemen, and is burning fast! The mobs control more than half of the city and are moving in on what's left of the Lawrence Plastics Works. Fire departments of four local communities have unsuccessfully tried to fight the flames, but they were either stoned, shot at, or even killed. I saw the bodies of three firemen who were killed fifteen minutes ago after their driver was shot and their fire truck crashed into a gasoline station. The crash touched off a gasoline explosion and burned those men alive. . . .

"I have another important development: Congressman Shannon is still alive and well, except for a deep cut on his hand from flying glass. His sister, who has as much guts as her brother, is still with him. A small group of Negro businessmen who tried to calm the crowd offered to escort the congressman and his sister out of the city, but they refused. It seemed the congressman is with two or three Negro leaders and a clergyman who are desperately trying to reason with the rioters. According to a businessman whom I spoke to only a few minutes ago, the congressman and his party were making some headway with the mob when another group came down the street with boxes of liquor. The mob went crazy. There were a number of shots fired, but the congressman and his sister and his party fled through a tenement in the direction of the plastics plant, which was almost destroyed some months ago in a fire police insisted had been set by arsonists. A complex of the factory near the loading section and some of the stone office buildings still remain. The man I spoke to said he believes the congressman and his party will try to make their way there. It looks like that factory will be the last stronghold against the mob. My informant said some of the executives of the plant are hiding there. Police fear the mob is now making its way to the plant to kill the executives and set fires to the last of this ravaged, symbolic factory.

"The National Guard is now at the junction of routes 19 and 32; they should be here within the hour. All I can say is, Thank God. The city is now a vast sea of flames. The air is filled with the wail of sirens, shots exploding like firecrackers, and the roar of the mob that chills your blood. In my personal opinion there won't be much left of Lawrence by dawn. I saw only televised films of Watts, Harlem, Philadelphia, and the other cities torn by riots, but I can say this: They were minor disturbances compared to Lawrence. This is Don Keith . . ."

We sat in silence for the rest of the trip, listening to the young reporter who would eventually win an Emmy for his superb, courageous job that night, as he emerged again and again from the ravaged city to give his listeners the latest tale of violence and death. The known toll was a hundred dead, and scores wounded by fire, bullets, and flying debris.

Then the awed voice of Luke broke in on our thoughts: "My God! Look at that!"

The city, as young Keith had said, was a sea of fire with billowing towers of heavy black smoke. As we drew near, what appeared to be a church steeple toppled in a shower of sparks. Our state-police escort brought us to the ball park on the outskirts of the city that had been turned into a command post by the state police and National Guard. Tents were going up, and the place bustled with cars, jeeps, police, firemen, and grim young guardsmen who surrounded us with bayonets as we stepped out of the car.

After we had been identified by our state-police escort, we were taken across the field to the colonel in charge. In a half hour, he told us, his guardsmen would be moving into the city from three directions with orders to shoot to kill all snipers, armed rioters, and looters.

He was a brisk, middle-aged man whose very air seemed to say that war is my business and business is good.

"We'll be moving in from the east end, from the west, and with my MTO trucks coming up—"

"Have you heard anything about Congressman Shannon or his sister?" Josh asked impatiently.

"No, but I damn well better find them in a hurry," the colonel said. "Washington and Albany have been screaming that same question at me for the last hour." He looked over his shoulder at the flaming city. "Back there I don't give you much of a chance if your skin is white."

"Will this be Central Communications?" Luke asked.

"The other side of the field is Communications until we get set up," the colonel replied. "The state police are over there."

"Luke, you stay here with the colonel," Josh said. "Finn and I will go over to the state police to see if we can find out anything."

"You know you're not going into that city," the colonel put in sharply.

"I wouldn't think of it," Josh said, "but I would like to find that WZRA reporter."

"We're going to stop him from going in again," the colonel replied. "He has five stitches in his head now. He's a damn fool, but I'll say this for him: he has guts." He turned to a young guardsman. "Driver, take these men down to the state-police roadblock on Harding Boulevard— I think that's where that reporter is—and tell the captain nobody—I don't care who they are—is to enter that city again without my written permission!"

We found Keith, the reporter, just finishing another broadcast. His eyes were bloodshot from the smoke, his jacket stained, and he had a large bandage across the top of his head. He was surrounded by a group of Negroes and guardsmen, some of whom he had just interviewed.

When Josh asked him where he thought Kelly could be found, he shook his head.

"According to the man I spoke to, the congressman, his sister, a Negro clergyman, and a few other Negro leaders were standing on a stoop trying to talk to the mob. From what he said it appeared the congressman was making some headway. The crowd had seen him on television and seemed impressed he was up there. There was a young Negro with him—"

"Was his name Abernathy?" Josh put in.

"You got me," Keith said. "Well, everything was going along fine until these monkeys came running up with boxes of beer and booze. They had guns. From what this guy told me, they passed the bottles around and things started to pop. Some shots were fired, but he said he didn't think the congressman or anyone with him was hit."

"What happened then?"

"The businessman said he and some of the others warned the congressman they had to leave at once, they couldn't be responsible for what happened. They left through a tenement and a backyard in the direction of the plastics factory."

"I thought it was burned down," I said.

"Most of it was," Keith explained, "but there are some smaller buildings the company still uses. There's also a small brick office building at the entrance to the main gate. That's where the plant's executives are holed up—"

"We heard you on the radio coming up," I told him. "You said they might be in danger."

"You can believe it," Keith said. "This is the only thing the mob hasn't burned. I think they're on their way now."

"Suppose they remain in those buildings."

"Let's say I wouldn't like to be there," the reporter said with a shrug. "I don't have to tell you what a mob can do." He silently held up his hands, palms out in a gesture of despair. "And they won't care if he's a congressman. They won't care if he's Christ Almighty!"

"You going back?" Josh asked.

"Yes, and I'd better get hopping," Keith said with an uneasy glance at a Guard truck that was unloading. "They said they're not going to let anybody in again. . . . Why? You fellows want to go in?"

"We're going to find Congressman Shannon and his sister."

Keith looked at the burning city, and whistled softly. "You might get your head blown off before you go two blocks," he said. "You'll never make it."

"Oh, we're not walking," Josh replied. "We're riding with you."

"Are you insane?"

"You went in, didn't you?"

"That's my job."

"It's also ours. Let's go!"

The young reporter stared at him, but Josh grabbed him roughly and pushed him in the direction of his truck. "That chicken colonel just gave orders to his captain over there to make sure you didn't go back in. You do want to go back in, don't you?"

"I was hoping I could make an eyewitness tape recording."

"Good. We'll help you. Let's go."

The reporter's truck was a small paneled affair with the name of his station in gold letters on the battered sides. Josh slid into the driver's seat while young Keith and I clambered in the back, which was jammed with equipment.

"I still think you're nuts," he said.

"Okay, we're nuts," Josh replied hurriedly. "How do we go?"

"You go down Harding Boulevard for about ten blocks, then turn left as far as you can go; that will bring us into the heart of the city." He put on a heavy plastic construction helmet and gave us each one. They were black with gold block letters, WZRA.

"The boss got these made after we saw the pictures the New York photographers had made in Harlem during those riots some years ago. Like a jerk, I forgot to put one on, and they conked me with a brick. Oh, oh, let's move out. Here comes that captain. I guess your driver tipped him off we might be going back in."

The captain was approaching the truck on a run, but Josh threw it in gear and we took off, the officer's shouted commands lost in the squeal of rubber.

We followed Keith's directions as he squatted near his recorder at the open back door of the truck, giving a running eyewitness description of the scenes. We swung into what appeared to be a main street, and abruptly came upon the first signs of the riot.

A block-square supermarket and liquor store were being looted by a mob that poured in and out of the smashed windows like hurrying columns of ants coming and going from a spilled sugar bowl. They carried the most incongruous things: a broken adding machine, an armful of lettuce, a huge fish. A man whooping with crazy laughter pushed a shopping cart filled with bags of apples while another dragged a burlap bag of artificial plants.

When three men came out of the liquor store with arms loaded with whisky bottles, it was the signal for a mad rush toward them. They went down under a flying wedge of men, women, and even children who kicked and clawed at each other to get the whiskey bottles or cans of beer. One man had a screwdriver, and kept plunging holes in the tops of the beer cans, handing them right and left, shouting, "Get your beer, folks . . . whitey's beer . . . ain't no nigger beer today . . ."

We circled the mob and drove several blocks and came to two radio cars parked bumper to bumper across a wide street. Another, on the sidewalk, was overturned. Four policemen crouched behind the cars. We drove up to them and jumped out, Keith hugging his tape recorder.

"WZRA, Sergeant," he shouted. "Have you seen—"

The sergeant, who was on one knee, shouted, "Get down, get down! They're coming up again!"

"Any of your men hurt, Sarge?" Keith asked.

The sergeant jerked his head in the direction of the overturned radio car. "They got two of my men," he said bitterly. Then he pointed with his revolver and said savagely, "But we got three of the sons of bitches."

I followed the barrel of his revolver. In the gutter and draped over the curb were the bodies of three Negroes. Alongside the overturned radio car were two other figures covered by police jackets.

"Here they come, Sarge!" a cop shouted.

"The bastards have guns and Molotov cocktails," the sergeant said nervously. "We may have to pull out. The Guard come in yet?"

"They've just arrived," Josh said.

"Thank God. We can't control these maniacs any longer. Christ, there must be a million!"

The streets were now filled curb to curb with shouting Negroes, who danced with the disjointed gestures of puppets, held bottles high, shook fists, or waved sticks and clubs. Others came out of the tenements, and in a few minutes flames were licking at curtains and window frames.

"They're burning the whole block!"

"Let them burn the whole God-damned city down for all I care," the sergeant said.

"Shall we shoot over their heads, Sarge?" a young patrolman asked.

"Are you crazy?" the sergeant cried. "Kill the bastards!"

There was a crash followed by a gush of flames in front of the cars as Molotov cocktails exploded. Then, with a wild cry, a cry that will echo in my dreams for as long as I live, the mob came on the run.

The young patrolman who had asked the question leaned over the hood of his car, and his revolver spat flame. Suddenly he fell to one side, holding his throat. Josh and I ran over to him. The bullet apparently had hit him in the neck. He started to get to his knees, but blood gushed from his mouth and he sank back against the wheel of the car, staring in disbelief at his two open hands covered with his blood.

The sergeant was shouting incoherently and firing, as were the other police officers.

"Sarge! There's too many. Let's go."

A patrolman grabbed the wounded cop under the arms and dragged him into the radio car, backed up, and took off. A wild cry went up from the mob. "Whitey cops! Get them whitey head busters!"

Keith threw his tape recorder into the truck.

"Let's get out of here!" he shouted. "Come on, Sarge!"

Josh and I jumped into the truck. Fortunately, the engine had been left on, and we took off with a frenzied squeal of tires.

I'll never forget the scene I saw from the open end of the truck. The sergeant and the remaining patrolman were still firing when the mob poured over the hood and roof of the radio car. The sergeant was standing up now, and in the glare of the burning building I could see he was a big man. The other cop never got to his feet. He went down under the kicking, punching figures. The sergeant hurled his revolver at the mob and lashed out with a billy club. There was a rattle of shots, and he went down. The mob had begun to stomp the dead or dying men.

Several blocks to the west the fire departments were having better success with their high-powered hoses. As we drove up, the jets of water had just hit the spearhead of another mob. The leaders were sent hurtling through the air. Like a phalanx aimed with stiff, watery battering rams, the firemen moved forward, driving the mob back. Men and women crawled up stoops, only to be knocked over railings by the jets. Some tried to raise shields of wooden doors and ash-can covers or even baby carriages, only to have them flung high in the air and sent tumbling down the gutters.

From three patrol wagons came policemen with several dogs.

"Take 'em off their leashes," one shouted.

The cops bent down, fumbled with the collars of the dogs, and at a command, the powerful animals rushed forward, fangs bared, snapping and snarling. The rioters sprawled on the ground stumbled to their feet, only to be hurled again to the ground by the raging animals, who tore at them like wolves.

But the mob had guns, and several cracked. One dog yelped and dragged his hindquarters around on the ground, howling pitifully. But the animals knew no fear. Like monstrous sheepdogs herding human cattle, they drove the mob back down the street, while it was battered from all sides by the relentless streams of water, until it shattered and its members fled.

Three dogs lay dead in the street among moaning, torn, and lacerated human beings.

"The factory is somewhere on the other side of the tracks," Keith said. "Do you want to take a chance?"

"Let's go!" Josh shouted.

We bumped across some railroad tracks and entered a street lined on both sides with burning buildings. Our truck was a moving target, with the sides battered by everything from bottles to ash-can covers. Once a big man rushed from the shadows and slammed a heavy iron across one of the fenders, which crumpled under the blow. Now the tire scraped the metal, and Josh shouted we might have a blowout unless we could stop and straighten it out.

There was no time to stop. We turned and twisted through the burning streets. The windshield was smashed, and Josh kicked out the glass so he could see. Something came whistling through the now open windshield and sent me reeling. The construction helmet saved me from a fractured skull.

We had turned into a wider street, presumably an avenue, when the truck began bumping along. We had a flat. We were stopped in the middle of this avenue when a hooting, jeering mob poured from a narrow side street. I thought we were finished, but they seemed to be running from something or heading in the direction beyond our truck. We were like a tiny island in a human flood. As they came nearer we could hear them chanting. Then they were running past, banging the sides of the truck with their fists, sticks, or bars of iron. Some stopped to shake the truck violently for a few minutes, then ran on. All we could do was sit there helplessly.

"They're shouting something about taking care of whitey's factory," Josh yelled over his shoulder. "It must be the plastics works."

During a momentary break in the rush, Josh pulled to the curb.

"Do you have any idea where the factory could be?" he asked Keith.

The reporter pointed vaguely to the west. "I have an idea it's over in that direction. I recall a little bridge and a shopping square."

"We'd better make a run for it," Josh said, pointing down the street. "They look mean."

Rounding the corner was a gang of about twenty, mostly teen-agers. As they ran, they tossed Molotov cocktails at every house or into any tenement hallway that caught their fancy. Several of the group who were pushing a large drum before them dumped it over. The liquid ran down the steps of a basement. One of the youths running ahead turned and hurled a bottle.

There was a deep, clumping sound. Flames billowed out of the basement and caught two of the youths, turning them into torches. The others tried to beat out the flames, but it wasn't any use. The burning kids rolled back and forth in the street, screaming in agony while the others looked on helplessly.

The main group had stopped, then turned and came forward. The leader, a powerfully built young man with a tattered white shirt and a black bandanna tied around his head, shouted to the others when he caught sight of us.

"Let's go," Josh said, and pushed me ahead of him into a foul-smelling hallway. Keith was struggling with his heavy tape recorder, but Josh yanked it from his hand.

"The hell with it, kid," he cried. "We have to move—fast!"

We ran down the hall, through a broken back door, and out into a grubby garden that consisted of a pigeon coop and some rows of corn. Josh kicked aside the rotting fence, and we dashed across another small yard and down an alley. It led into a street bordering on a small square of stores and a short bridge spanning an oily stream. The stores were all looted; fires seemed to have been started but died out in some of them. The street was littered with clothes, bottles, cans, clothing dummies, smashed furniture, office machines, and display cases. Near the bridge was a smoldering bus. The blackened figure of a man hung half out the driver's seat. A heavy pall of smoke hung over the place.

"I think this is Dooley's Square," Keith shouted. He pointed to the bridge. "The factory is over the bridge somewhere."

We crossed the bridge at a run that left me blowing like a whale at the other side. After I had caught my breath, we hurried down a narrow side street, crossed a few more, and then were at the plastics works.

Or what was left of it.

Buildings saved from the previous fire now roared like burning oil wells, the flames, taut, white, consuming. At brief intervals there were sharp explosions, and the flames would gush into gigantic fiery blossoms. Several freight cars were burned to the wheels, and others were smoldering.

"Are the police here? Is anybody in charge?" Josh asked an old man who was staring at the burning buildings.

He gave us a dull, slack-jawed look.

"They're all down at the Barley Building."

"Where the hell's the Barley Building?" Josh demanded.

"The office—just inside the main gate," the man said.

"Was the mob here?" Keith asked. "Did they do this?"

"Can't you see they was here?" the man said. "Oh, yes, they was here. . . ."

We ran down the street skirting the hurricane fence that shut off the factory property. Once I stumbled and reached out to grab the fence, and yelped with pain; it was white hot from the blaze.

The Barley Building was a squat red-brick structure that once had been covered with ivy. Apparently a fire had been started there but had been put out. With the leaves of the ivy burned away by the heat, the naked vines looked like a grotesque network of electric wires covering the walls. The windows and glass doors were gone; an ash can was wedged in the frame of one.

A small group of people, white and black, stood in front of the glass-littered steps. One or two were bending over a still figure sprawled in the street. As we came nearer we recognized one as Kelly, another as Lacey. Two state troopers, cradling guns, squatted beside them.

Kelly's shirt was in tatters; his pants were stained with grease and blood. The top of Lacey's dress appeared to have almost been ripped off. She was wearing one of the trooper's jackets. Both looked incredibly weary and drawn.

Between them was the body of a young Negro. At first I thought he was unconscious; then I saw the red stain, big as the spread of a man's hand, on the left side of his shirt.

It was Gene Abernathy, and I didn't need a second glance to tell me he was dead.

"Kelly," Josh said.

Kelly looked up. Slowly he rose.

"Are you hurt, Kelly?"

"No. I'm all right. Did the Guard arrive?"

"They're moving in now. It will be all over soon."

"All over?" Kelly said bitterly. "This is only the beginning."

"Lacey, are you hurt?" Josh asked as he put his arm around her and held her tightly.

She didn't answer, only put her head on his shoulder and closed her eyes.

"Gene's dead," Kelly said, almost mechanically. "He was walking toward them and they shot him."

"I got one of the guys that did it," one of the troopers said grimly. As he pointed across the road to the wire fence, I could see the crumpled body of two Negroes, a rifle near one outstretched hand. "Sanderson and I were in the building when he fired, and this one went down." He nodded to Abernathy's body. "I got him with the first shot; Sandy got the guy next to him."

"Benny's dead," Kelly said in a strained voice. "We heard it on the radio. And Molly."

"It was a madman, Kelly," I said. "You can't blame yourself."

"Dead," he repeated, half to himself. "And I wasn't there."

Two men came out of the building. Their faces were a sickly white. One man was smoking a cigarette, pulling at it with short, rapid puffs.

"You okay, Congressman?" one asked Kelly in a high-pitched, strained voice. Without waiting for an answer he turned, shooting the words at us like bullets from an automatic clip:

"The Congressman did the God-damnedest thing I ever saw. He and this guy"—he nodded at the dead Abernathy—"walked out and started to talk with them. But there was no stopping them. They just kept tossing those Molotov cocktails at the storage rooms. Boom! Boom! Boom! It doesn't take but a match with all that plastic. But gasoline! Christ, she went up like a bomb! Then they shot this one."

He looked down at Abernathy.

"I better go in and see if Sanderson got the phone to work," the trooper said. He turned to Kelly. "You sure you're all right, Congressman?"

"Yes, I'm all right, Trooper. Thank you."

"It was one hell of a day," the man with the cigarette said; then he and his companion walked back into the building. "One hell of a day," echoed faintly from the doorway.

One of the Negroes who appeared to be a clergyman had opened his Bible and was reading it, mumbling to himself.

"We must take care of him, Reverend," Kelly said.

"The Lord has him now . . . He has His lamb. . . ."

An old Negro beside me said in a high, singsong voice, "God gave him his glory, a great big glory."

"And I had to leave that damned tape recorder," young Keith said. "Congressman, can you give me some kind of a statement? What do you think happened here?"

Kelly stared at him for a moment, as if seeing him for the first time.

"What happened here today?" he said, slowly repeating the question. "I don't think that any of us here will ever discover the answer. I think to do so you would have to tear this town apart piece by piece and spread the pieces on a table. Then select one by one. Take one: unemployment. Another: bad housing. There's another we can call bad schooling or another heartsickness." He shook his head and said in a weary, harsh voice, "Then you might pick up a rusty link of chain and find it came from a God-damned slave ship that docked five hundred years ago and five thousand miles away. . . ."

He fumbled with a crumpled package of cigarettes and took one. It was dirty and bent. A man gave him a light, and he bent his haggard face to the tiny flame, then lifted his head to inhale deeply.

"You study what you picked up; you give it to the experts, and perhaps you might get an answer as to what happened here tonight. But even then there's no guarantee. Too many have tried it, too many have never succeeded."

He stood there staring at the flames across the road with bitter eyes. Keith shuffled his feet awkwardly, self-consciously studying the notes he had scribbled on the crumpled piece of copy paper—notes I don't think he understood. Then Kelly seemed to rouse himself, and turned to Josh, who was still holding Lacey.

"I want Mullady subpoenaed today. I want that son of a bitch on the stand on Monday. Monday, you understand?"

He dropped the cigarette and ground it out very carefully.

"I think you all should know I wasn't disappointed in Gene Abernathy."

Then he slowly walked away as the first khaki-colored National Guard jeep entered the road. Suddenly there were many—jeeps, cars, armed half-tracks—and Luke and the colonel who seemed to like war so much had their arms around Kelly's shoulders and were leading him to a car while Josh was holding tightly to Lacey and saying nothing—just looking at Kelly walking toward the car in the glare of the fire that seemed to have burned away his youth.

THERE DIDN'T SEEM TO BE time to eat, to rest, to sleep that week. Following the debacle of Lawrence, we worked constantly on the hearing. Within an hour after we had returned to the city, Mullady was served. I had the pleasure of pushing my way into his bedroom and slapping the paper in his hand and reminding him he looked more like a toad than ever before.

That grimmest of weeks you couldn't turn on television or twist a dial on a radio set that you weren't either listening to Kelly or someone talking about him. His White Paper on Lawrence, America's Time Bomb City, was released the morning after the destruction of the city, and it is a vast understatement to describe it as a national sensation.

Josh made sure that with each copy were excerpts from Kelly's speech on the floor of Congress in which he had predicted Lawrence would explode unless something was done to correct conditions. Many of the major newspapers used the grim quotation as a big box, sometimes columns wide.

A WARNING THAT BECAME A REALITY IN BLOOD AND FIRE was the headline one Midwestern paper used.

The report was divided into several sections; some had severe reactions, favorable and unfavorable.

For example, one section broke down the instability of the Negro family in Lawrence, which made it difficult for the Negro father—if there was one—or the sons and daughters to cope with the disadvantages already heaped upon them. One of the points Kelly's report made was simply that there were too many children, and if the Negro family in Lawrence was reduced to the size of the white's, many would automatically move into a better economic status. The larger the family, the more impossible this is, was the argument, and the report suggested strongly that birth-control information and techniques be made available to the poor of Lawrence. This, of course, raised a furor, and some of Kelly's own church leaders came out against him.

The summing up was a fine chapter on Lawrence, which, some commentators pointed out, could be many American cities in miniature; the tragedy of Lawrence wasn't all in that final, bloody night, but in the indisputable fact that the Negro had moved into this one-time busy, middle-class industrial city at a time when the community was settled and tightly organized; when its assimilatory process had declined after it had absorbed the Poles, Italians, Germans, and Irish after World War I.

These were barriers that the Negroes of Lawrence could never hurdle. They were not only poor, despairing, and without hope; they were poor, despairing, and without hope in a period of America's greatest affluence.

The Lawrence Time Bomb exploded when its Negroes in lonely misery faced the truth of this.

The last page of the report warned the government that other American ghettos would continue to explode with each long, hot summer but that someday the uprisings would no longer be isolated but would be part of a chain reaction of terrifying violence and bloodshed across the country—unless stumbling federal and state programs were radically altered.

The *Times* wisely started its account—Josh had made sure a friend in their Washington bureau received a copy several hours before the formal release—on page one, jumping it inside for a solid page of text. The Washington papers gave it impressive displays, and the L.A. *Times* ran the report in full, with a page of pictures of its own Watts. The White House remained silent; but the fat cats in the various poverty programs poured out their banal releases, depicting in glowing terms what had been done and what lay ahead in the rosy future. But no one was fooled. No one. The scar of Lawrence would not heal for a long time.

Of Lawrence there wasn't much left. For two days a pall of smoke hung over the area. The plastics factory was finally burned to the ground; of the slum sections of the city only heaps of charred ruins and red-brick foundations were left. After the mob had set fire to the factory, its anger, hate, and violence seemed to have oozed away, and it began breaking up into segments. I guess the bayonets of the Guard helped; three men who attempted to crash a Guard barricade with a car and then pull a gun were run through. The tough young Guardsmen and their brisk colonel seemed only too glad at the chance of a bit of realistic training. There was one last act of violence before the mobs disbanded. They stormed Lawrence City Hall and the police station and would have burned them if the Fire Department hadn't driven them off with their hoses. As it was, some of the mob got into the lower part of the station and left it a shambles, knocking out a lieutenant and a sergeant and locking them in their own cells.

"They should have burned it to the ground," was Kelly's only terse observation.

"It's a different Kelly, Josh," I observed, but he only nodded. Since our return from Lawrence he had been strangely silent.

It was also the saddest of weeks. We buried Benny and Molly in the quiet Jewish cemetery on a gentle rise not far from Wexford Hall. The Shannons, Josh, and I were the only mourners.

Then the next day we were in the huge Grace Temple of Harlem, listening to the Negro clergyman who had been with Kelly at Lawrence read the service for Gene to the packed auditorium that echoed with cries of "Amen" and "Hallelujah." The eulogy was given by Kelly, a moving, eloquent tribute. Then we followed the casket in a procession that numbered in the thousands. Negroes came from every community in the state, and from Philadelphia, Watts, and Chicago.

There were no tears shed at either funeral. There was only a sense of smoldering anger. While he never showed it, you could sense it in Kelly, too.

In between there was the news of the hunt for Willy. The morning after he had shot his way out from under the Grand Central area, a physician near Rutherford, New Jersey, reported that a man had forced him at gunpoint to remove two bullets from his body. The man, he said, had suffered the loss of a great deal of blood but seemed to have iron nerves. All he could administer was a local anesthetic; but the man, he said, never winced as he probed for the slugs nor did the gun in his hand waver. The *Daily News* had a page-one picture of the doctor, holding the slugs in the palm of his hand and the picture of Willy, which he had identified. The doctor said Willy had been armed with the revolver and a silencer and a rifle with a scope.

That produced a flurry. Roadblocks were set up on the highways and the area was sealed off for hours while the cops made a house-to-house search, but Willy again had made his escape.

Then on Friday there was another piece of startling news. The Associated Press reported that Saunders had arrived in Buenos Aires. He was quoted as saying he was there only for a vacation, but it was obvious he had skipped. Our investigator who went up to question Remington found him sitting in his office drunk. It was evident we would have no trouble with Mr. Remington once he took the stand.

The judge was a trembling old man who had taken his "vacation," as he called it.

Remington, the Chief Justice of the Federal Court of Appeals, Barney Mullady, one of the biggest and most powerful politicians in the United States—along with the police chief, the local political boss, and a few others from Lawrence, including the madam whose whorehouse had been raided only once in ten years . . . Quite a hearing. We would have no trouble with the ratings this time.

The hearings, the final of the series, were to be held in two parts, New York and Lawrence. New York would hear Remington, the judge, and assorted witnesses, but the big show would be in Lawrence. Jones, who realized the entire country would be watching, tried to get Kelly to agree to hold both hearings in the plush hearing room in New York's Bar Association Building, but Kelly brushed him aside.

The New York hearings would be heard in the same courtroom where Benny Jello had last testified, he said; the other hearing would take place in Lawrence.

"The Lawrence hearings will be held on the third floor of that crummy old City Hall," he said. "It's going to be in the Council Room where Gene said only the thieves had a voice. . . ." He gave us a grim smile. "Remember when Patton made the Germans come into Dachau and carry the bodies to the open graves?"

I wondered how Josh would explain Willy. In a statement he dismissed him as a schizophrenic who had given the committee information and apparently decided to kill off the witnesses when he wasn't called. It was accepted, particularly in Washington, where any public hearings attract hosts of nuts, some of them so violent they must be ejected. Kelly, who was numb after Lawrence, didn't question the story, but those of us who knew it tiptoed about the subject.

I wondered what would happen if Willy was captured and volunteered the whole story.

Josh just shrugged when I brought it up. "Just light a candle they kill the crazy bastard," was all he said.

On Sunday night, the eve of the hearings, Lacey and I sat alone by the side of the pool at Wexford. It was a mild, soothing night, with the stars brilliant as diamond chips against the sky.

Luther, Luke, Frank Shea, Josh, and the senator were back in the house, corralling the last of the evidence that we had gathered in Lawrence. Ironically, most of it, or the best leads, had come from Willy's investigation. Luke and the others had taken coffee breaks or stolen a few minutes for a quiet drink, but not Josh or Kelly; they had started before dawn, and were still at it.

Once you learned the total impact of the material, you realized under what shocking conditions the people of Lawrence had lived—survived, rather. It was a classic example of what could happen to an American city once the thieves and corrupt politicians gained control of the municipal government. We found crooks in every department—Police, Housing, Health, Sanitation, and Building—anywhere a dishonest dollar could be made.

With Barney we had a weapon of total surprise; he still didn't know he had been turned in by young Abernathy, whose signed and notarized statement we had. Obviously, Barney knew we had something—the hatchet-faced secretary to whom Gene had given the valise of money and Barney's chauffeur who had picked it up had both been subpoenaed. Our investigators had their initial statements in which they admitted the existence of the valise, but undoubtedly they had alerted Barney.

I had never seen Kelly so intent. He had insisted we go over Abernathy's statement line by line. Investigators had worked tirelessly to get independent evidence to corroborate Abernathy's charges. In a way I felt sorry for Barney. By the end of this week he would be destroyed, a political wreck, well on his way to prison.

"Kelly has the bit in his teeth," Josh said quietly, "and I'm letting him run with it. Next comes the lust to win. He doesn't know it, but it's there and getting stronger day by day."

Now, out on the lawn, Lacey and I sprawled by the still pool. I guess I hadn't realized just how weary this old body was; for the first time the thought had been entering my mind that perhaps this would be the last image I would help Josh create. As I leaned back I unconsciously sighed.

"Tired, Finn?" Lacey asked.

"The devil's sucked the marrow from my bones."

She laughed. It was the first laughter I had heard this week.

"Did you always live on the West Side, Finn?"

"Until I went to Washington with my first committee. I think we were investigating boondoggling on the WPA. We caught many a straw boss taking the names from the tombstones for his payroll."

"And you never married?"

"Never. Many a girl's the happier for that."

She leaned over and squeezed my hand. "I think they were fools."

"Josh always threatens to get me a young thing from the reservation."

"He spoke about the ranch a few weeks ago. I was sitting here and he came out. He talked about it for a long time."

"Don't tell him I told you, but he once said you were the only woman he would bring there."

Her hand found mine. "Finn, he asked me to marry him."

"He loves you very much, Lacey."

"I love him, Finn," she said. "I really do, but I'm afraid—"

"Afraid? Of what?"

"His obsession to put Kelly in the White House. I don't think you, I—anyone or anything, mean as much to him." I could sense her smiling in the darkness. "I guess that's the little girl still inside me—always hoping for Camelot and waiting for the untarnished knight."

"Was your first husband like that?"

"He was the gentlest man I've ever known, but we never should have been married. In a way he was like Josh, but instead of votes and candidates it was fossils and Indian burial grounds. Once when I thought I was pregnant—I wasn't, thank God—I never told him—"

"Why? Didn't he want children?"

"Oh, he loved children but I picked a bad evening. I went out to the site where they were digging and found him deliriously happy. They had uncovered a big Zuñi pueblo that had to do with the origin of the Rain Dance. He talked until dawn. I don't think he heard a word I said."

"I hope you wouldn't want a God's innocent, Lacey."

"Of course not. But I certainly want a man who has some human compassion—"

"Josh not compassionate? Oh, come, Lacey—"

"I don't believe dedication to politics is a prerequisite to redemption, Finn," she said dryly.

374

"Josh isn't interested in the means, Lacey, only the end."

"I just can't believe our gain will be that great."

"I do."

"Then I shudder to think of Kelly's responsibilities."

"I wouldn't worry about Kelly, Lacey. From the first time I met him I felt he was different from us. Call it an old man's romanticism if you will, but I believe it was destined we should all meet."

"I guess I never really understood what Josh meant when he said a man must not only want high office—he must lust for it."

"All change costs something, Lacey. In the end you must compare the costs against the gain." I leaned over and took her hand; it was slender but strong. "Take him as he is, Lacey; you'll never make him over, and if you could, you wouldn't be happy."

"Not the way he is," she said, "I can't."

"Josh isn't the kind to kneel down and put his head on your knee. In his world there's not much time left to finish what he's set out to do. He's helping to shape a man for great things in the future, Lacey."

"I don't want a future-shaper," she said fiercely. "I want a man who loves me as much as I love him. More than politics or high offices or hearings or conventions. Or even my brother!"

"Do you love him that much, Lacey?"

She stood up, tall and slim against the stars.

"You know I do."

"Then take him," I said.

"I don't know what to do," she answered. "I just dread this week. I dread it for all of us."

"The whole country will be watching Kelly," I said.

Her voice was full of resignation. "Yes, I guess that's important."

The clerk called the names, and it was a summoning of the condemned. Remington was first. He was full of bluster, but after a short time looked beaten, his face drained of blood, his Adam's apple bobbing up and down like a pump.

Kelly started off slowly, almost solemnly, gravely. He let Remington have his way, describing his education, his honors, degrees, and finally the awards that hung on the wall of his office, every last one of them a tribute to the influence of politics.

Then Kelly leaned forward and started with the questions, beginning with the first night Benny Jello had pleaded with him to fix an SLA violation. The answers were at first nonchalant, then hesitant, then fearful. If one wasn't answered, Kelly reframed the question.

By noontime the jug of water at Remington's side had been filled three times. He was obviously growing more nervous by the hour. Kelly was now snapping out the questions. Jones said little. Like everyone in that silent, packed room, he sensed that this was personal.

375

Q.　You say you never met Jello?

A.　I said I don't recall.

Q.　Let me refresh your memory. At 10:20 A.M. you said in answer to my question, 'I assume I never met him.' Which is true?

A.　I am not sure.

Q.　This is a luncheon check. Your name is signed to it. Is it your signature?

Remington studied the check laboriously, as though he had never seen his own signature.

A.　I guess that's mine.

Q.　Are you sure?

A.　I guess so.

Q.　No "guess so," Mr. Remington. I show you this signature. Is it yours?

A.　I guess so—yes, it is.

Remington was excused, and the waiter who served them was called. His testimony was brief; he simply identified Remington, the picture of Saunders and Jello as the men he served. Then Remington was recalled.

Q.　The waiter says he served you, Saunders, and Jello. What do you say to that?

A.　I don't remember.

Q.　Is he lying? Would you care to go before the grand jury and say so?

A.　(*Shouted*) I don't know! I'm not sure!

Kelly was merciless. He brought Kenneth Beering, the head salesman of Delafield Motors, to the stand and subjected him to a merciless cross-examination. By the time he had finished, Beering was a stuttering, confused man who knew he was hovering on the brink of a perjury indictment. Less than a half hour after he had testified, the AP man sent a note to Kelly quoting a dispatch from his bureau that the Delafield Company had dismissed Beering. Kelly read it slowly and carefully to the television audience.

There was no letup. The next day the waiter was recalled, then Remington, his secretary, the cabdriver who drove Jello up to Remington's office, and finally Noodles, who had been located after Kelly had told the Bureau in no uncertain terms he wanted this thug found.

He was, as Benny had described him, a tall man with thick old-fashioned sideburns that emphasized the thinness of his face. He was a professional thief who wasn't taking the rap for anybody. He told his story simply and directly; he had come to Jello to fix the Singer case. Benny had told him it could be done for a price. He went to the family, raised the money, and took it to Benny's office in a valise where together they had counted it. Then they had taken a cab ("Louie, the flat-nosed guy who always hauled Benny") to Remington's office, where the valise of money was turned over to Remington.

"I gave Benny the money; he gave me the fix," was his answer, accompanied by an elaborate shrug.

Q. Did you see Remington take the valise?
A. Sure. He came out of his office and Benny gave it to him.
Q. What did he do?
A. Went into his office. Benny said he was a suspicious guy and probably wanted to count it.
Q. Then he came out?
A. He came out and we shook hands.
Q. Did you consider the fix in?
A. What else? The kids called me and said they got off.

Kelly brought Remington back to the stand in the afternoon. He hurled only three questions at the lawyer before he broke down, swearing that he would tell the truth and that it was true he and Saunders had fixed many cases. Had bribed judges, sold contracts. He babbled on, a shattered figure. But Kelly bore in, demanding more evidence, more names, more dates. Remington left the stand, barely able to walk, clearly on the verge of collapse. A few more witnesses were called; then, just before a recess was called, Kelly, smiling grimly, read an announcement from the New York County district attorney's office that Remington had agreed to sign a waiver of immunity and appear before a grand jury.

It was the first major break; the implications of what could follow in the wake of his testimony were tremendous.

There was a bit more icing on the cake that day; Gentile issued a statement that night to disclose that Saunders had sent him a wire of resignation and had said he would not return from the country that was the traditional refuge of fugitives from United States Justice.

Meanwhile the parade of witnesses continued: city officials who had handled contracts; executives of the Delafield Company who admitted they had manipulated city contracts through payoffs and elaborate parties; magistrates who crawled to the stand to confess they probably had made mistakes in judicial judgments when it came to handing out suspended sentences to mobsters or policy bankers.

It was a grand parade, and to believe Frank Shea, there wasn't a set in the country that wasn't tuned in.

Federal Judge Tucker was a pitiful figure. He came to the stand trembling so badly he could barely raise a glass of water. For two days he was on, vague, indistinct, stuttering his explanations of the Transcontinental Trading Corporation, putting on his spectacles with shaking hands to read his own decisions until in the end he sat with bowed head, whispering he just didn't remember.

At the end of the second day Kelly read into the record a letter from the presiding justice; the judge had resigned; a federal grand jury had been convened; the Internal Revenue Service was reexamining the returns. It was the usual cry of the hounds closing in on the public man on the run.

On Wednesday we traveled to Lawrence. Kelly now, I noticed, didn't need any coaching. Now he seemed to know all the questions to ask—and the right answers.

The Lawrence hearings started off with the police chief, the same stupid chowderhead Kelly and I had met on the night of the plastics factory fire. His vacant smile soon disappeared under Kelly's questions.

Q. Are you aware there are disorderly houses in your city?
A. Well, the detectives tell me there are. But I can't find any.
Q. Have you tried?
A. Well, I had one place under investigation for ten years.
Q. How many times have you raided it?
A. Once. (*Laughter*)
Q. Did you make any arrests?
A. Well, no.
Q. Why not?
A. We kept ringing the bell, and they wouldn't open the door.

There was a roar of laughter. Kelly threw a sheaf of bank-deposit slips to the chief.

Q. These deposit slips show you have $8,500 in the bank in Lawrence and $5,000 in an Albany bank. Your salary is $5,500. Do you have any explanation?
A. I saved it all up.

And then, to our complete surprise, he blurted out that he had $15,000 more hidden in his wife's dressing table.

Q. Why do you keep it there?
A. There's been a lot of robberies lately. You know, junkies . . .
Q. Why didn't you put it in the bank?
A. I guess I never got around to it.
Q. Of course you never declared this money.
A. Well, maybe. Maybe I forgot it.
Q. How did you get this money?
A. Like I said, I saved it. A dollar here, a dollar there . . .
Q. And this money is in your wife's dressing table?
A. That's right. In a tin box.
Q. I would say that's traditional, wouldn't you, Chief?

The chief gave Kelly a blank look.

Kelly gradually brought the questioning about to the number of arrests of Negroes compared to those of whites, and the chief innocently insisted that was because all Negroes were engaged in the numbers racket. Kelly showed that fifteen arrests had been made three months before in a sit-down demonstration, yet they had been charged with violating the lottery laws. The chief continued to look blank.

Kelly also produced hospital records which showed that ten demonstrators, white and Negro, had been hospitalized after a demonstration, and the chief blandly insisted they were all Communists who should be deported.

Kelly, in a quiet, grave voice led the chief down the path of wanton ignorance until he took pity on him and ordered the chief to return when called.

Through his questioning of the captain and later his lieutenant, Kelly carefully dissected the Lawrence Police Department, uncovering a hard core of incredible ignorance, bigotry, and class hatred. He showed through his questions that these were the products of a machine that had sold them their jobs and a way of life that made me shudder. The lieutenant blandly told the committee he was sure 90 percent of all Negro demonstrators were Communists or in organizations sympathetic to Communism, "and I think the best thing to do to solve all the trouble is to send the leaders to Africa."

I believe the man was sincere when he testified he did not believe he was a prejudiced man. He pointed out very proudly that he had Negroes on his force, and Kelly agreed; he produced records of three Negro porters who cleaned up the station, a colored matron, and an ancient crossing guard. But the lieutenant stoutly denied the "incidents" of the past several months could have been racial in tone, then revealed very proudly that the department had been taking steps to prevent any serious outbreaks. No, they hadn't appointed any Negro officers to the area; they had bought several German shepherd dogs and hired a handler! After Kelly had on the record what we all knew were some of the reasons for the riot, he dug deeper and crucified the police lieutenant, the captain, and the police commissioner on the cross of their own corruption.

Statements from the local loan company showed how recruits paid for their jobs on the installment plan; three policemen who had police records for burglary and assault had lifted their own records after they had been appointed to the force. Because of their records they had to pay $15,000 to get the job! One cop's record showed he once ran a brothel. Their bank accounts and safe-deposit listings were produced and read into the record. In the end they sat there, mute, glaring until Kelly disgustedly waved them off.

By two o'clock they had been dismissed by the county commissioners, and the local district attorney had convened a grand jury. But more significantly, the Internal Revenue agents from Albany left with our records after the noon recess, and the governor's office sent a representative for the complete transcript of the hearings.

The afternoon, the next day, and the following day were devoted to politics in Lawrence, as corrupt as I have ever heard. City contracts were given to companies owned partially by the city officials; the poverty program was shocking; a few Uncle Toms had been used as fronts, and the other high-paying jobs were distributed to friends and relatives of politicians; the Head Start program was relegated to a gloomy, damp basement under a garage, with such a strong smell of oil and gasoline the few children who attended became nauseated. The housing of Lawrence was almost unbelievable; witness after witness testified there was no heat, no hot water—only rats and roaches. In one building five of seven families shared one bathroom, and the sewerage ran into the backyard.

The human statistics were sad: in one year in Lawrence twelve infant children died of lead poisoning, eating paint and plaster flakes. A state authority told the committee several children were now in homes for the mentally retarded because of the poisoning.

The head of the Housing Department resigned before he could be called to the stand, and when he did appear, solemnly took the Fifth on the advice of his attorney. Kelly refused to let him go, but read off his bank deposits for one year and ordered them delivered to Internal Revenue. Most of the checks were from corporations that owned Lawrence's rotting tenements.

There was no more laughter now; the crowds that packed the small hearing room and ringed City Hall listened in bitter silence to the outrageous testimony. Only when two of the officials of the big real-estate companies that controlled most of the housing in the slum sections of Lawrence were called did the hearing almost get out of hand. The crowd outside surged forward as the two men left the building, and it took all the reinforced state police available to hold the citizenry beyond the barriers.

The last day before Barney's appearance was devoted to witnesses from the slums, some humorous, some passive, others belligerent or bitter. Their testimony showed vividly that the economic status of Negroes in Lawrence had deteriorated in ten years in sharp contrast to that of the whites. As a result there had been a massive piling up of explosive misery in this horrible ghetto that erupted, as Kelly had said that night, into human violence.

I don't want to go into all the testimony, but I do have to tell about an old woman who waddled to the stand.

"I scrub people's floors all day," she testified, "Then I go home and take off my shoes. But I have to give people my money. I'm tired of giving people my money. I'm tired of being walked on in this town.

Tired to God of it. Tired of being treated like a dog. Tired of fighting off the rats. Tired of being nothing in Lawrence. Tired of walkin' with my head bowed when I should be raisin' it to the Lord."

Then she paused, and ended with these great piercing lines that have remained with me to this day:

"Maybe, Mr. Congressman, our heads were bowed when we was born."

Then Kelly said quietly: "Not any more, ma'am. We're here to raise them up."

The phrase caught on, and neither Josh nor I, Frank Shea or Luther, had a hand in it. You heard it on the streets, in buses, in factories . . . "Look up, man. The congressman says to look up!"

Look up! It spread around the state. *Time* and *Newsweek* took it up, and *Life* sent their best team up to Lawrence to do a cover story on Kelly and the hearings.

Frank Shea said he was willing to bet now only two sets out of ten were not tuned in on the hearings. By the time Barney Mullady took the stand, I did not doubt this was true. For three days and nights of hearings Kelly had carefully laid the groundwork for his entrance; he had shown Lawrence to be the most vile city in America, the Time Bomb City that had exploded. He had spread the reasons across the country—not only official corruption but also ignorance, poverty, and a cynicism hard to believe.

What was coming out of Lawrence had a sobering effect in Washington. Josh and I had heard from friends that some of the federal programs were quietly being reorganized. The FBI was sending in agents who wanted to know what had happened to the federal funds, and there were many who were now saying that the famous poverty program had been anything but a huge success.

But now would come the big reason: political machinery dominated by a ruthless man who had come to power by using the poor, who, Barney had said, are never grateful.

Barney had not been idle during the week. He had pulled every possible string in Washington, and the calls came from powerful political voices, but Kelly hung up on most of them. Jones began to feel the pressure, and when he told Kelly the chairman of the full committee—a politician who had never bothered his head about it before—had called to say he was coming down with the full committee, Kelly told him bluntly he would call off the hearings and issue a statement he was taking this action only because the party's high command had sabotaged the hearings. He also swore to campaign against every member of that committee if he had to travel from New York to Wyoming to do it. Jones beat a hasty retreat, and the committee never appeared.

On Wednesday, Barney arrived in Lawrence. He was still the affable, back slapping little beer barrel, and when he saw me he rushed over, hand outstretched.

"Finn! Finn McCool, the great man from Washington!"

I shook hands and warned him that my wallet was in my shoe.

But that didn't faze Barney. He just slapped me harder on the back and told his stooges how I was a great man for jokes.

Barney took the stand promptly at nine o'clock. He was dressed in conservative gray and looked like a brisk little banker ready to take over a board meeting. He was accompanied by his lawyer, a former governor, white-haired and distinguished. The first thing he did was protest against television. This was granted, and the cameras were ordered covered. But Josh had a large print of Mullady tacked to the door of the hearing room, and the audio was kept on.

Then Barney's attorney asked permission for Mullady to read his statement into the record. It was granted, and Barney carefully put on a pair of horn-rimmed glasses and began reading what appeared to be an endless statement.

He started off: "As a born New Yorker I have taken an active role in New York and national politics all my life. My father before me was an active organization Democrat, and he left me a heritage of loyalty to my party of which I am proud. I don't have to remind this committee of my position during the last national convention and the subsequent presidential election."

Barney shrewdly was reminding the party leaders of his position and his strength. He then went on to recap his whole political career, from the time he had been first appointed to the State Athletic Commission by the governor, then on up to the secretary and chairman of the Election Committee of Tammany Hall. He sketched the founding of the Tusk Club, carefully leaving out the role played by the McCools, of course, and then went on to picture himself as the only man who had realized the plight and tragedy of the minorities who poured into the West Side of Manhattan. He read letters of gratitude, produced a picture of a gallant young Negro officer for whom he had gained an appointment to West Point and who later died in Vietnam.

He went on to eulogize Gene Abernathy and other young Negroes who had been helping the minorities in the big cities, and of course he denounced those politicians who, unlike himself, ignored the poor and helpless.

It was a great speech, and if you didn't know Barney I guess you could believe most of it.

Kelly listened until Barney had finished. Then he began his questioning, letting Barney describe his friendship with Abernathy, step by step.

Q. He was your trusted right hand, was he not?

A. I couldn't do without him. He was a fine boy with a great future, Congressman.

Q. You say you couldn't do without him. Just exactly what did he do for you?

A. A million and one things, Congressman. He was always there when I wanted him.

Q. That's not answering the question. I want to know specifically what he did.

A. He handled things.

Q. Like what?

A. Well, take for example, someone would come in to the club and say they couldn't get any heat. I would let Gene follow through.

Q. What did he do?

A. Call the commissioner's office and let him know this lady wasn't getting any heat.

Q. Oh, the commissioner?

A. We always deal with commissioners, Congressman.

Q. In other words, Abernathy was doing one of your political errands?

A. Nobody does any political business for Barney Mullady but Barney Mullady.

Q. How about crooked business, Mr. Mullady? Would you say Mr. Abernathy was your bagman?

Mullady looked stunned, but his attorney leaped to his feet, shouting objection.

Kelly gave him a grim look and picked up Abernathy's statement.

"I have here a statement signed and notarized by Eugene Abernathy, which I will now read," he said.

I had read and reread Abernathy's statement, and it was devastating. It detailed how, when he had been sent to Lawrence to build their machine, Barney shared in every thievery existing in that rotting city. Abernathy told of meetings, named names, gave dates, described the interior of hotel rooms, motels, and clubhouses. He also described how each month he delivered the valise of money to the small office of the construction company on the West Side of Manhattan.

As Kelly continued reading, a wave of brick red rose from under Barney's collar.

His attorney at first listened unbelievingly, then jumped to his feet again.

"In the light of your own statement, Congressman, that a witness before your committee must not be regarded as a defendant, I submit that this statement from a dead man who no longer can be subject to cross-examination is not valid!" he shouted. "My client is one of the most prominent figures in American politics, and I submit that a great number of persons could be linked to a common purpose without necessarily being involved with one another in the sinister sense."

"Suppose we let the facts develop, Counselor," Kelly said. "If they don't show Mr. Mullady is a thief and a disgrace to American politics, I will publicly apologize to him."

"I will hold you to that, sir."

Q. Mr. Mullady, do you deny you met any of those people?

A. I do. If Abernathy was making any deals with them, it was without my knowledge.

Q. In other words you believe Mr. Abernathy had been acting on his own?

A. I hate to say it about the deceased young man—but it looks like he was a thief.

Q. You never received any monies from any illegal enterprise in Lawrence?

A. No, sir.

Q. You never had any money delivered to a company in which you had an interest?

A. No, sir.

Q. You never personally called the superintendent of the state police and asked him to go easy on the bookmaking spots in Lawrence?

A. No, sir.

Q. Do you deny the police chief of Lawrence called you to ask your help to try to find out if a wiretap had been placed on his phone by the state police?

A. Yes, sir.

Q. Did you ever take steps to determine if a tap had been placed on this political leader's home and office?

A. No, sir.

Q. Did the police chief of Lawrence ever complain to you that he had to tell the boys to lay off gambling after 5:00 P.M. because an unfriendly sergeant was on the desk?

A. No, sir.

Q. Did the police chief ever tell you the state cops were getting on his tail and you had better pull some wires?

A. No, sir.

Q. Did the political boss of Lawrence ever call you and ask your help in getting federal funds released for a low-cost housing project and at the same time tell you construction companies were all lined up and it would mean a big score for "all of us"?

Barney now was squirming. He obviously remembered the calls and was probably wondering how far he could go in his denials. His answers became: I don't know . . . I don't recall . . . I can't remember . . . As the afternoon wore on, his jaunty air vanished. By recess he was a worried man, his usually ruddy face pale and sweaty. By noon of the next day Barney was clearly on the ropes. Kelly was relentless. The only sounds in that crowded room were the reporters sending out their bulletins and the creaking of the fans as they moved back and forth. I couldn't help feeling this was more than an angry young man determined to destroy another man's evil power; it was also a new voice in American politics, a clear young voice that could herald the end of entrenched machine politics.

Mullady was excused on noon of the next day after his attorney told the committee his client was getting so hoarse he could barely whisper. This was true; Barney had tried to shout down some of the questions and accusations, and his naturally rough voice was getting scratchier by the minute. He was excused, but promised to return the next day.

That night Josh began his psychological warfare campaign against the police chief. He waited until dinnertime, then called the chief's home. It was the AP calling from Washington, he said, checking on the report that the attorney general had ordered an investigation into the chief's affairs through the United States Attorney, Eastern District. . . .

On the extension I could almost hear the man's hard swallow.

"Investigate me? What for?"

"Oh, it's probably to check the usual stuff before he convenes a grand jury," Josh said casually. "Do you have any comment, Chief?"

"No. No. I don't know anything about it," he blurted, and hung up.

"We'll wait about ten minutes," Josh said, glancing at his watch. "Just in time to catch him at dessert. I hope it sticks in the bastard's throat."

In ten minutes Josh called the chief's home again; this time he was the Washington UPI Bureau. Now you could almost reach out and touch the man's fear.

"No. No. I told the other fellow, I don't have anything to say."

Two more calls. On one, Josh posed as a reporter for an Albany paper, on the other, for a big New York City daily.

"He's ripe now," he said after the last call. "Let's hit him."

We drove over to the chief's house, a beautiful split level with a carefully trimmed lawn, gravel paths, shrubs, and a swimming pool in the rear. An expensive late-model car was parked by the curb.

"He not only keeps it in tin boxes; he spends it," was Josh's comment.

Inside, Josh put the decision before the chief: testify truthfully and receive the blessings of the committee or take his chances with the other corrupt officials.

"Do you think the government is going to investigate me?" he asked. "Some reporters called me from Washington and said they had heard—"

"They will not only investigate you but indict you," was Josh's brutal reply. "The IRS field agents are probably going over your returns right now. Within a week they'll be testifying before a federal grand jury, while some eager-beaver assistant stands by with every line of the transcript of your testimony before the committee." He leaned forward and added softly: "They're going to cut you up in little pieces, Chief, and your friends up here will run like deer when they hear you're coming around to say hello. Believe me, there's nothing more vulnerable than a cop who has been caught with his hand in the till. Every s.o.b. in the community wants to stand up and cheer, and every creep that ever got a ticket or was jugged will pass the word they always knew he would sell the gold in his old man's teeth."

The chief kept licking his lips and nodding, while his wife, a small, pale woman, laced her fingers in her lap as though in prayer.

Josh stared hard at the woman. "We can give him a break if he answers the committee's questions—but it's up to him: fish or cut bait." Then, to the chief: "If you decide you want to cooperate, Chief, give us a call at the motel before the hearings start in the morning. You can ask for me or Mr. McCool." He gave the woman a look of sympathy and said in a low, gentle voice that he was sorry.

It was a great piece of stage business.

"I bet she's been prodding him all day," Josh said in an undertone as we walked down the gravel path. "Just for the hell of it, let's sit in the car for a few minutes."

We had just settled down when the front door opened and the chief hurried down the path. Josh rolled down the window.

"Will you fellows come back in for a few minutes?" he said nervously. "The wife and I have been talking."

Later he did the same thing with the local politician. He wasn't as naïve as the chief. He told us his lawyer had recommended he talk—to a point, which he would.

"And what's the point?" Josh asked coldly.

"You guys bugged?" the politician, short, well fed, arrogant, asked with a knowing smile.

We silently opened our jackets; he gave us a sharp look, then nodded.

"I'll testify I called up Barney in Washington, to use"—he smiled—"his influence with the legislators to get our poverty funds sprung so we could get the programs started up here."

"Forget it," Josh said as he rose. "We don't want your cooperation. We're going to crucify you. We got you nailed to payoffs from your God-damn construction companies and to Barney's outfit. Who in the hell do you think you're kidding?"

We were at the door of his apartment when he stopped us.

"Wait a minute, fellows," he said pleadingly, "Let's have a drink."

"You can shove your drinks," Josh snarled. "You want to talk or don't you?"

The man stared at Josh for a minute. "Let me get my lawyer over here."

"Get him here fast," Josh said, throwing his coat on the chair. "We haven't got all night."

We left at three o'clock in the morning with another "cooperative" witness scheduled for the next day's hearing.

The chief was the first witness. He testified he had called Barney and asked his help in finding out if his phone was tapped by the state police. A week later he said he received a mysterious call advising him not to use his telephone—a private, unlisted number. The chief also admitted he called Barney and asked him to use his influence to stop the state police raids on gambling places in Lawrence. Barney, he said, promised they would stop within a week. Kelly then introduced records showing how the state-police raids tapered off shortly after the chief had made this call. The chief was on the stand for hours, unraveling a picture of corruption that was almost physically sickening.

The local political leader was next. He was so frightened he could scarcely be heard beyond the first row. He testified he had called Barney and got his promise to "spring" the federal funds for the city's low-cost housing projects and poverty programs that Washington had held up. Three weeks after the call, Barney phoned with the news the funds would be available shortly. Willy's wiretaps provided the basis for the next series of blockbusters that really rocked the hearing room. The leader, wiping his face and twisting and turning in his chair, admitted that three of the companies who subsequently received the bids for the $20,000,000 in projects were companies owned by himself, Barney, and several of the city's commissioners and politicians. He said that $300,000 in "consultation fees" had been paid to Barney's New York construction company.

After their testimony we could sense the panic running through the city. Lawyers were constantly calling, offering their clients as "cooperative" witnesses. It seemed there was no secret so deeply hidden that the committee couldn't drag it out.

"Gifts from a madman," Josh murmured wearily during a brief recess. "Now do you realize how valuable Willy was?" He added impatiently, "I know, I know: you're going to ask Was it worth it? Well, dammit, I say it was. I think what's coming out here is helping to balance the scale."

The testimony of others described how the "cream" was taken from the top of the rackets and brought to the basement of City Hall, adjacent to police headquarters, and brazenly divided. As one witness said, there was always a "satchel for Barney" that was collected by Abernathy in the first week of every month.

The hatchet-faced secretary swore Barney's chauffeur picked up the satchel which she carefully had placed in the office safe, but insisted she didn't know what it contained. Why did she put it in the safe? She didn't like to have things lying around on the floor, she explained primly.

The chauffeur, who wisely had quit driving Barney, swore he got the satchel and took it to Barney's apartment.

Barney's sweet chocolates really had paid him well. But now I didn't think there would be any left in the box.

I guess this was in the back of Barney's mind when he summoned me to the hotel where he was staying. I told Josh and Kelly, and they said By all means go; let's find out what he has on his mind.

I found Barney alone in his rooms. It wasn't much of a hotel and the rooms were not exactly the Waldorf, and this wasn't helping his disposition. He lay on the bed, his shirt open, a can of beer in his hand.

"The least you could have done was hold your God-damned hearings in the city," he said, waving me to a chair. "Want a beer?"

The can did look cool and inviting, so I accepted. He went into the bathroom and came out with one.

"I filled the basin with ice and keep them there," he explained. He flopped on the bed and eyed me morosely.

"You know you got me on the run?"

"We figured we would."

"I want to make a deal. Don't worry—the place isn't bugged. I'm not like you bastards. What does your boy want? Delegates? Help in the campaign? You can name it now."

"And in return?"

"Recess the hearings. No more testimony."

"You'll still be in the soup, Barney. Internal Revenue made us turn over your bank records. Every DA in the state will be after you."

He eyed me shrewdly. "Let me take care of that. It's my headache. But I don't want any more trouble."

I put down the can. "I'll deliver your message."

"And you'll put in a good word, old friend?"

I stared down at his pale, anxious face, and remembered the mob pouring over the police car, the sergeant going down, the leaping dogs, and the slimy hallways when I first came up here looking for Kelly and Lacey. His hoarse voice flung bewildered questions after me before the door shut them off. Given a thousand years, Barney would never understand.

Back at the motel Kelly had only one instruction for me. "Make sure he's back on that stand tomorrow morning," was all he said.

Barney returned in the morning, but this time it was a different Barney from the one I had seen in the hotel. The swagger and air of confidence were back, and he had a smile for everyone as he walked down the crowded corridor to the Council Room.

"I just want to let you know the answer, Barney," I said. "We—"

He held up his hand.

"Let's say we don't need it today," he said. "Let's say maybe we should repeat what that grand American George Washington said, 'Let's put only Americans on guard tonight.'"

388

Frankly he left me standing there with my mouth open.

We soon knew the reason for Barney's confidence. As he took his seat with a smile as broad as the Cheshire cat's, his attorney rose and announced his client had an important statement to read. After he was given permission, Barney, with many elaborate gestures, took a long typewritten statement from a folder and began reading.

After the first minute I went cold all over. When I glanced over at Josh, he looked stricken.

Slowly, distinctly, Barney was reading portions of the Gentile file which he said would be the heart of Tuck Larsen's Washington column and broadcast. Kelly never moved a muscle, but Jones kept turning up his hearing machine, darting bewildered looks at Kelly, and leaning over to whisper to him.

After he had finished reading the excerpts of the file, Barney went on to describe how Kelly had deliberately suppressed the file, and hinted at a political deal. There was more: Larsen also charged that the committee had been given information on Eva Schmidt and how she had been used by New York politicians to make their deals but that the leads had been suppressed because "the names of persons in high places in Washington had been uncovered in the committee's investigation."

New York City Homicide detectives, Barney went on, told him that undoubtedly there was some connection between the murders of Eva Schmidt, the young German immigrant girl found in Eva's Central Park West apartment, and Jello's woman friend Molly Shapiro, who had been slain in the Westchester motel.

It went on like this at length, and Barney made sure every word was read into the record. Like Larsen, he kept coming back to the Gentile file, hinting at the most serious of charges.

Barney kept the best till the last: Larsen had told him only this morning that much of the information he had received came from Willy in a registered letter a few days after the Foley Square "massacre," as the papers had called it. He had enclosed copies of reports he had made for Josh Michaels and the committee along with a detailed financial statement that he had signed. Barney agreed that Willy's letter to Larsen had been rambling and unintelligible, but Larsen's staff had independently confirmed most of the facts. They had finally located Suzy Forest and her husband in Hong Kong, where they were making a television pilot. Her husband, as Suzy's spokesman, had confirmed the whole story of Gentile's association with his sister-in-law, her subsequent suicide, and Gentile's assistance in getting Ching's bail lowered. . . .

I almost groaned out loud when I remembered how I had tongue-lashed that vicious young blowhard at the airport. As Josh had warned, all he had left was his wife's story and how we had bought it.

When he had finished reading, Barney carefully, almost methodically, put the papers back into his folder while the bulletins flew from the room.

I closed my eyes and let the headlines flash across my mind: CHARGES SHANNON SUPPRESSED GENTILE FILE ON PEKING AGENT, or some hogwash like that.

When I opened them, Barney was putting on a good show of trying to suppress his righteous anger. As an old pro he was well aware of the smoke screen he had sent up that now obscured, at least temporarily, the shocking facts of his own criminal acts.

"I must tell this committee that I believe Congressman Shannon, for purely personal and political gain, has deliberately suppressed a document of vital significance to our whole security program."

The hoarse voice grated on. "I further charge, gentlemen, that at a time when we are locked in a tremendous diplomatic struggle with Peking, he has—"

Kelly didn't shout, didn't bang the desk in a fury. I believe it was his even, calm voice that made Barney break off.

"You, sir, are a thief and a fraud and a disgrace to American politics. You will return here tomorrow. This committee is recessed until that time."

Kelly rose, walked from behind the desk, and down the aisle, followed by a pack of shouting, tugging reporters whom he ignored, and left the building.

"Come on, let's get him," Josh said, and we ran out.

We caught up with him at his car. Reporters were shouting questions, thrusting microphones in front of his face, pulling at his arm, waving copy paper as they angrily demanded answers. As we came up, Kelly was shaking his head and calmly saying "No comment."

"Get everyone over by six at the motel," he said in a low voice to us. "I'll see you there."

Then he slowly pulled away from the curb.

With Kelly gone the reporters turned their wrath on Josh and me, demanding to know the score. Were these charges true? Where was this file? Who was the Peking agent? What about those whores on Central Park West?

Josh, always quick on his feet, gave them a fast statement, full of double-talk that reminded everyone that Barney had been exposed as a thief who would probably be indicted shortly. Josh tried to create news, but the press was not buying today; they wanted answers to Barney's charges. Finally Josh promised them a statement later in the afternoon, but it did little to satisfy them. But then Barney came out, puffed up like a pouter pigeon. They left us in a hurry as Barney welcomed them with open arms.

"Stay here for a while and get an earful of what he tells them," Josh said. "I want to attend to a few things."

"Like what?"

"Like a few things," he said shortly. "I'll meet you back at the motel."

I stayed for a half hour on the fringe of the crowd listening to this human beer barrel weep for his country, which was being victimized by scheming politicians and Washington's "fast guys"—Barney's phrase—who were using the sacred arm of Congress to tear down reputations made, by, etc., etc.

It was garbage, but, truthfully, if I had been a bloody spectator who didn't know the real background of this thief, I would have been inclined to ask questions.

Barney saw me as he passed. "Present company not included in my comment on those fast guys," he said. "Finn McCool here is a grand man, right out of the great West Side story. . . ."

I looked about at the reporters who were scribbling down the immortal words. "I've known this man for more years than most of you have lived on this earth," I said, "and all I can say is to repeat Congressman Shannon's words: he is a thief and a disgrace to American politics."

I walked away, leaving Barney so mad he was in danger of swallowing his uppers.

CHAPTER TWENTY-TWO: THE SCAPEGOAT

PROMPTLY AT SIX we all gathered in Kelly's suite at the motel: Luke, Luther, Frank Shea, who had hurried in from Washington when he had heard the news, and Lacey. Josh arrived after me. He seemed tense and pale, but at the time I didn't think it was unusual after that horrible afternoon.

There were no amenities, and when Josh closed the door Kelly began. "I have some facts I think all of you should know," he said. "As you recall, when Josh and Finn brought me that report on Gentile, I hesitated to use it. I felt there was something missing. Finn, I think you had the same feeling."

"I did."

"In fact, Josh, just before you left for bed I told you I was uneasy; I felt something was missing."

Josh nodded but remained silent.

"When I went to my room I lay awake, I just couldn't sleep. That damn Gentile report kept floating about my mind. The one thing I couldn't reconcile was why? Why Gentile? After a while I got out the report Josh and Finn had prepared on what they had found, along with the copy of the original from the files of the government agency. I must have read them a thousand times. Finally I decided I had to do one thing—face Gentile and demand an explanation."

"Face Gentile with his own file?" Luke said in an unbelieving voice.

"I had to take the chance, Luke," Kelly said calmly. "This was a devastating report. Once it was released, Gentile would be destroyed, politically and personally. His patriotism would be suspect; he would become the target of every crackpot organization, every John Bircher; and in addition he could become the target of scores of investigations, many politically inspired. I just had to make sure there were no last-minute pumpkin papers lying around."

"Did you see Gentile?" I asked.

"Yes. I went downstairs and found Lacey going to bed and you and Josh leaving for the city. When I told her, she wanted to go after you and let you know what I was doing. But I stopped her—"

"Why?" Josh asked.

"I felt this was my responsibility, and mine alone. Lacey wanted to come along, but I refused." He turned to Josh and added, "I told you a long time ago, Josh, there would come a time when I would have to make my own decisions, my own choice, and come to terms with them."

"Did you meet Gentile?" Luke put in.

"Yes. I called his house and got him out of bed. Naturally, he was surprised, but he agreed to meet me. We met halfway in an all-night restaurant off the parkway . . ."

"Just you and Gentile?"

"Just me and Gentile."

"Well, what happened?"

"I put the whole thing to him. He was stunned. He excused himself and went to a phone booth. From the quarters he put in I knew he was calling long-distance, probably Washington. That's exactly what he was doing. When he came back he told me the whole story."

"Well, go on," Luke said impatiently, as Kelly paused.

Kelly rose and slowly walked across the room to the closed door of the bedroom.

"Mr. Gentile is here," he said quietly. "After what happened this afternoon he called me and asked to be allowed to come up and tell you the entire story. I agreed." He opened the door and said, "Will you come in, please."

Gentile walked in and stood by Kelly's side, looking down at us. His handsome face was drawn, and he looked as though he had spent a harassing day. Kelly briefly ran through the introductions, and Gentile sat down facing us.

"I brought them to the point where we had met and you had placed the call to Washington," Kelly said. "I believe you said you wanted to pick it up from there."

"That's correct," Gentile said in a low, emotionless voice. He took a deep breath.

"To begin with, Ching is our American agent in Peking. In fact, our most important one. If we expose him we must not only be responsible for his certain death but also for destroying the most important pipeline this country has into Peking."

"Ching—an American agent!" Luke cried. "How do we know? Who says so?"

"The CIA," Kelly interrupted. "I spoke to them."

"How many know who he is?" I asked.

"Up to now? No more than three persons. Before Mr. Gentile and I left the restaurant, a CIA agent arrived and drove home with me. In fact, Howard drove him back to where his car was parked shortly before Lacey and I took off for Lawrence. I told him I would have to tell you all the story if anything leaked out, and he agreed. Then when the news broke this afternoon, Mr. Gentile called me and suggested he come up here and give you the details at first hand." Kelly turned to Gentile and said, "I admire you for that, sir."

"It's the least I can do," Gentile said, "after what Mullady did to both of us."

"Don't worry about Mullady," Kelly said grimly. "We have not parted company yet."

"What about the girl who committed suicide?" Luke demanded.

"Oh, Luke," Lacey said, but Gentile held up a hand.

"That's quite all right, Miss Shannon. It's a fair question." A cloud crossed his long, aquiline face and he bit his lower lip before replying.

"That's a true story. I met Nina in China, and frankly we were very close for all the time I was there. When I came to Washington I met the woman who is now my wife, and we were married the following year. Nina and I had talked about our relationship, and I thought we had parted friends. I never knew she was expecting a child. In fact, I never heard from her after her father left the mainland."

"How did this whole plan come about?" Luke asked.

"It was after Nina's death that the CIA first came to me with the idea. I discussed it with Ching, and he agreed to go through with it." He slowly shook his head. "Gentlemen, that's the most courageous boy I have ever met."

"How ghastly!" Lacey said. "Didn't his sister know?"

"Nina? No. In fact the CIA thought it was best she was fed the cover stories."

"What about those parties that are in the report?"

"They were put on for the benefit of the man the CIA and the other agencies knew was the Peking agent in the UN. They knew he liked— shall we call them wild parties? I was well known in Chinese circles, and it wasn't too hard to get the message to him that I was staging pretty wild affairs attended by some beautiful Oriental ladies. It took a few months but we finally got him down."

"And what about Saunders?" Luke asked. "Wasn't he along?"

"Chuck Saunders was present," Gentile said, "but of course he didn't know what was going on."

"I asked the CIA agent if all Mr. Gentile's heartache and personal suffering and the courageous action on Ching's part were worth it," Kelly said, "and he gave me this example: Remember when State first released the news Peking was split by its own doves and hawks, with one side wanting to send a volunteer army to North Vietnam?"

We all nodded.

"Remember the effect it had on Moscow and how they threatened China until she denied it? Well, that came from Ching. It is obvious this intelligence helped to stave off another Korea. Is there any doubt it was worth it?"

I glanced over at Josh. I was disturbed to find him staring out the window, a strange, impersonal expression resting on his features, like the face of someone repeating a prayer under his breath. Then it faded quickly as Kelly asked again what he thought.

"I don't know," he said in a matter-of-fact voice. "It's up to you, what you want to do."

"I think you people have a lot to talk over," Gentile said, rising. "I'll say good night." He paused at the door. "I can't tell you how much I appreciate what you've done. I never believed there was this much civilization in American politics. Good night."

"Do you think it's a crock?" Luke asked. "It sounds like something out of Buchan or Le Carré."

"Every word he said is true," Kelly said. "In my opinion it took a lot of guts to come up here and tell this story."

"Kel, have you told Father?" Lacey asked.

"I gave him some facts. Naturally, he's disappointed, and still suspicious. He thinks State is covering up for Gentile."

"Maybe he has a point," Luke said.

"There are damn few people in State who know this story," Kelly said. "The Secretary and a few others. Call it what you want—it's true. Every word."

"Well, if you say so . . ."

"I say so."

"Suppose we had used this report in the first place?" Shea said cautiously. "You know, the one Josh and Finn produced . . ."

"You mean without going to Gentile?" Luke said.

"That's right. Suppose we had used it—what then?"

"I asked the CIA agent the same question," Kelly said. "The answer was —nothing."

"You mean they wouldn't have defended Gentile?"

"Of course not."

"And State?"

"State is another thing. They're starting to move now."

"Oh? How?"

"At eight o'clock the Secretary of State will hold a press conference. He will tell reporters that Gentile was simply acting on the orders of the then secretary, now dead, who in turn had received an urgent request to intervene in the case by persons high in the Chinese Nationalist Government. After all, the charges against Ching were based solely on the testimony of prostitutes. More importantly, those were ticklish days when we were doing everything possible to help the Nationalist Government at a time when it was moving to Formosa from the mainland. Such a request could not be ignored. Incidentally, at his press conference, the Secretary of State will be high in his praise of Gentile as a great American, a hero behind the Jap lines, and so on."

"That's just great for our side," Luke said bitterly.

"Would you rather have it the other way?" Kelly asked.

"All I can say is—if we were paid by Gentile we couldn't have done a better job for him," Luke said. "Do you realize what the Secretary of State's press conference will do to us?"

"I realize it's not going to help us—"

"Not help us!" Luke cried, jumping to his feet. "For Christ's sake, Kel, he could ruin us!" He turned to Josh. "Tell him, Josh! You know it!"

Josh gave him a calm, unruffled look. "I would think that was obvious."

"The only alternative we had," Kelly said, "was to have used that report on Gentile without checking it further." He appealed to Luke. "Would you rather we had used it that way, not knowing the true facts?"

"You're God-damn right I would," Luke said savagely. "I would have given it to him right between the eyes. The CIA wouldn't have told the true story? Fine. Let the bastard die on the vine."

At that moment, perhaps more than any other time in his life, Luke was his father's son.

"Fortunately, I was the one to make the decision," Kelly said. He turned abruptly to Josh. "What do you think, Josh?"

"I think you'll get a backlash from that press conference. How about the U.S. attorney who's quoted in the report? He sounded real hot. Suppose he gives Tuck Larsen an interview and confirms the whole report?"

"He won't," Kelly said promptly. "He has been told enough to make him realize he will only endanger his country. Fortunately, the man's an American first and a politician second."

"Shall we all stand up and sing 'God Bless America'?" Luke said.

"What about tomorrow's hearing?" Luther put in hastily. "Frank and I were just talking—you'll have to say something, Kelly."

"All I will do is to point out that the State Department has answered Mr. Mullady's ridiculous charges and that there is no need for any further comment." He threw a folder on the table. "The CIA thought they owed me a favor." He opened the folder and slid out a sheaf of photostats. "Here's Barney's numbered accounts in the Swiss bank: Dates, deposits, totals. He has over $3,000,000. As I told Gentile—I haven't finished with Mullady."

"I still wish Gentile was our target, Kel," Luke said fervently.

"If you have proof of any wrongdoing on Gentile's part, I will gladly use it."

Kelly shuffled through a sheaf of papers with a note of finality that silenced Luke.

"On the question of those murdered prostitutes. You all know Immigration had a copy of our report. I contacted the commissioner, and he told me his people were preparing deportation proceedings against the two women when news came of their murders. He wants to issue a statement explaining all this, and I agreed."

He returned the documents to a folder and looked up at Josh.

"Well, Josh, I guess it's your turn."

"Sure, I guess it's my turn," Josh repeated in a low voice. "What am I supposed to say? That I was a fool to approach that nut? That I should never have used illegal wiretapping or electronic bugs to obtain information? Sure Willy's unbalanced, but he also happens to be a genius in electronics. Government agencies used him to do their dirty work, and they paid him well. Obviously, if I had ever thought he would resort to violence I would not have stayed in the same city with him. But look at this committee. Look at the devastating picture of corruption and injustice it has exposed to the American public. We began with a thief's tale. Would you have put Benny on the stand without corroboration, Kelly? Do you think those poor fools and drunks of investigators for Jonesy's committee would have produced these facts—undeniable facts, for you?

"From the very beginning I have been interested in only one thing—Kelly Shannon. In the beginning I thought it looked like the money your father was offering was a windfall, but after I met you I began to believe there was a chance you could wind up in the White House, and I could be proud I had something to do with it.

"There just wasn't any time left to accomplish these things. We couldn't use the orthodox routine methods. We needed something big and dramatic to make your name a household word. We maneuvered the hearings but we needed the blockbusters, and that was where Willy came in. Sure he's a menace, and I hope they put the poor son of a bitch out of his misery. But as far as I'm concerned, what he produced was worth the lives of a thief who would steal his mother's wedding ring. If we have to be sorry, let's be sorry for Molly, who should have realized you can never take the larceny out of a thief's heart . . . and that marshal. If it means anything, I'll see that man's face until the day I die."

He stood up and faced Kelly. "As I said before, what do you expect me to say? That I'm sorry? Well, I'm not. As far as I'm concerned, the good that will come out of this will far outweigh the evil. Criminals and thieving politicians will no longer rule Lawrence. Justice isn't for sale any more on the barrelhead—at least for the time being. Ordinary citizens and honest businessmen will be assured they will get fair decisions from one of the highest tribunals in their government. And Mullady—finished, done with."

He nodded soberly. "As for tomorrow, don't worry about it. Let me take the blame for Willy. I know those wolves outside. Once I was one of them. Give them a scapegoat, and they'll be happy to tear him apart. And that's me."

He looked at Kelly. "You certainly can't say I didn't put up big stakes for you, Kelly. But I think it was worth it. Goodbye and good luck—all of you."

Then he was gone.

For a moment we were so stunned we just sat there. It was Lacey who gave a tiny cry and ran after him. I followed her. We hurried down the corridor to the lobby, but he wasn't there. The doorman said no one had come out within the last few minutes. When he suggested that perhaps the guest had parked in the rear, I knew that was the answer. When we reached the parking lot the attendant said Josh had left, took off with rubber, was the way he put it.

"Have you any idea where he's gone, Finn?" Lacey asked.

"Perhaps back to the hotel."

"Please—let's hurry."

But he wasn't there, only a letter explaining briefly he had decided to take the entire blame and had issued a statement to that effect. He had transferred most of the money the senator had given us into a bank account in my name—he enclosed the book—and gave me a notarized power of attorney to dispose of our business any way I wished.

"But why did he do that? Is he quitting politics?" Luke asked when I returned to the motel.

"Don't you realize what he's done?" Luther asked. "He's destroyed himself."

"But what about you, Finn?"

"He's left me more money than I know what to do with. But who cares about the money—it's Josh I'm worried about."

"It was my responsibility; I intended to make that clear," Kelly said.

"Apparently Josh thought otherwise," Lacey said.

"He has a mind of his own too, Kelly," I said.

"This is terrible, what he's done," Luther said. "Did he say who he gave the statement to, Finn?"

"I guess the AP."

"Can we find out, Finn?" Lacey said. "Maybe he said where he was going."

"I can call the AP bureau in Albany," I said. "Perhaps they—"

"Please, Finn," Lacey said. "Please call them!"

The voice of the AP deskman in Albany said they had not heard from Josh, nor had the UPI or the Albany *Times Union*. Suddenly I remembered one Sunday afternoon in Washington and Josh calling newspaper friends to get an old drunk a job on a copy desk. As he explained, you had to have been in the newspaper business to understand the strange loyalties it breeds.

I called Sissy Southworth.

Usually it takes a long time to get past her front lines of secretaries and copyboys, but this time someone called out my name, and immediately her rough voice was loud in my ear over the background of clicking typewriters and cries of copyboys. Sissy was in the city room of her paper, a place she visited only when she had a big, exclusive story. It was all part of her act, Josh once said, to sweep in like a queen, smile at the inferiors, rattle off the great news, and dare the managing editor not to lead the paper with it.

"Finn, where are you?"

"I'm up in Lawrence, Sissy. Have you heard from Josh?"

"Heard from him?" she cried. "I'm leading the paper with his statement! Where is he? I've been calling all over hell and creation trying to get him. What's going on?"

"Just read me the statement, Sissy."

"What's wrong? Is it okay? I'm leading—"

I seldom shout at a female, even Sissy's type, but this time I did. "Will you forget your stupid headlines and read that statement, woman!"

I could feel the shocked surprise; then Sissy read Josh's statement.

It confirmed my fears. Josh accepted full responsibility for hiring Willy without permission of Kelly or any other member of the committee, with the full knowledge that Willy would be using illegal wiretaps and electronic bugging devices to obtain evidence of official corruption. He completely absolved the committee of suppressing any part of the Gentile file, insisting it had been his decision and no one else's.

"After this, he won't be able to talk to the guard at the front door of that Pennsylvania address," Sissy said. "No more buddy-buddy. What happened up there?"

"It's a long story, Sissy. Someday I'll tell it to you."

"We're on the street with it now," she said. "They replated—"

"By the way, when did you get it?"

"A couple of hours ago," she said. "He called and dictated it and asked me to give it to AP and UPI with an embargo. We just finished reading it to the services. He gave me an hour beat—"

"Well, enjoy it, Sissy. I don't think there will be anymore."

The voice grew softer, more feminine. "Look, Finn, is there anything I can do? I really like the guy."

398

"Nothing, Sissy." I hung up.

When I told them they looked startled, Kelly included; then they were saying they would call him, they would stop him, that this was foolishness, and so on. I got up, blinded by tears, and pushed them aside, walking to the lobby, seeing nothing.

Kelly was beside me suddenly, with Luke and Luther just behind.

"What can we do to get him back, Finn?" Kelly was saying, his voice tight.

"There's nothing you can do or say. He's gone, and I know him well enough to tell you he won't be back."

"I'll talk to him. I insist, if there's any blame it's mine. I don't want anyone else taking it."

"It's too late. His statement is now part of the record, Kelly. You or no one else can erase it. He made himself the scapegoat, and—God help him—they'll tear him apart."

"After Larsen and his kind get finished, no politician will touch him with a ten-foot pole," Luther said bitterly. "They'll walk on the other side of the street when they see him."

"Dammit, I don't want that!" Kelly cried, "we'll prepare a statement—"

"It won't do any good, Kelly," I told him. "Somehow the first statement always seems to be the Gospel, all others carping or hedging. My advice is to let it stay as it is."

"And let Josh throw himself to the wolves?"

"That's the way he wanted it, and as far as I'm concerned that's the way it's going to be. Where's Lacey?"

"She's back in the room trying to make a reservation to North Dakota," Luke said with a glum look.

I found Lacey slowly hanging up the phone as she studied some notes she had apparently just made.

"There's a plane leaving at eight for Chicago. I have to change for Bismarck."

"How do you know he's going to North Dakota, Lacey?"

"The garage down the street called. Josh left his credit card there. Early this afternoon he hired two mechanics to give his car a fast checkup. He told them he was driving to North Dakota."

"If he's driving it will take at least three days for him to get there."

"I intend to be there when he arrives. Doesn't he have a man working the ranch?"

"Yes. He and his wife live there."

"I hope they're not shocked when I move in."

"So you're going after him, Lacey."

"I'm only following your advice, Finn. Didn't you tell me to take him as he is?"

"A week ago you would have suspected his sacrifice—that it might have been done to expiate his feeling of guilt."

"Why is no longer important, Finn," she said, her face soft with the remembering, "That he did it is."

She studied the schedules she had jotted down. "I don't know if you noticed, but they took something from each other," she said after a minute, meditatively.

"Josh and Kelly?"

"When he sacrificed himself, I think Josh was taking something from Kelly. And when Kelly threw down that folder with Mullady's Swiss bank accounts, for a minute he was like Josh—cold and ruthless. I never saw him like that before."

"Will you try to persuade him to come back?"

"No." She stood up. "I'll never mention it. If he comes back, fine. If he doesn't, we'll stay out there. Or anywhere."

I handed her the bankbook Josh had left me.

"I wish you'd give him this. I have all the money I'll ever need."

"When Kelly, Luke, and I reached twenty-one, father established a fund for each of us. I have more blue chips than I know what to do with." She gently pushed back the book. "And I don't think Josh is exactly starving."

She reached over and kissed me, the faint smell of her perfume bringing back the first time I had seen her, clearing the hurdles at Wexford a thousand years ago.

"Goodbye, Finn—wish you luck."

Then she was gone and I was alone, and for the first time in over a half century I felt scalding tears rolling down my cheeks.

The next day I had no heart for going to the City Hall and witnessing the final dismembering of Barney Mullady. It didn't seem important now. Instead I remained in the hotel room, ordered a double Jack Daniels, and sat back to watch the hearing on TV. From the first grim closeups of Kelly, I knew Barney was in for the most terrible day of his life.

State had done fine by Gentile: the secretary's story was plausible, and at the conclusion of the press conference he paid a glowing tribute to the Americanism of Felix Durant Gentile. Secretary of State, you just can't get anything better than that. It was page one across the country in the A.M.'s, and *The New York Times* in its lead editorial strongly criticized both Mullady and his attorney for releasing such a one-sided document. But on the other hand the *Times* editorial writer did take off on the committee, especially Josh, for his irresponsible hiring of an unbalanced man to collect information for a congressional body. There were pictures of Josh, and of course the Republicans gleefully went for him: as Josh had said, they wanted a whipping boy.

Immigration came through with a statement that the committee had indeed sent a carefully documented report on the affairs of Eva and her protégée and how they had been in the course of preparing charges for a future hearing against both women when they were murdered. They had also incorporated some Interpol stuff that was far from flattering to Eva; in 1947 she had been arrested and questioned in the murder of an American captain in Hamburg. Lily turned out to be one of those pitiful war orphans who existed all her life on the one thing she had to sell.

The New York police commissioner also got into the act—probably tipped off friends in Immigration that he was in a spot, admitting his office had received a copy of the report on Eva's activities and he had ordered an investigation to find out why her place had never been raided.

Kelly went all over this very carefully, in a grave, sober manner. And really watching him for the first time outside a courtroom, I could see millions of housewives from Manhattan penthouses to the kitchens of western farmhouses, nodding and agreeing.

The man had powerful charm, grace, and an attractiveness that engulfed the viewer.

Barney blustered, of course, and his lawyer did some grandstanding, but against the Secretary of State, and the official statements from New York and Washington their indignant cries were like BB shot against artillery.

Then, for the next few hours, I watched Kelly Shannon slowly, methodically, and mercilessly destroy Barney Mullady. He pulled out every stop, making Barney go over his story in detail, then bringing back witness after witness to stamp him a liar.

The last part of the morning session was devoted to the devastating Swiss bank records. Kelly read each item, then quietly asked Barney where he got the money to put there, how he got it, where his accounts were for such monies. Was the money taken out of Lawrence, out of the crumbling tenements, the policy racket, the commercialized houses of prostitution that had never been raided in ten years?

It went on like that, relentlessly.

By noon, TV was interrupting with bulletins about the announcement of the governor appointing a special prosecutor for Lawrence and ordering the immediate paneling of a blue-ribbon grand jury. IRS in Washington revealed they had been investigating Barney's returns for the last five years, and the Justice Department's press agent had finally awakened to the fact that his people better get into the act, for he soon had FBI agents and a team of Justice lawyers on their way to Lawrence.

Barney's last-ditch effort had boomeranged. There was no doubt the horns of the hunters were loud in his ears before the noon recess.

In the afternoon he left the stand, a stunned, frightened old man who saw innumerable appearances before grand juries, days in courtrooms on trial, and the possibility of jail hitting him in the eyes. Obviously he was now on the road taken by many other kingmakers before him, from Pendergast to Jimmy Hines. There just weren't any more chocolates left in Barney Mullady's box.

I tumbled into bed early that night after calling Kelly and offering my congratulations. He sounded weary and disheartened, and made a remark that has always stayed with me: "I guess I finally made it, Finn."

"What's that, Kelly?"

"Noble Crusader, Friend of the Minorities, Champion of the Poor— wasn't that the image?"

BOOK 6
☆☆☆☆☆☆☆
The Man ☆☆☆☆☆☆☆☆☆☆☆
in the Window ☆☆☆☆☆☆☆

CHAPTER TWENTY-THREE: THE CAMPAIGN

THE FORMAL HEARINGS of the committee ended at Lawrence with Barney Mullady the final witness. The following morning we all returned to New York, and the first call I received was from Max Dregna. At lunch he gave me the news that the Liberal policy-making committee had voted to endorse Kelly Shannon. For a time he said he would have sworn we were about to make a deal with Barney Mullady under the threat of subpoena. . . . I think I shook him up by telling him how near the truth he really was.

At the end of the week there was another piece of news. One morning just before dawn the phone rang and a nasal-voiced Western Union operator was reading me a message. It was from Lacey, sent from a place called Custertown or Custerville in North Dakota:

> When he arrived and found me here at the ranch, he turned right around and checked into a hotel at this place. I followed him. He called me all kinds of fools and was mad as the devil at you for not telling him. I rode it out and we had dinner. We argued all night, then called a truce. The next day I demanded he take me back to the ranch, pointing out he had invited me. He agreed after much arm pulling. We argued again—this time riding. He said I couldn't very well stay overnight because it would be all over the county by morning. He asked me to marry him. I accepted. We were married this morning in the tiny reservation church. Josh is still pulling wires. He had to get the chancery in Bismarck to waive the banns. His best man was an old school chum named Johnny Iron Star, whose sister was my attendant, Mary Fire Lily. Isn't that beautiful? The country out here is breathtaking. We are both very happy. Please

tell Kelly, Luke, and the others. I have sent a long wire to father. Love.

LACEY

P.S. Josh says now I have the job of picking out one for you, braids and all. When can you come out? Soon, please. Josh misses you terribly.

I guess we were all secretly waiting for the news, and it made me happy, although the senator grumbled that Lacey would soon find out that when you saw one mountain you saw them all. As for me, I knew where I was going to spend my Christmas holidays.

The following Monday, Kelly's name was formally introduced into the gubernatorial campaign at a packed news conference in Washington when he resigned from the House.

By this time there were four other hopefuls, the two usual party faithfuls, the upstate businessman, the majority leader who trumpeted he was the real leader of the party, now badly shattered during the past eight years by Gentile's victories and popularity, plus party apathy, dissension, and inner feuds.

Time, as important as money, was against us. Fortunately, Luke and Luther's teams had laid a firm foundation. Now they swung into action from one end of the state to the other. We spent money in a fashion that shocked me. There was the traditional promotion and publicity campaign; and highway posters with Kelly's warm smile, biographies, and handouts poured from our headquarters like snow to blanket the entire state. We doubled and tripled our teams so there was scarcely a community that did not have a Shannon headquarters.

Television was used as never before. We had jingles, mottoes, slogans, one-minute shots of Kelly expounding on this subject and that; shots of Wexford Hall and his family romping on the lawn—there wasn't an hour in a day that did not offer something on Kelly Shannon for the millions of viewers watching the idiot tube.

In the city itself we ignored the regular organization, splitting our campaign into three parts: First we created our own party, with the help of the Liberals, staffing it with an army of our own volunteers, plus a sprinkling of professionals. In the city we used money disgracefully—but not through the clubhouses. Second, we ignored the five county leaders and their so-called machines. Since the Republican-Fusion elements had swept Gentile into City Hall eight years before, the Democrats had slid steadily downward. Barney Mullady had been the supreme boss, and now that he had been discredited, kicked out of the national and state political picture, there was wild confusion. The Democrats were desperate, and we knew it.

"Let them hang for a while," I advocated, and Kelly went along.

The third part was this: In the last eight years the Republican elective superiority had been impressive, but now, while the Democrats were weak and splintered in their loyalty, the Republicans were also badgered and harassed by many issues. Gentile himself was one. While the Secretary of State had vindicated him, there was still doubt in many minds, although Kelly had issued firm orders to avoid any suggestion of this.

As an organization, even despite Gentile's excellent Liberal record, the Republican Party has traditionally been white, middle class, and comfortable. In the past they have enjoyed dubious martyrdom and quasi-intellectual separatism, as one writer had so ably put it.

With the terrible tragedy of Lawrence still burned on the conscience of most of the country, Kelly took the lead as the champion of the oppressed, the minority, the workingman who had been deprived of justice because the Republicans had ignored him and the regular Democratic Party had sold its soul to the Devil.

Abernathy's embryonic organization burst into full flower immediately after the conclusion of the Lawrence hearings and the announcement of Kelly's candidacy. While it was small, it was vigorous and loud in support of Kelly. They swept into Manhattan and, supported by our money, virtually took over Mullady's machine. He was still full of fight, but he was no match for Abernathy's enraged, bitter friends. There were many incidents, but one night three of Barney's musclemen were sent to the hospital after having been pummeled unmercifully by a mob that chased them onto an Eighth Avenue bus. Only the presence of a riot squad saved them from being torn apart. That was the first indication the tables had turned. Barney's organization had fallen to the swift, the aggressive. Gene Abernathy had taught his men well.

Kelly announced in the beginning that he was not running as a regular organization man; he was running as Kelly Shannon rather than as the Democratic candidate. There were frantic calls from the leaders of the faithful, even Washington, but we turned deaf ears; if you want to get on the bandwagon, they were told, now is the time to jump.

As anyone in urban politics knows, the key figure in a political machine is the district captain. The Republicans had developed a fine program of having a captain and an assistant, plus needed troops to throw into a questionable district; we went further, and this is where the Shannon money proved the grease of politics—we hired not only a captain but also an assistant and three others to help, thus forming a cohesive team. Not a Democratic district lacked these units. Each team was flexible. As Election Day drew near, the teams were expanded to twenty-five or more.

The convention at Poughkeepsie was only a formality. A week before it, as I had predicted, the party leaders had come to us, hat in hand, to beg permission to jump on the bandwagon. They knew when they were beaten; there were just too much money, too much youth, too much popularity. And as I always maintained, professional politicians are realistic men; they would kick their brothers aside for a hated in-law if that in-law was a sure winner. There were no deals, no favors. They were told that if they wanted to come along they were welcome.

Even though it was all in the bag, the senator insisted on putting on a fabulous show at the convention. On the last night I just couldn't take it anymore, and stayed behind at Wexford with him. I don't think I'll ever forget the tears on his cheeks when Kelly stood on the platform, facing that hysterical, roaring mob while millions of colored balloons (for the color TV sets), each one marked with a gold S, floated down like giant goblets of colored rain. We now had such a finely welded team that our researchers, political record books open, were supplying the press with the news that this demonstration was fifteen minutes longer than any other on record, including those of national conventions.

Kelly's speech was magnificent; he had a superb sense of timing, and by now we had a stable of the best writers, so it just sent that packed auditorium into another great demonstration.

But despite the frantic adulation, Kelly kept his head. When he called his father after the nomination, he made sure he spoke to me; Josh and Lacey had wired their congratulations. They had to drive a hundred miles to buy a color TV set, but Josh told Kelly that every Indian on the reservation had watched him.

CHAPTER TWENTY-FOUR: SETBACK

THE HUNT FOR WIRE WILLY died out, as most manhunts do after the initial burst of violence and the official hue and cry that follow. After the story of the New Jersey doctor who had been forced to remove the slugs from Willy's body at gunpoint, Willy seemed to drop from sight. There had been various reports about him from time to time, but all proved false. However, in mid-August there were indications he was still in the metropolitan area when a policeman of a small upstate village reported he had chased an eccentric-looking man, whom he later identified as Willy, but had lost him in the woods. Willy had been living in a closed summer house for weeks until he had been surprised by the owner and his wife on their return from Europe. Several hours later a truck driver told state police he had given Willy a ride into New York City.

The village was just north of Wexford Hall, and I had the eerie feeling the madman had been shadowing us. Inspector Marrick had the same opinion. After a meeting with the state police superintendent, it was decided to place a guard around Wexford, especially over Pam and the children.

I had met Marrick several times since that unforgettable afternoon when we had hunted Willy under the city; once he had hinted that the department was pressing the DA—an organization Democrat of course—for a grand-jury investigation into why Josh and I had never notified the police Willy had guns. I informed him I was more than ready to cooperate with the authorities at any time. In fact, I would offer to appear before the grand jury, and sign a waiver so I could submit a copy of the report prepared by the Committee for Immigration on Eva's activities in case the jurors were interested in why this notorious woman's establishment had never been raided.

Marrick was a fine officer, one of the best in the department, but he also knew the score, and he wanted no part of an investigation that might taint the honor of his department.

As for the DA, we made sure he received a broad hint that the committee was still studying all of Benny Jello's statements and testimony, among them affairs dealing with a member of his office.

Both got the message: no investigation.

Gradually Willy and the nightmarish memories connected with him were pushed into the background by the feverish pace of the campaign. The morning after Kelly's nomination, our program started to move along the guidelines prepared months ago by Luke and Luther. As Josh had said so many months ago, if there are two men in a men's room, Kelly had to be between them.

We were constantly on the move. Our planes shuttled between the big cities, and our cavalcade of station wagons reached every township, village, and hamlet. Kelly spoke until he lost his voice, then croaked a few words until his doctors insisted he rest or risk permanently damaging his vocal chords. He shook hands until his arm was so sore he tossed with pain at night. By mid-September we were all stumbling with weariness.

But something had gone wrong. Frank Shea and Dyke Short got their first indications in the late summer polls; it stunned us all after Labor Day.

Gentile had dramatically gained his lost ground. He was slowly emerging as a formidable candidate; some areas in the north country were almost overwhelmingly for him. I had been uneasy about Gentile for some time. The Republican Convention should have been the traditional straw in the wind; he had been given a rousing, unexpected ovation. He was their man of the hour. His comeback had to be attributed to that unprecedented press conference held by the Secretary of State to explode Mullady's charges. Also, Gentile had his own image makers, and they weren't slow to take advantage of a good thing. They inundated all avenues of communications, TV, newspapers, and radio with excerpts from the secretary's statement. When the secretary came to the UN to make an anniversary speech, it was Gentile who greeted him at the airport— to the chagrin of that idiot who had taken his place at City Hall—it was

Gentile who shared the secretary's limousine and who posed with him. Gentile had been a member of the Establishment, and it hurried to his rescue.

The image was subtly put across. Gentile had the unequivocal confidence of the Secretary of State, and in fact had foiled a Communist plot. Gentile did everything to encourage the image; his staff never failed to point out his wartime exploits, and even delivered a warm letter from one of the leaders of the Chinese Nationalist Government.

Then they scored a superb coup: a gathering of the prisoners of the horrible World War II Shanghai prison. I am sure it was all organized and financed by Gentile's people. Radio, TV, and the newspapers gave extensive coverage to the small gathering of now middle-aged Americans, some with eyes still haunted by the terrors they had suffered and witnessed so many years ago.

The timing was excellent; it was the late summer doldrums; a two-week heat wave had just ended, and the news was dull. No matter what the reason, New York and the country took this handful of men to heart.

Of course Gentile, the first man to enter the prison, was the keynote speaker. The next day we spread the nation's big dailies out on the floor and looked at one another.

"What do the polls say, Frank?" I asked Shea.

He gave me a distressed look. "I hate to say them aloud."

"Give it to us," Luke snapped.

As Frank read off the results, it was apparent Kelly had slipped from a fifteen-point lead over Gentile after the convention to a three-point edge after Labor Day. In the last few months, Frank said, a cross section of the state's voters had shifted to a point where they now stood 46 percent behind Kelly and 43 percent behind Gentile. Shortly after Kelly had been nominated he had 52 percent and Gentile 37 percent in a similar canvass. Eleven per cent, then as now, was undecided.

"Dammit, what's happened?" Luke growled. "We took off like a jet, and now we're bumping along like a Model T."

"We seem to have lost our spark," Shea said gloomily. "We had something dramatic with the hearings; they caught the public's attention." He shrugged. "Maybe it's the letdown."

Kelly, who had been staring at the floor, looked up. "You're right, Frank. I can feel it in the audiences. They're apathetic."

"You mean they don't give a good God damn," his father said bluntly.

"Well, what do we do?" Luke asked. "We just can't sit here!"

We looked at one another in the tight silence. I sensed we were toying with the same thought, but I had vowed I would never say it aloud.

It was Kelly who did. "We're sitting here like a circle of dummies," he remarked briskly, "all with the same thought. Why don't we say it? We need Josh!"

Immediately after he spoke, the whole room seemed to relax.

"Now that you mention it," Frank Shea began cautiously, "I'm only sorry I didn't say it sooner. Well, what do we do—call him and tell him we're in trouble?"

"Not on this phone," Luther told him. "It's too delicate for that."

"Do you want me to go up there?" Kelly asked.

"You can't, Kel," Luke said. "First of all, if it got out it could be ruinous. But, more importantly, your schedule is filled from morning to night. Where you made one speech, you'll have to make five. Where you visited five dinners it must be ten from now on."

"Well, who's going?"

One after another they turned to me.

"You're his closest friend, Finn," Kelly said.

"That's just it. I feel I'll be putting him on a spot."

"Will you go as a personal favor to me?" Kelly asked.

"We would all appreciate it, McCool," the senator said.

"I hate to leave right at the peak." I knew it sounded lame as hell.

"Another week and we'll be at each other's throats." Luke was pacing the floor. "Luther got so mad at me yesterday he almost swallowed his pipe."

We didn't have to be told by the polls that our early lead was slipping away, and this had increased the tension; we were pressing much too hard. Even Kelly was on a razor's edge, and the walls of those upstate motels weren't thick enough to muffle the fierce arguments between him and Luke.

If we hadn't known it before, we knew it now: Kelly was our beloved, cherished prize, but Josh was the genius at organization that had bound us together.

"I just happen to have reservations on the four o'clock to Chicago," Luke said with elaborate nonchalance. "Don't forget your cowboy boots."

They were all smiling at me. What I had thought was my secret had been obvious to everyone. I wanted to see Josh and Lacey—desperately, as though they were my own children.

CHAPTER TWENTY-FIVE: THE PRODIGAL

To a New Yorker born and raised in Manhattan, whose mountains are the Catskills and whose plains are the Jersey flatlands, the sight of the deep American West is an awesome experience. The air is so clear it seems polished; the mountains are brooding, majestic; the plains, endless. It made me feel big as an inch, and I suddenly realized what Josh had meant when he said that for a long time after he had first arrived in the city he had a deep feeling of uneasiness, almost claustrophobia.

Josh and Lacey met me at the nearest town to the ranch—Custertown, more a crossroads than a village. There were a gas station, a general store, church, post office, and an almost incongruously beautiful new school glittering with glass and surrounded by carefully trimmed lawns and shrubs. I half expected to see cowboys and Indians, and secretly I had hoped I would, but while the smiling, rawboned man who drove me to Custertown wore boots and had the skin of old leather, he casually asked me if the Paramount Theatre was still doing business on Forty-third Street. He had been born in Jersey City, and as a teen-ager had spent many an illegal afternoon at the Paramount listening to the bobby-soxers howl and swoon as Frankie crooned.

Josh and Lacey looked superb; Josh had lost that slightly flabby look and was lean and hard. Lacey, in Levis and as dark as a Sioux, would have been a stranger to New York. I had a devil of a time holding back the tears when Lacey hugged me and Josh kept pumping my hand.

We piled in the station wagon and had a hilarious trip back to the ranch, with a stopover at a highway motel bar that had a breathtaking wall-size mural of a voluptuous woman. Josh said it once graced the back of a bar owned by Bob Ford, the man who killed Jesse James.

What more could a tenderfoot ask for?

We were a bit stoned when we reached the ranch—by this time I was calling it a spread—and the main house. It was an impressive place, built of stone and hewn timbers, with a huge fireplace, a kitchen that glowed with copper pots, and bedrooms with waxed plank floors. Guns and a buffalo head hung from the walls. The rancher and his wife, whom Josh had persuaded to stay on, served a steak dinner that would put the finest in New York to shame.

As darkness fell, a chill crept across the land, bringing the first hint of winter, and Josh started a fire. We took our drinks and sprawled out on the huge, half-moon sofa. It was now time to get to the business of my visit.

"I sent you a telegram I was coming," I explained, "because I didn't want to go over anything on the phone, Josh. But the truth is, we need you."

"The campaign isn't going very well, is it?" he asked, staring into the fire.

"No. Have you been keeping track of us?"

"Oh, I try to—"

"Keep track of it!" Lacey exploded with an indignant snort. "He tears in here when the news is on, and cursed us all out the other night because he missed the early part of Tuck Larsen's broadcast."

"He gave you boys a real going over, Finn," Josh said. "You know, he's right. Kelly's last three or four TV appearances were as dull as anything I've seen."

"After Tuck Larsen's broadcast, we reran Kelly's TV spots. There was no question Tuck was right. They were the same issues, only rehashed and served up in a different way."

I asked him, "What do you think is wrong, Josh?"

"The obvious. You're pushing too hard and singing the same old tune. You certainly blanketed the state, which is what we all wanted to do months ago, but now Kelly must turn to something else."

"Do you have any ideas?"

"He just happens to have a few thousand notes," Lacey said.

He picked up a notebook from a table next to the big color TV set.

"Well, let's take—"

"Josh, not here. Come back and tell all of us," I said.

"How does Kelly feel?"

"He asked me to come to see you as a personal favor."

"Please, Josh," Lacey said softly.

"Lacey's been after me to at least call you, but I felt—"

"It was pride, Josh; you know that."

"So it was pride—"

"Well, Kelly's swallowed his pride, and now he's asking you to come back," I said.

"If I did, I would have to stay in the background," he said slowly, as if turning the idea around in his mind. "Wouldn't Larsen try to make trouble with that item!"

"Will you both come back with me?"

Josh knelt down to stir the coals, and carefully put on a few logs. "Let's talk about it at breakfast," he said.

Across the room, Lacey winked.

The following day we left Bismarck on the afternoon plane. I guess Josh planned a long stay back east. I overheard him tell the rancher he probably wouldn't see him until the Christmas holidays.

Back in New York it was the return of the Prodigal. The senator threw one of the best and most expensive parties I have ever attended in a suite in the Hilton that Cleopatra would have loved. It was one of the few times in my life that my bedroom slowly turned as I clung to the covers. We had enough champagne to float a Hoboken ferryboat. Every time I hiccuped, I swear I could inflate a balloon. It was a great night. We had missed Josh, and now that he was back we were happy.

By noon the next day we were gathered, slightly pale, and drinking countless pitchers of ice water, as Josh read us his notes and ideas. It was refreshing because now we had a professional observer, all these weeks someone who had been on the outside looking in, telling us what we had done wrong and suggesting what we could do to get the campaign back in stride.

Fundamental issues, organization, and personality could be among the keynotes to a victory, Josh told us, and then he described elections won on these tides. The 1958 issue was bad income, and the Republicans lost Congress. Personality was in Eisenhower's grin, and no Democrat, not even Adlai Stevenson, could lick him.

"Remember, Albany is fine," he went on, "but we want to put Kelly in the White House. We must weigh actions on long-range goals. We can't be afraid to go for the high risk, the high gain issue. From where I sat in North Dakota you all seemed to be afraid to move out into the center of the arena. We must not only talk the issues; we must dramatize them. Take the narcotics problem, for example—"

"Kelly spent three speeches on narcotics and what should be done," Luke put in. "He really clobbered the state's program."

"I heard it, and believe me, it sounded just like every other politician's speech about the subject. Elaborate plans to try that new drug, the promise of more beds, reshape the old state laws . . ." He consulted his notes. "I think you all missed Gentile's crack about how the state should try the English plan. It was only a sentence, but I think his writers painted him into a corner with that one. First of all, it would cost a fortune. Second, the idea would be abhorrent to most parents. Third, simple research would have uncovered the Butler Report, issued last year to Parliament, which showed how much of a failure their program really is. Now suppose we do this . . ."

His plan was for Kelly to spend a weekend in London to see for himself the disillusionment, the tragedy of the so-called English system to combat narcotics, then return with a TV eyewitness report to the people. Kelly, with a planeload of reporters, flew to London, made several appearances in the tough Soho district, talked to physicians, public figures, appeared on the BBC, and then made a devastating report back home. He gained worldwide publicity, and made Gentile look foolish.

Youth was our next target. As Josh pointed out, Kelly had to be the spokesman in an age when youth was combating conformity and computers, ghetto warfare, the irresponsibility of labor, cynicism and corruption in officialdom, and a crippling disillusionment about Vietnam.

Luke and Luther were sent hustling across the state to arrange a speaking tour of daily, sometimes twice daily, appearances for Kelly at colleges. None was too small.

"You are not like the last generation," he told a wildly cheering audience of young people a few weeks later. "You demand the answers to questions; deep within you is the spirit of motivation, of dissatisfaction— and of protest. Never let it die. Shelter it, fan it, make it glow, cherish it always—this spirit that I call the spirit not too sure it is right. . . ."

Josh made sure the phrase caught on: millions of small colored buttons with it were distributed across campuses; countless placards with the phrase in bold, black letters appeared on poles, fences, walls.

By early October we were conferring with our brain trust several times a day. There were times when we revised Kelly's speeches over the phone minutes from the time he appeared before a microphone.

Our contacts—a polite word for spies—in Gentile's camp informed us we at first had puzzled them, later worried them as Frank Shea's polls showed we were slowly edging back—but there was still a long way to go.

It was then that Josh came up with his idea of holding a series of debates "on great issues" across the state in "classic" spots, as he called them. (They have since become known as the Classic Debates.) There were to be five in one week, Monday to Friday, in that many historic and well-known locations: the Saratoga Battlefield Park, outside the State House in Albany, the square at White Plains, the World's Fair Grounds Park, and ending on the steps of New York's City Hall.

The debates would be nationally televised, and we would foot the bill.

Josh felt we had successfully presented Kelly's image, dramatically but episodically. The debates would give Kelly the opportunity of crystallizing his ideas, particularly on a statewide level. He suggested we produce a series of speeches on the growing urban crisis and a program to solve it. These would include "major and bold proposals for Negro education and employment for the poor, both white and black, but concentrating on an analysis of the poor.

"Remember what you told us one night in this library, Kelly, about the breakdown of the Negro family and the terrible lack of motivation for the poor?" Josh asked.

"But I thought we had covered that very well," Kelly protested.

"Of course you did, but that was months ago," Josh said. "I recall you had to compete for space with a big ship disaster at sea. You were really buried that day. It's always like that in a campaign: sometimes the voters know what you're saying; sometimes their attention is claimed by something more dramatic, more meaningful to their own lives than what a politician says."

"Someone will have to approach Gentile," Luke said.

"I think Lacey should approach him," was Josh's surprising proposal.

"Lacey!"

"Have you all forgotten that Lacey worked for Gentile in his first campaign and dug up a big score for him." He turned to Lacey. "Right, beloved?"

"Josh, I can't go to Gentile!"

"Why not? He's still friendly. Didn't he send us a wonderful wire?"

"I think Lacey will get further with him than any of us," Luther said.

"Come on, Lace, this is the last goal," Luke said.

"Kelly agrees with me," Josh said.

"You two talked it over without telling me?"

"Over a grilled-cheese sandwich and a beer at three o'clock this morning," Josh said cheerfully. He handed her a slip of paper. "Here's Gentile's private number. Just give your name to his secretary, and I bet he'll see you this afternoon. He has only one appearance at a Lower East Side rally, then a dinner tonight."

Lacey gave us an exasperated look, and turned to Kelly.

"I wish you would, Lace," he said.

Of course Lacey called, and a surprised Gentile promised to see her after his afternoon rally.

From the beginning, Gentile's camp was split by our proposition; some thought it was a fine opportunity; others warned him he was stepping into a beartrap. But Gentile not only had courage; he also possessed a gambler's instinct. His own polls showed Kelly had gained lost ground and would probably forge slowly ahead with the unprecedented TV appearances we had scheduled for the last few weeks before election. It was no secret that Shannon money was pouring into networks. And no matter how often and loudly he would cry unfair and unethical, there would be thousands of viewers. The debates could be an opportunity to pull us up short and score another coup. In addition, win or lose, this national exposure would be invaluable, because Gentile now more than ever had his sights on Pennsylvania Avenue.

And besides, the Shannon group was paying the bills.

He accepted in a telegram to Kelly after first calling Lacey. He was a politician, but also a gentleman.

At a secret meeting, Luke and Luther and Gentile's staff worked out the ground rules, the necessary but frustrating details, such as policing, crowd control, federal, state, and local approval for the sites and TV schedules.

The furious week of debates attracted national attention. Kelly and Gentile were crowd pleasers; both were poised, charming, witty, and articulate. The crowds increased, along with the audience, as the feeling grew of two powerful figures on the American political scene coming down the final stretch, neck and neck. The polls showed it this way, although being as objective as I could, I thought Kelly was slowly forging ahead. Josh thought so too, but Lacey pointed out that Gentile was tackling larger issues and that his programs were bolder than ever before.

Josh and Kelly worked around the clock on the speech for the fourth debate, and it was powerful. Lawrence was re-created; and although Kelly protested, Josh insisted the "I saw" could never be topped. In this speech Kelly told for the first time the role played by Gene Abernathy and how he had died.

The fifth and last debate could very well determine the outcome.

It was obvious, as the London *Times* man wrote, that we were not only witnessing the debates of two gubernatorial contenders but probably America's next presidential candidates waging preliminary skirmishes.

The final debate on the steps of New York City Hall would take place on Friday, one week before Election Day. It would include each man's program of what could be done: ghettos, housing, taxes, transit, crime in the street. After a general outline, each man would take the planks of his platform, one by one, and describe them in detail. The program was to last ninety minutes, and would be held at high noon—an hour expected to attract one of the biggest crowds in the history of New York City. Shea and Short predicted the TV audience would be in the many millions.

CHAPTER TWENTY-SIX: THE SHOWDOWN AT
                      CITY HALL PLAZA

ALL THAT WEEK it seemed even the weather had favored Kelly. The crisp, melancholy days were for football rallies, cheering crowds, waving pennants—youth. But that last Friday betrayed us. The ugly gray day held the first raw threat of approaching winter.

There was high excitement in our suite at the Roosevelt when the grapevine ticked off the news that the President would be among our TV viewers. City Hall Plaza was to be roped off from Park Row to Broadway and as far south as Barclay Street. Tickets had been issued— first come, first served—but the supply vanished in hours.

Since he had returned, Josh had carefully remained in the background, but this time he told me he would be among the guests on the platform. "I'll wait until it's just about to start, then slip in the back," he said. "Before they finish I'll disappear. I want to see Kelly square off in the flesh—just once," he added.

It was arranged for Lacey to be in the front row of VIP's on the platform, and I would hold a folding chair in the rear for Josh.

I arrived early at City Hall. There were countless details to be worked out with the other side, ridiculous items like makeup men, what papers could be held by the debaters, the length of time for summing up, and so on. At last the bickering ended, and we waited for the principals to appear. I was walking across the Plaza to the platform raised at the foot of City Hall steps when I met Inspector Marrick. I gave him a raise of the eyebrows. "Trouble?"

"A cop was shot and wounded by a holdup man he said had broken into a TV store on Sedgwick Avenue early this morning. He said the guy was as big as a house, and wearing sneakers." He made a motion to the crowd. "Just to make sure, I have plainclothesmen all over the place."

"Was it Willy?"

He shrugged. "It was dark. Maybe it was only a big kid wearing sneakers." He added, "Then again maybe it was Willy." He studied the platform. "This is the last one, isn't it?"

"The last one, Inspector."

"Politically they were interesting, but they gave me ulcers on ulcers." He raised his hand. "I'll see you after the show."

I forgot Inspector Marrick and his fears when Kelly and Gentile appeared. The crowd was the largest in the series. The roar that greeted both men reminded me of a fight mob welcoming the champion and the contender as their seconds pried apart the ropes for them to enter the ring.

Eyeing that sea of upturned faces, they were superb examples of American statesmen: Gentile, tall, confident, aristocratic as he smiled down upon them; Kelly, almost boyish, his half-wave, half-salute saying this is where the action is, and I love every minute of it.

As I watched him I wondered what this extraordinary magic was that glowed so warmly about Kelly Shannon this last week. Could those intangible human ingredients that had attracted so many of us to him been curiously blunted during the tiring campaign? I don't think so. Nor can it be said that the dedication, the purpose had worn thin. No, they were always there. Then what was it?

Perhaps it had been unconscious envy for the things so many of those who listened had wished for themselves: elegance, wit, courage, even the vigor of a graceful youth; then, again with unconscious bitterness, they had determined he must not win too easily—he must be tested.

Kelly had shown us that the grace, charm, wit, and courage were all part of his very bones, buried deep in the marrow. During the debates millions watched him make this brilliantly visible, as he reached out to stir their humdrum lives. Perhaps for the first time they had seen him clearly, without the image we had made for him.

My thoughts were interrupted as they prepared to toss the coin, and Josh slid in the chair beside me. He was wearing sunglasses and had his topcoat collar turned up.

"I feel like a refugee from a spy movie," he murmured.

"Anyone spot you?"

"I saw Marrick when I was coming across the Plaza. He did a double-take but only waved."

"He thinks Willy held up a place in Brooklyn this morning."

"Poor Willy," he said. "I hope they don't have to hurt him."

"A couple of months ago you were lighting candles they would kill him," I pointed out.

"I did, and said a lot of things I'm sorry about now," was his answer. "Well, here they go! Gentile won the toss."

418

They told me Gentile gave one of the best speeches of his career; frankly I caught only words and phrases. Marrick had made me uneasy. I kept craning my neck, peering out over the crowd until Josh whispered that I looked like a nervous old gander.

Kelly also scored high, but Gentile held a slim edge.

After the general debate there was a brief intermission. Then they returned to sum up.

Finally Kelly was up at the microphone. A wave of sound of cheering, whistles, and stomping feet rolled across the Plaza. I knew the damn speech by heart, and although I tried to follow it my mind wandered. What would I do after this last Election Day? What would Josh and Lacey do?

A great many scenes from the past months pushed and elbowed to the front of my mind: the first day here at City Hall when the senator faced Gentile as he resigned; how I had met Barney Mullady and Gene Abernathy only a few feet from where I was now sitting; then the call I received in our office just across Broadway.

I guess it was this last thought that made me raise my eyes to the windows of our office on the fourth floor of the Woolworth Building. With half a mind I studied it, remembering the first day we had rented it and Josh had insisted on buying a bottle of champagne, which left $15 between us. . . . My mind and bones are not what they were once, but thank the Lord I never needed glasses, so I could see our windows on the Broadway side that overlooked the Plaza. I suddenly realized one was opened four or five inches. Idly I wondered why. Suddenly the thought struck me.

It was as if lightning had hit. When I saw the rifle barrel slowly appear in the window, I jumped up with a hoarse shout. Josh who probably thought I was suffering an attack, leaped to his feet. Lacey, up front, had turned to stare at me, bewildered. A few feet from her, Kelly was at the mike. Luke, who had heard the noise, turned with a frown, as did the others. Now on my feet, I could see the upturned faces of the crowd that seemed endless.

They said I kept shouting. All I remember is pointing to the window. Josh jerked his head around and looked up. He caught it at once. There was a line of folding chairs in front of us, but his leap cleared them. He hit Kelly in the back with his outstretched hands as the rifle cracked with the sound of a dry stick being broken. Then again and again, with split-second speed.

Josh caught the bullet meant for Kelly; the second tore through the fleshy part of Kelly's right arm, then freakishly crossed his back to come out of the left side of his jacket, wounding one of Gentile's aides in the hand. The third slug nicked the right side of Kelly's neck and plowed into the wooden rail of the platform.

Kelly and Josh crashed against the front of the platform, and both fell in a tangle of wires and microphones. Kelly rose to his knees and reached over to Josh. I saw Pam fight her way to him.

The platform was a wild melee. I can recall almost being knocked from my feet by Inspector Marrick, who plunged through the tangle of over-turned chairs, shouting men, and screaming women. I don't remember getting to Josh's side, but Lacey was already kneeling down, her face next to Josh's, whispering, whispering, whispering. My heart stuck in my throat as I watched the pool of blood slowly widen about the back of his head.

There was bedlam in front of the platform, with men and women fighting to flee from the Plaza or shouting and pointing to the window. Marrick was barking orders for an ambulance when a round little man with a moustache pushed his way through, shouting that he was a doctor. He knelt down, made a quick examination, then pulled off his jacket, ripped his shirt in two, and wound the crude bandages around Josh's head.

"Get me a radio car, quick," he snapped. "Beekman Downtown is only a few blocks away."

"Is he alive?" someone asked.

"Just about," was the blunt reply.

The radio car wailed across the Plaza. Gentile and Luke carefully lifted Josh's unconscious form and carried him down the few steps to the radio car, while Luther and Pam helped Kelly. In minutes they screeched out of the Plaza and down Park Row.

I found myself in the cleared space in front of the platform where the police were battling to push back the crowd. Then Inspector Marrick was running across the Plaza, followed by plainclothesmen and uniformed men, all holding revolvers and rifles.

"We kicked in the front door but he was gone," he said. He held up a rifle with a scope. "Willy's?"

I nodded.

Suddenly I remembered the day I had been alone in my office and Willy had paid me a visit. I could see him standing at our window cursing City Hall; I recalled going to the windows on the Park Place side and on the Broadway side, but never seeing Willy come out.

"He's not there," I said. "He's back underground."

Then Luke and Luther came to take me to the hospital where the human being I loved more than anything else on earth was barely clinging to his life.

Strange how the crucial hours in the life of someone very dear always leave memories of little things: the startling white petals of the embroidered daisy on the top of Lacey's blue dress; the simple diamond ring she kept twisting round and round; the tiny scar on Luke's right cheekbone that I had never noticed before; and the strands of gray in Josh's thick black hair.

During the five-hour operation Josh's heart stopped twice, and twice that fat little doctor massaged it back to beating again. By eight that night one of the most important brain surgeons in the country had arrived, and Josh was back in the operating room. All we could do was pray, they said. His wild leap had not only saved Kelly but had probably saved his own life; a fraction to one side, and the bullet would have meant instantaneous death.

If he survived, the brain surgeon told us, it would not be without consequences, perhaps partial paralysis of one side. He was a kind man, and let his words trail away.

"I don't care," Lacey whispered. "Just let me keep him, dear God."

Kelly's wound was not serious in the sense that it would be fatal, but the slug had torn through muscles that would take a long time healing. With Pam gripping his hand, he had sat in his shorts on a stool in the emergency room, the freakish trail of the slug visible across his back. It appeared as if someone had taken the hot tip of a poker and run it carefully across the skin. The other slug had only superficially nicked his neck.

As Marrick said, if Josh hadn't leaped the slug would have torn Kelly's head to bits.

After he had been treated, the doctors wanted to put him to bed for the rest of the day, but Kelly waved them away. He stayed with us that afternoon and into the night—waiting. Finally, at my insistence, he let Pam take him home.

Lacey and I stayed through the next day and the next night. Hours passed one into another, all obscured by weariness and fear. I didn't know that Kelly had returned several times. It was touch and go for Josh; but he was in the best of condition, and that, plus his youth, kept him alive.

On Wednesday we had a flicker of hope; he emerged twice from his deep coma. On Thursday morning he opened his eyes. On Thursday night the surgeon said he had a fighting chance. There would be some paralysis on the left side, but with months, even years, of therapy—well, the outlook seemed brighter.

When the surgeon left us in the room at the end of the hall, I was not surprised to discover tears on everyone's cheeks.

On Friday morning Pam and Kelly arrived to take me back to Wexford, but I insisted on returning to the Sheridan. It would be only a brief taxi ride down the West Side Highway to the hospital if they needed me. Lacey stayed; she looked surprised that anyone would believe she would leave Josh.

Now he was conscious most of the time, but though the odds were with him, he was still in intensive care and on the critical list. Before I left I tiptoed into his room under the disapproving eyes of his nurse and held his hand for a moment. It was enough, and I returned him to Lacey's good care. As we walked down the corridor, Kelly told me he felt fine, but Pam whispered that he was in constant pain and that he slept only a few hours at a time.

In the lobby we were greated by the biggest crowd of newspapermen, photographers, and TV people I have ever seen. It was a wild scene, and if I told my story once I told it fifty times, as did Pam and Kelly.

When we finally reached our car, Marrick was at our elbows, saying he might as well ride with us uptown. On the way up the West Side Highway he gave us a running account of the manhunt for Willy. During the early part of the week the city had virtually been sealed off; highways, tunnels, and bridges all had patrols, while a small army of city and Transit policemen moved about underground. Evidently since his return Willy had been living beneath the city. Police had located a little-known, abandoned subway spur near the Brooklyn Bridge Station where they found milk containers and scraps of food. The loose bricks of the spur had been noticed by an alert trackwalker. When he investigated, they fell in; Willy had carefully replaced brick by brick when he left to kill Kelly at the City Hall Plaza.

"He's somewhere under the city," Marrick said, "but he's got to come up sometime." He turned to me. "Are you going up to Westchester or staying in town?"

"I plan to have dinner, then stay at the Sheridan if the hospital calls."

"Finn, don't you think you should come back with us to Wexford?" Pam asked.

"No matter where you go, my men will be along," Marrick said.

"You think it's necessary, Inspector?" Kelly asked.

"Necessary?" he exploded. "My God, man, there's an assassin waiting for a chance to kill you! I even doubled my force. If I want you people I know where to get you. Just call Communications at headquarters, and I'll be on the phone in a minute—you can let me out anywhere around Times Square—I'm going to drop by the West Forty-seventh Street house."

"We're going to let Finn off at his place. Is that all right?"

"Fine. It's only down the block."

We swung off the highway at Fortieth Street, and they dropped Marrick and myself at Forty-seventh and Eighth. He said goodbye and walked down the street to the old precinct where more than half a century ago they had booked Lieutenant Rosenthal and Gyp the Blood in another violent era.

I was infinitely weary when I reached the top of the stairs in the Sheridan and opened my door. The place was stifling, and I flung up the windows. For a long time I lay in a warm bath to restore my numbed mind and let my tired old body relax. I don't know how long I stayed in the tub. I know I dozed because the water was cold when I finally got out. I was tempted to have dinner at Sullivan's, but I was so weary

I decided to call the hospital, have a spot of Jack Daniels, and slide between the sheets. I spoke to Lacey, who reported all was well. The Jack Daniels slid down neat and warm. When I noticed the hands of the clock, it was three sharp.

For a moment I stared at those hands and listened to the steady ticking like the pulsing of a human heart in my quiet bedroom. I was puzzled as to why I should study the time. Suddenly, I remembered!

Three o'clock, Friday! The day Willy never forgot to visit the grave of his son.

After I flung on my clothes, I searched for the phone number of the old precinct, but I was so jittery I couldn't find it. The old desk clerk must have thought I had taken leave of my senses when he saw me fly down the stairway. In the precinct the desk sergeant undoubtedly shared his opinion when I burst in.

"Sergeant!" I shouted, "where's the inspector?"

The sergeant raised his hand and gave me a grave look.

"Just a minute, sir. I'll be with you—"

"For God's sake, where is Inspector Marrick?"

He was a wise old bird. One look at my face was enough. "He just left for West Fifty-fourth Street. . . ."

I started out on a run, but he shouted to a young cop to get me to West Fifty-fourth Street in his radio car. The policeman yanked open the door of his car as his partner looked on bewildered.

"We have to get this guy to the Seventeenth in a hurry."

They did the seven blocks in seconds. I was out and running across the street before they had come to a stop. Marrick was on the first floor talking to some police brass when I burst in. When he saw me he ran over.

"Willy? Did he call you?"

"No, but I just thought of something," I said, and rapidly told him about our meetings in the Queens graveyard. He interrupted me before I had finished.

"Captain, call the Tenth in Queens and have them get as many men as possible ready for when I get out there." He snapped to an aide: "Notify Traffic I want the exits on the expressway near that cemetery and the whole area shut off. Send a policewoman out there with some flowers. Have her get to the caretaker if there is one. I don't want anyone in that cemetery—if he's there, there's bound to be shooting."

He grabbed me by the arm.

"Let's go."

THE MOST DIFFICULT THING IN THE WORLD is to keep orders confidential in the New York City Police Department. Josh once told me there was an old story among newspapermen that some cops were paid by the city's newspapers to tip them off to big doings. This may be, but I believe the department is so huge, so complex, only the most sensitive of investigations can be kept secret. Routine police orders, such as went out that afternoon, are bound to leak out. So it was no surprise when we reached the Queens precinct to find reporters, both the writing press and TV, beginning to arrive.

In the upstairs detective squad room Marrick explained his plans to the hastily assembled police brass with the aid of a huge map of the area. I showed him the entrance we had taken and the approximate route we had traveled on foot to reach the grave of Willy's son. Marrick wasn't satisfied. He got the policewoman on the phone, who reported that the three persons who had been in the cemetery had left. Marrick insisted that the caretaker search his records for the exact location of the boy's grave. He listened to her report, then checked it on the street map.

"How many marksmen do we have?"

"Four. Two more are coming from the Seventh and the Nineteenth."

"They have vests and masks?"

"All fully equipped."

"How many men downstairs?"

"About twenty. There'll be more in about a half—"

"I don't want any more. We'll only be shooting each other out there. Give me about fifteen of the best shots." He pointed to the map. "Three teams of five each. I want them spread out, taking advantage of every tombstone and monument. This guy is a sharpshooter with plenty of ammo."

"Bring along the bullhorn." He looked at me. "How about it, McCool, want to take a chance of talking him in?"

"I'll try."

"Okay. Mr. McCool will try to talk him in. If he refuses to drop his guns, and fires, fire in return. This man is dangerous. I don't want any cop widows tonight. Another thing: I don't want any TV people or reporters in that graveyard! That's an order! Okay, let's go down and get those cops squared away."

It was like trying to chase bees from a honey pot to lose those TV reporters and the others. While Marrick cursed savagely, they followed us in streams of panel trucks and cars. At the entrance to the graveyard, Marrick ordered them back down the street.

The policewoman, dressed in a black dress and hat and incongruously carrying a wilting bouquet, reported she had seen Willy kneeling at the grave of his son.

"Did he see you?" Marrick demanded.

"I don't think so," the girl said. "I was several rows back of him and, frankly, I tiptoed away."

"Is he armed?"

"I couldn't tell. He was just kneeling there with a geranium pot in front of him. I checked the hothouse over there, and the owner said he always comes here on Friday at this time."

"Okay," Marrick said shortly. "Let's move out. Now remember—wait for my orders! We're first going to try McCool here; then let's see what happens. We may have to play it by ear."

I followed Marrick into the cemetery and down that gravel path. I can't recall when I was more frightened; the thought of facing that madman again made my mouth dry.

The teams of cops, the marksmen looking like ancient swordsmen in their iron masks and awkward metal vests, hurried across the graveyard. There was a deadly silence. The afternoon was so still I could almost taste the heavy fall air. I could hear, beyond the fence, the distant whine of the traffic on the expressway and the impatient honking of horns. From down the street the TV crews and reporters watched silently. We crossed the rows of tombstones and angels with sorrowing stone faces. Beyond us I could see the other cops moving in a crouch behind the gravestones.

Suddenly Willy was there.

I touched Marrick's sleeve, but he had seen him. He was the same— huge, silent, head bowed, dirty, torn sweater, soiled sneakers. In front of him was a pot with a solitary geranium. For a moment we watched him; then Marrick motioned us to move up.

We crept from tombstone to tombstone until the inspector held up his hand. He waved the cop with the bullhorn to come forward. Before I knew it I was holding the heavy horn in my hands, now slippery with sweat.

"Take your time," Marrick whispered. "Don't shout; talk softly. The horn will carry. And don't stand up!"

On my knees I held up the horn with both hands. I was directly behind two time-worn stones, both topped by weatherbeaten stone angels. Their backs were to me, their hands outstretched, almost beseechingly, in Willy's direction, as if the tiny broken and chipped fingers were begging us to have compassion.

Then the mouthpiece was at my lips and I was talking.

"Willy . . . Willy, this is Finn McCool. You are surrounded by police

425

officers. They want you to throw down your guns. You won't be harmed."

The amplified words echoed across the silent graveyard and gradually died out.

Willy never moved.

"Try again," Marrick whispered.

I tried again. Again the words died away, and the tense silence of the still day returned.

It was after the third time I tried that Willy slowly, almost laboriously, rose to his feet. He dwarfed the tombstones. His head was slightly thrust forward; he seemed to be peering at us.

In his belt were two revolvers. He slowly drew one, carefully removed the silencer, but let it hang at his side.

"Talk to him! Talk to him!" Marrick ordered.

"Willy! It's me! McCool! Don't shoot, Willy! There are cops all around you! Drop your guns."

He shook his head and ran the sleeve of his sweater across his eyes.

I talked until I ran out of breath. Willy kept staring at us, the gun still at his side.

"I think he's got one of his spells," I told Marrick. "They seem to knock him out."

"Move up," Marrick said. "Maybe we can rush him."

Then suddenly we heard it overhead. A helicopter, the blades churning furiously, was zooming down. Marrick cried, "Get off . . . move off!" as he waved frantically, but the plane dived downward. I could see the TV cameraman leaning out, holding a hand camera.

The noise seemed to jerk Willy back to consciousness. He stared up at the hovering helicopter. Then he let out a roar, shouting incoherently as he fired rapidly at the plane, which zoomed upward, as if yanked by an invisible heavenly wire.

I grabbed the horn and shouted something, but it wasn't any use.

"Here he comes!" a cop cried.

Willy was moving in on us. He had both guns and was blazing away. I hugged the dirt as the bullets ricocheted off the tombstones and whined angrily overhead. From between the narrow slit of the two stones I watched Willy advance. Rifles cracked. He dropped a revolver and grabbed an arm, but he kept moving forward, the gun in one hand still working.

The cops had no choice. Rifles cracked. I could see tiny puffs of dust rise on the tattered old sweater. Somehow, God only knows how, that wild, monstrous man kept advancing. He was about fifteen feet from where we lay when he slowly started to crumble. His last shot chipped the grimy robe of one of the angels perched above me.

As he sank slowly to one knee, a cop jumped up and fired. The heavy slug flung Willy back, and he sprawled motionless in the dust. The

426

echo of the last shot died away as the cops slowly emerged from behind the tombstones. It was an eerie scene of men with guns and mesh masks rising up, it seemed, from the very graves.

We gathered in a circle about the dead man. Blood seeped from scores of wounds about his body. The shot that had killed him had taken off one side of his head. A dirty envelope was tucked inside his belt. Marrick picked it up, studied it, and handed it to me. There was a list of names, some with a line of red ink running through them: Benny Jello, Molly Shapiro, Eva Schmidt, Kelly Shannon, Felix Gentile . . .

"Funny," Marrick said, "neither you nor Michaels is on the list."

Then the helicopter came out of the blue sky again, and the TV trucks were roaring madly up the road with reporters leaping over the stones like runners on an obstacle course.

"Let's go," Marrick said shortly. "I don't feel in any mood for these guys."

We walked down the path. As we passed the grave of Willy's son, I saw that the solitary geranium pot had been shattered by a bullet.

CHAPTER TWENTY-EIGHT: DAY OF TRUTH

It was Election Day, the politician's Day of Truth.

It was also a day when, like politicians all over the country, we realized we could never resolve the last-minute tangle of problems or do all the things we had planned.

Early in the morning Kelly and Pam voted in the beautiful little village of Crestview. I pulled the machine handles down in a shoemaker's shop on West Forty-eighth Street.

There was nothing more for Kelly to do, so he and Pam remained at Wexford. The one big remaining job was organization, and that was Luke's and Luther's task, with me sitting back and taking the bows and letting them accept the barbs and arrows. And there were plenty of those before ten o'clock.

We had taken over the old carriage house, where Kelly and Luke and their friends once had played basketball, and installed banks of computers, hundreds of telephones manned by operators, and three teletypes. In the library we had an additional teletype and several phones for the senator.

As Josh had planned months before, Wexford would be the nerve center for the statewide network of polling and survey teams, most of them based in Josh's "Indicator Cities." The findings of these teams would be fed into the banks of computers. If the results were adverse, Luke and

Luther would be on the phone within minutes to set into motion one of their teams standing by in that particular area.

The first good news was word of a record turnout not only in the big cities but also in the rural communities upstate, which are traditionally conservative Republican. Reports soon flowed in from Buffalo, Albany, Utica, Syracuse—the Negro vote would be a large one.

At Lawrence they were standing in line at dawn.

There were straws in the wind in the early morning. In one upstate solid Republican county, the local chairman and publisher of one of the best of the upstate dailys came out with a page-one editorial urging his readers to vote for Kelly, who he said he viewed not only as a politician but as a conscience of our time.

Bookmakers favored Kelly, but Gentile was still liked by many. One big question never left our midst: If Kelly won, would he squeak in as a heretofore unknown novice who, through the medium of TV and dramatic events, had captured enough of the public's imagination or would he come in strong?

In the last week I had ordered a three-part survey taken in which several thousand voters across the state—political leaders, labor-union officials, newspaper editors, businessmen—were to be questioned in an attempt to try to determine if we had reached that most important voter —the undeclared; what effect Kelly had on the housewives; if this had been a battle of personalities or of issues; and finally, what Kelly's public image was as against Gentile's.

Shortly after noon, Frank Shea and Dyke Short arrived with their reports. Copies were distributed, and we all settled down to get the results.

It appeared we had captured the imagination of the undeclared voter, not only in the big cities but also in the rural areas, where they apparently had been glued to their TV sets.

Kelly's score among housewives was impressive; there was little doubt he had won them over whether they were Liberal, Conservative, organization Democrats or even Republicans.

Issues, the survey developed, had not been the heart of the election, except possibly among the minorities; this had been a contest between two attractive personalities who had been the center of recent and dramatic events. This was underscored many times by the survey teams, who reported they had difficulty in getting voters to express opinions on what the issues were.

The heart of the survey showed the public images the voters had of Kelly and Gentile.

The prevailing image of Kelly was that of a boyish figure intent on driving out corruption in public office, of helping the needy and the oppressed, and seriously intent on using his talents and inherited fortune to

428

serve the public interest. He was regarded as a nonpolitical, regular line candidate with many good ideas and a genuine rather than a simulated liking for people.

The survey showed the prevailing public image of Gentile to be that of a fine public servant who had done much for this country and who probably had more experience than Kelly. However, he was usually associated in the minds of voters, the team reported, with symbols of a period that was history to many of the younger voters.

There was unshakable evidence Kelly had won tremendous support among minorities. Many voters recalled how he had predicted on the floor of Congress that Lawrence, the Time Bomb City, would explode; nearly all recalled how he had lived in the ghetto.

This was singularly dramatic: a millionaire's son sleeping with rats?

The survey showed how right Josh had been in the beginning to use television as the medium to mold our image of Kelly in the limited time available to us. More than 90 percent of those polled said they had never missed the committee's hearings, especially that grim day he destroyed Barney Mullady on the witness stand in Lawrence.

It would have been naïve to ignore the effect the tragedy at City Hall Plaza had on the election. Every voter polled admitted that he viewed Kelly as one of the heroes of that terrifying afternoon and that that would influence his vote.

True, it had been an act of a madman; but no matter what alibis I whispered to myself in the darkness of sleepless nights, I knew in my heart we had helped to set the events in motion on the first Friday afternoon in that forlorn cemetery.

Yet it was strange that while our retribution had been swift and ruthless, ironically, the evil we had introduced would help us win a victory for Kelly Shannon. Had Josh been right after all, that day in the Lawrence motel, when he predicted that the good emerging from these terrible months would far outweigh the evil?

The question would haunt me for the rest of my years.

In the late afternoon Kelly, in slacks and sport shirt, wandered over to the carriage house to report that Lacey had just called and said that Josh was sleeping like a babe but at one point had awakened to ask if there had been a trend yet.

We all cheered.

By 6:00 P.M. the tempo in the carriage house began to quicken. The phones never stopped ringing, along with the frenzied clanging of those damn bells on the teletype machines. I could not help being aware how Luke and Luther stood out in noise and confusion: both were calm and precise, and for an old professional it was a joy to see them operate. There was little doubt in my mind that, God willing, they would be moving out across the country in a few years to sell Kelly Shannon to the nation.

The local committees they had formed, the labor editors they had wooed, the dejected businessmen whose projects they had helped, paid off this day. The first results were encouraging. Kelly swept in to a fast lead. There was plenty of whooping, but I warned them no election is over until the vote is so huge there is no question of a victory.

On television the experts were predicting a Shannon victory. In the library Kelly watched the screen impassively, for the most part silently, while the senator and Pam jubilantly kept tally. I dropped over briefly when an upstate community announced it had gone for Gentile. Pam looked worried, and the senator announced they were a pack of fools, but Kelly simply said he should have spent more time there to try to discover their problems. It was a professional's comment.

As I walked back to the carriage house, I told myself that here was the man; there was no longer an image.

After a few hours of the leads seesawing back and forth, Kelly began to move ahead. In an undertone Luther Roberts predicted it was the beginning of the end for Gentile, and while I agreed with him privately I warned the others to keep the champagne on ice.

At one point Kelly, in slacks and a windbreaker, wandered over, studied the teletypes for a few moments, then left. I followed him. We walked in silence to the rim of the valley behind the stables and stared out across the windy darkness. The late afternoon had turned ugly; now there was a smell of snow in the air.

"A few months ago you could see the roof of Molly's house through the trees," he said. Then, "Now Molly's gone and so is the house. You were in it, weren't you, Finn?"

"Yes, when Josh and I talked to Molly."

"I remember when we were kids. I never went over there with Lacey that Molly didn't climb a chair and take down the Kentucky Long Rifle that hung over the fireplace so I could look it over. There was a date burned in the stock. Once I looked it up. It was the day Burgoyne surrendered at Saratoga. While Lacey was riding, Molly and I used to make up stories about that rifleman."

Then time came back into focus.

"I guess we'll know before morning," Kelly said abruptly.

"The way it's going now, there'll be no need to wait until morning, Kelly," I replied.

He said, "I think we should all wait it out."

Then we walked across the dead lawns to the main house, and I returned to the frantic, clicking teletypes that soon told me Kelly wouldn't have to wait. Morning could only tell us how big the tally was.

But Gentile wasn't conceding. He appeared on television to read a brief statement that he intended to wait out the verdict. I was watching him when Luke tapped me on the shoulder to say Kelly wanted to see me.

Rain mixed with sleet was falling when I left the carriage house. I found Kelly and Pam dressed and waiting at the front door. I didn't have to ask them where they were going. I found my coat and joined them in the car.

The hospital corridors were deserted, quiet. It had been a torturous drive down from Wexford. The roads were slippery, and the intolerable West Side Highway had been like glass.

Now we were walking down the corridor, led by the night nurse, who wasn't a bit impressed that she was in the company of the next governor of the state and even possibly a future President.

All she gave us was two minutes—no more.

I have many scenes harbored in my heart from those last few months, but the most unforgettable was in that dimly lighted hospital room where Lacey was sleeping in the chair near the bed, her fingers intertwined with Josh's, who was in a deep but serene slumber.

Kelly carefully closed the door, but the soft click awakened Lacey. She stared up at us, uncomprehending at first; then, as her mind cleared, she managed a smile. She slowly untangled Josh's hand and placed it on the coverlet. Pam leaned down, and for a moment they clung to each other.

"They had to knock him out about ten o'clock. He insisted on keeping that damn TV on," she whispered. "I must have fallen asleep. How is it going, Kel?"

He shrugged. "We'll know when we get back. How's Josh?"

"Now he's starting to have pain." She bit her lower lip. "He keeps sending me out for things, crazy things from the gift shop that he says he wants to bring back to the rancher who's taking care of our place. But the nurse told me he cries"—a sob caught in her throat—"like a baby when a spasm comes."

"Lacey, I'm sorry," Kelly whispered.

The anguished voice made me turn to him. I was startled. Perhaps I hadn't really looked at Kelly very closely the last few days. Before City Hall he had been a bouncing, vigorous, handsome young man, the light of youth glowing in his face. Now that face was lined; the body that had always seemed so erect sagged with weariness. There was a haunting sadness in the eyes that had sparkled so much with zest for living.

And poor Pam. She too had been seared. I suddenly recalled how in the last few days she seemed to be always watching Kelly, touching him, giving him tiny, secret smiles.

And Lacey. That chiseled face was worn—how worn I would never forget—but curiously, beneath the deep layers of fatigue and anxiety, I sensed a strangeness, something I didn't recognize for a moment, then suddenly it was there before me. Lacey was a stranger. She now belonged to a world in which we all were aliens, a world of family built dream by dream, hope upon hope, prayer on prayer, whispered, promised, and begged during those desolate hours in this room in which no one else existed except this ashen-faced man to whom she clung so desperately by a slender thread of love. The walls of this world could never be breeched by us—it was only for her and Josh and the unborn child she had seen so vividly in the lonely, antiseptic gloom. Even kin and tested friendship were shut out.

I had been too long on this earth, had seen too many men and women, had experienced too much of life not to read in her face how she had already established this world of family, glowing with infinite love, in the majestic land Josh loved so much, a land that had its own heritage of violence, death, and new beginnings. Here there would be no more conspiracies, no more maneuvers, no more petty men with tin hearts and twisted visions, no more of the raucous life of communications where immediacy is the heartbeat and every day is tomorrow. No more Pennsylvania Avenue.

Only family. And now we were only friendly intruders.

Tears, glistening in the soft light like tiny seeds of pure blown glass, rolled down her cheeks as she reached for my hand.

I knew it was goodbye.

The haggard old face peered out at me from the mirror across the room as the dead hours, each with its own special horror, sped across my mind in a weird kaleidoscope of scenes and faces, to tell me, if I never knew before, that this was the way it must be.

No man can toy with other lives and destinies, and remain untouched. My heart echoed with the cry: Dear God, we have paid. None of us will ever be the same.

None of us.

HORAN'S BOONDOCKS
May 10, 12:35 P.M.